UNYIELDING

BOOK THREE OF THE BLACKSEA ODYSSEY

J.A. VODVARKA

To those who never saw themselves in the books they read growing up
and had to create their own universes.

By J.A. Vodvarka

The Blacksea Odyssey

Unworthy
Unbound
Unyielding

Whiskey & Wagers – A Blacksea Odyssey short story

Author's note

Unbound is an epic fantasy book that is intended for mature audiences (18+). For a list of content warnings, please see the last page.

Synopsis

NYSSA BLACKSEA is the only adept at her guild who is not able to use magick, compensating for her perceived weakness by becoming a formidable fighter. She's now twenty-five and has been waiting some time to receive her post in service of the Empire. Doubt festers in the back of Nyssa's mind—will she ever be seen as anything other than an anomaly?

When an adept, QUINN, runs away from another guild, Nyssa is tasked by the master of that guild, CERIL ANELOS, with bringing his fugitive back. She travels to the city of Ocean's Rest with her protective best friend and fellow adept, ATHEN FENNICK. Here they meet up with a tracker who will help them find Quinn, ARYIS DEVITT, an eager but naive adept and member of royalty. Aryis is keen to prove herself, and looks up to Nyssa. While in Ocean's Rest, Nyssa gets into a scuffle with a brother and sister from a guild of assassins and spies.

With a line on their fugitive thanks to Aryis, Nyssa and her comrades venture out to find Quinn on the first night of a winter festival. Their mission goes horribly awry when they are attacked by wraiths—a mindless undead threat not seen in the Empire for thirty years. Nyssa is almost killed staving off the attack, narrowly surviving. But she comes out bearing the poison mark of a blood wraith—a more sentient creature that seemed to mysteriously recognize her.

Nyssa continues her quest to find Quinn, which takes her, Athen, and Aryis across the ocean to the island of Jejin. They capture Quinn, finding not a dangerous adept, but a scared and walled-off woman. Quinn tries to escape several times, finding that while her magick doesn't affect Nyssa, challenging Nyssa's sense of duty and honor is the way to get a rise out of her. Quinn reveals how she was mistreated by Ceril, planting seeds of doubt in Nyssa's mind, and accuses her of being a blindly loyal lap-dog. Is the system that raised her as noble and uncorrupt as Nyssa thought?

On their way back to return Quinn to Ceril, their ship is attacked by the pirate ELIAS, and the four adepts are taken for ransom. While being kept prisoner, Nyssa grows closer to Quinn, and continues to doubt whether she's doing the right thing by bringing her back. The delay in returning to the Empire and achieving her goal angers Nyssa, but she and the crew are forced to work together when the blood wraith from the winter celebration attacks the ship. Knowing that the powerful creature will tear the ship apart, Nyssa drags it overboard into the icy Black Sea, drowning in the process.

Quinn risks her life to save Nyssa from the sea and Elias revives her. As Nyssa recovers, Quinn reveals more dark secrets about Ceril, and Nyssa begins to wonder if the undead things attacking her and her friends could have been sent by him--a dangerous accusation to make without proof. Nyssa and Quinn settle into a begrudging peace with one another, with Nyssa trying to ignore the budding spark of attraction she feels towards Quinn.

Once back in Ocean's Rest, Nyssa is awarded her post and Quinn is to be returned to her guild and Ceril. Nyssa can't help but feel she's failing her responsibility to protect a fellow adept, and seeks counsel from her guild master and adoptive father, ERON. Shortly after, Eron is assassinated by a woman wearing Nyssa's face.

Grieving Eron's death and scared for Quinn's safety, Nyssa makes the decision to go after Quinn and her escort before they arrive back at the guild, choosing her own code of honor over her duty. Finding that Quinn has escaped into the woods, Nyssa convinces Quinn that she's not a threat and is there to help. They are attacked by the assassin siblings Nyssa encountered back in Ocean's Rest. They admit to killing her mentor, Eron, and reveal that it was Ceril who created the wraiths, confirming Nyssa's suspicions.

Nyssa and the siblings fight to the death. She kills the brother, but the sister manages to escape. Quinn and Nyssa head back to Ocean's Rest, where they plan to escape by ship. They are found and captured by Ceril and Imperial Justiciars, who carry out the Empress's justice.

Nyssa is found guilty of treason and presented with a horrific decision - will she sacrifice her own life to stop Quinn's execution? She decides to adhere to her code of honor and sacrifice herself. The Justiciars are disappointed in her decision, and instead of killing her, mark her Unworthy, making her a cursed pariah.

At the moment of Quinn's execution, Nyssa has a magickal awakening, and is consumed by a great power that she can scarcely control, feeling Quinn awaken as well. Together, they kill the Justiciars in self-defense, escaping from Ceril, knowing the Empire will now hunt them down for their crimes. Nyssa is forced to leave her friends and her life behind, headed towards an uncertain future. She has decided to betray her guild and to cast her own shadow.

THE EVENTS OF *UNBOUND*:

NYSSA BLACKSEA and QUINN become fugitives after the deadly events in Ocean's Rest. As they flee, they are ambushed by Obsidian Rule assassins, leaving Quinn gravely injured. Desperate to save her, Nyssa unleashes her dangerous, magick, killing the assassins but accidentally taking the lives of innocent dock workers as well.

Rescued by the pirate ELIAS and the Hannah's Whisper crew, Nyssa and Quinn learn what they are: Cursed Gods, powerful and feared beings not seen for over a thousand years.

On the run with a massive price on their heads, Quinn proposes a daring plan: kidnap the Empire's greatest enemy, QUEEN SUVI RELL of Thu'Dain, and trade her for their freedom. However, Fontaine—now transformed from chicken into a human—insists they must first master their new godly powers. She takes them to the hidden island of Monk's Cove, where they spend a year honing their abilities—Nyssa's control over lightning and the manipulation of magick, and Quinn's mastery of shadow and the negation of magick.

In Ocean's Rest, JUSTICIAR MEDIAS reveals her prophetic abilities to ATHEN, REECE, ARYIS, and LILLIANA. Despite animosities, a fragile alliance forms between Medias and the others, with a plan to protect Nyssa from afar. As they work together, old tensions begin to abate, leading to unexpected friendships...and perhaps a bit more.

Athen and Aryis's relationship deepens, and Aryis confides that she is EMPRESS KALLA'S chosen successor. But when she is summoned back to the Wayland Conservatory as a guest lecturer, her students are turned into terrifying mindless killers. Narrowly escaping, a traumatized Aryis returns to Frosland, her claim to the throne rescinded by Kalla.

Nyssa and Quinn's time on Monk's Cove comes to an end, and they're ready to enact their plan to kidnap Suvi. But everything falls apart when Nyssa's own guildmates catch up with her, forcing her to take their lives, shattering her heart into pieces. Spiraling into a dark place, she fights with Quinn and unspoken resentments rise to the surface, driving a painful wedge between them.

With tensions on Hannah's Whisper high, they meet a familiar face at sea—Aryis. But a warm reunion turns deadly when Aryis and her navy take Quinn and Nyssa prisoner. Frosland, now independent from the Empire, has allied with Suvi Rell, who demands the Cursed Gods as part of the alliance. Aryis, as Queen-in-Waiting of her nation, is forced to put her people's welfare ahead of her friendship and betray Nyssa.

Once Suvi returns to Thu'Dain with two Cursed Gods in her custody, she reveals a horrible truth about Nyssa's parents: they were hired by the Empire to kidnap Quinn as an infant. Kalla intended to use her as an Imperial weapon. Nyssa's mother begged Liliana to take Nyssa too, in a last-ditch effort to save her daughter's life. Lilliana agreed, and both infants were returned to the Empire—Quinn given to CERIL ANELOS to raise, and Nyssa given to ERON GREYE.

After the truth of the past is revealed, Suvi's sinister plan becomes clear—she wants to control a Cursed God. She forces Quinn to strip Nyssa of her magick, condemning her to a slow death. Nyssa is sent limping back to Ocean's Rest while Suvi locks Quinn away.

Bitter and hurt after confirming the truth of Suvi's story with Lilliana, Nyssa flees the city, losing herself in drink and gambling as she waits to waste away and die. Medias, still loyal to Nyssa and Quinn, sends Aryis on a vision-spurred mission to Wayland to recover an artifact to help Nyssa get back to Quinn.

With the tension between the Nyssa and Aryis thick, Aryis unveils her idea—use the artifact she stole from Wayland to open a portal to the dangerous, mysterious Realm of Shadows and rescue Quinn. Nyssa agrees to the insane plan, if only to see Quinn one last time and set her free.

Their journey to Thu'Dain takes them through the haunted Umbra Woods, where Nyssa encounters the Ancient God, Koras, after stumbling upon the Realm of Night. Unscathed but shaken, she senses a connection between her magick and Quinn's within the four-eyed stag god.

Joined by Athen, who will do anything to help his best friend, the trio opens a portal to the Realm of Shadows, infiltrating Suvi's mansion without being seen and finding Quinn alive. As they escape, the god of the Realm of Shadows traps Aryis, and she sacrifices herself to save Nyssa.

Nyssa, Quinn, and Athen barely escape back to the Umbra Woods, but Nyssa's condition deteriorates rapidly. Quinn reveals that instead of extinguishing Nyssa's magick, she drew it inside of herself, where it began to fester and turn against her like a cancer.

With Nyssa hours away from death, the three of them are visited by guests from the Realm of Night, who beckon them to follow. In the Realm of Night, Koras's herald, Cyphon, senses a spark of magick still within Nyssa, one that she can ignite and use to pull her magick out of Quinn and back into her own body. The risk of death is great...one mistake and she'll kill them both. The process is excruciating, but with Quinn's support, Nyssa succeeds.

As they recover, Nyssa and Quinn finally confront their feelings for each other. Nyssa takes a leap and declares her love for Quinn, delighted to find the feeling is mutual.

Athen, Nyssa, and Quinn return to Hannah's Whisper, where they're joined by Medias and Reece, and hatch a new plan—rescue Aryis and capture Suvi. They assault Suvi's mansion, with Nyssa diving back into the Realm of Shadows to confront its god, Tajal. Nyssa strikes a deal with Tajal, saving Aryis before rejoining the battle against Suvi.

In the climactic showdown, Suvi, controlling Quinn's body, fights Nyssa in a fierce battle of gods. Just as Suvi is about to kill Nyssa, Nyssa lets go of her fear and summons a lightning strike that finally brings Suvi down. Nyssa and the others take Suvi and flee from Thu'Dain. They got what they came for and Suvi represents their best shot at freedom.

Back aboard Hannah's Whisper, Nyssa and the crew take a moment to celebrate Winter's Fire, savoring the warmth of friends, family, and a bit of rum. Quinn reveals to the crew the surname that she has chosen for herself—Emerrath, an old name for the Umbra Woods. Nyssa, Quinn, and their friends embrace the brief respite, aware that their battle with the Empire looms beyond the horizon, beyond the calm of the sea.

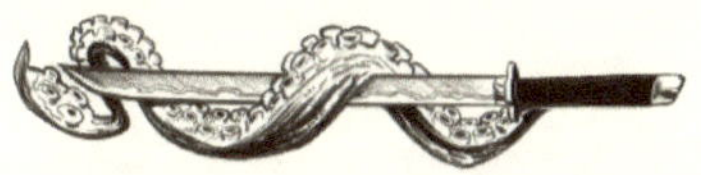

Two souls, forever entwined, chaos dancing in eyes and blood, born
between realms and belonging to the stars.

Two souls, forever entwined, clash with fists and blade, dragging the tips
of their swords across the world.

Two souls, forever entwined, dance and howl, as ancient magick unfurls
and envelopes the light.

Two souls, forever entwined, bend and break, hurling to earth to die and
be forever reborn.

THE SUN PALACE

R eckless. Idiotic. Impetuous.

There were a number of ways to describe what Nyssa and Quinn were about to do. And Nyssa was certain Justiciar Medias would settle upon a few choice words once they returned to Hannah's Whisper.

If they returned.

Nyssa tugged at the collar of her jacket. The Empire was still in the grips of deep winter, but that didn't stop the morning sun from blazing down on them, reflecting off the pristine white snow.

A bead of sweat meandered down her back, and she shivered, glancing over at Quinn. "You ready?"

Quinn ran her hands through her wavy dark hair, drawing it away from her face. She took a deep breath before answering, "Ready."

Nyssa took her own deep breath, a feeble attempt to calm her quaking nerves.

"Nyssa Blacksea and Quinn Emerrath to see the Empress." *No turning back now.*

The guards at the front gate of the Sun Palace—the seat of power of the Areshi Empire—craned their heads.

"We come offering a gift. We bring Queen...well, ex-Queen...Suvi Rell." Nyssa pulled down the hood of the woman standing between her and Quinn, revealing a shock of blonde hair and Suvi Rell spitting muffled venom behind her gag.

The guards murmured among themselves. Nyssa sighed, pushed her hood back, and yanked down the scarf covering the lower half of her face to reveal the Mark of the Unworthy.

A guard started laughing. "You two do look the part. Better than most of the cranks that come here trying to get in to see the Empress, I'll give you that. Go away. You're wasting our time." He dismissed them with a wave of his hand.

Nyssa hummed out a grunt of disbelief. Next to her, Suvi chuckled. No gag could disguise that indignity.

"Would you care to reconsider?" Nyssa held up her right hand and called forth her magick. Azure lightning rippled across her skin, sparks arcing from finger to finger. She sent cords of crackling energy along the ground and zapped the feet of the guards, making them jump back as the bolts licked at their toes.

No impostor could mimic the manifestation of a Cursed God's power. One look at her glowing eyes would prove her status.

"You want to see what she can do?" Nyssa asked, jerking her thumb at Quinn. "Or do you want to get someone out here with some measure of authority to address Cursed Gods?"

A second passed before one of the guards took off running toward the Sun Palace.

Nyssa squinted at the sprawling building, all white marble and soft-green ivy, each vine and leaf seemingly curated to present the perfect picture of vulgar grandiosity. Intricate threads of gold were laid into the stone, forming patterns of swirls and geometric shapes that curved and twisted across the surface of the Palace. Where the sunlight hit the gold embellishment, it danced and shimmered ever so slightly, to the point where Nyssa wondered if her eyes were playing tricks on her.

Across the top of the Palace, sloping white stone roofs rose into the sky, their edges curving upward and adorned with carvings of various animals, demons, spirits, and old gods. Talismans of tribute and protection. Sharp, slender spires dotted the top of the massive structure, the Areshi flag—solid midnight-blue with a golden tree of life in the middle—flew at the top of each one, waving high above them in the winter winds.

Nyssa exhaled and expanded her senses, letting the magick around her fill her view. Brilliant orange, red, and blue wards of various designs lined the tall, thick stone wall and metal gate surrounding the Palace. Some swirled in circular patterns, others formed stationary webs. A few pulsed and vibrated, their patterns changing in waves. The wards, layered on top of each other, reminded Nyssa of the neon bar and eatery signs competing for business back in Vane, where she had spent countless nights away from the Emerald Order to drink, fight, and flirt.

She lowered her gaze to the guards. The glowing essences in the center of their chests—their souls—were bereft of the unique energy that magick-wielders possessed. Inside the gates, a woman tended to a row of flowers, green and white magick flowing from her hands into the plants around her.

"This place is giving me a headache," Quinn grumbled with a frown. Dark shadows wafted off of her, and her green eyes glowed with power. "So much magick. Ward upon ward."

"Overcompensating," Nyssa snorted.

She knew that if Quinn wanted, those wards could be destroyed with a touch. A whole system of protection rendered null by one very specific, very dangerous power that only Quinn possessed.

Two colossal gold doors at the entrance of the Sun Palace opened, and a stream of guards ran out, surrounding one lone Justiciar clad in the familiar deep-red leather uniform of her order. She walked across the expansive, well-manicured courtyard, taking her time, her escort numerous and well-armed. And each one had the glow of magick about them.

The danger of coming to Cardin came into crisp focus.

Nyssa was now even more certain it was the right decision to not involve Elias, Medias, and the others in the last steps of their journey. Medias had assured them that Empress Kalla Simac-Areshi was a fair woman who dealt in good faith, but Nyssa wasn't willing to risk the lives of her friends. Her *family*.

And that fairness and good faith were all they had to go on now.

Medias had planned to go by herself to broker a meeting, but she'd likely have been arrested on the spot, with her execution looming soon after. She was seemingly willing to forfeit her life for them. That simply wasn't an option Nyssa would entertain. The Justiciar had proved her loyalty. A precious commodity for a Cursed God.

When Nyssa had pulled Quinn aside and posed the idea of sneaking Suvi off the Whisper and coming to the Empress alone, citing her desire to keep her friends safe, Quinn didn't hesitate.

The lone Justiciar made her way through the front gate and stopped ten feet from Nyssa, Quinn, and Suvi, her eyes scanning the three women as her guards fanned out on all sides. Her expression—though obscured by the white mask of her station—didn't change. Stoic. And there was a familiarity about the woman that Nyssa couldn't place.

The woman rested her hands on her hips, inches away from the daggers she wore strapped to her thighs, and spoke. "I am Arch Justiciar Decia."

They sent the fucking Arch Justiciar?

Nyssa waited, hooking her thumbs under the sword belt across her chest that held Winter's Bite firmly to her back, and tapped her finger against the dark leather. She hoped her hands didn't shake in the presence of the Arch Justiciar. The Empire's highest-ranking Justiciar had come out to greet them, perhaps as a show of respect or maybe fearlessness. Yet Decia offered nothing. Didn't even blink.

"I'm Nyssa Blacksea. That is Quinn Emerrath. And this is—"

"Suvi Rell," Decia replied. She stepped closer, eyes narrowing on Suvi. "Is it really you? Your face has barely changed in thirty years."

"It's her," Nyssa said. Had Decia faced off against Suvi in the Mire War at Kalla's side? "We would like to offer her in trade for our freedom. We request Diplomatic Parlay."

The Arch Justiciar took a step back and considered Quinn and Nyssa, her gaze disconcerting. Every Justiciar seemed to have perfected the art of intimidation with a mere look. Nyssa couldn't stop herself from swallowing, her nerves buzzing.

Decia scowled. "Diplomatic Parlay is not applicable."

"The parlay is for anyone in conflict with the Areshi Empire. I'd say we qualify," Quinn replied.

The request for Diplomatic Parlay had been Aryis's idea, who'd done as much research as she could, summoning piles of books to study Imperial law. It was a welcome distraction after her ordeal with Tajal the Curious in the Realm of Shadows.

According to her, too many warlords in the past had tried to use negotiations as a smoke screen for assassination attempts, so rules were put in place to protect all parties. Rules they could now use to their advantage and hopefully stay alive.

A parlay meant safe passage in and out—for everyone. But only if the Empire agreed to terms and didn't try to kill them on the spot.

Justiciar Decia took a step back, her eyes drifting across Nyssa and Quinn before coming to rest on Suvi.

Several tense moments lumbered by before the Arch Justiciar spoke. "I cannot let you see the Empress without your magick under control. You will need to be collared."

Though Nyssa hated it, collars were an expected requirement according to both Aryis and Medias given their powers. "Collars in exchange for everything on Imperial record," she replied. "And the blood signature of the Empress." She tapped her finger on her sword belt, waiting. This was their only shot at freedom, and now it rested on an amenable Empress and her head Justiciar.

Decia glanced at Suvi. Had such a prize ever been offered before? Surely putting the last Rell in Imperial custody was undeniably tempting.

"I will deliver your request to Empress Kalla. You will wait here."

Nyssa nodded, watching Decia turn and walk back to the Palace, her pace a little quicker on the return trip.

"Well, we haven't died yet, so that's a good sign," Quinn remarked.

Nyssa attempted to laugh but found her humor absent. "Ah, still plenty of day left."

AN AUDIENCE WITH THE EMPRESS

Quinn's stomach rumbled, having snuck off Hannah's Whisper before the sun rose, leaving only a note behind for Elias and Fontaine to find. She inwardly cringed when she thought of the crew's reaction to their skipping off the ship, abandoning their original plan, but this was for the best. No one else would have to risk their freedom or lives. Elias and the others had already done so much. Lost so much.

Nyssa arched her back, stretching out on the uncomfortable stone bench beside Quinn, where they waited in the expansive park that surrounded the Palace. The city of Cardin lay on the other side of the park, full of life and activity, but up at the Sun Palace, the din of the capital felt leagues away.

An hour passed before Decia returned to the gate. At her side jogged a short woman, doing her best to keep up with the Arch Justiciar's long strides. By the time Decia reached where they sat, the woman was winded and pushed the glasses she wore up on her face several times.

"Your request for Diplomatic Parlay with the Empress has been granted. This is Archivist Baran Sennaq, our Senior Imperial Registrar. She has the parlay order signed by the Empress. I will need your signatures and blood to ratify it."

Nyssa shot to her feet, causing a collective flinch from the assembled guards, a few hands moving closer to weapons. She gestured to Baran, who approached cautiously after a nervous glance at Decia for approval.

Nyssa took the paper, sat back down, and Quinn leaned over to read the contract. It was simple and straightforward, and everything looked in line with what Aryis had told them to expect. In black ink at the bottom of the page sat Kalla's signature and a small triangular seal. A blood mark.

The Archivist produced a flat triangular coin and a pen from a case she wore at her waist. She had Nyssa and Quinn sign the paper and two identical copies, one for each of them. Then, placing the triangle on the paper, she said, "Your palm, please."

Quinn pressed her palm down on the triangle. Icy to the touch, it pricked her hand and drew a sharp hiss out of her, but she let the object do its job until Baran asked her to remove her hand. A triangle of blood sat next to her signature. Baran repeated the process for the other copies and moved on to Nyssa, then signed them all herself to ratify the contract.

"This Diplomatic Parlay is now officially part of the Imperial Record and as such, all parties signed are under its contractual stipulations until the end of the day, marked by midnight," Baran explained before hurrying back to safety behind Decia.

The Justiciar waved a guard forward who had followed her out of the Palace carrying two very familiar things that sent a blazing trail of hatred through Quinn's veins and made her pulse quicken. Void collars. She ground her teeth, trying to keep calm. For so many years, a collar was used to punish her, cutting her off from her magick until Ceril Anelos needed her to dampen spells for him. Seemed she couldn't avoid the damn things.

"Void collars before you step into the Palace. And your weapons," Decia said.

Nyssa glanced to Quinn. The collars were unavoidable if they wanted to get into the Palace. Quinn nodded her agreement.

"We put the collars on but keep our swords. You can't render us defenseless," Nyssa said.

"You are under my protection while entered into parlay. I will let nothing happen to you."

Quinn wanted to laugh. Without that one piece of paper, Decia and her Justiciars would be at their throats.

"Swords stay or we leave," Nyssa said.

Decia stared at her. Several uncomfortable moments ticked away before she replied, "Very well."

The agreement didn't surprise Quinn. A woman like the Arch Justiciar would already know what risks the two of them posed and have weighed her options accordingly. Nyssa was an expert fighter, and herself passable, but magickless and facing the numbers Decia had backing her up, they posed a containable threat.

"Give me those." Nyssa grabbed the void collars from the guard and put one on herself, her face twitching up. "This is the last time one of these will be around your neck, I promise you," she whispered as she affixed the void collar on Quinn.

A wave of nausea hit Quinn as her magick went dim inside of her, a numbing sensation filling her chest. She sucked in a breath—the first touch of a void collar never got easier to endure. Not for her. Being without her power in the midst of her enemies made a dark fear creep over her.

She exhaled and reached up to adjust the collar, brushing Nyssa's hand. The touch was light and quick. A reassurance. "It's okay," Quinn said.

"Follow me," Decia said.

Quinn and Nyssa pulled Suvi along as they entered the Sun Palace. Quinn had never seen it before, but all the rumors were true—the Palace was massive, ostentatious, and annoyingly white. Its pristine milky marble, imbued with flecks of gold or trimmings of gold or leaves of gold, created a gaudy, pale monstrosity. She far preferred the bright, varied colors of Ocean's Rest, its blues, reds, greens, and oranges feeling well-worn and spirited. Alive.

The foyer inside the Palace's main entrance dwarfed most homes. Chalky white columns lined the space, while rays of multicolored light streamed in from the domed stained-glass roof. Alcoves dotted along the walls housed massive statues, some as tall as twenty feet. Quinn had read that all the Areshi Emperors and Empresses had a statue in the Palace to honor the leaders of the past.

Heads turned, eyes widened, and jaws went slack as Quinn, Nyssa, and Suvi walked through the main corridor surrounded by guards, a buzz of tension hanging thick in the air. There likely wasn't one person in the place—from Imperial Advisor to Elite Guard to kitchen cook—who wasn't fully aware of who was in their midst. Nearly two years of being wanted outlaws earned them quite a bit of infamy.

Not that Quinn much cared about reputation. As long as they exited the Sun Palace at the end of the day with their freedom and pardons for everyone who had helped them, she would be content. She had stashed the last bottle of honey whiskey that she had found on the Whisper, likely plundered off of some unfortunate ship, in the bottom of her foot-locker to celebrate. The drink was Nyssa's favorite, and Quinn longed to crack open that bottle and get obnoxiously drunk as a free woman.

The thought cheered Quinn as they walked through the Palace and ignored the whispers and looks. Occasionally, amid the low din of hushed voices, she caught the word *Unworthy*. Nyssa stiffened at each mention. Quinn hated that Nyssa bore the Mark of the Unworthy, a punishment meant to shame and ostracize her. Some superstitious fools even considered it a curse.

Decia finally led them into a spacious room that was warm and intimate, its marble floors covered with multicolored rugs. Shelves rimmed the walls, filled with all manner of books and decorations, and a few chairs and round tables dotted the room, looking ridiculously small in such a large space. The back wall was comprised entirely of floor-to-ceiling windows, the midmorning light streaming in and creating squares of sunbeams on the floor.

A contingent of Elite Guards waited for them, designated by the red stripes down each arm of their stark white wool uniforms. They were rumored to be skilled fighters, second only to Ashcloaks, and dedicated to the protection of the Empress, the Sun Council, and other high officials, like the Arch Justiciar.

Decia crossed the room and disappeared through a door in the back corner. Quinn did a quick count of guards. Only twelve, though all had enough magick to stop them in their tracks should they move an inch toward the Empress. And just outside the door, the other guards waited after escorting them through the palace.

After several awkward minutes, Decia re-entered the room, followed by a short, middle-aged woman who strode to the middle of the floor and stopped by Decia's side. Quinn immediately recognized her from a painting that hung in Arcton.

"The Honored Empress Kalla Simac-Areshi, thirty-second of her House," Decia announced.

Quinn didn't know what she expected from the Empress, perhaps a woman in a long silken gown sitting on a throne, but Kalla didn't seem ostentatious at all. She did, however, have a regal air about her, commanding every bit of reverence she was shown over the years, her head held high and a simple golden crown of interwoven antlers nestled atop a shock of spiky white hair. She wore a tailored white coat accented with shiny black fur at the collar, the coat open to reveal a loose white shirt and black pants. Understated yet elegant.

The guards all took a knee.

Decia stared at the Cursed Gods. "You are meant to kneel in the presence of the Empress."

Nyssa didn't hesitate to respond. "We don't kneel." She pointed to the mark on her chin. "And I think this precludes me from having to do so."

Decia started to respond when Kalla held up her hand. "It's fine. No need for such formalities."

The Empress took a moment to look Quinn and Nyssa up and down. Being under her gaze was disconcerting, her expression gave away nothing...until her eyes lit upon Suvi. "Remove her gag."

Nyssa complied and Suvi flexed her jaw.

"It's been a while since we last met, Rell," Kalla remarked.

Suvi smirked. "You've put on a few years."

"Ah, well, not all of us have illegal longevity magick tainting our blood."

"A pity. You could have two hundred or more years of Imperial rule in you with such *awful*, illegal magick. Now you'll die a common mortal."

Kalla laughed softly. "You seem to think that's the worst fate one could suffer. I've grown immeasurably in my middle-aged years. Mortality gives one wisdom and perspective, I believe."

Rolling her eyes, Suvi sighed. "If you're going to pontificate about the wonders of growing older, could you execute me sooner rather than later? I'd prefer to not hear you drone on."

"Aren't you a delight?" A restrained smile turned up Kalla's mouth.

The door at the back of the room opened, and a young man entered, hurrying toward the Empress. "Are these the—"

"Safin, you were asked to wait in my study," Kalla interrupted, a slight tinge of annoyance coloring her tone.

Safin. Quinn recognized the name. Safin Vonner. Medias had mentioned Kalla's new Imperial successor—and Aryis's replacement. He had to be in his late teens, his boyish looks giving way to that of a man. A sparse scraggly beard graced his dark-brown face, his hair twisted into thin locs down to his shoulders, silver bands dotting the strands, catching the light.

His dark eyes were wide and curious. "I wanted to see the Cursed Gods."

Safin took a step toward Nyssa and Quinn, only to be stopped by Decia, who looked to Kalla for guidance.

"Stay and observe, but remain silent," the Empress instructed, then swung her gaze back to the women before her. "Now, on to the business at hand. Decia has informed me you wish to trade pardons for your prisoner."

"That's right," Nyssa replied.

"And how do I reconcile the death of six Justiciars and nine guild adepts?"

Nyssa stiffened. "Self-defense. We didn't seek to do harm, we were provoked." She let out a heavy sigh. Quinn knew better than anyone that those deaths wore heavily on Nyssa's soul. "We just want to live free without having to look over our shoulders. You've made that impossible with the bounty on our heads and sending Order and Rule adepts after us. You sent my own guild after me. Kids who weren't even Ashcloaks yet. Kids I helped train, for fuck's sake."

A cloud of anger passed over Kalla's face, and she shared a glance with Decia. It struck Quinn that something didn't sit quite right.

"That should never have happened," the Empress said. A surprising admission that got Nyssa's finger tapping slowly against her leg.

Quinn straightened up. "Who ordered them to chase us?"

Another glance shared between the Arch Justiciar and the Empress spoke volumes.

"Ceril Anelos?" Quinn spat, his name like ash in her mouth. It had to have been him.

Kalla didn't answer, stepping toward Nyssa until only a few feet separated them, two guards moving with her. "I held a great deal of respect for Eron. He always spoke so highly of you, Nyssa. What would he think of you now?"

Quinn swallowed—did the Empress truly wish to provoke her anger?

Nyssa's shoulders tensed. "I know you probably think I killed Eron, but he was my father. I would never hurt him. *Ever.* Ceril has an Obsidian Rule adept in his pocket, Efla Eld'on. She can change her face to look like anyone she's studied for long enough. She disguised herself as me and killed Eron."

"Do you have proof of these accusations?" Decia asked.

"Bring Efla to me and I'll beat it out of her."

Decia shook her head and sighed. "So it's just your word—the word of a traitor and murderer."

"Eron raised me to follow the teachings of Sakei and gave me a code of honor. Don't ever presume to know what he would think of me after what I've gone through and what I've had to do because I've been pushed into a corner."

Nyssa and Kalla stood staring at one another, the air between them thick with tension. Nyssa deserved justice for her assassinated father, but she wouldn't get that by antagonizing the Empress.

Quinn interceded. "Shall we return to discussing the terms of our tra—"

The door at the back of the room opened again, and all the air left Quinn's body.

Arch Master Ceril Anelos entered the room and froze in place, his eyes widening.

Quinn willed her knees to remain steady despite her heart ricocheting against her rib cage. In the stark silence of the room, she was certain everyone could hear it.

Hear her fear.

Ceril straightened himself and strode across the room, followed by four dark-green-clad Obsidian Rule adepts.

He stared at Nyssa, radiating pure contempt. A look Quinn was more than familiar with and it turned her stomach. She knew he would likely be in the Palace, but the reality of his presence, after everything he had done and gotten away with, added an air of danger. Quinn could practically feel Nyssa's anger and Ceril's disdain.

When his eyes lit upon her, he smirked. Hatred pulsed through her body, her nails biting into her palms. The pain kept her moored in place while she fought the desire to beat him senseless.

"I just received word we had guests," Ceril said, his voice dripping with distaste. "And what guests they turned out to be. Murderers and traitors. And one displaced queen, it seems."

His smirk grew wider as he drew closer, stopping next to Kalla. Safin moved away from the group, his eyes on Ceril. Maybe he sensed the danger the man posed.

"They are not prisoners," Decia said, curt with him. "We have signed a Diplomatic Parlay with the Cursed Gods."

Ceril's face fell. "That's...ill-advised."

"In your opinion," Kalla replied, "but they are offering Rell in exchange for their freedom."

He paused and cleared his throat. Even that sounded like an admonition. "You can't seriously be considering this offer."

"I am."

For the first time that day, Quinn dared to hope.

Ceril grew more agitated, his face reddening. "They are murderous outlaws. If you let them walk free, you will look like a fool."

"I don't concern myself with appearances when I have Suvi Rell before me."

Ceril let out a small, dismissive laugh. "You have them all collared. You don't need to negotiate. You put them in prison cells and set a date for their execution."

"I adhere to the laws of parlay," Kalla replied, her demeanor growing stiff next to the man almost twenty years her senior, though he used magick to appear younger. A vanity of his that Quinn was all too familiar with.

No warmth seemed to exist between the Empress and her Arch Master, each bristling in one another's presence. He was not an easy man to endure. He wore a sheen of polite civility that was entirely put on, poorly hiding the undercurrent of arrogance and disdain.

Peering down at her, Ceril said, "You would have tea with these traitors and then guarantee them safe passage out of Cardin at the end of the day? I should think you'd discuss this with me before taking such a risk."

"Did you get your feelings hurt, Ceril?" Nyssa asked. "I guess you didn't expect us to walk right up to your front door."

Quinn clenched her jaw tight. Nyssa couldn't help herself, could she? She just had to poke at Ceril. Part of Quinn reveled in it, loving seeing him have to endure the indignity of Nyssa still drawing breath. But she didn't want their chance at freedom derailed by the chip on the woman's shoulder.

"As usual, Blacksea, your mouth does you no favors," he replied.

"And yet I always seem to get under your skin. Why is that, Ceril? Is it because I'm not afraid of you because fear and intimidation are your only currency? Or is it because I thrived under Eron?"

Quinn swallowed, the void collar heavy around her throat.

Ceril frowned. "You became Eron's arrogance, his pride. He gave you more than you ever earned. A magickless daughter of lowlife criminals should never have been an Emerald Order adept."

Nyssa laughed. "You once told me that I should have followed my parents to the bottom of the sea. I now know exactly what you meant by that. I know everything about that night on the Demon's Wail." Nyssa's eyes flicked to Kalla. "I know you contracted my parents to steal Quinn out of Thu'Dain. She was to be your weapon for the Areshi Empire. And I know you ordered my parents' deaths."

She paused. Kalla and Decia glanced at one another, but Ceril's reaction was galling—a slow smile spreading across his face.

Nyssa continued, "Quinn and I could have come here looking for revenge for what you did to us, but...we're tired. Just *fucking* tired. Take Suvi, grant us our freedom, and we'll piss off far away from the Empire. You never need to worry about us again."

The statement drew a scoff out of Ceril. Of course it did. "Are we truly to believe you don't seek revenge?"

Quinn finally spoke. "Do you think we care about what you believe?"

A withering look accompanied the words he spat out. "You are an ungrateful cur. You were fed, clothed, given a proper education at the Citadel, yet it wasn't enough for you."

Anger billowed through her. "You would have me live the smallest possible life, always on your leash. You are a *monster*."

Ceril's lips curled up in a snarl, the first sign of truly naked, unvarnished emotion. Behind him, Safin's eyes were wide. Did he know of the evil his Empire was capable of or was this his first harsh lesson in underhanded Imperial actions?

"Enough!" Kalla said, holding her hand up. "This is getting us nowhere. Ceril, you are not needed in this negotiation. Take your leave."

Ceril stiffened, his face going blank.

And Nyssa laughed.

Quinn fought back a smile. She loved Nyssa's sheer fearlessness and how it fucking rankled Ceril.

But he didn't move. "As your Arch Master, I disagree. I simply don't see an advantage for you here."

Nyssa gave Quinn a glance before addressing Kalla. "You say that you respected Eron. What if I can prove that Ceril had him killed? And that he was responsible for the wraith attack on Ocean's Rest and the incident at Wayland?"

Ceril scoffed. "Your allegations are pure desperation."

"I have someone who can show you memories, Empress. She can form a connection between you and Ceril, and you'll be able to see all his dark, dirty secrets."

A flicker of doubt in Ceril's eyes made Quinn's heart jump into her throat.

Arch Justiciar Decia stepped in. "Memory magick is no longer practiced. No one has such skills."

"Our friend Fontaine does," Quinn said. "She's Old Folk."

Silence fell over the room.

"Nonsense," Ceril finally replied.

Nyssa approached him. "I have Lilliana Fennick's memory of that night you stepped foot on my parents' ship. Even though it was spring, it was still cold on the Black Sea and the stars were shining bright. There was a demon's head pendant around my mother's neck, and she told you that Quinn was named after the Pirate Queen from *The Cry of the Sea*. My mother begged Lilliana to take me, and she almost didn't. You didn't want her to. I believe you said, 'This pirate's spawn isn't our concern'."

Kalla looked to Decia, something unspoken passing between them. The Arch Justiciar's hand slid to the dagger worn on her belt, her eyes shifting to Ceril.

"I would like to meet this Fontaine," Kalla said.

Ceril shot her a simmering look. "You can't be seriously entertaining these lies."

Kalla didn't waver. "We can put this issue to rest once and for all, Arch Master Anelos."

His expression changed, haughty confidence giving way to something far different.

Fear.

"You didn't have to kill Eron," Nyssa said, her voice tight and restrained. "The Arch Master position was already yours. He declined. He wasn't standing in your way."

He snarled at her, his face exposing his pure hatred. Finally, the face Quinn was all too familiar with revealed itself. How many times had he flashed that anger at her at Arcton Citadel?

Ceril stepped back, his face growing calm. He rolled his shoulders and stared at Nyssa, his pale-blue eyes set with disdain. He let out a low chuckle before saying, "Eron was killed for one reason only—to break you, Blacksea."

The room went still. Quinn let out a soft gasp. Had he really just confessed in front of everyone? Next to her, Nyssa tensed and exhaled a strangled breath.

"Arrest him!" Decia shouted, her hands flying to her daggers.

Ceril scrambled back. The Obsidian Rule adepts collapsed on his position, drawing their weapons to protect him. Was the whole guild behind him?

"I will destroy everything you love, Nyssa Blacksea," he seethed. "I'll find your friends—Athen, Reece, your precious pirates—and kill every last one of them." He leaned into the adept next to him. "Now!"

The adept disappeared.

Quinn flinched as something wet splattered across her face. Kalla's mouth fell open, a deep red gash across her throat. She crumpled to the floor, blood pulsing out of her neck, the Obsidian Rule adept standing over her body.

FLOWERS

Nyssa choked out a breath—the assassinated Empress lay dead at their feet. She scrambled back, dragging Quinn with her, unsheathing Winter's Bite.

"Kill them all! Including the boy!" Ceril ordered. "But save Rell for me."

His Obsidian Rule assassins moved, lighting up with magick. The adept who had killed the Empress blinked out of sight, reappearing beside two Elite Guards, his knife slashing and stabbing before either of them could move.

"Fuck," Nyssa whispered, reaching inside her jacket and pulling out a small sphere. "Find Athen and take the direct route. Message as follows: I need fucking help. Now!" she ordered. The orb flew out of her hand, shot across the room, and crashed through a window. Athen was their contingency plan—one she had hoped not to need.

"You will rot in a prison cell for this treason!" Decia shouted, yanking Safin behind her, white magick flashing at her fingertips. A thin column of light shot toward a Rule adept, hitting him in the chest. He flew across the room and hit the wall with a sickening thud.

Swirls of light and angry shouts exploded from everywhere as the Elite Guards rallied around Decia. Ceril retreated back toward the door, his fingers moving, purple energy pulsing from his hands. A low drone rippled through Nyssa, becoming an ache that clawed at her whole body.

The assassin who had killed Kalla turned to her. She sprang at him, her sword slicing through the air as he disappeared.

"Nyssa, behind you!" Quinn cried out.

Nyssa whirled around, her sword finding purchase in the teleporting adept's thigh. He blinked out of view, reappearing on the other side of the room before dropping to a knee from his injury. Behind him, through the door, came more Rule assassins. The traitors set their sights on Nyssa.

She had trained against her fellow Order warriors, using all the tools she had to fight against magick while she had none. She was right back in that situation, the void collar around her neck rendering her magickless. But not powerless.

Never powerless.

Nearby, steel clashed against steel as Quinn met a Rule adept's blade with her own, her eyes wild. The man fell back, black energy coalescing around his fingers. Nyssa's hand flew to the belt across her chest, clutching one of the small throwing knives sheathed there.

Hurt. Distract. Confuse. Those had been Eron's lessons to Nyssa on how to fight those with magick. Break their will and concentration.

Break.

Nyssa hurled the knife at Quinn's attacker, and it sank into his neck with deadly precision. He reeled back and pawed at the small weapon, the magick at his fingertips dissipating. Quinn took advantage and drove her sword into his belly, her expression hard and resolute.

The floor beneath Nyssa trembled and Kalla's body shuddered as if still alive at her feet. Nyssa shifted backward, comforted by Quinn's sudden touch on her lower back as they came together.

The low drone that Nyssa had felt before rippled through her body, making her skin prick up and her muscles ache. The mark on her chin began to throb.

Quinn's grip on Nyssa tightened. "Nyssa," she breathed, "do you feel that?"

The dead Empress's eyes fluttered, and she started to shake violently.

"Fuck," Nyssa whispered. The magick thrumming through her body had to be forbidden magick, Ceril's magick, transforming Kalla's corpse into a monstrosity.

Kalla sat back on her haunches and stared at Nyssa and Quinn, quivering, the pupils of her eyes turning a sickly, anemic white.

An acrid scent filled Nyssa's nose, and she gagged as the dead woman's skin began to sizzle and turn black, her body transforming into a wraith. She tore the crown off the top of her head, ripping it off with hands that had become claws.

Claws that could rend the flesh off of bones with one swipe.

Nyssa lunged forward, driving the tip of her sword into the monster's throat. Blood poured out of the wraith's mouth. It coughed and wheezed, pawing weakly at her blade before its arms fell to its sides. Nyssa pulled her sword out and the body of the wraith slumped over.

The thrumming continued, and the dead guards began to twitch and buck—they were about to suffer the same fate as Kalla. Nyssa slid back, her eyes darting around the room. They were outnumbered and outpowered.

She retrieved a bag from her jacket and sent up a whispered wish, opening the bag and spilling its contents on the floor. Small orbs bounced and rolled in all directions. Nyssa stomped on one, and it cracked, releasing a high-pitched whine. A cascade of more shrill whines filled the air as, one by one, the other orbs followed suit.

"Stop them now!" Ceril ordered.

The crushed orb at Nyssa's feet sprouted a flower, and it grew, expanding to eight feet tall in the matter of seconds. The other orbs popped and cracked, flowers springing out, growing to ridiculous sizes.

"What the fuck?" Nyssa hissed. Had she stolen the wrong orbs from Fontaine?

The flowers began moving. And changing. They sprouted branches filled with thorns, and the faces of the flowers morphed, massive mouths with sharp, jagged teeth taking shape, the high-pitched whines becoming low growls.

Pandemonium erupted in the room, flashes of magick hitting the flowers as they moved toward Ceril and his Rule adepts. The flowers—while not quite what Nyssa had expected—were the perfect diversion. Fontaine had been experimenting lately with illusions that held a tangible form but were ultimately harmless. It wouldn't take long for Ceril and his lackeys to figure that out. They needed to escape. Immediately.

"Go! Now!" Nyssa said, pushing Quinn back toward the door.

Through the whirling flowers, Nyssa spotted Justiciar Decia and her ward, Safin. They were surrounded by assassins.

"Shit," Nyssa whispered. She started back in the direction opposite of their escape.

"What are you doing?" Quinn asked, catching Nyssa's arm.

"Decia and the kid, I can't leave them."

"Alright, come on!" Quinn said, dashing toward Decia and Safin, weaving between the stems of the flower illusions.

Nyssa swore under her breath and followed, bumping into flower stalks as she went. They had no problem bumping back, causing her to stumble. Their thorns poked at her, but lacked a sharp point.

Decia stood in front of Safin, two daggers out, trapped against the wall by two Rule adepts. A bright splash of blood marred her Justiciar mask.

Quinn dashed toward them and attacked, one adept barely parrying her blow. The other sidestepped and threw out a glowing red dagger attached to a chain. The dagger flew past Quinn, then shot back, wrapping itself and its chain around her throat before the adept yanked hard, dragging her to the ground.

Nyssa snarled and vaulted over Quinn, smashing her knee into the adept's chin and severing the arm that held the chain strangling Quinn. A cry of pure terror left him, but Nyssa didn't care as she followed him to the ground, turning Winter's Bite over and ramming its tip into his chest.

Quinn gagged and choked, her face red. Nyssa grabbed the chain and let out a sharp hiss—the metal burned her fingers. She ignored the pain and unwrapped the chain. It left a charred imprint on Quinn's pale skin.

"Quinn?" Nyssa's heart thumped wildly.

Quinn rubbed at her throat. "I'll be okay," she rasped.

A body fell next to Nyssa. The other adept, her throat pumping blood, her eyes still moving, still aware for a few precious seconds before they stilled. Decia stood over the dead adept, bloody daggers dripping but at the ready.

Pulling Quinn to her feet, Nyssa barked at Decia, "Follow us, now!"

The Arch Justiciar made no move to leave, putting the butt of a dagger against Safin's chest to stop him.

The damn stubborn woman.

Nyssa growled, "Come with us. Or die here and lose the Empire."

A heartbeat passed before Decia gave them a terse nod.

"Get to the doors," Nyssa directed. "I'll be right behind you."

"What are you doing?" Quinn asked.

"Ceril wants Suvi. I'm fucking getting her back."

Flowers whirled around the room, their groans and roars frightening. Nyssa pushed through, ricocheting off of them, her head on a swivel searching for Suvi.

Athen paced back and forth, eyeing the gates of the Sun Palace. He glanced over his shoulder to make sure the horses they had rode up from the docks were still tied to a post at the entrance of the park that surrounded the Palace, separating it from the city proper. He wasn't usually so...twitchy, but rarely was he in a position to provide backup to two insane friends who had decided to walk to the enemy's doorstep and *knock*.

Waiting also wasn't his strong suit, and the plan he and Nyssa came up with made him worry regardless of her confidence. Confidence tinged with a hint of trepidation. He had grown to recognize Nyssa's quirks and the tone in her voice when she proposed something that could be dangerous or insane. Or both. Today seemed to qualify as both.

No, it was *definitely* both.

Putting aside his apprehension, Athen fingered the large bag in his pocket. Fontaine likely knew by now her stash of practice orbs had been stolen. Athen hoped these things held something frightening but, moreover, distracting. Fontaine had a penchant for whimsy at times.

"You fidget like a five-year-old waiting on dessert," his companion said.

Yuha appeared calm as she sipped on a tea bought from a park vendor and puffed on her thin brown cigar, its sweet, earthy smoke now a familiar scent after weeks aboard the Whisper.

"This has to go the right way," Athen said, scratching at his eyebrow, his eye patch irritating the skin around his right eye.

Yuha spit out a speck of tobacco. "After everything Nyssa and Quinn have done, you doubt them?"

"No. Yes." He sighed. "Fuck, I don't know. This is insane, right? We should have stopped them."

"Stop Nyssa? Have you met her?" She chuckled. "I find this rather exciting."

"You're only here because you caught us sneaking away."

"You worry too much. Had a man like you once."

Athen raised the eyebrow over his good eye. "Oh? What happened to him?"

"Wore him out."

Yuha took one long inhale of her cigar and dropped it at her feet, putting it out.

"I'm in need of a new man, if you're up for it," she continued, eyeing him over the steam of her tea.

Athen was certain he turned three shades of red at the thought of taking a tumble with the woman. "I'm...uh...things are complicated with Aryis right now," he choked out.

"If you change your mind, you know where my stateroom is."

Athen turned back to the Palace, and something plunked into his eye patch. "Hey!" he hissed. An orb hovered in front of his face. He quickly snatched it out of the air, and Yuha stepped close.

"Message for Athen Fennick. Speak the code."

Pulse pounding, Athen said, "Lemon tart."

Nyssa's voice, tinny and distant, came from the orb. "I need fucking help. Now!"

"Shit." *Shit, shit, shit, shit, shit.*

He glanced at Yuha.

She drained the rest of her tea. "You heard the woman."

HEADS WILL ROLL

Quinn ran after Nyssa, keeping her eyes on alert as they searched for Suvi through the confusion in the room, giant flowers ambling about.

"Here!" Nyssa yelled, and Quinn followed, barreling into a flower stem. It leered down at her and shoved her. Not hard, but enough to make her stumble off balance. Fontaine's so-called illusions were goddamn annoying.

Suvi was huddled against the wall, hiding next to a leather reading chair. Nyssa hauled her to her feet—

A loud *boom* shook the room, the ground shuddering beneath them.

Shrieks pulled Quinn's attention to her left, her eyes landing on Ceril as he stood in the back corner of the room. Dead bodies twitched at his feet, beginning their transformation into wraiths, the magickal resonance vibrating deep in her body, raising every hair on the back of her neck.

Seeing Ceril again had rocked Quinn. Made her feel small and vulnerable. Now, something else pulsed through her blood.

Hate.

"There!" Ceril shouted, pointing her way. "Kill them now!"

Gripping her sword tight, she peeled away from Nyssa and Suvi and ran toward Ceril.

"Quinn, no!" Nyssa called after her.

If she could get to him before the wraiths fully turned...

A Rule adept appeared in front of her out of thin air, wisps of blue smoke clinging to him. The same damn one who could jump from place to place in the blink of an eye. Hobbled though he was, he lunged at Quinn, his jagged knife aimed for her gut. Instinct took over, and she was able to block the blow with her forearm, the knife cutting through her jacket and into skin.

Behind him, the wraith rose to its full height, its sickly white eyes darting back and forth, landing on Quinn.

Another *boom* shook the room, and a klaxon sounded, loud and shrill.

Someone grabbed the collar of Quinn's jacket and hauled her back. Nyssa's blade arced down at the adept, hitting nothing as he blinked away again.

"Get back," Nyssa shouted.

"I have to stop Ceril!" Quinn cried out.

"You'll never get close enough."

A wraith started stomping toward them. Magick flared, and a bolt of fire shot straight at them from beside Ceril. Nyssa wrapped herself around Quinn.

A flash of white light streaked past them and splintered the fireball into pieces. They turned back to Suvi. Decia was beside her, white magick coiling around her hands.

"Come on," she growled, her hand around Suvi's arm. They disappeared into the roiling mass of flowers. Quinn and Nyssa followed. The illusions were beginning to flicker and fade, their magick waning.

They bolted to the door where Safin waited, his body pressed up against the wall as if he wanted to sink into its surface and disappear. Decia pulled open the door, and they spilled out into the corridor.

Men and women cowered in alcoves as guards ran past toward the main entrance, shouting for help. In the distance, in the exact direction they needed to go, wraiths moved up the corridor.

Quinn sucked in a breath. "Are those—"

The wraiths shrieked at guards and bystanders but didn't attack. Were they real, those people would be dead, the wraiths tearing through them. Those illusions had to be Athen's doing. He must have gotten the right orbs.

"This way," Decia said, heading in the opposite direction.

"No," Nyssa replied, "that's our distraction. Get to the front gate!"

Despite her hesitation, Decia nodded and pulled Safin along as they ran toward the wraiths. Nyssa and Quinn sandwiched Suvi between them, and thankfully, the woman cooperated.

"Stop them!" a voice shouted from behind. "They murdered the Empress!"

In the pandemonium, it seemed the prospect of getting slaughtered by a wraith was an unattractive option because none of the guards showed any interest in chasing them.

A *boom* thundered down the corridor. A massive stone head tumbled toward them, its nose causing it to hop as it rotated. It belonged to one of the large sculptures in the main foyer of the Palace. Its body came skidding after it, cutting a groove in the marble floor.

Nyssa darted out of the way and veered to the side of the hallway, hugging the wall as she ran, pulling Suvi and Quinn behind her. Decia and Safin followed suit. The last thing any of them needed was to get hit with the errant head of a long-dead Imperial politician.

Beads of sweat ran down Quinn's back. The cut on her arm burned, but she pinned back her fear as they waded into the wraith illusions. She had fought them a year back, before she knew they were illusions created by Fontaine. These wraiths seemed to be more simple than the flowers. They ran about, hissing and roaring at anything that moved, but they didn't attack.

When Quinn and the others entered the foyer, they found Athen and Yuha doing their best to cause mayhem. Athen twisted the head off a felled statue, stone splintering around his hands. The floor was littered with colorful shards, the dome above completely devoid of any remaining glass. Yuha tossed orbs out of a burlap sack down the hall, where they hissed and popped, a wraith rising out of each enchanted ball.

Athen dropped the head when he saw the five of them, and it shook the marble floor beneath them, cracking the white stone.

"We need to go!" Nyssa said without breaking stride. The entryway's massive doors were torn off their hinges, the stone frame shattered. Outside, guards lay unconscious or barely moving. Athen had created havoc, but Quinn knew he'd done his best to not seriously hurt anyone.

"What happened?" he shouted as he and Yuha turned to run with them toward the main gate.

"Ceril happened. The Empress is dead."

"Fuck."

"Fuck is right," Nyssa replied. "We have to get to the ship now or we're dead. I hope Elias took my note seriously."

Nyssa had left a note on Elias's door: *Be ready to shove off when we get back*, underlined thrice for emphasis.

The klaxon had brought onlookers to the park that surrounded the Palace, their mouths agape. Athen and Yuha took the lead as they weaved past trees and bushes, the large woman dumping the last of the orbs out of her satchel.

Quinn's heart pounded in her chest. She dared a glance over her shoulder to see if they were being chased. Despite her fear, no massive army of guards or Imperial mages streamed out of the front entrance of the Sun Palace. Their distraction had done its job, and they had lost their pursuers in the chaos...for the time being.

The last of the orbs began exploding, producing more fake wraiths. The illusions had the desired effect on the onlookers—wreaking sheer panic.

They reached their horses rented from the stables at the docks, and the beasts looked on, their tails swishing about. They didn't fall for the wraith illusions. Quinn breathed a sigh of relief. She wasn't great with the animals as it was and getting bucked would be disastrous.

Yuha swung up onto her horse in one fluid motion, her agility impressive for her size, and she pulled Suvi up by the scruff of her jacket, placing the woman in front of her. Athen helped Decia and Safin onto another horse, then he mounted his dappled mare while Quinn tried to get up on the last horse. Her body was uncooperative, her strength waning. She looked down at her wounded forearm, blackish trails of what could only be poison radiating out in all directions.

Her blood ran cold. "Nyssa, I need help. Poison," she said, trying to keep her voice steady, holding up her arm.

Nyssa laced her fingers together, and Quinn stepped into her hands and heaved her leg over the horse. It moved beneath her impatiently, its nerves matching her own. Nyssa swung up behind her, wrapped one arm around her waist, and took the reins in the other, nudging the horse forward with her heels.

"Hold on, Quinn," she said, her voice buzzing next to Quinn's ear, the low vibrating tone strangely comforting as they left the destruction in their wake. Just as the Cursed Gods' lore had warned. Not their fault, things went to shit when Ceril arrived.

Quinn grabbed onto the horn of the saddle, her arms tight to her body as Nyssa brought the horse up to a run, its hooves clacking against the stone streets of Cardin. Men and women hurried out of the way, gawking at their passing, no doubt catching sight of Nyssa's marked chin, along with the successor to the crown and the Arch Justiciar racing toward the docks.

Everything had gone so terribly wrong.

Their chance at safety and freedom had evaporated the second Ceril assassinated Kalla.

The malice in his eyes matched Quinn's own, and she knew he would never rest until she and Nyssa were in chains. Or dead.

They couldn't keep running. The world wasn't big enough to escape his hate.

Trying to stay upright despite the throbbing pain in her arm, Quinn hung onto the saddle and leaned back into Nyssa. She let her head loll back to rest on Nyssa's shoulder, hoping they would set foot the Whisper again before the poison reached her heart.

THE JUSTICIARS

Nyssa ignored the dockmaster yelling at her to stop, riding her horse onto the docks, with Athen and the others following. The Whisper sat at the end of a long pier, the best position to get out of port quickly.

A loud, shrill whistle sounded from behind Nyssa, and she didn't have to turn around to know it was Yuha signaling the ship. The crew from the Whisper ran down the gangplank ahead, looking ready to help—and, Nyssa knew, ready to fight if need be. She hoped they didn't have to. Risking their lives over and over racked her with worry and guilt.

She pulled up on the reins, Quinn swaying before Nyssa tightened her grip, her arm numb from holding Quinn fast against her. Athen ran to them, and Nyssa lowered Quinn down to him, the woman deathly pale and slick with sweat.

"Get her to Buck!" Nyssa ordered.

Elias tromped down the gangplank. "You better have a great *fucking* excuse for leaving the *fucking* ship!"

The angry tone gave way to concern as Athen rushed past him with Quinn. "She going to be okay?" His face contorted into confusion when he saw Decia. "That is not Medias. And who is the kid? What the fuck did you guys do?"

"Get on the ship. We need to get out of here!" Nyssa yelled.

Elias gave her the deepest frown he was capable of, but he ran back aboard the Whisper, barking orders to his scrambling crew. Decia and Safin stood on the dock and stared up at the ship.

"I am not getting onto a pirate vessel," Safin said.

Nyssa pointed up at the Whisper. "Get your asses on the boat."

"You need help wrangling these two?" Yuha asked, letting go of the grip she had on Suvi's arm and cracking her knuckles.

"No, I got this." Nyssa grabbed Safin by the back of his collar and hauled him to the gangplank. She had far greater things to worry about than a teenager—if Quinn was seriously hurt—

"Let go of me, Unworthy!"

"Fuck you, kid. Get on the ship. Now."

Safin yanked away from Nyssa and rounded on her, and a fist meant for her face collided with her waiting palm. She popped him in the nose with a light jab, not enough power behind it to put him on his ass, but enough to sting and warn him off.

Or it should have.

Instead, Safin doubled down and tried to hit Nyssa again, but his aim was far off, missing her by a foot.

This time, she dropped him to the dock.

"Get the boy on the ship, or we leave him!" Nyssa ordered to Decia. Why hadn't the Arch Justiciar lifted a finger to stop her?

"Safin, please get on the ship," Decia said, pulling him to his feet and directing him up the gangplank. Thankfully, he didn't protest. Nyssa waited until they were safely aboard before looking back down the dock. Save for a few onlookers, no one gave chase.

She bowed her head and exhaled a heavy breath, her heart pounding. "Yuha, please get Suvi back in a locked stateroom."

"Go see to your woman," Yuha replied before giving Suvi a shove.

Nyssa ran up the gangplank, and as the crew untied the Whisper from the dock and hurried back up to set sail, she followed Decia and Safin and found Athen kneeling on the deck next to Quinn, whose hair was wet and plastered to the side of her head. Buck had cut away the sleeve of her shirt, revealing an angry black spiderweb of poison already stretched up her shoulder and peeking under her collar.

"Fuck," Nyssa whispered.

"Safin," Decia said, her voice low. "Can you help her?"

"You're a healer?" Nyssa asked.

Safin didn't answer. She grabbed him. "You fucking heal her unless you want to swim back to the dock and have Ceril slit your throat."

"You don't give me orders."

Nyssa seethed, her face nearly touching his, towering over him by a few inches. "Help her or I start breaking your fingers."

He stared back at her, this throat bobbing. "You are an extremely rude woman."

"So I've been told. Help Quinn. Now." She gritted her teeth, stomach in knots. "Please."

Safin's face softened, and he knelt next to Quinn. His hands began to glow with purple magick, little sparks of light dancing down his fingers. He closed his eyes and bit his lip, palms hovering over Quinn's arm. Waves of glowing purple energy rippled up and down Quinn's arm, the dark poison receding and her sliced flesh stitching back together.

While Safin worked, the Whisper moved away from the dock, Elias taking them out of port. The sea wind whipped across the deck as the ship's short-burst acceleration enchantment got them moving quickly away from Cardin. The air around the ship shimmered as its invisibility veil activated, hiding them from view.

Athen crushed the locks on the collars Nyssa and Quinn wore and slid them off their necks. Nyssa's magick flooded back, accompanied by a wave of nausea. She grabbed ahold of Athen's arm to steady herself. She turned her attention back to Quinn.

After a few moments of healing, Quinn's eyes fluttered open.

"You okay?" Nyssa asked.

Quinn nodded and sat up with Nyssa's help, her color coming back. "Yeah. I'm feeling much better."

"I guess you're not a half-bad healer, kid," Nyssa said, eyeing Safin.

He sat back on his haunches, looking pleased with himself. Nyssa had to give him credit, his healing was fast and effective.

A shadow moved over her. "That is the last time you will conduct yourself in such a manner with Safin. You will learn your place, Unworthy," Decia warned.

Nyssa stood and faced the Arch Justiciar. "You don't have any fucking authority—" She paused, taking a step back. The spark of recognition from earlier caught fire, and her mouth went dry, her breathing growing ragged. "Your face. I've seen you before today."

"Nyssa?" Quinn asked.

"You were on the Demon's Wail," Nyssa whispered. "You killed my parents."

Decia's lips parted as Nyssa's pulse pounded in her ears. Magick exploded across her body, and she lunged at Decia, electricity sparking off the fist she smashed into the Arch Justiciar's chin.

Decia reeled back, somehow not felled by the punch. Nyssa roared in anger, balling her fist up to deliver another blow.

Arms wrapped around her, holding her back from committing the murder in her heart. "Nyssa, don't do this," someone rumbled in her ear. Medias.

"You and your Justiciars slaughtered my mother and father," Nyssa yelled, her voice cracking as she strained against Medias. She grabbed the Justiciar's wrist, lightning licking at her fingertips, sparking off them both. "Let me go."

"Stop," Medias hissed, in obvious pain.

Nyssa trembled. "Decia murdered my parents. She needs to answer for that."

"Harm her and make a mortal enemy of me, Blacksea." Medias let her go, stepping back. "She's my mother."

All the air left Nyssa's lungs.

She shot forward and punched Medias, landing her squarely on her ass. "You bastard!"

Quinn pulled Nyssa back. "Medias is a friend, calm down."

Nyssa tore away from her. "She's a goddamn liar!"

How didn't she see it? The same regal posture and mannerisms, dark-brown hair pulled back into a topknot. Fuck, they were even the same damn height. The only difference was eye color—Medias's odd red eyes an anomaly.

"I'm sorry, Nyssa," Medias said, standing and wiping at her split lip, blood smearing across her chin. "I had my reasons for not telling anyone."

"Reasons," Nyssa scoffed, her chest tight. She placed her faith in others and expected loyalty back, only to get her heart ripped out more than once. "Everyone has their reasons for their secrets and betrayals. And I'm fucking sick of it."

"I was protecting my mother. I'm a seer, and that fact could have been used to hurt her. I couldn't risk it."

Decia didn't move, her eyes boring into Medias. "What have you done, daughter?"

"Nyssa and Quinn are not like the Cursed Gods of the past. Father saw them in his visions and trusted them...trusted their hearts." Medias looked to Nyssa, her eyes unwavering. "As do I."

"You betrayed the Empire," Decia replied.

"Yes."

"Oh, Medias..."

"Do not lament me, Mother. I made my choice."

Nyssa exhaled and unfurled her hands, her knuckles burning.

Medias turned to her. "Give me your word, on your honor, that you won't harm my mother."

The idea that her parents' killer was within arm's reach and she could do nothing was galling, but she couldn't fracture her bond with Medias. The woman had risked everything to protect her and Quinn without asking for anything in return.

Nyssa couldn't let anger direct her now. She nodded.

Medias took a deep breath. "I need to hear it, Blacksea."

"On my honor, Decia is safe." The words felt like dust in her mouth, but Medias was too important to Nyssa. She was, strangely enough, a friend. "Sorry about the lip."

"It will heal. Please, can someone explain what's happened? When we all woke this morning, you were gone," Medias said, staring at Safin. "Who is this?"

"Safin Vonner. And now, Safin Vonner-Areshi, the new Emperor," Decia provided, her voice quiet. Adding *Areshi* to the kid's surname was traditional for every Emperor or Empress, cementing his title—he was the sole leader of the Empire.

Medias blinked, then slowly scanned the faces around her. "What happened to Empress Kalla?"

Nyssa hung her head. Someone stepped up next to her and gave her shoulder a gentle squeeze. Aryis.

It was Decia who answered the question. "Empress Kalla is dead. Assassinated by the Obsidian Rule at Ceril Anelos's order."

Medias shook her head. "No. That's...that's impossible."

Elias jogged toward them from the quarterdeck, trailed by Fontaine. "Did I hear that correctly? Kalla is dead?"

"Yeah." Nyssa exhaled sharply, then did her best to recount the events of the morning. Quinn and Athen added any details she missed.

"Why did you go without us?" Elias asked after their story was relayed, his face dark.

"That's on me," Nyssa confessed. "Every last one of you has risked your lives for me and Quinn. I couldn't ask you all to do it yet again. I..." She took a moment to quell the hitch in her voice. "I wanted you all safe. This was *our* journey."

"Then explain Athen and Yuha," Medias said.

"Athen got suspicious. I've never been good at hiding anything from him. And Yuha," Nyssa sighed, "caught us trying to sneak off the ship and insisted she come along."

Fontaine stepped forward. "You took all my orbs?"

"We figured they'd make a great distraction. And...they did. Though you'll have to explain those nightmare flowers."

"Those were my spellweaving experiments, not meant to be used! What if I had wiped the enchantments and they did nothing?"

"Luckily, I had a mentor who taught me how to detect magick."

The woman didn't look pleased. Nyssa had screwed with her enchantments a few too many times, tearing through veils, and now stealing her supplies. "I'll make it up to you, Fontaine."

Shaking her head, Fontaine sighed, her scowl giving way to a begrudging smile. "My heart is just glad to see you alive."

"You should have taken me with you. I could have circumvented all of this," Medias said.

"You were the last person we wanted with us," Quinn replied.

"Why? You still don't trust me? Did you think I would have betrayed you?"

"No." Nyssa grasped Medias's shoulder, half expecting to be pushed away. "You would have been arrested. And killed. And that would make me very angry. Angrier than you keeping secrets from me."

Medias swallowed and bowed her head.

Safin stumbled to a crate and sat down hard on it. "Empress Kalla is dead," he said. "And I'm the Emperor."

Arch Justiciar Decia knelt down next to him. "You are, Safin. And I pledge my life to you now."

"I'm the Emperor..." His brows knit up.

Nyssa exhaled, feeling for the kid, knowing he must be quaking inside. She looked around the deck. Worry and sadness hung on the faces around her. Their shot at freedom—one they risked their lives for, one that had cost others their lives, including their own crewmates—disappeared with one vicious cut of a knife. An assassination that they'd inadvertently made possible.

"Did we just give Ceril what he wanted?" Nyssa whispered.

More deaths she was responsible for. Like the dead dock workers in Ocean's Rest...

"What happens now?" Quinn asked.

"Let's talk this through," Aryis said, finally breaking her silence. She chewed on her thumbnail and her eyes darted back and forth, a sign of her mind turning the situation over every which way to examine it. Nyssa had come to miss that familiar look, absent after she had betrayed her and Quinn to Suvi, though now slowly coming back as she recovered from her encounter with Tajal the Curious, the Ancient God of the Realm of Shadows and one high-grade asshole. "With Kalla dead, I suspect Ceril will do everything in his power to contest Safin's claim to the throne. I listened closely to your story, aside from the five of you, Ceril, and his

Obsidian Rule adepts, did anyone else who witnessed what Ceril did survive?"

Nyssa swallowed, thinking back. "No, I don't think so."

"Well, shit," Aryis said, her rare use of profanity putting a fine point on their situation. "He can claim that you and Quinn schemed with Decia and Safin to kill the Empress and take the power for yourselves. That you created the wraiths."

"That's insane," Athen protested. "Who would believe him?"

"Aryis is right," Quinn said, though it must have killed her to admit it. "Look at us. Two of the Empire's most wanted outlaws escaped from Cardin on a pirate ship, in the company of the Arch Justiciar and Kalla's successor. This looks like a botched power grab."

"He's currently the most powerful person in the Empire," Aryis replied. "With the throne empty and the Arch Justiciar gone, leadership defaults to the Arch Master."

Nyssa's stomach turned. Her half-cocked plan to win their freedom had slid into unmitigated disaster. "What do we do now?" She searched the faces around her, finally landing on Aryis.

"Ceril's in charge, but I don't think his lies will hold up for very long once the Justiciars regroup and start to investigate," Aryis replied. "He's bought himself a little time, but that's about it."

"Could he claim the throne for himself?"

Aryis shrugged. "With no clear successor, he would be Emperor until the Sun Council chose a new one. Which, now that I consider it, could take a long time given their propensity for infighting."

Nyssa couldn't leave fate in the hands of Decia's Justiciars. She didn't trust anyone in the Empire, not when Ceril held so much power now. "We go back and stop him before he does more damage."

"Absolutely not," Elias replied.

Nyssa frowned. He had spent the last two years helping her and Quinn, why the sudden caution? "Since when do you back down from a fight?"

Glancing around to the others, he raised his arms and let them drop in frustration. "Cardin is on high alert and no doubt everyone believes you killed Kalla. We go back, we all die."

"We can't just fucking let him get away with this." Nyssa began pacing, flexing her hands into fists, then relaxing them repeatedly. "We go back."

"I agree," Safin piped up.

"Shut it, kid. You don't have any authority here."

He stood, raising up to his full height, which barely came to Nyssa's chin. "We're on the same side here, Unworthy. You should be—"

"Shut. Up," she seethed, power crackling around her. Her magick had risen to the surface without thinking, her hot emotions drawing it out.

Safin's eyes went wide, and he stepped back as Decia slid in front of him, putting her body between them.

Did the Arch Justiciar really think she'd hurt a kid? Nyssa's shoulders slumped.

Fuck.

"I cannot allow this ship to return to Cardin and further endanger Safin's life. He's my only priority now," Decia said.

A gentle hand touched Nyssa's arm. She turned to find Fontaine frowning at her. "You know we can't go back. It would be suicide. Don't make Elias set himself against you, Nyssa."

Nyssa turned to the only person who could understand how badly she wanted to draw her blade across Ceril's throat. Quinn's face was dark. Tense. But she shook her head and mouthed *No.*

All the time training, biding her time, waiting...had it been for nothing? Patience wasn't her strongest trait, but she couldn't let anger and desperation push her into a corner.

Sighing, Nyssa gave in. "Fine."

"We'll figure out what to do once we're clear of Imperial waters," Elias said. He turned to Safin. "You look like you could use a hot meal, Emperor. Come with me to the mess. Buck will whip something up for you." He led the young man below deck.

Decia approached Medias, who pushed past her mother and walked across the ship to the starboard rail. Instead of pursuing her daughter, Decia followed after Safin. The others dispersed, though Reece wandered round the deck, quietly watching Medias.

Nyssa glanced at Quinn. "I'm so sorry." She had fucked up and had no idea what they were going to do next.

THE LONE JUSTICIAR

Reece joined Medias at the rail as the Justiciar stared out to sea. Though her emotions were impossible to sense, Reece had become somewhat adept at reading her moods. Medias would set herself apart and appear to be strong and unaffected, but it was pretense to a heart that could ache just as deeply as any other.

"Are you okay?" Reece asked, moving closer to the woman. She cupped Medias's chin in her hand, examining her split lip. It had stopped bleeding, but it needed to be cleaned. "You should get Safin to heal this."

Medias took Reece's hand and pulled it away from her face, lingering before letting go. "I am fine."

Reece sighed and decided that fighting to get Medias to tend to her wounded lip would be a losing battle. "My heart is glad that your mother is safe. And I understand why you kept her a secret."

Medias's gaze drifted out to sea before settling on Reece. Those red eyes once made Reece take pause, apprehension at being in a Justiciar's presence fighting with her desire to exude fearlessness. Their early encounters had often left Reece quaking inside.

"Decia is indeed an exacting creature. We do not have much in common."

"Same chin dimple, I noticed, like the top of a peach," Reece replied, trying to draw a smile out of the grim woman. She seemed sorely in need of a little respite from the morning's events.

Medias grunted and narrowed her eyes. "You never fail to grate on me."

"I can't sense your emotions, so I have to bring them out in other ways." Justiciars were frustrating blurs to Reece, changed at Ambershine to obscure their emotions. She had gotten used to Medias's warm, fuzzy presence. Not an emotion to sense, but at least it was *something*. A pleasant something at that.

"What do we do now?" Reece asked when Medias stayed silent. "With the Empress dead?"

Medias chewed the inside of her lip, a habit she seemed to partake in when thinking. But there was something different, something new. It seemed like a sadness clung to her, and Reece kicked herself—she didn't even think to ask how Medias was dealing with the death of Kalla.

"I wish I knew, but I have no fucking idea," Medias responded, scowling. "Pardon my language."

Reece chuckled. "Nyssa rubbing off on you?"

"In all the worst possible ways."

A backhanded compliment in Medias's unique style. It was one of the many little things that Reece had come to enjoy very much.

"Everything is so screwed up," Reece said, a chill running down her spine. Her thoughts turned back home to Ocean's Rest. Despite her argument with Lilliana and her uncertain future, a homesickness nipped at her. "It's strange, I didn't realize how much I'd miss Ocean's Rest."

"I miss it too. I came to feel at home there." The Justiciar's tone was soft as her gaze seared into Reece.

Reece swallowed, refusing to allow that look to undo her. "Come back to the room. Get a mug of hot tea while I tend to your lip with some hazel oil. You need a distraction from everything that's happened today. Maybe relax for a bit with a book. I have a new one for you."

"Another shamelessly filthy romance?"

Reece chuckled. "Like the one you devoured in mere days? No, this one is a collection of five horror stories. Unless you lack the temperament for such a thing?"

A heavy sigh left Medias. "I could use a cup of tea."

THE DEEP BLUE SEA

Nyssa leaned against the quarterdeck steps and smiled up at Fontaine standing at the ship's wheel. They were a day out from their debacle in Cardin. "How far away are we from Unbound waters?"

Fontaine tilted her head to the side and shook out her white hair. "Two days, at most, but we have weather coming."

"I know."

Elias sat cross-legged next to his quartermaster, chewing on the end of a pipe, a map spread across his lap. "I'm thinking we should go south, see if we can't find some help in the Fingers."

"Pfft," Fontaine replied. "We didn't leave there in good standing."

"Do we leave anywhere in good standing?" he asked, running his pale, whitish-blue hands through a mop of dark-blue hair. He eyed Nyssa. "The life of a pirate, eh?"

Nyssa laughed, turning her attention back to Fontaine. "Are you not cold up there?"

The farther they got out to sea, the colder the weather had become, but Fontaine didn't seem affected. She wore leather pants, a loose white shirt halfway open down the front, and no shoes. Her long, shimmery hair flowed in the wind.

Did she try to look gorgeous or did she stumble into it every damn day?

"Cold is a state of mind," Fontaine replied with a smile.

"At least she's not naked," Quinn interjected from where she sat on the quarterdeck stairs.

"Yeah, there's that," Nyssa said. She perked up when she saw Safin come up from below deck. An idea sparked. "Hey, want to have a little fun?"

A low rumble came from Quinn, somewhere between a sigh and a growl. Nyssa had come to love the sound. "I'm afraid to ask what this 'fun' is."

Cheering up, Nyssa bounced on her toes. "Watch me." Once, she had been hazed by the crew not long after being taken hostage for ransom. *Time to test the kid's mettle.*

"I'm suspicious at how gleeful you are," Quinn replied, perking an eyebrow.

"Be honest, a part of you loves to watch."

Quinn clicked her tongue. "A little."

"I *love* watching," Fontaine said.

Snorting, Nyssa grinned and waited for Safin to complete his lazy stroll across the deck, Decia trailing close behind. The kid had been told to be on deck after breakfast but still managed to be very late.

An expression of simmering condescension had settled on his face. Nyssa was familiar with the rich assholes of the Empire, having had a few to contend with during her time at the Emerald Order. Their haughtiness tended to disappear while learning Ithais-Toru, when fist met face. That training humbled everyone.

"I see you found some suitable clothes," Nyssa remarked, giving Safin a once-over. The worn gray denim pants and a dark-navy peacoat topped off with a scarf suited the young man.

"Plundered clothes. I'm wearing plundered clothes," Safin replied, frowning deeply. "Did someone die in these?"

"Well, you look like you belong, dressed properly for the sea and the cold. And I don't think those are a dead man's clothes." She peered up to the quarterdeck. "Fontaine?"

The woman shrugged down at them.

Nyssa bent over and picked up a mop, handing it to Safin with a smile. "Look alert, sunshine. While you're on this ship, you pitch in. Seeing as Ceril would have killed you, I think a sparkling clean deck is the least you can do for us as recompense."

Safin blinked in the overcast haze of midmorning. "I am not mopping your deck."

Nyssa let out a belly laugh. "Oh yes, you are. You stay on this ship, you earn your keep." She took him by the wrist and shoved a mop into his hand.

Safin scowled at her while Decia looked on. The Arch Justiciar didn't seem interested in defending him against every slight, which was a good instinct. He needed to fight his own battles. Just like Nyssa did growing up.

"We asked the same of Nyssa when she came aboard," Elias said.

"You mean when I was kidnapped on the high seas by a scurrilous pirate and his crew of ruffians?" she groused over her shoulder.

"*Handsome* pirate," he corrected.

"She mopped the deck?" Safin asked.

"She started a fight with the crew and then got her ass kicked by a chicken," Elias replied, giving him a wink.

Safin didn't appear amused. "I am the Emperor of the Areshi Empire. I do not scrub boat decks."

Nyssa stepped closer to Safin, drawing a look from Decia, who appeared ready to strike if need be. Arrogance wasn't an unfamiliar trait. Nyssa had been accused of it plenty of times, though she preferred to refer to it as *pride*.

"What I learned out here on this ship is that we all depend on each other for survival. We work together to make the Whisper run fast and efficient. You keep the boat clean. Max oversees the crew on deck and the sails. Buck cooks for us and tends to our wounds. Everyone here earns their place. Even an Areshi Emperor." Nyssa stuck a finger against Safin's chest to drive her point home.

"Nyssa," a voice said, a slight tone of warning as if to insinuate an overstep on her part. She turned to find Medias behind her. When had she snuck on deck? "Please remove your finger from the Emperor's chest."

Nyssa smiled and clapped Safin on the back. "You'll catch on, kid."

"You should address me properly."

Patience waning, Nyssa caught Quinn's eye. Quinn shook her head in warning, as if telling her to stay out of trouble.

And yet, trouble seemed a fine thing to step into this morning. Nyssa felt downright frisky. "Listen, kid, I have ten years on you and you're not my Emperor, so lose the attitude."

Safin glared at Nyssa and dropped the mop, letting it clatter on the deck. She couldn't help but smirk at the audacity.

Medias held up a piece of paper, her eyes grim. "We have more pressing matters."

Nyssa's smile disappeared. Something's wrong. "What is it?"

Medias hesitated, bowing her head before addressing Safin. "We received a message just now via the ship's messenger bowl. Emperor, your mother is missing."

Safin's face went slack, his arrogance and bold defiance melting away. "No…" He rounded on Nyssa. "This is your fault! You brought your Unworthy curse to the Empress and now my family!" He tried to shove her, but she caught his wrists, holding fast. He trembled under her grip.

"I'm sorry," she said, letting him go.

"We need to go back. What if…what if Ceril did something to her?" His anger was understandable. But it was fear that hung on his face.

"You heard Elias. Going back is suicide. I wish we could, trust me…I want Ceril to pay for everything he's done to me. To Quinn." Nyssa took a deep breath, her heart softening toward Safin. "We'll figure out what to do next."

"You truly are cursed, Unworthy."

Nyssa hated that the damn insult actually hurt. Safin was immature. Naïve. But also in an impossible, insane position.

Nyssa hooked her thumb into her belt, glancing around, tapping her finger, trying to preserve some measure of patience. Their argument had garnered some attention, with Medias looking on and Athen and Aryis huddled by the mainmast, helping the crew.

"I want to keep you alive."

Safin's eyes darkened. "I have a responsibility to act. I can't honor Kalla's memory by running away."

Nyssa gritted her teeth, her stomach twisting. "You want to honor Kalla's memory?" She stepped back and turned her gaze to Decia. "Let me tell you about Kalla and your Arch Justiciar. Twenty-seven years ago, Kalla found a couple of smugglers willing to kidnap a baby from Thu'Dain—a baby they were told was special. And when the job was done, Ceril, Decia, and a group of Justiciars killed those smugglers and sank their ship at Kalla's orders."

Decia narrowed her eyes at Nyssa.

Nyssa turned to Safin. "Those smugglers were my parents. And Quinn was that baby. They gave her to Ceril to raise, but all he did was keep her isolated and use her power to poke around some very forbidden spell books. Your precious Empress Kalla had the blood of my parents all over her hands. Before you laud her memory, understand what she was capable of."

Safin looked over at the Arch Justiciar. "Is this true?"

She nodded once.

Nyssa stepped closer to Decia. "The only reason you're alive is because I respect Medias too much to kill you."

Decia's eyes wavered, the only sign of any emotion. How Nyssa burned to hit the woman, to make her *hurt*.

A rumble of thunder echoed across the sky. A number of those gathered around looked up. In the distance, lightning skittered along the underbelly of the dark clouds above, and the scent of rain hung in the air, promising a storm.

"Nyssa?" Elias said, his eyebrows arched.

"That's not me. We're headed for weather," Nyssa said, the ache in her leg confirming as much.

"Just had to check," he replied.

Stepping back, she addressed Safin. "You need to know exactly what we're dealing with. Ceril isn't just a threat to your throne. I fear for the whole Empire and its people. The wraiths that attacked Ocean's Rest? The possession at Wayland that almost killed Aryis? That was all him."

"And now that monster could have my mother." Tears welled up in the young man's eyes. He was quick to wipe them away.

Nyssa took a big breath and looked at Quinn, at a loss of what to say.

"Safin Vonner," Fontaine called down from the quarterdeck, "you are in excellent company. Some of the most courageous people on this earth, myself included, are on this ship with you. We will see you through this, understand, child?"

He looked up at Fontaine. The woman could be flighty, frivolous, and downright bewildering, but when she put a bit of bass in her voice, Nyssa was reminded that she had lived for countless centuries and knew more about the world than anyone she had ever met. The Old Folk were among the oldest, most mysterious races on earth, and fucking daunting when they wanted to be.

After a moment, Safin bowed his head and turned away, walking over to the side of the ship. The water was fairly calm for winter, but Nyssa knew that would change quickly once the storm rolled in. Winds and rain would roil the sea, and Elias would steer them safely through it, as he always did.

Nyssa ran her hand through her hair, considering their plight. They would have to figure out where to go and what to do, but for now, the only fight they could engage in was a war of information. She looked to Decia. "We need to send out a message. Tell our side of the story, claim the throne in Safin's name. It may not do much, but...maybe it will plant a seed of doubt and get your Justiciars poking around. Any danger in doing that?"

Decia glanced over at Safin. "Combating lies with the truth is always dangerous when confronting men like Ceril. No telling what he'll do."

"We're already in danger and on the run. That kid is the rightful heir to the throne, according to all your precious Imperial rules, so let's create a little strife."

Decia stood silent, her eyes fixed on Nyssa. Finally, she nodded. "I will craft a message and send it wide across the Empire."

"No. Send it across the world. Make Ceril sweat when Imperial allies start asking questions." He would likely lie himself out of any immediate trouble, but pressure, even a small amount, would be something.

"Fine," Decia replied, her tone terse. Taking orders from Nyssa likely didn't sit well with the Arch Justiciar, but Nyssa didn't much care.

The wind kicked up, and Nyssa rubbed her leg, wincing from the ache of an old knife wound. "You should both get below deck. I figure the storm's here in half an hour."

Done helping the crew, Athen beckoned Safin to follow, offering the young man a smile. "Come on." Perhaps he, with his more measured, gentle ways, could give Safin some comfort and confidence, even when they had no idea what to do next.

The crew got to work preparing the Whisper for the winter storm on the Saldurn Sea. It would pale in comparison to the storms on the Black Sea, but it would at least ease Safin into what one on the ocean felt like. She took one last look out at the waves before heading below deck with Quinn.

They returned to their stateroom where Nyssa pulled off her jacket and Quinn sat on her bunk, flexing her left hand.

"I can feel the storm coming in these fingers," she remarked, indicating her ring and little finger, both slightly crooked. Broken courtesy of Suvi Rell's guard when Quinn was her prisoner.

The boat rocked gently beneath them, but it would get more violent in an hour or two. Nyssa did a quick scan of the room to secure loose items before taking a seat on the floor at Quinn's feet, leaning back against her legs. It didn't take long for Quinn to start weaving her fingers in Nyssa's hair.

"I don't know what to do about our boy Emperor," Nyssa grumbled, telling Quinn about his plan to return to Cardin.

"You feel tense."

"I'm angry."

"At Ceril?"

"At Ceril," said Nyssa. "At myself. At fucking everything." She balled up her fists and tilted her head back to rest it on Quinn's knees.

Quinn gathered up Nyssa's curly auburn locks and moved them aside, exposing the back of her neck, rubbing and working away the day's tension, sending shivers down her spine

Nyssa closed her eyes and sighed, taking comfort in Quinn's warm presence. They settled into silence. The wind picked up outside the Whisper, its rocking becoming more pronounced as the storm drew closer.

Quinn hummed a song and feathered her fingers down Nyssa's neck. "You know in your gut what we need to do. We have to protect Safin."

"I thought you wanted nothing to do with the Areshi Empire?"

Quinn worked her thumbs into Nyssa's neck, making the tension in her muscles slowly release. "He's just a kid. I didn't have anyone to protect me when I was his age. If I'd had someone like you looking out for me..." Quinn's hands stopped moving, her voice faltering. After a moment, she leaned over and kissed the top of Nyssa's head and her hands resumed rubbing Nyssa's neck. "But I didn't. Safin needs us. He needs *you*."

Nyssa swallowed back the lump in her throat. She had already messed so much up. Perhaps it was better if Safin had nothing to do with them?

"When we save others, we save ourselves," Quinn said, repeating what Nyssa's father had taught her. It was his reason for adopting her.

Quinn taking Eron's words, his lesson, to heart meant so much.

Nyssa caught her hand. "I love you."

"I know," Quinn replied, a playful lilt in her tone.

Cheeky woman.

They settled in, waiting on the storm. Nyssa enjoyed Quinn's soft fingertips on her neck and shoulders while she ruminated on what Quinn had said. Nyssa owed Safin nothing, and Decia even less, but Ceril could do real damage if he claimed the throne. He would have the means and the drive to pursue them across the world, of that she was certain. They would never be safe.

A half hour later, when the storm hit, Nyssa moved to the middle of the floor and sat cross-legged, letting her magick flow and her senses expand beyond her room, through the ship, and over the small patch of sea the Whisper occupied. She unfurled herself into the sky as the storm surged around her, thunder and lightning rolling within the clouds. The colors of the ambient magick of the world swirled and flowed—bright blues, deep purples, and a thrumming, pulsing gray that sang in almost imperceptible low tones.

While she floated high above the sea, she did her best to keep the worst of it away from the Whisper. If needed, she could dissipate it entirely with some effort, but Fontaine had once told her that the world needed to express itself and it was best she stand to the side and marvel at its power.

And marvel she did.

As she strove to dive into the storm, to feel its sharp intensity, another energy enveloped her. A smile crossed her face at the dark coiling magick mixing with the blue energy that crackled in the clouds.

She felt Quinn's hands slip into hers.

Quinn's presence twisted around Nyssa, and they dove deeper into the storm. Something just beyond Nyssa's grasp toyed with her, like a mote darting and shifting as she tried to zero in on it.

The deep thrumming grew louder, settling into a rhythm with her heartbeat.

The song of the sea.

The power was something she had felt before, under the waves of the Black Sea. When she drowned two years prior, something was with her, there in the deep waiting.

"Where are you?" Nyssa whispered as the thunder rumbled within her soul.

CALM

Medias leaned over the starboard side of the ship—*or was it port, she could never remember*—and drank in the chill night air, the brine nipping at her nose. The previous night's storm had passed, its last remnants carried on the stiff wind.

When she'd first set foot on Hannah's Whisper, she claimed to dislike boats, but she couldn't deny the calmness that the sea brought her.

She needed that calm now. She had betrayed the Empire, and Decia, as Arch Justiciar, couldn't ignore her duty. Treason called for punishment. And Decia could be counted on to enforce the law, as she had always done.

Medias would do her last duty as a Justiciar when finally summoned to answer for her choices. Best the Cursed Gods and their friends not find out, otherwise they would try to interfere.

Nyssa would grab her and yell.

Quinn would cross her arms and scowl, and then scold her without raising her voice.

And then Reece...Reece would have *words*. So many words, some that would likely test her resolve to perform the Crossing. With the others, she could be strong, but with Reece, it was proving harder and harder. Those dark eyes unraveled her.

Medias raised her gaze to the sky. The night's stars twinkled high above her, cold and distant but so gorgeous, dotting the blackness. The almost full moon washed the deck of the Whisper in soft illumination. She found herself loving the sounds of the boat at night: the rustling of the sails as they filled, the dings of metal against wood, the creaking of the ship itself as it parted the sea, and the slap of water against the side of the boat.

Here, she found a modicum of temporary peace.

Medias tightened her hands around the perfectly polished handrail, letting the cold air help clarify her thoughts. She had done the right thing by protecting Nyssa and Quinn and their friends, hadn't she?

Footfalls on the deck roused her out of her thoughts, and she turned to find Quinn.

"Taking a break?" Medias asked. Several people had crammed into Elias's stateroom to work up a plan of what to do next. No solutions had offered themselves up, and soon the alcohol had begun to flow, Fontaine insisting that rum could dislodge a brilliant idea or two.

"I used to lament my time in solitude at Arcton Citadel. Now, surrounded by people all the time, I find a small part of myself missing a bit of stillness." Quinn sighed, her breath fogging the air in front of her. She shivered in the cold, her freckles standing out on her reddened cheeks.

"Why is it whenever I find myself alone, either you or Reece show up?"

Quinn laughed, her emerald eyes twinkling in the warm light offered by the orbs strung over the deck. "I like you, Medias. If you prefer some privacy, please tell me to fuck off."

Strangely enough, Medias didn't mind Quinn's company. The woman was like herself—a bit of a quiet watcher, someone who liked to sit back and observe. There was a bevy of information to be gleaned from almost every situation by simply being quiet.

"I do not mind your company," Medias confessed. "You are less tedious than most others."

Another chuckle. "That's quite effusive praise. I feel as though you and I have just become best friends."

Medias grunted. Quinn was far easier to endure than Nyssa, who seemed to take delight in poking and prodding. Though as much as she huffed and made a show of being annoyed, Medias didn't mind. The Cursed Gods and their friends proved to be a welcome addition to her life, even if it took her a year or two to admit as much to herself. Though she'd never admit it to others.

Who is this woman I've become?

Quinn sighed and looked out toward the ocean. "I can never quite understand how the sea is this magnificently beautiful. It's breathtaking."

Instead of fumbling for a response, Medias merely grunted again. But Quinn was right—there was something enchanting about the sea.

"Quinn! I thought we sent you for more rum. What are you doing up here?" a jovial voice called out.

Nyssa strode across the deck, her feet bare under her leather pants, a smile plastered on her face. She wore a thin cotton blouse that billowed as she approached. Such a garment surely didn't afford much warmth.

"Are you looking for me or the alcohol?" Quinn asked.

Nyssa narrowed her eyes. "That's a trick question and I refuse to fall for it."

"Blacksea," Medias said, "how are you not freezing?"

"Well, that's what the rum is for, Justiciar." Nyssa came to a stop beside Quinn. One need not be an empath like Reece to see how the two women beamed when together. "If we have more rum, perhaps we'll figure out what to fucking do about our Ceril problem."

"I'll get your rum from the storeroom," Quinn said, leaning into Nyssa to give her a nudge.

"Please don't touch me so suggestively, Medias will get the wrong idea," Nyssa joked.

"I already have the vision of you two 'making tea' burned into my brain," Medias said. Quinn, quite predictably, looked intensely uncomfortable. Nyssa, on the other hand, donned that smirk of hers meant to charm.

"Is it, now? Revisit it often, do you?" she asked with a wink.

"You are, as always, without shame, Blacksea," Medias said.

Shrugging, Nyssa pulled at Quinn. "Let's go hunt down that bottle of rum. Elias and Fontaine are running through their connections on the

Eastern Continent, trying to figure out if there's anyone who can help us. And it turned into them regaling us with their ridiculous adventures."

Quinn cocked her head. "I think they embellish a bit."

Nyssa held her fingers an inch apart. "A wee bit, I'd reckon. But even Safin smiled for a second. I think the kid is warming up to us."

"Come on," Quinn said, tugging at Nyssa's sleeve. The two women started to head back to the stairs leading below deck. Quinn stopped and turned around. "Hey, come back to Elias's stateroom when you've had enough fresh air. I know at least one person misses you."

Medias narrowed her eyes at Quinn, though it was Nyssa who wore a sly grin. Laughter accompanied both women out of her sight.

These were the two gods she had pledged her loyalty to, their fate and hers tangled up, as her father believed. Much of what she had done, vowing to protect them and their friends, she owed to her father's urging that she forge her own path. It was the one argument she could remember her parents having: her mother insistent on her joining Ambershine to become a Justiciar, her father wanting to wait, to find out what drove Medias's passions.

Unfortunately, her mother won out, but her father was always there to support her, even as she turned inward. Even when she knew some of his visions included her and what she would eventually do. How she would hurt people. But he kept telling her that her path lay with the Cursed Gods.

Her father never truly understood how being a Justiciar would make it impossible for her to split her loyalties. How could he? When she chose to pledge her loyalty to Nyssa and Quinn, her legitimacy as a Justiciar ceased, and soon she'd have to contend with the consequences of her choices.

Medias shoved the weight of her decisions to the side, drinking in the night air instead. Though the thought of sleep was tempting, she found herself wanting to go listen to Elias and Fontaine spin their tales of adventure. Turning away from the sea, she came face-to-face with Nyssa.

"Nyssa? Did you forget—"

No, not Nyssa. The eyes were wrong....

Her magick flicked at her fingertips, but a hood flew down over her head, cutting her off from the world. Something sharp pierced her arm, and she tried to yank away from the pain, but it ripped at her skin and everything became fuzzy.

Medias cursed, admonishing herself for letting down her guard, even out in the middle of the sea. As she sank to her knees and hands grabbed at her, a thought crossed her mind...

Mother would be so disappointed.

Nyssa drained the rest of her Basai rum, happy to be below deck and warm again after checking on Medias and Quinn. She had grown used to the liquor—sweet and potent and as good for cleaning out a wound as drinking—and slid her mug toward Athen.

"Top me off, big man," she said, giving him a wink. Dawn was a few short hours away, but they had gotten no closer to a solution of where to go to keep Safin safe. Decia had originally objected adding alcohol to the mix, but all of them needed something to relieve the tension of the last few days.

After the drinks started flowing, her objections faded, and she settled in, nursing her own glass of Elias's blackberry wine.

They were celebrating a victory of sorts. They had received a message from Ocean's Rest that morning, sent wide to everyone with a messenger bowl on this side of the world. In the message, Lilliana had declared Ocean's Rest's loyalty to Safin Vonner, refuting Ceril's claim to the Areshi throne. It was a bold, perhaps reckless decision, but one Athen and Reece were certain Lilliana would make after they messaged her a rundown of what had happened in Cardin.

Nyssa would take the small wins where they could get them, though she still didn't know what action Lilliana's declaration would garner from Ceril, the Sun Council, or any of the lesser Houses spread across the Empire. They'd wait and see in the morning if anything had changed, but for now, they drank.

Fontaine spun one of her stories, going off on a tangent whilst trying to remember the name of a minor royal family member she once knew in the Strings, off the far south end of the Eastern Continent. She was once stuck in the body of a small boy after she'd botched a transformation. The Old Folk were rather mysterious about their ability to change forms, and Nyssa didn't press for details, but if anyone could find entertainment in a massive fuck up, it was Fontaine.

"She was stuck like that for a week. Worst week of my life, with all the complaining about how she couldn't reach anything. All the while, we were island-hopping, trying to evade pirates that wanted the Whisper for themselves," Elias said, squinting at the label of a bottle of liquor he pulled down off a shelf in his stateroom. "Thu'Dainian whiskey? We really need to get back to pirating if we're relegated to this swill."

Quinn laughed and shot a sly glance at Nyssa that made her heart thump. Quinn knew damn well what she was doing, flirting without saying a word, though she would deny it later. Nyssa shook her head and shot a smile back, fighting fire with fire. Drinking and flirting were the only distractions from the growing realization that they had dwindling options and few allies to fall back on...and none that would risk harboring fugitives from the Areshi Empire.

Athen glanced across the room to where Aryis sat, his one remaining golden eye fixated on the woman as he absentmindedly stroked his bushy brown beard. If he was trying to hide his concern for her, it wasn't working.

Not that Aryis seemed to notice. She was busy chatting Safin up, building a rapport with the young man, who nursed a glass of wine. Safin had tried to convince them that he could handle Basai rum, but Elias refused, giving him wine under Decia's watchful eye.

Safin made himself busy with a piece of paper, folding it over and over again. Finally, he held it up. He had created an osprey, the sigil of House Devitt. He handed the small paper hawk to Aryis, drawing a big smile—one of the few Nyssa had seen on her face since getting back from the Realm of Shadows. Though her confusion had faded, she was far more withdrawn than Nyssa would have liked, talking to herself more frequently.

"Where did Medias get off to?" Elias asked. "I actually miss her looming in the corner and staring at us all."

Reece laughed. "Shall I go get her?"

Medias appeared at the door and held up a bottle.

"No need!" Nyssa clapped. "That's my girl! Give it here."

Fingers dug into Nyssa's arm, and she turned to find Reece grasping onto her, her eyes wide.

"That's not Medias," she hissed.

Before Nyssa could move, the room exploded in light.

STORM

Nyssa roused to darkness. No sight or sound. Everything dulled, including her magick. The only thing she felt was the warmth in her chest that let her know Quinn was near. She tried moving, aware she was lying down, but her arms were trapped behind her, bound.

A horrible memory sparked in the back of her mind. She had experienced this before—dulled senses, the world not within reach—at the Emerald Order when the other adepts thought it would be fun to fasten a blackout hood over her head and take their shots at her. She had tried to fight but hyperventilated and passed out. Eron had found her, a crying, blubbering mess when he got the hood off of her.

Nyssa's heart began to pound in her chest, and she struggled against her bonds, shaking her head violently. A scream ripped out of her as she gave in to sheer panic, deadening immediately within the hood.

Hands gripped her shoulders and legs, restraining her to stop her flailing.

A few moments later, the blackout hood was removed, and sound flooded in, assaulting her senses and making her head pound. Lying on the deck of the Whisper, her eyes slowly adjusted to the dim light of the orbs flickering above her. She found herself facing Quinn, who blinked, her eyes moving slowly. A void collar around her neck.

Nyssa's fingers curled, biting into her palms.

From the tightness around her neck and unresponsive magick, she knew she had been placed in a void collar too.

"Quinn?" she choked out, breaking into a coughing fit, the bitter taste of ash and bile lining her mouth. She could guess what had happened, recognizing the lingering aftertaste of Coldlight smoke, her tongue thick with it. She had been hit with Coldlight bombs once before, when their ship was ambushed by the Obsidian Rule.

"Quinn," she repeated. Quinn blinked, furrowing her eyebrows and struggling against her bindings.

"Nyssa?" Her voice was strained.

"You okay?"

"I think so."

A line of blood trickled from Quinn's hairline and dripped onto the deck.

Nyssa's eyes focused. Her heart leaped into her throat when she saw her friends across from her, bound and gagged on their knees. Athen, Aryis, Medias, Reece, Elias, Decia, and Fontaine, all in void collars. But the crew...where was the crew?

If they're dead...Nyssa gritted her teeth, fighting against the black fear rising within her.

Adepts in dark-green leather pants and jackets milled around the deck. Obsidian Rule. Of fucking course.

It was at that moment Nyssa knew they were going to die.

"Let my friends go," she said, her words slurred. She locked eyes with Athen. He struggled in his bindings, but with a void collar around his neck, he was helpless.

"On your knees, Unworthy," a gruff, unfriendly voice said.

Rough hands yanked Nyssa up to her knees, and she instantly bent forward, clamping her eyes shut. The sudden movement made her stomach lurch, and she did her best not to fall over from dizziness. Quinn was pulled up to her knees, wincing.

Black boots appeared in front of Nyssa. Suddenly, the cogs of her memory snapped into place and she recognized the voice. A hot blaze of hate shot through her. She turned her gaze up at the woman standing over her. An Ashken woman of reddish-pink skin, unruly black hair, and filed-down horns.

Ina Ruggen. An Emerald Order adept—now Ashcloak—who had tormented Nyssa for years. She was the one who had shoved Nyssa's head into a blackout hood. And when Nyssa was nine years old, Ina had wrenched her arm behind her back and used magick to shatter her bones. Once older, as Nyssa started to master Ithais-Toru and seek retribution, Ina found herself in the dirt with two broken fingers and Order Masters prying them apart before Nyssa could break a third...and a fourth...

"Ina?" Nyssa mumbled.

"Master Ashcloak Ruggen," Ina corrected. "You will address me as such, Unworthy."

So she is a Master now. "I'm not a guildie anymore. I don't have to do shit," Nyssa replied, trying to clear the cobwebs in her head. She locked eyes with Ina and gave her a wicked smile. "How are those fingers of yours, Ruggen?"

Ina's fist smashed into Nyssa's temple.

Not the first time her smart mouth had got her punched in the face.

"Stop!" Quinn ordered, her voice weak and raspy.

Her protests only served to get Nyssa punched again. The skin over her eye split—an all too familiar feeling from her time as a kid fighting back. Hot blood streamed down her face and dripped to the deck. She wavered on her knees, afraid she'd topple over.

"Untie me and try that again, Ina," Nyssa said. "Let's see how many fingers I can break this time before you beg me to stop."

Ina crouched down until she was eye level with Nyssa. "You've earned this, traitor. I only wish your death would last to get some measure of justice for what you did to First Master Greye."

Nyssa swallowed, fighting back tears at the mention of his name in an enemy's mouth. "I didn't kill him. Think what you want of me, but he was my father. I didn't—"

A swift fist to Nyssa's midsection made her sputter, blood misting before her face. She tried to take a breath but choked, her muscles seizing. Ina stood and walked a few feet away.

"Breathe, Nyssa," Quinn said. "Just slow down and breathe."

Quinn was trying to keep her calm, talking Nyssa through her anger and pain. She loved Quinn for it, but in the end, it wouldn't matter.

Nyssa bowed her head. "I think we're screwed, Quinn."

"Yeah, coming to that conclusion myself." There was a pause. "Nyssa?"

Nyssa raised her eyes and looked over at Quinn, her jaw tight. She tried her best not to show fear, but she was trembling.

"I'm sorry, Freckles. I promised that you'd never be in a collar again."

"This isn't your fault."

Tears rushed at Nyssa again, and she blinked them back. "I'm still sorry."

Quinn nodded, her bottom lip quivering. "Nyssa…I'm scared," she whispered.

A breath caught in Nyssa's throat, and she tightened her fists until her knuckles burned. "I am too."

Nyssa swiveled her head, trying to see how many Obsidian Rule adepts surrounded them. Not that they could do much in void collars with their hands bound behind them. There were at least twenty, but only one Ashcloak—Ina.

So she's betrayed her oath and turned traitor to follow Ceril.

The Rule adepts stiffened, turning their attention to something behind Nyssa. She glanced over her shoulder. Two assassins stood, Safin between them. And lashed to the port side of the Whisper, was a large Imperial vessel. A warship. Several gangplanks hung between the two ships. But how? No one on their crew had raised an alarm.

Nyssa breathed deeply and waited.

Ceril Anelos swept aboard the Whisper, his black cloak billowing around his legs. The Archivist they had met at the Sun Palace, Baran Sennaq, trotted at his side.

Two Rule adepts shoved Safin forward, his hands bound, but lacking a collar. Perhaps Ceril didn't think a teenage healer posed much of a threat. The Rule adepts pulled the young Emperor over to stand next to Ceril.

Safin kept his chin up and put on a brave face, but his hands shook. He locked eyes with Nyssa and gave her a terse nod. The kid was smart, he had to have an inkling how this all would end.

Ceril glanced over at Athen and the others before turning his attention on Nyssa, his pale-blue eyes roaming across every inch of her before landing on Quinn for the same examination.

"The Cursed Gods," he said, his voice low. "You have much to answer for."

"You killed the Empress. And it seems you've turned one Ashcloak into a traitor." Nyssa growled before addressing Ina. "Honorless dog."

Ina stared down at her, eyebrows wrinkling. So the bitch didn't like being shamed. Nyssa didn't care. Eron had tried to instill a code of honor in all his adepts. Seemed it didn't take with Ruggen.

Ceril slowly scanned the ship before settling back on Nyssa. "How you've managed to survive this long possessing such deficient intelligence is astounding. You two marched right into the heart of the Empire and inadvertently handed me an astounding opportunity. You might as well have slit Kalla's throat yourselves."

Ina's head whipped from Nyssa to Ceril.

She...she doesn't know the truth, does she?

Ceril raised his eyebrows at her. "You have a decision to make here, Master Ashcloak Ruggen. Raise your sword against me or become the First Master of the Emerald Order. I've yet to fill that role as we're...still in mourning over Eron Greye." He smirked.

Nyssa roared, her anger incoherent and guttural. The rope around her wrists bit into her skin as she strained to rip his fucking throat out. Someone started laughing and stepped out from behind another adept.

Efla Eld'on. Eron's assassin.

"I'll fucking kill you," Nyssa growled.

Efla stared down at her, cold hate radiating off of her. Nyssa had killed Efla's brother Tann in a fight for her life. She would have ended Efla too if she hadn't almost died herself.

"I've waited two years for this, Unworthy," Efla said.

"What did he promise you?" Quinn asked Efla, before looking at the rest of the Rule adepts. "What did he promise the lot of you to turn your back on your duty?"

Ceril answered for them. "The Obsidian Rule has languished in the shadow of Ambershine and the Emerald Order for centuries. They do the hard, ugly, dirty work to keep the Empire safe and in power. Gathering intelligence, eliminating threats, existing in the darkness. It's time they be recognized."

"Like you, asshole? You fucking entitled bastard, jealous and envious of everyone that has ever moved ahead of you," Quinn replied. "You tried to kill Nyssa because she didn't fit your ideal of an adept. And you killed Eron for it. Petty retribution from a small man." Her voice dripped with venom, a pure hate that Nyssa had never heard so ferociously expressed before.

Ceril moved quickly, quicker than Nyssa would have thought him capable, and grabbed a handful of Quinn's hair, yanking her head back, thrusting his face inches away from hers. Nyssa tried to get to her feet, but Efla shot forward and buried a fist in her midsection, crumpling her to the deck.

"You are an ungrateful wretch," Ceril spat at Quinn. "You want to be free? Your pathetic life was never your own to begin with, girl."

Ceril let go of Quinn and stepped back. "I debated sparing you from death, as you still have some use, but alas, the Empire needs justice. Otherwise, you'd be on a leash."

"This is who you serve now," Nyssa said, locking eyes with Ina. "Eron would be ashamed of you."

"What is your decision, Ashcloak?" Ceril asked.

Ina looked around the deck before a smile crept onto her face. "First Master Ruggen does sound rather fitting."

Ceril laughed, the sound scraping against Nyssa's ears. "I had heard you were an ambitious woman. You will make an excellent First Master."

"Fucking bitch," Nyssa breathed.

"You were always going to end up like this," Ina said. "On your knees, awaiting death. You should have left the Order as a child, spared everyone the embarrassment of your presence."

"How did you even find us?" Nyssa asked.

Ceril smirked and gestured toward Decia. "I had help."

Decia's voice was cold, yet certain. "I would never help you."

"Not knowingly. But you grow lax in the presence of others, Arch Justiciar." He nodded at Baran. "My faithful scribe here has your blood on file. Easy to track you using it and a few blood spells."

So Ceril had corrupted an Imperial scribe. Who else did he have doing his bidding? Baran looked up at Ceril with a smile and he caressed her cheek.

"You've done well, Baran. Now it is time to serve me in a far different way."

He stepped away from her, a purple glow forming around his hands, his fingers moving in intricate patterns.

Spellweaving.

"The term *blood wraith* is a misnomer, did you know that? They're not created with blood magick at all. Bone magick is responsible for such fearsome creatures and it's a wonderful, terrifying discipline. Difficult to learn and almost impossible to truly master. The key to creating a blood wraith out of a living being is patience."

A low drone filled the air, making Nyssa's blood run cold. Something was *wrong*.

Her skin pricked up a moment before pain crashed into her in agonizing waves. She doubled over. Even with void collar around her neck, she could feel magick in her bones, scraping across her body like a filleting knife. The mark on her chin burned.

Beside her, Quinn cried out, tensing up.

"You two can feel that?" Ceril asked with a smirk. "Fascinating."

The purple energy glowed brighter and began to pulsate. He lifted his hands up, murmuring something under his breath. "I've found creating a blood wraith is best done over time, like a slow-moving infection. The subject doesn't even realize what's happening. Then, it's simply a matter of tugging at all the strings at once."

Tendrils of purple magick wove around Baran. She shook her head, looking to Ceril, her mouth opening and closing. The purple tendrils spun around her for a moment before collapsing in on her and disappearing, as if they sank into her body.

Baran dropped to her knees, heaving and retching. She pulled at her clothes, her head whipping back and forth. A shriek tore from her throat, and her arms distended, growing longer in strange, jerky fits and starts, accompanied by the sickening *pop* and *crack* of bones. The rest of her body followed suit, her jacket and clothes ripping, falling away. Her skin turned black, splitting under the pressure of the grotesque growth, healing over just to split again. Her blood dripped to the deck and hissed as it burned the wood.

Another crushing wave of magick slammed into Nyssa, and she collapsed forward. Panting, she turned her gaze up to Baran, whose face was barely human anymore save for her eyes. Baran let loose a silent scream, staring at Nyssa, panic clear in her eyes. Her jaw popped and unhinged, ripping her mouth open. Teeth burst out of their sockets and tumbled to the deck, pushed out by sharp fangs that grew in their place.

The human was gone, transformed into a blood wraith. It lunged across the deck toward Nyssa.

"Wait!" Ceril ordered. "She's not for you."

The creature stopped, its body rising and falling as it breathed deep, its fangs bared. Its pupils turned red. Nyssa struggled back up to her knees, keeping her eyes on the wraith, her heart thundering in her chest. It didn't make a move toward her, obeying its master.

The low drone of the bone magick grew louder, cutting through Nyssa like a blade. The newly-born blood wraith shuddered and drew up to its full height. It locked eyes with her and unfurled its wings, dark and leathery. Nyssa gritted her teeth as it opened its mouth and roared at the sky.

The magick around Ceril's hands dissipated, and when it did, the excruciating pain slid away. Nyssa slumped over, her body buzzing. Next to her, Quinn wheezed. The blood wraith lumbered along the deck until it was standing behind Ceril. The Rule adepts shifted nervously, their eyes darting between their prisoners and the terrifying monster in their midst.

"It is so satisfying to see one's hard work come to life before your very eyes. I wove that enchantment for months. Baran thought I was using forbidden magick to address her heart murmur, more than willing to look the other way when it benefited her."

Nyssa swallowed. "You have no soul, Anelos."

Ceril let out a heavy sigh. "This has played out long enough. I have an Empire to rule and reshape. It's time you answer for your crimes."

REMEMBER ME

Quinn took quick, shallow breaths, the edges of her vision turning white. After everything, even after taking down a goddamn queen, they were reduced to shivering on their knees in the middle of the night, facing their deaths. She wanted to scream, to beat her fists against anything that would stand up to her rage, the indignity of freedom so close yet slipping away from her yet again.

She swallowed and squeezed her eyes shut, a buzz in her head drowning everything out.

Don't pass out…fight it…

"Breathe." Nyssa's voice cut through the noise. "Quinn, look at me and breathe."

Slowly, loath to take her eyes off the blood wraith, Quinn turned her head to Nyssa, who locked eyes with her as blood flowed from a cut in her eyebrow. "Focus. Find the calm in the chaos," Nyssa said softly, repeating Fontaine's words to her from when they trained together on Monk's Cove.

Quinn swallowed and took a shaky breath, not looking away from Nyssa's deep-blue eyes, using her as an anchor. The sea air washed over her, the breeze cold against her skin, making her shiver. The familiar sounds of the ship—the dings of metal, the creak of wood, the wind fluttering the sails—became her focus. All things she had come to love; things she would fall asleep listening to at night aboard the Whisper.

Ceril sniffed, peering down at Nyssa. "You were truly Eron's biggest mistake, Blacksea. What a fool he was to ever think he could make something of you."

A strangled sound left Nyssa, her face pure rage. The despicable use of Eron as an insult made Quinn burn with loathing, hatred etched into her bones. She had seen how broken Nyssa was after her father's death.

Nyssa panted and bowed her head. "Let the others go. Let the crew and my friends go. Safin is just a kid, he can disappear, not give you any trouble. Just...let him go. Please."

It pained Quinn to hear Nyssa ask Ceril for anything, but she knew the woman's damn honor wouldn't let her do anything less.

"They're good people," Nyssa continued. "Our lives for theirs."

Ceril smirked. "Your lives are already forfeit."

The deck went silent.

Nyssa began trembling. "Athen, I love you, big man. I'm sorry I dragged you into this."

Across the deck, Athen shook his head and yelled into his gag, his arms tensing. The others struggled against the ropes binding them. The only one who didn't move was Fontaine, who sat with her eyes closed. A soft whimper left Quinn's throat, and she gritted her teeth to slow her tears and tamp down the panic rising in her chest.

She had slowly grown to love these people and couldn't bear the thought of any harm coming to them.

"Aryis, I forgive you," Nyssa choked out. "Don't keep hating yourself, that'll piss me off. You don't want my spirit haunting you."

Ina Ruggen chuckled, drawing the attention of Ceril and the Rule adepts. She drew her sword and strode toward Athen and the others huddled around him. "I'm going to enjoy killing your traitorous friends, Unworthy."

"You don't need to bloody your blade, First Master Ruggen. The blood wraith will tear through them before it destroys this ship."

"You bastard," Quinn seethed. "I'll end you."

Ceril gestured at Nyssa and Quinn. "Enough. Kill these pathetic so-called gods."

Efla drew her dagger and circled behind Nyssa. Another Rule adept stood behind Quinn. She heard him draw his weapon, the soft scrape of blade against leather making her breath catch in her throat.

In her last seconds, she looked to Nyssa. The only person she wanted to see before death.

"Head up high, Quinn Emerrath," Nyssa said. "We die free women." The look in her eyes was steady, calming. A deep blue sea she could sink into forever.

Impossibly, Quinn was ready to accept her fate with Nyssa by her side. She nodded and did her best to smile through her quaking. "Remember me, Nyssa Blacksea. Remember my face and find me in the stars."

Quinn raised her eyes to the night sky. *Remember me.* The stars flickered above, floating in infinite space, promising peace.

A loud, rumbling roar from the other side of the ship startled her. Quinn's eyes snapped back down.

Athen, free of his bonds, swung his fists, crushing any Rule adepts that sprang forward to attack him. Fontaine was free as well, on her feet, hands weaving a spell.

Ashcloak Ruggen darted around Athen, yellow magick sparking off her hands as she touched the collars around Elias and Medias's necks. The metal cracked and crumbled, falling to the deck.

"Kill them!" Ceril's voice rose above the confusion.

A jumble of bodies and magick filled Quinn's vision. Cold, sharp metal pressed against the side of her neck, just above the collar, and she hissed at the pain.

"No!" Nyssa crashed into Quinn, saving her from the assassin's blade, and they tumbled together. A fireball blazed over her head, hitting the adept poised to kill her, his screams frantic. Quinn wrenched around. Nyssa lay next to her, struggling to get to her feet.

Across from them, Athen launched into the blood wraith. Fireballs slammed into bodies as the Rule assassins scattered. Elias shouted orders, Fontaine crouched at his side, golden magick threading around her fingers.

Quinn worked her way to her knees and looked up at Nyssa, who swayed on her feet. Movement caught Quinn's eye.

Efla!

"Nyssa, behind you!"

Nyssa whirled around and twisted away from the dagger aimed at her, kneeing Efla in the gut as she did. Efla stumbled back but stayed on her feet. She stalked forward, and Nyssa's forearms strained against her bindings. Neither of them was a match for an assassin with their arms tied behind them.

A blur of white crashed into Efla, and she and her attacker sprawled across the deck. Safin flopped around, trying to find his footing and get away from Efla, but with his hands tied up too, he couldn't gain purchase.

Someone snatched at Quinn from behind, yanking her hands back, wrenching her shoulders.

"Sorry about that," a voice hissed in her ear. *Aryis?*

For a moment, there was pressure on the rope binding her wrists, then suddenly she was free. Aryis scrambled to Nyssa and grabbed her. Nyssa turned, ready to defend herself.

"It's me! I'm cutting you free!" Aryis yelled.

Quinn got to her feet, her head pounding, and darted to Safin, pulling him up and backing away from Efla, who struggled to her knees. The kid had guts, she'd give him that. He'd saved Nyssa's life with his frantic tackle.

Aryis cut Nyssa free, and Nyssa lunged for Efla, but she crashed into the deck, only catching air.

Efla had disappeared.

"What the fuck?" Nyssa growled, springing to her feet, hands curled up in fists, her head whipping around.

Quinn scanned the deck. Ceril was gone. Efla and another Rule adept reappeared in a blink near the gangplank leading to the Imperial ship. It was that fucking assassin who could teleport across short distances. The one who had attacked her in Cardin.

A bloodcurdling, inhuman shriek pierced the air.

Quinn whirled toward the sound. The blood wraith picked Athen up by his neck and slammed him into the deck, its wood splintering. Threads of golden magick wound around the beast, trapping it. The wraith tore at the thin fibers of magick between it and Athen, the threads breaking and reforming with each swipe.

Across the deck, Fontaine held her hands out, sinking to her knees as she tried to keep the wraith tied up with her magick. Brilliant pops of light, one after the next, exploded across the deck, Rule adepts reeling back to avoid the attack. Quinn found the source of the magick—Medias. She stood over a prone Reece, fighting back. A Rule adept dodged a light explosion and lunged at the Justiciar, knocking her down. Barbed vines of magick sprang out of his hands.

Quinn rushed to Aryis, ripped the dagger out of her hands, then sprinted down the deck.

The Rule assassin crouched over Medias, dark vines of jagged energy wrapping around her neck, cutting into the wrist Medias had tucked there to protect her throat.

Quinn yelled, and the assassin turned to her a moment before she sank her dagger into his gut. She bared her teeth and jerked the blade up. His hot blood gushed over her hand. He stiffened and collapsed into her, but she stepped back, letting his body fall with a heavy thud.

The vines constricting Medias's neck disappeared, and she gasped for air as Quinn helped her stand.

Quinn turned to find the next traitor to attack. To *kill*.

The Rule adepts retreated, crossing over the gangplank to the other ship.

"They're running," Medias croaked, her bloody arm hanging at her side.

"The hell they are," Quinn whispered.

She moved to chase them, to stop them, but someone pulled her back. The collar around her neck grew cold. She spun and came face-to-face with Ina Ruggen, pale-yellow magick sparking at her fingertips.

Quinn grabbed the woman and jabbed her blood-slicked dagger at the traitor's midsection, but Medias caught her arm. "She's not the enemy," the Justiciar said.

"The fuck she isn't—"

The void collar crumbled, its pieces falling all around Quinn as magick flooded back, raging through her body. Ina backed away, holding up her hands, her pale-pink eyes trained on Quinn.

Behind them, Athen shouted. The blood wraith had freed itself from Fontaine's magick, and it darted around Athen, raining down punches. Beyond them, the Imperial ship was retracting its gangplank.

Maybe she could stop them, wrap her shadow around its mainmast and sever it—

Athen cried out. Quinn cursed, tearing her attention away from the retreating ship. She sprang forward, ropes of darkness twisting around the limbs of the blood wraith, pulling it away from Athen who staggered back under its blows. The wraith turned toward her and shuddered, almost vibrating, before it crashed into her, its preternatural speed impossible to counter.

It snatched Quinn up by her throat, and she gritted her teeth, grabbing its wrist. She drove her power deep inside it, sending wave after wave of negating magick through its body, but doing her best to not kill the wraith. She had faced one of these things before and had stopped it for a few precious seconds, but not before seeing a glimpse of its once-human face.

This time, though, her abilities were far different, more powerful.

Ceril had taken a woman and twisted her into an unspeakable monster. Quinn wanted to reclaim that life and turn the monster human again.

As she carefully shrouded its soul, dark and ravaged by bone magick, the wraith's face began to change. Its jutting features softened, and its red eyes gave way to the visage of a human, becoming green again. As the wraith shrank, it screamed, its voice a mix of monster and human. The claws that dug into Quinn's neck became soft and weak.

Baran, naked but human, fell to the deck, weeping and quivering. Quinn sank to her knees, shoulders slumped.

"Quinn?" Nyssa knelt next to her.

"Ceril?" Quinn asked. "Where is he?"

"Gone."

Quinn swallowed, her knuckles burning as she tightened her fists, fighting back the desire to rage, to strike out and destroy. She wanted him dead.

"Holy crap," Athen said, dropping next to Baran, poking at her cautiously. "You turned her back."

The pounding of feet distracted Quinn from her burning rage, and she glanced around to see the faces of the crew appearing around her.

"Is everyone okay?" Yuha asked. "Bastards locked us below deck. We had a hell of a time breaking out."

Elias grasped Yuha's shoulder. "I'm glad to see you all alive."

Fontaine and the others—free of their bonds and collars—surrounded Baran. Fontaine dropped to her knees and swept Baran's hair off her forehead while Elias removed his jacket and draped it over the woman's body.

"Quinn," Fontaine said with a grave face, "you need to extinguish her soul."

"Why? She's human again," Nyssa interjected.

Fontaine shook her head, her glossy eyes giving away her heartache. "Bone magick, Nyssa. Remember your mark."

Quinn had once tried to negate the Mark of the Unworthy on Nyssa's chin before understanding it couldn't be done. The dark line had disappeared...for a few moments before slowly reappearing, its agonizing magick tearing through Nyssa.

Quinn looked up at Fontaine. "Are you sure?"

"I'm sorry."

Quinn ducked her head, her eyes filling with tears. For all her power, she couldn't save this woman. Her magick meant nothing in the face of Ceril's depravity, his willingness to use spells that should have been destroyed centuries ago when the Rells were driven from the Empire.

A circle assembled around them.

Fontaine took Baran's hand. "I am sorry, child."

The woman blinked back tears and swallowed, throat bobbing. "I thought...I thought he was helping me."

"Close your eyes."

Fontaine nodded at Quinn.

"You don't have to do this," Nyssa said.

"No, it should be painless. She deserves that," Quinn whispered. She moved forward and took Baran's trembling hand, holding it tight.

Baran whimpered. "I-I can feel myself changing again."

"Safe journey." Quinn called her magick forth, snaking darkness around Baran's arm. She closed her eyes, expanded her senses, and found the bright core of the woman's life. The bone magick had spread deep within her, crackling and groaning like ice, an infection that couldn't be burned away.

Taking a deep breath, Quinn encased the woman's soul with her shadow and snuffed it out.

Baran's hand stilled, the last breath sighing from her lungs.

Quinn choked out a soft sob.

Fontaine straightened up, her jaw clenching and easing several times before she spoke. "Thank you, Quinn Emerrath, for your mercy."

AN OLD RIVAL

Nyssa groaned as she stood, helping Quinn up. She held her breath and scanned the bodies dotting the deck. All Rule adepts. Her friends were alive and safe.

For now.

"Blacksea," a voice called behind her.

Nyssa turned to find Ina Ruggen. She snarled and whipped a fist across the woman's face, crumpling her to the ground.

"What the hell, Nyssa?" Athen asked, bending over the Ashcloak.

"She sided with *Ceril*."

"I played along to buy time, otherwise you'd all be dead," Ina said, sitting up with Athen's help. "Once I realized what he had done—"

Nyssa scoffed. "Efla and the other adept had daggers at our throats. How long were you going to wait to act? You're exactly what Ceril thinks you are. Ruthless. Ambitious."

Ina shook her head. "Yeah, I'm ambitious, why shouldn't I be? But I'm not like him."

"I remember damn well what you did to me."

"Nyssa, we were kids." Ina stood up and rubbed her chin.

"*I* was a kid. *You* were five years older than me." Nyssa looked around the deck. Everyone was watching. The last thing she wanted was to bring up her past, to let everyone know how she had been bullied for years at the Emerald Order. "You go in a collar until we know for certain you're not with him."

"Nyssa, she's telling the truth," Reece said, Medias beside her, holding the empath steady.

Ina exhaled. "I've never made it a secret that I want to be First Master of the Order. Ceril played on my ambition, but there was always...something underneath his polite manner that set my teeth on edge."

"Doesn't hurt that he probably knew you hated Nyssa," Athen said. "Word spreads about bad guildie behavior, Ina."

"That was years ago."

Nyssa resisted the impulse to level the woman again. The passing of years didn't erase the hurt. Nor was it a substitute for an apology.

"The void collar. Let me shatter it." Ruggen reached for Nyssa, and Nyssa instinctively moved back. She had grown to hate the sight of Ina. How many times had Nyssa stared at those light-pink eyes when the woman had pushed her around as a kid?

Nyssa exhaled and stilled, allowing Ina to come closer. Vibrant-yellow magick sparkled off of Ina's fingers, flowing toward the collar around her neck. The metal turned cold before it cracked and fell off. Nyssa gasped as the warm rush of her power came back and her skin ignited with blue lightning.

Ina's eyes went wide.

"I dare you to fuck with me now," Nyssa said.

"Nyssa, are you hurt?" Medias asked.

Nyssa shook her head but noticed blood dripping from the Justiciar's wrist.

"Shit," she whispered, turning around. "Where's Safin? We need his help."

"I'm over here," the young Emperor replied. He stood with Elias, his purple healing magick at work. "I'll see to everyone."

Buck ambled up next to him and said, "I'll—mmm—help the boy."

Safin frowned, but to his credit didn't correct the man.

Nyssa exhaled and stared down at her hands. She had to concentrate on not shaking, the night's events settling in her weary bones—the memory of Efla drawing her knife and staring into Quinn's eyes one last time...

She glanced up to find Quinn approaching. "Nyssa," she said, her hands curling up in Nyssa's shirt, tears welling in her eyes.

"Freckles? Are you okay?"

"I almost lost you." Quinn's hands moved up to her face, pulling her head down for a gentle kiss. She wrapped her arms around Nyssa, holding tight, her head nestled under Nyssa's chin. "Can I stay here for a while?"

Nyssa buried her face in Quinn's hair, taking a deep breath. The faint scent of winter orchids and juniper soothed her. She closed her eyes and held onto Quinn, trying to put the day's events far from her mind. To just be in the moment.

She didn't know how long they stood there, but it was exactly what she needed. When Quinn finally pulled back, Nyssa groaned, missing the contact immediately. She noticed Decia, Safin, and Ina watching.

Nyssa and Quinn had kept their relationship discreet, Quinn cautioning against displaying affection around others not in their inner circle, preferring to protect their privacy and each other. It was a smart decision.

"We have an audience," Nyssa whispered.

Quinn turned to give Safin and the others a look. "I don't care."

Leaning close, Nyssa said, "This is something they could use against us."

"Oh, in addition to everything else? The ledger is getting long, Nyssa, and right here, in this moment, I needed a goddamn hug."

A smile crossed Nyssa's face. "I...needed it too."

Around them, the crew started to clean up the mess on deck. The dead had to be seen to.

"Wrap the Archivist in a sheet," Elias said, walking up. "For her, we'll say some words. Fuck the others. Dump them in the sea."

"Whatta we do with this one?"

Heads turned to the voice. Yuha had a Rule adept slumped over her shoulder. "He was guarding us in the mess." She hoisted him off and let him drop unceremoniously to the deck. Poking the body in the midsection, she said, "He's still alive. Might prove useful."

"Very useful. Put him in a void collar," Decia replied.

"Useful?" Nyssa asked.

"We have one of Ceril's conspirators. And multiple witnesses to his crimes, including turning a woman into a blood wraith before our very eyes."

Nyssa wrapped her arms around herself, her body suddenly reacting to the bitter winter cold. "What good does that do us?"

"Do you trust me, Blacksea?"

Nyssa looked at Quinn before glancing around the deck. The faces of her friends and crewmates were all waiting. She crossed over to Decia, not missing how Ina moved closer to Safin, to protect him if need be, her Ashcloak instincts well-honed.

"No. I'll never trust you," Nyssa replied, swallowing back the lump forming in her throat. "How can you even ask that after what you did to my family?"

Decia met her with an unwavering gaze. "I have one goal, and that's to return Emperor Safin to his rightful place in the Empire. I think you want what's best for him, whatever your reasons are. In that, we are aligned."

"There's only one outcome I want here: Ceril's execution for what he's done to me and to Quinn."

"He will pay for all his crimes by standing trial."

Not once did Decia look away from Nyssa or try to make an excuse for her past. The one thing Nyssa couldn't dispute was Decia's fealty to the Empire and its leader. She had done awful things for Kalla and now seemed willing to die for Safin if it came down to it. That loyalty was a trait Nyssa could respect, even if she couldn't respect the woman behind it. But that had to be enough. They were out of fucking options.

Nyssa turned to Safin. "Are we aligned, Emperor? I will help you re-take your throne, but I can't risk our freedom. We were declared enemies of the Empire. Is that still true?"

Safin considered her for a moment. "Our interests are aligned. On my word, I will issue pardons to all of you." He held out his hand to Nyssa.

She thought for a moment—was a handshake enough to force a boy barely able to grow a few whiskers on his chin to keep his word? They didn't have much of a choice, did they?

She grasped his hand. "I expect you to honor your promise."

Safin's grip was strong and his gaze didn't waver. "And I will."

Though still cautious, Nyssa addressed Decia. "Then I trust you in this instance and this instance alone."

Decia nodded, a small trace of a smile gracing her lips. "Then we sail to Ocean's Rest and summon the Sun Council."

HOMECOMING

Nyssa checked and rechecked Quinn's sword strap to ensure its scuffed-up buckle was clamped and secure. Scowling at the dented metal, she kicked herself for not insisting on buying a new one somewhere along their journey.

Quinn reached up and stilled her hands. "Nyssa, it's fine."

"This thing has a wonky clasp. Maybe we can find a new one in the Keep's armory."

"But I like this one."

"You have an affinity for broken, second-hand things." Nyssa raised an eyebrow. "Like me."

Quinn gave her a stern look. "You are by no means broken. Though you are a bit rough around the edges, which I happen to love."

Nyssa leaned forward until their foreheads touched and closed her eyes. She let the moment settle, drawing the calm in to center herself. "I wish we could just stay in this room. Take a nice long bath. Make love all day."

The corners of Quinn's mouth twitched. "That does sound lovely. But the world awaits."

"Fuck the world," Nyssa whispered, wrapping her arms around Quinn and pressing against her, drawing her in for a kiss. Quinn laced her fingers in Nyssa's hair, and for a second, they were alone, without the concerns of Safin or Ceril or the Empire to weigh them down. Never mind what reception might be waiting for them on the docks.

Grumbling, Nyssa reluctantly pulled away. She plucked her scarf off her bunk and wrapped it around her neck and chin, ensuring it covered the Mark of the Unworthy. The damn mark drew attention, and with it came the stigma of being an enemy of the Empire. A traitor.

"We should get going."

Quinn scowled. "Nyssa, stop for a moment."

"Hmm?"

"I can't make this decision for you, but I don't think you should hide your face. You shouldn't have to."

Nyssa blinked at her. "I see how people look at me. The mark is a curse."

"No, it's not. You know better. That's superstition."

She didn't move, letting Quinn pull the scarlet scarf off her face. Quinn ran her thumb down Nyssa's chin, tracing the mark, sending shivers through her body.

"Please don't hide," Quinn whispered. "It's beautiful."

Nyssa sighed, giving herself a moment to be still, to feel Quinn. "If you keep saying that, I might believe it one day."

A somber look settled on Quinn's face. "You earned this mark by saving my life. It's a symbol of your honor."

Nyssa blinked and cleared the lump that sprang into her throat. "Don't you dare make me cry right now."

Quinn's piercing green eyes didn't waver. "I want a future for you where you wear the mark with pride. And that has to start here, in Ocean's Rest, the city you defended once. Show them you're not ashamed."

Nyssa let the scarf hang loosely around her neck, fighting the habit of affixing it over the lower half of her face. "C'mere, Freckles." She pulled Quinn in for a quick, rough kiss. Quinn smiled against her lips. Gods, Nyssa wanted to will the world away and it just be the two of them, together, with no concerns. No fears.

Sighing, she stepped back and gave Quinn's sword buckle one last check for good measure. She tapped her finger on it and made a mental note to get the damn woman a proper sword. She deserved far more than a cast-off weapon from a dark storage room of a pirate ship.

"You ready for this?" she asked.

"Being back in the Empire with only Safin's word that we won't be harmed? No, not in the damn least," Quinn replied. "But there's no turning back now."

Nyssa glanced around the room and absentmindedly stuck her hands in her jacket pockets. Her fingers grazed a small piece of paper, and when she brought it into the light, she stifled a smirk. It was shaped like a Kraken, its delicate tentacles folded against its body. Safin's doing. How he had snuck it into her pocket was a mystery, but she put it back in her jacket, breaking into a smile. If being Emperor didn't work out, he had a future in expert paper folding.

She bent over her bunk, packing one last thing into her rucksack—the small tea tin gifted to her by Cyphon—and turned back to Quinn. "Let's go."

The sight on the docks made Nyssa's blood run cold, nervous energy nipping at every inch of her body. The spectacle before her was daunting, to say the least.

At least a hundred Justiciars lined the dock.

Watching.

Waiting.

"You're sure we're safe with them?" she asked Decia.

"I put out the call and the Order of Justiciars came, as is their duty," Decia replied. "They are here to serve and protect the Emperor. The *true* Emperor."

Putting her life in the hands of Decia was a big risk—but she hoped saving Safin had granted her and Quinn, and the others, some grace. A great deal of grace.

But another group of black-leather-clad warriors concerned Nyssa far more. Ashcloaks. They numbered a quarter of the Justiciars' ranks. More would come. Ina had called them to the city, but many were too far away to get there in time to greet the ship. The same was true of the Justiciars. Their group would swell in the coming days and weeks.

Being surrounded by so many Imperial adepts set Nyssa on edge. She had killed Justiciars and Ashcloaks. To them, she was a traitor worthy of death.

Despite the chill of deep winter, sweat made her shirt stick to her back, and she fidgeted, waiting for the gangplank to be lowered.

At the front of the Justiciars, surrounded by a number of guards, stood Lilliana Fennick and her right-hand man, Pol Cress. An impeccably dressed woman waited next to Lilliana. Judging by Safin's smile, it had to be Lyra Vonner, the young Emperor's mother. Nyssa ducked her head and exhaled, happy to see her for the kid's sake. His father had died of cancer when Safin was ten, and being an only child, all he had left was Lyra.

Beyond the Ashcloaks and the Justiciars, a large crowd of onlookers had gathered. The last time she was on these docks, workers had died by her hand. An accident, but their deaths plagued her, knotting her stomach.

A hand on her back startled Nyssa, and she turned to find Reece next to her.

"You're churning like a storm," Reece said.

"Everyone down there has a reason to hate me."

"But that doesn't mean they do."

Nyssa sighed. "How are you so calm right now?"

Reece stepped closer to Nyssa and lowered her voice. "This scares the piss out of me, but Decia wouldn't have insisted on coming back if she didn't think we'd be safe. And Medias...Medias trusts her mother. Somehow, that's enough for me."

In the days after Ceril's attack, Decia had been using Elias's messenger bowl like mad, ordering the arrest of Ceril Anelos and all Obsidian Rule adepts. She also called for the Sun Council to meet in Ocean's Rest, guaranteeing their safety under Lilliana's watch. And she ordered her

Justiciars to gather to provide protection for Safin. They had all come at her call, a testament to the Order of Justiciars and their unwavering loyalty.

Also among the messages sent was an order, signed by Safin, that Nyssa and Quinn and their allies were not to be harmed.

If the Justiciars and Ashcloaks would honor the order remained to be seen.

The crew lowered the gangplank. Athen, Reece, Elias, and Fontaine disembarked first, at the ready should danger present itself. The Lion's Guard and Lilliana went to Athen's side, greeting him. Nyssa had no love for Lilliana, but her heart warmed to see the embrace between Athen and his mother, who gently stroked her son's face before turning to Reece.

Their reunion was awkward, a hesitant embrace. Though Reece was considered Lilliana's adopted daughter, Lilliana had rebuked Reece's desire to become the next Regent of Ocean's Rest instead of Athen. Athen was happy to step aside for Reece, but his mother wanted her own blood to succeed her. Reece didn't talk much about the rift between them, but Nyssa knew it had to be tearing at the empath's big heart.

Nyssa glanced over at Yuha, who had one hand around Suvi's upper arm, another around their captive Rule adept. Yuha smiled back and disembarked in the company of Decia. A rumble of voices met Suvi's appearance. The woman was a spectacle to be gawked at—she had marched on Ocean's Rest over thirty years ago with the aim of razing the city.

Nyssa, Quinn, and Medias were the second-to-last group to leave the ship. The rumble of voices grew louder, and the group of Ashcloaks leaned in, whispering to one another. Nyssa scanned the mass of Justiciars, their eyes on her and Quinn—and Medias. Though they were usually hard to read with their masks on, Nyssa sensed their restrained animosity.

Suddenly, the Justiciars and Ashcloaks moved in unison, all taking a knee. Lilliana, Pol, and the Lion's Guard followed suit. The distant rumble of voices from the gathered crowd quieted. Nyssa turned. Safin descended the gangplank. He looked uncertain, his gaze darting about, his face locked in a serious expression. Nyssa caught his eye and smiled, a small reassurance. The kid had no idea what he was stepping into.

Neither did she, for that matter.

Safin rushed toward his mother, and Lyra embraced him, kissing the top of his head and asking if he was certain he was unharmed. She had the same rich, dark skin tone as her son and wore her hair in long locs with similar silver bands. Unlike his mother, Safin had a lanky frame, and with another growth spurt, would easily bypass his mother's height, pushing six feet.

Lyra wrapped an arm around her son and stared at Nyssa and Quinn. Nyssa knew the woman by reputation, a retired Master Ashcloak who had fought valiantly in the Mire War. She defended the southern Areshi territory, as her House had done for centuries. They were always the first line of defense against Thu'Dain and honored wardens of the south. Standing in her presence, under her withering gaze, made Nyssa's nerves buzz.

Lilliana rose from a knee and offered her hand to Safin. "Welcome, Emperor Safin Vonner-Areshi. You are among friends here."

Safin nodded. "Thank you, Regent Fennick. Has the Sun Council arrived?"

"They have, but I insisted they not come down here to greet you for security's sake. They're all at Ocean's Keep, eating my food and drinking my wine."

"We appreciate your hospitality, Lilliana," Lyra Vonner said, finally smiling. They seemed to be friendly enough with one another.

"I have arranged rooms for you in the Keep's guest quarters," Lilliana said. "You will be surrounded by Justiciars and Ashcloaks. In addition to our Lion's Guard. You'll be safe."

Safin smiled. "Surely over a hundred Justiciars and Ashcloaks has your home bursting at the seams, Regent."

"Not at all. The Keep was built to house an army. A few hundred new occupants are barely noticeable."

Safin exhaled, looking about. "I'm amazed at this reception."

"The people remain loyal to you, Emperor. The news of your ordeal had us all worried. Ceril's lies don't hold much sway in this city, nor with your loyal Justiciars and Ashcloaks."

Lyra eyed Nyssa. "It is only your current company that has given many pause."

Nyssa narrowed her gaze.

Safin pulled away from his mother and looked at those gathered on the dock. He walked over to Nyssa and Quinn and took a deep breath. Tension flexed along his jaw line.

Nyssa felt the eyes of everyone on her and Quinn. Waiting for one wrong, threatening move.

"Nyssa Blacksea and Quinn Emerrath are Imperial allies," Safin announced, his voice carrying down the dock. "I will officially pardon them in two days' time with the Sun Council as witness. Anyone who moves against them moves against me."

Lyra's withering stare could have set Nyssa aflame were she made of kindling.

Yet, no one said a word. No one would dare challenge their Emperor, not even a teenage boy who had barely worn the mantle. But judging by the charged tension that ran through the Justiciars and Ashcloaks—and their hushed murmurs—the pardon wasn't the most welcome news.

"That was bold, kid," she whispered.

"It's the right thing to do."

"You're not going to win friends."

"I...I know, but I made you a promise."

The news of their pardon would travel through the city's gossips like wildfire...and spread across the expanse of the Empire with one message: the Cursed Gods were allies of the new Emperor. And off-limits.

Athen gestured at them. "Let's get to the Keep."

THE PRISONER

Though only settled into the Keep for a few hours, a restless curiosity led Aryis to the cells beneath the massive stone fortress. As much as she hated every step she took to get down there, she needed to have a conversation.

Suvi sat up and smiled as Aryis came to a stop in front of the ex-Queen's jail cell. Though Aryis had gotten used to that smile—self-possessed and predatory—it made her stomach churn. She had no defense for it.

Suvi swung her legs off her bunk and smoothed down her hair before folding her hands in her lap.

"My dear Aryis Devitt, what brings you to my illustrious prison? I'm afraid I'm a terrible host. I have no wine to offer you."

Aryis bit her tongue. After negotiations between Thu'Dain and Frosland had resulted in a treaty that forced Aryis to betray Nyssa and Quinn, Aryis felt nothing but shame. And a deep, painful inadequacy for her own shortsightedness. Suvi had played her—and her father—at every step, exploiting a country in need to forge an alliance.

Each moment at Wayland studying the art of governance and every second under Lilliana Fennick's mentorship felt wasted. Had Aryis really learned nothing?

She pulled over a stool and sat down.

"My answer is no," Suvi said.

"Excuse me?"

"I assume you'd like to annul my marriage to your brother. I refuse."

The wretched woman has been dethroned!

Aryis ground her teeth to stifle the urge to scream. A scream that would likely start and never end. Betraying Nyssa and Quinn had been heart-wrenching, but falling into Tajal's clutches left her reeling. Lost. Now, listening to Suvi's arrogance drip from her voice threatened to unmoor her completely.

Compose yourself.

She took a deep breath. "I'm not here to talk about that."

"Oh, so am I to guess what you *do* want to talk about?"

Aryis sat there, suddenly finding herself unable to vocalize the words. She shifted in her chair and stared down at her hands, shame burning inside her.

Go ahead and ask!

Aryis shook her head.

"I see. You want to know how you could have avoided betraying Nyssa and Quinn," Suvi said.

Aryis had no reply. Suvi read her perfectly, every time, as if she were an open book.

Suvi leaned forward. "You seem reluctant to inquire, so I will tell you. Your father negotiated from a position of desperation. Your country *needed* food or it faced starvation. I could have just opened a direct trade route, charged a premium for wheat, corn, and beef, but his need created an advantage for me to exploit. I wanted more—an alliance of nations. And that's precisely what your father gave me. I pressed further and asked for Nyssa and Quinn. What did your father care about two strangers? He agreed. And then, to ensure he honored our agreement, I sent ships full of food to sit off your shores and wait until Nyssa and Quinn were delivered to me. And deliver them you did."

Aryis gnashed her teeth.

Suvi placed her hands on the cot behind her and leaned back, casual and wholly unconcerned. "Where did you study, dear sister-in-law?"

"Wayland," Aryis answered, bristling at the familiarity.

"Ah, the Wayland Conservatory. Where unimaginative scholars and tepid statesmen are born. It seems you learned very little during your stay. In our negotiations, I had wants. But your side had needs. You were bargaining from a position of weakness from the start."

Sweat pricked up on Aryis's forehead. Suvi's unkindness was truly stunning, justifying the small, dark ball of hate growing in Aryis's heart.

"I didn't come here for you to insult me," Aryis said. The notion that she didn't learn anything at Wayland was offensive. Of all people, she was arguably their best scholar.

"I have very little else to do," Suvi said before making a dramatic show of yawning, not taking her pale-green eyes off of Aryis. "Do you really want to know what it takes to be a queen?" Suvi smiled a wolf's smile and didn't wait for an answer before continuing, "The truth is, you know what it takes to be queen. The crown settled on your head *perfectly* the minute you betrayed your friends and gave them to me."

She has a point.

Aryis lowered her eyes, trying to form a valid retort to Suvi's words. She found none.

"And then you recoiled, didn't you?" Suvi continued. "Horrified by your own actions. You found out what you have to do to be a queen and realized that you don't have it in you. It requires a strength you simply do not possess."

"Cruelty isn't strength."

"Women like you quibble over distinctions without difference. It gives you some false comfort as you lay your head on your pillow at night. Tell me, do Nyssa and Quinn care where your head lies? Or your man, Athen?"

Aryis refused to answer, staring at Suvi.

"He hasn't invited you back to his bed, has he? And Nyssa used to be your friend, but you barely know Quinn, as I understand. I had my men beat her when she tried to escape, and I have to give her credit, she was *persistent*. You know who she'll come to blame for her pain? I don't know what my future holds, but you'll still be in her eyeline, darkening her thoughts. Don't forget, I was in her mind for a bit. There's a deep well of hate in her with nowhere to go, barely sealed over with scars. One day, Quinn will come for you. And she'll kill you for what you did to her...and to Nyssa."

Aryis bolted to her feet, the chair beneath her tumbling backward. Suvi didn't flinch. Aryis sneered. "You will do one good thing in your life, and that's die when Safin executes you."

There she is, the ruthless queen...

"Shut up!" Aryis yelled, her hands flying to brace the sides of her head. "You're not helping!"

I'm supposed to be helping?

"Leave me alone," she muttered.

The smug, self-satisfied expression disappeared from Suvi's face, replaced by confusion. Aryis's heart hammered in her chest as she backed up to the door and slipped out of it, running down the dark corridor below the Keep.

That didn't go well, Aryis. But I do like this Suvi Rell.

TORN BETWEEN TWO DICKS

Quinn opened her eyes to the murmur of a low conversation and the unmistakable aroma of dark coffee. Nyssa and Reece sat at the largest table in Nyssa's room, breakfast sitting between them. Still groggy, Quinn took a quick peek under the covers, relieved she was wearing bedclothes.

The previous day was hazy, a whirlwind of activity. Lilliana had extended her hospitality, insisting that Nyssa and Quinn stay in the family wing of the house. Quinn didn't mind, not exactly wanting to stay in the midst of a large contingent of Justiciars and Ashcloaks. The family wing was separate from the rest of the Keep. Quiet and private, just as she liked it. She had done her best to ignore the gawking Keep attendants who hustled to get their rooms ready.

The apartments in this wing were massive and far more luxurious than Quinn was accustomed to. They contained richly colored rugs, eclectic furniture, and unique décor from all over the globe, and the most comfortable bed she'd ever had the pleasure of sleeping in. A fireplace crackled away on the opposite wall, flanked by full bookshelves that Nyssa would likely scour for a good read. Enormous floor-to-ceiling windows overlooked an expansive stone balcony and beyond, down over the city of Ocean's Rest.

Tucked back in the corner of the room was a hallway leading to a pristine bathroom stocked with all manner of soaps, bath oils, and fluffy towels, and a claw-foot bathtub in the middle. A tub Quinn hoped to explore with Nyssa again, should they get the chance later. Next to the bathroom was a wardrobe bigger than her room at Arcton Citadel, full of clothes that seemed curated for Nyssa from her previous stay.

Reece suggested giving Quinn the room adjacent to Nyssa's—connected by a secret door near the wardrobe to allow them to move back and forth while maintaining their privacy to keep their relationship discreet. It was a considerate gesture, one Quinn greatly appreciated.

The previous night was fuzzy by a fair degree, a couple empty bottles of wine still on the nightstand next to the bed. All she knew was she felt quite a bit better, the rest having recharged her, though the dreaded downward pull of a hangover made her softly groan as she sat up. She wasn't prone to drinking a lot, but she had indulged. And now hated herself for it.

"Hey, sleepy," Nyssa said, beaming at her from the breakfast table and munching on a piece of bacon. She looked far too chipper for Quinn's liking. What happened to the grumpy woman who hated getting out of bed in the morning? Nyssa pulled a mug off a serving tray and filled it with coffee.

Reece stood and grabbed the cup. "Allow me, I'm the interloper. Quinn, I hope you don't mind the intrusion," she said, bringing Quinn the coffee, but also holding up a paper-thin wafer between her fingers. "For your hangover."

"Thank you," Quinn replied. After a sip of the sweet, delicious coffee, she felt a little more alive. She eyed the wafer before popping it in her mouth, nearly gagging when it burst and coated the inside of her mouth with cold, tingling magick. The wafer tasted inexplicably like stale air. Why were healing enchantments so damn...unpleasant? Was it just a sham to get people to pay healers instead of buying quick remedies from the corner store?

She got up and pulled a robe around her, joining the two women at the table, warming her hands with the mug of coffee. The aroma of eggs, bacon, toast, pastries, and a large bowl of sugared strawberries made her stomach growl, and she served herself breakfast.

The room, the food, Ocean's Rest...it all felt surreal to once again be in the Empire. Two years of living in hiding and now suddenly and very publicly back in society, such as it was, took some getting used to. Nyssa seemed rather happy to be back and had luxuriated in a hot bath last night, pulling Quinn in to join her. But as much as Quinn wanted to trust they were safe, she vowed to remain cautious.

Reece smiled at her before stabbing a roasted potato off of Nyssa's plate.

"Hey! Get your own," Nyssa groused.

"I was just telling Nyssa that news of your arrival has spread," Reece said around a mouthful of potato. "More people have trickled into the city since yesterday. Some dignitaries, a handful of Imperial advisors, including one rotund little man named Mikai Vawdrey who seemed to brighten Safin's mood."

"Any word of Ceril?" Quinn asked.

"None. Nor of the Obsidian Rule adepts with him. In fact, all Rule adepts have gone to ground save for a few, according to our sources across the Empire. Decia has suspended the Obsidian Rule guild and ordered all their adepts be arrested."

"Where is Safin?"

"He's huddled up in his apartments with Vawdrey, his mother, Decia...and a number of other advisors, preparing for tomorrow's Sun Council."

"Should we...be helping?" Though with what, Quinn had no idea.

Reece shook her head. "No, you're off the hook today."

"Good. I'm not exactly well-versed in Imperial politics," Nyssa said.

Reece sighed. "Did you simply skip the important lectures at the Emerald Order?"

Nyssa scoffed. "I was sometimes distracted."

"Writing your poetry?" Quinn asked, popping a strawberry in her mouth. She dodged the spoon Nyssa flung at her.

"Nyssa? You write poetry?" Reece asked, raising an eyebrow and looking rather pleased to have a new bit of information.

"No, I do not."

"Ah, that was a lie."

It was often easy to forget that Reece was an empath. One who would have made a frighteningly powerful Justiciar if Lilliana hadn't kept her out of Ambershine. In a private moment aboard the Whisper, Nyssa told Quinn the real reason Lilliana had brokered the deal to kidnap her out of Thu'Dain. If Lilliana had refused to help the Empress, Reece would have been taken away from her and trained to be a Justiciar. In the end, Lilliana's reasoning was simple—a mother protecting her daughter.

It didn't take the sting out of the woman's actions—Nyssa's parents had died at the hands of Justiciars. One last act to ensure loose ends were tied up. No witnesses to the Empire's crime.

"How do you know I was lying?" Nyssa asked.

"A bit of a tremor there in your emotions, a ripple that I've gotten very adept at sensing," Reece explained. "Can I read one of your poems?"

Nyssa's face scrunched up, not exactly angry, perhaps more flummoxed by the fact that another person knew her secret. She had let it slip while rather drunk two years back.

"The Winter's Fire poem that Quinn recited? That was mine," Nyssa said.

Reece smiled. "Ah. I guess that did sound like you. Your massive heart on the page."

"Could we not do this ever again?" Nyssa grumbled.

Reece sipped her tea. "Sure," she replied with a wink at Quinn.

The empath was pushy, trampled boundaries, and was somehow still eminently likable.

"You were busy yesterday. Have you gotten any rest?" Quinn asked her.

"A bit."

"And where is Medias?"

"Over here."

Quinn practically jumped out of her skin, whirling around in her chair. Somehow, Medias had found the darkest spot in the room to roost on a couch cloaked in shadow.

"What the fuck, Justiciar?" Quinn barked, clutching her pounding heart.

Nyssa leaned back in her chair and laughed. "Your situational observation skills need work. I thought I trained you better."

Quinn contemplated hurling a spoon at her. "I'm barely awake and my hangover isn't receding as quickly as I'd like."

Reece laughed into her coffee cup.

A knock at the door made Quinn startle again, and she could swear she heard a soft guffaw out of Medias. Nyssa jumped up and answered the door. An attendant rolled a cart inside. It was piled high with clothes.

"Ah, good!" Reece said, thanking the attendant. "I thought you both could use some new clothes. My clothier owed me a favor. She'll want to do more precise measurements for better fittings in the future, but this is what she came up with for now."

Nyssa pulled a black leather jacket off the top of the pile, cocking her head. "Is this mine?"

"Yes, it is. I know how much you love that thing and would wear it until it was a patch of leather held together by thread and sadness, so I had it repaired. Tay is a very skilled seamstress and has mastered some impressive restoration enchantments."

Slipping into the jacket, Nyssa let out a contented sigh. She loved that damn thing, claiming it met all the criteria she had for a quality leather jacket: it fit like a glove, had plenty of interior pockets, and she looked good in it.

Quinn couldn't dispute that last point, letting her eyes linger. Heat rose in her cheeks. Nyssa *did* look rather good in the jacket.

"The cuts and scuffs are gone, but it's still got that lived-in feel," Nyssa said, smiling.

"Yes, Tay fixed it up rather nicely for you. But not without telling me, rather dramatically, how she had worked through the night weaving her enchantments to salvage the thing. She got the blood and smoke out too."

"Just when I was getting used to the smell."

Quinn rolled her eyes and got up to inspect the other garments.

Reece gestured to her. "There's something there for you too."

In the stack of clothes was another leather jacket. Black, like Nyssa's, but with a white stripe down the left sleeve.

Quinn picked up the note stuck to the top of it, the ink sparkling with magick, oscillating between purple, red, and blue shades.

For Quinn Emerrath. Please endeavor to treat this with care.
Regards,
Tayalt Zaher, Master Clothier

The leather was buttery under Quinn's fingers, the jacket sturdy and structured much like Nyssa's. "I can't accept this, it's far too nice."

"You *can* and *will*. The fit should be okay, I told Tay you're around my size," Reece said, taking the jacket out of her hands and gesturing for her to turn around. Reece slipped it on her. "How does it feel?"

Quinn held her arms out and admired the new garment, its interior warm, soft, and cozy. She walked over to a mirror and couldn't stop the smile that crossed her lips. Even with her bedclothes on underneath, she looked *good*.

"It's...perfect. Thank you, Reece."

"I'm glad you like it. There are clothes there for both of you. Anything that doesn't fit, we'll have altered. Leave them on the cart, an attendant will be by to hang them for you in your closets."

"I had forgotten how spoiled this place makes me. I don't have to lift a finger," Nyssa remarked.

With a smile, Reece said, "You've both been on the run for two years, so we can spoil you a little while you're here. Now, I have to get back to Lilliana and Decia before I meet with the five faction heads. They are beyond curious as to what's happening with Safin and the Sun Council. Politics...a delicate dance of bullshit." Reece exited the room, waiting for Medias in the hallway.

"Blacksea. Emerrath," Medias said by way of farewell as she left the room. Quinn tried boring a hole into the Justiciar's back as she left. She'd need to remember to check all the corners of any room she was in, just in case Medias lurked about.

Quinn sat on the bed, still wearing her new jacket. She loved the soft creak of the leather when she moved. At closer inspection, it had several interior pockets, a perfect place to hide all the gold marks she didn't possess.

"You look fucking sexy in that jacket," Nyssa said, warming Quinn's cheeks again.

Compliments were still hard to accept, even from Nyssa. "Thank you."

"Let's get you a bath and get ready."

Quinn cocked her head. "Ready for what?"

"Everything is a little too cozy right now. We have to remain vigilant. Ceril turned a whole guild into traitors. Anyone could be in his sway. He's a threat no matter where he is."

"So we keep our eyes open."

"And we stay on our toes. Let's find a little nook and train, get our minds and bodies aligned."

Quinn returned to the table and dropped into her chair, trying to not dwell on the danger that Ceril posed. "Fine. Breakfast first. I'll need my strength. Then a bath."

Walking through the Keep, Quinn was reminded that she and Nyssa were different.

Very different.

People stopped what they were doing as they passed, eyeing and whispering amongst themselves. On the ship, Quinn was never made to feel as though she stood apart. She scrubbed the deck or worked the sails like the rest of the crew. Fontaine and Elias didn't show favoritism, and Quinn had the calluses to prove it.

The Cursed Gods lore that preceded them meant many already had a notion of how dangerous they could be. Unfortunately, their predecessors had been *assholes*. The worst ones were warmongering murderers. Nyssa and Quinn were burdened with a tarnished reputation they themselves hadn't earned. Which was entirely unfair. Nyssa could be a bit of an asshole, but Quinn was at least polite. Sometimes.

She smiled to herself, wondering if Nyssa would be proud or offended being unabashedly called a situational asshole.

Nyssa stopped and grabbed Quinn's arm, her face bursting into a bright smile. "Hey, look."

She followed Nyssa's gaze. A pair of open doors led out to a very large, sunlit courtyard paved with stone and rimmed with fragrant winter cherry blossom trees. A high stone fence, remnants of the fort that Ocean's Keep was built upon, surrounded the yard, and it was full of about twenty men and women going through synchronized movements. Movements that Quinn could follow with her eyes closed. The Third Form of Ithais Toru.

"That's got to be the Lion's Guard," Nyssa said. "Come on." She pulled Quinn along as she stepped out into the courtyard to watch. The Lion's Guard fell out of rhythm when they noticed Nyssa and Quinn approaching. The large man leading the training turned and straightened up to his full height. His students stilled.

Nyssa waved. "You're Brick, right? Athen has spoken highly of you. I'm Nyssa Blacksea. And this is Quinn Emerrath."

Brick scowled at her. He was a massive man, had to be taller than Athen, his dark skin a stark contrast to his short-cropped white hair. His wide nose was slightly askew, much like Nyssa's. Probably the victim of a fight or two. He wore his shirt rolled up to his elbows despite the winter chill, revealing muscular forearms and leather wrist cuffs. "Blacksea. Athen's told me a little about you. You've been away for a while."

"For good reason. I like keeping my head on my body."

"It's a fine head, I suppose." Brick squared up to Nyssa and put his hands on his hips, puffing his chest out. "Athen contends you're a good fighter, but you look a bit scrawny to me."

Quinn raised an eyebrow and waited for Nyssa's response.

"Scrawny? Well, I was dying for a bit there, but I think I put the weight back on. I eat my fair share of dessert," Nyssa said, poking at her midsection.

Brick ran his eyes up and down her. "I bet I could beat you in a fight."

What the hell? Did he know what his mouth was walking him into? Murmurs spread through the Lion's Guard. Brick picking a fight with Nyssa seemed like a deliciously terrible idea. Quinn couldn't wait to see how Nyssa handled it.

Nyssa scoffed. "Are you sure Athen told you about me? Because if he had, you wouldn't be making that bet."

"And I bet I could beat you with your own martial art."

The murmur behind Brick turned into an excited rumble.

Crossing her arms over her chest, Nyssa cocked her head up at Brick. He was a massive man, no doubt, but Nyssa didn't back down from anyone, a trait Quinn found wildly attractive. Anticipation fluttered in her belly. This would at least be fun to watch, though she feared for Brick's safety.

Nyssa smiled at him. "Wait a minute. Is this a dick-measuring contest?"

"Nyssa's woefully unequipped for such a competition," Quinn said, drawing a snort out of her.

"I'll take your word for it," Brick said. "This is my practice yard when Athen isn't here, and I want to challenge the best."

Nyssa shook her head. "While I'm flattered—and you're right, I am the best—you don't get to demand a fight. You earn your shot first. So let's make it student against student. Athen's student against mine," Nyssa said, gesturing to Quinn.

Quinn whipped her head toward Nyssa, the flutter in her belly turning sharp and biting. Before now, she had only sparred with Nyssa, and when she fought real foes, she was always fighting for her life, no time to think, just react.

A scowl planted itself on Brick's face, and he eyed Quinn. "Fine."

Nyssa turned and walked over to a wooden bench, sat down, and spread her arms across the backrest. Quinn followed.

"I'm sorry, but what is going on here?" she asked. Was she really meant to spar Brick?

"Dick-measuring contest," Nyssa replied. "Time to see how you fare against someone who isn't me."

"Why? I've fought Emerald Order. Suvi's guards. Obsidian Rule. Twice."

"Technically, three times. You did jump on Efla back at the mill. I thought you wanted to continue to learn. Is that not true?"

Quinn frowned. "It is, I just—"

"You are my student, you represent me. Do me proud, woman."

Quinn shook her head, took off her sword and brand-new jacket, and handed them to Nyssa. "You'll pay for this later."

"Ah yes," Nyssa said, leaning forward and lowering her voice. "I dread being thrown down on the bed so you can teach me the error of my ways."

Quinn ground her jaw. The woman was infuriating. Quinn wished she didn't find herself enjoying it so damn much. "Any fighting tips, Master?"

"Beat his ass."

Quinn sighed. Nyssa was taking the piss, but honestly, Quinn relished testing her skills. And Brick fit the bill perfectly.

Quinn strode over to him and bowed. She moved back and shook out her arms. It was a brisk day and she didn't want to stiffen up in the cold. Brick cracked his neck and then started in on his knuckles, each *pop* echoing in the large yard.

Brick's Lion's Guard gathered in a small group, chattering among themselves, an undeniable sense of excitement hanging in the air.

"Fight already!" Nyssa groused.

Quinn smirked. Well, if Nyssa wanted to push her buttons, she would push back.

Instead of settling into the stance drilled into her during her training sessions, Quinn adopted a new posture—arms dangling at her side, shoulders slumped, head cocked. She imitated one of Nyssa's lackadaisical stances, a tactic used to throw off opponents. The stance looked careless and lazy, possessing an undertone of disrespect. It was meant to annoy and distract.

Quinn glanced at Nyssa. The confusion on her face melted away, turning into a sly grin.

The intended effect of the stance worked perfectly on Brick. He set his jaw and attacked with a punch. Quinn dodged Brick's fists and danced away from him, creating space that he was a little too eager to close.

Nyssa had taught Quinn to relax and let the fight come to her. But instead of counterattacking, Quinn kept moving away from Brick, ducking and dodging his attacks, using her speed to her advantage.

Quinn ran the risk of a lecture later about getting too cocky and playing with her opponent, but if Nyssa was going to push her to fight, she would fight her own way, even if it meant adopting some of Nyssa's bad habits. And Quinn wanted to see how far she could take it.

She spun and danced away from Brick again when he attacked, his face growing more intense as his breathing deepened. The strength behind his blocked strikes was scary. If any of his blows connected, he'd send her flying.

"Alright, stop being an asshole and finish this!" Nyssa yelled.

Quinn immediately summoned her magick, formed a ball of shadow around her fist, and smashed Brick in the midsection. He hurtled through the air and hit the ground, skidding across the stones. The assembled Lion's Guard rumbled with approval despite Brick's defeat.

"That's cheating!" Athen yelled from across the courtyard, striding toward them.

"It's not cheating," Quinn said. "My teacher taught me to use every advantage that I have."

"And how to toy with your opponent too, I see," Athen replied as Quinn walked over to Nyssa. "Did your teacher give you her bad habits?"

"I was torn between two dicks," Quinn said, "so I improvised."

"What does that even mean? Fuck's sake, Nyssa, what the hell is going on here?" Athen asked. He sank onto the bench next to her, making it creak under his weight.

"Your student challenged me to a fight. I said he has to earn it by going through my student first." Nyssa smiled and shrugged. "Boulder there has good form but has to learn not to give chase. So impatient."

Brick stood up and dusted himself off. "That's one nasty punch, Miss Emerrath."

"Yeah, what was that? Shadow punch? That's new," Nyssa remarked.

Quinn crossed her arms. "I've been working on it a bit on my own." When Nyssa had left her alone on the Whisper for a week, Quinn staved off her loneliness by experimenting with her magick under Fontaine's watch. She had learned a few new things, some of which she kept to herself to surprise Nyssa with one day.

"I like it." Nyssa winked.

Heat rose in Quinn's face. She turned to Brick and bowed.

"You're fast. Pulled me in," he said. "Athen's been telling me to stop rushing, but what can I say? I like to punch things."

"I like to punch things too," Quinn said, smiling up at the big man and shaking his hand. "And please, next time, just call me Quinn."

"Brick, why are you challenging a god to a fight?" Athen asked.

"I was trying to test myself."

"Yeah, well you don't walk up and try to punch a shadow. Or a lightning bolt. Though I admire the moxie. Don't let it go to your head." Athen eyed Quinn. "You're a helluva fighter under Nyssa's watch."

"She gets a lot of one-on-one attention," Nyssa said with a sly glance at Quinn. There was a lightness to her now that she was back home with Athen. Quinn felt lighter too. She was never closer to being free. For the moment, she could forget the threat Ceril posed, wherever he was, and just enjoy life. At least before facing down the Sun Council.

"Use this yard to continue your training with Quinn, then. The more you're seen out and about, the better. Pretend to be regular people. Just...don't start trouble."

Nyssa put her hand to her chest and gasped. "I would never."

Athen narrowed his eyes at her. "A week after we met, you stuffed a roasted carrot up another adept's nose in the dining hall."

"First off, I was ten years old. Second, that bastard licked the piece of cake I was saving for later. *Licked* it, Athen."

Quinn snorted at the mental picture of Nyssa sticking a vegetable up some poor boy's nose.

"First off, age never seems to make a difference with you," Athen countered, "and second, that asshole did mildly deserve a carrot up his nose. But my point stands."

"Okay, I will behave," Nyssa said, settling back on the bench.

Athen pointed his finger at Quinn. "You too."

Quinn let out an exasperated breath. "What did I do?" She rubbed her arms, smiling at Athen. He was damn easy to like, and she understood how he and Nyssa complemented one another as best friends.

He stood and stretched. "I have to get back to arguing with the Ashcloaks about guard rotation for Safin. Brick, you're doing a good job with these recruits. Keep it up."

Brick nodded, and Athen took his leave. Nyssa leaned forward, focused on something across the yard. "What the fuck is she doing here?"

Quinn followed her gaze.

Ina Ruggen was watching them, her eyes glued to Nyssa. After a moment of staring her down, Ina turned and walked back into the Keep.

"You alright?" Quinn asked.

"Don't worry about her," Nyssa replied.

"I'm not worried about her, I'm worried about *you*."

Nyssa had told Quinn about growing up at the Order, how cruel the adepts were. Though she never got into specifics, Quinn understood. Her own time at the Citadel taught her that some wounds ran deep, twisting under the surface, and didn't make for polite dinner conversation. She had never pushed Nyssa to share. But Master Ashcloak Ruggen could become an issue.

"What are you standing around for?" Nyssa asked, putting on a smile and poking Quinn in the shin with her boot. "Fifth Form. Go."

Quinn scowled but nodded, walking over to an empty corner of the practice yard. Fifth Form—the Orchid Form—was slow and delicate, relying on precision and balance. And her worst form by far.

She hoped getting back into training would keep Nyssa's mind off of Ina and the past.

UNWORTHY

Quinn exhaled and pulled at the toldoku that she wore around her wrist. A Winter's Fire gift from Nyssa. She never removed the woven leather talisman. It was too precious to her.

Her nerves were peaked this chill night, for good reason. She had been contemplating this decision for weeks aboard Hannah's Whisper, but in the last few days back on land, she had become certain this was the right choice. But still...there was no going back once done.

Am I insane?

She swallowed and rolled her shoulders back. The air in the small, private courtyard was sweet with the scent of honey firs—small evergreen trees that exuded a sweet sap in the depths of winter.

"Quinn?"

Nyssa and Medias stepped through the frosty patio doors and out into the garden.

Quinn took a deep breath and smiled her best smile, despite what she was about to do. "Thanks for coming."

Nyssa held up a small piece of paper as she crossed the courtyard to Quinn. "What's with this mysterious note to grab Medias and meet you here?"

Turning her attention to Medias, Quinn said, "I know you'll probably be forced to resign your position as a Justiciar, right?"

Her lips in a tight line, Medias nodded.

Quinn took a step forward. "If I may, there's one last duty I would ask you to perform."

Nyssa scowled. "What are you doing?"

"Yes, Quinn, what are you doing?" Medias asked, her eyes boring into her.

A thought had been churning over in Quinn's mind a great deal of late. "The Areshi Empire stole me as a baby, and my life has never truly been my own since. I want to be free."

Nyssa stepped up next to Quinn, putting a hand in the small of her back. "But you are free."

"Even if pardoned by Safin, I wouldn't *feel* free. Not truly. Pardons can expire. There is only one way to shed the Empire and its claim over me forever. Nyssa, do you trust me?"

A rush of air left Nyssa, her brow wrinkled, but she said, "I do."

Perhaps it was folly, but Quinn was determined. She lifted her head and steadied herself, taking a deep breath. "I renounce my allegiance to the Areshi Empire," she said in a loud, clear voice. "Justiciar Medias, I want you to declare me Unworthy."

Nyssa grabbed Quinn by both arms, her fingers tight. "What the hell are you doing?"

"I'm setting myself free," Quinn said, "and sharing your burden."

"Quinn, I..." Tears sprang up in Nyssa's eyes.

"On your back foot again, eh, Blacksea?" Quinn whispered.

"You don't have to do this."

"Yes, I do. I want to be bound to *you*, not the Empire."

A gasp of air left Nyssa, and her face softened with a vulnerability that only Quinn got to see. Nyssa cleared her throat. "Are you really sure about this?"

Quinn cocked an eyebrow. "You should know better by now. Of course I'm sure."

Her declaration drew a hum of laughter from Nyssa.

Quinn turned back to Medias. "Will you do as I ask?"

A small smile graced Medias's face. "I would be honored to declare you Unworthy." She unzipped her jacket and pulled out a short silver dagger, her red eyes trained on Quinn. "Step forward, Quinn Emerrath."

"Do I need to kneel?"

"It is part of the ritual," Medias said. "Plus, your legs will give out from the pain."

Quinn blew out a breath and knelt in front of Medias.

"Nyssa, will you steady her?"

"Of course." Nyssa knelt down next to Quinn. "Freckles, this is going to hurt."

Quinn nodded as Nyssa placed one hand on her shoulder, the other on top of her head. Her stomach turned over in knots, not knowing what to expect, remembering Nyssa's cries during her own marking.

Medias peered down at Quinn. "I don't know what to say. I can't declare you a traitor."

"Just say what you think is right," Quinn said.

Medias narrowed her eyes and paused. "Quinn Emerrath, Cursed God and pirate of the Unbound Sea, under the gaze and authority of our Emperor, I declare you Unworthy. Your service to your guild and to the Empire is over. I brand you a free woman. On this day, you are beholden to no one, and you will live as such until you pass from this earth."

Quinn drew in a breath and smiled. "That was perfect."

"Hush, woman." Medias steadied herself and pressed her knife into the hollow below Quinn's lower lip, drawing the tip down her chin.

The blade's magick seeped into her, burrowing itself deep into her bones, like molten steel burning through her. Every inch of her body radiated with pain. She held out as long as she could, but a scream ripped out of her, reverberating through the garden and into the night sky. Nyssa kept her steady and still.

Medias pulled away once the mark was complete. Quinn's body trembled under Nyssa's hands. Medias dug out a dark cloth from her jacket pocket and wiped the blade clean. The pain was quenched immediately once her blood was gone from the magickally imbued steel, as if she had never been cut. But her body continued to tremble from the trauma, making it difficult to stand.

"I've got you," Nyssa said, wrapping an arm around Quinn's waist and helping her up.

Sucking in air, Quinn draped an arm over Nyssa's shoulders for fear of her legs giving out. "You really undersold the pain," she wheezed.

"I can't believe you did this," Nyssa whispered in her ear, eyes dipping to her chin.

Despite the pain and its aftereffects, Quinn smiled. "I'm my own woman now."

Nyssa tightened her grip on her.

"I will inform my mother of what transpired here," Medias said.

"Will she be pissed you did this without anyone's permission?" Nyssa asked.

Medias shrugged. "As long as I wear this mask, I will carry out the duties of a Justiciar."

Quinn grabbed Medias's arm as she turned to leave. "Thank you, Medias. Truly. You have been a good friend."

The Justiciar gave her a terse nod before leaving the courtyard.

Nyssa hesitantly cupped Quinn's face. "What you did, I..." Her gaze went to the mark, drawing a thumb down her chin. "You constantly astonish me, Emerrath."

"Careful, Blacksea. Anyone sees us like this and they might get the impression that you're hopelessly in love with me."

The smile that spread across Nyssa's face was beautiful. Easy and unguarded. "You should clean up. You're a bloody fucking mess."

Quinn grabbed Nyssa and kissed her for the first time as a *truly* free woman. Her heart soared.

THE SUN COUNCIL

Nyssa perused the library, trying to find the book her mother had cited as inspiration for Quinn's name. She had heard of *The Cry of the Sea* but never read it. The Keep Chamberlain had insisted there was a copy somewhere in the damn place...whether this library or one of the three others or tucked away in a random bookshelf somewhere, Nyssa had no idea. The Keep was too big, its contents handed from one owner to the next. What treasures had been misplaced or lost over time?

A disheveled pile of papers on a table caught her eye, and she leaned closer. Two familiar faces stared up at her—hers and Quinn's. Old bounty notices, tons of them, all rather...embellished.

A varied collection of mustaches, beards, horns, and spectacles had been drawn on every image with thick, black lines.

"What the fuck?" Nyssa grumbled, cocking her head at a picture of her sporting a beard and horns.

"I can't say that word," a soft voice said. Nyssa whirled around to find a small girl staring up at her. Tight, curly hair framed the girl's face like the seeds of a fluffy dandelion.

When the girl saw Nyssa's face, her vibrant blue eyes widened. "You're...you're her!"

Nyssa held up one of the wanted posters and poked a finger at it. "You mean her? Yeah, I'm her. Though with less facial hair. Did you do this?"

The little girl shook her head, a smile creeping on her face. Nyssa folded up the paper and stuffed it in her jacket.

"You're lying," she said. Studying the girl further, Nyssa noticed a resemblance—her dark skin, wide nose, and beaming smile giving her away. "You Brick's kid?"

"Delliah."

Nyssa put her hands on her hips and smiled. "You look like a Pebble to me."

"I'm not a pebble! I'm going to grow up taller than my father, I bet!"

"Don't argue with me, child," Nyssa said. "And a pebble can be very dangerous. One in a slingshot can put an eye out."

"Like Uncle Athen!" Delliah replied, immediately clamping her hands over her mouth.

Nyssa broke down in laughter. Someone must have scolded the kid for mentioning Athen's missing eye. Children were experts at pointing out differences in others. Her own childhood bore testament to that. "Yeah, just like Uncle Athen. Where's your father?"

"Training. I'm allowed to play in the Keep before my lessons if I'm nice and quiet. The Lions keep an eye on me," Delliah replied.

Nyssa eyed the two guards at the entrance, and they nodded at her. Guards littered the Keep, its security super tight.

She smiled at the girl. "Well, I think I'm taking you hostage. I reckon I'll get at least fifty thousand gold marks for you."

"Is that a lot? If it is, you should share it with me!"

"Prisoners don't get to make demands." Nyssa bent down and picked Delliah up, slinging her over her shoulder like a sack of potatoes. "I'll be able to buy an airship or an island for that much. And plenty of pastries. I'll be swimming in lemon tarts. And if I'm feeling generous, I might even share."

Nyssa hauled Delliah to the practice yard, drawing many curious looks. The little girl giggled and chatted her up the whole way, asking endless questions about what it was like to be a god, if the mark on her chin hurt, how sharp her sword was, if she ever swam with sea sprites, if she could talk to fish. Nyssa barely got an answer out before Delliah was on to the next question.

"Whose bothersome little gnat is this?" Nyssa shouted when she reached the practice yard. The Lion's Guard trainees all turned and fell silent when they saw her. Stopping and staring had become a common reaction when she or Quinn appeared.

Brick stood in the middle of the men and women, busy offering instruction. Quinn was practicing off to the side and gave Nyssa a confused look. Nyssa swung Delliah off her shoulder and put her on the ground. The little girl turned to smile up at her.

"Do magick!" she demanded.

"Do magick? You think you can order a god around?" Nyssa replied, putting a little bass in her voice. It only made the girl smile more and bounce on her toes with excitement.

Nyssa sighed. "Ah, fuckin' fine." She pulled her magick to the surface. Delliah squealed and clapped her hands. Nyssa created a small ball of lightning on her palm and tossed it to Delliah, who tried to catch it, but it exploded and sparkled when it reached her fingers. Nyssa made sure it only tickled, putting no real power behind it.

Delliah clapped again and took off running to her father. "Did you see? Did you see? Auntie Nyssa made lightning for me!"

Nyssa grimaced, not fond of the title.

Quinn walked up. "New friend?"

"She's a bit of an artist, like you," Nyssa said, handing over the folded bounty paper.

Quinn laughed. "The horns are kind of sexy on you."

"Oh, there's plenty of you too. You wear a mustache well."

"I imagine I do. I didn't know Brick had a daughter." Quinn frowned. "I'm not particularly good with children."

With a shrug, Nyssa nudged Quinn's shoulder. "Neither am I, but that one's a cheeky little asshole. Reminds me of me."

Brick walked up with Delliah in his arms. "Blacksea! You're calling my daughter Pebble?"

"You gotta problem with that, Boulder?" Nyssa smirked.

Delliah laughed and wrapped her little arms around Brick's massive neck. "Boulder! I'm going to tell Mother," she said with a bright smile.

"Delliah!" a voice called out. A woman stood in the one of the door-ways leading into the Keep. "Time for your afternoon lessons."

Brick bent down, and Delliah slid out of his grasp. She poked Quinn in the leg. "You have a chin mark too! Are you the other one?"

Quinn cleared her throat. "I'm Quinn."

"Father says you punched him with shadow magick."

"I did."

"Fun!" Delliah enthused before running toward the woman waiting on her.

Nyssa exhaled loudly. "She's got a lot of energy."

Brick's shoulders sagged and his face fell. "You don't know the half of it. And she has questions. *So* many questions."

"Right?" she replied, holding her arms out in exasperation. "Stick her and Aryis in a room and let them have a chat. I don't know who will come out alive."

Nyssa felt Quinn stiffen at the mention of Aryis. Still a sore subject, but Nyssa couldn't avoid talking about the woman living under their noses.

"There's a school in the Keep?" Quinn asked.

"Lilliana set up a temporary one for Delliah and some of the kids of the other Guard members. My wife is busy with her blacksmithing shop, so it works out well for us both."

Nyssa's interest perked up. "Your wife is a blacksmith? She any good?"

Brick cocked his head and rolled his eyes. "What kind of question is that? She's one of the best. Apprenticed in Malfi at the Bent Blade."

"An excellent smithy school." Nyssa nodded, impressed. "I need some work done on my sword. I'd like to pay her a visit...if that'd be okay."

A visit by an Unworthy could make people uncomfortable and cost Brick's wife customers, so best to ask first.

Smiling, Brick clapped Nyssa on the shoulder. "Becks will welcome you with open arms, she doesn't buy the Cursed God bullshit. People know what you did at The Masthead. Ocean's Rest doesn't forget. Be-sides, who's going to fuck with gods?"

"Didn't you challenge me to spar when we first met?" Nyssa asked.

"I had to, it was a matter of pride. Both for the Guard and my Triad."

"Equal parts ballsy and dumb," she replied. "Ivory Triad?"

"Yeah."

Nyssa knew very little about the factions that once ruled Ocean's Rest and that Lilliana had tamed over the last two decades. The Ivory Triad had a penchant for black market goods. From what Aryis had once told her, Lilliana turned a blind eye for a small percentage of their business. She had the same deal with all the factions save for Obscuras—the insular, mysterious clan that tended to the dead. They were left alone.

Nyssa smiled at Brick. "So, Becks and Brick?"

"Rebecka is her full name, but those that know her call her Becks. You'll take to her. Swears like a pirate, drinks like one too. Arm wrestled me on our first date. Gods, I love that woman," Brick said, sighing.

"I like her already," Nyssa said. "We'll pop in another day. We have a prior engagement."

"Meeting with the Great Houses?"

"Yeah."

"That should be fun."

Nyssa rolled her eyes. "I'd rather watch you fight Quinn again. Far less torturous than facing the Sun Council."

"Come on," Quinn said, tugging at her arm. "We don't want to be late and make a bad impression."

Laughing, Nyssa followed. "A bad impression would be a step up for us."

As Nyssa and Quinn drew closer to the Great Room, Nyssa's memories of the day she became a Cursed God crept back, dread creeping down her spine. After being marked, she sealed her fate by saving Quinn. She stood tall in those last moments, the seconds ticking down to Quinn's death. And her demise.

Then, something great and terrible shifted inside of her, an ancient power exploding through her body. How they escaped from that predicament still bewildered her. A mixture of dumb luck and desperation.

Now, little over two years later, approaching the room where she and Quinn were reborn into gods, her stomach twisted. Seeing the gathered Justiciars and a very sullen Lyra Vonner didn't instill confidence either. She was flanked by a short, rotund man in a black suit that looked expensive but a little worse for wear, the shirt he wore underneath wrinkled. His shoes were heavily scuffed, the laces frayed at the ends. Next to Lyra, he looked a mess.

Lyra also wore a suit, seemingly tailored to its very last stitch to fit her perfectly, its deep-purple hue gorgeous. Her sharp gaze settled on Nyssa and Quinn as they approached.

She stepped in their path, addressing Quinn. "I see the rumor is indeed true. You had Justiciar Medias mark you as Unworthy."

"I did."

"An...interesting choice." Lyra turned, her eyes examining Nyssa. "Your pardons are ready. Vawdrey will bring them to your rooms later today." She gestured to the man next to her. Decia had mentioned him, one of Kalla's most trusted advisors and, according to her, a loyalist down to his last drop of blood.

"Thank you, Master Ashcloak," Nyssa said, sure to add the honorific title before moving toward the Great Room.

Lyra moved to intercept them. "You won't be joining us today."

Nyssa glanced into the room, numerous people milling about inside, and quite a few interested persons craning their necks to the hallway where they stood.

"I don't understand," Nyssa replied, turning her attention back to Lyra. "Safin asked us to be here."

"I think it's best he maintains a distance from the two of you due to your...status."

Nyssa's pulse kicked up. "Status? You mean having an Unworthy in the same room as your son?"

Lyra maintained a polite smile, though it didn't reach her eyes. "By now, you understand any hesitation surrounding any association with two Cursed Gods. How would such a thing look, not only to our own people, but to our ally nations?"

Once again, Nyssa and Quinn were being viewed as weapons, not people. She let out a deep sigh. "We're here to help, Lady Vonner," she said, dropping the honorific of *Ashcloak*. "I'll protect Safin and make Ceril pay for what he's done."

The woman stepped closer. "You will get your pardons, as Safin promised, but that is all."

Nyssa considered Lyra, with her perfectly tied-back locs, piercing dark-brown eyes, and air of authority that was by no means put on.

Quinn stirred next to Nyssa. "We're going to stop Ceril, that is certain."

"Anelos is an Imperial matter now," Lyra replied, her eyes trailing up and down Quinn, dissecting her much the same way she had done to Nyssa as they walked up. "We will deal with him. Any personal quest for revenge is unacceptable."

"I have the right to go after Ceril because he killed Eron. Wasn't he once your friend, Lady Vonner? You should know the code of honor my father instilled in me. I can't let his killer get away." Nyssa dug her fingernails into her palms. "We're going to find him."

A beat passed, Lyra narrowing her gaze at Nyssa. "This isn't up for discussion, Unworthy."

The extra bit of venom in Lyra's voice tipped Nyssa's anger over the edge. She pushed past Lyra and marched into the Great Room, scanning the gathered people. The room reeked of wealth, with the tailored clothes and jewelry dripping off the Great Houses. All conversation hushed when she entered, followed by Quinn.

"It's true, she's marked," someone whispered, and a few fingers pointed at Quinn.

The room was bright, the giant drapes pulled back to let sunlight flood into the room. What had transpired here had been washed away, but Nyssa didn't forget the light waning into dusk as she killed Justiciar after Justiciar. The deep-red rugs were gone, replaced by blue ones. She swallowed at the memory of watching Master Justiciar Elken moving toward Quinn, his blade aimed at her heart.

Nyssa shook her head, pushing those thoughts aside.

Safin stood with Decia and Ina at the other end of the room. "Safin! What is this *bullshit* your mother is feeding us? We had a deal." Her voice reverberated off the walls, loud and bold. She advanced toward Safin with Quinn at her side. Nyssa tried to ignore the spot where they almost died, though her heart betrayed her, speeding up.

Justiciars descended upon them, surrounding the Cursed Gods. Just like that day when Nyssa's magick exploded inside her. The Great Houses of the Sun Council stilled, watching, their personal guards at the ready.

This was about to turn into a shit show.

Quinn moved next to Nyssa. "I'm right beside you," she whispered.

Nyssa glanced over. Determination hardened Quinn's face and she stood tall and strong, every bit the warrior Nyssa was training her to be.

Safin pushed through the line of Justiciars, followed closely by Ina and Decia.

"I'll be fine," he said, eyeing the Justiciars. He drew close to Nyssa and Quinn, but before he could speak again, Lyra rushed to his side.

"Your presence is not needed here," she said, her voice cold.

"We had an agreement with the Emperor. Not you."

Lyra turned her eyes down to her son. "Safin trusts that I know what's best for him as he starts his reign as Emperor." She directed her attention to Nyssa and stepped closer, lowering her voice so only she and Quinn could hear. "You weaken him in the eyes of the other Houses, Blacksea. There are considerations at play here that you cannot fathom. Accept your pardons and take your leave. *Now.*"

Lyra wrapped her long fingers around Nyssa's arm and attempted to twist her around, to prod her to leave, as politely as she could. It was the last indignity Nyssa was willing to suffer.

Shards of lightning sprang up on her skin, arcing around her body. A collective gasp emanated from the gathered onlookers. She lightly zapped Lyra, who flinched and released her, moving back to protect her son. The Justiciars lit up with magick, waiting to strike. Ina drew her sword.

Nyssa let her magick spill out, tendrils of electricity spreading in all directions along the floor, licking at the boots of the Justiciars. "Call off your dogs, Decia."

"Stand down, Blacksea," Decia replied, her voice low. Threatening.

Shadows spread across the floor, twisting through Nyssa's lightning. Quinn's darkness whirled around her.

"We've been here before, haven't we?" Quinn warned. "I don't think we're the ones that will get hurt this time." The emerald fire in her eyes blazed as she scanned the Justiciars. There was a danger to her in that moment that Nyssa hadn't felt before.

"No one moves against them!" Safin ordered, his head on a swivel. "Nyssa, Quinn, let's talk this out." His eyes pinned Nyssa in place, his spine rigid.

"We're here to help you. That's what I pledged to do," Nyssa replied.

Safin swallowed, his eyes darting to Lyra before settling back on Nyssa. "Your aid isn't required anymore."

Nyssa turned and examined the assembled Sun Council, all of whom were dressed in fine silks, wools, and furs. Most were in muted winter colors: grays, silvers, black, though a few wore lively oranges, deep reds, and bright greens. The display of wealth was not understated—a lot of sparkling necklaces, ostentatious watches, and rings embedded with gems glinted on the fingers of the Empire's richest Houses. The only entourage that stood out were those wearing white coats with black leather bands coiling around their arms. A traditional sign of mourning. Nyssa surmised that they must be from Kalla's House—House Simac.

"Do you really trust any of these people?" Nyssa asked, her voice loud. An angry rumble spread through the room. "How many of these so-called Great Houses are truly on your side, Emperor Safin?" Her gaze shifted. "Do you trust them with your son, Lyra Vonner?"

"Blacksea, you come here as an Unworthy, a Fallen Ashcloak," Decia said. "And yet you remain unharmed. You have been extended far more grace than *anyone* in your position should expect. Leave before that courtesy is withdrawn."

Nyssa stared at Decia. Whatever peace they had brokered aboard the Whisper fell away like ash. Another *fucking* betrayal. "Do your Justiciars and these Great Houses know that you killed my parents? That your precious fucking Empire kidnapped Quinn?" She took her eyes off the Arch Justiciar and scanned the room. "Do you all know the things your Empire does in your name?"

Lyra approached Nyssa, towering over her by a good four inches. Her bearing was that of a warrior now, not a mother. "You killed six Justiciars in this room. And now you threaten us?"

Nyssa dug her fingers into her palms. "Everything I've done...everything *we've* done...has been in defense of ourselves or another. I'm not a coward who sits back and waits, unlike those here who would gladly let Anelos hunt *your* son down and kill him, just as long as they didn't have to risk a hair on their own heads."

Eyes blazing with anger, Lyra took a deep breath, her jawline tensing.

"Anelos will be dealt with," Decia replied, inching closer, likely to intercede if Lyra decided to answer Nyssa with her fists. "I have issued an arrest warrant for the man. He will be brought back to Cardin to answer for his crimes against the Empire and the people of this city."

"Arrest him?" Quinn asked. "You intend to have him stand trial?"

"Yes. The victims of his crimes will get justice."

Quinn scoffed. "Justice? He's mine."

"Justice outweighs your vendetta against him."

Quinn sucked in a breath, drawing a sharp glance from Nyssa. "My *vendetta*? Is that all it is to you? I was a tool to him. He isolated me, put me in a void collar, whipped me senseless. All under your Imperial noses, and no one raised a finger to help me. This isn't a vendetta. His death is the justice *I* deserve."

Decia frowned but offered no response. The rest of the room remained silent.

Nyssa spoke up. "Ceril Anelos killed my father. You have no idea what that did to me." Her eyes filled with tears. *Dammit.* She didn't want to show them her pain, but mentioning Eron yanked all her hurt to the surface. These people didn't deserve to see her heart or the sadness and hurt that roiled inside her.

Find the calm in the chaos.

She exhaled, her sadness turning into a hot rush of anger flooding her veins. "Quinn Emerrath and I are going to find Ceril Anelos. Stay out of our way. Everything else—your Justiciars, your Great Houses jockeying for a modicum of power, the bangles you wear around your wrists to show off your wealth—I could not give a *fuck* about."

The room remained silent until Safin cleared his throat. "My decree is clear. Anelos is to be brought to me alive. He will face trial, not vigilante justice. Nyssa Blacksea and Quinn Emerrath, you will abide by my decree and the laws of this Empire."

Nyssa tried to maintain calm. Safin looked away. He no longer had the freedom to make his own decisions, that was very clear. His mother was forcing him down the path of a "respectable" Emperor, and Decia seemed on the same page.

It was bullshit.

"Blacksea! Emerrath!"

Heads turned. Justiciar Medias stood at the entrance of the Great Room, Reece at her side. A low rumble of whispers spread, the Sun Council and Justiciars bristling at Medias's presence. Decia seemed to grow taut, like a cocked crossbow string.

Medias took a few steps into the room, her eyes shifting between Nyssa and Quinn. "Emperor Safin has made his wishes known."

Several seconds ticked by, Nyssa's anger growing. What the hell was Medias doing?

Quinn shifted next to Nyssa, the darkness surrounding her fading. "Come on. We're wasting our time here." She headed toward the door.

Nyssa waited a moment before pulling her magick back, casting lingering glances at Safin, Lyra, and Decia. She should have known Safin was like the rest of the powerful figures in the Empire, loyal only to his own interests. And Decia was exactly who Nyssa thought she was: the woman who killed her parents without an ounce of remorse.

Fuck them both.

Nyssa followed Quinn. Medias waited patiently by the door, ushering them out, then closing it behind them. Reece stood outside, her face dark and pained.

"Reece, are you okay?" Nyssa asked.

Swallowing, Reece looked back at the Great Room door and shook her head. "I'm trying to read the Sun Council, but so many emotions are bombarding me. It's overwhelming."

"Protect yourself. Pull your magick back."

"Let me just…" Reece closed her eyes and balled up her fists.

Nyssa rarely saw her overwhelmed, save for when she experienced Nyssa's emotions firsthand. "Did I hurt you? My anger?" she asked, afraid of the answer.

"It's not painful, really. Just…intense. That room is filled with anger, mistrust, and hate. I'm afraid not everyone in there supports Safin, but it's hard to weed through so much emotion. And they won't let me inside. They know what I can do."

"They fear you," Quinn said.

"Yes."

Of course. The Great Houses could whisper and collude, make plans to overthrow Safin in secret, but they couldn't hide their deceit from someone like Reece for long. She could sense lies riding on the back of other emotions—a talent honed over years, but one that made her a particular danger in political circles.

Medias crossed her arms, scowling deeply. Nyssa braced herself for a lecture.

"You two have put yourselves at odds with everyone in power in the Areshi Empire. A feat to behold. I would honestly be impressed if you both weren't so damn stupid," Medias growled.

Nyssa pointed back to the room. "Safin, Lyra, and Decia ignored our offer of help. They think they can send us away with pardons and we'll just acquiesce."

Medias took a quick step toward Nyssa. "And you *will* acquiesce. Nothing here is what you think it is. Safin has to maneuver around the power brokers in that room. And the eyes of the Empire are on him. So control yourself and that deep well of anger in you. It isn't helping you here."

Quinn let out a sigh. "You saved us once again in there, Medias."

"Indeed. It's getting tiresome."

Reece did a poor job of containing a soft laugh.

Nyssa curved up an eyebrow. "Where are Lilliana and Pol?"

"Just as closed out of Imperial politicking as you and Quinn," Reece replied. "House Fennick isn't even a middling House. We're more of an…upstart House that doesn't have proper table manners."

Nyssa sighed and ran a hand through her hair, its loose curls falling back over her shoulders. The conceit of the Sun Council reminded her of what she used to face at the Emerald Order. The dividing line of arrogance that those like the Great Houses and Ina Ruggen sat behind rankled Nyssa to no end. "House Fennick has done more for this damn Empire than most in that room."

Reece shrugged. "Our heads aren't far enough up our asses to be considered a Great House."

The whole situation rankled Nyssa to no end. Safin had not kept his word, and she found herself startled at how disappointed that made her. But it was partially her fault—she should have known better than to trust anyone in power.

"But there is something you can do," Reece continued, pinning her shoulder-length silver-white hair behind her ears. She eyed Medias. "You're not going to like this."

"If Medias won't like it, I'll probably love it," Nyssa said, perking up.

"Word is Ceril's brother, Bennet Anelos, is up in the Northern Wilds. I know someone just as connected up there as Lilliana is down here who can probably give us an idea of where to find him."

Nyssa licked her lips, excitement rippling through her. Finally, a possible way to find Ceril. "Well, since we're not needed here, a little northern vacation sounds like a lovely distraction."

Medias immediately shook her head, tossing a frustrated glance at Reece. "You were told to leave Imperial business to the Empire. You go running off looking for Ceril, you're going to force Safin's hand."

"We're going, and you can be mad about it or come with and keep us out of trouble." Nyssa stared at the Justiciar.

Medias scoffed. "The notion that anyone could keep you out of trouble is—"

"Where to in the Wilds?" Nyssa interrupted. She could swear that Medias was close to rolling her eyes.

Reece smiled. "We're going to New Ibanis. Pack extra-thick socks."

AN UNWELCOME GUEST

Aryis paced amid the sunlight and books, wringing her fingers. Dust motes swirled in the air in her wake. Normally, a library would be her absolute favorite place in the world, but her nerves were frayed. Sweat pricked up on her forehead as her eyes darted to the clock. She was far too early. A good practice that now felt punishing. Too much time to think. To worry.

Tell him about me and I'll hurt you. Or him. I'm undecided.

Aryis stopped in her tracks. "You wouldn't dare," she hissed under her breath.

You want to tell Athen about me. I can't let you do that.

"What do you—ow!" Aryis's left hand began to throb, her forearm vibrating like it was home to a nest of wasps. She turned it over, opening her fist.

An eye stared back at her, embedded in her flesh.

Aryis screamed, clamping her other hand over her mouth.

The buzzing sensation intensified, pain amplifying until she was certain her hand was about to explode. The horrific eye in her palm blinked at her. And then it popped out of her hand and fell to the rug, leaving a dark stain on her palm.

Aryis reeled back into a table. Its heavy legs scraped against the wooden floor. She tried grabbing hold of it, but she fell, panting, certain her heart was about to hammer out of her chest.

The eyeball rolled to the middle of the floor, its pupil darting about. Aryis scrambled to her feet, ignoring her throbbing hand, and rushed forward, stomping on the eye.

Dark tendrils shot out from under her boot and spread all around her foot. It crawled up her leg, rooting her in place.

"What the...?"

Tendrils wound around her body, and shadows curled and coiled out from under her foot, climbing up the bookcases, ensconcing the tables and chairs nearby, and snaking up the tall windows in the back of the room, blocking out the morning sun.

A long, thin strand of dark matter sprouted from the floor, and the eyeball popped out of the top and focused on Aryis.

"You will keep my secret," that voice rumbled—only, it wasn't in her head anymore. It came from...all around her.

"Tajal," she whispered.

The eyeball blinked at her. "In the flesh."

Aryis swallowed. The Ancient God had spent a month picking at her fears, hopes, dreams, and shames in the Realm of Shadows. When his voice haunted her outside his domain, she feared that she had gone insane.

But this...this was worse.

"You're real."

Somehow, Tajal's eye scowled at her. "Of course I'm real."

"How are you here?"

"I left a little bit of myself in you, a small speck of a god. Most of me is back in the Realm of Shadows, busy with...god business."

"Wha..what do you want from me?"

Tajal's eyeball bobbed at the end of its tether, blinking at Aryis. "You and your friends were the first people I'd seen in my realm for...I don't know how long. Then they left you behind, so tasty and pained, and they expected me to just...not want more?" A tendril extended from the eye stalk and poked Aryis on her nose. She tried to wiggle her arms free, but Tajal tightened his grip on her.

"I won't let you hurt my friends."

Tajal sighed, sounding frustrated. Over the weeks he had been in her head, Aryis had come to recognize his moods, though not how to navigate them. "I'm not here to hurt, Aryis, you silly bean. I just want to know more."

"Know more what?"

"*More.*"

"Tajal the Curious," Aryis whispered.

"Now you're getting it."

There was a part of him that Aryis sensed was reasonable. "Please, help me understand what you want with me."

The black substance spread across the library expanded, then contracted, and Tajal's sigh filled the room. "You're supposed to be the smart one?"

"You...you would assume I could understand the mind of a god?"

"Flattery. I approve," he replied. "There's something bothering me, Little Bird—isn't that what Nyssa used to call you?—and I want you to help me untangle my quandary."

The situation wasn't ideal, but him needing her proved somewhat intriguing. "Explain."

Tajal fell silent—a silence that seemed to stretch for days. Aryis eyed the clock. If Athen came into the library now, she feared for his life. Tajal was unpredictable. Temperamental.

"I want to know what life feels like. Mortal life. All of you are so full of emotions that ping about like lightning bugs in a jar. I want to understand these emotions," he said. "There's something in me I can't explain. When I had you and Nyssa in the Realm of Shadows, a feeling...a memory...grew closer, almost tangible. It's right there, then it's gone. And it's only getting worse since our time together." Tajal's gaze drifted before flicking back to Aryis. "I need to spend more time with you to uncover this phantom that haunts me."

Even though he could snap her in half like a dry twig, she needed to capitalize on his need if he had no intention of leaving her alone. "I can help you, but you have to make me a promise."

"I am an Ancient God and do not answer to mortals. Especially one as slight as you, birdy."

Aryis took a deep breath and waited.

A cautious note rumbled out of him. "Proceed."

"My friends are off-limits. You cannot harm them."

"Fine...as long as you keep me to yourself. No yapping that you have a god rolling around your brain."

"Agreed," she replied. "And you have to leave once we figure out what's troubling you."

"We shall see."

"N-no," she stammered. "That's not good enough."

"It will have to be for now."

The eyeball in front of her split, revealing a row of fangs just under its surface. A gruesome grin curled up its makeshift mouth as the black mass all around her quivered, then rushed back toward the eyeball, disappearing into it in a heartbeat. The thin stalk holding the eyeball up dissipated, and the orb fell to the ground, bouncing once. It flew into her palm, and she watched in horror as it sank back into her hand, not a trace left behind, her light-brown skin unmarred.

She flexed her hand, turning it over. "Where did you go?"

Tajal didn't answer her. Didn't matter, Athen would be there any second. She got busy tidying up the table she almost upended, its stacks of papers strewn about the floor. She let out a soft burst of laughter when she saw they were bounty fliers of Quinn and Nyssa, their faces featuring drawn-on mustaches and horns.

Someone has an artistic eye, Tajal rumbled.

The door to the library opened, and Aryis straightened up, turning to find Athen striding in. He looked worried.

"Is everything okay?" she asked.

"Did you know that Nyssa, Quinn, Reece, and Medias left in the middle of the night?"

She scowled. "No."

"They didn't leave word as to where they went, unless they told you?" He looked at her, hopeful.

"No. They don't talk to me much," she admitted.

His face fell. "Dammit. I hope they don't get themselves in trouble. I hear it didn't go well with the Sun Council yesterday."

Indeed, the rumor spreading around the Keep was that Nyssa and Quinn were cut off from Safin, summarily dismissed and told their help wasn't needed. It was shortsighted, but Aryis had no say in any Imperial decisions. Not anymore. Not since Empress Kalla removed her as successor to the throne.

"Anyway, you wanted to see me?"

She stiffened. *Shit*. She was going to tell him about Tajal, but now she had no reason for calling him to the library.

No, that wasn't entirely true.

"I wanted to talk to you about us. About how we move forward, together."

Athen stared at her, his face sedate. He said nothing.

The kindness, love, and humor that Aryis had been so used to seeing from him wasn't there now. She swallowed. The tension between them grew, and she felt herself getting hot.

Your boyfriend got himself a haircut. You could mention that, Tajal intoned.

"No, that's dumb," she whispered.

Shit. That was out loud.

Athen frowned. "Excuse me?"

"You got a haircut!" she blurted.

He bristled. "What did you call me here for, Aryis?"

"I...I..."

Sighing, he turned around and headed toward the door.

Aryis hurried after him, grabbing his arm. His muscles tensed under her fingers—a far cry from how he used to respond to her touch.

"Wait," she said. "I don't know the right words here...but I want to heal this divide between us."

He pulled away from her. "There are no right words, Aryis."

The rejection slammed into her, twisting her stomach. A chill ran over her skin. "I still love you, Athen." Pouring her heart out to him had never felt more dangerous.

Athen swallowed heavily, looking down at her. There was pain behind his golden eye, but also a glimmer of the man she had fallen in love with. "I've never been good with anger. I'm not like Nyssa. She can turn it into a fine-point weapon and wield it with precision, but with me, it just sits around in my gut and festers until it turns into resentment. And I hate how that feels inside me," he said, his voice low. She missed its vibration against her chest when they snuggled in each other's embrace and he'd tell her stories of growing up at the Emerald Order.

"I'm so, so sorry, Athen."

"Our relationship was built on respect and trust. We don't have that now." He shook his head. "I'm sorry too."

"I'm not giving up," she declared.

"You don't get to decide that for the both of us."

"I know your heart. If I believed for one moment there wasn't a chance to find our way back to each other, I would let you go. But we—"

"There is no *we*!" he growled. "I wanted to be there for you after what you went through at Wayland. My heart ached for you, but you left instead of letting me in. I can't..." Athen shook his head, turned on his heel, and left her in the library.

As Aryis fought back the tears that threatened to flow freely, a heavy sigh echoed through her.

That went poorly. You're bad at contrition.

"You can't force forgiveness, Tajal," she whispered. Athen had never spoken to her in such a way. After her betrayal, he had grown quiet and watchful. He had looked after her when healing from her time in the Realm of Shadows, but it was obvious he was nowhere close to coming to terms with what she had put everyone through. Perhaps it was merely a sense of obligation that drove him to help her and now that they were back, he'd slip away, out of her life.

A sharp, frigid shard of regret surged through her.

She glanced down at her palm, curling it into a tight fist. Athen, Quinn, Nyssa...she had hurt them all so deeply. She had to find a way back to them. *All* of them.

THE NORTHERN WILDS

If Cardin and the Sun Palace were the example of pristine wealth, all clean and white and sharp corners, New Ibanis was the opposite: loud and bright, with more than a hint of a dark underbelly. Neon signs cast their glow on the streets where men and women ricocheted drunkenly from bar to casino to eatery. Brilliant colors mixed with the cacophony of hucksters and street musicians, further tinged with the scent of charred meat and stale beer. It was an assault on the senses.

Quinn didn't know quite what to think of the city, though beside her, Nyssa was all smiles. Just her kind of place, Quinn guessed. She pulled her scarf tighter, careful to cover the Mark of the Unworthy, just as Nyssa had taught her. No need to attract unwanted attention until it was necessary. Or unavoidable.

Despite the name, the Northern Wilds didn't appear to be wild so much as just rough around the edges. Quinn found the atmosphere of the city seductive, though she imagined danger lurked right under its radiant surface.

Walking through the streets to their destination, buildings rose and fell, their signs advertising what lay within. Casinos were everywhere. One promised acrobats and illusion, another an operatic soprano, yet another advertised seers and fortune tellers. The raucous noise that spilled out into the street whenever a door opened drew Quinn's curiosity. There was simply too much to look at and hear; too much vying for her attention.

The busyness of the streets allowed her and the rest of their party to pass through the city without garnering much attention, the particular time of night given to drunken festivities. The winter air held more of a chill this far north. Quinn nestled into her scarf, thankful that her new leather jacket was holding up against the bitter wind that tried to sink its teeth into her.

Nyssa had a little bounce in her step, her head on a swivel. Reece also looked in her element, waving to the topless women who tried to tempt customers to come into their clubs by calling down from their second-floor balconies.

Meanwhile, Medias kept her hood drawn down over her face. New Ibanis didn't seem to be her type of place, but she had insisted on coming along. Likely to keep an eye on everyone, but particularly Reece, if Quinn had to guess.

Was I as obvious when I was falling for Nyssa?

Loud pops and whistles made Quinn jump. Fireworks streamed across the sky, splintering and exploding into brilliant reds, golds, and blue streaks of light. The men and women filling the street cheered.

"This city is insane," Quinn said.

"This city is *amazing*," Nyssa replied, smiling at a group of men and women outside an establishment that promised a live sex show, their leather harnesses and sheer clothes leaving very little to the imagination. It was as if New Ibanis had the spirit of a more raucous Ocean's Rest, with a whole lot of sex and whiskey smeared all over it. A sudden spark of uncertainly hit Quinn. Was Nyssa tempted by what this city offered?

"Ah, here we are," Reece said, their group coming to a stop in front of a massive building. A bright-red sign featuring a constant shower of golden sparks falling from its letters announced their location—The Mystique. The building towered in the sky, the sharp edges of its roof glowing bright blue.

The casino looked a bit more upscale than some of those they had passed, though the whole city seemed to be a confusing mix of class and crass, offering everything in between.

Large men and lithe women in black suits stood outside the doors of The Mystique, a heavy display of security. The guards eyed Nyssa and the sword on her back as Quinn and the others passed through the front doors. One of the men whispered into an orb, and it flew past their group and into the casino, no doubt alerting someone within to the presence of odd-looking people with weapons.

The main floor of The Mystique was a whirlwind of activity, chips clinking on tables, laughter ringing throughout the casino, drinks flowing freely. A sweet smoke hung in the air, a combination of incense and tobacco, reminding Quinn of Elias. Topless women roamed the floor, as did men in impossibly tight black shorts and nothing else, serving drinks and food and chatting up patrons.

"Gods, they must be cold," Quinn whispered, trying to swallow. There was far too much to look at. And part of her didn't know if she *should* be looking. She tried not to gawk, but the moment she averted her eyes, they landed on another scantily clad server.

"Judging by the quantity of nipples that could put an eye out, I'd say so," Nyssa replied with a sly smile. She had to be loving this.

Despite the half-naked staff, the rest of the floor was rather understated—elegant, even. Clean, shiny, colorful. Bright letters hung in the air, guiding guests to the gambling tables and attractions in other areas of the sprawling building. One of the lounges promised dancers—Quinn guessed they'd be nude, given one of the other advertisements promising a live sex show. Yet another attraction promised a singer named Finna, the sign outside the doors indicating her show was sold out for the next month.

Servers hurried by, their trays full of brightly hued, glowing drinks—a far cry from the humble dram of whiskey or pint of ale she preferred. One of the drinks had smoke billowing off of it with an impressive display of tiny fireworks above the glass. Showmanship seemed to be of the utmost importance at The Mystique, and Quinn's curiosity was piqued despite how over the top it all was. Never in her time at the Citadel had she even dreamed of a place like this.

Next to her, Nyssa eyed the gaming tables. She had to be itching to try to take people for their money. They might have to resort to such a thing, given how they were living on borrowed funds. Reece had paid for the train tickets that brought them up to the Northern Wilds and she had filled their wallets with gold marks. Quinn didn't like to be in House Fennick's debt—or anyone's, for that matter—but they didn't have much choice.

Reece pulled them to the side. "Wait here. I'll go see Trick first and gauge what sort of mood the bastard is in. Keep your eyes open and keep to yourselves. New Ibanis is dangerous. The people in the Wilds don't fuck about."

"Medias, go with her," Nyssa said.

Medias nodded, and they weaved their way across the casino floor.

"I'll be at that Five Warlords table," Nyssa said, her eyes twinkling as she watched the card game that seemed to revolve around how well the players could lie about their hands.

Quinn wandered to the main bar to people-watch, though her eyes were drawn to the hundreds of bottles behind the bar, the myriad of liquor colors dazzling in its own right. She slid onto a barstool.

"What'll it be?" a bartender asked.

Quinn leaned forward. "The drink that smokes and sparks, what is that?"

"Elixir of the Cursed Gods."

"W-what?"

The bartender frowned at her. "It goes with our promotion. You want one? It's delicious."

Quinn nodded. *Why the hell is there a drink named after us?*

The bartender prepared the drink, mixing liquors and dropping a small cube into the glass that caused smoke to billow over the sides. She finished the mixture off with a sprinkle of powder that produced bright-blue sparks that flashed and popped above the surface of the liquid. The bartender slid the concoction in front of her.

Quinn took a cautious sip, thankful that the sparks were mere illusion and didn't zing her. The damn thing was delicious. And rather strong. She retrieved a few gold marks out of her pocket, and the bartender eyed them appreciatively. "Keep the change."

Quinn lifted her drink and turned to people-watch, the Elixir of the Cursed Gods going down smooth. Nyssa was a few tables away, intently watching a card game.

A commotion a few barstools down captured Quinn's attention. A large man pulled at a server, his bulky hand damn near wrapping around the smaller woman's bicep.

"C'mon, Jess, I'm off the clock. Give me a taste."

The man was dressed in the same dark suit as the casino guards outside. The woman covered her naked breasts and tried to pull away from him, but he yanked her arm, causing her to cry out.

Quinn stood, heat rushing to her face. "Hey, let her go."

The man turned to her and laughed. "Mind your business."

Quinn set her drink on the bar. "She doesn't seem to want your attention, so mind *your* business and stop groping at her."

He scowled. "Tourists need to keep their fucking mouths shut if they don't want their teeth knocked out of their skull."

Quinn balled up her fists.

The woman squirmed in the large man's grip, her eyes pleading with Quinn.

"Let. Her. Go."

The man yanked the poor woman closer. "Or what, girl?"

People around them stilled, their heads craning to see what the commotion was about.

Quinn swallowed. "Or you'll lose a finger."

"Ah fuck off," the man said.

The woman tried escaping him one last time, but he just laughed and threw a smirk at Quinn, giving her a dismissive wave.

Quinn's blood turned to fire. She reached up and pulled her scarf down, exposing the Mark of the Unworthy. Her magick exploded out of her. She flicked a razor-sharp shard of shadow at the man's hand, slicing his little finger clean off.

The finger fell to the carpeted floor, bounced, and rolled under a table. The man watched it disappear before lifting his hand up. Blood spurted out of the small stump where his finger used to be. His face went white.

Quinn exhaled. *Shit. Did I really just do that?*

The woman started screaming first. Then the man pushed off his barstool and rushed at Quinn, taking a swing at her with his fully-fingered hand. She blocked his punch and slid to the side, burying her own fist into his lower back. A kidney shot. He crumpled to the ground.

Pandemonium erupted around her. Bodies crashed into one another, men and women springing to their feet and throwing punches. She dodged one man reeling toward her, glancing up in time to take a fist to the face. Rocked by the blow, she barely dodged a swing from a different attacker. There was absolutely no telling who was fighting who. People flew past her and slammed into tables, scattering chips everywhere.

A woman lunged at Quinn, laughing, her punch missing by at least six inches. She teetered back and examined her fist, frowning as if it was defective before giving it another go. This time, she missed Quinn by at least a foot, and Quinn popped her in the face. The woman looked around and stumbled over to a table and picked up a drink, as if she had just lost interest in the fight.

Quinn glanced up to see Nyssa dash forward and vault over a gaming table with one hand on its blue felted surface, landing deftly on the other side. All in one smooth, effortless motion. Quinn grinned madly as she admired Nyssa's ability to make fighting look sexy. *Very* sexy.

Nyssa turned to her with a raised eyebrow. "You started a bar fight?"

"I guess?"

"That's my woman!" Nyssa reared back and punched a man who stumbled at her, his hands full of chips that were likely not his own. "There's only one rule in a bar fight—no magick!"

A strange rule, but Quinn didn't mind. She rather enjoyed throwing fists.

Diving back into the fray, she punched anyone and everyone that got close, which seemed to be another rule. She gave in to the chaos as Nyssa's laughter rang in her ears.

TRICK

Two Froslandian war wolves stared at Nyssa, low growls meeting her whenever she shifted in her chair or dabbed at her split lip with a damp cloth. She had seen chromoimages and illustrations of war wolves in books, but in person they were far larger than she had imagined. She wondered briefly if Aryis's family owned any.

"Ryd's finger had to be fished out from underneath a table. It had lint on it," Trick Baasham said, pulling at the lapels of his dark, pinstriped suit. "Fucking *lint*, Reece."

The large man sat at his desk and swept an errant strand of his thinning gray hair out of his face, frowning deeply at Nyssa and Quinn. Reece sat beside them, calm and smiling while Medias stood behind her like her very own Justiciar bodyguard.

"You not only bring a Justiciar into my casino, you bring the Cursed Gods too, and the first thing one of them does is cut off the little finger of one of my guards?"

Fair point. Not exactly the definition of lying low. And a bit of a shock that Quinn went that far.

"Do I need to be worried about you, Freckles?" Nyssa asked, glancing over at Quinn. "You took that man's finger off."

Quinn stirred in her seat. "A healer will get that pinkie back on. Maybe next time he'll be more mindful, lest he lose another."

"To be clear, he didn't *lose* a digit so much as you unattached it from his body," Trick growled.

"Let me ask this," Quinn started, staring Trick down, "if I made a threat and didn't follow through, how does that play out up here in the Northern Wilds?"

Trick leaned back, eyeing Quinn before sucking at his teeth. His face softened. "Ah...I can't necessarily disagree. You'd get eaten alive. But did it ever occur to you to mind your own damn business?"

"No. Your asshole guard was pawing at a woman who wanted no part of him," Quinn said. "He should have been minding *his* business instead of harassing her."

"Gonna cost me a nice chunk of gold to get a healer to reattach that finger," he said, sighing.

"You always take good care of your people. It's one of the things I admire about you, Trick," Reece said, the woman's voice like honey. Oh, she was *laying* it on. Nyssa had never seen this side of the empath before. She liked it. "Now, can we talk about the awkward little thing these two don't know about yet?"

Nyssa cocked her head. "What awkward little thing?"

Sighing, Trick opened a desk drawer and pulled out a slip of paper, handing it to Nyssa. "Before you think about detaching a finger from my body—or any other appendage, for that matter—let me assure you, it's a big hit."

Nyssa glanced down at the paper.

"The Cursed Gods, An Erotic Revue — Every Night at Midnight at The Mystique"

Below the headline was a chromoimage of two scantily clad women, one with a black mark on her chin. Men and women lay at their feet, their arms wrapped around the two women's legs. Everyone looked rather...lusty.

A strangled breath left Quinn.

"What in the flying fuck is this?" Nyssa asked.

"Now, ladies, it's rather tasteful. No onstage sex, if that's what you're worried about," Trick replied. "I've got other shows if you want to see the real thing."

Nyssa's mouth hung open. "They don't even look like us."

"He's using us as sex-show fodder and your objection is the actors don't *look* like us?" Quinn scoffed.

Nyssa shrugged.

Trick chuckled. "You two are the hottest commodity since you bumped off Kalla."

"Wait, we didn't kill Kalla," Nyssa said.

"Yeah, yeah. Whatever. No one up here really cares, they just want a good show that gets the juices flowing."

"I...I don't..." Nyssa looked to Reece, whose calm expression had not changed.

Reece leaned over and took the advertisement out of Quinn's hand. "So you're using their likeness and exploits to sell shows?"

Nodding, Trick smiled and tapped his finger on his desk. "Sold out every single night for weeks."

"Seems like the Cursed Gods are rather lucrative for you." Reece slid the flyer back onto the desk. "Since you're capitalizing on their notoriety, they should get at least a twenty-five percent cut of the door."

A laugh exploded out of the man. "You have some balls on you, Reece!"

Reece sighed. "Twenty-five percent."

Trick leaned back and placed a meaty hand on one of his war wolves' heads, giving it a scratch. The wolf's eyes closed a little, obviously enjoying the attention. "Fifteen percent. And I expand the show to The Feather. Fifty-fifty cut for that one between you and me. You can give the gods a taste out of your half if you wish."

"Twenty percent of your show here with a guaranteed six-month run, and for The Feather, we use local talent, none of your northern imports."

Trick took a deep breath, narrowing his eyes at Reece.

"Oh, and we don't touch tips," Reece added. "The performers deserve everything they earn."

Licking his lips, Trick smiled. "Done. Deposits straight into whose account?"

"Until Nyssa and Quinn have accounts with a bank—and a nation—of their choosing, deposit to House Fennick for now."

"You know, I happen to have a stake in a bank here—"

"No," Reece said sternly. "Trick, you know better. I won't let these women keep their money with scoundrels."

Trick gasped and pressed his hand to his chest. "You wound me, Reece Ae'Shen."

Nyssa bit her bottom lip, enjoying the back-and-forth. This was their form of sparring, each one trying to get the upper hand. Each one a master at their craft.

"We all square on the finger and the sex-show business, then?"

"Yeah."

"That brings us to why we're in New Ibanis. We're looking for a man named Bennet Anelos."

Trick's eyebrows shot up. "Ah, I see. He involved with that nasty business with his brother, the Arch Master?"

"That's what we're here to find out," Nyssa said. "By the way, Ceril's the one who killed Kalla, not us. Did you not see Arch Justiciar Decia's arrest warrant?"

He shrugged. "Am I supposed to care about those?"

Medias stiffened and crossed her arms. Trick shifted in his chair and smiled up at her.

The Northern Wilds had a well-earned reputation for being a bit unruly, not really adhering to Imperial laws when those laws didn't suit the Northerners. Nyssa couldn't begrudge the spirit of the North after being burned time and again by the Empire.

"And when there was a price on our heads? Did you pay attention to our arrest warrant?" Quinn asked.

Trick shrugged. "A million or more gold marks did have me sit up and take notice. But for Anelos, a warrant with no reward doesn't interest me."

Nyssa sighed. "Bennet Anelos. Where can we find him?"

The tone in her voice didn't seem to please the war wolves. The white one growled at her.

"Control your dogs," Quinn said.

Trick didn't heed Quinn's admonishment, neither did the wolf. It rose off its haunches and stalked around the desk, approaching Quinn.

Nyssa pressed back into her chair. War wolves were not creatures to fuck with. "Call him off, Trick."

Trick waved his hand. "Kai is a good boy. He won't attack unless I tell him to. Now, Flower? She might take a chunk from your ass." He stroked the head of the black wolf next to him, her dark eyes trained on Nyssa.

Kai sat in front of Quinn, his pale-blue eyes locked on the woman. He then rested his massive head on her knee.

Trick scowled. "Kai, come."

The wolf ignored his master.

Nyssa stared. *What the hell?*

Quinn laid her hand on Kai's head and proceeded to give him a good rub. "Bennet Anelos, where is he?"

Trick sucked at his teeth. "He lives a half-day's ride north along the coast. He limps down here whenever he has two silver marks to rub together and frequents the seedier casinos on the edges of New Ibanis."

"There are seedier casinos in this town than yours?" Quinn asked.

Trick raised an eyebrow. "I require five hundred gold just to sit at a table at The Mystique, and trust me, plenty of people have the scratch for my establishment. But Bennet? He can only afford the cheap tables. Whatever fortune House Anelos once had dried up long before Bennet squeezed the last drop from the family teat."

Interesting. Nyssa leaned forward. "House Anelos is bankrupt?"

"Has been ever since the end of the Mire War, I'm told. Middling Houses in this Empire are often one bad investment away from financial ruin."

"Can you get us some horses and directions to Bennet's house?" Reece asked.

Trick sighed and threw up his hands in mock resignation. "Anything for you, my dear. Tomorrow morning work?"

Reece nodded. "And comp us rooms? Your best, if possible. The week-long train journey was cramped and tiring. I know we could all use a hot bath and very soft bed."

"Why does a visit from you always take skin out of my hide?"

"Because you like me and our interests are often aligned. Hasn't House Fennick been good to you?"

"Of course. And I have been good in return. I hope for many more years of our informal...relationship." He drummed his fingers on his desk. "Fuck it, sure, four rooms. And come to tonight's show, yeah? See what you guys are making money off of."

Reece stood up. "Always a pleasure, Trick."

"Don't fuck with my people or my guests anymore, yeah? I don't have a ton of finger-reattachment money." He looked pointedly at Quinn.

Quinn shrugged. "No promises."

DINNER AND A SHOW

Hands slid over Nyssa's body—or the actress playing Nyssa—and wandered to places that made Quinn sink back in her seat on the deep couch next to the *real* Nyssa.

"I thought this was not a live sex show," she whispered.

"I'm not sure I know the difference between a sex show and an erotic revue," Nyssa replied. "Her hair color isn't even right...nor is it consistent with the...uh...rest of her. She has nice breasts, though, I'll give her that."

Turned out that *The Cursed Gods: An Erotic Revue* was somehow both deeply embarrassing and titillating at the same time. At least the dim lighting in the room hid her blush.

Reece and Trick sat at the table in front of them, their heads together, chatting. What exactly they were talking about, Quinn couldn't imagine. Medias sat with them, her arms crossed, a permanent scowl on her face. A few curious heads turned when they entered, but it seemed having a couple gods and a Justiciar in their midst didn't measure up to the action on stage.

The show's storyline was weak, the music passable for a small string ensemble, and the acting rather cringe-inducing, but it was undeniably sexy.

Quinn hated that she didn't hate it.

The actor portraying her sauntered over, dancing around Reece, Trick, and Medias, her hands lingering on the shoulders of Reece. Smart not touching Medias. She'd likely be responsible for the second finger mishap of the day.

Swirling around to their couch, the dancer smiled at Quinn and Nyssa before sitting in Nyssa's lap.

"You're awfully brave," Nyssa said.

"Which one of you lopped off Ryd's finger?"

Nyssa nodded toward Quinn.

The dancer reached over and lazily drew a thumb down Quinn's lips and over the Mark of the Unworthy. Quinn froze, unable to move. "The girls and I want to thank you. You see anyone you like, man or woman, just ask." She smiled at Nyssa. "You too, sweetie."

The woman caressed Nyssa's cheek, drawing a smirk out of her, and departed, returning to the stage.

Quinn swallowed hard. "Are you tempted?"

"Are you?" Nyssa replied, watching her carefully. Quinn's stomach tightened at the playful inquisitiveness in Nyssa's eyes, a curiosity that threatened to steal her breath.

"You're answering my question with a question, Nyssa."

A sly smile crossed Nyssa's face, but her gaze didn't wander. "Why do you ask?"

"Another question," Quinn mused. She decided to plow forward or they'd dance around the subject all night. "I know you've been with other men and women before me, and I'm not sure if you still want to...explore."

Nyssa let out a wistful sigh. "Oh, Freckles. While I find many different people attractive, I'm hopelessly monogamous. I don't want anyone else." Nyssa moved her knee until it touched Quinn's thigh, giving her a small nudge. "You're it for me, Quinn."

The admission made Quinn's breath catch.

"And you?" Nyssa asked. "I'm your first and only. If you want to see what it's like to be with someone else, man or woman or otherwise, I won't stop you."

Quinn scowled, not sure if she liked the lack of possessiveness on Nyssa's part. "You would be okay with me exploring?"

Nyssa grew serious, a stark change from her playful self. "I can't say I'd be okay with it. But you've been told what to do your entire life. I may hate the thought of you being with someone else, and we would have to have a very serious discussion, but I would never try to control y—"

Quinn leaned in and kissed Nyssa before she could finish her thought. For the moment, she didn't care that they were in public. No one would notice the two of them kissing while the real show unfolded on stage.

She pulled away, enjoying the surprised smile on Nyssa's face. "You're it for me too, Blacksea," she said, making Nyssa's smile even brighter. "Though if Reece appeared at the foot of our bed, I would give it some thought."

The look on Nyssa's face made Quinn break out in laughter, unable to keep up the ruse. "I had you for a second."

"You most certainly did not," Nyssa scoffed.

Knowing she was Nyssa's woman—and the only person she wanted—made Quinn's heart beat quicker. In the midst of all their trouble, Nyssa was the one constant thing she could depend on. Her home.

Nyssa laid back on the couch, and Quinn scooted next to her. She held her hand up, and Nyssa did the same, lightly brushing their fingertips together. A shiver ran through Quinn's body, indulging in the feather-like sensation. She wove her fingers between Nyssa's and pulled her hand down, kissing it.

"You are downright cuddly in public today."

Quinn gestured to the stage. "We are hardly as good a show as they are. No one's giving us a second thought."

"I know how we could make them notice us," Nyssa whispered in her ear, the low rumble of her voice alone enough to make Quinn blush. "I could slip my hand into your pants, slowly tease you until you beg to come..." She trailed her hand up Quinn's thigh.

Quinn stood, her pulse pounding in her throat. Nyssa was maddening. And exhilarating.

"My room. Now," Quinn rasped.

Nyssa dug into her pocket, pulling out gold marks and letting them spill on the table as a tip. She stared up at Quinn giving her a lopsided smile. "Yes, ma'am."

Nyssa hurried down the hallway, having gone scavenging for a bottle of whiskey before she and Quinn got far more comfortable. The silly Cursed Gods sex show had gotten them both downright flustered. She stopped in front of Quinn's door and knocked lightly, waiting a few seconds before entering.

She scowled at what she found. "Really? You've replaced me in your bed already?"

Quinn looked over and grinned. Kai was stretched out next to her in bed. He raised his head to look at Nyssa, yawned, then nuzzled his nose against Quinn's arm.

"He just sort of pushed past me into the room and made himself comfortable," Quinn said. She wore a sheer silk white camisole, low cut and stretched over her breasts.

I can't wait to take that off of her. But first things first...

"Is the other one in the bathtub having a soak?" Nyssa walked over to the bed and sighed at the massive wolf. "Come on, puppy. Move over."

The wolf didn't budge. Quinn snapped her fingers at him and pointed to the end of the bed. He immediately obeyed her, moving and then lying back down.

Nyssa laughed. "What the fuck? Do you have some sort of affinity for Froslandian war wolves?" She sat down and poured Quinn a glass of whiskey. Quinn sipped at her drink, her unwavering, searing emerald gaze made Nyssa down her glass quick. The liquor's sweet warmth spread through her belly.

Quinn put her glass down and nuzzled her face into the crook of Nyssa's neck, peppering it with soft, slow kisses. She pulled up Nyssa's shirt and caressed her stomach before inching her hand down into the waistband of Nyssa's pants.

As much as Nyssa desired what was about to happen next, she grabbed Quinn's wrist.

"Do you want me to stop?" Quinn asked, her breath hot on Nyssa's neck.

"I want you *very* much, but not with *him* staring at me." Nyssa nodded at the wolf at the end of the bed. His black eyes bored into her. It was unnerving.

Groaning, Quinn got out of bed and shuffled toward the door. Nyssa appreciated the view of the woman in her underwear.

"Come on, Kai."

The wolf hopped off the bed and followed Quinn to the door. She let him out, and he promptly flopped down outside the room. Quinn closed the door and shrugged. "I guess he just likes me."

"You're highly likable." Nyssa stood. Quinn laughed, and Nyssa caught her as she tried to get back into bed, walking her backward and pinning her against the wall. "Highly. Likable," Nyssa whispered as she pressed her body against Quinn and kissed her.

Quinn slid her hand under Nyssa's shirt and bra, making Nyssa gasp as she caressed her breast, lightly pinching her nipple. Nyssa's plan of taking control of the situation was slipping away when Quinn started working on her neck again. It was her weakness, one Quinn was more than happy to take advantage of and lavish with kisses and light touches of her tongue.

Not to be deterred, Nyssa pressed her thigh between Quinn's legs, drawing a soft moan from the woman whose body moved in concert with Nyssa's rhythmic grinding. The unmistakable blush of arousal spread across Quinn's upper chest underneath her sheer camisole.

Nyssa dipped her head and brushed her lips across the freckles dotting Quinn's shoulders. Quinn's hands wove into her hair, keeping her mouth against her skin. Nyssa didn't mind one bit. She pulled Quinn closer.

"Shall we move this to the bed?" she whispered.

"Please."

Nyssa slipped her hands under Quinn's thighs, boosting her up. Quinn laughed and wrapped her legs around Nyssa, greedily trapping Nyssa's lips under her own. The kiss turned greedy, desperate.

Ever thankful for her muscles—and always aware of how Quinn's eyes roamed her body in appreciation of them—Nyssa walked them both back to the bed and they tumbled into it, laughing.

Nyssa slid her hand up Quinn's leg, running her thumb along her inner thigh, and stopped. Quinn's pupils dilated. The heat between them made every inch of Nyssa's skin flush.

How did I ever live without this?

She trailed her hand further up Quinn's leg, her hand moving under the camisole's fabric. The hitch in Quinn's breath lit a fire in Nyssa's veins. She wanted nothing more than to make Quinn feel amazing, and she knew exactly how.

"Tonight, the focus is on you. You don't need to get me off. But if I want to...then I'll do it myself." She slid her hand between Quinn's legs. "And you can watch."

Quinn's lips parted in a gasp. "Fuck, Nyssa."

Nyssa caught those lips with her own, slowly teasing with her tongue, not in any hurry. Cocking a smile, she pressed ever closer, wanting to eliminate all space between them. Tonight, she wanted nothing more than to unravel Quinn and hear her gasping her name over and over.

HOUSE ANELOS

Nyssa yawned, still tired from the night before with Quinn. No regrets, though—she'd do it a thousand times over. She sucked in some cold air and shook her head to wake herself up, the half-day ride out to Bennet Anelos's property almost lulling her to sleep atop her horse.

They found the house easily, even with Trick's crudely drawn map. It was a drab, brown structure on the edge of a forest, overrun by age and the surrounding brush, a mix of dead foliage and a few scraggly bushes that struggled for survival. The ruddy brick exterior was crumbling in places, a hole pocking an upper corner of the building below its snow-covered roof. A thin wisp of smoke rose from the chimney, the top of it jagged and sharp, like a wolf's teeth.

The women approached the house cautiously, Nyssa calling her power forth to give it a good once-over, checking for traps, wards, or any other bits of nasty magick. Dull scraps of energy dotted the exterior, including the patch of grass Medias was about to step on.

Nyssa caught the woman by the collar of her jacket and pulled her back. "Hold up."

"What is it, Blacksea?" Medias asked.

Nyssa let her magick flow, sparks of electricity crawling along the ground, ready to twist the strands of magick that comprised the protection enchantment.

"Leave my wards be, Unworthy," a reedy voice called out.

Up at the house, a sliver of a man stood on the stoop.

"Bennet Anelos?" Nyssa called out.

"Been expecting you. Come on in. Mind your step."

The four of them steered around the wards protecting the property, most likely sticky traps to ensnare trespassers. They entered the house, and Nyssa's eyes adjusted to the dim light. The inside was shabby but clean, the furniture dingy and threadbare.

"Have a seat, let me put a pot on for tea. I don't have much else to offer," Bennet said as he moved toward the kitchen. His denim pants were a size too large—or perhaps he had simply shrunk as he aged—and his cream sweater was equally ill-fitting. Whatever hair he might have had was shaved close to the scalp. Nyssa studied him, finding similarities to Ceril. The sharp, hawkish features were there, but less severe, and they had the same light-blue eyes. Yet there was a mild warmth to Bennet that Ceril wholly lacked.

Nyssa and Reece sat down on the couch while Medias wandered the room, pulling books off shelves to rifle through them, opening up a small wooden box to poke around its contents. Quinn situated herself in a corner, her eyes not leaving Bennet as he tended to making tea.

"You were expecting us?" Nyssa asked.

"News reaches me. Slow, but eventually. Figured someone from the Empire would be out here poking around. Ceril isn't here. Never has been," Bennet answered from the kitchen.

Several uncomfortable minutes passed before the kettle whistled and he returned with a pot of tea and a stack of mugs, most chipped and discolored.

"We brought you some supplies from New Ibanis," Reece said, lifting up a knapsack packed with food, soaps, and warm socks. She had insisted on a small shopping trip to bring their host a few gifts. "Gifts are currency in the Wilds," she had explained, "and a sign of respect." If the items helped get information out of the man, good.

Bennet's eyes widened at the bag, and he nodded. "Much appreciated." He offered Nyssa and Reece tea. Their hesitation drew a sigh from the man. "I didn't poison it. I may be old, but I don't have a death wish."

Taking a mug, Nyssa took a sip, surprised to find the tea earthy and smoky, quite different from the kinds in the south. Different, but good. Nyssa made quick introductions for everyone while Bennet sat on a rickety dining room chair that creaked under his meager weight.

"I heard about a couple gods popping up. You them?" he asked, eyeing Nyssa.

"Yeah," she replied. "Do you know what your brother's done?"

"Accusations of assassinating the Empress." He waved it off, lackadaisical.

She glanced at Medias, who kept her eyes trained on the man. "Not an accusation. I witnessed it with my own eyes. He also had my father killed and branded me as a traitor. He wants us dead and he's not going to stop until we are."

Bennet chuckled. "Ceril has always been dogged in his pursuit of what he wants."

"There's nothing amusing about what he's done," Quinn said, her voice cold.

Bennet studied her. "You're the girl he was given to raise?"

"I'm the woman who was kidnapped by the Areshi Empire so they could have a god on a leash. Let's not romanticize it, as if he took in an orphan and gave her a good home."

The man studied her. "Ceril did say you had a spirit about you."

Quinn's face darkened. "What?"

"Before we had a falling out, he would often write to me." Bennet looked down into his tea mug. "He called you curious and odd. Exhausting. But he's never been very giving of praise." Bennet shrugged. "Haven't spoken to him in decades. I'm not his favorite person. You see, House Anelos fell on hard fortunes. I have a problem with gambling. Well, I have two problems with gambling. One, I can't stop; and two, I can't win. I drained all the money our family had."

"This was a waste of time," Quinn grumbled.

Nyssa eyed her, giving her a subtle shake of her head. Bennet was the only connection they had to Ceril. They had to probe deeper, get more information, maybe find something they could use. "Tell us more about Ceril, if you would."

Bennet shifted in his chair, and it groaned underneath him. "My father and Emperor Nillis were at Wayland together. Thick like brothers. So when it came time for Nillis to pick his successor, he chose Ceril as a favor to our House."

Nyssa scoffed. "That's how Ceril was named successor? A fucking favor between school chums?"

Sighing, Bennet continued, "Sadly, yes, but such is the way of modern Areshi politics: the Great Houses circling one another, vying for favors. Imagine their disdain when a lesser House was chosen to ascend to the throne. Yet, Ceril accepted the honor, but he had to swear off marriage and children. It's a solitary life of servitude to one greater good—the Empire. Unfortunately, Ceril was already betrothed to a woman."

"That's true then?" Quinn asked. She exchanged a glance with Nyssa. "That was a whispered rumor at Arcton. But I couldn't imagine anyone willing to marry that man."

"Her name was Gylias, if I recall correctly. Ceril was given a choice by our father—become Emperor and restore our House and its fortunes or remain a common adept but marry the woman he loved and raise a family. Nothing in his life meant more to him than his woman, but in the end, he chose duty to our father and our House over her."

Bennet paused and poured himself more tea, a sadness clinging to him like cobwebs. "After that ultimatum, something hardened in Ceril. He was never the warmest man, but with Gylias, he was happy. But being forced to give her up made him bitter. He replaced love with ambition—it became his sole focus."

"A deadly focus," Medias remarked.

"Ceril left Wayland to apprentice under Nillis for seven years to prepare for the throne. Then, on the cusp of the Mire War, that idiot of an Emperor drank himself to death. And what did the Great Houses do? Did they mourn his death and honor his wishes for my brother to ascend to the throne? No, they cast him aside and chose a girl to lead us."

Nyssa sat back, exhaling, familiar with that part of the story. "Why did they spurn Ceril?"

"The Great Houses look down on anyone not in their circle. Nillis came from a middling House. House Anelos was held in even lower regard. Everyone knew we were on the verge of bankruptcy. The Great Houses likely felt it was time to bring the throne back into the inner circle, so they chose a girl from House Simac."

He took a deep breath. "After the Mire War, Ceril was made First Master at the Citadel, a consolation of sorts, I suppose. He hated that he was pushed aside and he just grew darker, more bitter. Like a shade was drawn over his life. And me and him, we fell out. I suspect he blames me for his poor fortunes."

Nyssa glanced at the others. "Could Ceril be looking for Gylias? Do you know where she is now?"

"Long dead," Bennett replied.

"Does he have allies he can turn to?"

Bennet shrugged. "I know nothing of his life anymore."

"Is there anything you can tell us?" Quinn asked, looking troubled. "Does he have anywhere to go? Property anywhere? What's left of your House's estate?"

Bennet waved his hands around. "There is no House Anelos anymore, aside from this crumbling estate, if you can even call it that. Our family is from the Northern Wilds, though Ceril hates to admit it. The north was never proper enough for him. But he knows the territory. If he wishes to hide anywhere, it will be somewhere up here, in the Wilds."

Nyssa finally looked to Reece, who sat in rapt attention. "Well?"

After a moment, Reece replied, "He's telling the truth."

Bennet eyed Reece, blinking slowly. There seemed little else left to glean from the man.

Nyssa stood. "Thank you. We'll take up no more of your time." The others stood too, edging toward the door.

Bennet remained in his chair. "If you catch up to Ceril, what do you intend to do?"

"Kill him," Quinn answered.

A somber look settled on Bennet's face at her honesty. "He wasn't always the man you have come to hate."

"That doesn't matter to me," Quinn said. "He's killed countless people and imprisoned me for years. That darkness came from somewhere. It was always inside him."

"You have it in you too, don't you? That darkness."

Quinn's face twitched.

Nyssa needed to get her out of there before something bad happened. "We'll take our leave now." She and the others exited Bennet's house, walking back to their horses. "Let's get back to The Mystique."

A cadre of red-clad Justiciars awaited Nyssa and the others outside The Mystique—and in their midst stood Ashcloak Ruggen. New Ibanis was usually a safe haven from Imperial eyes and interference, and the lack of a crowd in the street was telling—word had likely gotten out to avoid the area at all costs.

Nyssa swore under her breath and readied herself for a fight. *Fucking fuck*. "What're you doing here, Ina?"

"You will address me as Master Ashcloak Ruggen. I earned this title and didn't piss it away," Ina replied, squaring her shoulders in the waning light of the day. "You four are under arrest for disobeying an Imperial order."

Nyssa dismounted, followed by Quinn and the others. "I'm not an Imperial citizen. I don't have to follow orders."

"When you are guests of the Emperor, you do not go against his wishes. He was very explicit that you were not to go after Ceril Anelos."

"Do you see Ceril in our custody? We're here to gamble and take in some shows," Nyssa replied. "I highly recommend the Cursed Gods erotic revue that they have here at The Mystique. They really don't look like us, but the choreography has some—"

"Your smart-ass charm likely works on other people, but not me," Ruggen snapped.

"You think I'm charming?" Out of the corner of her eye, Nyssa saw Quinn take a deep breath.

"You need to come with us."

Nyssa's teasing mood evaporated, and she balled up her fists, advancing on her old rival. The Justiciars shifted ever so slightly, hands inching closer to weapons. "You don't get to tell me what to do. Neither do these Justiciars." She stared at Ina. "For fuck's sake, Ina, Ceril killed Eron. Don't you care at all about that?"

Ruggen's jaw tightened. "Of course I do. But he would direct me to follow my orders and arrest Anelos so he can face Imperial justice."

Heat flushed through Nyssa. "Imperial justice?" she spat, raising her voice. "I've seen Imperial justice. It cut this mark into my chin and hunted me down because I chose honor over mindless duty. Fuck your *Imperial justice.*"

A perceptible shift in the tenor of the Justiciars raised Nyssa's hackles. Decia's lackeys were prepared to fight.

And it would be a bloodbath. Nyssa and Quinn had killed Justiciars and adepts before and she hated it. The memory of it churned her stomach.

Medias stepped up next to Nyssa. "We will return to Ocean's Rest with you."

"The hell we will," Nyssa growled.

"A word, please." Medias pulled her to the side, red eyes drilling into her. Quinn and Reece closed ranks. "You're going to go to war against the Empire if you do anything to harm Ruggen or these Justiciars. I won't allow you to do that."

"Allow me? *Allow* me, Justiciar? I'm not someone to be controlled," Nyssa snarled through bared teeth.

"You have been on the run for two years. Be smart. If there's violence today, you'll be on the run again, and your friends don't want that for you. They need you in their lives. They need Quinn too." Medias's face softened. "We just got you both back. Please, Nyssa. Don't let your past with Ina push you to make a dire mistake."

It was hard to deny Medias's words. Nyssa's eyes roamed to Quinn. "What do you want to do?"

Quinn took a deep breath and squared her jaw. "We need to be smart. Medias is right."

"Of course I am." Medias smirked.

Nyssa rolled her eyes. *Smart-ass.*

She turned back to Ashcloak Ruggen and ground her teeth. "We will return with you to Ocean's Rest."

A Justiciar stepped forward, a bag at his side, the all too familiar outline of void collars evident in its shape. Quinn tensed. Nyssa had promised her she'd never be collared again. She'd already failed when Ceril attacked them aboard the Whisper.

She would not fail again.

"You come any closer with those *things* and you'll die here in the street," Nyssa warned, flexing her fingers.

Ruggen held up her hand. "No need for the collars. They're coming willingly. Discretion is our friend when dealing with the Cursed Gods."

"You're an Ashcloak, this is not your call," the lead Justiciar said.

Everyone tensed. Ina's eyes flicked to Nyssa, quickly running up and down her body. She was doing as Eron had taught the adepts at the Emerald Order—assess the enemy and be ready for violence. And violence would ensue if they insisted on collars.

"Who wants a fucking drink?" Reece asked, clapping her hands once.

Heads turned to the empath. Nyssa blinked, confused.

"Nyssa and Quinn are coming along peacefully. You can choose to turn that peace into a bloodbath or you can have a drink. I'm buying." Without waiting for a response, Reece pushed past Nyssa, brushed by Ina, and walked through the gathered Justiciars. She didn't hesitate or step around them. She made them move for *her.*

And they fucking did.

Medias gestured for Nyssa and Quinn to follow. Not one Justiciar so much as flinched in their direction.

HOUSE ARREST

Quinn sat in a dim, sparsely furnished room in a remote wing of Ocean's Keep. They had been escorted there by Decia and at least twenty Justiciars the second they arrived after their week-long train journey back to Ocean's Rest. At first, she had no idea why they were taken to some rarely used part of the Keep, but she realized it was to isolate them from the rest of the sprawling estate. To contain the danger should Decia's forces push the Cursed Gods to violence.

Dark-red threads poked out of the arm of her chair, and Quinn pulled at them, her mind drifting off, an unfocused restlessness plaguing her.

"Quinn?"

She blinked and glanced up. Nyssa, Medias, and Reece were looking at her. "I'm sorry, did you ask me a question?"

"I asked if you're listening," Medias said through her frown. "And obviously you're not."

Quinn sank down a bit in her chair, tugging on another thread. "Sorry." She had barely listened to anything after Decia declared that she and Nyssa were under house arrest by order of Emperor Safin Vonner-Areshi. Nyssa had argued against it, Medias had calmed her down, and Reece stuck herself in the middle, trying to mediate. It all seemed like a waste of time. A waste of energy. A waste of anger.

Now they were stuck in Ocean's Keep, punished like children. Not that they had any bright ideas of where to look for Ceril next.

"You need to let Decia and the Emperor calm down. They will reassess this house arrest in due time," Medias said.

Nyssa paced back and forth, her face red. "This is bullshit and you know it."

"It is indeed bullshit, but it is the bullshit you must endure for the time being."

"Is this you protecting your mother? Playing the dutiful Justiciar to get back in her good graces?"

Medias tensed, her spine ramrod straight.

"Nyssa, that's not fair," Reece said, a note of admonishment in her tone.

Nyssa ran her hands through her hair. "Then why is she telling us to just put up with this, Reece?"

"Why don't you ask me, Blacksea?" Medias said. "You're quick to anger, but I'm not going to coddle your impulse to hit something."

Fearing they'd come to blows, Quinn stood and pulled Nyssa towards the couch. "Go sit down. You're making them nervous." She nodded to the two Justiciars that stood at the door. Another feature of their house arrest—new personal watchdogs.

Nyssa pulled away and sat down, anger radiating off of her.

"You have a very short—and I mean fleeting—margin of error here," Medias said, emphasizing every word, her voice low and steady. "Decia is showing you as much grace as she can. Safin's reign is in its fragile infancy, and she needs to protect him. Right now, he has to look strong and decisive in regard to you two dangerous, renegade gods. And when you keep ignoring his wishes, you put him in danger, but a far different one now than what he faced from Ceril at the Sun Palace."

Nyssa leaned forward, gesticulating with her hands. "Need I remind everyone in this room that we saved his life?"

"And need I remind you of this?" Medias took a deep breath. "*Two souls, forever entwined, chaos dancing in eyes and blood, born between realms and belonging to the stars. Two souls, forever entwined, clash with fists and blade, dragging the tips of their swords across the world. Two souls, forever entwined, dance and howl, as ancient magick unfurls and envelopes the light. Two souls, forever entwined, bend and break, hurling to earth to die and be forever reborn."*

The scowl deepened on Nyssa's face.

Medias continued, "Yes, I memorized it. The lore of the Cursed Gods is on the tip of everyone's tongue. All they know of you two is your reckless actions and that lore, which serves very much as a warning. They are heeding that warning in the face of your volatility. That you are not in void collars in a cell deep within this Keep is a *fucking* triumph."

Sharp ire tinged every one of the Justiciar's words. She wasn't given to much outward emotion, save for annoyance, and anger on Medias was downright frightening. Nyssa took a deep breath, and Reece sat silent but her eyebrows perked up.

"Okay," Nyssa said, leaning back, her finger tapping on her thigh. "I get your point. But we can't stay under house arrest forever. Something has to give."

"Two weeks," Quinn said. "Tell Decia the Empire has two weeks to act or we will."

Medias shot her a look. "The Empire will not bow to your ultimatum."

Quinn shook her head. "Come on, Nyssa. We're done here."

Medias moved in front of her. "Let me be clear about this: Ceril is to be arrested, not killed. He will face justice."

Unbelievable. Quinn let out an exasperated breath, feeling her face go hot. "That word again. Where is my justice for what he did to me, hmm? Or my justice for Aryis's betrayal? Or my justice for being hunted like a dog by your Empire?"

Medias put her hand up. "Ceril is responsible for the deaths at The Masthead two years ago and the Wayland attack. Twenty-six children died that day. Their families deserve justice too." Her hand dropped, and she moved closer to Quinn. "I'm sorry for what you've been through, Quinn."

Medias's eyes didn't waver from Quinn's gaze, but it all was a cold comfort.

"I want to keep you out of a prison cell," Medias continued. "The order to arrest Ceril comes from the Emperor, and Decia will carry out his wishes. If you go against them, you risk your freedom."

Nyssa popped up out of her chair and closed on Quinn and Medias. "I was raised to be an Ashcloak—we honor the spirit of justice as much as Justiciars do. We'll see Anelos pay for his crimes...but we can only sit on our hands for so long."

Unmoved, Medias shook her head. "Patience, Blacksea."

Quinn took a deep breath. "Just relay our message to your mother. Two weeks."

"Quinn—"

"Justiciar Medias, do as I ask. I'm done talking." She leaned her head back and pinched the bridge of her nose. "I'm just...I'm tired. I need a bath, a cup of tea, and a warm bed."

She turned and walked out of the room, her thoughts dark. Let the Empire insist on arresting Ceril—in the end, she had no interest in justice.

THE MASK SLIPS

T he masked visitor at Medias's door was not unexpected; this scenario had played out in a vision weeks prior aboard the Whisper. She steeled herself. *I thought I would have more time...*

"The Arch Justiciar and your peers will await you in the main garden tomorrow night for your Crossing," the Justiciar said, delivering his message and leaving her breathless in its wake.

It was a simple directive, one Medias understood all too well. She closed the door and unzipped her jacket. Free of its tight restriction, she rolled her shoulders, trying to work out some tension. Bisecting the room, she sat down hard on the narrow windowsill, her legs suddenly unsteady.

She peered down at the small greenish-blue plant that had appeared in her room one day. A gift from Reece. According to the empath, it was a succulent that needed very little water or attention to thrive.

Medias found herself contemplating the little thing often. Tonight, she realized she would miss it when she was gone. A foolish sentiment, caring about a plant that didn't care for her in return.

Medias brushed her fingertips over its leaves. Its fat, fuzzy foliage brought a slight smile to her lips. She grew careless and accidentally pricked her skin on the side of a leaf, where small, sharp spines grew.

Hissing, she stuck her finger in her mouth.

She was on her way to the bathroom to wash the blood away when someone knocked on her door. Medias answered it.

Reece waited outside, dressed in overalls and a fuzzy cardigan. Even dressed casually, she was somehow effortlessly stunning.

Medias could pinpoint the two moments she started seeing Reece differently. First came the harrowing emotional attraction that made her heart thump wildly when Reece considered leaving Ocean's Rest. The physical attraction came later, after Medias beat Reggie Cox senseless for threatening the empath's life. Once they were alone, Reece had asked her to remove her mask and Medias refused. She had never felt more vulnerable in the presence of another person.

An insidious thing, this affection, growing from an improbable seed of shared disdain and mistrust. It now wound around her like ivy, its roots invasive and deep.

Reece walked through the door, rarely waited for an invitation. "You weren't at dinner. Is everything okay?"

Medias sighed and turned back into the room, sitting on the bed. "I'm fine, empath."

"I have learned not to take that assertion at face value, Justiciar."

"You remain as excruciating as ever." Medias absentmindedly stuck her finger in her mouth.

Reece crossed over to her. "What did you do?"

"Your plant stabbed me."

"Ah. One second." Reece hurried into the bathroom, turned the water on for a moment, then returned with a small towel.

"I-I don't need assistance," Medias said, but that didn't deter Reece, who knelt before her.

"Why do you refuse help? It won't enter you into some blood debt with me," Reece said, her tone impatient.

Medias did the exact opposite of what her brain screamed at her to do and relented, offering her pricked finger, blood bubbling up from the small puncture. Reece took her wrist, her touch light and gentle, and pressed the towel against the wound.

"Just keep pressure on it for a minute or two," Reece said, rising to her feet and smiling down at Medias. "Careful with that plant. It looks harmless, but it does have a bite."

Medias scowled up at her. "I don't need your plant advice."

Reece's dark eyes bored into her, a frown overtaking her face. "Why are you so damn ornery? Could you just let people help you?" She reached forward, her fingers brushing away a few stray hairs that fell over Medias's mask.

Heat rushed to Medias's face.

Reece's touch, the intimacy of one simple gesture, carried an electric charge that hit Medias square in the chest. In that moment, something shifted. Her heart, body, mind…they were all Reece's for the taking if she but asked, of that Medias was sure. The change was undeniable.

And Medias had to put a stop to it. Immediately.

She caught Reece's wrist. "No," she whispered, her voice dangerously close to giving out as some unnamed thing inside her stomach fluttered.

"Medias." Reece moved closer. The empath looked down at her, face soft and open. "You are harder and harder to get out of my thoughts, Justiciar."

The admission set Medias's brain spinning. It was irrefutable that what she felt for Reece had tumbled on its head over the past few months, but Medias couldn't pursue anything with her.

Not with her own death looming.

The Justiciars expected retribution. Medias's Crossing would be the next night, and she would not allow Reece to watch her die. Better to turn the empath away now, to harden her heart.

"You need to leave." Medias kept her voice steady and swallowed back her regret.

Reece's response was soft. "You can't deny there's something here between us."

Medias opened her mouth, her heart leaden as the lies spilled out. "We are allies, nothing more."

Sadness flickered across Reece's face before it settled into a polite, guarded smile. A bit of armor the empath donned, perhaps to conceal her hurt. Medias had seen that armor often when they had started to get to know one another, Reece so mistrustful and angry at first. And now, it felt like Medias just unwound all the progress they had made together.

"I see," Reece said. "Goodnight, Medias." She turned and headed for the door.

Medias wanted to grab her and pull her back. But then what?

The door closed and her heart recoiled, aching from her own necessary coldness. She ripped the Justiciar mask from her face and threw it against the wall. The mask didn't shatter or break. Not one chip or dent.

No, the mask stood fast. Of *course* it did.

The woman once underneath it, however, slumped forward, burying her face in her hands.

THE MASK FALLS

R eece pinched the bridge of her nose and swallowed the remaining dregs of her cold coffee, her eyes cast down on the crisp, white paper on her desk. The paper that bore the seal of Emperor Safin Vonner-Areshi. A pardon for her "crimes" against the Empire. Lilliana had brought it to her that evening.

She spun her chair around to face the window, a row of plants adorning her windowsill.

In addition to the pardon, she received a letter from Decia, written in impeccable script, asking Reece to stay away from Safin and the Sun Council. First it was Nyssa and Quinn's house arrest. Now, she was ever so politely told to fuck off. The thing that made her famous—her empathic magick that made her valuable—now ostracized her.

It was a stupid decision. She could be helpful and wade through the negative emotions swirling around the Sun Council to possibly help Safin avoid danger. Lilliana had listened patiently to her frustration with Decia and the others, but in the end, asked Reece to fall in line.

Lilliana had become a source of frustration, making no mention of Reece quitting The Feather months prior, as if their argument about becoming the next Regent of the city had never happened. As if Lilliana rejecting her had never happened. Was she punishing Reece? Rarely did the woman ever not tackle a problem head-on, though Reece could say the same for herself. How had they turned into cowards in each other's presence?

Reece's errant thoughts left Lilliana and meandered to Medias. Their encounter from the previous night still stung. Reece had struggled to keep herself in check as her own emotions roiled. She wanted to rip that mask from the Justiciar's face just once and read her expression. To watch her try to lie about her feelings again.

Lately, she'd been pulling away—not just from Reece, but from everyone. The change was subtle, but ever since Decia's arrival aboard the Whisper, Medias seemed somber.

"She's...difficult. But not in an unrewarding way," Reece informed the succulent that sat at the end of the row of plants, turning her eyes to the moon high in the sky outside her office window. "She's always buttoned up, rarely a hair out of place in that topknot of hers. I just wanted to..."

Reece frowned at the plant, remembering how Medias almost killed Reggie Cox, the leader of the Razinu faction, for threatening Reece over money she owed him. When he struck Reece, the Justiciar had moved with deadly purpose and barely restrained anger in one moment, then made sure Reece wasn't hurt in the next, her touch tender and almost...affectionate.

Had she misread Medias? Not being able to sense the Justiciar's emotions made Reece rely solely on her gut. It had happened once before, with another, and she had promised herself to not let anyone rip her heart into pieces like that again. But after two years' worth of friendship building between them, Medias's high walls lowering a bit had to mean *something*. Or maybe Reece simply wasn't worthy of Medias's affections.

And so, her life of late had just...stalled. No one in her bed, no job, and no promise of a future. Lilliana had to see her as weak. How could she not after years of letting others' emotions wash over her, reading them, giving them counsel? It was all she had been good for—her magick making her one-dimensional. She had been a unique toy for Lilliana to exploit, her empathic magick so very rare.

Reece flexed her neck and let out a small, shameless moan when it cracked, giving her some relief.

The clearing of a throat startled her. She whirled around in her chair to find Medias standing in the doorway.

"Shit," Reece hissed. "How long have you been standing there?"

"A moment."

It felt like a lie meant to put Reece at ease.

"What do you want?" Reece asked, her voice clipped.

Instead of an answer, Medias walked into the room, immediately moving to the bookshelf. She picked up a book from a haphazard stack, scanned the rows, then reshelved it undoubtedly where it belonged. In nearly two years, Medias had stubbornly created order out of the disarray of Reece's modest library.

Medias exhaled heavily, tension clinging to her like a taut wire about to snap.

She finally spoke. "My mother acquiesced and agreed to let me see you. A final act of grace, I suppose."

"A final act?" Reece asked, confused. She rose from her chair and approached. "What's going on?"

Medias turned, her eyes shiny, and a darkness clung to her. Reece had never seen the Justiciar like this. Her mouth went dry.

"I wanted to thank you for your...friendship during my time here in Ocean's Rest. You didn't trust me at first, but you put your reservations aside and were kind to me."

"Why are you talking like this?"

Medias stepped closer to Reece, closer than she'd ever dared get. She bowed her head and reached up, her fingertips lightly touching the smooth white Justiciar mask she wore. She inhaled a sharp breath.

Moments ticked away before Medias pressed her fingers against the mask and pulled it from her face, raising her gaze to Reece.

Medias's features were softer than Reece remembered from the brief time she had seen her without her mask before. She was bare. Vulnerable.

Beautiful.

A thin black line ran across her cheeks, from temple to temple, arching over the bridge of her nose. The Mark of the Justiciar, branded so she could never be free of the mantle, even without the mask. The middle of her chin bore a small dimple—a family trait that Decia shared—that Reece found endlessly endearing.

Without the mask, Medias's composure seemed to crumble, her bottom lip trembling and deep-red eyes filling with tears.

"Did I do the right thing?" she whispered, closing her eyes. "Helping Nyssa and Quinn?"

"Yes, you did. You *always* do the right thing."

Reece smiled and took Medias's hand, surprised when the Justiciar didn't pull away. An unspoken struggle played out on Medias's face. A deep, grating fear rattled within Reece, her heart pounding.

Medias's eyes opened and took her in. "Reece, I'm so scared."

"Wh-what's going on?" Reece could barely swallow, her stomach dropping through the floor. Medias wasn't a woman who was *ever* afraid.

Something was wrong. Horribly wrong.

Medias paused, studying Reece, as if trying to commit her face to memory. Medias gave her a smile, a rare and treasured thing.

"Thank you for your friendship, empath," Medias said, her smile tingeing with sorrow. She reaffixed her mask and then hurried to the door to make her escape. Reece tried to open her mouth and beg Medias to stay, but she froze.

It felt like the earth shifted beneath her, her legs suddenly unsteady.

Medias opened the door to a sea of red uniforms and white masks. Without looking back, she disappeared into the middle of them, and they escorted her away.

Reece knew very little about Justiciar traditions, but the one thing that had always hung over Medias's head was the consequence of her so-called betrayal of the Order of Justiciars and the Empire.

Dammit. They had grown complacent, thinking Safin's pardons meant acquittal for Medias too. A chill ran down her spine.

They're going to kill her.

Reece fell back against her desk, stifling a gasp. Her mind raced. She had to stop them from executing Medias. She needed help.

Reece shot out the door and ran, her heart pounding in her ears.

Medias stripped down to her underwear, folding her red leather jacket and pants and placing them neatly on her bed. She put on the white cotton pants and shirt her mother held out to her. At least they hadn't taken her mask. Not yet. They would when she was dead, her time as a Justiciar—and her life—at its end.

This moment was inevitable, clear from a vision she had not long after Ceril attacked the Whisper. She had woken up in the dark of her stateroom, sweating, to the image of her mask turning to ash.

"Leave us," Decia demanded, and the Justiciar assigned to keep watch over Medias in her waning moments departed the room, leaving mother and daughter alone in silence. They rarely spoke of anything other than Imperial business, their personal lives completely walled off from one another. Growing up, Medias never felt a great deal of love from her mother. What love she didn't receive from Decia was given to her tenfold by her father, who had kept her from Ambershine as long as he could. His own marriage to Decia was a secret from everyone save Kalla. It was the nature of the role. A Justiciar's private life, the people they loved, made them vulnerable. Corruptible.

The separation, the forced aloofness, made mother and daughter veritable strangers. It pained Medias more than she could express, trying to love a woman more a stranger than a parent; a woman who had chosen Medias's path for her, turning her into a Justiciar. And as a Justiciar...the things she had done, the monster she feared she had become...

Medias broke the silence. "I'm not sorry for what I did for Nyssa and Quinn. Father would be proud, of that I'm certain. All he ever wanted was for me to carve my own way in the world, to be more than just a Justiciar. And I did that. For a while, anyway."

Decia watched her. "I barely know who you are." She reached forward and gently removed the mask from Medias's face, stroking her cheek.

"You grew up, and I made no effort to understand the woman you'd become."

As much as Medias craved a kind touch, she pulled away. Her mother's remorse felt trite and was delayed far too long to mean anything now. She retrieved her mask from her mother's hands and placed it back on her face, its magick holding it fast to her skin. They would remove it from her once dead. "Let's get this over with."

Willing her legs to support her, Medias left her room and walked down the narrow hall to the main corridor that ran through the guest quarters of Ocean's Keep. Head up and back straight—she wouldn't give them one glimmer of weakness or shame.

A legion of Justiciars awaited her, staid and silent. They turned and moved through the hall, Medias following, her mother trailing behind. What a sight it must have been for those in the Keep, over a hundred Justiciars marching one of their own down to the East Garden, moonlight casting shadows of stark, leafless trees onto the fresh snow. Medias inhaled the crisp, cold air and shivered. It was a breathtaking night.

The Justiciars brought her to a large paved clearing rimmed by stone benches and flowerbeds that lay fallow save for the few that contained winter lilies. Reece's favorite flower. Medias's breath caught in her chest. Any attempt to put Reece out of her mind had failed. The woman hung in the back of her brain, persistent.

A tall, gaunt Justiciar stepped forward when Medias reached the center of their gathering. In his hand lay a small cylinder. Ashara's Vengeance—named after the first Justiciar, its poison slow-acting. And fatal. She took the container from him.

Few Justiciars in the history of the Empire had been executed. All of them for breaking their code. And for those crimes, the Justiciar was expected to willingly take Ashara's Vengeance. Medias was no different. As much as she tried to pry herself out of the Justiciar mask, to leave it behind, she still had to answer for her crimes.

Decia stood next to her, eyes scanning the crowd. "Tonight, Justiciar Medias, you will give yourself over to the Order of Justiciars in a final act of repentance." Decia turned to Medias. "Due to your betrayal, the last act of grace we can offer you is the Crossing. We will administer Ashara's Vengeance if you cannot bring yourself to do so."

Medias met her mother's gaze and pushed up her sleeve. Without hesitation, she pressed the cold cylinder against her left wrist. She barely felt the needle prick.

"It is done," Medias rasped, her voice as hollow as her heart.

Decia's eyes wavered. "When you breathe your last breath, your mask will be burned to ash, erasing all memory of you from our Order."

A small greenish-black spot appeared on Medias's wrist. At first, she felt nothing. Far different from her Turning, when she was given Amberis to complete her transformation into a Justiciar—the gold liquid changing her, obscuring her thoughts and feelings against magickal abilities. The Amberis had burned hot and long. Some of her peers wailed and begged for death before the hours of agony slowly waned. Medias had closed her eyes and simply endured, seeking respite through meditation. She didn't find it. The only thing that kept her from crying out in pain those years ago was pride.

Stubborn, idiotic pride.

Medias's heart began to pound as the poison started to move up her arm. Strangely, she wasn't overtaken by fear. Only regret. She would die in this damn garden, surrounded by strangers. She almost wanted to laugh at how pathetic it all was.

At least the East Garden was beautiful, strings of golden light orbs strung between trees, casting a warm glow over everything. Shadows stirred along the ground as the trees above her swayed gently in the breeze.

As the poison began to burn, Medias fixed her gaze on a thick, massive oak that stood in the distance, wishing she could go lie under it, close her eyes, and drift off into dreams.

"Stop!" Reece shouted, bursting into the East Garden. A hundred masked faces turned her way. But she was only concerned with one of them.

A small crowd of spectators had already gathered, curiosity bringing them forth. A mix of Ashcloaks, Keep attendants, and numerous members of the Great Houses looked on.

"What the fuck is this?" Nyssa demanded as she hurried next to Reece. Quinn, Athen, and Aryis followed them.

Reece had run to find them, barely getting two words out as she panted for air: "Help! Medias!" Nyssa and the others wasted no time, following her, no questions asked.

Several Justiciars moved to intercept Quinn and Nyssa. Quinn called her power forth, twisting dark tendrils of energy around the Justiciars who dared approach. She shoved them to the side with her shadows and walked into the middle of them, trailed by Nyssa.

"This doesn't concern you, Cursed Gods," Decia said, her voice cold.

"The fuck it doesn't," Quinn snapped. "Medias is our friend."

*This is why Medias came to my office. She was saying goodbye...*Reece pushed aside her anger at the situation—and at Medias for not telling her the truth—and tried to cling to hope.

A commotion drew her attention. Safin and his mother moved through the crowd, a small retinue of Ashcloaks at his side, including Ina Ruggen.

"What's happening here?" Safin asked.

"Justiciar Medias has broken our sacred laws. Her betrayal of the Areshi Empire demands she pay a price," Decia answered, raising her voice for all to hear.

"And something tells me that price isn't just a stern talking-to," Nyssa said. "This is an execution."

Not waiting another moment, Reece pushed through the Justiciars, coming to a stop in front of Medias. Her stomach twisted. Medias's breathing was ragged, and the sides of her neck glistened with a sheen of sweat, tendons straining. Reece couldn't imagine what she was going through, how scared she must be.

"What did you do to her?" Reece demanded, her voice breaking.

"You weren't meant to see this," Medias breathed, her tone hollow. "Nyssa, get Reece out of here..."

Reece tensed. "I'm not going anywhere, goddamn it."

"No one is leaving," Athen said, walking up, the bass of his voice rumbling. "And you are not executing her. Safin, please, this isn't—"

"This is Imperial law," Decia said. "A law that transcends the power of one man, even the Emperor."

Anger flashed in Nyssa's eyes. "Anelos is out there somewhere and this is what takes precedence?"

"My Justiciars will deal with him."

Reece balled her fists up. "You're her mother. How can you do this?"

"I'm a Justiciar, first and foremost," Decia said, her gaze unwavering. "I am Imperial justice."

"Stop this execution or you'll have a very big problem on your hands," Nyssa replied, turning to Safin. "You want to see how destructive Cursed Gods can be, Emperor?"

Reece swallowed. The last thing she—or Medias—would want was a bloodbath. Nyssa could go too far if pushed. Her anger made her dangerous.

Lyra Vonner stepped past her son. "You dare threaten my son? I'll have your head."

"Try me. Better people than you have failed," Nyssa growled.

Medias shook her head and gritted her teeth. "No, Nyssa. Don't. I don't want...anyone hurt."

Nyssa's eyes settled on the Emperor. "Safin, come on, this isn't right. The good kid I got to know on the Whisper wouldn't allow this."

Safin stilled and silence, loaded like a coiled spring, descended on the garden.

Could he not see that Medias was worthy of grace? Reece opened up her senses, letting the young man's emotions wash over her.

He was anxious; scared; conflicted.

She threw caution aside and approached him. The Justiciars didn't move, but the Ashcloaks shifted slightly, their hands creeping closer to their weapons. "I know you doubt that this is the right course of action. Let compassion guide you."

Safin held her gaze as a storm of emotions roiled within him.

"Is there no other recourse here?" he asked Decia.

Without waiting for the answer, Medias took a shaky step toward Nyssa. "Please, don't...don't make this worse. Take Reece. Leave."

Nyssa exhaled loudly. "This is idiotic. You can't—"

Medias wavered on her feet and lurched forward. Nyssa and Reece rushed to her, each catching an arm to steady her.

"Too...too late," Medias murmured, glancing down.

Sickly green veins glowed on her right hand, shimmering in the dim light. Nyssa pulled Medias's sleeve up. The veins spider-webbed up her arm.

"Poison," Nyssa rasped.

"No," Reece whispered, her head swimming. "Oh gods, no."

"It's okay, I can barely feel it." Medias tried to muster up a smile, but her legs gave out. Nyssa and Reece sank to the ground with her to break her fall. She began to make quick, short breaths, her eyebrows stitched up. "My blood...it's on fire."

Tendrils of darkness billowed off of Quinn and coiled around Medias, sinking into her chest. She gasped, chest lifting skyward.

Reece held her breath. Quinn could stop this—she could find the poison and negate it, saving Medias's life.

Quinn stared at Medias, her face locked in concentration. Her emotions shifted from anger to...despair.

"It's not magickal. The poison isn't magickal, I can't destroy it." Quinn whirled around to Safin. "You're a healer, help her!"

Safin swallowed and looked down at Medias. She quaked in Reece's grasp, and her shirt stuck to her skin, damp with sweat.

"It's okay," Reece whispered, slipping her hand into Medias's and giving it a squeeze. "You're going to be okay."

Nyssa sprang to her feet and stepped up to Safin. Ina moved quick, her sword in one hand, taking a defensive stance at the Emperor's side.

"No, Nyssa...they'll kill you," Medias choked out.

She was right—the Ashcloaks would strike at any sign of an attack. If Ina or another one of them misread Nyssa's anger for aggression, people would die.

"Safin, I beg you to show mercy," Nyssa said.

"She is a traitor," Safin replied, keeping his voice low so no one outside their small gathering could hear. "Mercy would make me look weak."

"Mercy is never weakness. Axioms like that chip away at your humanity and give you an excuse for apathy and cruelty. Mercy is an act of strength," Reece implored.

Nyssa exhaled, her vivid, roiling emotions vibrating hard against Reece's senses. "Mercy saved my life. More than once."

"And mine," Quinn said. She crouched next to Medias and took her hand.

"Help me," Reece said, shifting to sit behind Medias and cradle her head in her lap. The woman moaned and shivered. Her red eyes drifted, unfocused. Reece wrapped an arm around her upper chest, holding on tight.

"I didn't...didn't want you...to see this, empath," Medias murmured, the words coming out slow and stunted.

"Why didn't you tell me?" Reece couldn't stop the tears that came.

Medias swallowed. "Couldn't...bear the look on your face."

"Medias, you're going to be okay," Quinn said.

"That's a lie...we both know it."

"I need someone who will lurk in corners to frighten me and stare daggers into Nyssa when she does something inadvisable."

Medias smiled weakly. "A...rigorous job." She paused, her breathing tattered and desperate. "I will miss you...idiot gods..."

Medias's shivers gave way to shaking. A woeful groan rattled out of her chest. Reece trembled herself, unable to stop.

Medias didn't have any more time.

Reece looked up at the Emperor. "Safin, please. Heal her. I'm *begging* you."

Safin's eyes darted around the garden. Reece sensed his indecision growing, and it was a thread of hope that she clung to.

"Justiciar Medias risked her life for me, for this Empire. But this isn't a poison a healer can stop. It's blood magick," he said.

"You mean forbidden magick," Nyssa snarled. "Why do Justiciars get to use this weapon to punish their own? Why do we all stand around and overlook the fucking hypocrisy right under our noses?"

A hum of low conversation filtered through the garden. Safin fidgeted, shuffling his feet. He looked to his mother, but she offered nothing. She was nearly unreadable, no doubt tightly controlling her emotions with an empath of Reece's talents in their midst.

"If this is what Imperial justice looks like, it's inhumane," Safin said, his emotions shifting to indignation. "Decia, stop this. Now. Use the antidote."

He might be a worthy Emperor after all.

"Safin, this isn't your business," Lyra said.

Reece held her breath.

He turned to his mother. Apprehension wound through him, but Reece sensed a stubbornness rising. "I'm the Emperor. Everything is now my business. Justiciar Medias risked her life for the Empire aboard the Whisper when Ceril and his traitors captured us. She's earned the same pardon as the others." His voice rang out clear in the night, his tone confident.

He was doing an admirable job of faking it.

A rumble of disagreement spread through the gathered Justiciars. Superseding laws that were centuries old rarely happened. Could the Justiciars simply ignore Safin? His heart was in the right place, but he had such a tenuous hold on the throne...

"Arch Justiciar Decia, do as I command and stop this execution," Safin said. This time, a steady and resolute calm descended over him. "Now."

Decia dropped to her knees, pulled a red cylinder out of the interior of her jacket, and pushed it against Medias's wrist. After a small prick of a needle, golden liquid glowed under Medias's skin, pulsing up her arm.

Seconds passed. Then Medias cried out and began to convulse, her eyes rolling back into her head.

"What did you do?" Reece hissed at Decia.

"Hold fast to her and let the antidote do its job, empath. It's not pleasant, but she'll live. Just hold her," Decia said. She grasped Medias's hand and pressed her lips to it.

Medias's arms began to flail, looking for purchase.

"Grab onto me," Reece said.

Medias seized the arm Reece had laid across her chest. Athen sank to his knees and secured Medias's legs, and they both held on tight as she struggled.

"We have you," Reece assured her, though she feared the antidote might have been delivered too late to make a difference.

Medias shook and suffered while the poison and its antidote battled it out in her body. She stared up at the sky, her red eyes unblinking.

For Reece, the world shrank to the point of a pin, and she shut everyone's emotions out to just concentrate on Medias. She bent over her and whispered assurances in her ear, tears falling from her face, dropping onto the Justiciar mask.

After several long, agonizing minutes, Medias's shaking ceased. Her skin was flush and slick with sweat. Reece let out a heavy breath, and the world crept back in, becoming loud and bright with emotions once again.

"How do you feel?" she asked.

A groan was Medias's only response, but the slight smile that accompanied it made Reece's heart feel a million times lighter.

"Thank you, Emperor," Nyssa said.

"I think I have about a hundred Justiciars mad at me," he said, his voice low.

"Welcome to the party," she replied, shifting closer to him. "Today, you cast your own shadow. And you did so with honor."

Safin took a big breath and scanned the Justiciars. "There is no true justice without mercy. Ashara never meant the Justiciars to blindly apply Imperial law without discretion. Justiciar Medias failed her duty, but she put her life in danger for the Empire. I witnessed her valor firsthand against the traitor Anelos. I will not be a leader who punishes valiant hearts that stray from their path. If there are any Justiciars or Ashcloaks among you who cannot serve me knowing that, you may leave the service of the Areshi Empire without penalty."

Reece held her breath. Safin had already broken from convention, giving a pardon to Cursed Gods. If the Justiciars and Ashcloaks abandoned him now, the Empire as it was known would cease to exist.

Ina Ruggen moved first, taking a knee in deference to her Emperor. The other Ashcloaks and Justiciars followed suit. None remained standing. None raised their voices in dissent.

Reece let the Ashcloaks' emotions wash over her. They were sincere.

"Nice speech, kid," Nyssa whispered, flashing Safin a smile.

"Justiciar Medias's life is spared, but she must lose her status as a Justiciar. Tomorrow, she will be stripped of her mask."

Decia let out a breath and sat back.

"Arch Justiciar, will she be okay?" Reece asked.

Decia nodded. "She will be feverish for a few hours. Now, she needs to rest."

"I've got her," Athen said, gently scooping Medias into his arms and standing.

"I can walk," she said, her voice weak.

Athen twisted up the side of his mouth. "You would reject a handsome man's generous offer of help?"

"Point me to a handsome man," she replied.

Athen chuckled. "Is that the first joke you've ever attempted?"

Medias didn't answer and just closed her eyes.

"Take her to my room," Reece said. "I won't have her in the guest quarters."

With a nod, Athen turned and walked toward the Keep. Reece followed, along with the others. She barely felt her legs and wondered how exactly her body was moving. The shock of the night's events—and what had almost transpired—threatened to fell her. But she kept moving. Kept her eyes on Medias as she lay in Athen's arms, still alive.

Gloriously alive.

THE MASK SHATTERS

Quinn and Nyssa escorted Medias into the garden. Though exhausted and a bit shaky from the previous night's thwarted execution, Medias couldn't help but finally be hopeful.

Few Justiciars had ever been stripped of their mask. Leaving the Order of the Justiciars happened through retirement, death, or execution for crimes against the Empire. And no Justiciar had ever been administered Ashara's Vengeance and lived.

If not for her friends pleading for her life, she would certainly have died.

Friends. Such a strange term. Even weirder to consider those that once viewed her with fear and distrust were now loyal companions. And once her connection to the Justiciars was severed, they'd be her only world.

Medias's breath hitched at the sudden realization. The guilds—especially Ambershine—imprinted themselves deep into an adept, becoming their only life. Now what the hell was she supposed to do?

"You ready for this?" Nyssa asked.

"Yes," Medias lied. Somehow facing a new life was more daunting than staring down her execution the night before?

Torches blazed around the giant circle of Justiciars surrounding Medias's mother, illuminating their bone-white masks with an eerie flickering glow. A brazier burning with a low blue flame stood next to Decia.

Medias pulled her jacket tighter, the winter night seeping into her bones. She was dressed in her red guild leathers, the last time she would wear them and the mask.

A crowd of curious onlookers had gathered, the crew of the Whisper among them. Elias didn't like Imperial customs, but they had come to support Medias—at least according to Fontaine, who seemed to have an aversion to Justiciars at the best of times. Aryis was present as well, though standing apart from everyone. Small groups consisting of the Great Houses and their entourages looked on, staying far enough away to avoid getting too close to Nyssa and Quinn.

Medias searched for Reece, finding her standing beside Athen and Lilliana. They waited just outside the circle of Justiciars. Safin was next to Decia, in a black suit, light-blue tie, white wool coat, and shiny black boots. He looked more and more like an Emperor every day. He wore a warm smile, far from the stern seriousness of his mother or the faces of the gathered Great Houses.

Lyra Vonner left the company of the other Houses and approached Nyssa and Quinn. "I hope tonight will be bereft of violence, threatened or otherwise."

"We're here for Medias, that's all," Nyssa replied.

"Good."

Nyssa waited a beat. "Your son showed great leadership last night."

Lyra stepped closer. "He has a generous heart, but his mercy doesn't win him favor with the Sun Council."

"You know, Lyra, Eron spoke of you on occasion. Bravest Ashcloak he ever fought beside—his words. You're not the same as these other rich assholes, so why are you so scared of what they think?"

Medias braced for an angry response. Nyssa's shameless desire to poke at those who thought themselves her betters was ingrained from a young age. Medias herself had been on the receiving end of her brazenness and understood it, but she also knew it could get them in trouble.

Lyra took a deep breath but offered a smile. "Your arrogance doesn't do you any favors."

"Yeah," Nyssa replied, "but I don't much care. I don't put on airs. You'll always know where you stand with me. Can you say the same of your *friends* in the other Houses?"

With a withering glance, Lyra took her leave, joining Safin's side.

"Honey just drips off your tongue," Medias whispered.

"And dry sarcasm drips off yours, my friend," Nyssa replied with a wink.

Medias scanned the gathered Justiciars as she walked among them. The vast garden quieted, save for the chill breeze that rattled the bare branches of the massive oaks. Reece caught her gaze and offered a soft, warm smile. She had stayed by Medias's side the whole night, making sure she was comfortable. Sleep had come in fits and starts, and each time Medias opened her eyes, Reece was there with a kind word and a sip of tea.

Decia stepped forward and studied Medias for a long time. At last, her mother spoke: "Medias Levesque, your life has been spared through the mercy of our Emperor. But you have betrayed your oath to the Order of Justiciars. For this, you can no longer serve the Emperor as his hand of justice." Decia moved toward Medias, extending her hand. "Your mask, daughter."

Medias lifted her hand but stopped. She had never considered this moment, the last moment she would wear the mask of the Justiciar. The thin black line that ran across her cheeks and nose would forever signify her past, but to be finally free of the mask...she would be naked and exposed.

Hiding behind it had become too easy over the years.

She took one last glance at Reece before she bowed her head and removed her mask, placing it in Decia's open hand.

Decia stared down at the symbol of the Justiciars, her face unreadable. She held the mask up for all to see, then placed it in the brazier. Blue flames licked around its edges catching it aflame. As Medias watched, the white Mask of the Justiciar turned black.

"You are released from the Order of the Justiciar, Medias Levesque," Decia announced.

A chilly quiet settled on the garden, the only sound the crackles of flames from the brazier and torches.

Medias stole a glance at Reece, whose eyes were on her. Heat rose in her cheeks under the empath's gaze.

"Medias!" Elias's booming voice broke the silence. "Let's get you a fucking drink!"

The cheer that went up from the Whisper's crew broke the tension in the garden. Even the members of the Great Houses seemed to be glad to be done with this business in favor of drinking Lilliana's expensive liquor.

Everyone started returning to the warmth inside, including the Justiciars. If they were satisfied with the outcome of Medias's punishment, it was impossible to tell. Both Safin and Decia had broken from tradition, putting aside the law in favor of mercy—a decision they both might pay for politically in the future. The thought of it put Medias on edge. But thankfully, for the moment, the Emperor, the Sun Council, and the Justiciars prioritized hunting Anelos down and bringing the Empire back to some measure of stability. The political backbiting would follow soon thereafter, no doubt.

Medias stayed in the garden, not ready to go back inside. Her legs were unsteady, so she found a bench near the brazier that consumed her mask and sat. Reece approached while Nyssa and Quinn lingered nearby. Medias didn't miss their curious glances, or how they leaned into one another and whispered as they watched.

"Medias Levesque," Reece said, her voice bright. "It's nice to see your face, finally free of the mask forever."

Medias's cheeks burned hotter, and she silently cursed her reaction.

"Are you coming in?" Reece asked.

"In a moment."

Reece's smile reached her dark eyes, and she nodded. "See you then."

She rejoined the Cursed Gods and walked off with Nyssa, but Quinn approached Medias, sitting next to her on the bench. "How does it feel, this freedom?" she asked.

"Drafty," Medias replied. "My face is cold."

"You're marked like us. Bone magick?"

Medias gave a terse nod.

"It's a detail about you I didn't remember when Nyssa and I made our retreat from Ocean's Rest a few years ago."

"You mean when she punched my mask clean off my face?"

Quinn chuckled. "You know, you and I, we were trapped in different ways by our guilds. We are bonded, in a sense. You're not like Nyssa, Athen, or Reece. You're more like me. And I...need a reserved presence at times. A bit of calm."

Medias stood and walked over to the brazier, its low blue flame almost gone. No trace of the Justiciar mask was left, and its absence created a weird pang of longing in her chest. "You mean I don't express every emotion I have the moment I have it?"

"I suppose that's a way to put it."

"This emotional reserve you speak of that we share...how do you move past it?"

"What do you mean?"

Medias glanced back at her, choosing to cut to the chase. "You and Nyssa. It took you two years to finally..."

With a cock of her head, Quinn laughed. "Sleep together?"

"I didn't mean to be impertinent. If the question is too personal, I apologize."

"I admit, it's strange to talk about with anyone," Quinn replied. She sat forward and rubbed her hands on her thighs. "Look, Nyssa and I both had things to work through. And I..." A smile took over her face. "I didn't know what to do with her."

"Didn't seem like it in my vision," Medias remarked, arching an eyebrow.

Quinn buried her face in her hands. "I still can't believe you saw that."

"Indeed. It's seared into my brain." Medias straightened. "I don't get to choose what visions I see and when, but I feel a strange need to apologize for the invasion of your privacy."

Quinn shrugged. "There's nothing we can do about it now. What's seen is seen, I suppose."

"Indeed."

"You asking about my relationship with Nyssa is...unexpected."

"Perhaps the empath's forwardness is rubbing off on me."

"Not that I mind." Quinn ran a hand through her raven-colored hair. "It's...sometimes hard to not have someone to talk to about more private matters, especially concerning Nyssa. Fontaine became a bit of a confidant for me, but here in Ocean's Rest, I lack her counsel."

Medias nodded. She knew the feeling all too well, lacking any true close friends of her own. Save for Reece, and this wasn't something she could share with her. "How did you overcome your reticence with Blacksea?"

"When I say I didn't know what to do with Nyssa, the feelings I had for her, the...physical attraction...I wasn't exactly experienced in the ins and outs of love. But I took a leap and figured it out rather quickly. And Nyssa was...instructive." Quinn blushed, far more forward than expected. It was strangely nice to be trusted with such information.

"I'm not well-versed in how to form and hold friendships, Quinn. The mask kept the world at a distance, and now, I find myself...a bit lost."

Quinn smiled. "Oh trust me, I understand. All types of relationships were foreign to me. But Elias, Fontaine, and the crew of the Whisper took me in as family and showed me how to be a friend. And Nyssa, for all her bluster, was extremely patient with me. Gentle. She allowed me to grow into myself. Still is."

"I'm glad you and Nyssa are together. You seem happy." Something about their relationship gave Medias hope.

"I am." Quinn laughed softly. "Might I suggest you work out what's holding you back with Reece?"

Medias froze. Had she said too much? "She and I are merely friends. I-I..."

"You are a shit liar, Medias Levesque."

Medias bowed her head, searching for a response. Lying had never been one of her strengths, a poor fit for the person she was raised to be. And Quinn...well, she seemed to see through bullshit all too well. Medias swallowed, choosing to trust the woman. "I wasn't honest with Reece. I told her I didn't have feelings for her. The look on her face after that almost crushed me."

"Oh?" Quinn's eyebrows stitched up. No judgment, just curious. "Well, that seems counterproductive."

"A woman facing her own death shouldn't burden others with hope."

Quinn grunted. "Yeah, Nyssa did that to me once. When she was dying, she tried to spare me the pain of knowing how she felt about me. You don't have to protect Reece. She's a grown woman. Trust her."

Medias shook her head. "I have done things in my past as a Justiciar...things I'm not proud of. I am still that person, and I could hurt her so deeply."

"I don't know what you've done, Medias, but you can't let your past hold you back."

"And if I don't feel worthy of her?"

Quinn smiled. "We all deserve happiness. I think you make her happy, from what little I know of her. She looks for you when she enters a room, stealing smiles that maybe she thinks no one notices when she spots you. You do too."

"I see you've been spying on us?"

"Once Nyssa pointed it out, how could I not?"

Medias took a deep breath. "I realize how awkward this is for the both of us, speaking on such a subject."

"Your desperation must be at an all-time high to come to me with this, considering that I may have no idea what I'm talking about."

"Regardless, your possibly clueless counsel is helpful."

"Thanks for trusting me with this."

Medias leaned her head back, casting her eyes to the sky. "You are becoming a good friend, Quinn."

Friend. The word still felt strange in her mouth, lumpy and unearned.

"What are your plans now?"

Medias stared down into the brazier's flame. She hadn't considered life past her death, but now, speaking with Quinn and remembering her father, it seemed clear. "I pledged myself to you and Nyssa the moment I marked her. It was my father's will that I help shape fate rather than merely observe it play out from a distance." She smiled, her cheeks crinkling up, free of the constriction of the Justiciar mask. "Seems I rather enjoy it, being in the thick of things. So I think I shall remain in the thick of things."

Quinn got to her feet, joined Medias next to the brazier, and did something rather unexpected—she pulled Medias into a hug.

"I'm sorry about this," she whispered. "This isn't like me."

After a moment of surprise, Medias returned the hug. "This is awful."

"We'll never let this happen again." Quinn pulled away with a smile. "Now let's go celebrate you getting fired from your shitty job."

SHAYLIN VANCE

Medias retreated to a shady alcove on the side of the Keep's entrance, her eyes trained on the brazen woman shouting at Ocean's Keep.

"Reece Ae'Shen! Where the fuck is Reece Ae'Shen? Get her ass out here now!"

Medias scowled at the short woman pacing back and forth in the massive gravel driveway. She wore a tight white shirt that showed off her toned muscles, though it seemed a rather foolish choice in winter. Her leather pants were tighter than Medias thought possible and still be able to move. She had the tanned skin of a pirate, messy, shoulder-length dark-purple hair, and several piercings in her nose and eyebrows.

The woman held her head up high and flashed an annoying smirk, suddenly reminding Medias of Nyssa. They wore the same easy confidence that spoke of a danger if pressed.

"Are you lurking?" Nyssa asked as she and Quinn approached from the Keep, drawing an eye roll out of Medias. "The attendants are in a tizzy about fetching Reece. What's this all about?"

"I was on my way to see my mother when I heard this...person shouting."

"She's well-armed," Quinn noted.

Nyssa raised an eyebrow.

Quinn sighed. "Weapons, not actual arms, you idiot."

"She does have nice arms, though. I know you like arms," Nyssa teased.

Medias coughed.

Athen's deep voice startled her. "Oh no."

"Is this woman a problem?" Nyssa asked.

Athen groaned. "She's multiple problems. That's Shaylin Vance. Pirate, thief, and goddamn backstabber. Bad news all around. And Reece's ex. That bitch stole ten thousand gold from Reece and disappeared, breaking her heart."

Medias let a low, discontented growl rumble in her chest. This had to be the person behind Reece's debt to Reggie Cox. A startling urge to smash the woman's face into pieces took Medias aback. Fists before words seemed more Nyssa's style, not her own. Though Medias's ability to ignore the slights of the world in favor of calm rationality fell away the instant Reece was in an ounce of trouble.

Nyssa wrapped her hands around the sword belt across her chest, her index finger slow tapping away at the dark leather. "Back at the Order, Athen and I would spend time in the bars in Vane, and I'd run into women like Vance there. The type of woman who would try to drink me under the table or fight me or fuck me. Sometimes all three."

"Oh, I remember," Athen said. "It's nice that you've grown out of troublemakers."

"Have I?" Nyssa asked, her grin jaunty and aimed directly at Quinn, who inhaled a deep breath, though her slight smirk gave her away—she didn't exactly mind the teasing it seemed.

"Reece can't read Shay's emotions," Athen said. "She was happy to finally have someone be a mystery to her."

"She's like me?" Medias asked, surprised and desperately wanting to know more about this woman's history with Reece. It wasn't her business, but she couldn't help herself.

Athen turned to her. "Most decidedly *not* like you. Reece can't read Shay because she doesn't *have* emotions. She fakes it. Whatever she needs to be for you, Shay will be it. Then she'll stab you in the back. That one's a snake. You aren't like her at all."

The anger in Athen's voice suggested there was more to the story, but before Medias could probe further, Reece came striding out of the Keep. When she saw who was creating the commotion, her face grew dark, and she stalked toward Shay.

"Shit," Athen said, "Reece is going to kill her." He bolted out of the alcove to intercept her, gently pulling her to a stop.

"What the fuck are you doing here, Shay?" Reece asked. Her voice held a tone Medias had never heard from the woman before. Raw, unbridled anger. No...not just anger.

Hate.

"Hey, darlin'. Miss me?" Shay smirked. "You must because you've impounded my goddamn ship! Fifteen thousand gold to get it out of dock?"

"You stole ten thousand gold from me. Consider the extra five interest," Reece said through gritted teeth. She straightened up and shook her head. "You know what? The price is now twenty thousand gold to get your rickety piece of shit out of my docks."

"Didn't figure you'd hold a grudge," Shay said. Her eyes slid over to Athen. "Hey, sexy, nice to see you too, though somethings different about you...can't quite put my finger on it." Shay winked at him.

"You shouldn't have come back to this city," Athen said.

Shay shifted her weight and rested her hands on the hilts of her short swords. "I had goods to offload, and I'm sick of avoiding this continent's busiest port. There's a simple solution to getting rid of me. Release my ship, and I'll finish up my business here and sail out."

"You need to leave. Now," Reece said, her voice cold. Hard.

"Not without my ship. This doesn't have to get nasty, babe."

Babe? Medias pushed past Nyssa and Quinn, her eyes set on Shay.

"Oh shit," Quinn hissed behind her.

An understatement. Medias raised her hand, sending a burst of her light magick directly into the pirate's skull.

Shay cried out and grabbed her head, falling to a knee. No permanent damage done, but she'd have a nasty headache. Medias bent over Shay and hauled her to her feet. It took Shay a moment to recover herself, ready to throw fists. Reece rushed to Medias's side and pulled her back. "Stop!"

"I do not like this woman."

"Yeah, well, neither do I."

"Fuckin' weird company you keep now, Reece," Shay said, her eyes taking the women in, one by one, as Nyssa and Quinn came to stand behind Reece. "You have a thing for women with facial markings? These two gods and this ex-Justiciar asshole are quite the topic of wagging tongues on the docks." Despite the pirate's bravado, her eyes betrayed something...not exactly fear, but a realization that perhaps coming to the Keep was a poor calculation on her part.

"Get the fuck out of here," Reece said.

"What about my ship?"

"Twenty thousand gold and it's yours."

Medias smiled. Reece wasn't going to budge.

"You really want me to be back here same time tomorrow, hollerin' on your front step?" Shay's face softened and she smiled, a smile intended to charm.

Medias wanted to wipe it off her face. "You come back tomorrow and you'll need to hold your teeth in a bag."

Shay's eyes slid to her and she cocked her head, her smile turning predatory. "Ah, did you replace me with this one, Reece? A Justiciar? You do like your women to have a bit of an edge, don't you? She's but a pale imitation of me."

Athen stepped forward and wrapped his hand around the back of Shay's neck. "Time for you to leave."

"Oh, you know I like it rough, Athen."

He steered her away from the women and through the gates of the courtyard.

Reece trembled, her breath ragged, and turned to Medias.

"What she said about you...you're nothing like her. She's a fucking monster." She swallowed hard, averting her eyes. Not like the Reece she knew. "I'm sorry..."

Medias's wanted to comfort Reece but didn't know exactly what to do. She felt so ill-equipped for these situations. "No apology necessary. That woman is detestable."

Athen returned to them. "Don't worry, Reece, if she returns, I'll deal with her."

When Reece looked back up, she had tears in her eyes. "I never thought I'd see her again. I can't..." She let out a shaky breath and pushed past Nyssa and Quinn, retreating to the Keep.

Medias took a step to follow, but stopped.

Nyssa drew close and gave Medias's shoulder a squeeze. "Yes, I realize I'm touching you, but we're friends, so this is what I do. I'm touchy. But more importantly, Reece needs someone right now. And that's you. Go after her."

Not caring about appearances, Medias took off into the Keep, following an instinct that told her the empath had probably withdrawn to her office, to the comfort of her books, knickknacks, and—most importantly—her plants.

As she strode to Reece's office, those in the corridor gave her a wide berth. If she was frightening to them as a Justiciar, what exactly was she to them now? A fallen Justiciar? And what was she to Reece? Just another disappointing woman with a dark past? The marks on her face meant she could never hide who she used to be from anyone, and that would be a burden anyone close to Medias would also have to face. Justiciars were feared. Ex-Justiciars were hated and no longer under the protection of the Emperor.

When she got to Reece's office, she knocked softly on the door. Without waiting for an answer, she tossed decorum aside and entered anyway.

Reece sat on the windowsill behind her desk beside her plants. Medias slipped through the room and sat on the corner of the desk. Reece stared at her hands as she laced them together in her lap over and over again.

Medias let the silence linger, waiting.

Finally, the empath spoke. "I haven't seen that woman in five years. Five fucking years and it might as well have been yesterday. I shouldn't feel this way."

Medias couldn't help her curiosity. "How *do* you feel?"

"Broken all over again. And not just by Shay's betrayal, but by my own damn stupidity. Athen warned me about her, but I didn't listen. I thought he was bitter because she moved on from him to me."

"Wait...Athen and Shay?"

"Yes. It's messy business all around. They had a drunken tryst once before I even met her. It didn't mean anything to either of them. And Shay made me feel...like I was the center of the universe." Reece sighed and raised her eyes to meet Medias's gaze. Her dark gaze was alluring in the shadows of her office. "Have you ever been in love, Medias?"

The question took her aback. It was so personal. At Ambershine, she had tried to form connections with her peers, to chase that elusive thing she had read about in books and her father had hoped she would have for herself one day—a deep, abiding love for another.

She never found it. Not that she didn't try, indulging in a few discreet trysts with peers. But feelings never stirred inside her, not even sexual attraction. It was a confounding problem, so she shut that part of herself off and focused on her duties. But after coming to Ocean's Rest, Medias most unexpectedly did find a connection. One she had rejected days earlier.

One she didn't feel worthy of.

So she lied about ever being in love, knowing the empath couldn't detect the fib. "No, I haven't."

"I don't recommend it."

Medias shook her head. "I don't believe you."

Reece pointed to the door. "That woman made me question everything when she left me. I swore off relationships for years. The only person I gave myself to was Nyssa, and that was just sex. For...for a while, anyway."

Medias swallowed, not sure how deep she wanted to go. "You fell in love with Blacksea?"

"The spark was there, but she was meant for another. So I stood aside and let the spark fade. I moved on. Nyssa and Quinn have something special. And I *want* that. I won't compromise anymore, allowing women like Shay into my bed. She didn't want me, she just wanted what House Fennick could give her—a soft bed, a closet full of the finest clothes I could lavish her with, and my fucking heart to kick about for her own fucking entertainment."

Medias shifted on the desk. They had never had such an intimate conversation. Were it anyone else, she would have found an excuse to leave, but she couldn't fathom leaving Reece in this state. And this Vance asshole...she was a monster, but was she so different from Medias? How could Reece want her?

She swallowed back her shame. "I will not let that woman anywhere near you."

"You don't have to...do that for me."

"I want to."

"You're not to hurt Shaylin, Justiciar. Ah, fuck. Sorry."

Medias smiled. "That will be a hard habit to break, empath."

A small crack in Reece's dour expression, a hint of a grin, gave Medias hope of pulling her out of her bad mood. It was the same grin that had greeted Medias the other morning when she woke from a night of recovering from the poison meant to kill her. Waking up in Reece's bed was disorienting, but she was met with soft words of concern and a hot mug of tea.

The scent of lavender from the empath's pillows had lingered on Medias's clothes for the rest of the day. Gods, how she loved the smell.

Reece, Quinn, and Nyssa had all stayed that night, sleeping on chairs and couches, watching over her after her ordeal. Medias had never had that type of concern before. She'd barely fought back tears after seeing them there for her.

Reece stood and reached for a small orb on her desk, drawing close and making Medias's pulse quicken. Reece paused, her eyes locked on Medias, before she spoke into the little ball. "Dock master, release Shaylin Vance's ship. Message me when she's gone." She palmed the orb and wrapped her fist around it.

"What about the money she owes you?" Medias asked.

"It's...not worth it. I'd rather never see her again than try to punish her for what she did."

"That's rather mature of you." Medias didn't mind if Shay never showed her face in Ocean's Rest again, given how her mere presence upset Reece.

Reece sighed. "Shay enjoys the game. She can't get any pleasure from it if I just don't play."

Reece picked up another orb. "Ankur, please prepare the room next to mine for Justic— For Medias Levesque." She walked over to the door and cracked it open, and the orbs zipped out of the office. "I hope you don't mind. I think it's best you're on the family wing and away from the Justiciars in the guest quarters. I don't trust them around you."

Medias scowled. "They will not touch me." She tried to give Reece a reassuring smile, but she feared it came across as an awkward grimace. Without her mask, she was so conscious of her damn face now. At times, it felt like an unbroken horse, prone to buck and bolt out of her control.

"Regardless, pack your things and bring them up after dinner. The room will be ready by then."

Medias didn't need a fancy new room, but going against Reece rarely ended in her favor. "As you wish."

SHARED CUSTODY

Medias stood in the doorway of her new room, her small rucksack of dwindling possessions strapped over her shoulder, her only other possession in her hands. The scent of incense gently pricked at her nose, a mix of pine and warm spices that reminded her of her room at Ambershine, small and modest compared to the apartment Reece insisted she occupy in the Fennick family wing. It was full of fine furniture, worn books, aromatic candles, and a bowl filled with foil-wrapped chocolates. And there, nestled among the lavish amenities, its large bed looking impossibly inviting, with far more pillows than seemed necessary.

A fire crackled in the fireplace across from the bed, Reece lit by its soft glow, a halo of gold making her look otherworldly. Medias meant to let Reece know of her arrival, but she closed her mouth and simply watched the empath. A dark-blue velvet dress clung to her body, accented by an expensive-looking wool jacket laced with gold and scarlet threads forming patterns of leaves. Her silver-white hair hung just above her shoulders with thin multicolored ribbons woven throughout.

It struck Medias that she would simply be happy to study Reece for endless moments. She had watched her throughout her stay at the Keep, their mutual distrust at the beginning of their time together making keeping an eye on one another necessary. But something had shifted in Medias.

She had pushed it far down, stuck it in the back corner of her brain so it wouldn't be a distraction, but she couldn't deny the alarming hunger of attraction for Reece. While Medias could admire the objective beauty of others, she had never found that beauty sexually appealing. But with Reece, there was an undeniable desire that threw her far off-kilter and was distressing in how exciting and forbidden it felt.

And then there was her past as a Justiciar. How could a gorgeous woman like Reece want a monster who hid behind a mask and her duty? She wasn't worthy of—

"You cut your hair!" Reece said, shaking Medias out of her dark thoughts.

Medias swallowed when she realized Reece had caught her staring. She self-consciously ran her hand along the top of her head, her topknot and long hair gone, cut off that afternoon as a way to leave her old life behind.

But she still felt like an imposter, a shadow of a person pretending to human.

What hair she was left with was an unruly mop of dark curls that barely reached her chin and fell over her shaved temples, the oddest of sensations. And a lone, stubborn curl that insisted on getting in her face. No amount of trying to push it back kept it away for long.

Smiling, Reece waved Medias forward. "Come in. It's your room now."

Medias took a hesitant step inside and closed the door behind her.

"Is that my plant?" Reece asked, her face lighting up as she approached.

Medias looked down at the small bluish-green succulent in her hands. "I don't know if you can claim possession of something you entrusted to my care." As Reece drew closer, Medias became keenly aware of the absence of her Justiciar mask, now more than ever in the low light of the room alone with Reece.

"I had to sneak into your room to care for that plant more than once."

"I prefer to think you intruded upon my privacy, using the plant as an excuse."

"You are rather paranoid, Justiciar."

Medias flinched at the title. "I'm no longer a Justiciar."

Reece cringed. "Apologies. It's such a habit now." She took the little succulent. "I have the perfect place for our jointly owned plant." Crossing to the back of the room, she placed it on a small table near the window where it could get plenty of sun. Medias trailed behind her, taking in the massive windows and the night sky beyond them. The plant wouldn't lack for sunlight. Nor would she.

"How do you like your new room?" Reece asked the plant, smiling as she rotated it on the table.

Medias ventured farther into the apartment and made a show of inspecting it, but kept an eye on Reece, amused at how she doted on the little succulent. Medias wandered over to the bookshelf and began to scan it, a low growl rattling in her throat. They were disorganized. "Did you have the Keep attendants purposely rearrange the books in here just to rankle me?"

A low chuckle from the other side of the room made Medias's stomach flutter. She took a deep breath. She would not be riled by a damn laugh.

"While that is a rather delicious idea, I did not mess with your books. They've been that way for years. No one has used this room for ages," Reece replied. "By the way, I've taken the liberty of having your closet stocked with clothing I think you would like. Tasteful and understated. Not a speck of red."

Nodding, Medias stopped at the bed and put her bag down. "I don't even have my guild leathers anymore since I'm no longer..." She stared down at her bag. *No longer myself.* "Anyway, thank you for the room and the clothes."

Medias opened her bag and pulled out a white mask—an extra one from her time as a Justiciar. She had conveniently forgotten to return it. "The impulse to put this on is almost overwhelming," she admitted.

"So you can hide again?"

Medias glared at Reece. "You mock me."

"I do not. It's insulting that you think so."

Medias tossed her mask back in her bag, which now only held it and a few pairs of underwear. Those items and her co-owned plant were her sole possessions other than a bank marker, stuck in the pocket of her denim pants, and her daggers, worn on her hips. Her pants, cotton shirt, and wool coat were not her own—scavenged out of Nyssa's closet in a pinch.

She shrugged out of the coat and laid it on a chair next to the bed, turning to find Reece's dark eyes following her every movement. After two years of seeing her in her Justiciar mask and leathers, covered from neck to toe, it must be odd for Reece to see her so…casual. Honestly, she barely recognized her own self in the mirror as she dressed in the morning. Her mask was gone, but the thin black line running from ear to ear was still there, rising and falling as it traversed her over nose. The Mark of the Justiciar, one she could never shed, sunk deep into the flesh and bone, just like the Mark of the Unworthy.

"Why didn't you tell me about the Crossing?" Reece asked, sitting down on the corner of the bed.

Medias removed her rucksack from the bed, letting it fall to the floor, and sat on the other corner. "There seemed no point in worrying you," she replied finally, a bit of truth, a bit of a lie.

Reece turned and let out an exasperated breath. "Worry me? Worried is the most…inane word you could conjure up to downplay a Crossing. Medias, you were going to skip happily along to your death, and none of us would have been okay with it, don't you get that? I would have been…"

The look on Reece's face was rare but familiar from their early inter-actions—anger. But this was different. There was an intensity to her ire that signaled something behind it.

Medias swallowed. "You would have been what?"

"You're so goddamn blind. Or is this merely feigned ignorance? Either way, I have no patience for it." Reece shot to her feet to march toward the door.

Medias stood and intercepted her, catching her arm. "You would have been what, empath?"

Drawing Reece closer, Medias studied her face. She seemed on the verge of collapse. There was hurt behind her eyes, hurt that Medias knew she caused, their encounter from the other night hanging thick between them.

"Devastated," Reece breathed. "I would have been devastated if you had died. But what do you care? You let your lack of feelings be known." She pulled out of Medias's grip. "You were ready to give the Justiciars your life. Did you ever stop and think about what your death would do to your friends? Or...to me?"

A sudden rush of heat flooded through Medias, and she tensed, taking a step toward Reece. "All I've done over the last two years is think about the rest of you and how to keep you all safe."

"That's not enough!" Reece said, her dark eyes shiny. "You have to care about yourself. And care about what *you* want."

Medias didn't answer. She couldn't think with Reece standing so close, the familiar scent of lavender lingering and her anger so palpable. Medias's breath caught in her chest, the tension in her stomach coiling.

Reece shook her head and sighed. "I think you need some time to get settled. Have a good night."

She backed away from Medias and strode toward the door.

Dammit.

Medias rushed after her and caught her wrist, the empath's skin hot under her fingers.

Reece's eyes blazed. "What are you doing?"

"Don't leave."

"I thought you preferred to be alone."

Medias stepped closer. "Don't leave."

Reece's gaze narrowed, dipping to Medias's lips. "Then make me stay."

The thin thread of restraint holding Medias back snapped. She advanced on Reece, pushing her up against the wall, crushing her lips in a searing kiss that was breathtaking in its intensity. In Medias's experience, kissing had always been a chore, a necessary step to get clothes off and the sex over with.

This...this was different. The sensation of Reece's tongue exploring hers made her whole body flush with a heat she had never felt before, pooling in her belly. The sound that rose in Reece's throat made Medias's breath catch—it was low and primal.

Reece grabbed at Medias's waist and pulled her close, her hands desperately yanking Medias's shirt out of her pants. Medias caught Reece's hands and pinned them to the wall, deepening the kiss and moving her thigh between Reece's legs. Reece gasped and pressed her body against Medias.

The friction, the fever between them, threatened to drag Medias under.

The intensity of her own desire startled her, but she didn't stop. And Reece didn't either, grinding against her, desperate kisses causing all the heat in Medias's body to pool between her legs.

She let go of Reece's wrists and took Reece's face in her hands, her touch turning tender. Reverent. If she could capture this moment, when she had everything she wanted right in front of her...

Reece slowed her pace and their kisses grew passionate instead of desperate. Eventually Medias drew back and opened her eyes to find Reece smiling at her. Reece shrugged her jacket off, letting it drop to the ground. Then she started undoing the buttons on her dress, not taking her eyes off of Medias. Those eyes that were once distrusting and wary, now hooded and filled with something far more dangerous.

When the dress slipped away, Medias let her eyes dip to take Reece in, clad only in black underwear, her breasts bare. Reece's clothes didn't do her soft curves justice.

The desire to run her lips over the dip of Reece's shoulders and the hollow of her throat was almost overwhelming.

Reece reached forward, her hands settling on the buttons of Medias's shirt, undoing them and pushing the garment off her shoulders, then deftly unhooking her bra, tossing it aside. Medias had the ridiculous urge to bend over, pick up the discarded clothes, and fold them. She smiled at how her penchant for neatness crept in at inopportune moments.

"You have a gorgeous smile," Reece said, brushing the curl that hung over her brow to the side. It fell back in place immediately, drawing a soft rumble of laughter out of the empath.

They kissed again, skin pressed against skin, Reece's hands wandering and caressing and making Medias gasp until they settled on her belt and started to unbuckle its clasp.

Medias captured Reece's hands in her own. "You're not in control here. I am." The assertion forced a sharp *oh!* out of Reece that made Medias's heart pound. She leaned forward, their lips grazing each other. "I will take my pants off when I wish, but right now, I want to touch you. Taste you."

Reece's breathing quickened, and Medias dipped her mouth to her throat, running her tongue from one collarbone to the other. Reece sighed under her touch. Medias glided lower, trailing kisses down Reece's body, stopping to pull one nipple between her lips, then the other, each time eliciting a strangled moan out of Reece.

Medias grinned.

She painted kisses down Reece's torso, sinking to her knees and making quick work of the woman's underpants. Reece arched her back, growling a sound that Medias vowed to commit to memory. Her eyes flicked upward, watching Reece's face, how her eyebrows knit up at the first taste. She smiled at the empath's response, how the woman's body submitted to her tongue.

How every lick, every tease, made Reece quiver.

Reece, who so often prodded Medias to elicit a reaction or emotion, who withdrew bits and pieces out of her to examine, was now completely at Medias's mercy.

She smiled and wrapped her arms around Reece's thighs, committing herself to the woman's pleasure, her tongue exploring what made Reece react. Each moan, each movement, each tightening of hands in Medias's hair served as a map to Reece's pleasure. A map Medias committed to memory.

As she sensed Reece getting closer to release, she doubled her efforts, swirling her tongue faster and harder. Reece dug her hands further into Medias's hair and trembled, coming undone, her moans becoming a strangled cry of pleasure.

Medias rose to her feet and kissed Reece, keeping her pinned to the wall, bracing her as she came down from the high of her climax. Medias kissed Reece's flushed skin, the taste of arousal still clinging to her lips. "That's my good girl," she murmured against the empath's ear.

She pulled back, bringing Reece with her, and splayed a hand on her stomach, turning her until her back faced the bed. Medias walked her to the bed and pushed Reece down onto it. The empath's gaze never broke from her own, her lips parted, breathing hungrily.

Medias climbed atop Reece and settled over her. She spent an inordinate amount of time teasing, her lips roaming across Reece's lips and neck, dipping lower to her breasts. The heat between them had never abated—it just kept building.

Medias willed herself to not grab Reece's hand and guide it into her pants. The anticipation was too delicious, suspended there, wanting but waiting. She moved up to kiss Reece, teasing her, dragging her teeth across her bottom lip. She finally slipped her hand between Reece's legs, turning the woman's breaths short and raspy. In a soft, low whisper, Medias asked, "Do you want me to fuck you again?"

Reece opened her eyes, meeting Medias's gaze. Fire danced behind her eyes. "I think it's your turn now."

The smile on Reece's face was pure mischief, one that Medias had seen before, but never in this context. She swallowed when she realized Reece had already unbuckled her belt. The empath flattened her hand against Medias's abdomen and moved it lower into her underwear where she stopped, teasing.

Gods, this woman...

Reece's lips turned up in a smile the moment her hand ventured farther. Medias shuddered as if hit by an icy wind. No one had ever made her feel this way before, nor had she ever been so intimately in tune with another person. She swallowed, trying to maintain focus, but she couldn't ignore how her body was moving, responding to Reece's touch. Her breathing turned heavy, hitching as Reece explored her.

Reece's fingers worked Medias into a full-body euphoria. She practically vibrated at the touch. She grabbed hold of Reece's forearm, her muscles tensing and flexing. Medias swallowed, her throat dry from breathing hard. "Don't...don't stop."

Medias hovered over the empath, trembling, her lips brushing Reece's neck. She closed her eyes, the intensity of Reece's movements making her tense before she tipped over the edge, coming so hard her whole body quaked.

Her breathing ceased, everything going fuzzy and white. A low groan of release escaped her lips.

She collapsed next to Reece and rode out the aftershocks, her gasping turning into light laughter. She felt the bed shift as Reece stood.

"I need to see all of you," Reece said, making quick work of Medias's pants, her eyes roaming. No one had ever looked at her with such hunger.

"Come here," Medias rumbled, taking Reece's hand and hauling her back onto the bed, flipping her onto her back. She pressed into Reece, slotting their legs between each other. Medias dipped her head and kissed Reece, slow and deliberate at first, becoming more needy as Reece's hands pulled Medias's hips closer. She slipped her fingers behind Reece's neck and up into her hair, holding her fast as they moved in concert.

Medias paused the kiss, needing to breathe. She couldn't help the moans that escaped her. The intensity of Reece's gaze and her hands digging into her hips was almost too much to endure.

"Medias..." Reece whispered, her grinding growing more desperate.

Medias exhaled hard, barely able to clutch onto coherent thought. When Reece arched up against her and a strangled sound rumbled in the back of her throat, Medias tipped over the edge again. She held on to Reece tight as she came, eventually collapsing next to her on the bed.

They lay there without talking, the only sound their breathing.

Reece turned to her, running her fingers through Medias's newly cut hair. Medias hummed out a sigh, captured in the woman's gaze. The empath's dark eyes and smile consumed everything, and she wanted nothing more than to be devoured.

Reece splayed her fingers over Medias's belly. Lips soon replaced those fingers, Reece painting lazy kisses down her body. "I have to taste you," she said before settling between Medias's legs.

Medias gasped when Reece's tongue finally reached her core. She closed her eyes, relinquishing control, her back arching as Reece touched and teased her until her breathing turned into desperate gasps. She dug her hands into Reece's hair, willing to let the empath unravel her again and again.

VANISHED

Reece woke, a heavy sigh rumbling out of her when she ran her hand along the empty space where Medias should be.

She's gone.

Was it too much to want to wake up next to the damn woman? It was barely dawn, judging from the hazy shafts of daylight poking through the window.

She let out a low growl. No use trying to go back to sleep—not after the memories of the previous night sauntered back into her brain. She could still feel Medias's lips on every part of her. Closing her eyes, Reece recalled Medias's face, body, tongue, and hands, all hungry for her, driving her insane with desire. And how Medias had trembled uncontrollably when Reece made her come, the deep, unrestrained moans and grateful kisses afterward. That all had to mean something...so why was Medias gone?

What were they to each other, exactly? They had merely expressed sexual desire for one another, nothing more. And Reece didn't know if Medias would want more. She was impossible to read at times. Though last night was the first time there was no question as to what Medias wanted, as she pressed Reece up against the wall, her passion almost primal.

Reece flushed again just thinking about it. "Fuck," she whispered. She was angry Medias was gone, but also knew if the woman walked back into the room at that moment, Reece would tear her fucking clothes off.

She got out of bed, finding her clothes neatly folded and left on a chair. After dressing, she let herself out the door, closing it slowly behind her and peering down the hallway. She let her walls drop and reached out to sense the emotions around her. Two very bright signatures—Nyssa and Quinn—vibrated in the room across the hall, soft and calm. Sleeping. She didn't sense anyone else, and no sign of Medias's soft, warm presence.

Not about to go searching for the woman like a lost puppy looking for affection, Reece tugged at her jacket, smoothed her hair down, and headed to her office. The corridors of the Keep were busier than usual, plenty of Justiciars, guards, and attendants milling about. As she passed the dining hall, she caught sight of a few faces she recognized from the Sun Council eating a very early breakfast.

She turned down the hallway to her office, almost running into Brick and a small group of Lion's Guard members.

"Reece! Perfect timing!"

Brick caught her hand and spun her around before stepping close and dancing with her. The sweet smell of winter ale clung to him. The group laughed as the big man whirled her about.

He smiled. "They didn't believe I'm a good dancer."

"It's dawn...have you been drinking all night?" Reece asked with a giggle.

Brick held his thumb and forefinger less than an inch apart. "A little bit." He spun her again and let go, waving as the group continued on. It was good to see him taking a break from training. He and Athen were going to burn themselves out if they didn't rest.

Reece laughed to herself and stumbled into a Keep attendant, still dizzy from Brick's impromptu dance. "Oh, sorry!"

The attendant caught her in his firm grasp. "Are you okay?"

"Yes, just a little tired."

He smiled and let go. "You're up early this morning. Can I bring you breakfast in your office?"

"Oh, no, that won't be necessary."

"Good morning, then, Miss Ae'Shen."

She nodded to him and continued down to her office, half expecting to see Medias inside when she opened the door. She let out a sigh of disappointment when the woman wasn't there. Of course she wasn't. Why would she be?

Reece flipped on the lights, their warm yellow glow comforting. There were few places she felt truly comfortable, and her office, surrounded by the things she loved, was once such place.

She walked to her desk, noticing a fresh pile of papers. New communications to catch up on from all over the Empire. Lilliana's whisper network was working day and night, trying to find clues to Ceril's whereabouts. The work never seemed to end. Hadn't she quit her damn job? Only to have another unofficial one with zero pay?

She reached her desk and—

Pain, bright and sharp, smashed through her senses.

She grabbed at her side, and when her hand came away, blood coated her fingers, glistening in the soft morning glow. *H-how?* That attendant...the one she stumbled into...

All breath left her. "Fuck."

With a grunt, she ambled around the desk, her side roaring with a shocking, screaming pain. She stumbled into a plant, pushing it off the side of her desk, its pot shattering on the floor. Dirt spilled everywhere, exposing the small plant's roots.

"Sorry, little one," she mumbled, opening a desk drawer. She searched the underside of her desk with trembling, bloody fingers for a few frantic moments before she found what she needed.

She pressed the hidden button, and a second later, a klaxon began to ring through the Keep.

She stumbled to the other side of her desk and opened another drawer, pushing aside pencils, paper, brightly wrapped candies, and other clutter.

Where are they? Where...where the fuck are they?

She swallowed. Her life crystallized into sharp focus as she wavered on her feet, her strength waning. She silently cursed the disarray in her desk drawers, wondering if her messiness would be her downfall.

Her hand closed around a small object as she sank to her knees and slumped over behind her desk, pain overtaking her.

DISTRACTION

Quinn and Nyssa sprinted through the halls, a klaxon blaring throughout the estate and jolting them into action. There was only one explanation for it—someone or something threatened the Keep and everyone in it.

"Go find Lilliana—protect her!" Nyssa shouted. "I'll get Safin."

Nyssa veered off, heading towards the Emperor's quarters. Quinn pushed forward towards the administrative wing where Lilliana, Pol, and Reece kept offices. Attendants backed up against the wall as she rushed past.

"Quinn!" Medias ran toward her from the direction of the East Gardens.

"Come with me!" Quinn ordered, happy to see her. "We're getting Lilliana to safety."

Medias followed without question. They turned the corner to the hall that led to the executive offices and skidded to a halt. A group of guards and Keep attendants ran up, Suvi Rell gagged and blindfolded in their midst.

"Why do they have Suvi?" Medias whispered.

Quinn's stomach dropped. A second passed. No one moved as the groups stared each other down. Then, in the blink of an eye, the hallway erupted in light and smoke, blinding Quinn. Something crashed into her, and she was lifted off her feet, then slammed to the ground, all the air forced from her lungs. She choked, trying to breathe, tears streaming down her face.

Footsteps thundered past her, and she reached out with her magick, blindly sending out her shadow in all directions, making it corporeal and using it to trip up their attackers. She rose to her hands and knees—

Something heavy came down on the back of her head, and she collapsed against the cold stone floor, her magick dissipating. With a groan, she rolled onto her back.

"Bring her!" a voice commanded.

A dark shape moved over Quinn and clutched at her.

Panicked, her hand flew up to grab the attacker's arm, and she sent sharp, hard shards of darkness through him.

She heard a surprised grunt, and the heavy body of her attacker fell on top of her.

A loud *crack*, followed by another, made Quinn try to push the man off of her, but her arms didn't respond. Another *crack*. The unmistakable sound of flesh and bone violently meeting stone.

Fuck. FUCK. She would be next.

Quinn summoned every last ounce of energy to push the dead weight off of her. A blur of movement caught her eye. A woman flew across the hall and collided with the wall, blood spattering the light-gray stone. Another body thudded to the floor next to her.

Quinn blinked tears out of her eyes and held her hands out toward the advancing attacker.

Lilliana Fennick came into focus, blood streaked across her face. She held up her hands. "Don't attack, Quinn, it's me."

A man darted out from behind Lilliana, his tall, lanky frame unmistakable. Pol, Lilliana's right-hand man. He bent over her.

"Miss Emerrath, are you okay?"

"Suvi...they took..." Quinn fell back, panting. Her head felt like it had been hit with a boulder.

"Come on," Medias murmured beside her, helping her sit up. Quinn took a quick scan of the hallway. Several dead bodies lay bloody, a testament to Lilliana's strength and ruthlessness.

"Where's Suvi?" Quinn asked.

Lilliana crouched down, panting. "Gone."

"What are you doing? Go after them!"

"Those bastards tried killing me in my office, and they paid the price with their lives. I'm not going anywhere until I know my children are safe."

"Fuck it, I'll go." Quinn grabbed onto Medias's shoulder. "Help me up."

Medias stood and pulled Quinn to her feet. Quinn started in the direction her attackers went until a cruel wave of dizziness overtook her. She stumbled to the wall and leaned down, losing the contents of her stomach.

Quinn turned around. Medias slid down the wall opposite her, breathing heavily and looking worse for wear. *Dammit, their magick packed a punch.*

Distant screams made Quinn's stomach drop.

Nyssa!

Not a second later, the ground trembled. Quinn's heart pounded in her chest. She braced herself against the wall, pushing off of it, her feet unsteady beneath her.

"Nyssa," she whispered.

"Go," Lilliana urged. "We're secure here."

"Quinn, wait!" Medias called out.

Ignoring her, Quinn started jogging in the direction of Safin's quarters.

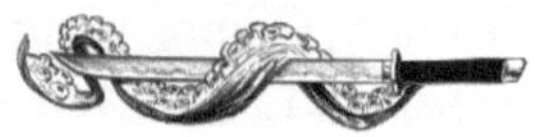

Medias rested against the wall, her breathing labored and painful—no doubt a bruised rib or two sustained in the attack. She turned her attention to Lilliana and Pol. A man lay dead near him, blood pooling around his body. Pol bent down and pushed him over, pulling his scarlet Keep attendant jacket open. Underneath, he wore dark green.

"Obsidian Rule," Pol said, standing. He pointed toward one of the other lifeless bodies. "I recognize him. That's Reggie Cox's nephew."

"Dammit. Razinu faction must have sold us out to Anelos," Lilliana said. "Pol, I want every last member of Razinu found and arrested."

Medias exhaled. "Razinu?" She struggled to her feet, stumbling as if she were drunk. Reggie would have killed Reece if Medias had not intervened months back. "Where's Reece?" Ice ran through her veins as she started toward Reece's office, clutching her ribs, breaking into an awkward loping gait.

"Medias, wait!" Lilliana called after her. More distant screams and tremors made her stomach ball up. But whatever was happening outside the Keep didn't matter. Not now. Not with Reece missing.

Medias reached Reece's office and she took a cautious step through the door.

A pained whimper left her throat.

A body lay on the ground next to the desk in a pool of blood.

"Reece!" Medias choked out, tearing into the room and dropping to her knees. Reece's dress was ripped open at the side, the fabric stained dark with blood.

"No," Medias whispered, reaching out with a trembling hand. No. Please no. Her heart stalled, refusing to beat.

She fumbled at Reece's dress, pulling it open where it had been torn, wiping at the blood. The skin underneath had a fresh red scar.

"Th-there you are," Reece's weak voice muttered. She opened her eyes and groaned. "I was...looking for you, Justiciar."

Medias sucked in a breath. "Y-you're alive?" she gasped.

Reece blinked. "Remind me...to organize my drawers," she grumbled softly. "Almost couldn't find a healing disk. I...I have at least three, I think..." Her voice drifted off, though she tried to muster a smile.

Medias let out a strangled laugh and brushed errant strands of hair out of Reece's face, stuck to her skin with sweat. Her heart resumed beating, its pace frantic and pounding.

"She needs a healer," Lilliana said, gently moving past Medias. "Let me take her."

"Hurts," Reece murmured.

Lilliana took a moment and caressed Reece's cheek. "Oh, my daughter, I'm so sorry."

"Come," Pol said, gently taking Medias's arm and urging her to stand.

She complied and moved out of the way, letting loose a deep exhale. Lilliana tended to her adopted daughter with a tenderness Medias never would have expected out of the Lioness of Ocean's Rest. Lilliana slid her hands underneath Reece and picked her up effortlessly, the strength she'd used to slam attackers against the walls earlier now turned gentle. She walked out of the office with Reece, Medias scrambling behind her.

Brick waited for them in the hall, an unconscious body at his feet.

"I got one, Lady Fennick," he said. "Caught him before he could get away." He knelt over the face-down man and tapped him on the temple.

Lilliana stopped. "Thank you, Brick. My son chose wisely trusting you."

"Hey," Reece said weakly, looking down at the unconscious prisoner. "He ran into me in the hallway...knifed me."

"Brick, go to my office. I have a void collar in the back set of drawers. Get it on him and take him to the cells. Then get outside and help defend the Keep."

Brick nodded and took off down the hall.

Medias clutched at her midsection, grimacing from the pain of her bruised ribs. She stared down at Reece's would-be assassin, her jaw flexing, murder in her heart.

ASSAULT ON OCEAN'S KEEP

A massive explosion rocked the Keep, making the ground under Nyssa's feet shake. Distant screams pierced the air, turning her blood to ice. She ran in the direction of the explosion. Whoever was attacking took precedence—she had to trust that Decia and Ina would keep Safin safe.

More explosive impacts sent tremors running through the Keep, and Nyssa tried to stay focused. Quinn, Athen, and the others occupied her mind—if anything happened to them, she would be sick with guilt. But Athen was a warrior, and she had trained Quinn, giving her the skills to take care of herself.

Faith. Nyssa needed faith that her friends would be fine.

As she sprinted past the Great Room, she skidded to a stop. Outside of its massive windows hovered the source of the attacks.

A dark, metallic airship.

Balls of fire rained down from above, exploding when they hit the garden grounds. Nyssa ran through the Great Room and exited to the terrace outside.

The warship floated above them, its underbelly illuminated by the fire it shot down at the grounds below. People scattered in all directions, their morning meditations interrupted. Huddled next to the trunk of a large oak tree was a woman with three children. One Nyssa instantly recognized.

Pebble!

Nyssa shot out toward the tree.

She sensed a massive spike of power flaring from the airship just before a ball of fire hit the ground in front of her and exploded, sending gleaming shards flying in all directions. Nyssa hit the ground hard, covering up, but not before debris sliced her cheek.

Turning her eyes back to the airship, the red blaze of another fireball filled her vision. A large mass moved over her as the air burst into flame and light. She hissed and curled away from the heat.

"You're okay." Athen stood over Nyssa. He had blocked the fireball from hitting her with his body, his invulnerability saving them both from harm.

Nyssa sprang to her feet and let a lightning bolt fly toward the ship. It struck its underside and rippled across the surface, dissipating harmlessly.

"Dammit." There had to be a protective ward at play.

Athen pulled his coat and shirt off and cast them aside, their fabric half burnt and shredded.

"Are you okay?" she asked.

"Yes. Be careful, those glass bombs contain mage fire."

Glass bombs could cut anyone to ribbons. She bolted for the tree and the kids, ignoring Athen's shouts behind her.

A flash from the sky drew her attention.

Nyssa swerved to her left, escaping a collision with another fireball. It crashed into the hard winter grass, peppering her with shards of glass. The fire stuck to the ground and spread like liquid. She veered away from the flames licking at her boots.

A bone-chilling shriek came from the direction of the tree as another attack rained down from above. Nyssa had to shield her eyes from the burst of light. When she got to the tree, her stomach turned. A dead body lay smoldering.

"Pebble!" she yelled.

"Nyssa?" a small voice whimpered. Nyssa circled around the tree, finding the girl and two young boys. "Miss Hampstone saved us. Is she okay?"

Nyssa bent down and wrapped an arm around Pebble, hoisting her up. "Hug my neck, sweetie." The two boys cowered from her. "Take my hand," she commanded. The boys recoiled further. "Fuck, I don't have time for you to be scared of me."

"Boys, take my hands," a soft voice said.

Nyssa whirled around to find Safin at her side. "What the fuck are you doing here, kid?"

"Helping!"

There wasn't a Justiciar or Ashcloak in sight. *Why is he alone?*

Gritting her teeth, she grunted. "Stay behind me and—"

A fireball burst in front of them. Nyssa instinctively curled her body around Pebble and sent out a wave of her magick. Shards of glass hit her and the others, but the mage fire hung midair, suspended by her power, drops of it dripping onto the ground and sizzling in the snow and ice on the grass. She collapsed the fire into a small sphere, shattering its magickal components. It disintegrated, the ash floating to the ground, no longer a threat.

Pebble tightened her grip, whimpering. The boys were crying, huddled behind Safin and pressed up against the tree.

"Keep your heads down, eyes covered!" she yelled. "Safin, take Pebble."

"No, Nyssa!" the little girl pleaded.

"I have to fight back, and I don't want you getting hurt by my lightning, okay?"

The little girl nodded, her eyes full of tears.

"That's my brave girl." She handed Pebble to Safin.

The garden was a wasteland of fire and glass, men and women darting about, taking up positions behind cover.

Athen led a smattering of the Lion's Guard. "Fire!" Crossbow bolts arced up into the sky, striking the bottom of the airborne warship, its magickal shield sparking where the arrows hit, holding fast.

Nyssa faced the ship, azure lightning raging over her skin. She strode out from under the tree, bringing her hands together, gathering energy between her palms, bright blue and crackling with as much power as she could cram into a sphere of pure magick.

Fontaine once said that a large quantity of magick forced into a small space was a recipe for disaster, but if Nyssa could create something powerful and highly unstable, it could perhaps get through the wards of that damn ship.

Her hands and forearms vibrated, aching from the concentration of ancient power gathering at her fingertips, the thrum of the balled-up energy reverberating through her body. As the power grew, it began to *hurt*. Nyssa ignored the pain and kept shoving more and more magick into the ball, blue arcs of energy jumping off her fingers and hands in all directions.

"Nyssa?" Safin called out.

"Get behind the tree, Safin! Now!"

More fireballs fell around her, though most seemed aimed at Athen's gathering of Lion's Guard warriors. Screams continued to pierce the air.

Nyssa gagged on the smell of burning flesh but held her focus. Her Ancient Magick hummed, then roared, howling its power into Nyssa's bones, every last muscle trembling. Eyes flicking upward, she gathered the last of her resolve and hurled the lightning ball at the airship. The orb shrieked through the air, the sound of it setting Nyssa's teeth on edge, like metal straining and bending, about to break.

The lightning exploded against the warship, filling the sky with blinding sapphire light. Its shock wave hit Nyssa, and she fell back to the ground, her skin buzzing with power.

Blue skeins of lightning rippled across the ship's ruptured golden ward, a huge black hole of fire and smoke where half of the ship's hull used to be. The vessel jerked forward, then listed to the side, smoke billowing from the hole. It didn't lose altitude, but it was dead in the air, incapacitated by Nyssa's violent attack.

A high-pitched whistle rippled through the air, and dark ropes unfurled from the warship, and figures rappelled down, abandoning ship.

Men and women hit the ground, drawing weapons. The Lion's Guard fell upon them, and the garden lit up with magick from the combatants.

Though Nyssa wanted to help Athen, Safin and Pebble were her priority. She pushed herself to her feet—

A massive man dropped in front of her and straightened up to his full height. By the looks of him, he had an inch or two on Brick, who had to be almost seven feet tall. Far more alarming were the pulsating plates of armor he wore and a sword that was almost as tall as she was.

She stumbled back and drew Winter's Bite. It sparked with blue lightning. *Huh, that's new.*

The armored man reared back and cleaved his sword through the air. Nyssa danced out of its range, and the tip of the blade bit into the frozen ground.

"Stop moving, bitch," he hissed.

In the corner of her eye, Safin circled to her left. *Dammit, what is he doing?*

"Safin, get behind the tree!"

"Watch out, Nyssa, that's power armor and—"

The man flung his arm out, and a shock wave of air sent Nyssa flying back into the tree trunk. She crumpled to her hands and knees, the wind forced ruthlessly from her lungs.

Instead of advancing on her, the man turned his attention to Safin, laughing. "The boy Emperor? I'll get extra coin for killing you."

Nyssa climbed to her feet, tossing out bolts of lightning at the attacker. They hit his armor and rippled across the dark-gray plates before sizzling harmlessly and petering out, as if the bursts of lightning were sucked into them. The man didn't even flinch. Nor did he halt his progress as he ambled toward Safin.

Nyssa darted at their attacker. His sword arced down again, but she parried the blow, knocking the hefty blade off course, its bone-jarring impact making her forearms hum with pain.

Gritting her teeth, she stepped inside the man's guard. He relied on his strength, but his size was a liability. Once she got close to him, he couldn't stop Winter's Bite from sliding between the plates of his armor and into his gut.

He howled and gritted his teeth. His meaty hand landed on Nyssa's shoulder and scrabbled to her throat. She grabbed his wrist and sent a shock of magick through him.

It didn't stop him.

Nyssa twisted Winter's Bite, and a hot spray of blood covered her face, but still, the man held fast.

A growl left her throat as she tensed, trying to withstand the force of his squeezing fingers.

He's going to snap my neck...I have to twist his soul...stop him...

She sank her magick into him, looking to mangle his essence and hasten his death, but she couldn't pinpoint his glowing life force. It was there, but obscured. She couldn't get a hold of it...couldn't stop him.

Strange power buzzed under her fingers, one she had never felt the like of before.

"You die with me, Unworthy," he hissed. His hand tightened around her throat.

Nyssa gagged, unable to draw air into her lungs. Panic shot through her as her eyesight dimmed.

Shadows slipped over Nyssa, a bone-deep chill running through her. The world slowed down, immersed in night. A welcome, glowing warmth rose in her chest.

Quinn's magick moved through her and the world around her, casting the garden into darkness.

Fingers clawed at Nyssa's throat, trying to maintain their grip, but the man was snatched away, his voice rising in a muted scream before going silent.

Nyssa folded forward, drawing in a desperate, icy breath, and opened up her senses. She found a little cluster of souls where the tree should be and moved toward them.

"It's Nyssa," she said, her voice echoing in the cold night that Quinn had pulled down over the garden. Shouts rose up around her, though it was impossible to tell how close or far away they were. Disorientation was one of the effects of Quinn's night magick, though Nyssa could navigate the darkness without issue.

"What's happening?" Safin asked, his voice laced with a note of fear.

"It's okay, Quinn has us." Nyssa touched him, and his hand flew to her shoulder to get his bearings.

Arms wrapped around her leg, and Nyssa bent over to pick Pebble up, whispering encouragement into the girl's ear, trying to calm her. "Auntie Quinn is protecting us, Pebble."

Nyssa shivered, holding the girl tight. In the cold grip of Quinn's darkness, she became aware of a myriad of cuts and bruises marring her own skin, the sting of their pain in sharp focus.

One by one, the voices raised in alarm all around her became quiet.

Shadows swirled around Nyssa, moving outward and up, the darkness giving way to light as the overcast day returned. Shadows dispersed from the man who had attacked her and Safin. He still stood upright, but his eyes...his eyes held no spark of life.

Quinn stood beside him, onyx tendrils spiraling around them both. She withdrew her magick from him, and he collapsed to the ground with a dull *thud*.

Nyssa's heart leapt at the sight of Quinn, her relief quickly replaced by caution as she scanned the garden for enemies, taking in the bodies dotting the ground. She held Pebble tight in one arm, the other holding Safin behind her to protect him. The two boys clutched at Safin's hands.

"Quinn, the other attackers—"

"They're dead," Quinn replied before sinking to the ground.

"Quinn!"

Quinn held up a hand. "I'm okay, just a little foggy. Got knocked about a little in the Keep."

Athen shouted out, a call and response to his commanders to make sure the garden was secure. His presence of mind in the midst of a fight and its aftermath would have made Eron proud.

"Pebble, are you okay?" Nyssa asked, giving her a once-over.

The girl just nodded, but Nyssa needed to get them all to the infirmary anyway.

A booming voice rang out. "Delliah!" Brick ran toward them, his face fraught with worry. He scooped his daughter up into his arms.

"I'm okay, Daddy," she assured him, wrapping her little arms around his neck. "Auntie Nyssa kept us safe."

He rubbed her back with trembling hands. "Thank you, Blacksea."

She nodded and crossed over to Quinn, sinking to the snow beside her. She was exhausted.

Athen came striding toward them, barking out orders. The Lion's Guard scrambled at his commands. "Are you okay?"

"Yeah," Nyssa breathed. "What happened?"

"Bunch of Razinu assholes thought they were a match for the Lion's Guard and a couple Cursed Gods," Athen said as he ambled up, shirtless and covered in sweat-streaked ash.

Quinn's eyes scanned Nyssa up and down. She gingerly pushed a chunk of hair away from Nyssa's face. "Nyssa, you're all cut up."

"I'll be fine." She looked down. Her white shirt was blotted with blood.

Quinn's eyes wavered and she rested her hand on Nyssa's thigh. "Infirmary, now."

Nyssa was usually the overprotective one in their relationship, but she didn't mind Quinn's worry or attention. Not one bit. "In...in a moment."

"This fucking warship appeared out of nowhere. It's an Areshi military weapon," Athen seethed. "Attacking civilians!"

"That ship was stolen last night," Safin said.

"You didn't think to share that news with us? So we could at least be prepared?" Nyssa asked.

Safin dipped his head, a deep frown creasing his brow.

Nyssa shook her head, her blood running hot. "Let us help you! Keeping us at arm's length and under house arrest is bullshit."

Safin was about to respond, but a wave of Justiciars rushed toward them, Ashcloak Ruggen at the head.

"Emperor Safin, are you hurt?" Ina asked, her eyes darting to Nyssa before returning to him.

Nyssa rose to her feet and grabbed Ina, twisting her fist in the Ashcloak's jacket. "Where the fuck were you and the rest of his guards? He was out here on his own!"

Ina bared her teeth. "Get your hands off me, Unworthy."

Arch Justiciar Decia pushed through the throng. "I see you learned the Keep's secret passages, Emperor?"

"I just wanted some time to myself. People are always around, pulling me in every direction." Safin sighed. "Nyssa, release Ashcloak Ruggen. I snuck out on my own, this isn't her fault."

Nyssa pushed Ina away. "Where were your brave Ashcloaks when we were fighting a hijacked warship?"

"Frantically searching the Keep for the Emperor. His well-being is our only priority," Ruggen answered.

"Innocent people were attacked out here. Our duty is to protect the people of this Empire."

"*Our* duty, Unworthy?" Ina stepped closer to Nyssa. "You're not one of us anymore. Don't speak to me of duty."

"Stop this," Safin ordered. "Both of you."

Nyssa's better impulses overrode the desire to flatten Ina where she stood. She turned away and surveyed the destruction in the garden. Bodies of men and women lay strewn about. Friends and foes.

"What was the point of this?" she asked, gesturing to the warship that hung lifelessly in the sky.

Quinn groaned and stood, unsteady on her feet. Athen wrapped an arm around her for support. "A distraction. Obsidian Rule assassins stole Suvi Rell out from under us."

Nyssa hung her head. "Fuck."

"They were helped by Razinu faction," Athen said. "My mother will have them all killed for this betrayal."

Nyssa walked over to the body of the large man who had almost choked the life out of her.

"Nyssa, you should know...the dockworkers that died during your escape? They were Razinu," Athen said.

Her stomach twisted. "Would they have done this if I didn't kill their people? Would they have turned their back on their city?" She examined the man's body. "This armor he's wearing..."

"Power armor. Gives the wearer extra strength. It's useful for moving big cargo around on the docks."

"It absorbed my lightning strikes."

He grunted. "It could have been magickally altered. Maybe an absorption or reflection enchantment?"

Nyssa ground her teeth. Rendering her magick almost powerless was not a swerve she expected. She'd have to be better prepared for surprises.

Athen moved next to her. "You're injured. Quinn looks a bit loopy. Let's get everyone to the infirmary. Lilliana will have the Keep on lock-down to sort all this out."

Raising her head, Nyssa watched as the Justiciars surrounded Safin and escorted him away. Only Ina lingered for a moment, locking eyes with her.

Oh, how the Ashcloak seemed to relish every fucking opportunity to spit the word *Unworthy* at her. One day soon, Nyssa would have to punch that word straight out of her mouth.

ROOTS

Reece slipped out of the infirmary, not wishing to be a bother after being tended to. When she left, Nyssa was grumbling at the healers, forcing them to look after everyone else before her, and Quinn was resting after being treated for a concussion. Reece would have stayed behind to help, but Aryis was already expediting, making sure the healers were seeing to the most injured.

Medias had been in the infirmary earlier after her ribs were healed up, lingering in the periphery, pacing, waiting for the healers to say Reece was fine before suddenly disappearing. Again. Seemed the woman was rather good at that. Reece tried not to be hurt.

She attempted to put Medias out of her head for the moment, trying to make sense of the day's chaos.

Lilliana informed her that members of Razinu had turned traitor and attacked with Obsidian Rule assassins, targeting innocents in the garden to distract everyone from their true purpose—Suvi Rell. They had wreaked havoc, killing over twenty people and almost killing Delliah and two of her classmates.

Reece swallowed. Almost killing *her*.

She had to pause and duck into an alcove on the way to her office to catch her breath. She pressed her hand to her chest, feeling her heart racing. An assassin had almost ended her. He had slid his blade so efficiently into her belly she didn't even notice. Medias mentioned that he likely used a numbing agent so she wouldn't feel the wound immediately, but Reece kicked herself anyway. How could she be so careless to let herself get hurt? She made it a practice to keep her walls up, to not reach out to sense the emotions around her, both to protect herself and to respect the privacy of those around her. And there was no place else in the world where she felt so safe as Ocean's Keep. Today shattered that safety. It made her angry. And fearful.

After Reece gathered herself and calmed a bit, she made her way to her office, steeling herself against the bloody mess she'd have to clean up. She shuddered at the thought.

The door to her office was ajar, and Reece slipped inside, finding Medias on her knees. Medias didn't notice her, too busy scooping up spilled dirt and putting it into a small pot before gingerly picking up the plant that had been smashed on the floor, trying to replant it. The look of concentration on her face, as if it were the most important duty in the world, made Reece's heart skip a beat.

I think I might love this woman.

Medias looked up and smiled, her whole face lighting up.

Reece forgot to breathe for a moment.

No, I know I do. I'm in love with her.

Fuck. Fuck-fuck-fuck-fuck-fuck-fu—

"What are you doing here? You should be resting in the infirmary, woman." The way Medias growled her concern tightened Reece's stomach. She was insanely sexy when commanding.

Reece cleared her throat, trying to pull herself together. "I'm fine, Medias. What are you doing with my plant?"

"I didn't want him dying on you." Medias stood up and put the plant back on the desk. "I had cleaners come in and enchant the blood out of the floor."

"This is what you've been doing? Getting my office cleaned and re-potting my plant?"

Medias frowned. "Is that not okay?"

Leaning against the doorframe, Reece shook her head. "No, it's fine. I just... Thank you. That's a she, by the way."

Medias scowled. "A she?"

"That Flat-Leaf Lathea you repotted is female."

Shaking her head, Medias glanced down at the little plant, gently stroking a leaf. "No, he told me you had it wrong. He's a *he*." She looked up with a tiny smirk that seemed designed to drive Reece insane.

The one word Reece never thought to associate with Medias was adorable. But right now, she was being fucking adorable. Amusing and alluring in equal measure. Reece cleared her throat, trying to refocus on the danger facing the Keep.

"Where are Nyssa and Quinn?" Medias asked.

"The infirmary. Quinn is resting and Nyssa is waiting for the healers to tend to everyone else before she'll let them touch her."

"Are you sure you're okay?" Concern blanketed Medias's tone. "Earlier...when we found you...I thought you were dead."

How refreshing it was to see her without a mask, to be able to read her emotions as they danced over her face. Her dark-red eyes didn't release Reece's gaze, holding her there, still. The distance between them was almost unbearable, but Reece stayed anchored to the doorframe, doing her best to ignore the pain that laced Medias's words.

Neither of them had broached last night, what it meant or where it left them with each other. Reece had always led with her heart, but the mess with Shaylin a few years prior made her cautious. Compounding everything was Medias herself, gone from the bed when Reece woke up. That never boded well.

Reece searched for something to say, anything that didn't sound completely inane. Suddenly, the small talk she liked to torture Medias with evaded her.

A Keep attendant saved her by running up with a message. "From Lady Fennick." He handed it off to her.

Reece's heart dropped as she read the paper. "Fuck."

Medias started forward, but stopped, waiting.

"Reggie Cox is gone. He used Razinu to attack our home and then ran like a coward," Reece said. "I'm sure Cox promised his people that once House Fennick fell, they'd rule Ocean's Rest. They're now paying for his treachery."

Medias finally moved, slowly approaching, as if Reece were a wild animal that was not to be spooked. "They made their choice, Reece."

"I don't understand. Why did Ceril target Suvi? They didn't even look for Safin." It didn't make any sense—Safin only found himself in danger because he tried to save others.

"I think they were intending to take Quinn as well if they could." Medias scowled. "I need to speak with my mother. Stay here, I'll be back." She was out the door before Reece could stop her.

Reece put her hands on her hips and looked around. Aside from remnants of dirt next to her desk, the rug had been cleaned thoroughly. She approached her desk and smiled down at the little plant that Medias had done her best to replant. She moved it to the other side of her desk, hoping it would be safer from any more knocking-over incidents.

"Reece."

Lilliana stood in the doorway.

Reece didn't have her walls up, and she sensed an overwhelming feeling radiating off of Lilliana—relief. And love. Reece hesitated, not used to experiencing such raw emotions from her adoptive mother. Lilliana had, over the years, learned to control her emotions around her empath daughter. But now, they were laid bare.

Reece's breath caught. She suddenly felt five years old again, looking for Lilliana's attention and affection, frustrated when the woman doled it out so sparingly. Now that love hit her in waves, unrestrained.

Lilliana crossed the room and wrapped Reece up in a hug. Reece melted into her arms, hot tears flowing.

"I've got you, Reece."

They stood like that for minutes, mother embracing her weeping daughter, allowing her to cry her fear, hurt, and anger out.

"I was so scared for you," Lilliana said, her voice barely above a whisper. "The sight of you lying in your own blood, I..." She squeezed Reece tighter.

She took a deep breath and pulled away, wiping tears from her eyes before smudging the tears off Reece's cheeks. "You saved a great many lives sounding the alarm like you did."

Reece sniffed, composing herself. "Cox was after us. What I don't understand is why the Obsidian Rule assassins took Suvi Rell and left Safin alone."

"The captured assassin will know," Lilliana replied. "I was just with him. He wouldn't talk to me. But Medias will certainly break him."

Reece scowled. "Medias? She's not a Justiciar anymore."

"She passed me on the stairs coming up from the lower levels. I assumed she was going to question him."

"Shit," Reece whispered. "I have to stop her."

"Reece, wait—"

Reece rushed out of her office, heading for the nearest winding staircase that would take her below the Keep to the cells. A creeping dread overtook her that Medias would go too far with their prisoner. He was the only one they had, and they needed answers. Something in the back of her mind was convinced that Medias would kill him for what he'd done to her.

Her fears were confirmed when cries of pain echoed from a cell at the end of the hall at the bottom of the stairs. Keep guards stood sentry at the door, glancing nervously at Reece as she hurried toward them. "Open it!"

A guard unlocked the door and pushed it open. "We're sorry, Miss Ae'Shen, Justiciar Medias ordered us to let her in."

"She's not a damn Justiciar anymore!" Reece entered the cell and stopped cold.

Medias stood over the Rule assassin, her back to Reece. When she turned around, her face fell. "Leave. I don't want you to see this."

A breath left Reece's chest. The assassin's emotions flowed over her. Pain and some last dying remnant of indignation hit her in crushing waves. This was the part of her gift that others could never understand. She could feel *everything* when she dropped her walls and reached out. And even the worst people's fear was raw and naked.

"What are you doing? Leave this to Decia and her Justiciars," Reece implored.

Medias stepped away from the man, the sparse lighting casting shadows that moved across her face. "This man is our only link to Ceril. He will tell me what I want to know."

"Stop." Reece was met with a scowl, but persisted. "You're not this person anymore. I thought you wanted to turn the page. I thought we..." She hesitated. There was no *we*. An empty bed told her as much.

"This bastard almost killed you."

Words failed Reece. She knew how this was going to go. She knew what Medias was capable of—she had seen the Justiciar's cold and deadly fury when she almost killed Reggie Cox months ago. Part of Reece found Medias's protective streak intensely attractive. But that protectiveness could be dangerous.

Medias held up her hand, white magick flashing across her fingertips, and the man cried out, doubling over. The ex-Justiciar had the perfect magick for interrogating a prisoner, able to explode light anywhere, including inside a body, causing immense pain but no actual harm.

"Where is Ceril Anelos?" Medias asked.

He looked up and smirked. "I'm Obsidian Rule. You know I'm trained to endure your questioning."

Medias stepped toward the man. "You won't survive me."

"I don't know where he is," he said.

Reece held up her hand. "He's telling you the truth."

"He knows something, and I will pry it out of him," Medias replied, circling the man. There was a grace to her movements, slow and deliberate.

It was that moment that Reece saw the predator Ambershine had created, perfect and deadly.

"Where is Suvi Rell?"

When he didn't answer, bright-white light flashed around Medias's hand and the assassin cried out. She repeated the question. His silence drew another flash of magick. Again, the question. And again, silence followed by Medias's punishment.

Each time he cried out, a spike of agony hit Reece and she flinched.

Medias drew her eyes up to meet her gaze. "You should leave, empath."

"No."

Medias's jaw clenched, but Reece couldn't leave. It was as if her feet were rooted in place. But she also knew she could help get the truth from the man who had almost killed her. "He knows something about Suvi, I can sense his fear."

Their prisoner panted, his voice weak. "Reece Ae'Shen. The empath of Ocean's Rest. I wonder what Ceril will do with you, hmm?"

Medias grabbed his head and yanked it back. "You almost killed her. Do you know how badly you will suffer for that? Let me show you, assassin."

Medias slammed a fist into the side of his head. Again. And again. Blood splattered against the floor, a massive cut opening above his eyebrow. She kept hitting him, each new strike followed by the sound of ichor hitting the floor.

Despite the brutality, Reece didn't look away. She couldn't. Medias was a force, terrible and deadly, her anger honed to a razor-sharp edge and wielded with violent purpose.

"You will tell me what I want to know, traitor," Medias said, stepping back from the Rule adept and shaking her red-stained fist.

The assassin's head hung between his shoulders, blood dripping onto his lap and the floor. He wasn't unconscious. Not yet. Medias rounded behind his chair and buried her hand in his hair, pulling his head back. His face was a mess, one eye beginning to swell shut, his bottom lip split.

"Where are they taking Suvi?"

Medias raised her eyes to Reece, her face etched with a different kind of pain. The pain of the naked truth of what she was capable of. A burst of white energy surrounded her hand, and she exploded it into the Rule adept, over and over again. His cries gave way to whimpers and his pain hit Reece in waves.

"Where is Suvi Rell?"

Reece could hear her own breathing, sensing the stubborn resolve of the adept crumbling. Before, pain and contempt were the strongest emotions coming off of him, but now, something else crept in.

Regret tinged the fear.

Reece put her hand to her chest.

Another burst of light exploded inside the assassin, and Reece bowed forward from the force of his emotions. "Don't do this!" she yelled. "Please."

The concern on Medias's face was washed away by cold resolve. She might as well be wearing her mask, the expression all too familiar. "I won't stop. Put your walls up, empath."

"I've already felt his pain. Putting my walls up won't stop me from understanding what he's going through."

Reece was met with a scowl. "You feel for the man who almost killed you?"

Exhaling, Reece straightened up. "You don't understand. I've felt this all before with men and women facing death, and it's always the same. I feel...I..." she stuttered, unable to explain how such strong emotions affected her. Wore her down. But gave her insight into people at their lowest, most desolate moments.

"I've come too far to stop now, Reece." Medias glanced down, hiding her face. "I'm sorry this hurts you."

"Fucking stop!" Reece yelled. Medias stilled, her eyes wide.

Reece approached the Rule assassin, and his brown eyes fought to stay on her as she knelt in front of him. "Why did you side with Ceril?"

When he didn't answer, Medias pulled his head back. Magick flashed at her fingertips, and he mumbled something.

"Wait!" Reece insisted. "Medias, please wait." She focused back on the assassin. "What do you want to tell me?"

"You're wasting your time, Reece," Medias growled.

"Fucking trust me." She raised her eyes to drive her point home before taking the assassin's trembling hand. "Tell me."

"Anelos...threatened to arrest my sister...accuse her of spying."

Reece swallowed. "Does he threaten everyone that's working with him from your guild?"

He shook his head. "No. Some...do it for power and riches. He didn't turn everyone...but enough gave...gave in."

"Why didn't you just say that from the start?" she asked.

The man's eyes filled with tears, his fear washing over her in full force. "You've seen what he can do. My sister...he'll kill her."

Medias spoke up. "Where is Suvi Rell?"

"A sh-ship."

Reece tensed. "What ship?"

"Wave Piercer," he mumbled.

All the air left Reece. How had she been so shortsighted? "Shay's ship." She stood up and stumbled away from the man. "This is my fault." She took one last look at her would-be assassin and fled the cell, hurrying past the guards to the stone staircase that wound back up to the ground floor.

Her legs refused to carry her up more than a few steps before she collapsed. Within moments, Medias found her.

"I...I lifted the lien on that fucking boat," Reece rasped. "They got Suvi out of Ocean's Rest on it because of me. *I* fucking let her go."

Medias offered her a hand. "It's not your fault."

Reece shook her head. "You must think me so weak. I didn't let Shay go to be the bigger person. I just...I couldn't face her again." She exhaled, took Medias's hand, and stood. "And in there, with that assassin, I felt his fear. And I was scared *for* him."

Pain flickered across Medias's face. "Now you know what I am. What I'm capable of."

"That isn't truly you."

Medias exhaled a sharp breath. "You don't know that. You keep pushing me, thinking you'll find something in me that'll make me..." She shook her head, straightening up to her full height.

"That'll make you what?" Reece asked.

"Worthy. Of you."

Words escaped Reece. She reached out, hesitant, before laying a hand against Medias's cheek, drawing out a sigh. "You're a *good* woman. What you do to protect those you love doesn't scare me."

She almost bit her tongue. She had said *love* far too casually.

Medias pulled away. "It scares me." With that, she stalked up the stairs, leaving Reece behind.

THE DEAD

Nyssa stood alongside Quinn in the East Garden, watching the faction known as Obscuras—their faces painted black and white to resemble skulls—collecting the bodies from the infirmary. Though Nyssa had heard about the mysterious group, she hadn't laid eyes on them until now. According to Reece, they tended to the dead and traced their lineage back to when necromancers were still allowed to practice their magicks.

The silent members of Obscuras moved with purpose, only pausing to glance at the Cursed Gods, no doubt curious. They handled the bodies with a reverence that made Nyssa's heart ache. When Eron was murdered, she didn't wait to see what had happened to his body, instead taking off after Quinn. Obscuras likely had seen to his cremation.

After some time, Medias found them in the garden, casting a quick glance over to the two Justiciars trailing them. Not even after the attack on the Keep did Decia relent on keeping an eye on them. "Reece would like to see us all in her office. We have information for you."

Nyssa and Quinn followed Medias to Reece's office, to find Athen and Aryis already there. Nyssa didn't miss the glare that Quinn shot Aryis.

"Close the door," Reece said, bending over her desk, pen to paper, quickly scratching out a note. She straightened up with a grunt, her hand going to her healed wound. Without a word, Medias moved next to her, bracing her arm. It wasn't just a helpful gesture, it was tender, but an undercurrent of tension hung between them. Medias helped Reece sit at her desk.

"Medias and I learned something from the man who tried to kill me. Suvi escaped on Shay Vance's ship, the Wave Piercer," Reece explained, her mood dark.

"Shit," Athen said.

"I'm sorry, guys. I lifted the lien on her ship."

"This isn't your fault," he replied.

Reece sighed. "That's debatable, but I have a plan."

Nyssa chewed her bottom lip and sat down in one of Reece's plush, worn armchairs. "What are you thinking?"

"Shay has a couple hours' head start, but I know from her own words that the Wave Piercer isn't the fastest ship on the water. We are going to get Suvi back. I've already messaged Elias, and he's game to give chase to Shaylin Vance. He said it would be his pleasure. I guess he's had run-ins with her before, which doesn't surprise me in the least. That fucking asshole bitch of a cunt pirate is trouble to anyone out at sea."

The room stilled for a moment. Then Athen exhaled a laugh. "You've been holding that in for a while, haven't you?"

"Gods, I hate her." Reece dipped her head and then composed herself. "Elias will give chase to Shay and Suvi, but he's going to need help finding them." She turned to Aryis. "That involves you."

Aryis looked at Reece before her head swiveled to the rest of the room, as if checking to see if she had heard correctly.

Reece continued, "Suvi's dagger. Elias still has it on the Whisper. You can use your magick to—"

"Yes," Aryis said, her face brightening. "I can use it to track Suvi, and we'll find Shaylin that way."

Nyssa raised her eyebrows. "Are you sure?"

Aryis pursed her lips and nodded.

"I'm going with," Athen said.

The news didn't seem to please Aryis. "I don't need a babysitter."

"I won't be babysitting you, woman. Going up against Shay, you'll need muscle. My muscle. I know how...devious she can be. We can't underestimate her." Though Athen was gruff with Aryis, his tone was familiar to Nyssa, having grown up alongside him—his protective streak was undeniable.

"It's rather arrogant to assume either Elias, Fontaine, or I would underestimate—"

Nyssa held her hand up and interrupted, "Settle down, both of you. We're all going, okay?"

Reece shook her head. "No."

Nyssa scowled, tapping her finger against her leg. "What? Of course we are."

"I know your first instinct is to jump into action, but you're under house arrest. You won't get two steps out the front door of the Keep without your Justiciar escort raising the alarm."

"Then we take the tunnels under the Keep."

Reece inhaled a long, loud breath. There was a note of restrained frustration to her whole countenance. "There are Lion's Guards and Justiciars guarding all the tunnels now. There's no sneaking anywhere, not for two gods who have been told to stay put."

"Stay put?" Nyssa dug her nails into the arms of her chair and sat forward. "Ocean's Keep was just attacked by a hijacked warship and one of this city's own factions. I think Safin has bigger issues than keeping an eye on me and Quinn."

"That's the thing, Nyssa. This Keep was attacked. Safin was in danger...and my family was targeted." Reece paused, her jaw tensing. "We need you here."

Digging herself in for an argument, Nyssa shook her head. "No, Shay has Suvi and can lead us to—"

"*I* need you here," Reece said. Her eyes didn't leave Nyssa, but they wavered. The woman had almost died that morning. Lilliana had been targeted as well.

Athen was quick to Nyssa's side, crouching. "I need you here too. We can't be certain that the danger has passed. And Safin is still vulnerable. Protect him. Protect my mother and sister. Please."

There were very few things Nyssa could ever deny Athen—he had looked out for her so often when they were kids, and they had vowed to always be there for each other. As much as she hated to stay put, she couldn't deny his or Reece's plea. "Okay. Quinn and I will stay here and keep an eye out. We'll be the...good little gods that don't rock the boat."

Athen tapped his finger on Nyssa's wrist. "I don't think you can exist without rocking the boat just a *wee* bit, eh?"

Nyssa hummed out a resigned sigh. He knew her far too well.

"Now that this is sorted, go pack some clothes. I'll have transportation to the docks in two hours. Elias needed extra time to get the Whisper ready to sail." Reece eyed Nyssa. "With Athen gone, Brick could use some help training the Lion's Guard. Can I count on you?"

"Trying to keep me busy so I keep the boat-rocking to a light sway?"

"Yes. But there's no one more qualified to fill his rather large shoes."

"Flattery. Not necessary, but appreciated." She glanced at Quinn, who gave her a nod. "Fine, you have one Unworthy god at your service."

"You have two," Quinn added.

A visible wave of relief washed over Reece. "Thank you both."

Before they all dispersed, Athen pulled Nyssa aside. "Come with me. I have something to show you."

"That sounds ominous," she replied.

"It's not. Just...long overdue."

She turned to Quinn. "I'll see you back in our room." Then, looking up at Athen, she said, "Lead the way."

Nyssa walked with Athen through the Keep. He was in a somber mood, a rarity for her best friend. "I know you probably don't want to be stuck on a boat again with Aryis," she said, "but we have to get Suvi back."

"I'll be fine."

Nyssa nudged him. "Talk to me."

"I'm not sure you want to hear about how I feel right now."

"I know you love her, I've never been mad about that or had illusions that your heart would suddenly grow cold."

Athen reached up and smoothed down his beard. He claimed it helped him think. "What am I doing, Nyssa? Why am I in love with someone who almost killed you?" He avoided looking at her. "Gods, it aches just to be in the same room as her."

Nyssa clucked her tongue. "Remember when you first came to the Emerald Order and you joined me for every meal in the dining hall? I didn't invite you, but you insisted on eating with me. Rather rude, Fennick."

"You refused to talk to me."

"Yup." Nyssa let out a short laugh, enjoying the memory. "And you would talk anyway while I sat mute as a rock. Telling me about your day, what you had learned, what you thought about what you had learned, just a never-ending stream of chatter."

Athen finally looked over at her, and she met him with a smile.

"And then six months in of me listening to you prattle on and trying my best to ignore you, you said something idiotic that I simply couldn't let pass. Do you remember what that was?" she asked, looking up at him. "You should. That was the day you got me to crack."

"A triumphant day," he replied with a grin. "I made a simple, yet correct, assertion that the pear tarts from the kitchen were better than the lemon tarts. And you yelled at me."

"As I said, idiotic."

Athen laughed. "I was just happy you finally talked to me."

Nyssa reached out and grabbed his hand. "You spent six months chipping away at me, insisting on being my friend. We were ten years old and you didn't waver. Six fucking months."

"I had nowhere else to be," he said, shrugging.

"You are the man that sticks it out. Immovable. And you call me stubborn?" Nyssa smiled at him. "You don't have a love that's blown away by a harsh wind. Your love is this massive craggy rock that splinters everything that thrashes against it."

He cocked his head at her and raised an eyebrow. "Your compliments need work."

"You sat with me for six months until I let you in. That's who you are, big boy. So don't lament your stalwart heart. That heart saved my life a couple times."

Athen sighed. "My heart is kinda weighed down by a lot of resentment for Aryis."

"Oh, I know that feeling. But you're not one to dwell in negative emotions."

"I'm just so...tired of feeling like this."

"I'm not saying resolving any of your feelings about her will be quick or easy. But give yourself a chance to work through it, okay?" Nyssa asked, pinning him down with her gaze.

"Okay."

"Good."

A heavy sigh, one she had heard many times growing up, left him deflated. "I don't trust her...not yet."

Nyssa glanced at him. "And that's fine. That's where you're at with her right now, and I think that'll change."

"Do you trust her?"

"I...I think I do? And that doesn't make things easier between Quinn and me. It's a big sore spot."

Athen grunted.

He led her back to the family wing of the Keep, coming to a stop at a narrow door in a dark alcove. Behind it lay a small, quiet courtyard rimmed with trees. Nyssa breathed deep. The scent of rare winter cherry blossoms filled the air, sweet and fragrant.

"I didn't know this was here," she said. "This is beautiful."

"It's only for family."

Nyssa looked up at Athen. He grew quiet.

"Athen, I don't understand. What are we doing here?"

Athen took Nyssa's hand and led her to a corner of the courtyard. A square block of shiny black onyx stood knee-high, winter lilies surrounding its base. It was clear of snow, though the whole courtyard was covered in a blanket of white.

Nyssa's breath caught in her chest.

Engraved on the black stone read:

WHEREIN
ERON GREYE
LIES IN QUIET REPOSE
STEADFAST WARRIOR
HONORED FRIEND
DEVOTED FATHER

On top of the gravestone lay a small round object. A wolf's head pin—the Emerald Order guild sigil.

"Is that...?" she murmured, pointing to the insignia.

"Yes, it's your guild pin. Medias gave it to Reece." Athen put his arm around her. "Reece planted winter lilies around his headstone. She visits often to ensure they're tended to. Sometimes Medias accompanies her, strangely enough. I think Reece looks after Eron to honor you."

Nyssa swallowed back the lump forming in her throat. "That fucking woman...we are lucky to have her in our lives." She wiped away an errant tear.

"I...I sometimes talk to him, to keep him apprised of what's going on in our lives. It was a comfort coming here while you were away."

"He'd be proud of you, Athen."

Athen sniffed, and Nyssa looked up at him. His lone eye was shiny. "I wanted you to have some time with him." He took her hand and pressed a key into it. "You can visit whenever you want. And thank you. I know staying here while we're chasing after Suvi isn't ideal for you, but I need to know my family has you watching out for them."

"Of course, Athen. I would never let anything happen to them. *Any* of them."

He seemed to understand the part she left unsaid—she would protect Lilliana too. He gave her shoulders one last squeeze and left the courtyard.

She glanced down at the key in her hand before slipping it into the leather cuff she wore on her left wrist. The key sat beside the flat river rock that Quinn had gifted her for Winter's Fire. Her cuff had come to now hold two very precious items.

A light breeze stirred the leaves of the winter cherry blossoms next to Eron's grave. Nyssa clutched at her thighs, seeking to wipe away some of the sweat on her palms. A reticence moved through her. She had never gotten a chance to say a proper goodbye, and it struck her that this moment *was* that farewell.

And she wasn't remotely prepared.

She knelt before Eron's gravestone, braced her hands on the ground in front of her, and bowed, touching her forehead to the cold stone at the foot of his grave. Closing her eyes, she reflexively recited the Emerald Order oath, words that no longer bound her to anything but remained a comfort, nonetheless. *"To my brothers and sisters, my bond. To my guild, my fidelity. To my Empire, my blood. Stand fast. Face the darkness. Fall without fear."*

Sitting up, Nyssa exhaled and centered herself, resting her hands on her thighs. She touched her chin, its black mark a stain on Eron's legacy. No matter his accomplishments, his bravery in the Mire War, or his service to the Empire, he was likely only remembered as the First Master who took in a magickless infant and raised her as an adept. And that adept turned out to be...whatever label they used to punish Nyssa. Unworthy? Traitor? A dangerous Cursed God who needed to be put down before she wreaked havoc?

She turned her thoughts away from the dishonor that the Empire had placed upon her, slipping her hand inside her jacket. She pulled out a small leather notebook from an interior pocket, unwinding the cord wrapped around it. Inside, tucked between the pages of an unfinished poem she had been struggling with for months, was a chromoimage of her and Eron, taken the night he elevated her to the title of Ashcloak.

A bittersweet memory. She had worked so hard to become an Ashcloak, but it came on the back of returning Quinn to the Empire. What should have been a victory had felt hollow, her heart aching that she had chosen duty over what she felt was right.

Nyssa stared down at the picture. Eron smiled up at her, pride beaming on his face. Her fingers gently lit across the surface of the chromoimage. The simulachrome device had captured him perfectly: the faded tattoos at his temples blending into the short gray hair on the top of his head, his bright and attentive hazel eyes, the way he and Nyssa had an arm around each other. The perfect picture of their little two-person family.

Gods, how her heart ached at his absence.

"It has been a while since we've spoken, Eron. I miss you, old man. I could use some of your wisdom right about now." She dropped her head and chuckled. "Seems I can't make anyone happy. I was hated when I didn't have magick. And now I'm hated because I do. Fuck me, right?"

She leaned forward to touch the gravestone. It was warm underneath her fingertips, likely due to an enchantment. Explained the lack of snow surrounding it.

She eyed her guild pin, shaking her head. It had once been the only thing she ever wanted, to attain the title of Ashcloak. To prove her worth. To *matter*.

"I have so much to tell you."

Nyssa sat back and told Eron the events of her life after his death. Her struggles, discoveries, and triumphs. How she found friends worth their weight in gold and a home with a crew of pirates.

And a deep, unexpected love.

"You would like Quinn. I'm a pain in her ass, but she seems okay with that. She's patient with me, like you were. And quietly kind in ways that keep me surprised. Fierce as fuck too. Unbelievably fierce." She laughed, feeling lighter. "And she loves me. That's the crazy part. Despite everything, she loves me."

THE WAVE PIERCER

S uvi roused at the *thunk* of a door opening. She had drifted in and out of sleep, unable to tell the time of day with the blindfold covering her eyes. Her shoulders ached from her arms being wrenched behind her and tied to the creaky chair underneath her. Wherever she was being kept smelled of old apples and dust. She surmised she was on a ship rather quickly, thanks to the incessant rocking and her unhappy stomach. The Rells had never been much of a seafaring family.

Footsteps closed in on her and a sudden pressure on her thighs made her flinch. The blindfold was lifted off her head, and she slowly opened her eyes to find a woman straddling her, the stranger's forearms draped over Suvi's shoulders.

"Wakey-wakey," the woman said with a smirk. She was far too close for Suvi's liking. Back in Thu'Dain, no one would dare touch her without fear of losing a finger.

"Kindly remove yourself from my lap," Suvi said.

A laugh rumbled out of the stranger. "Every queen needs a throne. And you just happen to be mine right now."

Suvi's lip curled up. "Who the fuck are you?"

The woman cocked her head. "Shaylin Vance."

"You say that as if it is relevant to me."

Vance leaned back and ran her hands through her dark-purple hair while keeping her violet eyes locked on Suvi.

Was she...*flirting*?

Suvi sighed. Women like this bitch were so damn tiresome. "If you're trying to seduce me, not interested."

Shaylin leaned forward and licked her lips. "You can call me Shay, Princess."

Princess. It was a term of derision her brother, Matthys, had used on her once. And only once. She'd put him in the dirt as a warning to never call her that again. There were no princes or princesses in the Rell family, just kings and queens.

Or at least there used to be.

"Could you do me a favor and untie me...Shay?"

The woman stared at Suvi.

Upon closer inspection, the pirate's tanned skin was riddled with scars of all shapes and sizes, a map of injuries. Even with the bad purple hair dye she was striking, but something about her was...off. The way her dark-violet eyes studied Suvi set her teeth on edge.

"I'll untie you, but you'll have to behave. Any tinkering with this and you'll be unhappy with the results," Shay said, tapping a finger on the void collar around Suvi's neck.

Suvi glanced around, searching for an escape route. They were in a small room, dim and mildewy, crates of apples stacked in the corner. A bed was shoved up against the wall, no bigger than the one in her cell in Ocean's Keep. At least there she had secured herself wine and paints. They were civilized jailers; a far more preferable situation than being in some moldy bucket on the churning sea.

"Where are you taking me? Are you going to ransom me off?"

"Oh, princess, I'm not holding you for ransom. Who the fuck would pay? I think your reign in Thu'Dain is at an end. They've already moved on, electing a governing body from what I've heard." Shaylin gave her an exaggerated frown to drive the bitter point home. "Are you sad? You look sad."

The truth stung coming from a stranger's mouth. Suvi was truly alone in the world, her family's legacy ending with her, thanks to Nyssa Blacksea and her idiot friends.

Shay went on, "I was contracted to transport you out of Ocean's Rest. Even had a pleasant little reunion with my ex. She was delighted to see me."

"Paid by whom?"

"Arch Fuck Anelos. Promised me a nice new ship."

Suvi brightened. The day was looking up. "Ceril Anelos is behind this?"

"Yep."

Judging by Blacksea's desire to kill the man and the bits and pieces of what she had gleaned since being abducted, he had proved to be a dangerous and resourceful man. Just the person Suvi needed. She could do with a new ally. Especially one who wanted to see Blacksea suffer.

"I look forward to meeting him," Suvi said. "We have a common enemy."

Shay shrugged and stood up, taking a step back. "We'll know where to rendezvous with him soon. Until then, sit tight, princess."

"Wait, I thought you were going to untie me?"

Shay bent over, her face inches from Suvi's. "That's cute."

Then she whirled around and pushed the door open, leaving Suvi behind to fume.

THE WHISPER

I've never been pirating before, Aryis Devitt. I must say, this is rather exciting.

"Hush," she admonished, keeping her voice down. Though she had to admit she was also excited as she watched the Whisper approach the Wave Piercer. But enough fear ran through her to make her hands tremble a bit.

The crew were all at the ready, weapons on their hips, waiting to get close enough to the other ship to ensnare it and board her.

Elias had assured Aryis and Athen that he had perfected capturing ships, his crew an efficient machine. They had the benefit of sailing aboard the Whisper, a ship unlike most others. Its invisibility veil alone made it more valuable than a decade's worth of plunder. The ship's other enchantments, like water purification, a small engine, and on-ship plumbing, just added a touch of luxury, one that Elias was rather proud of. He was a man of high standards.

I hope you do not die today. The sadness you feel whenever you stare at Athen Fennick is interesting. I find it brings me closer to that elusive memory. Perhaps sadness is the key? Please, remain as sad as possible, if you will.

Heat rose to Aryis's cheeks, and she glanced up at Athen standing tall next to her. He didn't seem nervous at all.

Aryis sighed and slipped Suvi's dagger into her belt. The weapon helped her find the pirate ship carrying their quarry. And when she did her job tracking Suvi, Elias and the crew deferred to her. They still gave her the cold shoulder over her betrayal and the lives they'd lost due to it, but it was something. And she would take it.

The Whisper silently closed in on the Wave Piercer, Elias using hand signals to communicate to his crew. The Piercer shimmered in the distance, the sun reflecting off the dark-blue waves of the Black Sea. Fontaine appeared next to Aryis, her wardrobe quite different than her usual choices. Gone were her simple flowing dresses. Now she wore leather and wool, a dagger at her hip, looking far more like a warrior than the Whisper's free spirit of a quartermaster.

Fontaine scowled at the Piercer as they drew closer, narrowing her eyes. The deck of the other ship was deserted.

"Where's the crew?" Aryis whispered.

Good question.

Aryis glanced up at Athen. He motioned with his hand for her to stay calm. Down on the rail, Elias signaled his crew to be at the ready. Yuha and three other crewmen hefted their large metal hooks, ready to shoot them at the Piercer to ensnare the ship, wrench it to the Whisper, and board.

Elias waited, his hand steady, as they got closer to the Piercer. Max stood at the helm, using their small engine to close the distance. They had one chance at this, the engine good for a burst of speed before it ran out of power and had to recharge for a day using the waves slipping beneath the boat.

Aryis gripped the rail, waiting, her eyes trained on Elias. The second his arm slammed down, Yuha and the others shot their grappling hooks at the Wave Piercer, each one finding purchase on the ship's rail. They began cranking the hooks' winches, pulling the two ships closer and ensuring the Piercer couldn't run.

Gangplanks were slid across and secured. Elias stopped them from crossing, his eyes scanning the other ship. Aryis's shoulders tightened.

Aryis, something isn't right.

"Where is the crew?" Elias stepped forward. "Something feels off."

The blue man is right.

Tajal had proved to have exceptionally bad timing, but in this, she shared his trepidation.

Elias held his hand up and everyone froze. Aryis stilled, the only sound was that of the ships—the groan of wooden vessels as they rocked in the sea, the clank of metal against wood, and the whip of the sails in the light wind.

She closed her eyes, calming. Focusing. A faint ticking pulsed in the air, becoming louder as they waited.

Tick.

Tick.

Tick.

It was slow and low at first, but the ticking sped up, growing louder.

Tick. Tick. Tick.

Tick-tick-tick—

Ticktickticktick—

Aryis, something's off about this. You can feel it.

"Shush."

Aryis, please, be caref—

A light flashed on the deck of the Wave Piercer, and something ripped through Aryis's coat. Searing pain bit into her side before Athen pushed her to the deck.

Aryis! Have you died?

Fontaine yelled and tumult followed, a battle cry ringing out in the air.

But not from the Whisper's crew.

Aryis turned and peered over the Whisper's handrail, in the direction of the flashes. Dark figures shimmered into view, men and women appearing on the deck. Aryis cursed under her breath.

The crew of the Piercer had been hidden by a spell.

A man stood at a round metal contraption, winding a crank. All the air left Aryis's lungs when she recognized the weapon—a rotary gun. Rare. Expensive. And deadly.

Athen moved quickly, pulling Elias, Fontaine, and Yuha close. "Get behind me!" he ordered, towering over Aryis. He formed a human wall, his body jerking as metal pellets struck him. How much punishment could he take before he was wounded...or worse?

The air around Aryis shimmered, little explosions of light making her flinch. Fontaine wove a ward to protect the ship and its occupants. Aryis wavered on her feet. Another pellet hit her in the shoulder. It stung but didn't get through her clothes. The ward was slowing the pellets down, but it began to spark and groan under the assault, its color and vibrancy fading fast.

"Attack!" a woman shouted.

"Stand your ground!" Elias yelled at his crew, throwing a fireball at the purple-haired woman leading the pirates' charge.

It's her! Shaylin Vance, has to be. She's shorter than I expected.

Tajal sounded far too excited as Aryis's stomach dropped. Elias's fireball dissipated in the air before it even flew five feet, blown apart by countermagick.

So, the other pirates had powerful magick too.

Shaylin roared and led her pirates over the gangplank strung across the ships, spilling onto the deck of the Whisper. Aryis hunkered down, hiding under the handrail.

Steel clashed against steel, and she flinched, the sounds of violence making her teeth vibrate. Flashes of magick lit up all around her. Aryis was not built for battle...but she wasn't going to give up on getting Suvi back from Shay. She shimmied along the side of the ship, reaching a gangplank. No one had seemed to notice her, and if they did, likely didn't consider her a threat. Athen, Elias, and the crew fought off the pirates, blades and magick singing.

"Be safe, Athen," Aryis whispered. She closed her eyes for a moment, working up her courage, before standing and vaulting up onto a gangplank. It wavered beneath her, forcing her muscles to tense.

What do you think you're doing? Tajal shouted, rattling her brain.

"We have to get Suvi," Aryis replied, fighting to find her balance.

We? You didn't even want me in your head and now we're a we?

"Yeah, you're in the thick of it now, Tajal. Enjoy, asshole," she hissed.

You're going to get us killed.

Aryis glanced back. No one made a move to stop her. The battle on the Whisper's deck raged. A perfect distraction to slip aboard the Piercer and find Suvi.

She hurried across the gangplank, dropping down onto the deck of the Piercer. A set of stairs caught her eye, and she darted over to them, nearly sliding down them ass-first. Barely catching herself on the handrail, her nerves a jumble, she regained her balance and took the stairs two at a time to the bottom.

You're going to get yourself killed and you will be dead, dead, dead and won't remember how helpful I'm being in this moment as I tell you to get your uncoordinated, spindly body off this ship.

Aryis ran down the dim hallway, trying every door. She lucked out at the fourth one.

Suvi sat inside, tied up. "Aryis Devitt? This is certainly a surprise."

Aryis cut Suvi free of the ropes binding her to her chair, but left her hands tied up behind her. Aryis didn't want to end up with a snapped neck. "I don't have time for your shit, Suvi, get moving."

"Are you rescuing me?" Amusement wove through her voice.

"Shut up." Aryis shoved her through the door and down the hall.

Suvi glanced back, eyeing the weapon in her hand. "Is that my dagger?"

Aryis hadn't realized she had used Suvi's dagger instead of Talon to free the woman. "How do you think we found you?"

"What makes you think I wanted to be found?"

"What makes you think I give a damn?" Aryis shoved Suvi again, hard. "Get moving or I'll slit your throat where you stand." It was an idle threat, but Aryis backed it up with a scowl and another hard shove.

You've got a bit of darkness in you, Aryis Devitt. I like it.

"Shut the fuck up, Tajal," she whispered.

A hiss of air next to her ear made Aryis flinch. A bolt struck the stairs ahead of her, the wood cracking and splintering. Her brains would have been splattered all over the interior of the Wave Piercer if it had been 2 inches closer.

"Go!" she ordered, driving Suvi forward. Behind her, a man reloaded his small crossbow at the opposite end of the hall.

This is less than ideal. You should have asked my opinion on this plan—

"Fuck off!" she yelled, forcing Suvi up the stairs.

Suvi spilled onto the deck. Aryis had a few more steps to ascend and then she would drag Suvi back to the Whisper by her hair if she had to.

A shadow fell over Aryis, and she barely glimpsed the boot before it collided with her head. She collapsed against the stairs, clinging to them. If she let go, she'd tumble to the bottom. Then she'd be dead, of that she was certain.

She set her feet on a step to steady herself and looked up.

Shaylin Vance stared down at her.

This isn't good, Aryis.

Vance grabbed Aryis and hauled her up the stairs and onto the deck, launching a fist across her face. Aryis collapsed, stars exploding in her view.

Oh, this is not how I wanted my brief time in a mortal to go. You are highly disappointing at fisticuffs.

Her left hand tingled and spasmed around Suvi's dagger.

Pokey, pokey!

Aryis coughed, tasting copper. Her fingers jumped and twitched.

Get her, Aryis! Poke her with the pointy bit!

"Shu…" Words formed in her head but didn't fully travel to her mouth.

Aryis, please! You're going to die here. I think that would make me feel bad.

A shadow moved over her again, and Aryis struck haphazardly, dragging her dagger across the shin of Vance. The pirate cried out and danced back, limping.

Good job!

"You little cunt," Vance spat. "I'm going to enjoy killing you."

"She's a Queen-in-Waiting," Suvi said. "Better alive than dead to you, pirate."

Aryis tried to blink the stars out of her eyes and focus on their voices. *Why is Suvi…*

"You queens stick together, eh, Suvi? I don't need an extra mouth to feed. Maybe I'll tie her to the mast and let the cold slowly take her."

Aryis lifted her eyes up to Shaylin. The woman put her fingers to her mouth and let out a shrill whistle before smiling back down at Aryis. Her eyes moved to the dagger Aryis still gripped in her hand.

"What is this, little Queen?"

Suvi stepped forward. "That's my dagger. That's how you found us, isn't that right, Aryis?"

"Oh?" Vance bent over and took the weapon. "I think it's best if we stop that from ever happening again."

"What, no—"

Cocking her arm back, Shaylin tossed the dagger, hurling it off the ship.

Suvi grabbed her. "No! What did you do? That's my family's dagger!"

Vance shoved Suvi back and shrugged. "Gone forever. Given to Narileh of the Deep, princess."

"You fucking bitch, that's the only thing I have of my father. I will—"

The pirate silenced Suvi with a punch. She crumpled to the deck.

Aryis...get up.

"What d'you care?" Aryis slurred. "You're still in your Realm...the lil speck of you in me will just...*poof*..."

I don't want to poof. *And I certainly don't want to see you freeze your stupid skin off. This Shaylin sounds serious about that...*

In the periphery of Aryis's awareness, a cry went up...it sounded far away. The Whisper?

Her heart sank.

Was the Whisper in danger? She shook her head, the world coming into better focus. Sound collapsed down on her, drawing close, getting louder. Clearer. She blinked hard.

Get up.

The thunder of footsteps and rattle of loose deck planks got Aryis to roll on her side.

Stand. And run.

"Prepare the harpoon! I want that ship sunk," Vance yelled, a frightening edge of laughter in her voice. She was *enjoying* this. "No more Ghost of the Sea. He'll drown with his chicken."

How rude. Fontaine is not a chicken!

"Get the little Queen up. We're going to slit her throat while Elias watches."

Gasping, Aryis tried to fight off the hands that descended on her, but she wasn't strong enough against two large men, the stink of their sweat pungent in her nose. They yanked her to her feet, her shoulders burning in their sockets as they dragged her toward the side of the ship facing the Whisper.

The air between the ships shimmered, groaning and straining when Elias's fireballs hit it and dissipated impotently. Someone on Shaylin's crew had raised a ward to protect their retreat.

On the Whisper, a fire raged on deck, and the crew scrambled about, dealing with it.

If Elias's crew didn't contain the fire, it could destroy the whole ship and condemn them to a cold death on the Black Sea. Athen would go down with the ship...

The pirates aboard the Piercer kicked the gangplanks off the rails, and Aryis let out a soft sob.

What do we do? Aryis, they're going to kill you!

Tajal's tone had changed. For the first time, something akin to humanity broke through his gruff, judgmental disposition. He sounded worried.

Aryis tried to ignore the sick irony of dying with an Ancient God as her only solace.

She searched for Athen. He stood next to Elias and Fontaine as the two of them shouted to the crew and tried to weaken the ward that kept their attacks from reaching the Piercer.

Shaylin approached Aryis, pulling a dagger from the sheath she wore at her thigh. "I don't get to kill queens often, but when I do, it's always fun." She turned and waved at Elias and the others.

The bitch *waved*.

With a roar of anger, Aryis drove her fist down into the crotch of the man on her right. He yelped and let her go, dancing away in pain. She ripped away from the other man and stumbled toward the edge of the ship, hiking a leg up onto the metal handrail, trying to shimmy her foot over. She wasn't going to die on this damn pirate ship, her blood seeping out of a slit throat.

You are full of bad ideas today. You'll freeze and drown. Or drown and freeze, I can't predict which horrible thing will happen first and—

"Will you shut the FUCK up?" she screamed.

She had one leg almost hitched over the rail. She just had to throw her weight—

"Where do you think you're going?"

Aryis was jerked backward and tumbled down to the deck, the force of the fall driving all the air out of her lungs.

She gulped for breath as she blinked up at the shiny blue sky.

"After that little stunt, I'm going to make this hurt," Shaylin hissed, looming over her. "I think I'll slice you open and let you bleed out like a gutted fish."

A guttural roar filled the air, and the deck shuddered from a heavy impact. Aryis rolled her head toward the sound, and her heart thundered in her chest when she saw the cause.

Athen.

He swung his arms, crushing all pirates within his grasp. He looked utterly possessed, his face contorted by a shroud of fury.

"Kill him!" Shaylin ordered. The dagger in her hand began to glow a radiant red. While Athen was resistant to injury, an enchanted dagger was a threat.

Aryis stood and stalked after Shaylin, wobbly on her feet.

Escape is in the opposite direction, my dear.

She pulled Talon from its sheath and threw an arm around Shaylin's throat, driving her dagger into the pirate's hip.

Shaylin bucked Aryis off and turned around, shock and amusement on her lips. "Did you just poke me with your stick, girl?" She lunged forward, her glowing red dagger aimed at Aryis's midsection. Aryis reeled back, the cut on her side burning. "Stand still, you little cunt."

Behind Shaylin, Athen loomed large, tossing pirates aside as he rushed toward Shaylin and Aryis.

Tick-tick-tick.

Aryis whirled around to the rotary gun, a ruddy man starting to spin its chamber.

"Athen! Look out!"

He was on her in a second, wrapping a massive arm around her waist and bolting toward the side of the ship. A moment later, they were airborne, hurling over the churning water of the Black Sea between the two vessels. Something hot and angry tore through her leg. She howled in agony, curling into Athen's arms.

Aryis, what's wrong?

They crashed down on the Whisper, Athen encasing her, protecting her from the brunt of the fall.

Aryis?

"Hit the deck!" Elias shouted.

Pellets *pinged* off of metal and *thumped* into wood, ripping across the deck.

Athen uncoiled from around Aryis, and his deep voice rumbled in her ear. "Are you okay?"

Such a dumb question, of course we're not okay! I can't believe you love this big idiot.

"I do," she mumbled.

Athen cut through the haze of pain. "Aryis?"

"My...my leg."

She glanced down. Blood leaked from her left knee. And the pain...it was unbearable. She laid her head back and tried to breathe, her body starting to shake.

"Buck! We need Buck now!" Athen shouted, fear in his wide eyes.

Ignore it. She had to ignore it.

Charred bits of cloth floated to the deck, the edges of the fabric glowing bright red. Above her, the sails held, the very bottom of the last one tattered but no longer on fire.

Yuha appeared over her, a smear of blood on her face. "I'll take Aryis below to Buck. Get her fixed up, yeah?"

Aryis caught Athen's arm. "I'm so sorry," she whispered through clenched teeth. Sorry for leaving him after her heart was torn out at Wayland. For giving Nyssa and Quinn over to Suvi.

For so much...

HOOKED!

Athen pushed Aryis's mussed-up hair out of her face, her apology hanging between them. "Stay alive," he ordered. His gut twisted up for her, but he shoved his worry aside. They would all die if they didn't escape.

He scrambled over to the side of the Whisper that faced the Piercer. The two ships had drifted apart, the pellets from Shay's rotary gun hitting water and the wood on the port side instead of ripping through the deck. Elias sat with his back against the rail, popping his head up to gauge their distance from the other ship. Fontaine sat next to him, her fingers furiously weaving a spell. She had ripped a hole in her ward to hurl Athen over to the Piercer before pulling him back again with her magick after he rescued Aryis. It was an insane idea, but they were desperate.

Athen fell in next to them. "What's the plan?"

"We're not equipped to fight like this. We're pirates, not a fucking warship, and they have a fucking rotary gun," Elias responded, squinting and wiping blood out of his eyes. "I'm going to get us out of here. We have to avoid them while our invisibility veil takes hold."

Those few minutes could spell disaster if they couldn't get away from the Piercer.

"I'll do my best to protect our stern," Fontaine said, worry etched on her face. "Who knows what other magick Vance has up her sleeve."

"I'm coming with you," Athen said.

Elias grabbed Fontaine's arm and pulled her close. "You be fucking careful, woman."

"Oh, Elias, you know I will. You steer us true." She smiled at him, but it didn't remove the worry from his face.

"Alright, let's go!" Elias pushed himself up and ran toward the quarterdeck, where Max stood steering the Whisper.

Athen followed Fontaine, the two of them crouching as they weaved to the back of the ship.

The Wave Piercer sat off the rear of the ship. Pops of light filled the sky and grew closer. Fontaine's hands went to work, weaving a spell. A shimmering golden lattice began to form at the back of the Whisper.

Fireballs exploded all around the ship, each one bursting with a blinding pop of light. Fontaine's ward sparked and groaned as it shielded them from the attacks. How long could it hold? Her magick was powerful, but her body bowed from strain.

Shaylin's crew continued their barrage, relentless. The ward quivered, a sign it was close to breach. Fontaine stood fast, reweaving the ward spell to shore it up.

A flash of light caught Athen's eye, racing toward the Whisper, and a high-pitched whistle filled the air. Athen's blood ran cold. "Fontaine—"

Her eyes went wide. "Brace for impact!"

A giant, needle-like spear hurled toward them. Athen grabbed Fontaine and pushed her down onto the deck and fell forward, shielding her body.

The spear slammed into the Whisper. The ship jerked and shuddered from the impact, and large splinters of wood rained down on them. Athen uncovered his head. A massive harpoon was embedded in the deck.

"We're snared!" he yelled.

"They want to sink us," Fontaine said, rolling out from under him and popping to her feet. "We have to get free."

The tip of the harpoon was sunk deep into the ship, the wood of the stern around it shattered. A thick chain trailed off the shaft of the spear, suspended midair like a dragonfly.

"The chain is floating," he said.

"Not for long, likely. Pirate trick—it's an enchantment that stops the chain from slowing the harpoon down before it reaches its target." Fontaine grabbed his arm. "Once it drops, the chain's weight and momentum will tip us, drag us down."

"That's not happening." Athen ran to the harpoon, jumped to grab the chain, and pulled it down. It was both heavy and light, its floating enchantment creating a strange, conflicting sensation. Athen gritted his teeth and tried to pry two links apart. Sweat popped up on his brow, his fingers burning as he struggled to break the chain.

"It's too strong!" He would just have to get rid of the fucking harpoon itself. "Move back!"

Athen cracked his neck and rolled his shoulders. He leaned his chest against the harpoon, and wrapped his arms around it, bracing with his legs. Exhaling, he relaxed for a moment before putting every last reserve of strength into lifting the harpoon out of the hole in the deck. Wood creaked and strained underneath him, but the harpoon barely moved. It was heavy and stuck in the ship, its massive barb making it impossible to pull out.

Almost impossible. Athen wasn't about to give up. They were dead if he did.

Exhaling a second time, he closed his eyes and focused. First Master Greye had taught him how to meditate—how to concentrate his will to a fine point—and he used that lesson now.

He pulled again, his shoulders and thighs burning as he dug his fingers into the smooth, round metal. The deck beneath him groaned, and an alarming *crack* made him pause.

If the deck collapsed, they were doomed.

The chain shivered while it hung in the air, as if ready to give out under the strain of its own weight.

"Hurry, Athen," Fontaine said. "The chain is beginning to fall."

Athen steeled himself for one last try. *Come on. Come on!*

A final burst of energy surged through him, and the harpoon moved. Ignoring the protest of the groaning wood, he hoisted the damn thing out of the deck, nearly tumbling over when its large barb was freed.

The harpoon was at least ten feet in length, and Athen wavered under its weight, sucking in air and blowing it out, his muscles trembling with the strain. He steeled himself, gathered up his strength, and heaved the harpoon over his shoulder and off the back of the Whisper.

Free of the weight, he dropped to a knee.

The harpoon splashed in the sea behind them, a wave of water drenching Athen. He smiled and shook his head, fat droplets of water dripping off his beard.

The air around the Whisper shimmered and crackled, the invisibility veil taking hold. Not a moment too soon.

"You did it, Athen," Fontaine said, laughing. Her smile matched his own.

Athen turned and looked out over the stern toward the Piercer, the ship getting smaller as the Whisper escaped, and he breathed a huge sigh of relief.

Fontaine gently touched his shoulder. "Thank you. This ship is my home, first I've had for centuries where I wanted to stay past a week. My family is here."

"I would never let anything happen to you guys," he replied. "I like you all too much now."

Heavy, quick footsteps approached. Elias looked harried, his eyes going directly to Fontaine. "You're okay?" he asked, the low bass in his voice tinged with worry.

"Of course!" Fontaine said. "You needn't worry about me."

"Woman, I'll always fucking worry about you." He grabbed Fontaine and pulled her into an embrace.

"Okay, you can worry about me a little bit."

Elias stepped away from her, bracing her face for a moment before turning to glance down into the hole created by the harpoon. A hole that led directly into his stateroom. It was full of debris, his drafting table a mess. He sagged. "My beautiful ship. My beautiful stateroom."

Yuha and a few of the crew inched closer to inspect the damage.

"All fixable," Fontaine said, wrapping an arm around him.

Athen sighed, his whole body sagging from exhaustion. "How is Aryis?"

"Buck is tending to her," Yuha said. The look on her face churned his stomach. "I think you need to go to her."

Nodding, Athen steeled himself and headed below deck. He ducked into Aryis's stateroom. Buck sat next to Aryis's bed, a bloody mound of towels next to him. Ebe, an old hand and the ship's main navigator, looked up when Athen came in the room, her hands holding Aryis's injured leg down as Buck worked. An uncorked bottle of Basai rum sat next to the old man. Steadied his hands, he'd say.

While Buck worked on Aryis's knee, Athen knelt beside her, gently moving her sweat-soaked hair out of her face.

"How are you?" he asked.

Her brown eyes blinked at him. "Athen? You're safe?"

"Of course I am."

She shuddered out a breath and closed her eyes, tears rolling down her temples and into her hair. "I...I screwed up. I thought I could get Suvi back on my own."

He scowled. "Getting Suvi back, that was the mission. You tried your damn best."

"If anything, I screwed up," Elias said from the doorway, Fontaine beside him. "I thought I could take Vance on the open water. I underestimated her."

"Vance is a different animal, Elias," Fontaine replied. "Unpredictable."

"Indeed. But you distracted her, Aryis. She took her eye off of our ship to deal with you just long enough to gather our wits and retreat, otherwise I think we'd be in chains."

Aryis closed her eyes. Sweat coated her skin. Athen picked up a clean towel and gently wiped her face.

"Buck, how bad is it?" Fontaine asked.

Athen looked at Aryis's left knee. It was a bloody mess, the skin ripped open, white bone exposed. He had to look away, wishing he could bear Aryis's pain for her.

"Ah, coulda been—mmm—worse. I gotta get the pellet out and stitch her up. But without a proper healer, can't say how it's gonna mend. A healin' disk is only going to do so much." Buck took Aryis's hand. "You gotta be brave now, girl. Braver than when you took to Vance's ship to retake that—mmm—bitch of a queen." Buck smiled, his eyes squinting in his goggles.

"What can I do?" Athen asked.

"Just don't leave me," Aryis whispered, her eyes closed.

As if he ever could. "I won't. I promise." He grabbed her hand and gave it a squeeze. The squeeze he got in return was weak. His stomach twisted. "Can you give her something for the pain?"

Buck blinked, his eyes large. "Already have. Gotta go in for the—mmm—pellet now, Miss Aryis." He gave the bottle of rum to Athen. "Make her drink."

Nodding, Athen took the rum and held it to Aryis's lips. "C'mon, Little Bird, have a swig." Using one of Nyssa's nicknames for her seemed to brighten Aryis up a bit. Athen smiled. She took a drink and sighed back into her pillow, her face scrunching up. "Ah, can't be that bad if Buck drinks barrels of this a day and is still kicking."

"Mmm—truth," Buck said, his eyes big and exaggerated behind his goggles. "You gonna have to hold her—mmm—down."

Athen swallowed and laid an arm across Aryis's chest, his touch light until he needed to press down to keep her from moving.

"Here." Buck handed him a worn piece of leather that Athen realized had bite marks in it.

"You ready, Aryis?" he asked.

She nodded weakly at him.

"Bite down on this."

Aryis did as told, and Athen smiled down at her. How brave she had been today, venturing into the bowels of an enemy ship with no other goal than to stop Ceril from getting Suvi. He wanted to tell her all of that but found himself lacking the courage to pull away from his own hurt.

Instead, he held her down and tried to keep a brave face while she moaned and shook from the pain, his heart breaking to see her so fragile.

At least Buck worked quickly, with Ebe at his side to help. By the time he was done removing the pellet, Aryis had passed out. Buck burned several healing disks to mend the muscles and skin around the injury, grumbling that he was doing his best. The small room had filled with crewmates, Yuha crouching next to Athen to steady him as he began to shake from the day's strain.

"Aryis was a damn fine pirate today," Fontaine announced to the small gathering.

Heads bobbed in agreement. Aryis had been through so much and suffered under the consequences of her own decisions, but he was proud of her. Trusting her after what she had done was hard, but loving her was the easiest thing in the world for him.

Aryis woke to the early morning sun streaming through a porthole. The events of the previous day slowly came back. The failed attempt to get Suvi back, Athen grabbing her off the Piercer, a bullet ripping through her...

She swallowed and tried to move her knee. It was stiff and sore, almost impossible to bend, but at least the pain was dull. A small mercy. Lethargy weighed upon her whole body, likely the effects from a painkiller Buck had given her.

You are alive.

"Yes, I am," she mumbled.

A soft snore made her turn her head. Athen was curled up on the room's other bunk, as best he could on the tiny bed.

He's been here all night. Snoring. He could have returned to his own room and let me be in peace.

A slow smile spread across Aryis's face. "Hush."

You are happy to see him here.

"Yes. It's something," she whispered.

Something? What is it, exactly?

Aryis sighed and closed her eyes, drifting back to sleep.

A VISITOR FROM THE SKIES

Nyssa sat atop a table in the Great Room, her feet stretched before her on a chair and her sword lying at her side. Quinn paced back and forth at the window, her eyes scanning the Justiciars who dotted the outskirts of the room. Medias hovered near a bookshelf.

"This is obnoxious," Nyssa groused to no one in particular.

"That is certainly…a word for it," Quinn replied.

"They're isolating us."

Nyssa, Quinn, and Medias had been called to the Great Room by Safin, but that had been hours ago, and Nyssa wanted to go to the docks to greet Aryis, Athen, and the Whisper. They were due back today, and according to their messages, things did not go well at sea.

The weeks the others were away had gone by without incident. Part of Nyssa lamented the wasted time—but she knew how shaken Reece and Athen were after the attack on their home. And she and Quinn were still under house arrest. Getting out of the Keep would have likely been impossible. There was always a Justiciar close by. Two were posted outside their rooms day and night.

They were now well past the two weeks that Nyssa and Quinn had promised to sit tight and wait. The grace period was over, but Nyssa had no idea what their next move should be. And Reece was sticking to her principles, not entertaining Nyssa's so-called *whining* about being stuck at the Keep under the Empire's thumb. The empath had dug in her heels. And Medias was equally immovable. An annoying duo they made.

"At least they fed us lunch," Nyssa grumbled.

"You get testy when hungry," Medias said. "Was merely self-defense on their part."

The doors to the Great Room opened, and Safin entered, escorted by Decia, Lyra, and four other Ashcloaks, including Ina. Nyssa tensed but didn't budge from her spot on the table.

"Thank you all for coming," Safin said, his eyes on Nyssa.

She scowled at him. "Do you care to tell us why you've kept us here for hours?" As they drew near, Nyssa gave him a closer inspection, her ire replaced by unease. "You look tired, kid. Are you okay?"

"I'm fine."

Nyssa couldn't help worrying about him, the circles under his eyes concerning. Lyra's cold stare bored into her. Nyssa shrugged. "Just get to why we're here, then."

Safin came to a halt in front of her. "We're waiting for the rest of your party to get here."

Sure enough, the doors opened again, and Athen entered, followed by Aryis and Reece. Aryis limped along, using a cane to walk.

"Aryis! Are you okay?" Nyssa hopped off the table, and the Ashcloaks surrounded Safin. The Justiciars rimming the room moved forward.

Decia held up her hand to stay them. She nodded at Nyssa.

Nyssa glared at Ina and rushed to Aryis and Athen. "What happened out there?"

Aryis shook her head, lowering her eyes. "Shay was ready for us. We barely made it out alive. I failed, Nyssa."

Without a word, Nyssa wrapped the young woman up in a hug. "You didn't fail, Little Hawk. But your leg..."

"She took a rotary gun bullet to knee," Athen said. "Buck removed it and used healing disks, but you know those aren't like a healer. We were just at the infirmary and the Master Healer did his best to fix as much as he could, but there's permanent damage."

Nyssa pulled away. "I'm so sorry. What can I do?"

"Walk a little slower from now on?" Aryis replied, offering a smile.

The lighthearted response made Nyssa laugh.

"Aryis Devitt, Athen Fennick, please come forward and account for your actions," Decia said. "You were not given leave to chase after Suvi Rell."

Reece stepped forward. "That's on me. I told them to go."

Decia turned her attention to Reece with a look that could freeze the sun. "I was not addressing you, Ae'Shen." She beckoned Aryis and Athen forward. "Come, give us your account of what transpired."

Athen and Aryis complied, unwinding the tale of what happened when they caught up with Vance's pirates. Nyssa clenched her fists as she listened. *I should have been there to help.* Worse yet was Aryis taking matters into her own hands. She could have been killed.

"You went after Suvi alone?" Nyssa asked. *What was she thinking?*

"Suvi was our priority. I didn't want her to get away," Aryis replied.

Nyssa put an arm around her and guided her to a chair, helping her sit. "What you did was stupid...and incredibly brave. You're lucky you're not dead."

"I have Athen to thank for that."

Nyssa didn't miss the slight grin on his face. Maybe he had taken her words to heart and decided to be patient with Aryis.

"How is the crew of the Whisper?"

"They're fine but the ship is in need of repairs," Athen said. "They'll be docked for a while and Elias is *not* happy."

Decia cleared her throat. "None of you are to do anything else in regard to Ceril Anelos, his family, or his associates. Blacksea and Emerrath were put under house arrest for a reason. Miss Devitt, you are now joining them."

Aryis's face scrunched up. "But—"

"And we censure House Fennick. Athen and Reece, do not test the Emperor's patience further."

Nyssa had heard enough. "This is bullshit!" She turned to Safin. "Come on, kid! We can help, you *know* we can. I get that Lyra and Decia are protecting you and your reputation, but your reputation will be shit if you don't get Anelos soon. And who knows what damage he'll do with Suvi at his side."

Safin frowned. "I've made my feelings about this known."

Scoffing, Nyssa shook her head. "I don't believe this. How can you—"

"Nyssa, enough." Reece's dark eyes and the insistence in her tone made Nyssa shut up. No small feat.

"I will be returning to Cardin in a few days, as will the Sun Council," Safin said.

"You're going back to Cardin? Is that a good idea?" Nyssa asked.

"Anelos has been on the run ever since he attacked us on your pirate ship. It's now clear to everyone that he was behind Kalla's death and that the Emperor had nothing to do with it," Decia replied.

Nyssa raised an eyebrow. "And that we had nothing to do with it, right?"

"Indeed. Your Imperial pardon indicates as much. And my Justiciars assure me the Sun Palace is safe. Any of that traitor's loyalists left in the capital have scurried into the shadows. It's time for the Emperor to begin his rule from the throne."

Back to Cardin? Maybe that would be a good thing. Nyssa and the others could leverage Lilliana's contacts to get a lead on Ceril, though, to date, there had been no rumors of any sort regarding him, according to Reece. And Reece, though she was straddling the line between the Empire and her loyalty to her friends, wouldn't keep anything from Nyssa.

"You are welcome to stay here in Ocean's Rest, but my requirements are the same. Do not interfere in Imperial matters," Safin added.

"When will we be off your leash?" Quinn asked, contempt dripping from her words.

"As the Emperor stated, you are to stay in Ocean's Rest for the foreseeable future," Decia said.

It was a warning—Nyssa knew they would be monitored and Decia would receive news of their comings and goings. She didn't like it at all. And by the look on Quinn's face, she hated being told to stay put.

Nyssa swallowed back her anger, her pride, her indignation, though resolved to figure out a way around their restrictions. "Very well."

Neither Safin, Lyra, nor Decia looked convinced, but it would have to be enough for them. Nyssa didn't have any more grace to give them. She was tapped out.

Safin extended his hand. "This is a temporary thing, Nyssa. I promise."

There was a sincerity to his gesture that Nyssa couldn't dismiss. She moved to shake his hand—

Glass shattered behind her and she jumped into action, her sword in her hand and magick at her fingertips. Justiciars and Ashcloaks surrounded Safin, ready to fight. Shards of glass fell from the hole at the top of the massive window facing the East Garden.

"Stay alert!" Nyssa ordered.

A voice assaulted her ears.

YOU ARE BECKONED.

Nyssa cried out, dropping to her knees, the voice driving a spike of pain through her skull. Quinn reeled back into a table.

DO NOT DALLY.

"Who is yelling?" Nyssa hissed, grabbing at her head.

Quinn shoved her hands against her ears. "Make it stop!"

"Nyssa, what's wrong?" Athen asked, hurrying to her side, his fists balled up.

YOU ARE DALLYING.

"What is that voice?" Quinn growled.

Safin and the others stared at them as if they were mad. A sharp, needle-like prick at her knee startled Nyssa. She leapt to her feet and glared at her attacker. A white and black seagull stood on the marble floor of the Great Room and blinked at her. It pecked at her foot.

Nyssa yelped and skipped back. "What the fuck?"

The seagull took flight and landed on the back of a tall leather chair.

ARE YOU SOFT IN THE HEAD OR DO YOU UNDERSTAND ME, CURSED GOD?

"What is happening?" Decia asked, her hand on Safin's arm.

Nyssa stared at the seagull, her head pounding. "*You're* talking to us? A fucking bird?"

DON'T BE A BIGOT.

"Could you please lower the volume of your goddamn voice?" Quinn implored, her knuckles bone-white as she gripped the edge of a table.

SORRY. I FORGET HOW FRAGILE YOU FLESHY IDIOTS ARE...IS THIS BETTER?

The voice was still loud, but bearable.

"Better," Nyssa said. "What do you want?"

YOU NEED TO COME WITH ME.

"Nyssa, what the hell is going on?" Reece asked, clutching at her chest, staring at the seagull. Medias, of course, looked nonplussed, but Nyssa knew she would spring into action in an instant if needed.

"Do you not hear the bird?" Nyssa scanned the faces in the room. All of them, save for Quinn, looked deeply confused. "Oh...wait, I think the voice is in our heads?"

YES, IDIOT.

Nyssa pursed her lips. "And he's exceptionally rude."

"Ah, that explains the waves of impatience and disdain I'm feeling. Rather unsettling coming from such a small creature," Reece said, shaking her head and shoulders like warding off a chill.

The seagull hopped across the back of the chair and squawked. *GET A MOVE ON, GODLINGS.*

Nyssa scowled. "What do you want?"

HAVE I NOT MADE MYSELF CLEAR, NYSSA BLACKSEA? YOU ARE EXCEPTIONALLY THICK IN THE HEAD.

Before Nyssa could answer, the door to the Great Room opened and Lilliana rushed in, Pol behind her, both wearing worried expressions. "Something's happening at the docks."

"What?" Decia asked.

"Something...extraordinary."

The seagull tapped his beak on the chair. *NOW WILL YOU COME WITH ME?*

A VISITOR FROM THE DEEP

The entirety of Ocean's Keep seemed to be hurrying to get down to the docks, the streets crowded and humming with excitement. Nyssa stayed on high alert—whatever was happening could be a trap set by Ceril, and Safin would need to be protected, since he had insisted on coming along.

Which was a whole pain in the ass in and of itself. The Areshi Emperor going anywhere, especially in public, required a great deal of security. The sight of city trams rattling along their tracks down the middle of the street, packed with Justiciars, Ashcloaks, and the Lion's Guard must have been quite the spectacle.

Nyssa wasn't prepared for what awaited them at the docks. Wave upon wave crashed into the ships, causing them to bob up and down in the water, straining against the ropes that bound them to their moorings. A dark, angry sky loomed above them, blue-tinged lightning licking at the bottom of the clouds. Lightning that reminded Nyssa of her own magick.

The air was charged with an electric buzz, exhilarating and frightening in equal measure. Nyssa sensed a...presence. She felt it in her chest, and by the looks of the people near the docks, they felt it too.

Something tremendously powerful waited off the city of Ocean's Rest.

The seagull flapped in the air and squawked at her. *COME.*

She followed the seagull, walking down a long, empty dock, flanked by Quinn and trailed by Athen, Aryis, Medias, and Reece. Behind them, the Imperial retinue—including Safin surrounded by over two hundred Justiciars and Ashcloaks.

The water in the city's port roiled, dark and blue with strange flecks of color, as if reflecting the stars above. But that was impossible—no stars shone during the day. And certainly none that could be seen through that thick blanket of clouds.

"I've never witnessed anything like this before," Lilliana remarked when they got to the end of the expansive wharf that was reserved for fishing, food carts, street performers, and small vendors.

Nyssa spotted Elias and Fontaine standing outside a cadre of guards. "Let them through," she said, pointing. "Let them through, dammit!"

Safin nodded, and the Justiciars relaxed their protective boundary, letting Elias and Fontaine pass.

"You ever seen anything like this before?" Nyssa asked.

"No. But if I had to guess..." Fontaine said, her eyes scanning the sea, "the Shimmer's been breached."

Shit. That could only mean...

The seagull flew around them in a flurry of black and white feathers, coming to land on a dock piling.

Nyssa crossed her arms. "What is this about, bird?"

MY NAME IS HOOKFOOT, AND I AM THE SENTINEL OF NARILEH THE PROTECTOR.

A rush of air left Nyssa, and her stomach fluttered while she tried to suppress a smile. The Ancient God's power ran through her veins, but she had no idea what to expect of the being.

Hookfoot ruffled his feathers and cocked his head. *DID KORAS OR CYPHON NOT TELL YOU OF ME?*

"No...should they have?" Quinn asked.

ASSHOLES. NOT EVEN A MENTION?

"No. Sorry?" Quinn tossed a glance at Nyssa, who shrugged.

MEH. The bird squawked again. *NARILEH THE PROTECTOR WISHES AN AUDIENCE. INTO THE WATER, GODLINGS.*

Nyssa looked to Quinn and smiled. A smile that the raven-haired woman returned, her fingers brushing against the back of Nyssa's hand. Though she tried to contain it, Nyssa couldn't help the bark of joyous laughter that escaped her mouth. She hopped around the dock as she pulled her boots off and stripped out of her jacket and sweater, leaving her only in leather pants and a light cotton shirt. She hurried to the end of the dock, balancing her bare feet on the edge, trying not to shiver when the wind picked up.

Her friends gaped at her, and Safin, Lyra, and the Arch Justiciar stared. What must they be thinking?

"Nyssa, careful! What are you doing? The water's still very deep here," Athen said, rushing forward. The look on her best friend's face was pure concern. He couldn't understand. She was about to meet the god who chose her.

Nyssa spread her arms wide. "Coming, Quinn?"

"Yeah, if you'd just give me a second—"

Nyssa smirked, blew Quinn a kiss, and fell backward off the dock. She sliced into the sea just like Quinn had taught her on Monk's Cove.

The water gave her a jolt, her body tensing immediately from the shocking cold. It was almost as icy as the day she drowned in the Black Sea. On that day, Quinn had dragged Nyssa's dead body back to the surface. Though that felt like a lifetime ago, she couldn't ignore the small shiver of fear that ran through her. She could swim now, but freezing to death was a very real possibility, even so close to shore. She was placing her faith in an Ancient God she had never met, hoping Narileh was friendly, unlike her asshole seagull Sentinel.

When Nyssa came up for air, the faces of Athen and Reece stared down at her, soon joined by Safin and Decia. Nyssa lay back and kicked her feet, drifting away from the dock.

"You can't swim! Are you insane?" Athen groused.

"Yes, I can! Quinn taught me," she called back up, "and I'm rather good!"

"And rather humble about it too," Quinn said, poking her head around Athen. She cautiously shimmied forward, her toes curling over the edge. Nyssa swam backward and watched Quinn dive into the water with hardly a splash. Was there anything that woman didn't do beautifully?

"Fuck!" Quinn swore when she surfaced. "It's freezing!"

She even cursed attractively. Her bright-green eyes blinked water away, and her raven-colored hair stuck to the side of her face. Nyssa swam away from the dock. The seagull stared down at them.

"Well, bird? What do we do next?" she shouted.

YOU WAIT. AND AGAIN, MY NAME IS HOOKFOOT.

Nyssa tried to calm her body as it trembled from the chill of the sea. "That bird is kind of an assho—"

Something yanked Nyssa under the water.

The glimmering surface raced away from her, her arms flailing as she was dragged downward at incredible speed, into the chilly depths. Her heart pounded and the rush of water assaulted her ears. She could never forget the agony of drowning as her body struggled for air and eventually betrayed her, sucking in the sea.

When the ocean turned from icy to warm, she was relieved she wouldn't freeze to death. She would merely drown.

A deep voice filled her head and thrummed throughout her whole body.

Breathe.

Nyssa shook her head violently.

Breathe, child.

No! her mind screamed back. *I'll drown!*

Nyssa dared to glance down. A giant tentacle was wrapped around her legs. Below her, roiling in the deep, more tentacles coiled in the darkness. They seemed to go on forever, illuminated faintly by sparks of blue lightning. The water sparkled and shimmered, like a clear night sky full of stars. It was clear—she was no longer in her own world.

Let go of your fear and breathe, Nyssa Blacksea. I have you.

Nyssa closed her eyes and tried to compose herself. It didn't seem she had much of a choice, trapped underwater. This required a leap of faith.

Nyssa opened her mouth and drew in a cautious breath. Water shot down her throat, burning everything it touched. She struggled as her lungs filled with the sea, panic overtaking her body.

How had she been so stupid?

Calm yourself, godling.

Nyssa closed her eyes and drew in another breath. Then another. And another. The pain and discomfort waned after each successive inhale. She wasn't drowning. Not even close. She opened her eyes, astonished to be alive. And breathing water...or whatever water was in the Realm of the Deep.

It's unpleasant at first, but you can breathe in my realm. Now you will have to convince the other godling to not panic as you did.

A tentacle raced past Nyssa and up to the surface. Quinn appeared next to Nyssa a few moments later.

Breathe, Quinn Emerrath, Narileh's voice rumbled in their heads.

Quinn shook her head, her eyes wide with terror.

Nyssa stretched toward her, reaching out with her mind, trusting that Narileh's connection worked between all three of them, the way Koras had linked their minds in the Realm of Night. *It's okay. Take my hand and breathe.*

Quinn grasped Nyssa's hand in a death grip.

Nyssa squeezed back. *Trust me. Just breathe. It'll hurt at first.*

Quinn resisted, her eyes full of fear, but she finally opened her mouth and took a breath. She panicked, like Nyssa anticipated, as her lungs filled with water. Quinn almost pulled out of Nyssa's grasp, but Nyssa held firm, waiting for Quinn to get past the worst of it. Quinn eventually calmed down and looked perplexed when she realized she, too, was breathing water.

It's so strange, her voice echoed in Nyssa's head.

See, you're okay.

I am.

A massive creature moved toward them—a giant, black Kraken, just like Nyssa's sigil. Narileh's skin rippled with shards of lightning, and her huge azure eye opened before them.

I see that you are both well. I am glad.

You were with me when I drowned, weren't you? Nyssa asked. *You feel...so familiar.*

I was watching.

Then why...why did you let me die? Nyssa bit her tongue. Was her question too forward? Would it anger Narileh?

It was not my place to save you, Nyssa. That was Quinn's job. You are responsible for each other, your lives entwined forever.

Nyssa looked at Quinn. Even this far under water, her emerald eyes were bright, vibrant. She floated with stars as her backdrop in the Realm of the Deep. *Stunning.*

Quinn smiled. *I heard that.*

I'm glad this mind connection only works when we're with the Ancients, then. It would be...distracting. Nyssa gave Quinn a wink before turning back to Narileh. *Did you light the spark of magick in me when I drowned?*

That was you, child. And you helped Quinn's magick rise.

All it took was me dying, Nyssa said.

A necessary catalyst.

Narileh, why did you summon us? Quinn asked.

Enormous black tentacles swirled around them, twisting in the water. There seemed to be no end to the Ancient God.

I wanted to see the Cursed Gods you have become.

Nyssa spread her arms wide. *You like what you see?*

Nyssa! Quinn chastised.

You're cocky, Nyssa Blacksea, even in the face of an Ancient God. I rather like that.

Nyssa turned to Quinn and grinned at her. *See? She likes me.*

Quinn shook her head. Nyssa took her hand, like she had done hundreds of times in the dark sea of her dreams before they ever met.

Narileh spoke again. *You both have been brave. Stout hearts, strong souls. You will need to remain steadfast for each other.*

Cyphon warned us that there are others like us, Quinn said.

Yes...and things even I don't understand have begun to stir. Darkness is growing. It will reach out for you. You must not become the monsters of Cursed Gods past. They were filled with hubris, greed, a disregard for life...they wasted their gifts and dishonored themselves.

How do we not become like them? Nyssa asked.

I don't think either of you are anything like them, child. We watched you, chose you both for reasons that are our own. Your connection to Koras and me is unique.

How? Quinn asked.

We felt your births into this world, the first Cursed Gods in a thousand years. There was something different about the two of you, a connection formed outside the confines of time.

Nyssa glanced at Quinn. What the hell did that mean?

Narileh continued, *To protect you, Koras and I hid your magicks down deep so others couldn't find you. Nyssa, your ability to manipulate magick and, Quinn, your ability to abolish it, are unique. That power in the hands of those with darkened hearts could wreak havoc on far more than your Earthen Realm.*

A chill ran up and down Nyssa's spine.

Quinn, a bit of the magick you were born with did stubbornly poke through.

Nyssa smiled. *Stubborn. That sounds about right.*

Quinn shook her head.

To protect you, we imbued you both with a spark of power from each of us. The storm. The night.

With every bit of information Narileh gave them, a myriad of questions popped up in Nyssa's head. She struggled to organize her thoughts.

Why are the realms appearing again? she asked. The realms had pulled away from the world of men almost a thousand years ago. Around the same time the last of the Cursed Gods died out.

The realms never left, just receded from your world, and the Shimmer dimmed. But now, ancient magick rises again, Nyssa. We are all a part of that. You carry the burden of the Cursed God lore. Your forebearers left a tarnished legacy, but we believe you two are different.

And if we're not? Quinn asked.

A bold question. Nyssa's jaw tensed as she waited for the answer.

Your world will reckon with its gods as it must.

Nyssa swallowed back the ball of fear in her throat. It wasn't a threat so much as a warning.

The man you hunt, the one who laid claim to you as a child, Quinn Emerrath, you must stop him.

That's our plan, Nyssa said.

He wants far too much. His ambition could destabilize the balance of magick.

Quinn frowned. *Can't you help us stop him?*

Narileh's massive blue eye closed and reopened. *Mortal affairs are for mortals to address.*

Nyssa didn't understand. *So you want us to stop him, but you won't help?*

Narileh didn't answer the question. There had to be more.

Why did you and Koras intercede with Quinn and me if mortal affairs are below your purview?

The giant form of Narileh moved all around them, the hum of her sea song thrumming deep in Nyssa's chest. *Ceril Anelos is not the only being who can disturb the balance of magick. The realms—yours, mine, and countless others—form a delicate nexus of existence. The Ancient Gods know how delicate that balance is.*

Quinn swam closer to the eye of the giant god. *Please, Ceril has disappeared and now he attacks from the shadows. We need your help.*

Narileh held Quinn in her gaze for a long while before she answered. *There are some battles only Cursed Gods can fight.* Narileh blinked, slow and languid. *The blood of the last Rell is powerful.* She went quiet.

After waiting a few long seconds for more information that didn't come, Quinn said, *Thank you.*

Dark tentacles swirled around the two of them, the field of stars in the Realm of the Deep shifting and twinkling. Narileh spoke once again.

Quinn Emerrath, you have the ability to wreak vengeance on those who have hurt you. But remember the power of mercy and grace.

Quinn and Nyssa looked at one another. Warning or advice, there didn't seem to be a difference.

And you, Nyssa Blacksea. Your blade needs to be as sharp as ever, protector. Your anger is a weapon, but it cuts both ways.

What does that mean? Nyssa asked.

Follow your code of honor, as you have always done. I've placed trust in you both for a reason. The giant blue eye blinked. *Now, daughters, it's time for you to rejoin your friends.*

Nyssa held her hand up. *Could you do us a huge favor? If you're willing, we know someone who would love to meet you.*

FLYING GODS

Quinn flailed as she flew through the air, whatever modicum of grace she possessed completely abandoned. She arced toward the wharf, people scrambling out of her way. She hit the dock and rolled to a stop at a pair of feet. Seconds later, Nyssa skidded into her.

Quinn flopped onto her back, and Medias stared down at her. Reece's head poked up over her shoulder.

"Interesting way to return," Medias said.

Quinn opened her mouth to respond, but clutched her chest. She couldn't breathe. Her body convulsed until she violently expelled the water from her lungs, splashing Medias's boots.

The woman let out a grunt of disgust.

Quinn pushed herself to her knees and leaned her head back, gasping, shivering in the icy air. Nyssa lay on the dock next to her, coughing up water herself.

"I would...have preferred a...softer landing," Nyssa choked out.

Narileh had jettisoned them out of the water a little too high and fast, perhaps forgetting that, despite their status as Cursed Gods, they were still human, rather fragile and soft and subject to breakage.

Apologies, Nyssa Blacksea.

The gathered crowd let out a collective gasp. From the looks on their faces, they all heard Narileh's voice too. The Justiciars shifted nervously, hands on their weapons. Even Lyra appeared taken aback. It wasn't every day—hell, it wasn't every millennium—that mortals got to meet an Ancient God. And they were all about to witness something spectacular.

Members of the Whisper's crew waved at them from the wharf while more spectators crowded onto the other docks.

Quinn stood and doubled over, expelling more water. It seemed endless. She shivered once and straightened up. "Fontaine...we have someone who...wants to say hi."

The dock began to vibrate under her feet, the water in the port growing turbulent. Fontaine cautiously approached. Nyssa popped to her feet and threw an arm around Fontaine's shoulders.

"You're soaking wet!" Fontaine admonished.

"Would you like to meet Narileh?" Nyssa asked with that cocky half smile of hers that Quinn loved.

"You can't be serious..." Fontaine's voice trailed off when the sky grew dim, becoming a beautiful shade of steel blue. Darkness fell and dots of faint light filled their field of vision.

The buzz of conversations ceased.

Boats rocked and clanged in their moorings as the sea came alive and the sky above took on the visage of night. Deep, threatening thunder rumbled all around them. Quinn could feel its vibration in her bones. Her shadow magick rose to the surface on its own, spreading around her, billowing off of her, as if called forth by Narileh.

She turned to Nyssa, whose eyes glowed blue and sparked with lightning. Energy rolled off of her in waves, tendrils of lightning twisting and combining with Quinn's own threads of shadow that sprawled across the surface of the dock and licked at the feet of those present. Lyra hugged Safin close, her eyes wide. Next to them, Ashcloak Ruggen's face wavered, her eyes darting from the magick winding around her ankles to Nyssa.

Quinn smirked. *Now they see what we truly are.*

A massive figure rose from the water to the collective gasp of those watching. Tentacles twisted around the docks and boats and extended out into the sea. Quinn exhaled at the sight. Narileh wasn't just huge, she seemed endless, a god who could reach out to the stars and back. Azure lightning arced around her body and rippled through the water and into the darkened sky, spreading over them like a dome.

A giant eye opened and stared at the assembled group behind Quinn, a tentacle rising from the water before them. The tentacle snaked across the dock and ever so gently nudged Fontaine.

You are Fontaine? The trees and the sea sing of you with great esteem. You raised my godlings, Old Folk?

Fontaine choked out a breath and nodded. "Yes, in a manner of speaking...I taught them. As best I could," she stuttered.

A commendable job, Old One. You honor your people.

"Thank you," Fontaine whispered. She reached out and touched Narileh. Her whole body tensed as blue energy crackled around them both. Quinn put her hand on Fontaine's shoulder, shadow mixing with Narileh's lightning, watching to make sure Fontaine was okay.

After a minute passed, Fontaine smiled and bowed her head. "It's my pleasure," Fontaine said and pulled her hand back, wavering on her feet. She slipped to her knees. Elias rushed to her.

Quinn crouched down. "Fontaine, are you alright?"

"That was...incredible. She spoke to me. I could hear her voice vibrating in every corner of my body," Fontaine said, her eyes shiny. "Like the most wonderful dream."

Nyssa beamed at Fontaine. "Figured you might enjoy that. It's the least we could do after everything you've done for us."

Narileh's eye scanned the group on the dock, settling on Medias. A tentacle slithered toward her and stopped, wrapping slowly around her legs. Reece rushed forward, but Medias shook her head. "I'm okay, empath."

This is the one, Hookfoot.

The seagull cawed, sounding angry. *THAT ONE? YOU'RE KIDDING ME.*

The color drained from Medias's face.

You, Medias Levesque, will serve a great purpose.

Medias's mouth dropped open.

I'M LODGING AN OFFICIAL PROTEST AGAINST THIS.

Your objection is noted, my friend, the massive god replied.

"What's happening?" Medias finally choked out, her voice tight and strained.

My gods need a Sentinel. I suspect the role will fit you nicely.

CURSED GODS DON'T GET SENTINELS. THIS IS A PRIVILEGE RESERVED FOR—

Shush, Hookfoot. Do you think my brethren were pleased I picked a loud, obnoxious seagull for the job?

FINE. BUT I HATE IT.

Quinn was perplexed, but Nyssa broke out in laughter, drawing a beady-eyed stare from the bird. "Narileh, what's happening?"

This seer is touched by ancient magick. Or had you not taken notice of her essence?

Quinn scowled and concentrated on finding the glowing core of magick inside Medias. Faint jagged spikes of ancient magick surrounded the soft center of her power.

Nyssa frowned. "Well, shit."

"I...I don't understand," Medias said.

You possess enough ancient magick to make you different, Medias. But not enough to make you one of them. Cursed Gods are nothing but ancient magick, child. Narileh's tentacle tightened around Medias, who did an admirable job of not losing her shit. *Do you accept becoming the Sentinel of the Marked Gods?*

Marked Gods? Quinn didn't mind the title. Far better than *Cursed* Gods.

Medias opened her mouth and closed it, scowling, her gaze fixed on the giant eye of Narileh. She finally spoke. "What does it entail?"

You will be their sword. Counselor. Ambassador. Confidant. A trusted friend. And, hopefully, one that keeps them on their path. Do you accept, Medias Levesque?

Medias broke her gaze from Narileh and looked to Quinn and Nyssa. "I accept."

Good. I had to ply Hookfoot with prawns to get him to agree to be my Sentinel.

I'M NOT EASY, UNLIKE THIS FLESHY FOOL.

A deep rumble of the god's laughter filled the port. It made the mark on Quinn's chin tingle.

Take care of my godlings, Sentinel Medias. The dark tentacle unwound from Medias's legs and found a new target—Aryis, who was busy scribbling away in her notebook.

Startled, Aryis stumbled and lost her footing, her knee giving out. Narileh caught her. Athen moved toward her, looking ready to strike if need be, his care for Aryis rather apparent.

Behave.

And with that, Narileh let Aryis go, withdrawing her tentacle from the dock and moving back out into the water, her giant body filling the harbor.

Quinn scowled. Behave? What the fuck did that mean?

Be safe, my daughters.

Narileh slowly sank below the waves. As she went, the water in the harbor calmed and the sky lightened, its roiling clouds disappearing. The absence of the Ancient God felt like a massive void, her sea song no longer rumbling in the deepest parts of Quinn.

As Narileh receded, so did Quinn and Nyssa's magick, coiling back inside them. The crowds of men and women on the docks chattered excitedly. Understandable, given what they had just witnessed.

Quinn let out a breath. Meeting Narileh was astonishing. But moreover, the god had given them a small clue about Ceril—and Suvi. And now that clue tickled at her brain. There were things about her time at Arcton that were starting to make sense. Her gut was telling her the answers were likely there.

Nyssa strode over to Medias to clap her on the back. Medias barely moved, her face slack. "Sentinel Medias." Turning, she smiled at Hookfoot, even as she shivered from being soaked through. "Does being a Sentinel include things like foot rubs and fetching me pastries whenever I wish?"

Hookfoot stretched his neck, ruffled his feathers, and took flight. *IDIOTS!*

"You're an asshole, Hookfoot!" Nyssa yelled after him.

Quinn smirked at her. "Only you could make a bird your nemesis." She turned to look at the gathered spectators, finding the one she needed to talk to. "Emperor Safin, a word!"

She left Nyssa and strode toward him. As expected, his Justiciars and Ashcloaks moved to protect him. Quinn stopped and didn't call forth her magick, as much as she wanted to. She would be polite. For now. "I know why Ceril took Suvi."

Safin didn't hesitate. "Let me through."

The Justiciars and Ashcloaks moved away, but Decia stuck next to him, as did his mother.

Quinn waited for Safin and the others to draw close, keeping her eyes on the distant Sun Council. They didn't need to overhear—who knew if any of them were secretly in league with Ceril.

"Narileh said something to us about the blood of the last Rell being powerful," she said.

Safin nodded. "Continue."

"Think about it. Without her throne and wealth, or an army to do her bidding, what possible value does Suvi have to Ceril? He doesn't want her as an ally. He wants her blood."

Judging by their faces, they didn't quite understand. Quinn pressed her hands together. "Every single Rell possession at Arcton is protected by wards and locked away in the Night Vault. Before I came along, only a Rell could get inside. Now, Ceril has one of the two people in the world who can access that vault."

"I have already sent extra security to Arcton," Decia said.

Quinn lowered her voice. "There's more. Ceril and I spent countless hours in the Night Vault. He didn't just study the spell books, he pored over Rell journals, often rereading the same material over and over, taking notes. He grew more frustrated over time. I got the sense that he was looking for something."

"Something that perhaps Suvi can help him find?" Safin asked.

"I know it's not much to go on, just a gut instinct, but...I can't shake the feeling that he wanted something *more*. He kept taking and retaking a detailed inventory of the vault. As if—"

"Something's missing," Aryis interrupted.

Quinn turned to her, cautious. "Yes."

Aryis leaned forward, clutching her wooden cane. "Emperor, if Ceril is after something belonging to the Rells, I think it's safe to assume he'll go back to the place with the biggest collection of that family's spells and research."

"And we need to find it before he does," Quinn said, addressing Safin. "What if there's something in Arcton that's more powerful than the Alabaster Books and there's a clue there to find it? Send us there to protect the one place Anelos could return to and look for whatever he's after."

Decia stiffened. "Absolutely not. Need I remind you that you're not to interfere with Imperial affairs?"

"You need to listen to them." Medias stepped past Nyssa and Aryis, taking a spot next to Quinn. "Mother, I've seen him at Arcton in a vision. He will go there."

Decia's mouth drew down, her jaw muscles tensing. She pulled Safin and Lyra aside to talk.

Quinn and Nyssa exchanged a look. If Safin didn't take this threat seriously, Quinn didn't know what else to do.

Safin took a deep breath. "I am going to treat you as allies to the throne, so anything you do now will reflect back on me. Understand?"

Nyssa and Quinn nodded, and a nervous excitement coursed through Quinn.

"Go to Arcton. You will have full access to the Citadel. Find what Anelos is looking for. And if he shows up, as you suspect he will, he's to be arrested. No vigilante justice. To make sure, I'm sending ten more Justiciars and Master Ashcloak Ruggen to be your escorts."

Nyssa let out a huff. "Ina? Oh, hell no."

"This isn't your decision, Unworthy," Lyra interrupted.

Nyssa tightened her jaw. "You're sending her to spy on us?"

"That's the only way this works," Safin replied. "Arcton holds the secrets of the Empire, so yes, you absolutely need to be watched. These are my conditions."

As much as Quinn hated the idea of Ina being anywhere near Nyssa, they would have to make concessions. "Nyssa?"

Nyssa groaned but nodded. "Fine."

"Good. We'll arrange for an Imperial airship to take you to Arcton," Safin said. He drew closer. "What happened here today will change some opinions about the two of you. There are many who still honor the Ancient Gods."

Nyssa leaned in. "Narileh popping out of the water and saying hi hasn't made your mother stop calling me Unworthy, though, has it?"

Safin merely offered a smile and a handshake for the two of them. He was smart enough to know what the gesture signified. It would further rankle anyone who had it in for the Cursed Gods, but for the time being, Quinn was satisfied.

"I am preparing to return to Cardin," he said. "The Empire needs a return to normalcy while we sort out this business. Good luck." With that, he turned, and the Justiciars once again fell in around him as he and his Imperial procession made their way up the dock.

Quinn let loose the breath she had been holding. "I didn't think he'd agree." She turned to Aryis. "You're coming with us."

Aryis blinked. "Wait, me? Why?"

"I can get us in the Night Vault, but you're the bookworm. You can dig around in there far better than we can alone."

The woman's face brightened. "Of course! Whatever you need."

Nyssa brushed Quinn's arm. "Are you sure about this?"

"Yeah. You heard what Narileh said."

Shaking her head, Nyssa turned serious. "Are you going to be okay going back there?"

Putting on her best confident grin, Quinn lied, "Yes, I'll be fine." She turned to Medias. "In your vision, what else did you see besides Ceril?"

Medias shrugged. "Nothing. I lied. I didn't have a vision of Ceril at the Citadel. My mother needed an extra push, otherwise you two would still be stuck under house arrest. She has never questioned my seer sight."

Nyssa chuckled and shook her head. "Lying now? We've been such a bad influence on you, Sentinel."

"Yes, you have."

Quinn turned and looked back at the city of Ocean's Rest. Crowds still milled about the docks, but a large contingent of Lion's Guards waited to escort Quinn, Nyssa, and the others all safely back to the Keep. In a few days' time, they would be in the air, on their way to Arcton.

The thought of it made Quinn's stomach turn. She would have to put on a brave face. The last place she ever wanted to see again was the Citadel.

AN INVITATION

Reece knitted her fingers together while she sat waiting for Lilliana to sign the last of a stack of papers. Pol stood patiently by Lilliana's side, his eyebrow arched as he watched and nodded, occasionally leaning down to clarify what was being signed.

Over the years, as much as Lilliana had served as a mother figure for Reece, Pol filled in the role of father. More often than not, as Reece grew up and struggled with her magick, it was Pol who watched over her and tried his best to guide her.

A heavy sigh emanated from Lilliana, and she pushed the last of the papers to the side. "Hosting the Sun Council is a rather expensive enterprise."

"One that you have executed with hospitality and grace," Pol intoned.

"I didn't have much choice when Lyra Vonner landed on my doorstep, followed soon after by the goddamn child Emperor. Not to mention the Sun Council," Lilliana replied. "Oh, and I stopped counting how many Justiciars and Ashcloaks are now here."

"The drain on our stores of liquor alone pains me." Pol winked at Reece.

Lilliana chuckled. "Me too, old friend. We'll have nothing left to drink to celebrate their return to Cardin." She continued to sign a few papers before finally raising her eyes to regard Reece. "I'm sorry to have kept you waiting. Thank you for coming."

Reece untangled her hands from one another. Lilliana rebuffing Reece's desire to become the Regent of the city still hung between them like a silent specter, their one unresolved issue.

"I suspect you and Athen were planning to go to Arcton with Nyssa and Quinn," Lilliana said. "But I'm afraid you're needed elsewhere." She pulled a small square envelope out of a drawer and slid it across the desk. It bore a golden stamp—a sun. The official sigil of the Areshi Emperor. Reece picked it up and opened it, extracting the card tucked inside. Minuscule golden specks orbited the paper, catching the afternoon light. A delightfully ornate bit of stationery.

Reece read the paper as the specks of light rotated around her hand. "An invitation to officially join the Assembly of Regents?" She glanced up at Lilliana. "Quite the honor."

"I'd like you to go in my place, as the representative of our House and Ocean's Rest."

The words stilled Reece. *Our* House. "You're not serious."

"Use your magick on me. What do you sense?"

Reece swallowed. "I'm not poking into your emotions. I rarely do."

Lilliana scowled. "You and I have always tiptoed around one another."

A true statement. Reece slipped Safin's invitation back into its envelope and stared down at her hands.

"I wasn't ready to be a mother when you came into my life," Lilliana said. She stood and circled her desk, sitting in the chair next to Reece. "You are a blessing, the last gift your mother gave to this world. I promised her that I would always look after you, but I haven't always been the mother you deserve. I'm sorry for that."

Reece opened her mouth, trying to find words. She didn't need to use her magick on Lilliana to know the truth. "I know I haven't always been easy."

"Raising an empath was a challenge when you were younger." Lilliana chuckled. "Your tendency to speak your mind started very early. Not much has changed." She turned serious. "I truly regret the things I said to you that night you learned the truth about my role in Nyssa's parents' deaths. I drove a wedge between us. A wise counselor had some very choice words for me after that."

Lilliana glanced up at Pol. He nodded, smiling. No self-satisfaction was evident. He and Lilliana had been friends for years. More than that, they were partners in turning Ocean's Rest into the shining city it was, calming the faction warfare and uniting those disparate forces in service to one goal—prosperity for all, even if some of that prosperity had illegal origins. Pol was always far more measured in his actions, a quality Reece had come to admire greatly.

"Nyssa will never forgive me for what I did to her parents, and I don't expect her to, but just know that what I did, I did to protect you."

Reece swallowed. Nyssa never mentioned it, but knowing that Lilliana helped set the events in motion that led to their deaths in order to save Reece from being taken by Ambershine and turned into a Justiciar had to sit in the back of her head.

Lilliana leaned in. "We need to heal this rift between us. You and Athen are the future of House Fennick. *You* are my daughter. When I retire, this city will be yours as its Regent."

Behind the desk, Pol picked up one of the papers. "The order to name you future Regent of Ocean's Rest is here," he said. Lilliana's signature stood out in bold, black ink.

"I—" Reece quickly closed her mouth. She stared at Lilliana.

A knock at the door saved her from fumbling for an immediate response.

Pol moved around the desk and headed to the door, opening it. "Come."

Athen entered the office, Nyssa trailing behind him. He sported a massive smile. "Did you say yes, Reece?"

"You knew? And you're okay with this?" she asked him.

"Of course. We all know I would have made a horrible Regent. Politics aren't my thing. Bores me. I need to be out in the sunlight, throwing fists."

"Athen has agreed to be the Vanguard of Ocean's Rest," Pol said.

Vanguard? That title hadn't been used for centuries, since Ashcloaks had taken over the duty of protecting Imperial lands. "I thought they might reinstate you as an Ashcloak?"

Athen shrugged. "Safin offered, I politely declined."

"Athen, you trained every day for over ten years to become an Ashcloak. You deserve the honor."

"And yet I lost it by doing the honorable thing and helping out my best friend. If the title is that easily taken away, is it really worth all that much?"

"But Medias stripped you of your title so Ceril wouldn't suspect her of colluding with us. It was all fake!"

Athen shrugged. "Ah, I'd probably do something stupid to lose it again anyway if I accepted my guild sigil back."

"Nyssa, what are your thoughts about this?" Reece asked.

"It's Athen's decision, and I respect his reasons," she said, an edge to her voice.

Reece gave a reluctant nod. She had seen how easy it was for the Empire to misjudge Nyssa and Athen, stripping them of their titles. Perhaps the role of Ashcloak was more of a burden than an honor.

"Athen knows that he needs to protect you when you're Regent, so I'm not terribly disappointed that he's no longer an Ashcloak," Lilliana said. "But for now, let Pol and I focus on this city. I need you both in Cardin to join the Assembly of Regents after the Ascension ceremony. The Emperor is leaving on an Imperial ship in a few days' time, and I've arranged for you to join him. You'll also have guest residence in the Sun Palace."

"I thought we were going to Arcton with Nyssa and the others?" Athen asked.

"Change of plans," Reece said, handing him the invitation to the Assembly of Regents. He scanned it, surprise evident on his face. Nyssa leaned against him and plucked the paper out of his hand, read it, and passed it back to Reece.

"I guess we're respectable now?" Athen grinned.

"Oh, never," Pol said with a chuckle.

"I'd prefer to go to Arcton and keep an eye on everyone. Keep them safe."

Reece knew damn well he wanted to keep an eye on Aryis most of all.

"Nyssa and I have already spoken about this," Lilliana replied. "That's why I invited her here, so you all know we're aligned on this."

Nyssa nodded. "And you're taking Medias with you."

Reece's stomach flipped. "I just assumed Medias would go with the two of you. She's your Sentinel, after all."

"We're going to be stuck doing research at the Citadel. Our noses will be buried in books with Aryis. Not exactly dangerous stuff. Medias is familiar with Cardin and Imperial politics. I'll feel much better if she's watching your backs."

An air of insistence wafted off of Nyssa—one that Lilliana mirrored. It was odd seeing them united...for the moment.

"Will I be welcome back to the Palace after my, uh, creative redecoration of the main entrance?" Athen asked, grimacing. Reece laughed softly, reminded of their childhood together as he learned how to control his strength. A few glasses, vases, pots...well, numerous things had been shattered accidentally through the years. Each time was followed by that grimace.

"Your full pardon exonerates you from everything. I've seen what passes for art at the Sun Palace. You did the Empire a favor," Lilliana said. "I could not be prouder of you, Athen. I know you'll represent this city with courage and honor."

Reece and Athen exchanged a look. Color rose in his cheeks. Lilliana was downright effusive in her praise this day.

Reece smoothed her fingertips over the invitation in her hands, deep in thought.

"Reece, what is it?" Pol asked.

He had seen enough of her moods over the years and knew her all too well.

"There's...something off about the Sun Council," Reece said. "The few times I've been in their proximity, I've sensed contempt. Greed. Even hate. I fear there's a threat on the Council."

Leaning forward, Lilliana brushed her fingers over Reece's knee. "Who?"

Reece let out a deep breath. "I don't know."

"This is precisely why I want Medias to go with you," Nyssa said, concern lacing her words. "If there's a threat to Safin, there's a threat to all of us."

Lilliana sighed. "There have been whispers of unrest on the Sun Council ever since Kalla named Safin as her successor."

Once again, Lilliana's whisper network came through. Years of building pleasure houses in Ocean's Rest and other cities had yielded a precious commodity—information.

"Safin is young and a new Emperor, so he's vulnerable," Reece replied. "Perhaps the Sun Council thinks he's making poor choices. But he's facing a world that's far different now with the re-emergence of Cursed Gods."

Nyssa rocked back on her heels. "There's other Cursed Gods out there, at least that's what Koras and Narileh have told me."

Lilliana sat back, pensive. "I haven't heard anything definitive, but there has been chatter from the East of strange occurrences."

"Really?" Nyssa asked, scowling.

Reece's stomach sank. More Cursed Gods wandering around the world wasn't great news, but they couldn't worry about that right now. "Safin could be in real danger, so any talk of other gods needs to be deferred for a time. No offense, Nyssa."

"One headache at a time," she said with a wink. She tried to put on a brave face, but Reece detected a thread of nervousness weave through her emotions.

"Agreed," Lilliana replied. She sat for a moment, then looked at Athen and Reece. "I don't like any of this. Ceril may be gone, but his influence lingers. He kept his circle of confidants extremely tight, but I find it hard to believe he didn't make a friend or two on the Sun Council. Go to Cardin and find out. The Assembly is the perfect pretense to get you in the Palace. Keep an eye out for Safin."

"Do we talk to Decia about any of this?" Athen asked.

"Not until you have something definitive. Making any allegations against the Sun Council could have unfortunate repercussions. Decia and I aren't exactly friends, but she, too, isn't in the most secure spot, given this business with her daughter. There's not a lot of confidence in her either, I imagine."

Reece was beginning to feel in over her head. "You don't think Safin could be in any real danger, do you?"

"Rulers have died for less in the history of the Areshi Empire," Pol replied. "Reece, trust your gut."

"And lean on Medias," Nyssa added. "She's prickly, but she's proved herself loyal. And she seems to hold you in high regard, Reece. Trust her." She punctuated her words with a mischievous smirk. There was no damn subtlety to the woman at all.

Lilliana leaned forward and took Reece's hand. "Keep your eyes and ears open while you're in Cardin. House Fennick will be viewed as upstarts among those pedigreed Houses and Regents. But remember, you're my daughter and son." She looked up at Athen. "Be careful. You'll find snakes lying in wait around every corner."

A FAREWELL

"**S**top staring and get back to work!" Elias barked at the men and women repairing Hannah's Whisper as they gawked at Nyssa and Quinn.

Nyssa chuckled under her breath. Seeing him dote over his ship was, at the very least, entertaining. The crew seemed mostly absent, save for Max and Yuha, both watching the workers hired from Ocean's Rest with their arms crossed.

"What are you two layabouts doing back on my ship?" Elias asked, striding up to Nyssa and Quinn with a bright smile. Fontaine skipped behind him, greeting them with a short wave.

"We're here to say goodbye," Nyssa replied.

Fontaine frowned. "Goodbye? We'll be in port for another few weeks. Elias is being very picky about the repairs."

"We're the ones on the way out. A couple of us are going to Arcton to poke around the Night Vault. Aryis and Quinn think there's something there that Ceril wants and will go back for."

Fontaine's frown grew deeper, and she turned to Quinn. "Oh, dear girl, do you think it's a good idea you return to that place?"

Fontaine wasn't asking a question that Nyssa herself hadn't considered at least ten times since the previous night.

"I will be fine, Fontaine," Quinn answered. "But I know where your concern comes from, and I appreciate it."

Crossing over to her, Fontaine stroked her cheek for a moment before giving her a hug. The two women shared a bond that warmed Nyssa's heart.

"We don't know how long we'll be gone. You'll likely be out to sea again before we return to Ocean's Rest," Nyssa said. "And we couldn't leave without saying goodbye."

Elias crossed his arms. "I'm not happy to see you go. I half expected you might rejoin us. You know you're a part of this crew." He raised an eyebrow at Quinn. "I need the Pirate Queen...and Nyssa can tag along, although she's a drain on our food stores."

Quinn laughed, her arm still around Fontaine. "Let us deal with Ceril and then we'll see. We could use some pirate money once all this is over."

"I do owe you two a couple thousand gold marks for your crew work on the ship," Elias said.

"Ah, keep it to cover these repairs. I feel like we're to blame for this damage," Nyssa said, eyeing the black tarps draped over the back of the ship and the stacks of wood piled nearby.

"A generous offer, but not necessary. House Fennick is footing the bill for this. You know I pay my debts...if you're working on this ship, you earn a cut."

"Well then, transfer the money to the Fennick account and earmark it. Reece is sorting all that out for us," Quinn said.

They did need the money. Being a Cursed God didn't pay all that well, aside from Trick's show in New Ibanis. Nyssa was grateful for Reece's quick thinking on that, but she didn't want to be dependent on House Fennick while waiting for their cut of the profits. There was something distasteful about accepting Lilliana's money.

"We want to thank you for how you and the crew have stood by us all this time," Nyssa said, a lump springing up in her throat. Trying to smile, she shook her head. "I'm...not good at this type of thing."

Elias didn't prolong the torture. He embraced her, squeezing tight. "You two keep trying to thank us and I keep reminding you that you're a part of this crew. You're family."

Nyssa stepped back and wiped away a tear. "Dammit, Ghost of the Sea, you're tugging at my heart."

"I do have my ways."

"You'll be back in port soon, right?" Quinn asked.

"As long as Lilliana will have me. She seems to have forgiven me for years of extracting ransoms out of her."

Nyssa laughed. "I will miss your dumb face."

"My extraordinarily handsome face, you surely mean."

Nyssa sighed. "Flirting with me will get you nowhere."

Elias gave her a deep, mocking bow. "I cannot simply turn off the charm."

Fontaine groaned and pulled Nyssa into a hug. "Farewell for now. I hope you find what you need at Arcton."

Quinn crossed over to Elias and hugged him. There was a time when she would merely endure affection—freely embracing Elias was a step in a very positive direction.

Before Nyssa and Quinn could leave the Whisper, Yuha barred their exit. "You will return to us."

Upon first meeting the imposing woman, Nyssa instigated a fight with her. It was another welcome change to call Yuha a friend now.

"We will," Nyssa assured.

Yuha inhaled a deep breath and narrowed her eyes, her gaze shifting from Nyssa to Quinn. "Good." Nodding, she stepped aside.

Once on the docks, Nyssa glanced back at the Whisper, her eyes growing misty.

"I'll miss them too," Quinn said, giving Nyssa a gentle nudge. "Let's get back to the Keep and pack."

Nyssa nodded, turning her attention to their next mission. They were leaving the next day for Arcton and she couldn't shake her apprehension over how returning to the Citadel would affect Quinn.

CERIL AND SUVI

Suvi shivered in her chair despite the fire licking at big, white logs in the fireplace of whatever long-abandoned mansion Shaylin brought her to after they docked in a flimsy seaside collection of buildings that barely qualified as a town.

The Northern Wilds were just as cold and desolate as she'd expected, though they bore a certain beauty. The gray-blue sky had loomed above, carrying a constant threat of snow as they rode for three days to a run-down estate.

Just grateful to be off the damp, rickety ship that Shaylin and her crew called home, Suvi scanned the large, barren room she sat in. The mansion was likely once fairly appointed and opulent, but its grayed-out, frayed furniture and threadbare rugs were signs of quite a turn of fortune.

Did House Anelos once reside here? She knew very little about Ceril and his family, hearing only bits and pieces about the Empire's efficient—albeit callous—Arch Master. But anyone who set themselves against Nyssa and Quinn had to be a worthy ally, if such an arrangement could be forged with the man. The two women had killed her brother, her only remaining family, and they needed to feel that loss intimately.

Shaylin paced back and forth, rubbing her hands together and mumbling. Suvi's treatment hadn't gotten better since Aryis had pulled her from her dim room aboard the pirate ship and tried to...rescue her? How

Aryis was still alive and had not fallen victim to her own incompetence was beyond reckoning.

Shaylin kept up her pacing, her thin coat ridiculously inappropriate for the weather at sea, let alone the barrens of the northern most territories of the Areshi Empire. The woman's vanity seemed to trump common sense, her shirt clingy and low cut, showing off perhaps her best assets, as her brains didn't seem to amount to much.

A tall older man entered the room, flanked by another man and a woman.

"Fuckin' finally," Shaylin hissed.

Ceril Anelos, had to be. He had an air of arrogance that Suvi was all too familiar with. Her brother once had the same affect, though she found it endearing on him. Matthys was charming and playful with his conceit, but Ceril seemed utterly bereft of humor.

"I brought you your queen, Anelos. Now I want my money."

Anelos turned a withering glance toward the pirate. Shay didn't appear to either notice or care. In the scant time Suvi had spent with the woman, it became apparent that something wasn't quite right with her.

Ceril's lips formed a thin line of annoyance. "Your money is currently tied up in other endeavors. You will get your gold in time."

Shay stopped pacing and took a deep breath, a twisted smile spreading across her face, her eyes cold. "You motherfucking cunt. That wasn't the deal. Suvi for two hundred and fifty thousand gold."

Two hundred and fifty thousand gold? That was the going rate for a queen? *Pathetic.*

"And I have explained I don't have it for you. Yet. You will need to be patient."

Edging closer to Suvi, Shay shook her head. "Then the price goes up. Three hundred thousand. A lesson for your lying ass."

Ceril began to laugh, a reedy sound, like the gust of wind through dead trees. "Adept Temo, if you will."

The man next to Ceril disappeared, leaving behind a waft of dark-blue smoke. He reappeared behind Shaylin, his dagger aimed at her neck. Her arm flew up, blocking the blade from slicing through her throat, but his dagger bit into her forearm, drawing blood.

"Mind your cock!" Shaylin cackled, her face alive with wild excitement. She pushed the tip of her dagger into Temo's crotch, forcing a hiss from him. "I'll cut you, boy. Ain't no healer out here who can reattach that limp worm you call a dick."

The woman's fearlessness was...impressive. She seemed to have no magick, but certainly didn't back down from those who did.

"That's enough," Ceril said.

Temo disappeared and reappeared next to him, glaring at the pirate. Shay laughed, pulled out a small disk from a pocket, and bit into it. It started glowing red, and she pressed it against the gash in her arm. Suvi had been the recipient of a few healing disks during the Mire War. They did the job, but they were far more painful than a healer.

Shaylin barely flinched when the disk's red healing tendrils dove into her arm and started its work. Instead, she laughed.

She's insane.

"I want my money," Shay said, licking her lips as she watched the cut on her arm close up. "Three hundred thousand now. Or the cock I threaten next is yours, old man."

With a sneer, Ceril nodded. "Fine, three hundred. You will get your money, but you will need to be patient."

That seemed to appease Shay, who clapped her hands once. "Just know that if you backstab me, Arch Master, I'll slice your throat while you sleep." She approached Suvi and ran her fingers down the side of her face. Suvi scowled, drawing a guttural laugh out of Shay. "See you in my dreams, Princess." Shay nodded at Ceril and took her leave, whistling as she left the room. A door slammed moments later.

Ceril pulled in a long breath, turning his attention to Suvi. "I apologize for Vance. She's effective but not exactly the type of woman I tend to associate with. But I find myself needing...alternative forms of problem-solving at the moment. Efla, will you please cut our guest free?"

Efla slid a dagger out of its sheath, approached Suvi, and with a flick of her blade, Suvi was unbound. She relaxed in her chair and rubbed her wrists. "I would appreciate losing this cursed collar as well."

With a smile, Ceril said, "Efla, if you will."

Suvi's head suddenly snapped back, a sharp explosion of pain rattling her teeth, the crisp *crack* of skin-on-skin contact ringing in the chill air of the room. Efla stared down at her, eyes cold. Suvi rubbed her jaw, slowly blinking. When she pulled her hand away, her fingertips were bloody. A split lip was hopefully the worst of it, but she poked her tongue at her teeth to see if any were loose.

"You will not be let out of that collar," Ceril said. He moved to the chair opposite Suvi and sat, smoothing out his dark cloak and picking at a minuscule piece of lint, a sour expression on his face.

A lump formed in Suvi's throat, and she swallowed it back. "That wasn't necessary."

His eyes examined her. They were cold. Expressionless. "You have gravely misinterpreted the situation here. You are not my guest. Or an ally. You are my prisoner."

Keeping her calm, Suvi gave him a polite smile. "We have a common enemy, Arch Master. Nyssa and Quinn have taken something dear from me. I can help you."

A laugh rumbled out of Ceril. "Oh, you will help me, my dear. Your family left quite a legacy at Arcton Citadel. I've been in the Night Vault more times than I can count. I've studied everything in that haunted place, but reached a dead end. One that you will help me with."

The Night Vault? It should have been impossible to breach without... Suvi swallowed. *Quinn.* Ceril had Quinn for over two decades. He had used her to get into the vault.

Ceril continued, "I know there is a sixth volume in the Alabaster Books collection. The fifth volume becomes increasingly theoretical, the magick within unstable. So I can only imagine what lurks in the sixth book. Where is it, Suvi? Where did your family hide it?"

Suvi broke eye contact with Ceril, glancing to Efla and Temo. Their expressions didn't change. Did any of them truly understand what he was asking? She couldn't give him what he wanted. Not for any price. "There is no sixth volume. That is a rumor that treasure hunters spread to give themselves something to do."

"You're lying, though I don't know why," Ceril replied, the expression on his face growing darker. "You will tell me where that book is."

"And I'm telling you there were only five Alabaster Books." The lie was necessary. Above Suvi's own desire to stay alive was the harsh, perilous reality of what that last, lost volume held. Magicks that her family had unlocked; soul magick that made her ability to control the will of others look trivial by comparison.

The Rell family had a long list of sins and secrets, but the existence of that last book was their worst. The damn thing should have been burned, along with everything in the Night Vault.

"I lost everything I ever truly wanted once, so I will not let an opportunity like this slip through my fingers. We will find that book together, and I will use you to unlock its power."

Suvi shifted in her chair, trying to keep calm, but her face went cold. If Quinn got Ceril into the Night Vault, he must have devoured every book, journal, and errant piece of paper in there. He had to know that some of the most powerful magick her family ever created could only be unlocked using the one thing she solely possessed in the world—Rell blood.

Ceril drummed his fingers on his knee and nodded toward Efla. She rounded his chair and stood over Suvi.

Suvi swallowed and smiled up at the assassin, trying to hide her growing fear. "Do your worst, woman."

TRAVELING TO ARCTON

Quinn's breath was hot and quick on Nyssa's neck, her fingers digging into her back. Nyssa kept moving, grinding, taking them both to the edge until Quinn muffled a cry against her collarbone, teeth scraping skin. Quinn buried her head in the crook of Nyssa's neck and held tight, Nyssa shuddering against her as she rode out the aftershocks of her orgasm.

The heat between them was a welcome source of warmth in the chill of the night aboard the Cloud Crasher. Winter still very much had its hold on the Empire, and Quinn's skin against hers made Nyssa feel alive and safe. And horny.

Nyssa tumbled off of Quinn, collapsing beside her with a low, grunting laugh. "I think I pulled a muscle," she said, sighing a contented sigh. "I'm too old for this."

Quinn groaned, and a lazy hand fumbled at Nyssa's face, pressing her lips shut. "Shush, you're barely twenty seven. And I was doing quite a bit of work myself."

Nyssa laughed and nipped at Quinn's fingers, drawing a yelp of laughter out of her. "Eh, you did alright."

"I can be on top next time."

This time Nyssa groaned. "We're not planning this out. Takes all the fun out of sex. I like spontaneity!"

"Noted. I'm still figuring all of this out. Slowly."

Nyssa flipped over on her side and propped her head up to gaze at Quinn's green eyes, vibrant in the low light of their cabin. "Look, we're both new to an actual living, breathing relationship with the scary word *love* involved. Between the two of us, we could fuck this up spectacularly."

Quinn chuckled. "I like how much faith you have in us. Really bolsters the confidence."

"Meh," Nyssa said, offering a sly grin. "Speaking of spontaneity, I love when you push me against the wall and fumble at my belt like you've forgotten how fingers work."

"You don't seem to complain about my fingers when they're between your legs."

A laugh burst out of Nyssa, and she clamped her hand over her mouth before stretching toward Quinn to plant a kiss on her cheek.

Quinn let a low hum of contentment rumble in her chest. The sound always drew a smile out of Nyssa. This time was no different. "You're sweaty. You put in a good night's work, warrior."

"I did." Nyssa smiled. She had first proposed they try something different when they were back on the Whisper. When Nyssa had half straddled Quinn, Quinn put her hands behind her head and waited patiently as Nyssa awkwardly tried fitting their bodies together like a puzzle. And when Nyssa rolled her hips, Quinn's hands shot to Nyssa's waist, a surprised "oh!" leaving her lips. The experiment had been a success.

Now Nyssa couldn't get enough, especially when no longer constrained to a small ship bunk and having the benefit of a larger bed afforded by the airship. She loved how intimate the position was, allowing them to lock eyes and chase their pleasure together. And Quinn was definitely a huge proponent as well.

Nyssa slid her hand across Quinn's stomach, lightly caressing her skin and drawing another hum of contentment out of the woman.

Gods, I can't get enough of that sound.

She wished they could stay in the air forever and not land in the last place Nyssa ever wanted Quinn to revisit. But it was time to address the issue. The part of her that wanted to protect Quinn demanded it. "We need to talk."

"That sounds dire."

"I know going back to Arcton is hard for you. And I hate that you have to do this. You have to come to me if you find yourself struggling." She tucked an errant strand of raven hair behind Quinn's ear.

Closing her eyes, Quinn rested a hand on top of Nyssa's. "Whatever Ceril wants is at Arcton. I'll tear the place apart to find it."

Nyssa pressed her palm against Quinn's stomach.

"That means letting Aryis do her work."

With a sigh, Quinn nodded. "I know. And I'll help her. You and I both will. There's too much in the Night Vault for her to go through on her own."

"Thank you," Nyssa breathed. That was all she could ask for. She didn't wish to dwell on the subject of Arcton or Aryis—both put Quinn in a mood. Best she keep the woman's mind off either for as long as she could.

She drew closer to Quinn. "It'll be days before we touch down. We'll have to figure out how to fill our time until then." She teasingly traced her finger up Quinn's stomach and between her breasts. That finger swirled over her nipple, then trailed down her side, tickling her ribs before lighting on her hip.

A rumble vibrated in Quinn's chest, a low growl only Nyssa could tease out. "I have an idea or two."

Sitting up, Nyssa swung her leg over Quinn to straddle her again.

"I was going to take a bath," Quinn said.

Nyssa raised an eyebrow. "I'm not done with you tonight."

"Oh?" The playful lilt in her voice meant mischief—Nyssa's favorite.

Smiling, she reached up and grabbed Quinn's wrists, pinning them to the bed. "Close your eyes."

Quinn did as she was told.

Nyssa brushed her lips against Quinn's before pulling back, making her wait. Next, she teased the base of her neck. Then an earlobe. Her lips roamed, ducking in to tease before pulling away again.

Nyssa bent close to Quinn, her breath hot against her neck. The way Quinn moved and moaned made Nyssa ache with desire as she whispered, "You're mine."

Quinn looked up at her, green eyes blazing. "Always."

THE CITADEL

Quinn shielded her eyes from the sun as the Imperial airship touched down on the outskirts of the Citadel's expansive grounds. She disembarked, followed by Nyssa, Aryis, and the Imperial contingent Safin had insisted on sending along—Ina and four other Ashcloaks, ten Justiciars, and at least forty soldiers who Decia felt were needed to bolster the thirty already assigned to watch over Arcton.

The Emperor was taking the threat of Ceril returning to the Citadel seriously. Good. But Quinn knew the Justiciars were also there to keep an eye on her and Nyssa, not just keep the Citadel safe. She would have to put up with them, same as Aryis.

Quinn turned her eyes to the stark white stone structure of the Citadel that rose in the distance. Perched atop the Eagle's Breath Mountains, it was unreachable save by airship or a three-day-long trek up a mountain pass. The only ways down were those same two avenues, plus the free-fall enchantment off a cliff at the back end of the small forest adjacent to the grounds—the way Quinn had escaped the damned place to begin her strange journey.

She pulled her scarf tighter around her neck. The winter up on Eagle's Breath was wholly different from anywhere else, its cold lonely and bracing in a way that no amount of clothes or blankets could ever truly dispel.

Gods, how she *hated* it.

Nyssa walked beside her, perhaps closer than usual. Quinn didn't have to look over to know the woman was keeping an eye on her.

The Citadel grew closer as they trudged through the snow. A long, round driveway made of paver stones encircled the front of the estate, the massive building rising behind it built partway into the mountain. In the center of the path sat a statue of a man studying a book, an inscription etched at his feet—*To Those Who Seek The Knowledge Of The Future, Those Of The Past Embrace Your Journey.*

The wing of the Citadel where her old room resided was off on the side of the building closest to the forest. The same dead, strangled garden sat at its base. How the seconds of running through those desiccated plants had stretched on for an eternity when she'd fled, her heartbeat pounding in her ears. The risk of getting caught had tugged at her heels as she escaped into the forest and leaped off the cliff into the unknown darkness.

Guards stood outside the entrance to the Citadel, waiting. Adepts young and old gathered in the driveway in small groups, their quiet conversations swept away on puffs of frosty air.

One man strode toward them through the snow, his shaggy hair a touch grayer from the last time Quinn had seen Master Ludov. She'd had little interaction with him in the twenty-five years they spent under the same roof.

Ludov raised a hand in greeting, pausing when he spotted Quinn, his hand drifting back down to his side. The blood drained from his face.

Ina led their entourage to the man, who stood nervously glancing Quinn's direction before straightening up.

"First Master Ludov," Ina greeted, shaking the man's hand.

First Master? What had the drunk done to earn such a coveted role?

"Welcome to Arcton Citadel. And welcome back to some," he said, bowing his head slightly to Quinn. "By the size of your group, I suspect you fear Anelos will return here?"

Quinn squinted at him. "Yes, most likely." She pushed past him and continued toward the Citadel's entrance. The rest of them followed.

Aryis spoke up. "We will need full access to the Citadel, First Master. Nothing is off-limits, including your office."

"My office?"

"It was once Ceril's, and anything of his, we want to see. Journals, papers, files...no matter how meaningless you think they may be. He was searching for something and likely kept a collection of notes that will hopefully point us in the direction he was looking."

At least Aryis was proving good for something—keeping Quinn from having to explain what they needed. The less she had to deal with the Citadel's personnel, the better. Most of them who were here at the same time as she was had turned a blind eye to Ceril's treatment of her. No one questioned why she was kept on a solitary wing of the estate. Nor did anyone raise the issue of why an adept was kept in a void collar—a clear violation of guild rules. But Ceril was imposing, a controlling First Master who was cold to everyone. So no one interfered or raised their voices on Quinn's behalf.

And once they got a taste of her weak magick-suppressing powers, they feared her. That was Ceril's doing as well, experimenting using her magick on others when she was very young. She never got a chance to make a friend because of it.

"I have prepared rooms in the guest quarters for everyone," Ludov said.

"Have your head of security and the commander of the soldiers see me immediately," Ruggen said. "I'm now in charge of keeping Arcton safe."

"Certainly, Master Ashcloak."

As Quinn and the others drew closer to the Citadel, the crunch of old snow gave way to the grit of paver stones. The conversations among the adepts ceased, their eyes all on Quinn and Nyssa. The youngest ones huddled together.

"Back inside!" Ludov said to the adepts. "Your studies have not ceased merely because we have guests."

The guildies did as they were told, filing back inside the Citadel, casting glances over their shoulders.

"This place shines like the sun," Nyssa said, her eyes lit up, glowing impressively herself, and blue shards of energy arcing off her skin.

Quinn followed suit, turning her attention to the building. Runes had been etched into the stones used to build the place, pulsating with whatever enchantment was laid atop the stone. Those runes held on to magick longer, strengthening the wards that protected the Citadel.

A myriad of colors swirled around the structure, lines crisscrossing its exterior. When needed, the estate could be locked up and the wards activated. Only a prolonged attack could make a dent in them.

"Do you see that?" Nyssa asked.

At the back of the Citadel, where it merged with the mountain, rose a tower that glowed blue. Definitely a much different magickal resonance than the wards clinging to the building.

"That's the Beckwit Tower," Quinn replied. "I've never been inside. It was always strictly off-limits to all adepts." She turned to Ludov. "What's in there?"

Ludov looked taken aback. "I...it's not..."

"Answer her," Ina said, stepping forward.

"I've never seen what's inside myself, but I was told it's not entirely of this realm."

Ina scowled. "That's not an answer."

Ludov shifted his feet. "It's a Primalith Shard. Are you familiar?"

Nyssa nodded. "Very. This one...I can feel it vibrating on the edge of my senses."

"It's the Spire of Heaven," a tinny voice said.

A golden sphere about the size of a small fist zoomed out of the front door and hovered in the air.

"Curator?" Quinn asked.

"Quinn?" The Curator asked. "Is that you, my friend?"

For the first time since arriving at the Citadel, Quinn smiled. "It's me."

"You've been away. I have missed you."

Aryis circled The Curator, her face lighting up with delight. "A self-aware construct? These are very rare." She reached out, but The Curator dodged her fingers.

"One does not touch if one does not ask with a polite tone of voice," the orb said.

"It looks like the Hummingbird a bit," Aryis said.

"Ah, you've met the Hummingbird? A rather one-dimensional tool he is, an honest construct would say. Not to disparage him, of course."

Aryis scowled. "Curator is an interesting moniker. The Lythrosii agents are called Curators...is there a connection?"

"My creator had no love for the Lythrosii. My name is meant as an insult to them. I do know when they come to visit, they seem less than pleased in my presence, though my name is befitting my role here at Arcton."

Quinn chuckled. "I'd like you to meet my...friends." Quinn introduced Nyssa and Aryis to The Curator.

"You have friends now, Quinn. How nice. There was a time I was your only friend."

Quinn kept her smile steady but couldn't ignore the heat rising in her cheeks.

Aryis seemed undeterred by The Curator's admonishment of her. "This Spire of Heaven—I had heard rumors of a Primalith Shard running through the mountain. I didn't realize it was visible from our realm."

"Visible and very dangerous," The Curator replied. "The tower was built around the shard that protrudes from the mountain in order to protect it. The Spire of Heaven is older than the Citadel, this mountain, and the very earth itself. It is the remnants of a dead star."

A breath of surprise left Nyssa, and she smiled up at the old tower. "It's beautiful." Quinn admired Nyssa's constant appreciation of magick, that world opening up for her the minute she exploded with power.

"We're here to access the library and the vaults, Curator," Quinn said.

The orb shifted in the air, moving back and forth. "All the vaults, my friend?"

"Yes."

"Ah, exciting times for The Curator, then! Come, let's get started!" It jerked in the air toward the Citadel, then waited.

"We have to visit the First Master's office and then get settled," Quinn replied. "But perhaps this evening?"

"I look forward to seeing you then, Quinn." The orb zipped back through the open doors of the Citadel.

"Ludov, please take us to your office," Ina requested.

The moment they stepped over the threshold to the Citadel, a chill ran through Quinn. She resented how her body reacted to the place, as if it controlled her. The main foyer and the hallways were just as she remembered them—woodsy and bright, light oak covering the walls, plenty of light orbs keeping the shadows relegated to the corners.

The soldiers they had brought with them peeled off with an Ashcloak under instruction from Ina to set up guard rotations. Two of the ten Justiciars who had flown to the Citadel with Quinn and the others accompanied them, those remaining dispersing.

As Quinn walked to the First Master's office, a place she had come to hate the very sight of, she could feel Nyssa's eyes on her. This was her reality now—attention keenly focused on her to make sure she was okay.

Okay. Such a fucking impotent word. She would never be okay inside these walls.

"We need to let Cardin know we've arrived and that the Citadel is secure," Aryis explained while she walked beside Ludov. "We'll be going through all your files in the office, so if there's anything Ceril left behind, we'll start there first."

"Understood. I'll do my best to stay out of your way, but understand we need to continue our adepts' studies. The events of the past few weeks have shaken some confidence in our mission here, given the Arch Master's—"

"He's no longer the Arch Master," Ina said, her voice cold. "He is a traitor and fugitive from the law."

Ludov scowled at her but nodded. "I know."

"If there is anyone here who holds any loyalty for that man, you will tell the Justiciars. We will not tolerate sedition."

Ludov stopped walking and turned to them. "Let me assure you, right here and now, that Ceril Anelos has no friends here. Even when he was First Master, he barely tolerated his own peers." His eyes lit upon the Justiciars before returning to Ina. "I'm insulted you would think anyone at this esteemed guild would be loyal to a man who used the very secrets we're supposed to protect to visit horrors upon the citizens of this Empire."

It seemed Ludov at least had some pride.

Ina's expression didn't change. "Regardless, we will be questioning everyone."

"We already had a Justiciar interrogate all adepts and staff."

"And we will ask our questions again," one of the two Justiciars who had accompanied their party said.

Ludov huffed and started toward his office again. When they arrived, the door stood open. The room was illuminated by a small fire glowing in the fireplace, its flames dancing off the glass of the opposite wall of cabinets. Gone were the books and various magickal items that Ceril had collected, replaced by a good quantity of liquor bottles.

The desk was messy. Ceril had been fastidious, not one paper out of place. Not one errant piece of lint to mar his sanctuary. Ludov was the exact opposite, which somehow made being inside the office somewhat bearable. It felt lived in by an actual person rather than the sterile space of a monster.

Quinn glanced to the bank of windows behind the desk that over-looked an interior garden bound by the walls of the Citadel. Her eyes drifted down, and she stilled. On a credenza underneath the windows sat a void collar. Even from across the room, Quinn recognized it. She had stared at it in the mirror for a decade, studying it, trying to figure out how to get out of it, finally using a purloined fork as a lockpick. It took her months of frustration to unlock the damn thing. Of course it was still here. Anything containing Coldlight was rare and valuable.

She moved around the desk and picked it up, the metal cold to the touch. Darkness flowed out of her without effort, and she wrapped the cords of shadow around the collar. It trembled in her hand and she gritted her teeth. A moment later, it shattered, its pieces clinking on the worn wood floor of the office.

Shadow billowed off of Quinn and filled the office, spreading out across the floor. Ludov's mouth popped open, and the Justiciars gripped the hilts of their daggers tight. They weren't just cautious—they were scared.

If she wanted to, she could shred the office to pieces. Instead, she calmed her magick, pulling it back into her core.

Quinn raised her eyes. Nyssa's face was darkened with worry.

"Let's contact Cardin, shall we?" Aryis suggested.

Quinn turned back to the windows, watching as the snow began to drift from the sky.

Nyssa trailed Quinn through the Citadel. She hadn't been invited along, but she thought it best to not let Quinn wander alone. After they had combed through the First Master's office, finding nothing they could use, Ludov had shown them to their guest quarters. Once unpacked, Quinn sat on the edge of the bed for a long time, staring down at her hands, before excusing herself.

The line between being concerned and overprotective was one Nyssa would blur while at the Citadel. She needed to keep Quinn safe from the demons that awaited her here. So Nyssa followed her, staying a good distance away. If Quinn found her overbearing, Nyssa would deal with that later.

The Citadel was nicer than she expected, clean and tidy. The place carried its age well, old but not dingy, though it buzzed with magick and it made Nyssa's skin tingle. Strong magick could be intrusive and push against her senses. Probably in the same way her emotions poked through Reece's barriers.

Quinn weaved her way through the corridors of the Citadel, heading to the rear of the estate. The temperature fell and the lights grew dimmer as Nyssa followed. She peered into the rooms she passed, some empty, others with sparse collections of furniture hidden under white sheets.

"Where the fuck are you going?" Nyssa whispered to herself. Quinn would eventually notice her, not that she was trying hard to remain hidden, but once she got too close, she would be found out through their connection.

At the end of a long corridor, only half of its light orbs illuminated, Quinn disappeared up a winding staircase. Nyssa followed, running her hands along the wall to guide her, the light almost nonexistent in the spiraling tower. The white stone was cold to the touch and vibrated slightly under her fingertips.

The top of the steps opened up into another corridor. Like the ones below, the rooms Nyssa passed were empty, save for a bed or two, dingy furniture, or storage crates. Quinn was nowhere in sight, and Nyssa began to worry.

As she neared the end of the hall, warmth spread through her chest. She smiled, the comfort of Quinn's presence a relief. Nyssa came to a stop in front of the last door. Inside stood Quinn, her outline framed against the window, sunlight barely piercing the dark interior of the room. Dust motes hung in the weak rays of light, swirling at the disturbance of their presence.

Nyssa leaned against the doorway and looked around the dim interior. There was a small bed, a chest of drawers, and a writing desk with a rickety chair. The walls were full of white squares, which she found odd. She narrowed her eyes, getting used to the low light, and hesitantly moved into the room to inspect a wall.

Pieces of paper were tacked on it, each one containing a sketch. One was a singular flower with delicate petals. Another was a fish under a ripple of water. And yet another was a sketch of a hand, its skin marred by small scars. Picture after picture hung on the wall, each one a treasure that made a lump rise in Nyssa's throat.

"This one is you," Quinn said, moving to the wall opposite the door and pointing to a square of paper.

Nyssa stepped closer and peered at the sketch. Two glowing blue eyes stared back at her.

"I had dreams of those eyes in shadow. But I could never make the face out. For the longest time, I thought it was a nightmare, or a warning of a monster I needed to watch out for. Now I know those are your eyes."

Nyssa turned to Quinn. "You never told me that."

"Because those dreams happened here, in this place. I didn't want to remember anything from Arcton."

"All this art...it's beautiful, Quinn."

Quinn moved away, back to the window. "They didn't change a thing about this room after I ran away. As if they were just waiting to bring me back. Collar me again."

"Are you okay?" Nyssa asked, hating the banality of the question.

"I will never be okay in this place." Quinn turned and pointed to the chair at the writing table. "That's the chair Ceril tied me to when he whipped me. I didn't even bother to scrub the blood off it. I figured, what was the point? Ceril could punish me again at his whim."

Even shrouded in shadow, Nyssa could see the pain on Quinn's face.

"I hate that we had to come here," she said. "I'm so sorry. I..." The words died on her tongue. What could she say to soothe any of the sting of this place? She moved to offer a hug, a touch...anything that would help.

Quinn put her palm on Nyssa's chest, stopping her. "No."

Nyssa swallowed and took a step back.

Quinn hung her head. "In this moment, in this *fucking* room, the last thing I want is the woman I love to see me like this. To see how much...hate is in me."

Her face wavered. She didn't cry often, instead choosing to suck in her emotions and present a calm, even face to the world, hiding her pain behind a wall. This Nyssa knew all too well, having spent over two years getting to know the ins and outs of Quinn's moods and expressions. And she had spent so much time clawing at that wall, trying to get to Quinn, to truly understand her. It felt as though that wall was going back up, making Nyssa's heart ache.

"I want to be here for you," she said, her voice soft.

"I know."

Silence hung between them, Quinn's eyes dim in the low light.

"I'll leave you, then. I'll be in our room."

Nyssa left and headed back down the corridor to the stairwell, lightning leaping to the surface of her skin in time with her building anger. What this place—what Ceril—had done to Quinn, pushing joy and love out of her, filling her instead with rage and hate...

Nyssa wanted to lash out. To *destroy*.

She ran her hand along the wall, lightning arcing across the cold stone, scorching its white surface, leaving a jagged black trail of anger behind her.

THE SUN PALACE'S NEW GUESTS

Medias had warned Reece about the opulence of the Sun Palace, but never having been in Cardin, she didn't quite know what to expect. The shiny white marble competed with the gleaming gold appointments that seemed to gild everything in sight. There was little by way of restraint to the Palace.

Ocean's Rest had a warmth to it, its Keep softened by Lilliana's decor and improvements over the years. It was a functional seat of power—and a home. But Cardin was almost sterile in comparison, its streets pristine, the buildings matching the ivory tones of the Sun Palace. The neon signs and loud streets of Ocean's Rest were absent here, replaced instead by understated blue and gold accents to draw the eye and hopefully shoppers' money to the shops, eateries, and attractions of the city.

Reece took everything in as she, Medias, and Athen trailed behind Safin, Decia, and each representative of the Sun Council.

The only flaw—and it was a big one—was the destruction in the foyer. Shattered statues and massive decapitated heads littered the corridor.

"Was this you?" Reece whispered to Athen.

"Oops," he replied with a grimace.

"They haven't been removed?"

"The Palace was locked down by the Justiciars and Ashcloaks after Kalla's death, running on a skeleton crew," Medias replied. "The staff has been called back now that the Justiciars have returned and there is a new Emperor."

"Who is that?" Athen asked, indicating a man who cut quite an imposing figure. Close-cropped, tight, white curls sat atop his head, and his skin was dark with lighter spots. He bowed low to Safin, righting himself with a smile on his face, welcoming the Emperor back to the Palace.

"Master Ashcloak Helo. An honorable man. He came up in the Order with First Master Eron. My mother trusts him implicitly. Don't let the affable smile fool you. He can kill you faster than you can blink. May be the best fighter the Emerald Order has produced in years."

"Nyssa might have something to say about that," Athen replied.

"You've never seen him in action. He can move faster than normal in short bursts—that's his magickal ability. Lethal in close combat."

As they trailed behind the Sun Council, several of its number kept glancing back at their little unwelcome party of three. A fallen Justiciar and two members of a barely recognized House from the wild city of Ocean's Rest must have felt like an intrusion in these halls of power. The collective body of the Sun Council had been courteous and smiled politely while taking up temporary residence in Ocean's Rest, but now that House Fennick and Medias were in their territory, their attitude had shifted. They were the dingy, chipped flowerpot beside a dazzling display of flawless vases.

But mistrust for a lowly House wasn't the only thing at play, of that Reece was convinced. She concentrated and opened her senses. Emotions washed over her, plentiful but muted, tinged by caution. No one in the Sun Council wanted her in their midst. Secrets were secrets, but *their* secrets were held tighter than most.

A few stronger emotions drifted her way. Not just disdain, but a simmering resentment. Even a bit of anger. And...something else. Fear? All the Great Houses had something to hide, but this felt like more than mere protectiveness of one's House.

It was impossible to zero on who was feeling what, causing a bit of frustration for Reece. There was most likely some low-level disruptor spell in play, easily enchanted onto jewelry, and much like Amberis, it could throw her off.

Reece glanced to Medias who met her gaze, lifting an eyebrow. Very few exchanges between them went without subtext, and Medias seemed to read Reece better than anyone. If only she could better read Medias in return. Since spending that one night together, entangled in pleasure, Medias had turned cold.

No, not cold exactly. Reece knew cold, having sensed it in prior lovers, affection slowly draining away. Medias was—reticent. What had she said? *You keep pushing me, thinking you'll find something in me that'll make me...worthy of you.*

Perhaps Medias was scared after what Reece saw her do in Ocean's Rest, systematically prying that Obsidian Rule assassin apart, getting him to confess his secrets. Did Medias think Reece now viewed her as a monster?

I don't. I never could.

Or maybe, in that cell underneath the Keep, Medias finally saw Reece as weak, her ability to sense emotions in others making her too sympathetic to their suffering. But even the worst people had a moment where they broke open and their fear and regret spilled out.

In times when a hard decision had to be made, could Reece be strong for Medias? Could she be depended on, or would she always err on the side of mercy?

"You have a look on your face, empath," Medias said, her voice low.

"Later," she replied, sharing a glance with Athen, who gave her a nod. His emotions were a low boil, but she didn't need to be an empath to know he was torn between his duty to his family and wanting to be with Aryis at Arcton, even if at arm's length from one another. Years of growing up together, brother and sister in all but blood, gave her a unique insight into the big man's moods. And into his massive heart.

Athen loved Aryis, Reece knew that. But alongside that love sat a resentment that ran deep. She couldn't blame him. Aryis had made her choice, but it cut both ways—at least that's how Reece saw it. Aryis had sacrificed Nyssa and Quinn to feed her people. A cruel, impossible situation to be forced into.

"What's this?" Athen asked as Palace guards stepped in front of the three of them, cutting them off from Safin, the Sun Council, and the rest of the procession while they moved deeper into the Sun Palace.

"This is as far as we are allowed to go," Medias explained, eyeing the guards who stood wordlessly in their way. "Once an Ascension date has been put in place, the Emperor sequesters himself in the Aura to prepare for his reign. The Sun Counsel will be busy as well."

The Sun Counsel would be meeting to set an agenda for the early days of Safin's rule, and such an agenda would entail a great deal of arguments and late nights. She had no doubt that Safin's patience and lack of experience would be tested during his first months on the throne. Every House's little pet project would be trotted out, demanding attention and funds from Safin. All the Great Houses desired to continue thriving, and that always meant finding ways to direct gold into their coffers.

A Palace attendant appeared behind the guards, who parted to let her through. Streaks of gray and a face mapped with well-worn creases, along with a sense of patience and order that flowed off of her, set Reece somewhat at ease.

"I am Chamberlain Vishan Pace. I oversee the management of the Palace. Should you want anything, there are a number of attendants at your service, so you need only ask. Now, please follow me to your rooms."

"Actually, Athen, could you follow the Chamberlain and settle in?" Medias asked. "I'd like to show Reece something."

Athen hesitated but didn't object.

"Please contain yourselves to the outer chambers of the Palace. The Aura is for the Imperial retinue and the Great Houses," Vishan said with a polite smile.

"Understood," Medias replied.

Reece found it galling. How were they supposed to get close to the Sun Council like this?

"What are we doing?" Reece asked as Vishan led Athen away, attendants scurrying after with their bags, their emotions roiling from caution to curiosity.

"Come."

Medias maneuvered through the Palace, Reece at her side. As they walked together, heads turned their way, Medias's status as a fallen Justiciar unheard of for centuries. No Justiciar since Eliza Rell had been labeled a traitor. One common emotion cascaded over Reece as they passed through the Palace: fear.

Even with her mask stripped, Medias still commanded fear.

Eventually, Medias led them to an exterior door that opened onto a path. It wound through a tall hedgerow and deposited them in an expansive garden on the backside of the Palace. In the middle of that garden stood a massive glass structure that spanned the entirety of Reece's view. The late afternoon sun's rays glinted against that glass, creating a kaleidoscope of colors that illuminated the snow surrounding what Reece realized was a gigantic arboretum.

The colors, caused by the stained-glass rim, took Reece's breath away. It sparkled in the sun like a jewel. Whatever craftsperson had designed the structure had a keen eye for beauty, and the effect was spectacular.

A smile she couldn't deny crossed Reece's face. "Is that the Garden of the Sun?"

"Yes. Would you like to go inside?" Medias asked, her eyes trained on Reece.

"I would love to."

Reece walked next to Medias, trying to remain patient and contain the excitement that rippled through her, but it was difficult. The Garden of the Sun had plants and flowers from across the world, some reportedly rather rare and exotic.

She also fought off the desire to thread her arm around Medias's elbow and pull her close while they walked. They weren't *together*. She had to remember that, Medias setting herself apart physically while always keeping an eye on Reece.

Her thoughts trailed away as they approached the doors of the Garden of the Sun. Medias led them inside. Reece stopped in her tracks, her eyes darting everywhere. There was simply too much to see. And the scents—*oh gods, the scents*—she closed her eyes and breathed deep, drinking in the rich fragrances surrounding her. A deep, earthy scent laid the foundation for fruit notes and the perfume from a myriad of flowers.

She opened her eyes and hurried forward, weaving between various beds, visiting each section, marveling at the beauty of each plant—some known to her, some completely foreign, others exceedingly rare. She could spend the whole afternoon going from plant to plant and only see an eighth of the arboretum. Orchids, roses, daises, violets...vivid purples and blues, bright yellows, pinks and reds, and pristine white. Green, her favorite color, was everywhere, vines and vegetation filling the spaces between flowers.

Several plants gave her pause, having never seen them before. And a few she recognized from chromoimages or drawings in the books strewn on her shelves in her office back home.

A particular flower caught her eye, its large bloom, mostly purple with whorls of white, shaped like a cat's head. Reece bent over it, taking a generous inhale of its scent—black licorice. Gods, how she loved it. "Is this a Spiral Poppy from the Insimia Desert?"

"You ask as if I would know," Medias replied from the end of the row.

Reece had felt the woman trailing behind her as she darted from one plant to another. Patiently watching, as always. Over nearly two years, she had grown accustomed to that gaze, unwavering and bold. Never had Medias shied away from direct eye contact—it had almost become a challenge between the two of them.

But lately, she would look away whenever Reece met her gaze.

The silent tension between them had become annoying. As much as Reece loved to be in the Garden of the Sun, among some of the most beautiful plants from around the world, she found her attention focused back on Medias.

"Why did you bring me here, Sentinel?"

Medias cleared her throat and let her eyes wander over the contents of the arboretum. "Given your fondness for plants and flowers, I thought you might find something of interest here."

"You brought me to this beautiful place knowing I'd love it?" Reece straightened up, brushing her fingers across a brilliant red flower with the white spirals, before capturing Medias in her gaze. "What exactly is going on between us?"

Medias set her shoulders. "We are in Cardin at Safin's behest. I would prefer we remain focused on—"

"Bullshit!"

The word rang out louder than Reece would have liked.

Medias scowled but didn't offer a response.

Maddening.

Reece stalked toward her and stopped, folding her arms across her body, ignoring the impulse to grab hold and shake her. Embrace her. Kiss her.

"Back in Ocean's Rest, you seemed very clear on what you wanted from me. That night, in your room, you could have let me leave. But you stopped me. And we...had sex, made love, fucked— I don't know what that was to you." Reece took a deep breath. "But it meant something to me. And when I woke up, you were gone. I can't explain how much that hurt."

Medias blinked a few times. Always so *fucking* measured and in control—though Reece had seen her unmoored, her control and calm abandoned in equal measure when they had their night together. Where had *that* Medias retreated to?

"I didn't bring you here to discuss...our past actions," Medias replied.

Reece almost winced. What an innocuous way to refer to their night together. A night she replayed in her mind often. Too often.

"Tell me what you want from me, Medias."

"We have some privacy here, away from the eyes and ears of the Palace. I'd like to know what you're picking up from the Sun Council so we can—"

"No, you're avoiding my question again." Reece let out a sharp breath and shook her head. "You can't keep avoiding the subject."

"A subject that I don't wish to discuss. A subject that has no pertinence to our purpose here in Cardin."

Reece stepped closer, her patience waning. "I bet you would love to put your mask back on right now so you could hide from me again."

A rush of air left Medias. "You need to put aside this issue for the time being so we can talk about how to proceed here at the Palace."

"I don't understand how you can be so callous."

"I warned you in Ocean's Rest, I'm not what you need."

Reece narrowed her eyes. "Are you trying to protect me?"

"You've seen what I'm capable of."

"You think I haven't known what you're capable of? I don't *care*. You must have a low opinion of me if you think I can't accept you as you are."

"No, I—"

"What are you two up to in here?" Athen's voice rang out.

Reece whipped her head around to find him striding toward them. She turned back around to Medias brightening, rescued from the conversation.

Reece ground her teeth, not thankful for the interruption at all.

"I was impressing upon Reece the need to be focused while here in Cardin. We have no friends in the Palace aside from Safin and my mother. We cannot afford to get distracted by trivial matters."

Athen sat on a nearby bench and spread his arms across the back of it, breaking out into a wide smile when butterflies fluttered around him, their iridescent blue and orange wings brightening the air surrounding him, giving off a slight glow.

He reached out toward them and wiggled his fingers, and the butterflies dipped and hovered just out of his reach. "We know Reece has sensed something unsavory from the Sun Council, we just don't know from whom yet. They're screwing with your magick, right?"

Reece nodded.

He continued, "With Ceril running free and Safin's tenuous position as a new Emperor, this could be the perfect storm for a political shift."

Reece scowled at Athen. "A political shift? That's a rather tame way to say coup. Or assassination. Or—"

Medias moved closer to Reece and lowered her voice. "You keep those words to yourself until we know exactly what it is you're sensing, empath."

Reece sighed. Medias would be cautious, but the situation called for action, not holding back and waiting for something to happen. Doing so could spell disaster for Safin. "What are we supposed to do, then? We can't get into the Aura and near the Council anymore."

"Well, I have an idea," Athen said. "It won't get us into the Aura, but you know who will have all the best gossip?" He smirked at Reece. "Every single person working at the Sun Palace who the rich assholes in the Council see as below them."

"The invisibles," Reece said. When Medias gave her a puzzled look, she explained. "It's slang among the staff of places like Ocean's Keep or this Palace. We did our best to not make them feel that way."

"Exactly," Athen replied. "And I'm going to see if I can make some new friends. Work my charm, maybe get a little information."

Reece considered it. "That's a fantastic idea."

"You two seem to have this sorted," Medias said. "I have to attend to some business." Without another word, she left.

The Sun Palace was a massive place, and Reece was sure there were plenty of dark corners for Medias to retreat to where she wouldn't be bothered and could avoid being alone with Reece.

"Bit of a chill between you two of late," Athen said. Reece frowned at him, and he shrugged. "What? I have eyes...well, *an* eye. But more importantly, I know you, sis. You're in love with our Sentinel."

He knew. Of course he knew. Hiding anything from Athen was impossible.

Reece's shoulders drooped. "Athen, I'm stuck. You're right about me, but love seems to mean fuck all to Medias."

"Well, have you...told her how you feel?"

"Athen! I...I just—" Reece shook her head and sighed louder than intended. "It's complicated."

"How do I always seem to be the one you women confide in?" He leaned forward and peered at a butterfly that had landed on his knee. "You know, I was in much the same position, watching Nyssa and Quinn dance around each other like idiots."

Reece blew out an exasperated puff of air. *Idiots.* It was too mild an insult to describe her and Medias. "I'm sorry, Athen. I know this must be hard for you, given your...what do you and Aryis have right now, exactly?"

He spread his arms wide. "A thing. I can confidently classify it as a *thing*." He let his arms fall, careful not to crush any butterflies as they drifted around him. "I don't know. Shouldn't we be worried about keeping Safin out of danger instead of our personal relationship woes?"

Reece shuffled over to Athen and dropped onto the bench beside him, disturbing the butterflies. They swirled in the air around her. "That sounds like you're avoiding the subject."

"Since when did my asking after you and Medias become about me? Who's avoiding the subject now?"

She leaned against him. "How is it Nyssa has the most stable relationship of the three of us?"

Athen chuckled. "Certainly not due to our example."

"Nope. We're failures." Reece unfocused her eyes, letting the butterflies and their soft glow lull her for a moment.

Athen turned serious. "What are we doing here, Reece? We're in way over our heads."

Imperial politics weren't exactly easy to navigate. "Lilliana has faith in us. We can help keep Safin safe." At least that was Reece's belief.

"Can we?"

She turned to him. "You're the one who keeps us all on task, Athen. Our foundation. Don't start doubting us now."

"I'm not the foundation, Reece." His eyebrows stitched up.

"You are. Don't ever doubt that we lean on you far more than you lean on us."

He sat back with a pensive look. After he returned from the Emerald Order at the age of twenty-two, Reece and Athen had settled into a quiet, slow rhythm of getting to know each other again—as siblings and as adults. He had spent so much time away at the Order under Eron Greye's watchful eye, forming a bond with Nyssa that Reece was, for a fleeting moment, jealous of. But Athen had grown into a man who she had come to admire more than she could say.

"You're a good man, Athen. A *good* man. Safin trusts you. What's more, his heart is in the right place—we saw that with Medias. He's got the potential to be a great leader, but if anything happens to him now, I'm scared of what the political ramifications might be. The struggle for the throne could tear this nation apart."

"Then we keep him safe as best we can. We be there for him and face whatever danger these backbiting Sun Council assholes pose."

"Yes, we will." Reece reached over and squeezed Athen's hand. She let her walls down and reached out, ever so slightly, with her magick, to take the measure of him. "And you'll be there for Aryis when she needs you. That's who you are. Even if you two aren't together, I know you still care for her."

He nodded, though doubt colored his emotions. Stronger, though, was the spike of love Reece sensed at the mention of Aryis's name.

AN UNRULY DINNER

S uvi picked at her food, tongue flicking over her split lip. Her time in Ceril's company had ranged from frustrating to intensely unpleasant. He had no compunction about letting his underlings hurt her as they tried to extract information from her, apparently lacking the will to do it himself.

Coward.

She denied the existence of a sixth Alabaster Book as Ceril's assassins kept trying to get the secret out of her. The secret her family had kept for centuries. Not that it made much of a difference now—she had no idea where Eliza Rell hid the damn thing, thankfully protecting the world from its dangerous, experimental magick.

Eliza had been one of the smart ones, understanding how the spells they'd created could be used and twisted to disastrous effects. She also sacrificed her legacy and life for the family, standing fast against Imperial forces as the rest escaped to Thu'Dain.

Now this arrogant fool sitting across from her, who could barely weave a passable cosmetic spell to appear younger, believed he had a right to Rell magick.

Ceril peered over his wine glass at Suvi. These little meals were nothing more than a power play. Him trying to whittle away at her, her denying knowledge of the book. It was a boring, predictable dance. One that she never would have bothered with were the situations reversed. Torture was always the best way to get what she wanted out of a reluctant subject.

Over many meals, she had wondered why a man like him, after what he had done—including turning a class of mere children into bloodthirsty, mindless killers—wouldn't torture her until she was more than willing to say anything.

Perhaps he was cautious because he needed her. No, not *her* so much as her blood. Rell blood would get past the wards and traps her family had woven to protect their magick. No one was more arrogant about protecting their property than her family—and it made sense, given the blood spilled and flesh shredded by her ancestors as they practiced their craft. Mistakes were often deadly.

"How long do you think you have before your Imperial friends find and kill you?" Suvi asked, sniffing her glass of wine. Pure swill. As befitting a fugitive hiding away in a run-down home in the middle of nowhere. She tipped her glass over, pouring the wine onto the floor next to her. Another stain to add to the others.

Fingers dug into her hair and yanked her head back. Efla stared down at her, the woman's patience fraying.

Finally.

Suvi smashed the top of the wine glass against the table and jabbed the jagged stem at Efla's throat. Efla caught her wrist, grabbed a handful of hair, and slammed Suvi's head into the table for her trouble. Stars swam before her eyes. Vaguely aware of her throbbing nose and hoping it wasn't broken, Suvi did her best to smile up at Ceril.

Give no quarter. Show no weakness. Words her father, Teodor Rell, had spoken to her right before the siege on Ocean's Rest that cost them the war and him his life. That sentiment led to his death. And she'd follow him before she gave Ceril anything. Even if her defiance hurt like a bitch.

Hot, metallic blood filled her mouth and was swallowed back.

Show no weakness…

"The magick my family died protecting isn't for men like you. Small men with their eyes set on power. That's all people like you seem capable of, your desires limited by a paltry imagination," she said, leaning forward. Blood dripped down onto the table in front of her. A shattered plate lay before her. *Ah, my face did that.*

"So you're keeping the sixth book from me. As I thought." Ceril smirked as if he had won and sipped his wine. "I have studied everything in the Night Vault five times over. I know that book exists."

Conceding its existence seemed necessary. Getting beat for denying it was becoming tiresome. A lie she couldn't keep up.

"I don't know where it is," she said, holding her head up even as she gripped the table to keep from falling over.

He smirked. "Now we're making progress." He sliced through a piece of chicken and stuck it in his mouth, chewing it as he considered her. Chickens seemed to be the only thing plentiful in this gods-forsaken place. Chicken and sewer wine. "Where is it?"

Suvi sneered, the wrinkling up of her nose making her hiss with pain. "I don't know."

"So you claim. Which one of your ancestors hid it?"

He didn't know? Good.

"Another bit of family history I'm not privy to," she replied. Keeping her voice steady to sell the lie proved difficult. Ceril's eyes shifted to Efla, who stood behind Suvi, ready to strike again. Like a good lapdog. Suvi turned her head to the side. "What has he promised you, woman?"

"Blacksea," Ceril replied.

"Oh? Seems a small prize for risking your life to betray the Empire."

Efla rustled behind her. "Blacksea killed my brother."

Suvi chuckled, risking the assassin's wrath. "Seems you and I are kindred spirits, my dear. Nyssa killed my brother as well. If you ever want to be *my* lapdog instead of Ceril's, you need only remove this collar."

A loud sigh rumbled out of Ceril. "Before I promised her Blacksea's life, I promised Efla a seat at the table. When I rule, I will make her Arch Assassin."

Suvi reached for the wine bottle and took a long drink. It wasn't good, but she was parched and needed the soothing buzz of alcohol. "Make no mistake, Efla, he will never give you what you want. Men like him do not share."

"Men like me..." Ceril shook his head, a self-satisfied grin on his face. "You would gladly accept my help if I extended it, Suvi. You were hoping we could be allies. Maybe take down Nyssa together?"

She smiled and took another swig of the gutter wine. It didn't get smoother. "I want Nyssa and Quinn's heads."

"Ah, yes, Nyssa will die."

"How do you plan on killing a god? I tried. She's far more powerful than you realize."

Ceril seemed unconcerned. "Efla will be more than ready for her this time."

"And Quinn?"

"Quinn I want alive. She is my prodigy. I will deal with her."

Suvi scowled. "You were willing to kill her before, were you not? What's changed?"

"Let's say I've taken a bit of inspiration from you, my dear Queen. You had the right idea, caging Quinn. She's a weapon to be used to make the world tremble, and I intend to do just that." The smirk and light laugh that accompanied his assertion sent a chill through Suvi. He meant to use Quinn. As he had always done since she was a child, from what intelligence Suvi had gathered while still on the throne.

Not that she cared about Quinn's welfare, having proved to be a stubborn, troublesome woman. But if Ceril had a Cursed God on a leash and Rell magick at his fingertips, he could do tremendous damage. Make others suffer. She had never fancied herself much of an altruistic person, for it was an untenable position to lead from, but she was, at the very least, a realist.

Rell magick didn't belong in the hands of anyone like Ceril Anelos. Hell, her own family had locked it away on purpose, understanding its danger. They weren't hungry for power as the Areshi Empire's history books claimed. They simply didn't know how to contain what they had created.

They feared the power—rightfully so—yet were still too proud to destroy what they had wrought.

Suvi chuckled at the damn irony. Pride had driven her family to wage war against the Areshi Empire, set on taking back their country. And that same pride had destroyed them all because they couldn't just burn a goddamn *book*.

Ceril peered at her over the top of his glass before swirling the swamp wine within. "Understand that I will find that book. Your usefulness wanes the more you impede me. On the other hand, your blood is extremely valuable. With a little help, it will lead me to what I want."

Suvi didn't react. No show of fear. She wouldn't give him the satisfaction of a queen trembling before him. But there was no doubt that he wouldn't rest until he found the sixth Alabaster Book. And once he did and used her blood to unlock it, her value to him would cease.

THE CURATOR

"**P**lease, do not touch. You didn't ask politely if you could touch."

The Curator followed Aryis as she limped from shelf to shelf, her excitement growing at each new discovery. This is where she should have been studying, not at Wayland. Wayland's library paled in comparison. She shuddered at the thought of her old guild and what had happened there. The lives of so many children snuffed out, and almost her own, at Ceril's behest.

She spotted a book she had only dreamt of reading—*The Collected History of the Ancient Gods and Their Realms*—and let out an embarrassing squeal of delight.

Tajal was quick to annoy her. *Is this what a human orgasm looks like? Should I leave you alone?*

"Hush!" If it was his attempt at a lewd joke, it was a horrible one.

The Curator zoomed in front of Aryis, stopping her cold. "Aryis Devitt, please respect the tomes."

Aryis laughed. "Do you have any idea how long I've wanted to see this library? It's..." She let out a breath, for once at a loss for words. Her fingers danced across the spines of books on the nearest shelf as The Curator bobbed up and down.

The sheer size of the Arcton Grand Library—the most important collection of books, items, and ephemera in the Empire—would have been enough to take her breath away. But the massive library was beautiful as well, its ceiling as tall as a six-story building, with floating shelves and moving staircases that shuffled position as needed.

When the floating orb wouldn't move out of her way, Aryis huffed, "I was just browsing."

"Browsing turns into books being misplaced, miscataloged, or stolen." *This ball doesn't know you very well. You misplace a book? Laughable.*

At least Tajal knew her propensity—no, respect—for the proper cataloging and shelf placement within a library as esteemed as this one.

"Can I see the vaults? I hear that only the Lythrosii archives are a true rival to the Citadel." The library was one thing of beauty, but the real secrets of the Citadel—and some would say the world—lay underneath, deep into the mountain.

"The Lythrosii would have some very cross words for you, considering their order is centuries older than the very Empire you stand in the midst of right now. They consider no one their rival."

She shrugged. "The vaults?"

"Follow me," The Curator said, almost with a sigh.

"Your creator instilled quite a bit of personality in you," Aryis remarked. Magick-wielders always wove a bit of themselves in a spell, everyone's magick leaving a unique imprint.

You have more personality in your little finger than this ball.

The surprising offhand compliment brought a smile to Aryis's lips. She and Tajal had settled into a polite coexistence. His questions were often rather perplexing, but she could do without his quips. At times, he seemed to poke at her deepest insecurities, though she was already fairly good at beating herself up about them without his help.

The Curator led her to the heart of the library and to Arcton's true treasure. Bookcases spiraled out from the center of the room. In the middle, a set of stairs coiled down, deep into the dark mountain.

The little orb headed down the stairs. "There are six levels in the Spine, each with an extensive system of corridors and vaults."

"The Spine?" Aryis gingerly tested her knee out on the stairs, taking them slowly while holding onto the railing. Her knee ached a little, but she managed, her cane clacking against the stone steps as they made their way down.

"Yes. A fitting name for the center of the Citadel and the location of its most precious gifts."

"And secrets."

"Yes."

As they descended, Aryis's eyes widened in wonder. The polished stone steps led to an expansive landing, revealing a space almost as big as the library above them.

She shook her head and looked around the first level of the Spine. Despite being carved out of rock, the walls were smooth, giving way to three main sections, like pieces of a pie. Bright veins of golden light snaked through the rock walls and ceiling above, illuminating each section. Shelves stuffed with books, cabinets of endless drawers, and boxes stacked on top of one another filled every last open space.

Aryis chewed on her lower lip, anxious to explore each level of the Spine. Farther down, as the stairs drilled deeper into the rock, came the locked vaults containing objects of greater value—and danger.

"And the Night Vault?" she asked.

"On the sixth floor—the very bottom."

"Of course it is," she groused. Why wouldn't it be so far down, given the state of her knee? "Shall we?"

The Curator halted and whirled around her. "I would...rather not. I don't go below the fourth floor. The deeper we go, the closer we are to a vein of the Spire of Heaven that cuts into the mountain, and it interferes with the magick that gives me life."

Life? Is that what this little disagreeable metal ball calls its existence?

"Stop," Aryis breathed.

"I have stopped. Please pay a bit more attention, Miss Devitt." The Curator ducked to the left. "Besides, without Quinn or the last remaining Rell, you will not get into the Night Vault."

"Tell me more about Rell blood, if you will?" she said.

You're so damn polite to this little ball. But with me you are ornery.

Aryis rolled her eyes.

The Curator bobbed in the air, doing a little loop. "The Rells were ethereal mages who made their blood an integral part of the magick they studied and developed. Many of their spells aren't originally their own but, like with a piece of music, the artist—or in this case, the mage—can put a unique twist on a spell. For instance, the wards on the vault recognize Rell blood and don't trip when touched by a member of that family—like Suvi Rell. Even proximity works, no need for pricking fingers."

"They used their own blood? Seems like they didn't want others to use their strain of magick."

A metallic hum came from The Curator, his version of a contemplative murmur, Aryis guessed. "It wasn't always that way, not for a great long while. The Rells were renowned scholars, some of the finest magickal theorists of the Areshi Empire. But the later generations of Rells became secretive, experimenting with dangerous lines of blood, bone, and flesh magick. And soul magick, if rumors were true. Not long after those rumors came to light, the Rells fled to Thu'Dain in what became known as The Schism."

Soul magick, Tajal rumbled. *Now you know how Ceril compelled your students to attack you at Wayland. Powerful stuff, that type of magick.*

Tajal wasn't completely useless at times, and now she silently thanked him for his insight. The ability to control and compel were said to be major branches of soul magick, a rare, complex discipline long forbidden throughout the world, not just the Empire. A ban that the Lythrosii themselves enforced should a governing body fail to live up to their responsibilities to regulate magick use.

"This Suvi Rell," The Curator said, "I hear she can control minds for a short while. Is this true?"

Aryis tensed, remembering the sinking helplessness of being under Suvi's sway. And what Suvi had made her do to Athen.

"Yes, it is. I experienced it firsthand and don't recommend it." Swallowing, she pushed past the memories. They needed to focus on immediate matters. She leaned back against the staircase railing and chewed on her bottom lip, contemplating the vault. Of course a Rell could get into the Night Vault, they had built it centuries back, but why would Ceril need her to get into a room he had scoured many times over? What was he looking for, exactly?

A Rell once wandered into my realm using your little Hummingbird.

"What did you do?" she whispered.

I pulled his arms and legs off of him. Then sent him back through the portal. In pieces.

Aryis swallowed, wishing she hadn't asked. She approached the banister and peered down the stairs, deep into the darkness of the Spine. "We have to get into the Night Vault."

"It is currently sealed and warded. You'll need Quinn," The Curator replied, making lazy spirals in the air.

I bet she cannot wait to be stuck in that vault with you for endless hours, days on end, Tajal said with a cruel chuckle.

"Could you not be an asshole?"

The Curator stilled. "Excuse me?"

Aryis cringed. "Uh, I was talking to myself. I do that. A lot."

"I see. Shall I summon Quinn to unlock the Night Vault? Her magick used to suppress magick for short stints, but now, as I understand it, she can completely destroy it?"

"Yes. Her previous abilities pale in comparison to what she can now do." As much as Aryis wanted to get into the vault, it wasn't up to her. Quinn had to be ready. "I think it's best to wait for now."

"Understood. Let us head back up to the main library, then."

Aryis took one last glance down the heart of the Spine, wondering what they would find in the Night Vault.

THE NIGHT VAULT

The door to the Night Vault was just as Quinn remembered. Its large, gleaming metal surface was etched with the scene of a dark forest and the sky above it, replete with stars, moon, and an ancient floating city in the distance. Beautiful artwork hiding untold power inside.

Now, something was different. *She* was different, full of rare power. A thrumming in her chest made her toes and fingers buzz—a wholly new sensation. Her magick was picking up on the power of the Primalith Shard.

"You feel that?" she asked, eyeing Nyssa.

"Yeah. It's like the Pillars of Mercy, but..."

"Stronger. Older." Quinn narrowed her eyes. "When I was an adept here, I used to feel something strange—distant, almost—when I was in certain areas of the Citadel, including down here in this vault."

"Likely your dormant Ancient Magick was calling to the shard, and it to you. Though weak, you still felt it," Aryis said.

Quinn swallowed. "I thought it was in my head."

Nyssa frowned and ran her gaze over the door.

Standing in front of the vault once again sent a shudder down Quinn's spine. How many times had Ceril made her unlock the vault to study the magick that lay within? How many times had the wards sparked against her hand, burning her before she was able to tame the protective magick, negate its effect for a bit so they could enter? Her hands bore the scars of all those visits, healed over and over.

Quinn reached out. She flinched in anticipation of the pain the ward would induce before she could dull it, an instinct from her time before escaping the Citadel. *That's not me anymore.* She stopped and called her magick forth.

Shadow wound out of her hands and sank into the metal door, its wards popping to life in front of her eyes as her magick came forward. A brilliant green enchantment wove through the door and into the rock beside it, an intricate web meant to keep everyone out. The Rells had done their best to protect their precious spells, but their safeguards couldn't withstand Quinn.

She concentrated and dimmed the wards. Destroying them completely would be easier, but given the magick that lay within, she had to ensure no one could get in after they left.

The green magick dimmed, and she reached forward, tensing before turning the handle on the door. For the first time, it didn't attack her back.

The door swung open with a deep groan, and stale air rushed out as the light orbs inside sparked to life, flooding the darkness with a warm white glow.

Quinn stepped aside, and Aryis nodded at her, limping past, her head swinging from side to side as she took in the contents of the vault.

"It's...so big," Aryis remarked when she got inside. The vault wasn't much different than the rest of the library—it was full of bookshelves, cases holding magickal and historical items, and three long tables to sit and research at. A few couches lined the walls. Nothing had changed since Quinn last laid her eyes on the room.

"The Rells were nothing but prolific," she replied. "But it's not all their work. They collected a lot of spell books, literature from around the world, histories...they were true scholars in their own way, I suppose."

Nyssa folded her arms across her chest and addressed the two Justiciars who had come down the Spine with them. "This door is to remain open so we don't need Quinn to get in every time we need access, but no one goes inside save for myself, Quinn, and Aryis, understand?"

"And everything stays in the vault," Quinn said. "No books or papers are to be taken out. If anyone unauthorized comes down here, you close the vault door immediately. The ward will seal it up tight."

The Justiciars nodded and took up a post on either side of the door.

Quinn swallowed and finally entered the vault.

The domed stone ceiling loomed high above them, and the opposite end of the room glowed with a dim golden glow, a piece of the illumination enchantment that ran through the entire Spine.

Aryis ambled toward a glass case that sat beneath the glow. "The Alabaster collection?"

"Yes," Quinn replied. She waited for Aryis to get closer to it before speaking up again. "Do not touch them." The resulting shock wouldn't have killed Aryis, but it would have been cruel not to warn her off.

"Right." Aryis looked around the room. "Let's get started."

Quinn took a deep breath and moved over to a shelf, its contents hidden behind a small metal door. She called her magick forth again, wound the tendrils of darkness around the lock on the door's latch, then hardened the shadow, shattering the lock. She slid the door open and let out a relieved sigh.

"They're still here." Ceril's notebooks full of research lay within. "He didn't want anyone seeing these."

A chill gripped Quinn. He kept them in the Night Vault and would never be able to access them again without her.

Had he really believed she'd be his forever?

Shoving the thought away, she pulled the notebooks out and tossed them down on the nearest table.

Aryis rushed forward awkwardly, grasping a notebook. She held her hand above it and called her magick forth.

Of course, she might be able to track him! Quinn tried to quell her excitement as Aryis called forth her magick.

A red tendril rose from Ceril's notebook, nestled in Aryis's hand, before it sparked and sputtered out. Aryis took a deep breath and tried again, with the same result. She tossed the notebook down and picked up another. Her frustration grew as she went through each tome.

"I can't find him. It's probably been too long since he touched these," Aryis sighed with disappointment. "Or he's shielded himself in some way. I'm sorry."

"Don't be sorry, magick isn't always the answer to everything," Nyssa said, her tone soft. "We're just going to have to roll up our sleeves and use our brains."

"Thank you, Nyssa," Aryis replied, taking a seat. She held her hand out, and in a shower of golden sparks, a book appeared in her palm. Quinn recognized the worn brown leather cover—it was Aryis's notebook, likely her most precious possession.

"I'll get the Alabaster Books," Quinn said, walking over to the display case. While the Night Vault held a lot of the Rells' research and plenty of spell books they had collected over the years, the Alabaster Books were their own creation. The culmination of centuries' worth of research, experimentation, and hubris.

They were bound in black leather, rather mundane, considering what they held inside. Every time Ceril brought her down here, she had been subjected to pain. Suppressing the wards with her paltry magick back then meant physically touching the books, pushing past the stings and burns that punished her hands for daring to ignore the protective magick infused into the tomes.

Ceril would yell at her if her focus wandered as he studied, forcing her to subdue the wards for as long as she could until she was drained and dragged herself back to her cold, lonely room to collapse into her bed and rest.

He wanted hours with the books, day after day. And it wore her down, her magick exhausted by his curiosity.

His ambition.

He would slam the books shut every time her magick fizzled out due to exhaustion, unable to keep the wards down for more than a few hours at a time. The very nature of magick itself, and how its power taxed the user and waned until replenished with rest, seemed a personal affront to him.

What she would have done to have the magick she now possessed, to have been able to snuff out the wards permanently. If she had the magick of a god back then, she would have extinguished Ceril's very soul without a second thought and watched the smug, self-important glint die in his eyes.

Quinn approached the case and let her shadows flow, destroying the wards attached to each volume forever—Ludov or The Curator could find someone to re-ward them if they wanted. She didn't care.

She pulled the books out and placed them on the table, sliding them down to where Aryis sat.

"What can I do?" Nyssa asked. She had been rather quiet, her eyes roaming the vault but constantly flitting back to Quinn. Checking on her.

"We need to read these notebooks and the Alabaster Books to start," Aryis said, flipping a book open. "More than one set of eyes on everything is ideal, so we can be sure we're not missing something."

"I won't be able to understand any of the actual spells, but I'll read any related notes. What should we be looking for?" Nyssa asked.

"Whatever isn't here," Aryis replied.

"Great. Vague and unhelpful."

"Truth is, we don't know what we're looking for right now. But according to Quinn, Ceril read and reread the Alabaster Books as well as the journals. He was searching for something."

Quinn patted the shelf behind her. "The Rell journals are here. I thumbed through a couple of them when Ceril wasn't paying attention. I didn't get much out of them, but he thought they were important enough to study."

She moved to another shelf. "Research notes on magick here. A bit disjointed, as notes tend to be, but the Rells seemed to write everything down, even innocuous spells that do little to nothing."

On to another shelf. "This shelf and everything down to the back wall is the Rell collection of spell books, magickal history, magickal theory, and even some realm research for good measure."

Aryis eyed the shelves, her gaze narrowing as she took in the sheer volume of material they would have to sift through. "Ceril went through everything?"

"As much as he could. He had plenty of time. And...he had me." Quinn felt Nyssa's eyes on her, and she straightened up. Though her stomach churned and she wanted to run back up the winding staircase never to descend into the Spine ever again, she steeled herself against her creeping dread. "Let's get started."

THE GARDEN OF THE SUN

Reece raised an eyebrow at the giant stone head in the middle of the Palace's main atrium. The workers stopped and stared as Athen approached. She reached out with her magick, finding them filled with curiosity. *Good. Better than animosity.* She nodded at her brother.

Athen stripped his jacket off and rolled up his sleeves. "I've got this."

Their forewoman held her hands up to stop him. "Lord Fennick, there's no need—"

"Can you please hold this?" Athen asked, handing his jacket to a Palace attendant. He strode over to a large stone head sitting in the middle of the corridor. The workers around it moved away, staring at him as he sized the obstacle up.

The forewoman trailed him. "Lord Fennick, I simply must insist that you needn't trouble yourself with—"

Athen turned and laid a meaty hand on the short woman's shoulder, practically engulfing the whole thing. He flashed a bright smile. "I made this mess, and I'm going to clean it up. Let me help, okay?"

Reece folded her arms across her chest and smirked. Frustration flowed off the forewoman, but she didn't argue. It was impossible to say no to Athen when he turned the charm on and backed it up with his bright smile. He went back to sizing up the head and then wrapped his arms around it, digging his fingers into an eyehole on one side and an earhole on the other.

Taking a massive breath, he hoisted the head up and walked it over to the flat trolley in the middle of the hallway. He put it down as gently as possible, but the trolley still groaned under the weight of the sculpture.

Athen straightened up and took a long look down the hallway. Five more severed heads lay strewn about. He cringed. "I was a bit reckless, wasn't I?" he asked of no one in particular, rubbing the back of his neck. Ever since he had his shoulder-length locks cut off, his short brown hair stuck up at awkward angles. He pointed to the next decapitated head. "Bring another trolley."

"Is this how you're going to spend your day?" Reece asked as she sidled up to him. She had hoped they could return to the Garden of the Sun and strategize about what to do next.

He moved closer. "I'm going to help them clean this up, then see if I can pry some Palace gossip out of them over drinks that I, of course, will pay for."

"Ah, smart."

"I'm not just a pretty face, you know," Athen replied. He put an arm around her and planted a kiss on top of her head. "I'll fill you in later, but I expect a late night."

"Have fun," she replied. He walked off toward the next head lying in the corridor.

Reece stood in the middle of the hallway, looking back and forth. *How the hell do I get to the arboretum?*

An attendant appeared next to her. "May I help you, Miss Ae'Shen?"

"I'm afraid I'm a little lost. Can you direct me to the Garden of the Sun?"

"Let me take you, Miss. The Palace is rather large and confusing to newcomers." The attendant smiled and took a few steps in the opposite direction Reece was going to try. She sighed and followed him.

As they wound through the Palace, her mind drifted, wondering what Medias was up to. Never would Reece have thought she'd miss having the woman silently watch her like she did in Ocean's Rest, just out of Reece's line of sight.

Fucking *infuriating*.

How quickly Medias had become integral to Reece's life. She hated it now. The silence between them held her hostage, unable to move for fear of unraveling the tenuous threads that kept them tied to one another.

Reece found herself standing outside, so lost in thought she barely remembered the route they took to get there. She sighed, knowing she'd have to ask again tomorrow.

The attendant blinked at her. "Is there anything I can get you? Perhaps tea and refreshments in the arboretum?"

Reece smiled. "That would be lovely. I appreciate your thoughtfulness."

A warm wave of satisfaction wafted off the attendant. He nodded. "I will see to your tea, then, Miss Ae'Shen."

"Reece, if you may. Simply call me Reece."

After a moment's hesitation, the attendant straightened up. "I'm not at liberty to address you so casually, ma'am. I hope you understand."

Oh, the formality of the Palace was going to annoy her, wasn't it? She sighed and nodded. "Very well."

With a quick bow, the attendant turned and disappeared through patio doors. Reece made her way to the Garden of the Sun. The moment she stepped inside, she closed her eyes and took in a deep breath.

She spent some time walking through the arboretum, stopping when a flower or plant caught her attention. The garden gave her a chance to think, away from the noise of the Palace. Even when in her room alone, she found concentrating difficult, wanting to knock on the door next to hers.

The attendant returned, flagging her down, and she hurried over to find him waiting with a tray of tea and an array of finger sandwiches and pastries sitting on a table next to a chaise.

"Perhaps you'd like to take your tea here, ma'am?"

"Yes, thank you."

With another one of his curt bows, the man left her alone.

Reece sat down and poured a cup of tea. She popped a morsel into her mouth and savored the burst of flavor. It was a small meat pie, warm and filled with spiced ground beef, the pastry buttery and flaky.

Lying back, she closed her eyes, allowing herself a moment to rest. Guests had already begun arriving at the Palace for the Assembly of Regents. Though weeks away, she supposed that the smaller Houses were eager to introduce themselves to the new Emperor before his Ascension.

The Assembly would officially convene two days after the Ascension, vying to get matters onto the legislative agenda presented to Safin and the Sun Council. Then more rounds of negotiation among all the Houses, great and otherwise. Weeks of politicking.

Thinking about it gave Reece a headache. Ocean's Rest always enjoyed a certain amount of autonomy, earned by Lilliana in the wake of the Mire War. But also, a city like Ocean's Rest simply didn't work under Imperial scrutiny. It had become a bustling seaport because of Lilliana's hard work and willingness to turn a blind eye to certain black market activities. She got her cut, the factions remained happy, and everyone prospered. Of course, there were rules—Lilliana warned the factions that if she caught even a hint of slavers using the city for their business, heads would roll.

A shadow fell over Reece. She scrambled to sit up, her eyes finding their focus, and opened herself up, letting her magick flow. She kicked herself for not staying vigilant.

Amused contempt pricked against her senses, causing an involuntary shiver.

Thomus Jansin smirked down at her. "Miss Ae'Shen. Have I startled you?"

Reece popped to her feet, forcing Thomus to step back. "I was just having tea."

His hazel eyes drifted around the Garden of the Sun before settling back on her, an uncomfortable silence stretching between them.

"You spend your afternoons here?"

Reece took a breath to calm herself and offered Thomus a warm smile. The last person she expected to encounter was the head of a Great House. "The garden is full of remarkable specimens. I find their company soothing."

He turned, pacing a few steps away, his shiny leather shoes creaking underneath his dark suit and black wool coat, his wide shoulders straining the fabric. Lilliana had her run-ins with the man as he tried to negotiate with House Fennick for cheaper dock rentals for his merchant ships. Lilliana stood firm, refusing to go lower than the merchant companies that didn't boast the wealth that House Jansin did.

And Thomus had been somewhat of a loud critic of Empress Kalla. Rumors of his displeasure with her choice of successor had rippled through Lilliana's vast whisper network. Now, that knowledge set Reece on edge—he was definitely not a friend of hers or Safin's.

"Nasty business back in Ocean's Rest. I hear you almost died." Thomus made a show of shaking his head, as if sorry for the strife she'd encountered.

Thomus wasn't making any attempt to mask or hide his emotions and his contempt twisted through Reece. A bold move, but who would take her word over a Great House that had held a seat on the Sun Council for over two centuries?

If he believed her to be harmless, he was sorely mistaken. But he was the first member of the Sun Council to give her the opportunity to get close. "I suffered a mere scratch, Lord Jansin. Is there something I can do for you?"

"The Sun Palace can be overwhelming for someone like you," he said, ignoring her question. "Empaths are so very rare. Tell me, Miss Ae'Shen, do you get overwhelmed when surrounded by so many people?" He stepped closer, confidence wafting off of him. He was much larger than her, his broad frame imposing.

But Reece grew up roughhousing with Athen, who had towered over her their entire lives, though she was three years older. A big man didn't intimidate her. Not that he needed to know that. She smiled up at him, placing her hand on his arm. "Lord Jansin, your concern is truly touching, but I assure you, I can handle a few politicians and their scattered emotions." Honey dripped from every word, but she detected a glint of frustration in Thomus.

She wouldn't be cowed by him—a fact he was finding out. Men like Thomus always expected a certain amount of awe and reverence for their position in the world and didn't seem to know how to deal with someone like Reece.

Thomus pulled back and straightened up. "You would do well to remember your place."

Stilling her anger, Reece replied, "And what place is that?"

He scoffed. "Do I really need to tell the daughter of a dead whore where you truly belong?"

Words failed Reece, her lips parting slightly. Over the years, similar insults had been slung at her on occasion, usually by faction members looking to get a rise out of House Fennick. Always behind Lilliana's back. Save for once. Lilliana had caught a Snaketail Triad man sneering out an insult—he'd called Reece a lowly whore—and she'd sent the man through a wall.

Twice.

No one dared insult Reece after that.

Lilliana wasn't here now, but Reece could draw on the lessons her adoptive mother taught her. And her unwavering strength of will. "Lord Jansin, my place is where I determine it should be. And the Sun Palace is fitting for a woman of my stature."

Anger washed through him, pushing aside the simmering contempt. He grabbed her arm, pressing his fingers into her flesh. "You would do well, girl, to remember you have no power here. Return to Ocean's Rest and leave the business of protecting the Empire to its leaders."

"I have every confidence in our Emperor as our leader."

Thomus's eyebrows twitched, but he let Reece's arm go. "Not all of us do. He'll find that out at his Ascension."

The statement chilled Reece to her bones. "What is that supposed to mean?"

Thomus stepped back and smirked.

"Thomus!" a voice rang out, booming through the garden.

Reece exhaled, thankful for the interruption. A stout, bald man wearing a split black skirt with a bright-orange silk jacket approached.

Thomus's mood grew darker.

Reece recognized the man as Kip Notario of House Notario, another member of the Sun Council. She expanded her senses, reaching out to Kip. He was the opposite of Jansin. Cheerful.

"Kip," Thomus said as the man drew closer.

Kip's eyes roamed the arboretum. "This is truly a glorious garden. I find myself missing its peace when I'm home." His gaze settled on Reece, and he offered her his hand. "Miss Ae'Shen. A pleasure to finally meet you. I caught fleeting glimpses of you at Ocean's Keep."

"Lord Notario," she replied, bowing her head.

The simmering anger of Thomus buzzed against her senses—an unpleasant distraction.

"Let me leave the two of you to become acquainted," Thomus said before he hurried off.

Kip watched him leave, a faint smile on his face. "I hope Lord Jansin wasn't too intense. He's a rather humorless man."

"He was...politely impolite."

Her answer drew a hearty laugh from Kip, his brown eyes warm in the fading afternoon light. "I know exactly what you're talking about. The not-so-subtle insults behind a thinly drawn smile."

Reece nodded. On the day before she left for Cardin, Lilliana had taken her through a bit of a whirlwind tour of the Great Houses, sharing all the intelligence she had gathered through her whisper network. From what Lilliana told her, Kip Notario had his toes in many different social circles, always eager to share a bit of gossip. And gossips were always looking for an opening to wag their tongues.

"I don't think Lord Jansin likes me," Reece said.

Kip took the bait. He leaned over the tray of afternoon snacks and plucked up a piece of toast smeared with cheese and fig jam. "Oh, he doesn't like many people, myself included. So you're in good company." He popped the toast into his mouth and snickered.

He sat down on a chaise and poured himself a cup of tea. Reece took a seat opposite him, and he refilled her cup. "I don't mean to talk ill of the man, but Thomus had much different expectations of who would be announced as Kalla's successor, and he's worn his disdain at Safin's appointment on his sleeve."

Reece sipped on her tea and studied Kip. His emotions were pleasant. Even his reaction to Thomus had been evenhanded, a note of patience in his demeanor.

"I've gotten to know Safin a bit," she volunteered. "I quite like the young man. With the right guidance, I believe he could be a great leader."

Kip smiled, but his emotions were muted. He must have learned how to restrain himself, giving Reece very little to sense. "I don't disagree, but Thomus was expecting his House to get the nod from Kalla. After the ugly business with Aryis Devitt..." He trailed off, then said, "I apologize. From what I've heard, she's a friend of yours."

"No apology necessary."

With a nod, he continued, "Thomus has a daughter around Safin's age, and he had been in Kalla's ear, talking her up. A very bright girl who no doubt would have made a fine Empress, but things didn't go his way." Kip took a sip of tea, his eyes pinned to Reece. His demeanor turned serious, though his emotions barely shifted. "Be careful with House Jansin."

The warning wasn't necessary. Thomus Jansin radiated negativity and her hackles were already raised. But she placated Kip. "Thank you. I'll watch myself around them."

Kip stood with a smile. "I enjoyed sharing a bit of tea with you, Miss Ae'Shen. With House Fennick joining the Assembly of Regents, I suspect we'll be working together soon. I do have some business interests I'd like to expand into Ocean's Rest."

"Certainly, I look forward to speaking with you about it once the Ascension Ceremony is complete."

"Ah yes, the bit of pomp and formality before we get down to the real work of governing. The ceremony will be quite the spectacle. Are you invited?"

Reece shook her head. "No."

"A shame. You would be stunning in formal attire, my dear."

"Thank you, Lord Notario."

He took a deep breath and smiled. "I need to get back, but it was a delight speaking with you."

Kip turned and walked off. He was quite a refreshing experience after the hard, cold emotions of Thomus Jansin, who made her skin crawl. Something was very off about him.

Something familiar.

Reece closed her eyes and collected her thoughts. Then it hit her—why his attitude and emotions felt so familiar. He exhibited the same coldness that Anelos did in the few times she'd encountered him in Ocean's Rest. A simmering disdain that set her on edge.

She swallowed. What could a man like Thomus be capable of?

Medias stood still, concerned at Reece's demeanor. The empath paced back and forth, far more frenetic than usual. Medias held her tongue and hoped Reece didn't give Decia cause to toss her out of her office deep within the Sun Palace.

"We have to do something *now*," Reece said, rounding on Decia, who sat impassively behind her desk watching the woman wear a rut in her floor.

"You make very serious allegations against House Jansin, yet have nothing to back them up with," Decia replied.

Reece stared at her. "I don't know how else to explain this to you both. What Thomus said, the way his words *felt*, he's dangerous."

"You did the right thing by coming to me. I will handle it."

"You're going to handle it? How?"

Decia folded her hands together on top of her desk. One of her few tells—she was growing impatient. "In matters like this, it's imperative that you let the Order of the Justiciars look into Jansin. Since you and your friends have a propensity for interfering in Imperial business, this is an order—you will not take any action against Thomus Jansin. You will make no public accusations. You will keep your mouth shut and mind your business. Do we understand each other, Miss Ae'Shen?"

Medias stilled, waiting. Reece could hold her own in any argument—Medias had stood toe-to-toe with the woman on many occasions—but now, the empath didn't say a word. The look on her face was, however, withering. She glanced at Medias, her frown deepening, then left the office, leaving Medias alone with Decia.

Medias took a seat in front of her mother's desk, smoothing down her jacket. How many times had she been in this office? Taking orders or reporting her findings of whatever she had been investigating, both of them ignoring their mother-daughter bond.

Bond. A rather generous a word for whatever their relationship had become. Part of her understood why Decia chose to keep a daughter a secret from the Justiciars. It was logical, although the forced distance was a painful reminder of how their relationship would never be marked by closeness.

Empress Kalla had kept their connection a secret as well when she was alive. It was a favor only earned through years of friendship and Decia's loyalty to Kalla.

"The empath is a very passionate woman," Decia said.

"She is. But you'll find that she is also rarely wrong."

"You believe her?"

"Yes."

"And trust her?"

"Yes."

Medias realized her answers came too quick. Nothing like her considered responses when speaking as a Justiciar.

An errant blink, out of rhythm with Decia's carefully curated expression, was the only clue, but Medias knew her mother well—she had noticed Medias's lack of hesitation when answering.

"This Reece...you are fond of her."

It wasn't a question, though Medias struggled for a response. She tugged at the bottom of her jacket, its location and texture, the weight of it in her hands, completely different from her old Justiciar uniform. Another stark reminder of what she no longer was.

"Reece is a bright woman, in both intellect and aspect. She softens you, Medias." Decia rose to her feet and wandered over to the window, stepping into a shaft of midmorning light. Her dark chestnut hair turned warm in the sun. The color was a trait they shared, though her mother's hair was bone straight. Left untamed, Medias's curls were unruly. But at least one person had whispered a love for her new chaotic hair into her ear...

Medias cleared her throat. *Focus.*

"You and I are hard edges and sharp corners. We pose a challenge to anyone who would deign to get close to us. Your father pushed past all of that and loved me anyway. Your heart is more open than mine. I see how you have found a family among your...odd collection of friends. And they respect you."

Family.

"Your empath, is she a worthy woman?" Decia asked.

"Worthy?"

Decia turned around, her figure framed in the light. "Is she worthy of your heart?"

Medias swallowed. "Her worthiness isn't in question. Not for a moment." A swell of sadness bunched up in the back of her throat, and she fought against the tears that suddenly formed in her eyes. "I'm the one who lacks worth."

Decia let out an exasperated breath and crossed the room, removing her mask as she moved, surprising Medias. Justiciars weren't meant to take off their masks in the presence of anyone.

She tossed it down on the desk, then sat in the empty seat next to Medias. The tiny lines around her eyes and mouth gave Medias pause. For her whole life, her mother had been a Justiciar, a paragon of justice. The white mask *was* her mother. Now, seeing her face after so many years made her suck in a breath. The woman before her had gotten older without her realizing it. The only thing that didn't fade was the Mark of the Justiciar running across her face, its black line a stark signifier of the status they would both wear to their graves.

A deep scowl overtook Decia's features. "Is that what you truly think of yourself?"

Medias laced her fingers together, fighting against the tide of emotions that welled up. Why was this happening? Why with *Decia*, of all people?

Perhaps the reason was simple—no one could understand what Medias had gone through, what she had done, save for her mother.

Despite the gulf between them, words came spilling out. "I've hurt people as a Justiciar. I've killed. I…"

Decia shook her head. "Being a Justiciar is difficult and thankless, but we are necessary. Medias, you performed your duties admirably."

This wasn't a conversation Medias wanted to have. Not now, not ever. So, she changed the subject. "Do you have any news from the Citadel?"

Decia scowled and stood, picking up her mask and placing it back on her face. "The Night Vault has been opened, but progress is slow."

"Nyssa and Quinn, are they alright?"

"My Justiciars have not noted anything is amiss, so we shall assume they are."

Medias simmered, not satisfied with the answer. *I should be there with them.* She stood. "If there's nothing else to discuss, I shall take my leave." She turned to the door.

"I know you lied about your vision."

Medias stopped cold.

"You were right to do so. I wasn't keen on letting two Cursed Gods into Arcton. But upon further reflection, I think it was the correct course of action."

"Then I will make no apology," Medias said.

"Medias, your father's only wish was for you to be happy, and he didn't think you would be as a Justiciar. But he never stopped me from taking you to Ambershine."

"Why? Why didn't he?" The fact that her father didn't fight to keep her at home was Medias's sole unresolved conflict with him. And it burned at her that he died before they could truly talk about it.

"He wanted you to decide what you wanted out of life, and he chose not to interfere."

"And you? You never gave me a choice."

"No, I did not," Decia replied. "But you made one anyway. This may not mean anything to you now, given all that's happened, but I'm proud of you. As your father would be."

The tears that threatened earlier sprang back into Medias's eyes, and she hesitated a moment before slipping out the door.

UNREST

Quinn shot awake, gulping in a breath. She covered her mouth, lest she make too much noise and wake Nyssa. As it was, neither of them were getting much peaceful sleep of late.

Nyssa mumbled in her sleep, stilling Quinn.

Be asleep, be asleep, be asleep...

Nyssa turned over and bunched up under their blankets, her hands fisted in the sheets, a sheen of sweat on her forehead shining in the low moonlight.

Dreaming. Like I was.

The desire to shake Nyssa awake, to save her from whatever dream was no doubt troubling her, was almost too great. But Nyssa needed her sleep.

Quinn got out of bed and quietly dressed, pulling on a large, warm sweater to top off her cotton shirt, leather pants, and half-tied boots. She didn't know where she was going, she just knew she couldn't stay in bed, lying next to Nyssa.

A restlessness, a need to *move*, set her on edge.

Her feet carried her to the one place she hated and yet couldn't stay away from—her old room. Crossing over to her bed, she sat down and exhaled. Her eyes skimmed to the door, half expecting Nyssa to be standing there.

In the weeks they had been at the Citadel, Nyssa had stuck close by. Watching. Protective.

Quinn loved and hated her for it.

The concern made her feel small, as if she couldn't take care of herself. The two of them had once fought over Nyssa's protectiveness on Monk's Cove, and Nyssa's solution was to begin teaching Quinn Ithais-Toru, to teach her how to protect herself like a true warrior.

But the Citadel wasn't a foe she could punch in the face. The guild and the specter of Ceril clung to her, sank into her bones, and there was nothing she could do to fight it.

Quinn gazed at the scraps of paper stuck to the wall. One of the few things she took from this place was a love of drawing. Of creating something just from her mind's eye.

She got up and stood in front of the sketch of Nyssa's eyes. Years after they had been together briefly as infants and years before they truly met one another as adults, Nyssa was etched into her very being. But being here, in this place, Quinn felt a gulf growing between them.

In this place, everything was darker. Even Nyssa. It wasn't just the specter of Ceril hanging over Arcton, it was Quinn's past. Its shadow blanketed everything, corrupting any bit of happiness she could find, sending its dark tendrils into the bond that held her and Nyssa together.

Quinn was deeply, inextricably in love with Nyssa, but Arcton turned everything...hard. Dim.

It's that damn Primalith Shard.

Its constant presence on the edge of Quinn's awareness was like a burr rubbing against tender skin. When she closed her eyes, she could hear it...its voice hollow and cold, calling to her from countless past millennia. And it was wearing on her. And Nyssa.

Quinn shook her head and stared at her sketch of Nyssa's deep-blue eyes, touching the paper before turning around and leaving the room, retracing the route she took out of the Citadel the night she escaped. How her heart had pounded that night.

She wound down the stone staircase. Even more light orbs were burnt out than when she was last here. At the bottom of the stairs, she pushed the door open and burst outside, sucking in a breath and letting it out, like coming up for air in the Black Sea.

The night sky hung above her, the scant slice of the moon giving away what little light it had to offer. Quinn shook her arms out, then rubbed them for warmth.

Find the calm in the chaos.

Fontaine had offered that advice to Nyssa, who needed it most, her inner storm constantly churning. But now, Quinn felt that storm raging in every muscle, nerve, and bone in her body. She hopped on her toes, copying Nyssa's method of loosening up, giving the pent-up energy somewhere to go.

Drawing up to her full height, Quinn exhaled a slow breath. She closed her eyes and centered herself, pulling up the mental image of the First Form of Ithais-Toru—the Bamboo Form.

Quinn rolled her shoulders back, paused, then began moving through the form, her boots sliding in the dirt as she transitioned from one position to next, making sure her stance was extended deep into the ground. Like bamboo. Strong, yet flexible.

The air held a map of her movements as her breath hung in the chill of the night. She closed her eyes and let her body follow the imprinted memory of the form. As she moved, her magick flowed out of her, coiling around her like a cloak of pure shadow, swirling until she completed the Bamboo Form.

She opened her eyes and walked over to one of the barren trees unlucky enough to share dirt with the dead garden. Its bark was cold and rough under her fingertips. Good enough. She threw a punch at the tree, hitting it with the precision Nyssa had taught her. Her knuckles stung for a moment. But only a moment. She landed another punch, the bark crunching under her blow. The skin on her knuckles frayed a bit, but the pain was bearable.

Pain.

Pain was an escape. It had been her companion at the Citadel growing up. And in Sarisan while Suvi's prisoner. Pain would wrap its arms around her and keep her grounded. She could retreat into it, concentrating on how *real* it felt.

Quinn punched the tree again. And again. And again—until her knuckles screamed in protest and angry streaks of blood marred her pale hands. She kept hitting the tree, even as a warm glow in her chest ignited and grew. She didn't need to turn around to know Nyssa was watching her.

The warmth that radiated in her chest—Nyssa's presence—was always so comforting. Part of their god bond. But now, it annoyed her. Nyssa was here to check up on her, to see if she was okay.

Nothing was okay. The cold shadows of this damn place had crept back in, taking up residence in Quinn's bones, filling every crack within her with hate. It felt like failure. Utter failure. And Nyssa was watching every second of it.

"That tree insult you or something?" Nyssa asked. It was the first joke she had cracked in weeks.

Quinn shrugged.

Nyssa moved closer, the waning moonlight casting darkness across her face, only her sapphire eyes holding any light. She took one of Quinn's hands and frowned. "Quinn, your knuckles are torn up."

"They're fine...something just got into me."

"I...get it. There are some practice posts at the Emerald Order with my blood on them." Nyssa rubbed the back of Quinn's hand with her thumb. "I guess you couldn't sleep?"

"No. This place weighs on me."

"I know...I feel it too." Nyssa glanced towards the tower that housed the Spire of the Heavens before looking back. "I'm here for you. Just...don't run from me. I want to keep an eye on you, even from a distance. For my own peace of mind, yeah?"

Nyssa's words, her concern, made some of the darkness clinging to Quinn recede. "Thank you." She bounced on the balls of her feet to get warm. "Will you help me work off some of this restless energy?"

A half-smile spread across Nyssa's face. "Now, sparring I can do." She cracked her neck and beckoned Quinn forward.

Quinn advanced on Nyssa, throwing a punch right at her face.

Nyssa blocked and moved back, her feet scraping against the dirt. Quinn attacked again, this time with an unblocked low kick at Nyssa's thigh, catching her off guard. A rare win for her.

"Good," Nyssa grunted, dancing back, favoring her leg a bit.

"I've learned a few things from my teacher."

"Have you?" Nyssa shot forward with a palm strike. Quinn barely deflected the attack, taking the brunt of the blow in her shoulder. The force rocked her. She stepped back, assuming a defensive stance.

They traded blows. Nyssa blocked Quinn's punches and kicks and countered, backing Quinn up until she hit the tree, its bark sharp and rough against her back. Quinn attempted a series of jabs, but these Nyssa deflected with ease. A short jab to the eye reeled Quinn, but it wasn't going to deter her.

She tried to counter-punch, but Nyssa caught her fist and didn't let go. Nyssa pinned her with her searing gaze, chest rising and falling with every deep breath. The air became charged between them and Nyssa's eyes dipped to Quinn's lips.

"Yield," she demanded.

"Never." Quinn twisted her other hand in Nyssa's sweater and yanked her close, kissing her with a desperation she could barely contain. Nyssa pressed up against her, devouring her, meeting her with an aggressive desire that awoke every nerve in Quinn's body, heat gathering between her legs.

She pulled back, head swimming. The chill of the air and the rush of the wind rattling the branches of the tree above them, Quinn's skin feeling every sensation. Verbena with an undertone of woodsy spice clung to her, Nyssa leaving her scent.

"Nyssa, fuck me," she rasped. "Make me yours."

Nyssa exhaled and didn't flinch. Her hands pulled at Quinn's belt, making quick work of her buckle and zipper, slipping under her underwear.

Quinn gasped as Nyssa's fingers settled between her legs. Her mouth parted in a feral moan when those fingers moved further, slipping inside of her. She buried her hands in Nyssa's sweater, holding on while Nyssa's fingers rocked inside of her.

Nyssa tipped her head forward, pressing her palm against Quinn's core. "You've always been mine," she whispered against her ear. The dual stimulation unraveled Quinn, her knees trembling.

She drank in the night air, the smell of Nyssa, the cold wind against her skin—before her whole body tensed up. She came hard and fast, burying her face in Nyssa's shoulder to stifle her cry.

"I love you, Freckles." Nyssa held onto her, tight, before pulling her in for a deep, long kiss. Its tenderness sent a flood of warmth through Quinn. They stood there, lips crushed against each other, for a long time. The restlessness that drove Quinn out of their bed abated.

Eventually, they parted and Quinn put her pants back in order, her head still buzzing from the high of her orgasm.

Nyssa reached forward and gently ran a finger under Quinn's right eye. "Shit. I caught you with a punch. This is going to bruise up. I'm sorry."

"We've done worse to each other when sparring." She grasped Nyssa's hand and grazed her lips across the knuckles, giving them a light kiss. "I'm fine."

Nyssa scowled. Those blue eyes searched Quinn's face.

Stepping forward, Quinn cupped Nyssa's cheek. "Really, I'm fine." Nyssa closed her eyes and leaned into the contact, a soft smile making Quinn's heart melt further. There was very little at Arcton that gave her any comfort, but it was clear that Nyssa was her sanctuary.

"Let's go back to bed," Nyssa murmured.

Quinn pressed her hand against the center of Nyssa's chest. "No. I still have too much energy. I'm going to bring some tea down to the vault for Aryis and see if she's made any progress."

"That's kind of you."

Standing on her tiptoes, Quinn gave Nyssa a quick kiss. "Go back to bed. I'll be up later."

Nyssa took Quinn's hand and they returned to the Citadel, parting in the main foyer. Nyssa disappeared up the stairs to the living quarters and Quinn made her way to the kitchen. She steeled herself for the descent down the Spine to check up on Aryis.

There was still a chilly distance between the two women. Quinn didn't trust Aryis and likely never would, not after her betrayal. Not after having to watch Nyssa waste away and almost die, taking her love with her.

SHOWDOWN

Aryis rubbed at her eyes and pulled a light orb closer. It trembled from the movement before stilling in the air above her. She poured herself a cup of coffee, a new pot sent down from the kitchens. In the weeks they had been at the Citadel, the staff grew accustomed to their schedule, sending refreshments to the Night Vault every few hours. It was kind of them, and Aryis needed every ounce of kindness she could get of late.

Sleep had become something of a fleeting ghost for her. Finding the missing piece of Ceril's puzzle wouldn't happen without a concerted effort, and if that meant cheating on sleep, well, she had spent many sleepless nights studying at Wayland.

Except now, the toll felt different. Something about the Night Vault drained her. And not just her. She could see the strain in Nyssa's and Quinn's faces. Even Ina, when she hung about watching them, seemed frayed around the edges.

Aryis shook her head to wake up and stood, straightening her right leg out with a groan. The stiffness in her knee only added to the pain, and the chill in the Citadel only made it all worse.

Is it a good idea to be up and about on that knee?

She sighed. Over the weeks, Tajal had grown to be a...comfort was probably not the right term for it, but he seemed to care about her in a way that grew beyond his mere need for her to remain alive to give him a playground in her head.

"I have to move around to keep it from getting really painful," she said, glancing at the door. The guards outside never seemed to hear her talking to herself, or if they did, didn't seem to care.

And all the coffee you're drinking. How you're not just one frayed nerve by now is beyond me. Thankfully, whomever decided to carve these vaults out saw fit to include bathrooms, otherwise you'd be relegated to eliminating in a—

"Mind your business."

Touchy.

Aryis paced the floor, working blood back into her leg and loosening up her knee. She had run out of the salve the healers at Ocean's Keep had given her and didn't bother to ask the healer at the Citadel for something to replace it. The damn stuff didn't seem to work anyway.

"Have you gotten any more inklings of your elusive memory?"

Tajal remained quiet for a while before answering, *It seems almost within reach whenever you're in distress.*

Interesting. Perhaps Tajal was feeding off her emotions and they sparked something in him.

"When that happens, focus. Dive into it, see if you can hold on to anything."

Genius. A revolutionary idea. I never would have thought of it. And you're supposed to be the smart one among your friends.

"I'm just trying to help. That's why you're in my head, right?"

Get back to your work. I find the mystery you're trying to unravel mildly interesting.

She chewed on her bottom lip, staring down at the stacks of tomes and papers on the table. The last volume of the Alabaster Books lay open, the last half of it baffling. Most of the spells were incomplete, notes jotted in the margins that made little sense.

"Could this be what's missing?" she asked, drawing in a deep breath. "Did Ceril want to find a way to finish these last spells?"

That's a bit too easy.

"Explain."

You mumbled something last night about a couple of them, feeling like the component parts were shoved together. Experimental.

Perhaps her strange companion wasn't just a pain in her ass. He could provide someone to bounce her thoughts off of. "My study of enchantments is limited, merely a hobby at Wayland before I left. I can pick apart the aspects of simple spells that make them work—theoretically, since I can't weave enchantments—but with anything more advanced, I'm just guessing."

Explain.

She sighed at his mimicking her. "I'm applying a limited set of knowledge to a much broader set of variables, hoping that extrapolating and making educated guesses isn't setting me off in the entirely wrong direction. I recognize snippets of familiar spell components, but I don't know enough to see the bigger picture. I'm just wondering if Ceril was stuck here too, trying to figure out what was missing from these spells."

The pieces don't fit.

"But what if they don't fit because there's another magick component needed? Like a spice missing from a stew that just makes it burst with flavor. Some bit of blood or bone magick that—"

She stopped. *Theoretical magick.* She limped over to the open Alabaster Book and flipped to the last few pages. Throughout the earlier volumes, she could trace the evolution of the Rells' magick. The enchantments started from a basic set, then spider-webbed out into offshoots and variants. But the magick wasn't just evolving, it was inventive. Creative in a dark way that Aryis struggled to grasp but found exhilarating, nonetheless. The Rells were extraordinarily talented mages.

Tapping a finger on a half-scribbled spell, she stared down at the notes in the margin. "These spells are incomplete because they were actively creating new spells. That's what these last enchantments are. Trial and error. Incomplete."

And yet that gets us nowhere.

Her shoulders drooped. "Yeah. Nowhere."

I was led to believe—by you, specifically—that you were a good student. A fast study. Smart. We've been stuck in this dreary Citadel for weeks and you're no closer to an answer.

"Well, we don't know what we're looking for."

I'm not impressed with your intellect at the moment.

Aryis blew out a breath.

"Too bad."

"What's too bad?"

Aryis whirled around, hissing as her knee protested. Quinn stood in the doorway, a teapot in one hand, a small cup in the other. She looked tired.

"Uh...just talking to myself, as usual." Aryis made her way back to her chair and sat down. She looked beyond Quinn for Nyssa, her notable absence setting Aryis on edge. "Have you slept at all tonight?"

Quinn shook her head. "No. I can't...sleep."

Over the past few weeks, both she and Nyssa had grown quieter. For Nyssa, that was a dramatic change. She didn't smile or crack jokes. And Quinn withdrew even further, spending whole afternoons poring through the same texts over and over again, not speaking a word, barely eating or drinking anything. And she would disappear for long periods of time. During those disappearances, Nyssa would fidget over her books, glancing to the door often, her mood only brightening when Quinn returned.

Quinn entered the vault and placed the pot and cup on the table. "For you." A kind gesture, considering everything.

Tajal piped up. *She looks odd. Does she look odd to you?*

Aryis cleared her throat and focused, noticing a bruise forming under Quinn's left eye. And her hands...her knuckles were raw. What had she gotten up to?

"Are you okay?"

Quinn scowled at first, then her eyebrows shot up. "Oh this?" She pointed to her right eye. "Nyssa and I got to sparring a bit. The results were what they usually are."

A smile—so rare of late—crossed Quinn's lips, brightening her face.

She drew closer and picked up the book open in front of her. "What's this?" Quinn scanned the spine. Her gaze turned on Aryis. The smile disappeared, replaced by anger. "What the fuck is this?"

The book—*The Blight of the Cursed Gods*—wasn't part of what they needed to study, but Aryis felt it important to fully understand what Nyssa and Quinn were. The lore was a warning. The Cursed Gods of the past were dangerous. And some were truly depraved. Aryis didn't believe Nyssa and Quinn were the same as the gods of the past, but knowing the history could be helpful.

"It's not what it—"

"Are you reading this to figure out how to stop us?" Quinn asked, her face dark.

Lie. Be smart and lie.

Aryis ignored Tajal's ill-conceived suggestion. How was he so dense at times? "I'm just trying to learn more about you."

Quinn held the book up before slamming it down on the table. "This book isn't about me or Nyssa. This is about the past." She drilled her index finger down on it. "We're not these monsters."

"I know that! But learning more about what you are can help you avoid...pitfalls that others have fallen into."

A gruff sigh left Quinn. "You really see us like everyone else does, don't you? We're a potential danger to be avoided...or destroyed, if need be."

"No, that's not it at all! How could you even think that? I wouldn't be here helping if I thought that." Anger bubbled up in Aryis's chest, shoving aside her sense of caution. She was trying to atone for her sins, her injured knee bearing testament to that. What more did she need to do to prove herself?

"You should have gone back to Frosland. Go be their queen and forget all of this."

Don't listen to her. You would be so boring there, wouldn't you? And I don't want to be bored.

Returning home would be the easy route, but Aryis had so much to make up for. She was resolute to prove herself worthy of friendship. Worthy of love.

"I've abdicated my duties to my brother. I'm no longer the Queen-in-Waiting."

A short gasp left Quinn. "You gave up the throne? After everything you did to us for your fucking country, you just...quit?"

"I'm not fit to be a queen. The things I did showed me how ill-suited I am to lead. And I just can't face my family after everything. They—"

Quinn rounded the desk and pulled Aryis out of her chair. Aryis's knee buckled, but Quinn shoved her up against the bookshelves.

"After what *you* did, you think *you're* the victim here?" she spat, her face red. She let go of Aryis and stumbled back, exhaling. "I was driven to my knees and forced to destroy Nyssa because of *you*."

Quinn turned back to the desk and picked up the book on the Cursed Gods. "Does this tell you about our soul-bond? How I can sense her when she's close?" She put her fist to her chest, tears in her eyes. "I *felt* Nyssa dying. Here, in the very core of my body, I felt her slipping away. You did that. *You* fucking did that."

Quinn flung the book at Aryis. It hit her in her stomach and toppled to the floor. Aryis held onto the shelf behind her, afraid she might fall, her knee aching like mad.

"You fucking did that," Quinn mumbled.

Suvi told you she's dangerous. I concur with the fallen queen's assessment. You best watch yourself here, she could kill you with a thought.

Quinn balled up her fists. She was trembling.

She's going to hit you.

Quinn lunged at Aryis, catching her square on the chin.

Aryis crumpled to the floor, books from the shelf tumbling down around her.

Told you!

It wasn't the first time she had taken one of Quinn's punches. Nor was it even the second. The woman had a lethal right fist.

Why do people insist on leaving their faces within Quinn's reach? She does this often.

A shadow moved over Aryis, and she blinked, still reeling from the punch. Fingers threaded in her hair, pulling her head up.

Quinn's face came into focus, tears streaming down her cheeks. "I felt her dying and I...I did that to her."

Aryis choked out a sob, her own tears springing to her eyes. "I'm sorry. I'm so sorry."

A look of utter sorrow washed over Quinn. She let go of Aryis and slumped forward onto her knees, breaths shallow. She lifted her eyes to Aryis. "I hate you for what you did."

This is the pain of love, isn't it? It's ugly and agonizing. Why would you ever subject yourself to this?

Swallowing, Aryis only offered a nod. She hadn't once considered what the soul-bond between Nyssa and Quinn felt like. For her, it was a mere detail, a piece of information to gather about Cursed Gods. She had been so thoughtless.

You can't keep letting others treat you like this. You made one mistake. Are you to pay for it forever?

Though loath to admit it, Tajal was right. Every apology yielded diminishing returns.

Aryis and Quinn sat on the floor, silent for minutes. Finally, Aryis spoke up. "You have to leave this place, Quinn. I know you hate me and we don't know each other well...or at all, really...but I can see you're hurting."

She's going to punch you again, woman!

"I won't leave until we know what Ceril is after. He will destroy everything I love if I don't stop him."

Aryis straightened out her leg and rubbed her knee with a low groan. "You're not in this alone."

Quinn laughed once and stilled, her face falling. She stood. "When I see Ceril again, he's going to die. That thought is the only thing that makes being here—and enduring you—bearable."

Your death would make Nyssa sad. Quinn isn't killing you as a favor to her. So, at least one person likes you.

Aryis grabbed onto the shelf at her back and pulled herself to her feet, not caring about how inelegant she looked or the groan it elicited. "I'm going to help you, no matter what it takes, but you *ever* think about assaulting me again, we're going to have an issue."

A low, rumbling chuckle met Aryis, along with Quinn's smirk. "I'm a god. I could snuff out your soul with a mere touch. What exactly are you going to do to stop me?"

Aryis, do not push her. Tajal's voice was devoid of his usual droll sarcasm.

Aryis hobbled over to the table and braced herself against it, tapping on the dark-brown leather cover of *The Blight of the Cursed Gods.* "You said you weren't like the gods in this book."

"I'm not, but don't threaten me."

"That wasn't a threat. That was a promise of consequences for *your* actions."

Aryis, please.

Quinn stared at her, something akin to surprise flashing across her face.

Aryis didn't know if she had pushed too hard, too far. It was obvious that the stress of being at Arcton was forcing Quinn—and Nyssa—into dark places. But Aryis was done kowtowing. Being pitiful wasn't a way back into Quinn's good graces. That had to be earned.

Too little sleep and skipping meals had made Aryis trembly and fragile, and a stiff wind could blow her over, but she stood as tall as she could on her protesting leg.

Without another word, Quinn shook her head and exited the vault.

Aryis waited a minute to make sure she was truly gone before falling into her chair, tears flowing freely as she grabbed her knee.

Standing up to Quinn, given the way she feels about you, seems like one of the dumbest things you could do. You're supposed to be smart!

"I had to," Aryis whispered. "You don't understand how we mortals work. We don't command respect like you do. We have to fight for it."

You...respect me?

"No, I fear you."

He fell silent.

She leaned forward and let her forehead rest against the cool surface of the dark wood table.

Finally, Tajal spoke. *Quinn is angry because you caused Nyssa pain. That's why she hates you.*

Aryis picked her head up. "She loves Nyssa deeply. That's what love is supposed to be about."

But the extremes are wildly unpredictable. I do not like it.

She laughed. "You won't understand until you're in the middle of it, and then nothing is more wonderful."

Sometimes I think I understand, but then, I...

She waited for his next thought, but it didn't come.

"Have you ever been in love, Tajal?"

What an odd question for an Ancient God.

"Answer me."

How dare you, you impertinent child?

"Answer me," she insisted, unbowed. She would stand up to two gods that night.

Finally, his voice came again, softer. *I...I don't remember.*

"Could that be the memory you're chasing?"

No. You're wrong.

"You seem awfully sure about something you claim to not remember." She stood, despite her screaming knee, and hobbled over to the back corner of the vault where a couple cots had been set up. Her body cried out for sleep, but there was no way she could maneuver up six flights of stairs. She lay down, gathering blankets around her.

Perhaps we can talk about love again tomorrow?

Her eyelids grew heavy. "Mmm."

Goodnight.

Aryis jolted awake to a figure standing over her. Nyssa smiled down at her.

"Is everything okay?" Aryis mumbled. She rubbed her face, eyeing the clock. She had been asleep for less than fifteen minutes. Impossible.

"Come on, you're not sleeping down here. You need proper rest in a proper bed."

"S'okay," Aryis replied, sleep tugging mercilessly at her. "Nyssa, I-I can't climb those stairs. I'm too tired, my knee—"

"That's why I'm here." Nyssa crouched down, slipping her hands underneath Aryis's knees and arms.

Before Aryis could protest, Nyssa stood. The action was effortless, as if Aryis weighed nothing.

"But I have more books to study," Aryis said, her head lolling against Nyssa's shoulder.

"The books can wait, Little Hawk," Nyssa rumbled, her voice low. "They're not going anywhere."

"Thank you," she whispered, exhausted, thankful that she wouldn't have to spend another night on a lumpy, thin cot in a cold corner of the vault. She stifled a yawn.

"Thank Quinn. She sent me for you."

Aryis's mind tried to mull over why Quinn would do that for her after their unfortunate encounter, but sleep overtook her as Nyssa carried her up the Spine.

A REVELATION

Aryis stacked the Alabaster Books in front of her, drawing a look from Quinn before she returned to the journal she was reading, a massive steaming mug of tea in front of her, the mint wafting off it making Aryis's mouth water. Nyssa sat nearby, slumped over in her chair, head resting on the makeshift pillow she'd made of her arms, sleeping.

It had been days since Quinn's scuffle with Aryis, and neither of them had mentioned it. The encounter seemed best left in the past, for now. They still were no closer to figuring out what Ceril could have been looking for.

The Alabaster Books were, by far, the vault's biggest treasure, but studying them yielded no answers. Certainly Ceril had ascertained their value, the sheer power of spells contained within. Including spells to create blood wraiths and theories on how to tap into Primalith Shards to amplify magick—which made the proximity of the Spire of Heaven worrisome. If the Rells had figured out how to—

You keep staring at those like they are going to suddenly change.

Tajal had an annoying penchant for stating the obvious and interrupting her stream of thought. She had admonished him enough for him to know better, but that didn't stop him, especially when she couldn't talk freely to him in front of others.

She ran her fingers down the spines of the books, counting them under her breath, a childish, comforting habit. Five books. The fifth one interested her the most. Its theoretical magick, incomplete and experimental, highly confusing. And infinitely exciting. No wonder Ceril had spent hours in the Night Vault studying everything the Rells had written.

The frustrating bit was the incomplete spells at the end of the fifth book, spells that needed more development. The Rells were making exciting discoveries, combining old and new components to make something new and different. Their discoveries were also dangerous. Harmful. *Awful.* Days earlier, she had frozen when she worked out which spell Ceril used to compel her students at Wayland to attack her. The magick was rare, and Aryis had only seen bits and pieces of it elsewhere in the books—soul magick.

If only the Rells had done more work, expanded on their theories. If only—

Aryis bolted upright in her chair, making it squeak against the floor. Nyssa jerked awake.

"If only there was a sixth book," Aryis said.

What? A hint of excitement tinged Tajal's voice.

Quinn closed the book she was reading and leaned forward. "What?"

Aryis gripped her cane and struggled to her feet. Pacing was always the way to energize her brain, made much harder of late because of her injury. But she needed to move.

"The magick in the fifth Alabaster Book gets strange, full of a bunch of incomplete spells. Questions and hypotheses scribbled in the margins of the last few pages. Spell components that I *think* are soul magick, if I had to guess. These...half-conceived spells lead somewhere. It wouldn't make sense for the Rells to just give up here." She pointed to the books on the table. "Maybe there's a sixth book where the enchantments are fully fleshed out?"

Nyssa rubbed her eyes and pinched the bridge of her nose. Dark circles had formed, her lack of sleep evident on her face. She was starting to resemble the dying woman she had once been after Quinn was forced to take her magick. And it worried Aryis.

Aryis looked to Quinn. "Could it be possible? Did you hear Ceril say anything that might indicate he came to the same conclusion?"

Quinn closed her eyes and rubbed her forehead. "I-I don't know. I mean, it could be possible, but if he considered it, that's not something he would have shared with me."

"Let's suppose, for argument's sake, that you're right. Where would this book be? Obviously it's not in the Night Vault," Nyssa said.

"I have no idea," Aryis said.

Well, shouldn't you look for it?

"Shush!" Aryis hissed.

Quinn cocked her head. "Excuse you?"

"I'm sorry, the thoughts in my head are pinging about like firecrackers in a jar." Aryis ran her hands through her unkempt hair. "We need to look everywhere we haven't yet."

Nyssa let out a heavy sigh. "The Spine alone would take weeks to go through chamber by chamber. And all the other locked vaults down here—"

"Wait," Quinn said, springing to her feet. "The Curator might know. But he won't come down here, we have to go to him."

Aryis nodded, her excitement reigniting. They exited the vault and made their way up the Spine's spiral staircase, Nyssa wrapping an arm around Aryis's waist to help her climb the steps.

Back in the main library, Quinn called out for The Curator. The small golden ball whizzed through the air and came to a hover in front of the three of them.

This little ball again. How annoying.

"Quinn, my friend, do you need assistance?" it asked.

"Yes. You have all the contents of the Spine—including the Night Vault—categorized, correct?"

"Yes."

"Is there a sixth book in the Alabaster collection?"

Aryis held her breath, excited. But The Curator didn't answer. Quinn caught her eye and scowled.

"Curator?" Quinn asked. "Please answer."

"I am afraid your question is outside my purview," it replied.

"Explain."

"I cannot comment on the existence of books, documents, artifacts, ephemera, or other such materials that no longer reside within the Citadel."

Aryis let out a short laugh of triumph. "There is another book, isn't there?"

The Curator wobbled in the air before righting itself. "There was, but as I stated, I cannot be certain of its continued existence once it exited the premises."

"Well, fuck me," Quinn breathed.

Tajal hummed in Aryis's head. *You figured it out. You are slightly less disappointing.*

"Ceril didn't want to come back here and get into the Night Vault! He snatched Suvi up so he could get that missing book," Aryis said, her heart beating faster.

"Is there any way you can you find it using your magick, Aryis?" Nyssa asked.

Aryis shook her head. "No. I haven't seen or touched it. I have to have a connection to an object, that's how it works for me. And I can't track it either. I'm sorry, I know that's not useful."

"Hey, it was a desperate shot in the dark," Nyssa replied. "And don't beat yourself up, you figured this out!"

"Where is this sixth volume?" Quinn asked the Curator.

"I cannot say. It was removed by Eliza Rell at the time of the Schism, and she never returned to the Citadel, to my knowledge."

Eliza Rell. That was an infamous name in a family known for infamous members. "The first Unworthy," Aryis said. "And a Justiciar."

"Lovely woman," The Curator replied. "Courteous and kind."

Quinn scoffed. "She was a Rell."

"Yes. You have been taught to hate and mistrust that name, but there was more to the Rells, and to Eliza, than the history books might wish you to believe."

Quinn glanced at Nyssa and Aryis. "Could you elaborate?"

The Curator whirled around in the air. "I'm afraid I cannot. We leave the past in the past."

Impudent ball. What good is it if it can't share what it knows? What it saw?

"Did Ceril Anelos ask you these same questions?" Quinn asked.

"The words didn't come out in the same order, nor were the word choices the same, so no. But I take it the spirit of your question is if his inquiries were directed to the same topic. And yes, he did ask if there were more Alabaster Books and for the location of said books. To be clear, there is only one additional volume, the one you inquired after."

"You catalog everything, don't you?" Quinn asked, walking small circles around The Curator.

"Generally speaking, yes. I know the topics covered in the Alabaster Books, since that is your current line of inquiry."

Aryis sucked in a breath, a question almost exploding out of her. "Do you know what's in the sixth Alabaster Book?"

"Written spells, whether functional, experimental, or purely theoretical, dealing with soul magick."

As we thought!

"Shit," she whispered.

But you were right!

"Soul magick?" Nyssa asked.

"High degree of difficulty. Rather dangerous if done incorrectly, and very illegal across the world, as you know," The Curator replied. "Few mages have unlocked its secrets, but the Rells did make progress. The magick branches into control and manipulation."

"The damn irony of Suvi being able to control minds." Nyssa looked to Aryis. "How bad is this?"

Aryis was loath to speculate, but the truth was dire. "Imagine if Ceril had the ability to enthrall a Cursed God. Or an Emperor." She swallowed back her fear. "Curator, did Ceril ever indicate that he had found the book or at least its location?"

"Ceril never shared that information with me. I am but a lowly construct."

I agree. What a rather insightful statement for such a clanky little thing.

Aryis ignored Tajal's petty grudge. "Now we know what Ceril wants. We have to look for clues where Eliza Rell may have taken the book, and if that information is in the Citadel, it's back in the Night Vault. Time to go through the journals, maps, contracts, memoirs...all of it again."

Nyssa visibly deflated. "All of it?"

Quinn nodded. "All of it, Blacksea."

They look like death dragged its balls over their—

"If I may suggest," Aryis said, "a night's rest first? It's late and you two are exhausted. We'll pick this up again tomorrow."

Quinn looked like she wanted to protest, as if getting back down to the Night Vault was her only priority, but she nodded. "Okay."

Aryis let out a sigh of relief, hope firmly taking hold for the first time in their weeks of searching.

THE SPY

Reece tugged on the hood of her cloak and kept her eyes on Medias. Sneaking around and following her was not something Reece was especially proud of, but Medias had become even more sullen and withdrawn after speaking with her mother.

Gentle questioning had yielded no answers, so Reece, filled with concern and frustration, resorted to an illegal disguise enchantment. Though outlawed, such enchantments weren't impossible to find, and Ocean's Rest had a thriving black market. Reece kept a small collection of useful enchantments, just in case. Lilliana had impressed upon her the importance of being prepared for anything.

Ahead of her, Medias stopped at a cart stacked with broadsheets and picked one up, flipping through the pages.

Reece ducked into an alcove. She slipped a small leather satchel out of her pocket and pulled out a smaller envelope. Inside was a square piece of translucent paper imprinted with a green eye. She took the paper out and quickly held it to the skin underneath her chin with her thumb. The enchantment sparked painlessly against her skin.

Dark purple smoke wafted out from under her chin and Reece leaned forward. The strange sensation of magick adhering to her flesh made her suck in a breath. The smoke wrapped around her head and after a few seconds, her skin went cold. The enchantment had set.

Popping out of the alcove, Reece followed Medias as she wound her way through the ivory streets of Cardin. Signs hung above the doors of the upscale shops that lined the street, housed in bright-white stone buildings covered with ivy that thrived in winter, greenish-blue leaves and pale purple flowers winding up the façades.

The affluent of the city brushed past her, their cashmere, wools, and furs adorned with ribbons of midnight-blue edged with sparkling golden thread, and homage to Safin in anticipation of his Ascension. Reece glanced down at her plain black wool cloak, hoping she didn't look too out of place among the rich.

Latching onto Medias's warm presence, Reece hung back, blending in as best she could with the city's denizens. Her mentor, Crusian Fry, had taught her a great deal about how to be an empath. Reece would always be grateful to Lilliana and Pol for finding Fry and hiring him to help her navigate her abilities when she was growing up. Without him, she would have been lost. He imparted the valuable skills of isolating one person's emotions and becoming familiar with what he had called their *emotional signature*. It took time and exposure, but she had gotten better at it over the years.

Each person's signature was unique, but Medias's was different. Where others' emotions were in flux, Medias's presence was devoid of any emotional variance. She was a constant Reece had grown to find a great deal of comfort in.

Medias wandered from one block to the next, keeping her head down and the hood of her cloak pulled tight. She didn't go into any of the shops. She just...walked.

After an hour, Reece realized they were walking in a circle as she passed the same shops.

What is she doing?

Reece's stomach rumbled, a reminder she had skipped breakfast in favor of trailing Medias. She sighed and continued forward.

A woman crossing the street caught her eye—Dinah Jansin, Thomus Jansin's wife. She strode into a shop named Luxe.

After her encounter with Thomus a week prior, Reece was shaken to her core. He was a dangerous man, and if he was the one who posed a threat to Safin, Reece was certain he wasn't alone in his ambitions. With the Imperial Ascension mere days away, Reece would take whatever opportunity she could to spy on Dinah.

She abandoned her fruitless pursuit of Medias and made a show of doing a bit of window-shopping before reaching Luxe. A small gasp left her lips. Precious metals and gems sparkled in the window, illuminated by the late morning sun.

Beautiful.

Ornate rings rotated slowly in their beds of purple velvet, the facets of their expensive stones catching the light. The intended effect worked—they were beguiling, gorgeous pieces of jewelry.

A sapphire-laden necklace caught Reece's eye, its thick silver chain rippling with magick, making it shimmer. Flitters floated above the display, held aloft by magick. The small metal figures were ornamental, meant to float over their owners' heads. Famous artists had begun designing them, making them a popular fashion statement. The three butterfly flitters in the window meandered in a circle, golden dust drifting off their delicate stained glass-like wings.

Reece used the window for a second purpose—checking on her disguise enchantment. She preferred not to be spotted by Dinah. If the Sun Council caught wind of her spying, Reece was certain she would find herself sent back to Ocean's Rest.

The face that appeared in the reflection of the glass was that of an older woman with dark hair—nothing like her true appearance. Nothing that could identify her seemed to show through, the sign of a good enchantment. Reece sighed with relief—sometimes magick obtained on the black market could be as sketchy as those peddling the illegal wares.

The back of the window display obscured her view into Luxe. Reece chewed the inside of her cheek and tossed caution aside, pulling the door open.

She was met with soft, lulling music emanating from a small golden box that sat on the main counter. The Melodicastrum likely cost a couple thousand gold. Owning one was a luxury.

A slightly sweet floral scent tickled her nose. White lilac. Not her favorite, but creating a posh atmosphere was part of Luxe's presentation.

Reece immediately went to a flitter display, feigning interest in the baubles. Luckily, Dinah was not the shop's only customer. A few other men and women milled about, so Reece didn't draw much attention.

Dinah stood at the counter. The store attendant disappeared into a back room, returning a few moments later with a purple velvet box. He opened it, and the golden flitter inside popped out and floated in the air about a foot above the counter. The figure was shaped like a wren—the sigil of House Jansin—with its short pointy beak and slight little body. The wings beat slowly, only there for show, since an enchantment gave it the ability to float. Its multicolor metallic finish was mostly orange with a few red circles on the sides of its face and white dots along its wings.

"It still needs attunement, Lady Jansin," the attendant said.

"Of course, Rodrick."

"If I may?"

Dinah nodded and held out her hand. Rodrick plucked the flitter from the air and gently placed it in her palm. He pressed his finger on the side of it, and Dinah sucked in a bit of air. The flitter shuddered, stilled, then rose into the air again. A tiny dot of blood sat on her palm, and Rodrick offered her a handkerchief to wipe it away.

Dinah stepped back, and the flitter followed. She took another step, and it stayed with her before it began a lazy circle over her head.

"Perfect," Rodrick stated. "I must say, this is a very unique piece. You have excellent taste, Lady Jansin."

Reece let the woman's emotions wash over her. Dinah was pleased, but there was an edge of anticipation there. She reached up and captured the flitter between her fingers, returning it to its case before handing over her bank marker to pay.

"Let me just wrap this up for you."

When Rodrick turned to the counter behind him, Dinah glanced around. Her hand darted out to a display of jewelry floating above the counter, and she grabbed a bracelet and snuck it into her pocket. A flare of excitement and fear spiked through her.

Reece had to lower her eyes to stop herself from staring in shock. She slipped out the door while Dinah waited for Rodrick to finish wrapping up the flitter and hurried away from Luxe out of fear of getting caught.

Dinah is from a rich House. What the hell is she doing stealing jewelry?

Reece turned down a side street, looking for somewhere to eat. Her stomach practically sang a dirge of hunger.

Someone grabbed her arm and pulled her into an alley. She spun around on her assailant.

"Why were you following me?" Medias asked.

"What? How did you know it's me?"

Medias sighed. Were she given to eye rolls, Reece felt she would have earned one.

"Do you honestly think a disguise enchantment would fool an ex-Justiciar?" Medias asked, a lilt of amusement in her voice. "The way you move and the way you hold yourself makes you obvious to the observant, empath."

Reece clenched her jaw. *She's enjoying this, isn't she?*

"I guess I don't need this anymore, it would have faded soon anyway," Reece said. She rubbed at the paper adhered underneath her chin. White smoke surrounded her face and it felt like millions of little bubbles were bouncing off her skin. Her face tingled for a moment. "Is my face back?"

Medias nodded then pinned her in place with a gaze. "You haven't answered my question—why are you following me?"

"Who says I'm following you? There is a garden shop I wanted to visit to buy seeds for home."

"A lie. A weak one at that."

Reece frowned. "I'm hungry and in no mood to deal with you." She pushed past Medias and exited the alley.

After a few feet, she chanced a glance back. Medias followed her, pulling down her hood and tightening her scarf. Much like Nyssa—and now Quinn—it would be hard to hide who she was. By now, news of a fallen Justiciar with distinctive red eyes had to have reached most of the Empire. Such was the nature of rare, salacious events. So-called journalists would scribble the story in their broadsheets and messenger bowls would be smoldering with the news. And Reece knew Medias hated such attention.

Reece kept walking, checking over her shoulder occasionally. Medias kept up with her. Eventually, she made her way to the end of the posh area of town and crossed over into the working-class neighborhood that rimmed the city.

She stopped at a food stand and sat on a stool at its small, pock-marked counter, plunking down a few gold marks. "Two bowls of noodles for me and my...friend." She gestured for Medias to sit.

With a sigh, Medias took the stool next to her. The food stand's proprietor, a very burly man with hairy forearms and a sweat-soaked handkerchief around his neck, slid large bowls in front of them. His eyebrows perked up when she saw Medias's face—the black line of the Justiciar unmistakable.

He placed two shot glasses and a small bottle of unmarked liquor on the table.

Pieces of what looked like meat floated at the top of the soup within a thin layer of shining grease. Medias leaned over the bowl and poked at the meat.

Reece clucked her tongue. "Who taught you how to eat noodles, Sentinel?" She grabbed two bottles sitting on the counter, squeezing the contents into Medias's bowl. First, a dark-brown sauce, then a few drops of a red sauce. Medias scowled but didn't say a word.

"Eat," Reece insisted, suddenly nervous.

Medias twirled some noodles onto a fork before giving them a tentative bite.

Reece followed suit, though far more enthusiastically, slurping noodles and broth off a large spoon. The broth was rich with flavor, so utterly delicious that she raised her eyebrows and nodded with approval. Then the spice hit her on the back of the tongue.

Reece glanced at Medias and flashed a self-satisfied smile. "It's good, right?" She tucked back in, her mouth watering in anticipation of her next bite.

The soup's meat was tender and delicious, smoky and sweet, warming her down to her bones, driving away a bit of the chill imparted by the last vestiges of winter. Deep, tingly spices infused the broth with a heat that numbed her tongue and made her cheeks grow warm.

The two ate in silence.

Finally, Reece turned to Medias, who eyed her with a gaze that could persistently unravel her. "Why did you wander around the city today?"

Medias frowned. "You shouldn't have followed me."

"I'm worried about you. You haven't been the same since we came to Cardin."

"My affect is none of your concern."

The *fucking* audacity. Reece slammed her hand down on the wooden counter, making their bowls rattle, drawing curious glances from the other patrons. "*You* are very much my concern. I care about you, even if you don't feel the same way."

Reece hadn't planned on being so forthright, just blurting out her feelings over a bowl of noodles at a street vendor, but such was the nature of their relationship now, since she couldn't pry one meaningful conversation out of Medias of late.

Reece sighed. "Look, we should—"

Movement from across the street caught their attention. A group of men and women stalked toward them. Reece reached out with her magick, and anger slammed into her senses.

"That's her!" a man cried out, pointing at them. "I told you she was here."

A short woman picked up her skirts and crossed the street. Her shirt was rolled up to the elbows, her hands covered in flour. Strands of rusty-blonde hair had escaped the haphazard bun atop her head and framed her ruddy face. As she grew closer, Medias scrambled off her stool, her eyes wide.

Reece rushed forward, putting herself in the path of the woman and her cohort, and held up her hand. The emotions spilling from them sent chills down her spine. "We don't want trouble."

The woman ignored Reece, her hard eyes stuck to Medias. "Justiciar Medias. Even without your mask, I know you."

"Bree Hadden," Medias breathed. She bowed her head—a sign of respect.

Hadden. Where had Reece heard that name before?

The woman shoved Reece aside and slapped Medias across the face.

Reece grabbed at the woman. "What do you think you're doing?"

Medias swallowed and straightened up.

"Why did you come here, murderer?" Bree balled up her fists.

"I..." Medias lowered her eyes.

Reece had never seen her act in such a way. And the look of shame on her face...

A large man in the small crowd with the woman stepped forward. "You want us to take care of her, Bree?"

"She's no longer a Justiciar. No one's going to miss her," another man said.

"Back off," Reece said, gritting her teeth, putting herself between the group and Medias, who tried to pull her back, but Reece eluded her grip. "What is going on here?"

"She killed my husband," Bree spat, glaring at Medias. "You dragged his name through the mud and then executed him. But he was *innocent*, you bitch."

The hate that bombarded Reece made her take a step back. Medias didn't move or offer a word in her defense.

Reece needed to get them out of there before things turned bloody.

"We didn't come here for trouble," she said. "We're leaving."

Another man behind Bree came forward, looming over Reece. "And if we want her blood, what're you going to do?"

Reece stepped up to the man, setting her lips in a hard, humorless line, even as her gut flipped with fear. "You'll be chasing your balls down the gutter," she said, her voice low, almost a growl. She glanced down. The man followed her gaze...to the dagger she held to his crotch.

The man snarled, but took a step back. "Who are you, girl?"

"I'm a woman, not a girl. And my name is Reece Ae'Shen of House Fennick."

The emotions around her shifted. Even if they had never heard of the empath of The Feather, they certainly knew Lilliana, the Lioness of Ocean's Rest, and House Fennick. Bree looked back at her cohort and shook her head at them before addressing Medias. "Don't come back to Waterside."

"I'm sorry," Medias mumbled. She pulled at the back of Reece's cloak.

Reece resisted the tug, holding fast. Her heart pounded in her chest, but Bree and her cohort left, their anger and hate receding. Reece watched them go, fearing they might change their minds and come back, intent on violence.

When she turned back, Medias was gone.

Reece searched the Sun Palace for an hour before she found Medias hunched over her knees and knitting her hands together in a dark sitting room far away from the heart of the Palace.

Medias rarely spoke of her past. When it came to her time as a Justiciar, she had been cagey, pushing away Reece's questions. Now Reece knew why. Justiciars were the Empire's swords of justice. Their decisions were swift and sure—but not infallible. They, too, made mistakes.

Whatever Medias had done, she seemed to pay for hers, again and again.

In the past, Reece had always cut a wide swath around Justiciars, polite in their presence when needed. Then Master Justiciar Elken bent her to his will to hunt down Nyssa and Quinn within Ocean's Rest. Her heart had turned swiftly, burning with hate for all Justiciars.

Until Medias.

The woman had done little in the beginning to abate Reece's loathing for Justiciars, proving prickly and difficult. But then she softened, little by little, showing Reece the woman behind the mask—a deeply complex, confounding, caring woman who wore her mask as armor to keep everyone from seeing the steadfast heart that beat in her chest.

"You continue to find ways to hide from me, Sentinel," Reece said as she closed the door behind her and leaned up against it.

Medias lifted her head. "I wish to be alone."

"Ah yes, this song again. It's a threadbare tune that grows more tiresome each time you sing it."

Anger flashed on Medias's face, but Reece ignored it, pushing off the door and making her way across the room.

Reece sat. "Hadden. I now remember that name from the broadsheets. A man accused of killing multiple women in Cardin. You found him guilty." She swallowed.

Medias closed her fists tight. "And he was innocent. I didn't question his guilt once we found evidence in his house. But the killings started again after he was executed. Hadden was set up, and I didn't see it."

"You were fooled. As were other Justiciars and the city Marshals. It wasn't your fault."

Medias shook her head. "I tortured him. He confessed. Reece, I..."

"You've spent the last five years punishing yourself."

"The Justiciars didn't find any fault for what I had done. How can that be? I murdered him."

There were no words to smooth over Medias's pain or absolve her guilt. But Reece had to try. "You can't keep letting this eat away at you or you'll lose yourself."

"I think I already have lost myself."

Reece scoffed. "That's entirely untrue."

The proclamation seemed to have the opposite of its intended effect as Medias's face darkened. "You don't really know me, empath. Stop taking liberties I don't grant you. You shouldn't have followed me today. You violate my—"

"Privacy? Fuck your privacy!" Passion and ire mixed in equal measure and cascaded through Reece. The words escaped her mouth before her brain could claw them back.

Medias shot to her feet. "How dare you?"

"How dare I?" Reece stood and pinned Medias in her gaze. "I've seen who you are, the beautiful and the ugly, and none of it scares me. You try to wall yourself into a dark little prison so you can punish yourself, and I hate that you do that. You deserve the light." She sighed, shaking her head. "I can't keep doing this dance with you. I'm not...strong enough."

Medias's face softened for a moment. "Strong enough? Reece, you're stronger than anyone I know."

Reece scoffed, thrown by the compliment. It couldn't be true—but Medias wasn't one to patronize.

Medias turned and stepped into a weak beam of sunlight that slipped through the heavy curtains hanging over the window. Dust motes swirled in the air as she moved. Reece exhaled, unsure what Medias would say or do next. A deep sadness clung to her—the same sadness witnessed in that stairwell in Ocean's Keep after interrogating the Rule assassin.

"Your strength isn't anger or ruthlessness," Medias said, her voice low. Those red eyes of hers, one time imposing, held such great intensity and heat. She had no idea the power she held over Reece. "You're patient. Watchful. You operate with intention. And you believe in mercy and grace. That's what makes you so different from the rest of us. I admire that about you, empath."

The praise once would have been welcomed. Rejoiced over, perhaps, coming from someone whose compliments were scarce. But now? Reece found her energy waning, her limbs heavy.

"I don't want your goddamn admiration." She sighed, her heart pounding hard in her chest as the blurry warmth of Medias's presence pressed into her. "I want more than that. I'm in love with you, Medias."

The woman dropped her gaze, her jaw tightening.

Reece waited.

After painfully silent seconds crept by, Reece finally drew in a breath, disappointed in the lack of response. "Ah, okay. I guess I should have known how you felt when I woke up and found you gone after we slept together."

A flash of anger washed over Medias's features. "Don't presume to know how I feel."

Reece held her hands out before her, letting them drop to her sides. "You know what? I'm not interested in waiting around to find out. Or being accused of violating your precious fucking privacy." She turned and began walking toward the door.

"Where are you going?"

Reece whirled around. "I'm wasting my time here. You took what you wanted from me for one night but won't accept love. I misread your intentions. I won't make that mistake again."

Medias stammered, looking lost. Hurt.

"I'm tired of getting my heart broken, of being taken for granted. I deserve *more*." Reece swallowed the cold lump in her throat.

She turned and left the room.

Reece cursed at herself as she ventured through the Palace. She had allowed Medias to become a bigger distraction than intended in the last weeks when she should have been concentrating on finding out if there was a danger to Safin on the Sun Council.

Looking out for the Emperor and rooting out any bad actors were the sole reasons Reece was in the damn Sun Palace to begin with.

Screwing around trying to pry open Medias's heart was wasting her damn time.

The Ascension was drawing near, and it was the one place where all the Great Houses would assemble and be in the same room as Safin after his sequester ended.

Reece stopped cold in the middle of the hallway, her mind seizing upon an idea, ignoring the stares from those rushing about their business.

There was only one person who could help her.

She turned around and hurried off until she found herself in front of Decia's office. Two Palace guards stood watch, eyeing her without looking directly at her, in the way guards did that she found disconcerting.

She took a deep breath. "Reece Ae'Shen of House Fennick to see Arch Justiciar Decia."

CRACK

Nyssa groaned and squeezed her eyes shut, trying to soothe her pounding headache.

Where am I?

She had woken up in the middle of the night and found herself in a hallway, recognizing it as the way to Quinn's old room. But she had no memory of leaving her bed, let alone getting so far away from the heart of the Citadel.

How did I get here?

Darkness swirled around her, shadows creeping out of the corners and crevices, swaying like seaweed in a slow tide. The tops of the walls curved in toward her, the hall warping as she moved.

Her skin buzzed with energy, but her bones ached. The feeling was far too similar to how she felt after Quinn was forced to strip her magick from her. Dying and unable to ever get warm. Nyssa never wanted to feel that way again.

A deep chill made her shiver. Beads of sweat rolled down her face and back, and her shirt stuck to her skin.

CRACK.

Nyssa stilled. She swallowed and leaned against the wall, confused and clutching her chest. Her heart raced wildly. *What is happening to me?*

CRACK.

She jumped at the sound. It was followed by a soft rush of air that whispered against her skin.

The darkness in the hallway began to move, crawling towards her. With it came an eerie echo of ice groaning and cracking as wisps of shadow swirled around her. When the wisps touched her, the familiar buzz of Quinn's presence filled her chest. But that presence was darker. Decayed. Corrupted.

CRACK.

A whimper followed.

Nyssa's blood turned to fire. *Quinn.*

She pushed off the wall and started toward Quinn's old room. Her limbs grew heavy with each step, as if moving through ice water. Gritting her teeth, she pushed forward against the force trying to ensnare her, dread pooling in her gut.

Quinn is in danger.

The shadows tried to hold her back, slicing into her skin, drawing blood. A bitter sensation gripped her chest—a chill radiating from where Quinn's warm glow should be.

CRACK.

The door to Quinn's room stood ajar and ripples of shadow spilled out, like smoke billowing off a fire. Waves of magick crashed into Nyssa, coupled with something else. Something darker.

Pain. Anger.

And *hate.* Cold, razor-sharp *hate.*

CRACK.

Quinn cried out.

Gathering every ounce of strength she could muster, Nyssa clawed at the doorframe and pulled herself into Quinn's room.

The darkness and shadow stilled. Silence.

Quinn sat backward in a chair, her arms clutching the wooden slats. She raised her face to Nyssa, tears of blood streaming down her cheeks. Nyssa gasped.

Behind Quinn stood—

No.

Nyssa stared into her own deep-blue eyes.

A replica of herself stood behind Quinn with a whip in her hand, azure shards of lightning arcing off of its black leather. Blood dripped off the tip, disappearing into smoke. Bright moonlight glinted off a piece of metal on her duplicate's chest—a wolf's head pin. The sigil of the Emerald Order. The scar down the left side of her face glowed blue and smoke leaked out, like a magickal fissure.

The Mark of the Unworthy was gone from her chin.

Shadows wound around the fake Nyssa, and she smirked, drawing her arm back and snapping the whip across Quinn's flesh.

CRACK.

Quinn cried out.

Nyssa raged. "Stop!" she screamed, lunging at her dark replica.

Suddenly, she found herself behind Quinn, replacing her evil duplicate, holding the whip. Lightning crackled at her fingertips. "No," she whispered.

She couldn't stop herself as she reared back and whipped Quinn's back.

CRACK.

Quinn's flesh split under the force of the strike. Nyssa choked, her stomach seizing up. She fell to her knees.

In a blink, she was back on her feet, propelled by some unseen force, her body not her own. Her arm moved again without her bidding.

This isn't me...

CRACK.

"Nyssa, please stop," Quinn pleaded. Her voice was weak, brimming with pain.

Nyssa's eyes filled with tears that rolled down her face, turning to ice before they hit the ground and shattered into smoke.

Her body moved on its own. Everything in her cried out to stop...but she couldn't. She tried to open her mouth, to say something, but only a silent scream came out.

Dread crashed into Nyssa like a wave, threatening to pull her under.

Something inside her shifted. Another presence forced its way through her, settling in her chest like frozen thorns.

They weren't alone. She raised her eyes.

A dark shape loomed in the doorway, its eyes glowing blue. It rushed at Nyssa, ripping through her. "This is who you truly are," its voice hissed, icy tendrils wrapping around her throat. As its grip tightened, her body flooded with strength and terrible purpose.

The whip burned in her hand. She drew her arm back again.

CRACK.

This isn't me...

This isn't me...

This isn't—

CRACK!

A RECKONING

Quinn jerked awake, roused by Aryis's scream.

Darkness and lightning swirled through the Night Vault, Cursed God magick running rampant.

Aryis was pinned against a bookshelf, shadows wrapped around her limbs and throat.

Quinn's shadows.

"Stop!" Aryis choked out.

Across from Quinn, Nyssa bolted awake and shot to her feet, her face filled with tears. Lightning rippled off of her, arcing through the room, entwined with Quinn's darkness.

Quinn threw her hands out, willing the darkness away. It disappeared from the vault, and Aryis fell to the floor, clutching her throat. Quinn rounded the table and grabbed Nyssa, wincing as lightning crashed through her. Nyssa's magick couldn't kill her—their bond prevented that—but the pain was excruciating. Still, she didn't let go.

"Nyssa, get control over your power," Quinn said.

Nyssa turned her head, her eyes blazing with azure fire. She looked absolutely lost.

"Get control!"

Gasping, Nyssa tensed and her magick collapsed back into her. She shrank away from Quinn. "What was that?"

Over the short time Quinn had known her, Nyssa had faced danger—even death—with courage. She had never seen the woman fall apart, but the look on her face now broke Quinn into pieces.

She had done this. She had made Nyssa fear her.

Quinn reached out. "Nyssa, I'm sorry, I don't know what happened. I-I think it's the damn shard. It's screwing with our magick. I was having a nightmare…"

Nyssa backed away from Quinn, wiping at the tears on her face. "And…you…pulled me into it?"

"I-I don't know…"

"What I saw in there…is that what you think of me?" Nyssa asked, her eyes pinning Quinn in place, anger replacing the fear in her gaze.

How could she answer that? Quinn thought she had shed the dream years ago, the misery of it finally fading, no longer replaying what Ceril did to her every single night as she slept with a cold void collar around her neck. But it had come roaring back, and she'd somehow pulled the woman she loved beyond life itself into her horror.

Making *Nyssa* the horror.

Why?

Nyssa backed away and rushed from the vault, past the Justiciars who watched them wordlessly.

"What happened?" Aryis asked.

"None of your *fucking* business." The thought of Aryis knowing what Quinn had manifested in her dream…the shame of it…

Quinn cursed under her breath. She should have stayed away from this place, from the darkness waiting for her.

No, the darkness is in me. And now Nyssa has seen it. The longer they stayed near the Spire of Heaven, the more intense its influence became, calling to her, and Quinn was certain it made her nightmares feel real. Did the shard's power somehow allow her to pull Nyssa into her dreams?

Why didn't she run? Take Nyssa and just run away and hide from Ceril and the Empire? They could have found a safe place somewhere in the world.

Nyssa. Nyssa was the reason. She would never abandon her family and friends. She would never leave Athen forever. Nor Reece, Aryis, nor Medias.

"We should go after Nyssa," Aryis said.

Quinn shook her head. "No. She needs time alone to calm down."

"She needs *you*."

After subjecting Nyssa to her nightmare, the idea was laughable. "I assure you, I'm the last thing she needs right now."

"What happened in your dream?"

Quinn glanced up at Aryis. Why couldn't the woman drop it? "I said—"

"That it was none of my business, yeah. But Quinn...you're suffering. I'm the only other person here that's a...friend." The earnest look on Aryis's face reminded Quinn of when they first met. Aryis had been so eager and curious, excitement rippling through her whenever there was something new to learn. She had lost that exuberance after coming back from the Realm of Shadows, but here, in the Citadel of all places, with a mystery to solve, it seemed as if she was becoming herself again.

What an utter fucking *joke*. After everything she had done?

"You're not a friend, Aryis. You're just someone I need to get what I want."

Aryis blinked and her face fell. She retreated from the vault, her cane clacking on the stone floor.

Quinn placed her hands flat against the table and let out a pained exhale. They needed to concentrate now, work harder to find Ceril, but things were spinning out of control. She looked to the vault's entrance, half expecting Nyssa to be leaning in the doorway, waiting for her.

It was empty.

VIOLENT BUSINESS TO SETTLE

Nyssa paced under the crescent moon, her breath hanging in the air. Quinn's nightmare—and her part in it—drove her to the First Master's office, where she broke the glass door to his locked liquor case. The first swallow of dark whiskey went down smooth, so she had another. Then another. And another. She wandered from his office and found herself outside, sucking in cold air, trying to gain clarity.

She held the bottle up to the moon before taking another deep drink. The liquor's effects shot through her, making her toes and fingers tingle with warmth.

She stumbled, cursing herself for getting drunk.

Fuck it, I don't care.

Quinn's dream left her roiling inside. Arcton itself made her skin crawl. The Night Vault, the Primalith Shard, the dream...it all felt like she was on the precipice of something awful. The effect on Quinn was worse.

This was how she grew up. Nyssa never could have truly understood until she saw the look on Quinn's face when they'd first stepped through the Citadel's doors. It was as if Quinn drew darkness around herself as a shield. But it blocked out her light. And Nyssa couldn't figure out how to combat the oppressive, awful memories Quinn had to deal with just being in this cursed place.

Nyssa kicked at a rock, trying to dislodge it and skid it across the snow. The rock failed to move, and she growled at it.

A dark figure came to rest in her peripheral vision at the entrance of the Citadel.

"I'm not in the mood to be watched, Ashcloak," Nyssa called, raising her eyes to Ina Ruggen.

"My orders were to do exactly that, Blacksea. You're here at Safin's request, but the reality is you're on a short leash." Ina descended the terrace steps, the silver jewelry adorning her horns catching the waning moonlight.

Nyssa bowed her head and laughed. The fucking audacity of Lyra, Decia, Ina...they all felt her a threat to their precious Imperial status quo. Don't rock the boat. Don't step out of line.

Don't. Don't. DON'T.

She was *sick* of them.

"I'm done with this foolishness, Ina. You and I have violent business to settle."

"You're drunk, Unworthy."

Nyssa snarled at the word and venomous emphasis Ina put on it. Another goddamn dig at her pride. "And? What's your fucking point? I'm challenging you to a fight. Get your ass over here."

Ina stared, her jaw clenching. "This will accomplish nothing."

"The fuck it won't." Nyssa grabbed the leather strap across her chest and lifted her sword off her back, tossing it aside. "No magick, no weapons."

"You're not in any state to challenge me."

Nyssa tossed her head back and laughed before leveling her eyes on Ina. "I'm better than you. Not just better. Superior. Even when drunk. And you know it."

"Nyssa, what is this?" Quinn stood at the entrance to the Citadel with Aryis and a number of Ashcloaks, Justiciars, and guards.

"This is Ina and me working things out," Nyssa said.

A few of the Ashcloaks started down the steps.

"Mind your business," Nyssa warned, stopping them in their tracks. "If I see one of you even touch a weapon or call your magick forth, I'll kill you."

"Nyssa, please, you don't mean that," Aryis said, limping down the steps with her cane.

Nyssa launched a lightning bolt that landed at Aryis's feet. "Stay back, Little Hawk. This doesn't concern you."

Taking one last pull of whiskey, Nyssa tossed the bottle at the statue in the middle of the Citadel's round drive. It shattered against the figure of the man holding a book.

"Fuck this place," she whispered.

Quinn stood next to Aryis, her arms wrapped around her body to ward against the cold. She hated the chill while Nyssa relished it...now it made so much sense. The Citadel was nothing but a cold, dark prison that had leached into Quinn and never truly let go.

"Nyssa, come back inside. I'll get you some tea and you can sober up," Quinn said.

Nyssa shook her head. "No."

"Please."

The last thing she wanted was to go back inside that damn Citadel. She wanted to get as far away from it and the Spire of Heaven as possible.

"No. I need this." Nyssa turned to Ina. "Come the fuck on. Fight me."

"I won't do that."

"Coward."

Ina's frown deepened and her jaw tightened. After a moment, she unbuckled her sword belt, wrapped it around her sheath, and placed it neatly on the ground.

Nyssa smirked. She knew all of Ina's tells and tendencies. Of course she wouldn't take to being called a coward. And she would likely lead with a left jab.

Nyssa slouched into a lazy stance and smiled. "Come on, Ina."

As predicted, Ina attacked with a left jab.

Too easy.

Nyssa spun her right arm up, blocking the punch with her wrist. She slid back when Ina followed it up with another strike. Nyssa grabbed her arm and pulled her forward, causing Ina to lose her balance.

Nyssa danced away and tripped on a bit of pavement, stumbling. She barked out a laugh and beckoned Ina on with a wave of her hand.

The other woman scowled and gave chase, just as Nyssa expected. Few fighters had the patience to wait and let their opponent attack first, a lesson Nyssa had learned quickly at the Order. So, she'd molded herself into a deadly counterstriker.

Ina attacked with a palm strike, precise and crisp. Nyssa stepped inside her defense, caught her wrist, and wrenched her little finger back until it snapped. With a yelp, Ina whirled away, trying to escape with a spinning elbow strike that Nyssa ducked.

"Let's break a few more of your fingers, Ashcloak," Nyssa growled.

"Stop this!" Quinn yelled.

Nyssa threw her a glance of warning. "Stay out of this, Emerrath."

Quinn and Aryis shared a look of worry that Nyssa instantly resented. Didn't they understand that this was a matter of honor? *Her* honor? She was *owed* this retribution. And she would fucking take it.

Turning back to Ina, Nyssa wavered on her feet. The whiskey sloshed around her stomach, and a wave of nausea washed over her.

Ina tugged at her broken little finger, letting out a grunt. "Breaking my fingers isn't going to make you feel better."

"The fuck it won't. That one felt pretty good. The Masters stopped me from paying you back for years of torment. Yet they never stopped you from hurting me. Not once. Not even Eron..." Nyssa's throat caught. She rarely thought about how Eron never lifted a finger to stop her bullies. If she did, it would permanently color her love for him, taint it.

Nyssa exhaled and shook her head, trying to drive those darker thoughts away.

Ina pointed at her. "Eron never stopped us because he knew the second he tried to protect you, you would be finished at the Emerald Order."

Nyssa huffed out a wry laugh. "That's a lie."

"You were his legacy. He needed you to succeed. And the rest of us? We needed you gone. You corrupted the honor of the guild with your mere presence." Ina walked forward and stopped in front of Nyssa, within a punch's distance. "The thought of you being elevated to the rank of Ashcloak was an insult to us all."

Nyssa balled up her fists. "And I was barely an Ashcloak for a week before that honor was stripped from me. I bet you and the others celebrated my failure."

"Failure," Ina scoffed. She grimaced as she shook out her hand, her broken finger barely bending when she tried to form a fist. "You might be Eron and the Emerald Order's greatest triumph."

Nyssa stilled. "Don't talk about Eron as if you knew him like I did."

"Your anger makes you blind." Ina sighed and held out her injured hand to Nyssa. "Break the rest if you wish."

Nyssa scowled. "You yield that easily? You're not even bleeding." Time to seduce the violence out of Ruggen. She shoved Ina and sneered, "Coward."

Ina's expression hardened.

Nyssa didn't even attempt to block the fist that collided with her jaw. It was precise and vicious, a blow meant to put her on her ass. Nyssa listed to the side before dropping to a knee. She spat out blood. It gleamed against the stark white snow.

I'm bleeding. Good.

Tremors of laughter, silent at first, wracked her body. Rage, regret, fear, confusion...so many emotions roiled through her, creating an irrational, dangerous mix. But she didn't care. She cocked a half smile at Ina. "Coward."

Another punch landed on Nyssa's jaw, and stars exploded in her field of view. She fell forward onto her hands, still laughing as blood filled her mouth. It dripped out of its own accord, brilliant and red.

"Master Ashcloak Ruggen, stop this!" Aryis pleaded. She sounded so far away.

"Fuck off, Aryis!" Nyssa yelled, sitting on her haunches and throwing her head back. Ina hovered over her, her fist cocked and ready to throw.

"Coward," Nyssa snarled.

Ina let her fist fly. Nyssa's nose gave way with a sickening *crunch*. Such a familiar sound, often dotting the violent milestones in her life. She toppled over, her body reeling from the blow.

Aryis lurched forward, as if she could stop any of this, but Quinn grabbed her arm.

Nyssa rolled and tried pushing herself up but collapsed. Two knees sank into the snow in front of her face. Ina bent over her.

"Fuckin' coward," Nyssa whispered.

"Do you yield?" Ina asked.

"No."

"I didn't think you would. You didn't when we were kids. Stubborn as ever." Ina squared her shoulders. "I know you're the better warrior. I concede that, but don't question my honor or my courage *ever* again, Blacksea."

Nyssa curled her fingers into the snow, trying to anchor herself to the ground as it spun beneath her. "Piss off, you Ashcloak fuck."

Ina dug her fingers into Nyssa's hair. Quinn's cry of protest arrived a second before one last fist drove Nyssa under the waves, darkness consuming her.

A WINDING PATH

Aryis reached beyond the jagged broken glass of the liquor cabinet of the First Master's office and pulled out a dusty bottle of Froslandian whiskey. It was an acquired taste, but its briny, smoky sweetness reminded her of home, when her father would let her steal sips of his dram as he worked at his desk and she read a book next to him.

She drank and watched paper burn up in the messenger bowl. Things had gone too far, and they needed reinforcements. Nyssa would be pissed with her for raising the alarm, but Athen, Medias, and Reece could help. And Aryis was tired. It wasn't enough to comb through the Night Vault for clues, she was also trying to keep Nyssa and Quinn from spiraling into darkness. If nothing else, Athen could calm Nyssa, or talk sense into her.

Ina and her Ashcloaks had carried Nyssa into the east sun room and dumped her on a couch to sleep off the alcohol. And Quinn had disappeared out into the back garden. Aryis could blame the effect of the Primalith Shard for their growing unrest and...violence...but it wasn't completely to blame.

Bringing Quinn back was necessary to get into the Night Vault, but this place was weighing her down, turning her mood darker and darker. And Nyssa was getting pulled down with her.

You are in a sour mood.

"Astute as usual, Tajal," she quipped.

And you are working yourself into exhaustion. And watching two Cursed Gods unravel.

"They'll be fine."

You haven't lived a life that spans millennia, Aryis. I've seen what Cursed Gods have done to your realm.

Books upon books cataloging the history of Cursed Gods had opened her eyes to their danger. Magick alone wasn't the problem—many of the gods had followers who believed proximity to gods elevated their station in life. A god with more powerful magick was one thing—a god with a cult following was something else entirely.

Your kind, with your lives ticking down from the moment you are expelled into the world, don't do well with power. Your mortality makes you needy and reckless, willing to do horrendous things in the name of being remembered after you die.

"Tajal, just..." She sighed. "You know what? I can't even argue with that. You have a point."

I...do?

"Yes. But Nyssa and Quinn are different. They're good people. You were in Nyssa's head, am I wrong?"

Tajal didn't respond. He would generally go silent when he lacked a quick comeback. And since she'd started challenging him a bit more, he was going silent often.

Maybe he was learning. It was a hope Aryis held on to.

"I have to find Quinn and make sure she's okay."

Why is that woman—who hates you, I feel I need to point out—your responsibility? She's not a friend. She's not family. You're not having sex with her. Leave her to Nyssa.

No, he wasn't learning, it seemed.

"I care about her. You can't just shove people aside, especially when they're hurting. And she's hurting."

Well, when she slits your throat, don't say I didn't strongly protest your incessant need to get her to like you.

"This is the difficult part of life, these emotions and desires we have to wrestle with."

You mortals seem insistent on sticking your hand in the fire repeatedly until it's nothing but a charred stub on the end of your arm. I fail to see the wisdom.

"Because the fire is where love is, Tajal. And redemption. It's worth a singe or two." She stood up and put the cork back into the bottle, replacing it on the shelf in the office.

You still think they'll forgive you.

"Maybe they won't, but I'm not giving up on forgiving myself."

Foolish.

"Yup."

Aryis left Ludov's office and made her way through the Citadel to the back garden, where Quinn was last seen. Decay surrounded her as she trudged through the scraggly dead things. Calling it a *garden* was lunacy—it hadn't been tended to for years. The barren stretch of land likely couldn't hold a healthy root anymore. *Maybe* Reece could work some magick, but the Citadel denizens had let it wither.

A rugged stone path wound through the garden and toward the forest that lay beyond the Citadel. Perhaps Quinn had taken a walk to clear her head. Aryis followed the trail, pulling her coat tighter. Something about the cold up in these mountains, and Arcton itself, chilled her to her very bones.

The whispers of magicks and ghosts of history long forgotten hung about the place. The adepts and Masters went about their days, studying, cataloging, and archiving. Once, she would have done anything to be an adept at the guild, but now, seeing how it seemed the caretakers of the place simply rearranged dust, the appeal fell away.

Aryis headed toward the dark forest, the footpath winding into the trees. She shook off a shiver as she entered the shadows.

Far down the path, she caught sight of Quinn with another person she recognized. But...it couldn't be...

Tajal perked up. *Aryis, how are you here and also there? Do you have special magick you haven't told me about?*

"Fuck!" Aryis broke into a slow, loping run, her heart in her throat and her knee screaming in pain. There was only one person she knew who could assume the faces of others. And that person was now wearing Aryis's damn face. "Quinn!" she yelled as she ran.

Quinn turned to Aryis.

The woman with her moved fast, striking Quinn in the throat.

Darkness billowed out of Quinn and wrapped around the woman, but the magick wavered and twitched before falling from the air harmlessly. Quinn dropped to a knee, her hand at her throat.

Run, Aryis!

Cold dread spiked down Aryis's spine. She pushed it away and drew Talon. The woman with her stolen face kicked Quinn in the head, and she collapsed. Metal flashed in the attacker's hand before encircling Quinn's neck.

"Qui—"

A hand clamped down on Aryis's mouth, and she felt a sharp sting under her chin. The trees began to swim and fade from her sight. More hands caught her as her legs gave out, her body floating beyond her grasp.

Aryis, what's happening? What's happening...I feel strange...

THE IMPERIAL ASCENSION

R eece did her best not to gawk at the sheer beauty of the throne room. While she found most of the Sun Palace ostentatious, this room, on this night, was pure breathtaking elegance. High above her head, a field of stars glinted through the soaring glass ceiling. Showers of tiny white sparks of light cascaded down from high above their heads, fading out and creating an otherworldly luminescence, as if the stars themselves were falling to earth in celebration of the new Emperor's ascension.

Crystal chandeliers floated overhead, glowing with soft light, creating a warmth that the rest of the Palace lacked in its white and gold presentation. The walls were draped with midnight-blue tapestries—the Areshi Imperial color—with the lotus flower sigil of House Vonner woven in golden thread. Safin's sigil sparked in the light, infused with an embellishment enchantment, making the lotus appear to be moving as if floating on the water it called its home.

Vines wound up the walls between the tapestries, resplendent with purple, pink, and white flowers, their gentle scent flowing through the room. In one corner, a string quartet played a song Reece didn't recognize—likely a new composition out of Hazelspine, the arts and music guild that once kicked out Brick for fighting. The mental image of the large man throwing fists among the Empire's most talented artists, writers, and musicians almost brought a smile to Reece's face—until she gave herself a mental kick in the ass.

Stop. No smiling. Fucking focus.

Nestled in the center of the violin, cello, and viola players was a man drawing a large bow across a ten-stringed treldice that spanned almost six feet, lying horizontally on his lap, balanced and stabilized by magick. A faint red aura surrounded his hands, his magick infused into the notes, giving them an ethereal quality that made Reece's spine tingle.

Reece cast surreptitious glances around the room. Servers weaved through the attendees with silver platters, delicately balancing flutes of golden champagne and delectable bites of food. Justiciars stood at attention along the walls, easily outnumbering the guests. Each one wore a black cape draped over their left shoulder and a black leather strap across their chest bearing a Justiciar dagger. Like the one used to mark Nyssa.

Other than the Justiciars and the servers, the only other occupants were members of the Sun Council and their guests.

The Great Houses had outdone themselves when it came to a show of wealth. The men wore tuxedos or expensive silken robes, wrists encircled by thick golden chains and fingers laden with rings beset by massive gems. The women were truly a sight to behold, their gowns either slick and elegant, or large and poofy, some almost to ridiculous excess. Fat rubies, sapphires, and emeralds dangled from necklaces and earrings. A few men and women bore flitters. The small, floating ornaments rotated above the heads of their owners, another accessory of the rich that served no discernible purpose other than extravagance.

Reece kept her eyes forward, darting on occasion to Thomus and Dinah Jansin. Dinah's lone flitter—the one Reece had watched her buy—circled above her head. The couple's emotions made Reece's stomach roil. Contempt. Anger. Frustration.

Kip Notario wore a bright silk jacket and dark pants. He smiled and chatted up some of the other Houses, sipping on champagne. The others in the room mingled, their emotions a mix of excitement, anticipation, and curiosity, though darker ones threaded through the room. Mistrust and doubt were also in attendance, but most of the negativity Reece sensed came from House Jansin.

Reece swallowed and tried to focus, but her nerves were getting the best of her, making it hard to concentrate.

She was suddenly aware of every bead of sweat that her body produced.

The door at the far end of the room opened, and Arch Justiciar Decia entered with a cadre of Justiciars, her black cape lined with gold trim. Behind her came Emperor Safin, flanked by his mother and Master Ashcloak Helo. He wore a sharp white suit, buttoned up to the collar. Down each arm and leg ran a thin ribbon of midnight-blue, and a golden sigil was pinned to his chest. A scarlet cloak was draped over his shoulders.

Safin looked every bit the Emperor, but Reece sensed his nervousness.

The string quartet began playing a serious tune—a strident piece entitled "O! The Areshi Nation Rises!"

Safin stood for a moment, overlooking the room before taking a seat on the throne. The string quartet's tune faded to silence.

Decia stepped forward. "Emperor Safin Vonner-Areshi welcomes the Great Houses of the Sun Council on the night of his Ascension. He asks we take a moment to turn our thoughts to Empress Kalla Simac-Areshi and to House Areshi here tonight, both in mourning and in celebration."

"May Kalla find peace among the stars," Safin said.

Heads bowed, and the attendees all repeated the blessing in concert.

"Your Emperor will now greet his Sun Council," Decia said.

The Great Houses approached. It was a show of fealty, bending a knee to the Emperor on his Ascension night, each House presenting Safin with a small box containing their sigil.

Reece kept a careful watch on the attendees. One by one, each House approached Safin, taking their time to give him their present and say a few words. House Jansin hung near the end of the line, going last. Reece swallowed, her eyes glued to them, trying to pick up every last stray emotion.

Thomus and Dinah moved forward. The emotions swirling about weren't right. Thomus and Dinah radiated resentment, but there was something else. As they got closer to Safin, Thomus pulled at the lapel of his suit coat, reaching inside.

Reece pushed off the wall, breaking the neat formation of the Justiciars rimming the room. She had been told to wait and watch, but something wasn't right.

"Stop!" she shouted, pointing at the couple.

Justiciars around Decia rushed forward, grabbing Thomus, pinning his arms to his sides. Surprise and fear replaced his resentment.

"What are you doing?" Thomus asked.

Decia approached him, glancing at Reece.

"Inside suit pocket," Reece said, her mouth impossibly dry. Had all the moisture in her body turned to sweat?

Decia reached inside and pulled out a small box, like the ones containing sigils from the other Houses. She opened it, finding the box empty. Her eyes returned to Thomus's face. "What is this? Where is your sigil?"

Thomus sneered. "Safin Vonner will get no sigil from House Jansin. I'm calling for a vote of no confidence."

The guests erupted into sharp whispers. Indignation and anger flowed over Reece.

Up on the dais, Safin stood and started down the steps that led up to his throne. "What's happening?"

Something in the room shifted. A volatile sense of anticipation drowned out all other emotions, entwined with a dark, murderous undertone. Reece spun to the source.

Kip Notario wore a smirk, his eyes darting from Safin to Dinah. His excitement grew as Safin approached the Jansins.

"Something's wrong," she muttered, drawing a glance from Decia.

Reece lunged, grabbing Dinah's arm. Dinah whirled away, confusion and fear on her face, teetering back toward Safin.

A metallic *click* sank Reece's stomach. Before she could move, the metal wren above Dinah's head shot at Safin.

"Athen!" she yelled. "The flitter!"

A large Justiciar on the opposite wall bolted forward.

The small silver bird sped toward Safin. In a flash, Ashcloak Helo put himself in the projectile's path, catching it in his hand.

He let loose a roar of pain as the flitter ripped through his palm.

The room filled with screams. Safin scrambled away from Helo.

A Justiciar lunged in front of his Emperor. The flitter struck the Justiciar with a sickening *thunk*, burrowing into the man's eye. He pawed at his face, letting out an unearthly shriek. He staggered forward, blood cascading down his white Justiciar mask.

The echo of a loud *crack* turned Reece's blood to ice as the flitter forced its way deeper into the man's eye. His mask shattered and clattered to the floor.

The Justiciar's body trembled while the flitter bored through his skull, a temporary detour from its true target.

Reece scrambled toward the Justiciar. The flitter had to be stopped at all costs before it killed Safin.

When she reached the Justiciar, he fell in a heap at her feet, the small metal weapon bursting out the back of his head, spraying blood across the white marble floor.

"No," Reece whispered.

The flitter bobbed in the air for a scant second, rotating back in Safin's direction. Reece dashed toward it, grabbing the metal figure. It was slick with blood and slipped easily out of her hand, viciously slicing through the soft flesh of her fingers. She bit back a cry.

Silver glinted in the golden light and the flitter dove toward Safin.

Athen dove to intercept, batting the trinket onto the floor. It skidded across the marble, coming to a stop.

The damn thing shot back into the air, pitching to the side with a loud, grinding buzz.

The flitter dove for Safin again. Athen jumped in front of the Emperor, sweeping him behind his massive body. The flitter collided with Athen's chest.

And started to bore into him.

Reece gasped. "Athen!"

Athen roared with pain and snatched the flitter from his chest. "This is over!" he shouted. He curled his fist around the metal trinket and gritted his teeth. His forearm tensed, and he crushed the flitter, its destruction accompanied by a small *pop*, like glass grinding underfoot.

He opened his fist and fragments of metal tumbled out, clacking against the marble floor. Wisps of red magick clung to the pieces before dissipating harmlessly.

Athen pulled off his Justiciar mask and exhaled. He turned to Safin, grabbing the young man's shoulders and giving him a once-over. "Are you okay, Emperor?"

Safin nodded, his eyes wide. "What...what was that? Why are you dressed like a Justiciar?"

Lyra was quick to his side, wrapping an arm around him, mouthing a "thank you" to Athen.

A light touch on Reece's shoulder made her jump. A familiar Justiciar was behind her.

"It's me," Medias said as she removed the mask she wore and gently lifted Reece's injured hand to examine the damage. Blood coated her fingers and palm. Reece sucked in a breath. She couldn't stop her hand from trembling. No, it wasn't just her hand. Her whole body vibrated from fear and stress.

"You look quite intimidating in red leather," Medias hummed under her breath before reaching up and pulling the white mask from Reece's face, freeing her from her disguise as one of Decia's Justiciars. It was the only way to get close to the Sun Council without them knowing. She hid in their midst and it paid off. Just not as she had expected.

"No one leaves this room!" Decia shouted to her Justiciars. "Arrest Thomus and Dinah Jansin immediately."

"No!" Reece said. "It's not them."

Decia's eyes narrowed on her. "Who?"

"House Notario."

Gasps hissed around Reece. Kip stared at her, pure hate radiating off of him.

His glare set something off in Reece. "What did Ceril Anelos promise you? What did your integrity cost?" A ripple in Kip's emotions gave her what she wanted. "Question him about Ceril. There's something there."

With a nod from Decia, Justiciars descended on him. "Take him to the cells."

Notario said nothing as the Justiciars escorted him away. Not one word of protest. The rest of the Ascension attendees huddled together.

Reece scowled and turned to Dinah, who stood trembling. She was consumed with fear. "The flitter you bought from Luxe, who knew you ordered it?"

Dinah blinked and stared at Reece, her mouth opening and closing. The woman was in shock.

Reece reached down and took Dinah's hand, giving it a squeeze. "It's okay. I know this wasn't you. You special ordered that flitter, didn't you?"

Dinah nodded.

Good, they were getting somewhere. "Did Kip Notario know you ordered it?"

"Y-yes. He knows I love Luxe, and I told him I was getting a special piece made for the Ascension."

"Good job, Lady Jansin." Reece smiled at her, but Dinah just blinked, her face pale.

Decia approached. "Is House Jansin involved in this plot?"

Reece turned to regard Thomus Jansin. The arrogance and contempt present at their first meeting was nowhere to be found. He, like his wife, was scared.

"Take note, Lord Jansin. This daughter of a dead, forgotten whore is about to save your life." Reece turned to Decia. "He doesn't like Emperor Safin, but he's not the murdering type."

Decia nodded, then cast her gaze across the guests. "I have vowed to protect one thing above all others—the Areshi Empire. A threat to the Emperor is a threat to this nation. And if anyone here has thrown their lot in with House Notario against our Emperor, we will extract names from him under interrogation." She glanced at Reece.

Taking Decia's cue, Reece closed her eyes and concentrated. Emotions, bright and vivid, dotted the room. Curiosity, fear, anger. A great deal of anger. Reece was relieved to find none of it was directed at Safin.

"Do you sense anything from the other Houses?" Decia asked, keeping her voice low.

"At the moment, no. But Kip seemed friendly to me at first, as well. I would remain vigilant."

"Take the Sun Council and their guests to Council chambers and hold them there. We'll debrief in an hour," Decia instructed her Justiciars.

If any of the Sun Council were reluctant to comply, none of them spoke up. They filed out of the room with a large cadre of Justiciars accompanying them.

Reece rushed over to Athen, who sat at the foot of the throne, blood trickling from the small wound in his chest.

He smiled up at Reece. "I felt that little bugger. It wasn't going to stop until it drilled through me and killed Safin."

She sank to her knees and threw her arms around him as best she could. "You saved him."

"We both did," he replied, stroking her hair before grimacing at her sliced-up fingers. "Oh, Reece, your hand."

"Let me see." Safin crouched next to them and took Reece's hand, his touch light. Purple magick flowed out of his fingertips, and the pain receded as Safin wove his healing magick into her flesh, healing her deep cuts. Safin then turned his attention to Athen, healing the shallow puncture wound. Finally, he tended to Ashcloak Helo, who barely flinched as the healing magick bound the hole in his palm.

"You will need additional care in the infirmary, but this will do for now," Safin remarked. When he was done, Safin stood, a frown darkening his face. "Now, will one of you tell me what exactly happened here and why I wasn't informed that Reece, Athen, and Medias would be disguised as Justiciars?"

Decia glanced Reece's way. "It was your plan, Ae'Shen."

Reece swallowed. "I sensed discontent on the Sun Council but could never zero in on who it was. When Thomus Jansin approached me in the Garden of the Sun and practically told me to wait and see what would happen at your Ascension, I was certain he was going to harm you. Emperor, he does not like you one bit."

Lyra made a show of her displeasure, sighing loudly. "Is this all about Thomus's daughter? He was lobbying for Kalla to pick her as the Imperial successor."

"I believe so," Reece replied. "I got concerned that Thomus was going to harm you, but without any proof other than my gut feeling, Decia was rightly cautious. So, I came to her with the idea of posing as a Justiciar. Big decisions and actions are always paired with big emotions. I was to intervene before anything bad happened if I sensed danger."

"But it wasn't Thomus who wanted to kill me."

Reece sighed. "That's my miscalculation. But my gut told me he was a danger."

"He was, Reece," Decia said. "A vote of no confidence destabilizes the Empire. You weren't incorrect, your scope was just limited to one House."

"Kip never gave me an inkling of what he was planning. He...he used me."

Lyra shook her head. "Kip is a very astute politician. He made you trust him by simply being as benign as possible. It's his gift."

"Why did he do this?" Athen asked.

"My Justiciars will find out," Decia said. The declaration chilled Reece.

"Who else knew about this ruse?" Safin asked.

"Ashcloak Helo. Decia, and her Justiciars." Reece almost cringed, forgetting to address Decia with her title. She didn't miss the tight line of the Arch Justiciar's mouth draw downward at the omission. "Athen and Medias, obviously. And your mother."

Safin turned to Lyra. "Why didn't you tell me? I could have been killed today. I should have at least been warned!"

"You were kept in the dark because you are not yet adept at masking your emotions. A skill you will learn in time, but we couldn't risk you changing your behavior," Lyra replied.

Safin's face darkened. His mother was right—he wore his emotions on his sleeve. Reece hoped it wasn't completely drilled out of him as he grew into the Emperorship. She found it a refreshing change from the usual stoic demeanor of those in charge.

A Justiciar approached Decia, the crushed flitter in his hand. "I can't be certain without a tracing enchantment, but I suspect this has been attuned to the Emperor's blood. I need an engineer or spellweaver to test this."

"Get it done, and send a team to Luxe tonight. I want every employee brought to me," Decia ordered. "I will deal with the Sun Council. Reece, I would like you to accompany me to see if there's any lingering danger you can sense."

"Yes, Arch Justiciar," she replied.

Medias extended her hand. Reece accepted, trying to ignore the electricity of Medias's touch or the way she steadied Reece as she stood. All sharp corners and aloof with others, Medias possessed a tenderness with her that made her heart race.

"Come, Miss Ae'Shen," Decia said, gesturing to the door. Once outside the room, Reece let out a long, slow breath. Decia had placed a great deal of trust in her, listening to her concerns and then agreeing to her insane idea of masquerading as a Justiciar.

Reece wondered for a moment how much of Decia's trust was Medias's doing.

NEWS FROM ARCTON

The stars made their lazy, imperceptible circles high above in the heavens, a rotation that Medias used to swear she could see as a little girl. She'd stare into the sky and listen to her father tell her stories about each star—about the heroes and myths that dotted the night, roaring to life at the end of the day.

She dropped her gaze to her companions. Athen sat on a bench, a bottle of whiskey in one hand, his other poking at the newly healed skin on his chest where the flitter had tried to drill through him.

Reece sat next to him, her head back and eyes closed. She had insisted on coming out to the Sun Garden after a long debrief with the Great Houses. The two of them still wore their borrowed Justiciar uniforms, though both had the jackets open and collars unbuttoned.

Watching Reece, Medias's mind turned back to the woman's confession of love and how it made her heart soar. And then made it sink. How had she grown to be such a coward? As a Justiciar, she had faced powerful men and women—faced mortal danger—and never flinched.

Now? One glance from Reece could unravel her thoughts and send her heart racing. But her courage fled in the face of owning up to her own feelings. She couldn't match Reece's fearlessness.

She took in a deep breath and pushed that forlorn thought away, drinking in a moment of peace. At night, the Sun Garden was truly serene, the workers gone for the day. Light orbs were strung throughout the glass structure, bathing the flowers and plants in a warm, golden glow.

Moreover, Reece visibly relaxed once inside the garden, the tension easing from her shoulders and face. According to her, the debrief with the Sun Council went fine. The Great Houses were concerned about Safin's safety at first, but then their thoughts turned to how House Notario's actions tarnished the reputation of the Council.

The moment called for self-reflection, but seemed an opportunity wasted on what was, at its heart, purely a political machine. Corruption didn't tend to flourish in a vacuum. The one good thing that came out of the evening was that House Jansin withdrew their demand for a vote of no confidence. Thomus understood it was in poor taste, temporarily at least. No doubt, he would reconsider after some time had passed. But Safin would be better prepared.

And Decia would be on high alert. Medias found a great deal of comfort in the notion. Decia may never have been well-suited to be the warm, loving mother that Medias wanted, but she was an excellent Arch Justiciar.

"Are we expected to wait in Cardin while Decia reschedules the Imperial Ascension?" Athen asked. He took a swig of whiskey, scrunching his face up. "Is all the liquor in this city suited to strip paint off a pirate ship?"

Reece sighed and held out her hand. He passed her the bottle, and she tipped it back, taking a deep sip. "Ah, this is Ilios whiskey. I can't keep it in stock at The Feather. Seems your palate is not suited to such a drink."

"Are you calling my palate weak?" he scoffed.

Reece opened her eyes and laughed. "Is that your takeaway?"

Athen shook his head and gave her a playful nudge of the shoulder.

"I have spoken to my mother," Medias said. "The Ascension is postponed indefinitely. She thinks it's best that Anelos be found and dealt with first."

"And?" Reece asked, eyeing her.

Perceptive, as usual. "And the delay will give her the chance to look further into the Sun Council and see if there are any other bad actors."

"The Sun Council won't be too happy about that," Athen remarked.

"The Sun Council will have no idea."

Athen's eyebrow perked up at that. He took the bottle back from Reece and held it up. "To formidable mothers and the poor souls who cross them."

Medias nodded, and he took another drink, his face scrunching up yet again. She tried to repress a chuckle, but she couldn't help it. Reece's eyes shot to her, not missing the small moment of fleeting mirth either. She missed very little where Medias was concerned, it seemed. Her intrusive eyes would have been galling were she anyone else.

"Well then, I propose we return to Ocean's Rest, regroup, and see if Nyssa needs help at Arcton. And maybe my mother has heard something about Ceril. He can't stay hidden for long," Athen said.

"Oh, but he can," Medias replied. She unfolded her arms and took a seat opposite Reece and Athen. "Ceril may be a traitorous bastard but, unfortunately, he's smart. He has contingency plans."

"Where do you think he is?" Reece asked.

Leaning back, Medias rubbed the side of her face. "My first instinct says he's still in the Northern Wilds. Many an outlaw has disappeared north of the Blighted Forest, including Eliza Rell centuries back."

"The first Unworthy."

"Yes. And the only reason House Rell survived the Empire."

With a groan, Reece stood up and stretched. "I've sat behind a desk for too long. I'm not used to being in a fight." She eyed Medias. "What are your thoughts? Should we return to Ocean's Rest?"

Medias looked beyond Reece. A group of Justiciars weaved their way through the flower beds, led by Decia. "I think maybe that will be decided for us," she replied, standing. A cold tingle made its way up her spine. Decia seeking them out didn't bode well.

As Decia approached, her Justiciars kept a respectful distance, their eyes constantly moving, watching for a threat. A threat coming from inside the Sun Council was a rare occurrence, and they prided themselves in being ever vigilant. That they didn't root out dissension within the Great Houses would be viewed as a failure by the whole Empire.

"I bring news from Arcton," Decia said.

Medias felt at her core that something was wrong. "What's happened?"

"Quinn and Aryis have been taken. Presumably by Ceril Anelos."

Athen shot to his feet, his face a dark cloud. "We need to get to them. Now." His gaze moved to Reece and Medias. "If Anelos does anything to Quinn and Aryis while we're here..." he growled.

Medias stilled and her mind raced, silently cursing. *I should have been with them.*

Tension bunched up Athen's shoulders and rippled across his forearms as he balled up his fists.

Decia continued, "Since Ceril's disappearance, we've been monitoring all shipping and transportation routes. A merchant airship has gone missing in the Northern Wilds. Many ships take on contract work, but the timing is suspicious."

"That's a place to start," Reece said.

"We can't dick around here anymore," Athen said. "Nyssa needs us to help find Quinn and Aryis." He swallowed, a pained look flickering over his face before he shored himself up, rising to his full height. "We need transportation, Arch Justiciar." It wasn't a request, and Medias found herself impressed by his insistence.

"Our dwindling fleet of airships have all been commissioned to protect possible targets against Anelos, but I've commandeered a commercial airship to take you to Arcton Citadel to rendezvous with Blacksea, Ashcloak Ruggen, and my Justiciars," Decia replied. "A mutual friend of us both, Lord Fennick."

CRASHING CLOUDS

Nyssa paced, her eyes glued to the gray skies. The days stranded at Arcton—knowing that Quinn and Aryis were Ceril's prisoners—were torture. Every second ground down upon Nyssa's hope. The only thing that gave her relief from her dark thoughts and kept her from taking off on her own was a message from Cardin:

> *We're coming.*
> *– Athen*

Ashcloak Ruggen and a small cadre of ten Justiciars waited, silent and unmoving. Were it not a profoundly stupid idea, Nyssa had half a mind to start another fight with Ina. Anything to take her mind off what could be happening to Aryis and Quinn.

Quinn.

She clenched her jaw, grinding her teeth. Her fingernails dug into her palms. The cold of the day had sunk into her bones, though she had no intention of returning to the Citadel to wait in its warmth. She didn't need the comfort of a roaring fire or a mug of tea. She needed to do *something*.

Ina had been the one to tell Nyssa of a airship spotted sailing away from the mountaintop Citadel when she eventually regained consciousness the night they fought. The dark whiskey and Ina's fists were a deadly combination that'd kept Nyssa out for hours. The Justiciars had already searched the grounds, finding only Aryis's blade, Talon, lying on a dirt path through the woods next to the Citadel. Quinn and Aryis had gone missing.

That night, the Justiciars messaged Cardin the news—Ceril Anelos likely had Quinn Emerrath and Aryis Devitt in his possession. Nyssa blamed herself for their disappearance. Her drunken, reckless behavior had been a distraction to everyone. The mere thought of it had turned her stomach, driving her to smash her fist into the First Master's desk out of frustration.

And fear.

The Citadel's healer had to deal with her broken hand and split knuckle.

Now, as Nyssa paced, she felt no less frenzied than she had that night. She had learned to keep in the chaotic storm of anger that roiled just underneath the surface, but if anyone or anything pushed at her, she feared she might fall apart.

"Nyssa," Ina said, her voice quiet and eyes turned to the sky.

Nyssa followed her gaze. In the distance floated an airship. Nyssa's stomach churned with nervous impatience. As it grew closer, she recognized the ship, its figurehead familiar—a rotund woman cloaked in robes, posed as if flying through the air and pulling the ship behind her.

The Cloud Crasher?

It had been the first airship she had ever been on, traversing from the Emerald Order to Ocean's Rest for the first time, sent on a mission to capture Quinn and return her to the Areshi Empire.

How long ago that seemed now.

A glowing orange ribbon unfurled off the port side of the vessel, becoming a column of light, its tip reaching the ground. It gently swung back and forth, bending in the air ever so slightly, as if pushed by the wind. Nyssa gasped as bodies dove off the Cloud Crasher, knifing through the air toward the orange column.

The crewmen hit the column one by one, and it slowed their descent, allowing them to float safely to the ground. They scattered in four directions, igniting red flares while they ran, each one sending up shrill whistles to one another, marking out a landing area for the Crasher in the Citadel's small clearing.

"You have to be a strange individual to be a Sky Diver," Ina remarked, drawing a few unexpected chuckles from the gathered Justiciars.

Their group moved closer to the Citadel, leaving plenty of space in the clearing for the Cloud Crasher to land. Nyssa stood still, her arms clutched tight to her body, the chill of the day pressing down upon her. She closed her eyes for a moment and willed herself to stop shivering, as she had done countless times at the Order when standing out in the winter air for lessons.

The four divers waved their arms, their flares guiding the ship in. When it landed, its gangplank was lowered to the ground for its passengers to disembark. The first figure at the top of the ramp was Athen.

Nyssa hurried to meet him at the bottom of the ramp, her eyes filling with tears as he drew closer. He didn't hesitate to wrap her up in his arms, his hug warm and reassuring.

"We're here," he said.

"Thank you," she breathed. "I've been going insane since..." A sob closed her throat, all her fear and hurt threatening to burst out at once.

She balled up her fists. *Stay. Strong.*

"It's going to be okay." Athen pulled away and braced her shoulders. "We'll find them."

Worry had settled on his face, mirroring Nyssa's emotions. Medias and Reece came down the ramp next, and Reece didn't hesitate to give Nyssa a hug.

"Oh, Nyssa, the storm inside you is ferocious. We're here to help now," Reece said.

Nyssa turned her attention to Medias. "Tell me you've seen something in your visions. I need to know—"

"I haven't had a vision in weeks," Medias replied. "Not since Narileh's visit."

"You better not be lying." She'd been shifty about her visions in the past. Now wasn't the time for Medias to get precious about her seer sight. They needed answers.

Medias's frown deepened. "My visions aren't yours to command, Blacksea. I swear to you, I haven't seen anything."

Nyssa bit the inside of her lip. Desperation to find Quinn was making her anger flare in all directions, and her attempts to tamp it down weren't working. "When can we leave?"

"That depends on how quickly we can get you aboard, my girl." The voice belonged to an older woman with a shock of white hair atop her head.

Nyssa sighed, happy to see a friendly face. Or was the woman friendly? Time had lapsed. And Nyssa...well, the mark on her chin and the stories circulating about her no doubt had set opinions in the minds of others. "Captain Legrand."

The short woman approached, reaching up and cupping Nyssa's cheek, her touch warm and gentle. Her eyes trailed down to the Mark of the Unworthy. "My girl, what have they done to you?"

Nyssa bowed her head. "You're not scared of me?"

"You still the same girl who is terrified of flying and flirted shamelessly with my crew?"

Nyssa managed a smile. "I suppose I am."

"Then you're still tops with me, sweets. The Cloud Crasher is yours. The Emperor and his Arch Justiciar insisted I taxi you and yours all around the Empire. I gotta gaggle of Justiciars on the ship waiting for you." She jerked a thumb over her shoulder. "Eating my food and drinking my liquor. Decia's gettin' a fat bill at the end of this venture, make no mistake."

"Thank you, Captain. I'm...I..." Nyssa shook her head, not knowing what to say. Tears sprang to her eyes, and she did her best to hold them back.

Anna approached and patted her on the back. "I'm here to help." She yelled up to her deckhands, "Got baggage down here. Need some hands, then get ready to sail. Quick turnaround, boys! And get Miss Blacksea here a stomach-settler."

The deckhands swarmed down the gangplank, and Ina took charge, pointing them to the luggage before conferring with the Justiciars and Ashcloaks remaining at the Citadel. The Night Vault had been closed, its wards springing back to life. No one was getting back in. The Arcton Masters had hurriedly started to weave another ward to secure the Spine just in case, but it would take another week to complete.

Ina approached. "We are ready to board."

"I don't appreciate you continuing to babysit me," Nyssa remarked.

"My job—and that of the Justiciars—is to see this through to the end and take Ceril Anelos into custody. You are not my concern." Ina glanced up at the ship before turning her gaze back on Nyssa. "We are going to find him, Blacksea. And your two friends."

Nyssa took a deep breath. "Just stay out of my way."

Ina lingered for a moment before walking up the gangplank.

The days after Quinn's abduction had left Nyssa hollow. Ina had shadowed her, always within her eyeline. Nyssa had wanted to scream to leave her alone, but she couldn't muster the will. So she let Ina follow and watch as she wandered the grounds or sat silently on Quinn's old bed or stared into the fireplace with a mug of tea growing cold in her hand.

A ship's attendant appeared in front of Nyssa with a small vial of pale-pink liquid. His throat bobbed up and down as he stared at the mark on her chin. "Miss Blacksea, a tonic to settle your stomach."

Nyssa downed the salty and bitter swill. "Thank you."

The man nodded and rushed back up the ramp, throwing her a look over his shoulder.

"The highlight of his year, sweets, meeting you," Anna said. "Now, we'll be up and in the air in less than half an hour."

Though the Cloud Crasher filled Nyssa with hope—a feeling she had been devoid of for a week—Ceril could be anywhere.

Anna began barking orders to her crew, and they scrambled about, getting luggage sorted and politely attending to getting the Justiciars on board.

Nyssa turned to Athen. "We have no idea where to go."

Athen put his arm around her. "Not entirely true. Decia told us that a merchant airship has gone missing in the Wilds. Lilliana reached out to Trick, and after a couple days, he got back to her. He says he has some information about the ship, so we'll be heading to the Wilds."

"Can't we just get the information from Trick now?"

"That's not how the man works, Nyssa. Information for a price, and part of that price is face-to-face. He's particular in that respect."

"Fuck. We don't have time to chase gossip."

"Trick's a lot of things, but if he says he knows something, then he does."

She tried to keep her nerves under control. "Okay, fine. I trust you."

"We'll find them, Nyssa. I don't know what I'll do if..." He shook his head, his eye growing glossy. He had to be torn up inside over Aryis.

"I hope you're right."

The big man sighed, his massive chest rising up and down. "We will be. We *have* to be."

Trick might very well have something to tell them, but what would his price be? She leaned into Athen. "Distract me. Please."

He glanced around. "Come here."

He steered them to a felled tree and cleared off the snow, offering Nyssa a seat. She sat down on the cold bark, a memory stirring of her time on Monk's Cove with Quinn and the tree that sat beside their practice ground. How many times had they sat side by side while Nyssa explained Ithais-Toru's philosophy? Or recounted one of the many times Athen had her back at the Emerald Order? Or when they simply sat in silence, letting the day's breeze wash over them?

Nyssa watched as Reece and Medias walked the grounds, waiting and giving her and Athen space to talk.

"Let me fill you in on what happened in Cardin." Athen took her through their time in the capital city, weaving quite the tale. It seemed their stay in the capital city had a bit of excitement of its own.

Nyssa was shocked to hear an attempt was made on Safin's life. She leaned forward and rubbed her cold hands together. "Reece really came through, didn't she?"

Athen chuckled. "She can barely throw a decent punch—and trust me, I've tried training her—but she's savvy in ways I can't even fathom. I think she's the best of House Fennick."

"And what part of House Fennick are you?"

"The handsome part, obviously."

That drew a faint laugh out of her. It felt alien after a week of frustration, worry, and anger. The laugh quickly faded, and she covered her mouth, stifling a cry. She had to be strong. For Quinn. Aryis. For *all* of them.

Athen nudged her shoulder. "Hey, I'm right there with you, Nyssa. I'm barely holding it together."

He dipped his head, and she moved to comfort him, rubbing his expansive back. For the longest time at the Emerald Order, they'd only had each other, and she was so grateful to have him now.

"We'll get them back," Nyssa said, trying with all her might to put conviction behind her words, but her fear injected a wedge of doubt. She didn't want to contemplate what that bastard, Ceril, would do to Quinn.

She slid her hand into Athen's and squeezed. "We'll get them back," she repeated, the hollow ache in her chest unrelenting.

AN IMPATIENT SENTINEL

Medias indulged in an activity she wasn't in the habit of doing—she paced. And ignored how Reece's eyes stuck to her every movement. She had sought out the empath in her room after the Cloud Crasher had gotten underway toward the Northern Wilds, though she couldn't articulate why she found herself needing Reece's company.

A deep, piercing sense of guilt had taken root in her chest from the moment she had learned of Quinn's abduction.

I should have been at Arcton.

The guilt came as a surprise. When she was offered the position—no, the strange honor—of becoming a Sentinel, she hadn't understood what it meant to be one. The gravity of the role didn't fully settle into her bones until she saw the look on Nyssa's face hours earlier. She was meant to protect them, and she'd failed.

I'm horrible at this.

"Your agitation is agitating me," Reece remarked, popping to her feet. She caught Medias's hand, guided her to a worn leather chair, and pushed her down into it. "Be still."

Medias didn't resist. What was the point?

Reece pulled her loose denim pants up at the knees and sat at Medias's feet, using Medias's thighs as an armrest, making Medias's heart speed up a bit. "You know what your problem is?"

The woman's impertinence seemed to peak after her performance at the Ascension ceremony, having gained more than a little self-confidence having saved the Emperor's life. A well-earned impertinence—not that Medias would ever admit to such a sentiment.

She hadn't addressed their argument in Cardin, choosing to concentrate on the dire situation at hand. But it didn't seem that Reece was pushing the matter either. She had welcomed Medias into her stateroom without hesitation and being in the empath's presence was a comfort.

Medias scowled down at Reece, whose dark eyes were focused and her silver-white hair pulled up. Messy strands had escaped her hair tie and drifted around her face.

The desire to tuck an errant strand behind her ear made Medias shift in her chair. "Tell me, what is my problem?"

Reece brightened. "You carry the weight of ridiculous expectations on your shoulders. And those expectations mostly come from inside that wonderful head of yours."

Medias's cheeks grew warm. Compliments from Reece sent her soaring. *I'm no better than a child getting a pat on the head.*

"You set yourself up for failure. You must enjoy beating yourself up over everything you perceive is even *slightly* your fault," Reece continued.

Ridiculous. Reece was simply ridiculous. And wrong. "I was made a Sentinel by an Ancient God, charged to serve Nyssa and Quinn, and what have I done? While they were at Arcton, I was playing politics in Cardin," Medias said. She picked at the worn chestnut leather on the arm of her chair. Warmth from Reece's arm spread across her thighs, the weight of her touch comforting.

"You were doing as Nyssa asked, looking out for me and Athen," Reece replied. "But somehow you'll spin that to being your fault." She shifted her arm, her hand coming to rest on Medias's knee.

That's not distracting in the slightest.

"I'm a seer, Reece. I should be one step ahead of our enemies if my goddamn vision was working correctly."

"How long has it been?"

"I haven't had a vision since I saw myself dying at the Crossing."

Reece sucked in a breath. "You...you died in your vision?"

"Yes."

Reece's hand tightened on her knee.

Death was a fate Medias had been ready to accept. Not happily, not in the least, but she had understood the punishment for her crime and forged ahead, aiding Nyssa and Quinn as her father had once asked her to do. It would have been an honorable death. She was used to her visions morphing when they concerned the Cursed Gods, forking off into variations. Troubling, though, that at least two of her visions in the past involved her death. Did it mark a trend or an anomaly?

"I'm more concerned with my lack of visions of late," she said. Visions had become such a part of her life that she now strangely missed them.

"Maybe we can figure that out together?" Reece asked.

"Why are you being so nice to me after our...disagreement in Cardin?"

Reece sighed, though a sly smile graced her lips. "Arguing with you is exhausting. I want to be, in the very least, your friend."

Even if we're nothing more. That was the unspoken bit that lingered between them and that Medias found discomforting.

"Besides, you came to me. Perhaps we need each other?" Reece mused.

Medias hummed out a resigned sigh.

It was an affirmation, and Reece seemed to take it as such, her face brightening. "We need to keep an eye on both Nyssa and Athen. Nyssa's in turmoil. Her emotions have always been intense and chaotic, but with Quinn missing, she's...angry. Constantly. And Athen is trying to keep up appearances, but he's falling apart inside."

Medias nodded. She didn't need to be an empath to know Nyssa was struggling. She wore her emotions openly. "I'm concerned about what Nyssa will do to Anelos. We're charged with bringing him back to Cardin for trial."

"I don't think Nyssa cares about what the Empire wants. I understand that justice has to be served here, but I don't think you'd be able to stop her if she wanted to kill Ceril. Do you really want to stand in her way?"

After everything that had happened and knowing the type of magick Ceril was after, it was hard to argue for arresting the man to face trial in the Imperial capital. As a Justiciar, she would have done everything in her power to ensure he answer to the families and friends of the people and children he had killed.

But now...

Now, she was no longer a Justiciar. Yet, she had to keep Nyssa and Quinn in mind—if they took justice into their own hands, she couldn't protect them from the Empire's wraith.

She unfolded her arms and rested them on her thighs, the tips of her fingers brushing against Reece's hand. "What do you want to do, empath?"

"I don't...I don't know. Is arresting him the right thing to do? I was there the night the wraiths tore through The Masthead. Over sixty people died. Sixty innocent people who were out to celebrate Winter's Fire. I watched them get slaughtered. I thought I was going to be one of them. It was—" Her breath caught.

The pain on her face sent chills through Medias. She reached forward and slipped her hand over Reece's. "I would have stood between you and those monsters."

The admission slipped out. Impulsive, but true. Denying her feelings for Reece was proving near impossible.

Reece placed her other hand on top of Medias's and gave her a smile infused with melancholy. "I know."

Medias's heart pounded. Reece had extended her trust and her heart to Medias, and what had she done in response? Shut her down every step of the way since their night together. And yet, Reece never stopped *trying*. She was tenacious. What if one day she did give up and turned her heart away from Medias? The very idea sent a wave of cold nausea through her. Maybe it was time to stop fighting so hard to drive the woman away.

"I'm scared," Reece said. "Ceril is a desperate man. We can't know what he'll do."

Reece was avoiding saying what they both feared the most. But Medias held on to hope. Anelos took Quinn and Aryis for a reason and she hoped that reason would keep them alive long enough to be found. "We're not going to stop until they're back with us, Reece."

Reece shifted closer to Medias and leaned against her legs. "Would you stay here tonight with me? Just...as a friend?"

Medias smiled, the warmth of Reece's touch driving her insane. "Of course."

NO QUARTER

Trick Baasham strode across the casino floor, flanked by his Froslandian war wolves and a small security detail that wore its weapons openly as a warning: Do not fuck with this man.

Nyssa, however, would fuck with the gods themselves to get Quinn back.

"My friends!" Trick said, his arms spread as wide as his smile. "Welcome back to The Mystique. Though I could do with a lot less Justiciars in my establishment." His eyes scanned past Nyssa to those with her—her friends and Ina, along with ten Justiciars fanned out through the room.

The casino had cleared out soon after they'd entered, its patrons hurrying for the doors, its staff sticking together behind the bar. Nyssa couldn't fault them. One Justiciar alone could send a room scurrying for the exits.

"Do you know where Quinn Emerrath and Aryis Devitt are?" Reece asked, sidling up next to Nyssa.

Trick pursed his lips and let out a huff of air. "Do I know where they are? Not exactly, but I've heard some things from my contacts here in the Northern—"

"Where the fuck are they?" Nyssa asked. Reece sucked in a sharp breath, body stilling.

Something akin to annoyance flashed across Trick's face before he settled back into a smile. "That's not how this works, Nyssa. You don't come into my casino and make demands, no matter who you bring with you. I have something you want. You give me something I want. This is a negotiation, not charity."

"You mother—"

Athen caught her arm. "Nyssa, let Reece handle this."

She clenched her jaw. "We don't have time to dance around with this fool."

"This fool is standing right here," Trick replied, his bushy eyebrows furled down. "Reece, is this how you wish to conduct our business?"

"Apologies, nerves are a bit frayed," Reece replied, shooting a displeased glance at Nyssa. She straightened up. "What do you have?"

A smile lightened Trick's face again. "I have information on what I think is Ceril's whereabouts. I can give you that information for a price."

"What's your ask?"

"I hear there's an open spot on the Sun Council, thanks to you, Miss Ae'Shen. I want that seat."

Reece rasped out a laugh. "A seat on the Sun Council. Is this some sort of joke?"

"I am a jovial man by nature, but not when it comes to business. I'm deadly serious."

"You have no idea what you're asking for." Reece let out an exasperated breath and looked to Athen and Medias.

"Oh, I've heard the rumors, Reece. You do hold a bit of sway in Cardin now, don't you? You can chirp into Emperor Safin's ear and get me that seat," Trick said. He walked forward, his head swiveling to look at all the Justiciars before stopping on Ina. "Who here can establish communications with the Emperor? I will negotiate directly with him. Surely the boy will want to capture the man who almost killed him. I can help with that."

"You will address him as Emperor Safin," Ina said, her voice cold and steady. "Never call him a boy again."

Trick chuckled, waving his hand. "Let's contact *Emperor Safin* and put the request to him."

"You don't demand a seat on the Sun Council as if it's a mere favor," Medias growled next to Reece. "There's protocol and—"

"Ha! Protocol, my ass. If Safin wants Ceril Anelos—and if you want your people back—you will make this happen."

Ina shook her head. "No."

Trick stopped his pacing and stared daggers into the Ashcloak. "We in the Northern Wilds pay our taxes, bow our heads in deference to the throne, but we've languished without representation on the Sun Council for a century now. That changes today."

"What you're asking for is impossible," the lead Justiciar said, approaching.

"Trick, please," Reece interjected, "there has got to be something else you want."

The argument continued. Trick didn't budge. Neither did the Justiciar or Ina, both insisting that Safin wouldn't even entertain such an outsized request. Reece tried her best to mediate, but the argument trounced over her attempts to talk sense.

Trick cocked his head. "If you want Ceril, you will give me what I want. Simple as that."

Nyssa's simmering anger turned to rage. *No more words.*

Lightning exploded across her skin. Trick flinched and his guards drew their weapons. She flung a hand toward them, concentrating on the glowing balls of light in their chests that only she could see. Bolts of energy flashed through the air as Nyssa used her magick to shove everyone around Trick back. His guards crashed to the ground. Jagged azure tendrils radiated in all directions along the floor. The war wolves whined and snarled as lightning licked at their feet.

Trick yelped and tried to jump back, but Nyssa caught him by the lapel of his silken pinstriped suit jacket and yanked him forward. His face was pure surprise and fear. He hadn't seen what a Cursed God could truly do.

Now he knows.

"You will tell me where Ceril is or I will bring this casino down on your head, Baasham," Nyssa growled.

Trick held his hand out. "Wait—"

Nyssa wound her lightning up his legs, his torso, his arms, tiny bolts of blue flickering across his face. He whimpered, flinching.

"I swear on everything I hold dear, I will *ruin* you," she warned Trick.

A hand came to rest on her shoulder. "Nyssa," Medias said, wincing as shards of electricity traveled up her arm. "This isn't the way."

"I'm not going to lose Quinn because this asshole wants to dick around." Lightning sparked off her body and hit nearby objects—glass shattered, tables and chairs splintered. She teetered on the edge of control, close to tipping into pure chaos. Power flowed through her body and raged under her skin.

Who the *fuck* did Trick think he was? "Do I look like a woman who wants to barter Quinn's and Aryis's life for a goddamn Council seat?" She shoved her face a few inches from his. "Do I?" she yelled.

He held up his trembling hands, lightning dancing from fingertip to fingertip. "Please, I didn't mean any harm."

Athen stepped forward. "Anelos has people I care about. You're going to tell us where they are." He brought a heavy hand down on Trick's shoulder, giving him a squeeze. Trick winced.

Nyssa's magick snaked up the walls and wrapped around the columns dotting the room. The air vibrated, and a deep rumble filled the casino.

"Nyssa, you're going to shake this building apart," Medias warned.

"I don't care," Nyssa spat, emphasizing each word, her gaze burning through Trick.

Medias's grip grew tighter. The message was clear—Nyssa was putting everyone in danger.

"Last chance, Trick."

"Okay! Okay. That merchant ship you're looking for landed near a remote estate on the outskirts of Dennbury, a tiny little burg that's on no one's shipping routes. That estate had been empty for a while, the last of its occupants putting it up for sale and moving to warmer climate. It's still up for sale. So who could be squatting in it?"

Nyssa exhaled, tamping down her anger. The low rumble abated as her magick calmed. "Is that all?"

Trick nodded. "That's it! That's all I know."

Nyssa didn't trust the man. "Is it the truth Reece?"

Reece stepped forward, hissing when Nyssa's lightning zapped her when she drew close. "Trick's exceptionally bad at emotional deceit. Always has been." She drew closer. "Do you trust me?"

A rush of air left Nyssa. "Always."

"Then trust me when I tell you that Trick isn't lying."

Nyssa eyed the man, then let him go. He gathered himself and nodded at Reece. "I've told you everything I know." The words rushed out, eager to convince. "You have to understand, negotiation is a way of life up here. It's a currency worth more than gold."

"Not when people's lives are at stake," Nyssa replied. "Not when it's people I love. You will never do that to me again, do you understand, Baasham?"

He nodded and pulled at the lapels of his suit, smoothing it out.

She brought her magick back under control, dissipating the lightning filling the room. The low, dangerous rumble ceased. Trick's war hounds crept forward, their eyes glued to Nyssa.

"I gave you the information you wanted, Blacksea, but now you owe me a favor," Trick said, his arrogant bravado apparently restored.

Heat flooded her face. "You dare make demands of me?"

"I have to get something out of this exchange, otherwise you shame me."

"Shame you? You're lucky you're still breathing."

Reece got between them, placing a hand on Trick's chest. She scowled at Nyssa. "A fair exchange is honorable, Nyssa."

"Honorable?" Nyssa scoffed. As if Trick knew the meaning of the word.

"You have your honor code. So does Trick," Reece said. "You will owe him a favor, understand?"

The edge in Reece's voice warned Nyssa to comply, even if she hated it. Owing Trick didn't sit right with her, but she wasn't in the mood for another argument.

"A favor. But one I approve of, Baasham."

"Nothing untoward, I promise." He offered a handshake.

Nyssa complied, grinding her teeth.

Trick turned back to his guards, who kept their distance. "You all are witnesses to this agreement. The Marked God, Nyssa Blacksea, has agreed to an undisclosed favor at a future date."

The men and women in his company nodded.

Nyssa wondered what she had gotten herself into, but for the moment, she couldn't think about it. They needed to get back on the Cloud Crasher and on their way to Dennbury.

"Let's go," she said, turning to the exit.

A crowd had gathered outside, but she paid them no mind while she and her cohort passed through the streets, making their way to the airfield at the edge of town.

Athen fell in beside her.

"You backed me up in there," she said. "You're usually the one to talk reason to me."

"I would have torn that fucking casino down around Trick's ears if he didn't give us what we wanted," he replied. "We're getting Aryis and Quinn back."

Her heart thudded in her chest, aching for both herself and her best friend. She grabbed his hand as they walked, giving it a squeeze. "It's going to be okay. It has to be."

Athen cleared his throat. "Let's get back to the Cloud Crasher. Anna will get us to Dennbury as quickly as she can."

Nyssa gave him a terse nod, her thoughts ricocheting through her mind. What if Quinn and Aryis weren't in Dennbury? Her stomach flipped, cold and hollow, when she considered another possibility...

What if they were too late?

SPILL NO SECRETS

Quinn grunted, tugging on the ropes that bound her wrists. Her shoulders and elbows burned from the effort. She bit down on the gag tied around her head as she strained. The pain made tiny white stars explode in the darkness that enshrouded her. The void collar they had clamped on her neck kept her magick away, a distant and dull fuzz in the center of her chest.

She had been kept in a blackout hood for most of the journey from Arcton to...to where? The blackout hood made time hard to keep track of, trapped in perpetual darkness.

Her captors had only let her out to feed her and force water down her throat while they traveled. The water was spiked with some sort of drug that made her thoughts turn sluggish and her body heavy. But she was aware enough to recognize Efla, the woman's face floating in and out of her field of vision for the scant amount of time she was free of the hood. The rest of the time, Quinn was secured to a bunk, drifting in and out of sleep.

They had traveled by airship, its dips and ascents a poor imitation of traversing the dangerous swells of the sea. Why didn't she just take Nyssa and return to Hannah's Whisper when she had the chance? Leave Ceril to Safin and Decia to deal with. She owed the Empire nothing, having given them so much of herself already.

No, not *given*. Her freedom, her magick, her childhood…had all been *stolen* from her.

After while—days or a week, Quinn couldn't say—their airship had landed, and she was transported by horse to another location. She had tried to stay alert, but the only thing she sensed was a deep cold burying itself in her flesh and bones as they rode.

When their journey finally came to an end, she was taken inside a house. That much was obvious by the feel of wood and stone beneath her feet and the reprieve from the winter chill. She had been locked in a room, fed once, and then tied to a chair.

Untold hours had passed. And then she was moved somewhere else. Her hands were strung up over her head so her feet barely touched the floor, putting constant strain on her joints. But whatever subduing drug they had been administering had worn off. Her arm muscles burned while her legs trembled from the effort of standing on the balls of her feet. The blackout hood was hot, making the hair stick to her sweaty face as she struggled.

Quinn stilled. The subtle vibrations of footsteps on the floor alerted her to another presence. Her breathing quickened, and she blinked sweat out of her eyes.

The blackout hood was yanked off her head. Light and sound flooded in, the sudden sunlight stinging her eyes. Her gag was removed and she flexed her stiff jaw.

She tensed when her vision cleared and she saw Aryis sitting across from her, hands bound behind her back.

"Aryis?" Quinn croaked out, her throat dry and crackly. She swallowed hard, making the cold metal of the void collar press into her throat.

Aryis blinked slowly. She looked about the same as Quinn felt.

Quinn glanced around—looking for avenues of escape, as Nyssa had once taught her—finding Efla Eld'on smirking at her from her perch on the back of a couch. The other assassin, the one who could shift from one location to the next in the blink of an eye, lounged on a purple velvet chair, two blackout hoods resting on the side table next to him. Pieces of furniture dotted the room, which looked to be a sizable study or salon.

There were others present as well. Even though they no longer wore the dark-green leathers of the Obsidian Rule, Quinn was sure they were all assassins. Each one a dangerous, coiled snake ready to strike, as they had been taught by their Masters. And now, they were Ceril's weapons.

"Where the fuck are we?" Quinn asked, drilling her gaze into Efla.

"You are in my possession now," a voice behind Quinn said.

Her blood ran cold.

Ceril.

The tall man swept around Quinn and cocked his head at her. "My errant daughter."

Daughter. A word he had never used with her before. A word now injected with pure venom. He was mocking her.

"I'm not your fucking daughter," Quinn hissed.

"I raised you. I shaped who you are today." The smirk that accompanied that bold, disgusting statement turned Quinn's blood from ice to fire.

She gathered what saliva she could and spat at him. And she found her mark. Ceril flinched, anger roiling across his features. He pulled out a handkerchief and wiped his cheek with a snarl.

"I should have broken you when I had the chance," he said, moving away from her. His light-blue eyes fixed to her face. "You grew up to be quite the headstrong woman, didn't you?"

Quinn ground her jaw.

Ceril narrowed his gaze. "When you were placed in my arms, knowing what you might become, I had such great expectations for you, Quinn."

"Yeah, I turned out to be quite the disappointment, didn't I?"

"Yes. Though I did find a use for you after all."

Quinn swallowed and decided to cut to the heart of the matter. "We know what you're looking for. The sixth Alabaster Book."

Ceril scowled. "Clever."

Something was off. Wouldn't he brag if he had the book? Quinn felt in her gut that he had no idea where it was. "You don't have it, do you?"

A slight twitch of the corner of his mouth gave her the answer.

Aryis caught Quinn's eye. If he didn't have the book, there was hope. And hope was something Quinn desperately needed to cling to if she was going to live through whatever Ceril planned for them.

A door opened and footfalls grew closer to her, some steady and at least one pair of uneasy feet, shuffling near.

A person was shoved between Aryis and Quinn. Quinn recognized the tousled blonde hair and green eyes immediately. Suvi Rell.

But...wearing a void collar?

Suvi straightened up, scowling at Quinn. A purple bruise bloomed under her right eye. The void collar, the bruise—did Ceril view Suvi as yet another tool for him to use?

Ceril slid his hand onto Suvi's shoulder. "I sent Efla and Temo to bring Aryis to me, but it seems I got a Cursed God as an unexpected special treat. What shall we do with our good fortune, my Queen?"

Aryis paled, her eyes darting between Ceril and Suvi.

Aryis? Why Aryis?

Suvi shot a look of pure disdain at Ceril.

He let go of Suvi and stepped back, clasping his hands behind his back. "I have a Rell, filled with all the blood I could ever need to unlock the last Alabaster Book." He smiled and approached Quinn, his pale-blue eyes drilling into her. "And if I'm right, the spells within those pages will give me the power to bend *you* to my will."

Quinn shot forward with what little strength was left in her limbs, a strangled roar stuck in her throat. Her bindings stopped her from moving very far. Ceril backed up and laughed. Fucking *laughed*.

"I'm going to kill you," she whispered, her body trembling from fatigue.

"You have no idea the power I will have," Ceril said. "The Rells were inventive mages, but they were scared of the power they—"

"My ancestors weren't scared, you pompous prick," Suvi interrupted, seething. "They understood the dangers of soul magick."

Ceril regarded her. Then he moved, slamming a vicious fist across her cheek. Suvi crumpled to the ground, drawing chuckles from Efla and a few of the assassins in the room. A queen brought low. It had been something Quinn wanted from the moment she'd met Suvi, but seeing her bear the brunt of Ceril's anger ignited a small flame of pity for the woman.

Suvi gathered herself, sitting back on her haunches, raising her head to stare daggers into Ceril. Blood dripped from a cut under her eye. Ceril bent over and wiped at it with his finger, smiling at the ichor as he straightened.

"This is the reason you're here, Aryis." He turned, his grin like a knife in Quinn's gut, twisting. "Precious Rell blood, the key to finding that last book and unlocking its secrets."

Aryis struggled in her bindings. "When Nyssa and the others find us, you're going to answer for your crimes."

A laugh emanated out of Ceril, his mouth turning up in amusement. "I should think not."

Quinn's stomach turned at how dismissive he was of the thought. He truly did believe himself above justice.

Ceril continued, "Your tracking magick is very interesting. You use a precious object to find its owner. I wonder if you can use a person to find an object? I suspect you can. Rell blood is in the ink and the magick protecting it, forming a very powerful, intimate bond."

"No...I won't..." Aryis stammered.

"You will with the right incentive," Ceril insisted, turning to Quinn with a wolfish grin. She had seen that grin before. Ravenous. She feared he would kill her, or Aryis. Even if he wanted to control Quinn, in the end she was merely a tool, as she always had been. And tools could break.

Efla hopped off her seat on the back of the couch and approached Aryis, taking a small cube out of her pocket. She touched it to Aryis's void collar, and it clicked open.

"No!" Aryis said, her voice strained.

The two Obsidian Rule assassins with Suvi seized her arms.

"What do you think you're doing?" Suvi hissed, struggling against them. One assassin grabbed her balled-up fist.

"Open your hand," Efla ordered.

Suvi set her jaw. The ex-Queen wasn't going to give up easily, of that Quinn was certain. She was a ruthless woman, and Quinn hoped that ruthlessness translated into a stubborn resolve to resist Ceril.

When Suvi didn't comply, Efla buried a brutal fist in her midsection, causing Suvi to double over and cough violently. Efla forced her fist open and unsheathed a short knife she wore at her waist. She drew the blade across Suvi's palm, and blood burst from the cut.

Grabbing Suvi's wrist, Efla yanked her toward Aryis and smeared the bloody palm over Aryis's face. Aryis tried to turn away to no avail. Blood covered her cheek and dripped down her neck.

"No," she breathed.

Ceril held his hand out to Efla. Efla let go of Suvi and walked over to a black satchel on the couch. She removed a round, coiled object and handed it to Ceril.

The air left Quinn's lungs.

A whip.

Ceril uncoiled the weapon, the end of it licking at the floor with a soft hiss of leather against wood.

Quinn tensed, all her muscles straining against the rope binding her wrists. Across from her, Aryis's eyes widened.

"Now, Lady Devitt, you will locate that last book using Suvi's blood or I'll strip the skin off of Quinn's back. Do you understand me?"

Aryis stammered and shook her head, panic flashing in her eyes as they darted from Ceril to Quinn. "No, don't hurt her, please." The tremor in her voice gave away her fear.

But Quinn needed her to stay strong and shut up. If Ceril found that last book, they were dead. And Nyssa...what would happen to Nyssa? And Athen? Reece? Medias? Ceril with access to powerful forbidden magick would spell disaster for everyone in the Empire.

"Aryis, don't you dare help him," Quinn said. "No matter what. Do *not* help him."

"Quinn..." Aryis breathed.

Quinn shook her head and did her best to keep her voice steady. "Stay strong. I can endure this."

Ceril glanced at Aryis, then back to Quinn. "One of you will eventually break. I have both patience and persistence." He snapped his wrist, cracking the whip against the wooden floor.

The sharp *pop* echoed through the large room.

Quinn flinched, unable to stop her body from reacting. She closed her eyes against the tears that burst forth. "Don't tell him anything, Aryis," she said, opening her eyes, locking Aryis in her gaze. "Promise me."

Aryis let loose a sob. She, too, was trembling.

"Aryis, fucking promise," Quinn hissed. They had to be of one mind. If one of them broke, Ceril would win.

With a sharp swallow, Aryis steeled herself, frowning. She nodded once.

Please, Aryis, stay strong.

A shadow drew down over Ceril's face. Quinn had seen that darkness before and borne the brunt of it. He licked his lips and slowly moved behind her, the tip of the whip trailing along the floor.

Stay strong.

Quinn braced herself.

Hot, razor-sharp pain exploded across her back, forcing a shocked cry out of her. She sucked in air through gritted teeth. The slash on her back pulled with each shallow breath. Every mote of dust floating in the shafts of light, every small sound whispering through the room came into acute focus, as if her senses had dialed up.

Focus. Quinn needed to focus. She locked in on Aryis. Rivulets of tears trailed down the woman's face, carving a path through the blood smeared across her skin. To her credit, she didn't look away.

Stay strong.

A pathetic half sob, half laugh escaped Quinn's lips. Of all the people to be stuck with in this situation, why not her betrayer?

The whip sliced through the air again, splitting another slash across her back. Her body quaked under the blow. A soft chuckle left Efla as she watched, twirling her knife around her fingers.

Stay strong.

Time passed, slow and painful. Ceril kept hitting her, his breaths turning heavy. It was all she could hear aside from the crack of the whip.

Crack.

Crack.

Crack.

After a while, Ceril stopped, walked around Quinn, and turned his attention to Aryis. "You can end this."

"I won't help you."

His face grew dark and he bared his teeth. "I'm glad the students at Wayland didn't kill you so I can watch you suffer, you entitled brat."

Aryis leaped out of her chair with a strangled cry, lunging at Ceril. He sidestepped her, and she crashed to the floor, unable to break her fall with her hands bound behind her back.

Laughter dotted the room, the assassins smiling at one another.

"You murdered *children*," Aryis mumbled.

Efla yanked Aryis to her feet and shoved her back down into her chair.

"You can stop this," Ceril said, his voice cold. "Use Suvi's blood. Find that book."

Aryis shook her head.

Good girl. Stay strong.

"I'm going to kill you, Anelos," Quinn choked out around ragged breaths.

Ceril merely smiled and circled around Quinn to continue his torture.

Her flesh gave way with every blow.

Blood dripped down her legs, puddling on the floor.

She couldn't stop the wheeze of pain that accompanied every breath.

How much could her body take before it truly broke beyond repair?

Aryis flinched with each snap of the whip. Tears streamed down her face.

The whip drew louder cries of pain out of Quinn. As much as she tried to control herself, tried to be strong, her body shook with each blow.

"Stop. Please!" Aryis whimpered.

Ceril persisted. The whip's sharp *crack* echoed through the large room, punctuating Quinn's pain.

A whisper left Aryis's lips. "Stop."

Quinn stared down at Aryis, pleading with her eyes to remain stalwart. To not give Ceril what he wanted. But it was obvious the woman's resolve was crumbling.

It only took a few more whip cracks for Aryis to shout, "Stop! Please stop. Please, I know where the book is."

Ceril paused.

"Aryis, no," Quinn croaked.

The tip of the whip swished against the wooden floor. "Where, Aryis?" Ceril asked.

"Skystrand," she whispered.

Ceril grunted. "How do you know?"

Aryis breathed heavily, drops of tears quivering on her chin before they fell. "The door to the Night Vault. It's a map."

"No," Quinn whimpered before her body went slack, her wrists, arms, and shoulders numb. She closed her eyes and retreated, trying to burrow deep inside herself. Where she could escape. Where Nyssa waited.

A TENUOUS PEACE

Aryis cleaned Quinn's back while the woman drifted in and out of sleep, careful to be gentle and go slow. She had thrown away any sense of pride and begged Ceril to let her tend to Quinn's wounds. If they got infected, Quinn could die without a proper healer or an antibiotic tincture.

Is she going to be okay?

Aryis flinched. Tajal had been fairly quiet since their capture, his silence disconcerting. "I hope so," she whispered.

It will be a shame if she has to die in the company of her betrayer.

"You are really uplifting, you know that?"

I don't deal in blind optimism. The fantasy of surviving that...detestable man is unhealthy. You should steel your soul for the reality that Cecil will kill you.

"Ceril," Aryis seethed.

I care not for the man, so why should I remember his name?

Aryis ground her teeth and dipped her cloth in a bowl of pink-tinted water. "Can't you do something to help here?"

Why would I?

"So, you won't help?"

Was that not clear?

She sighed. "Useless asshole."

"A bit harsh," Quinn mumbled as her eyes fluttered open.

"I-I was talking about myself."

"Hmm..." Quinn took a deep breath, wincing. Her green eyes focused on Aryis wringing the bloody water out of the cloth before dabbing it on Quinn's raw skin. Quinn hissed at her touch.

"I'm sorry," Aryis said. She bit her lip, nervous to be alone with Quinn. After everything that had happened, it was impossible to know what to say. Her mind settled on hope. They needed hope. "Nyssa's going to find us."

No, she isn't, Tajal rumbled.

Quinn tensed more under her touch. "I can't imagine what she must be going through right now."

What Nyssa is going through? Quinn should concern herself with her own predicament.

Tajal's annoyance was evident—clearly he didn't understand the bond between the two women. He was still so dense, even after studying Aryis's emotions while she was trapped in the Realm of Shadows. What had one of her Masters at Wayland said during a lecture? There was often a vast difference between observation and understanding.

Quinn and Aryis fell into silence as Aryis worked. Quinn's hands balled up in the blankets underneath her while she lay on her stomach and let Aryis clean her wounds. She stifled grunts of pain into the thin pillow below her face, being braver than Aryis would be in the same circumstance.

At least she's not glowering at you.

"I suppose."

Quinn turned her head to Aryis and narrowed her gaze.

Shit. "Sorry. I tend to talk to myself more when stressed." It wasn't a lie necessarily. She did talk aloud when under pressure—it soothed her, allowed her mind to work and find solutions to whatever problems she faced. Though, of late, her problem-solving skills had been put to the test. "Can you sit up?"

"Yeah."

Aryis stood, groaning from the way her knee twinged and ached. Quinn's eyes flicked up at her, a look of concern on her face. Aryis put the pain aside and dropped the cleaning cloth into the water bowl, then bent over Quinn to lend assistance. With Aryis's help, Quinn sat up, holding her blanket over her chest.

"Your knee, how bad is it?" Quinn inquired.

"Pay it no mind. I try not to." Aryis picked up a roll of bandages. "Ready?"

With a grunt, Quinn turned on the bed as much as she could to expose her back to Aryis, who began wrapping the bandage around Quinn's upper body. She worked in silence, going slow and tensing with each of Quinn's sharp intakes of breath. The pain must have been unimaginable.

This seems like a waste of time. That man is just going to flay that bandage off the next time he wants something from you two.

Aryis bit her tongue. He was right, and she knew it. She wanted to rant and rage against him, tell him it didn't matter, that she had to help Quinn. They could only depend on each other now and try to keep each other alive until Nyssa and the others found them.

If they found them.

A hand caught her wrist. Quinn blinked up at her. "Why did you tell Ceril where to find the book?"

Aryis swallowed. "He was going to kill you. I couldn't let that happen, Quinn."

The woman let her head hang. "He's going to use soul magick to control me."

The prospect of Ceril with Quinn under his thrall was a fearsome notion. "I think the Wayland tragedy was a test run. Ceril wanted to see if he could actually weave soul magick. The few spells that I found in the Alabaster Books at Arcton are a precursor to far more powerful magick. The spell that made my students turn on me took months to weave by the looks of it, and its effects would've only lasted an hour. Had any of the children lived that long..." Aryis felt sick to her stomach again, the image of all those dead children plaguing her.

What does this mortal think he's playing at with such foolishness?

Ceril wanted *control*. If he could enthrall Quinn, he could enthrall anyone, including an Areshi Emperor. Ceril didn't have to wage war on Safin to overthrow him.

Quinn's hand tightened around her wrist. "So he knows the book is in a sky city but not *where* in that city. Promise me you won't track it for him. My life isn't more important than keeping that deadly magick out of his hands, do you understand me?"

"I can't make that promise. You know I can't."

Quinn's jaw tensed. "The one goddamn time I need you to be strong, and you can't do it."

Aryis sat silent.

Quinn licked her lips and blinked slowly, raising her arm with a wince to point to the metal water carafe on the small table next to the bed. Aryis poured Quinn a glass and helped her hold it to her lips to take tiny sips. She shook her head to let Aryis know she was done. Replacing the glass on the table, Aryis stared down at her hands. They bore a slight pinkish tint from the bloody water.

"I'm sorry, Quinn."

From behind her, Quinn took a deep breath. "You keep telling me how sorry you are."

"I don't know what else to say."

"Stop apologizing. It wears thin after a while and grates on my ears."

"I'm sor—shit."

A light laugh rumbled out of Quinn. Aryis turned to face her.

"How did you figure out where the last book is?" Quinn asked, her eyes bright despite the dim room. "We scoured through the Night Vault. We found nothing."

"It came to me on the ship. I stood in front of the damn door so many times. The etching on it is a map." She extended her index finger and began tracing its etching in the air. "Remember the forest at the bottom?" She drew the figure of trees, then moved her finger up. "And a sky city floating above the forest in the distance? It's the city. The book is in the city."

"That could be any sky city, Aryis. There were thirty or so at one point. And half have fallen out of the sky, right?" Quinn asked. "That's a lot of locations to visit...and a lot of land to cover."

Aryis laughed. "I figured out which one." She dotted her finger in the air. "Remember the stars?"

Quinn nodded.

"I recognized the constellations. And right above the city, there's a star. Except, it doesn't belong. There is no such object in the night sky in the midst of those constellations."

The puzzled look on Quinn's face opened up to realization. "The Dawn Beacon?"

Oh, she's a smart one.

Aryis hummed a soft growl under her breath, warning Tajal off. "Yes, the fake star that's above Skystrand, the so-called City of the Dawn. The city itself was an engineering and magickal marvel of its time, though the Beacon was a bit of a pet project of its builder, who wanted it to—"

"Aryis, are you sure the book is there?"

"Completely sure? No. But I remember that the Night Vault was constructed after the Alabaster Books were written, overseen by Eliza Rell herself. No one would give the door a second thought, thinking the artwork was just that...merely art."

"Except for you," Quinn said. Her face softened for a moment. "Not bad."

You humans are so confounding, Tajal rumbled. *Don't believe for one moment she cares if you live or die. You merely serve a purpose.*

"Thank you," Aryis said, ignoring Tajal.

They fell into silence as Aryis helped Quinn into a clean shirt. Both women moved slowly. Quinn was barely able to get her arms into the sleeves, pain etched across her face.

When they were done, Quinn's body bowed forward from the exertion.

She looks pale. Well, paler than usual. She is practically translucent. Does the woman spend any time in the sun?

How Aryis wanted to rage and scream at Tajal. He wouldn't help when she asked, and his commentary was less than useless. But she calmed herself, for Quinn's sake.

Shouldn't you say something to bolster her confidence? Tajal asked. *Something...hopeful?*

He was right. Annoyingly so.

"Nyssa will find us," Aryis said.

Quinn raised her eyes and swallowed heavily. "You never waver in your faith in her, do you?"

"No." It was true. From the moment she met Nyssa, Aryis took a correct measure of the woman—she would bleed herself dry for those she loved. Aryis leaned forward. "She's going to find us. Know that."

Quinn nodded, her eyelids half shut.

A flutter of fear moved through Aryis, and she did her best to tamp it down. She needed to be strong, but that fear was cruel and persistent, whispering awful things...

Like she'd never see Nyssa again. Or Athen.

THE GREATEST FAILURE

Quinn opened her eyes, sensing someone else in the dark room with her. She had been drifting in and out of restless, pained sleep for days.

Quinn swallowed, wincing. Her throat ached for water. "Aryis?" she whispered.

"No," a male voice replied.

Cold fear flooded her veins, but she had no energy to move.

Ceril sat down in the chair next to her bed. He leaned forward, his sharp features coming into slow focus. He pushed a strand of hair out of Quinn's face. She flinched at his unwelcome touch. He sighed. "I wish things had turned out differently for the two of us."

She shrank away from him, trying to move to the opposite side of the bed, but her body protested. "You're a monster."

"And you were my greatest failure."

He sat back in his chair. Thin lines covered his face and his hair was grayer than ever before. Whatever cheap vanity enchantments he had been using to cover his age had long worn off. The irony—for such a powerful spellweaver, he seemed to have little talent in that particular line of magick.

"You were going to be my retribution. A god given to me to raise, one I could use to regain my place in the Empire as one of its leaders," he said, examining her with his pale-blue eyes. "I gave you a home and an education. Then you turned out to be...mundane. Not the god that was promised by the Mystics."

Quinn ground her jaw, her hand clenching the pillow underneath her cheek. "And for that sin, you punished me."

"You were a headstrong brat."

Quinn swallowed, her throat burning. "Still am, I suppose."

"I am going to take what I'm owed, girl."

"I owe you nothing."

He lunged forward in his chair, his face inches from hers, full of rage. "You owe me everything! I was promised the throne, and it was snatched away from me. Given to a fucking child. You were meant to be my way back into power, but you were worthless. I sacrificed my future for the Empire."

"Your future?" Quinn scoffed, indignation flaring in her chest. "Do you mean the woman you were to marry? As if I actually believe you loved her. You don't know the meaning of the word."

Ceril moved back. His face lost its intensity, once again looking old and worn.

Plucking up every last ounce of strength, Quinn pushed herself up, swung her legs off her cot, and sat upright. Her back stung and burned, its light bandage almost unbearable against her raw skin. She breathed shallow breaths, trying to stop her body from quaking.

I got through it before, I can get through it now.

"You made your choice." Quinn drew her eyes up to his. The pain lacing across her back turned into a dull throb when she sat still. "You saw a throne and everything else became unimportant. Do you know the real reason you were named successor? You weren't special or worthy of the throne. It was a fucking political favor."

In a blur of motion, Ceril backhanded Quinn across the face, his golden ring slicing through her cheek.

Wincing, she touched her trembling fingers to the cut. Another scar from Ceril Anelos.

"There was a time I wanted nothing more than a smile from you," Quinn said, swallowing back bile as her stomach roiled from the pain wracking her body. "I was such a stupid fucking child, confusing attention with affection. When you pushed me aside, I didn't understand what I did to make you hate me. You were the only person in my life who felt remotely like a father, and I came to understand far too late, and so cruelly, that you aren't even capable of love."

Ceril studied her. "Nyssa got the father you so wanted. How you must resent her for it."

Quinn laughed ruefully. He *truly* didn't understand love. "I'm glad she had Eron. He raised an honorable woman, and she saved me. Nyssa is a *credit* to him."

Ceril's face grew dark.

"I understand why you hate her so much," Quinn continued. "You didn't think she belonged at the Emerald Order, and yet she thrived."

He took a deep breath and stood. "This Empire embraces its tradition and rules. Even now, in the midst of upheaval, those fools are trudging forward with the Emperor's Ascension ceremony. They are desperate for normalcy. Safety. Everything in the Empire is bright, gold, clean. Orderly. Because it has to be. And the Emperors, Great Houses, guilds, and Justiciars make it so. I came to realize too late that it's all a façade. There's ugliness under the riches and privilege, and the scales can be tipped by the mere touch of a corrupt feather."

He smoothed out his jacket, picking at a small piece of lint on his sleeve. The man had always been fastidious about his appearance, vain even. Everything in its proper place. That was Ceril's expectation of the world, and once he was knocked askew, he never recovered.

Quinn chuckled, no longer caring if he hurt her. "You thought having me under your thumb would give you power, but I turned out to be a dud."

"Not anymore." Ceril spread his arms and cast his eyes about the dank room. "You're my prisoner, and once I get that book, you'll be mine. Completely. I'll turn you into a world destroyer. I'll make you kill everyone you love, while you watch from afar, trapped inside your own mind, under my thrall." He rubbed his fingers together, sucking his teeth. "You will tear Nyssa's soul to shreds for me, child."

Cold fear flooded Quinn. She lunged with a roar in her throat, fingers weakly scrabbling for Ceril's throat. He shoved her back onto the bed with ease. Moving so quickly, so violently, it felt like her back was tearing apart. The intense spike of pain made her stomach lurch, and she became lightheaded.

He loomed over her and raised his hand. Quinn flinched, an instinctive reaction honed through years of abuse. She hated how her body betrayed her fear of him.

He sneered down at her before striding to the window and pulling back the curtain. Sunlight burst into the room, illuminating his face. The small, satisfied grin on his lips made her burn with hate.

"Once you're stable enough to travel, we'll make our way to Skystrand and recover that book. And when that happens, the world is going to change."

Quinn stayed silent.

Ceril lingered for a moment, then crossed the room and left.

Quinn let out a whimper, her body bowing forward. It wasn't in her to cry, but now tears trailed down her cheek and dripped off the tip of her chin.

A DEPARTURE

Nyssa pressed her back against a towering oak tree and stole a peek at the sprawling estate that sat past a snowy clearing. Trick's intelligence turned out to be correct, and a cautious spark of hope lit in her chest.

Outbuildings dotted the landscape, a few in disrepair, but the main house looked in fine shape. An expansive wooden porch wrapped around the front of the house, its deep-maroon bricks overrun by ivy that snaked up the exterior, rimming large windows. White wisps of smoke trailed out of a chimney on the other side of the house.

This out-of-the-way manor was the perfect place for Ceril and his cohort to hide.

Past the estate, in a clearing, sat an airship smaller than the Cloud Crasher. A few people milled around a fire lit next to the vessel while others carried bags up the gangplank to the ship. The people were likely its merchant crew, but Nyssa couldn't be sure. As far as she cared, anyone associated with Ceril was an enemy. Those making money while abetting a criminal like him would get locked up right alongside him.

Nyssa's and the others' advance on the old estate had been under the cover of early darkness and through dense woods, masking their approach. She exhaled and closed her eyes, calling upon her power to search for any magickal traps or alarms.

Turning to face the tree, she flattened her palms against the rough, brittle bark and dipped her head. She exhaled and closed her eyes, calling upon her magick. Keeping calm was imperative—the last thing they needed was for her magick to flare up and alert their enemies to their presence. Fine control over her power could still be a challenge, especially when under stress. And a heady mix of worry and anger had been eating away at her since Quinn was taken, making it hard for her to focus.

Expanding her senses, she did her best to shut out the low roar that vibrated through her body, a roar that filled the space where Quinn's presence once was. An undeniable reminder that part of her was missing. A vital part that she needed almost as much as the air she breathed.

Nyssa let the cold winter wind, with its hint of evergreen, calm her. As she reached out, dots and lines and blobs of magick flooded her senses. She took a moment, concentrating on the soft glowing orbs of the living beings, their souls moving and flickering like a candle's flame.

"There's...maybe twenty people in and around the house. Another seven or so near the airship." *Shit.* Ceril had more Obsidian Rule assassins with him than they had anticipated. He had corrupted less than half of the guild, according to Decia—at least by her best guess. There were a number of Rule adepts who were unaccounted for, spread across the world, doing what they were trained to do: be spies. How many of them were unaware of what their guild had become?

Narrowing her focus, Nyssa zeroed in on each magickal essence in the house. There was one soul among them all that she knew intimately. Its resonance sang to her when she stilled. The bright-white glow surrounded by spikes of brilliant gold made her heart jump. It was the soul of a Cursed God.

Quinn.

"She's alive," Nyssa breathed.

"And Aryis?" Athen asked.

The familiar resonance of Aryis washed over her as she zeroed in on the other soul close to Quinn, its light-blue magick like a warm blanket. "Alive as well."

A rush of air left Athen, as if he had been holding his breath since he learned of Aryis's abduction.

A rustle of cloth pulled Nyssa's attention away from the estate. She turned to find Ina crouched next to her. Nyssa relayed what she had sensed.

"Are you sure?" Ina asked.

"You doubt me?" Nyssa replied, annoyed. She wasn't in the mood to argue anymore. She would have preferred to leave Ina behind on the airship with Reece, who'd argued mightily to come along. Even Anna had volunteered to help in the rescue, citing her younger days as a roustabout. She insisted she'd held her own in countless bar fights at the local pubs in Ruinoak, a frigid town along the Northern Wilds coast, even farther north than New Ibanis. Medias talked sense into them both, and the women ultimately acquiesced, though Reece was undeniably grumpy.

"Let's move back deeper into the woods and—"

"That ship is readying to sail," Nyssa whispered to Ina. "We can't let that happen. We need to move now."

"No, we need to have a plan. Let's assume we're walking into a trap."

Fuck a plan. Nyssa wasn't about to let Ceril get away with Quinn and Aryis. She darted out from behind the tree, crouching as she ran toward the estate, ignoring Ina and Athen's alarmed whispers calling after her. Adrenaline rushed through her body, her magick humming just under the surface, waiting to be unleashed.

She closed in on the house quickly, drawing the attention of the two lookouts on the front porch. Their magick flared, filling her vision. Nyssa threw her hands up, letting loose a bolt of lightning. She flung it at one of the guards, hitting him dead in the chest. The electricity boomed and crackled, chaining to the assassin next to him. They both died instantly.

Shouts pierced the air. "Intruders!"

Seconds later, a deep rumble shook the ground, vibrating through Nyssa's chest. A bellowing *CRACK* caused her to duck, and wood splinters rained down all around her. She turned to the noise, finding Athen and Ina close behind her.

"Shit," she whispered when she saw the source of the explosion. A massive gray stone giant, at least twenty feet tall, lumbered toward her, the garden shed that served as its hiding place razed to the ground.

"Nyssa," Athen shouted when he reached her, pointing at the airship. Dark figures spilled off the deck, scrambling along the ground and in their direction, like insects.

"Wraiths!" Nyssa shouted.

Magickal energy exploded all around her, coming to life as the Justiciars and Ina joined the fight. Nyssa rushed at the stone giant, drawing forth her power. When it spotted her, it stooped over and began galloping toward her on all four of its craggy limbs.

The thing moved fast. Too damn fast. Nyssa skidded to a stop and sent a wave of lightning at it, hoping to shatter it before it got closer. Her magick rippled around the behemoth's body and dissipated harmlessly.

Shit. The thing didn't slow down. Magick sparked at her fingertips, a spike of panic shooting through her spine.

A profanity barely formed on her lips when Athen shoved her out of the path of the stone construct, taking the brunt of the collision. The giant lifted Athen in the air, and they both slammed to the ground. It reared back to attack.

Bright bursts of white light exploded in front of the giant's onyx eyes, its pupils rimmed by a silver luminescence. Medias's magick did nothing to slow the creature. Its fist hurled down at Athen's head.

Athen caught it with a roar, twisting the giant's wrist. It tried to pull back, shards of stone flaking off of its arm from the pressure.

Nyssa rushed at the giant, reaching out with her magick to mangle whatever enchantment created the damn thing. Azure energy flowed out of her fist, and she drove a spike of lightning into its chest.

The instant her magick touched its body, a reflective shock wave of energy hit her, pulsing through her arm with so much force she flew back several feet. Nyssa hit the frozen ground with a *thud*, the impact jarring her to the bone.

Medias rushed over and helped her stand. She tried lifting her right arm, but it was numb all the way up to her shoulder. "I don't understand," Nyssa said, blinking at Medias. "I did nothing to it."

Athen was back on his feet, dodging blows from the deceptively fast giant and getting his own attacks in where he could. The thing was tough—and Nyssa's magick had no effect on it.

"Get Quinn and Aryis!" he yelled as he reeled back from a glancing blow. There was a smudge of blood on his face. "Go!"

"Come on," Medias said, grabbing Nyssa and heading to the front door of the house. "Where are they?"

"They're in the middle of—"

A black, shrieking wraith barreled through Nyssa and Medias, driving them through the front of the mansion, shattering its large door. Glass tinkled all around them, showering the ground. Nyssa struggled to move—the impact knocking the wind out of her. She pushed up to her hands and knees, jagged glass biting into her flesh. Sharp pain lanced through her side with each breath.

"Nyssa, close your eyes!" Medias yelled.

Nyssa obeyed, clamping her eyes shut. She felt Medias's pops of light exploding near the two of them. The wraith screeched and claws sunk into her flesh, sending a wave of stinging agony across her back.

Lightning jolted out of her hands as she blindly attacked the wraith, sensing its dim, corrupt soul, brought back to decayed life by Ceril's magick. Nyssa opened her eyes. The wraith crashed to the dark marble floor in the manor's foyer and twitched before stilling. Its milky white eyes stared blankly at her.

Nyssa rose to her feet. Each breath came with a wincing grunt. She hunched over, unable to straighten up completely.

"Here," Medias said, pulling Nyssa's arm over her shoulder to help her stand. Blood flowed out of a cut on her cheek, but she seemed to have escaped the brunt of the wraith's attack.

"Quinn and Aryis are close," Nyssa said and pointed to a pair of doors at the opposite end of the entryway.

Medias got them moving. A ball of blue energy sparked around Nyssa's hand, and she flung it at the dark wood doors, shattering them with a thundering *boom*.

The room beyond was large and filled with a few pieces of old furniture. Winter air rushed in through doors that led outside. Figures hurried away from the house toward the ship.

Nyssa recognized the tall figure leading them. "Ceril." Behind him, a woman in a hood struggled against the assassins who held her in their grasp—Aryis. More assassins dragged a limp form between them. Nyssa's heart leaped into her throat.

Quinn.

"Medias…"

"I see them," Medias replied, picking up the pace.

They crossed the room and exited the glass doors out into the back garden. The airship loomed in the distance.

"We have to stop them!" Nyssa said. "Let me go."

Medias released her hold, and Nyssa stumbled forward, breaking into a jog once her legs became steadier underneath her.

"Ceril!" she yelled. Magick pulsed at her fingertips, another ball of lightning forming.

The man turned, shrouded by the darkness of the early night. "Get the prisoners on the ship," he commanded. The assassins moved in concert, pulling Aryis along, though struggling with Quinn.

Offering up a silent apology, Nyssa hurled her lightning orb at Quinn and her captors. Her aim was dead-on, and she hit one of the assassins square in the back. Lightning arced and chained from one assassin, through Quinn, to the other assassin. The three of them dropped to the ground. None of them moved.

Oh gods…

A low thrum of magick washed over Nyssa, the sensation of it turning her stomach. The sound of leathery wings beating the air echoed in the night, and two wraiths landed next to Ceril. With a grunt, Nyssa let loose her power, bolts of energy flowing out of her outstretched arms and racing at Ceril.

The wraiths shot toward her, barreling straight into the lightning, taking the full brunt of her attack. Their screeches stung her ears before they fell to the dirt, writhing. Errant strands of glowing blue magick sparked and sizzled along the ground, lighting up the air around Ceril. He shouted and dropped to a knee as weak currents licked at his legs.

Nyssa gathered herself for another attack.

Ceril raised his hands. The air in front of him shimmered, filling with dots of purple light. He flung his arms out, and the points of light raced toward Nyssa with a high-pitched whine. It looked very much like one of Fontaine's traps.

Without thinking, Nyssa exploded with magick, flinging out a web of lightning in front of her. The purple light hit the web with a hiss, trapped by her magick. It vibrated for a moment before collapsing into a quivering ball.

But something wasn't right—Ceril's magick hadn't been destroyed. The ball hung in the air, growing brighter with each moment. Nyssa tried wrapping her magick around it, but she couldn't grasp ahold of it. Volatile energy cascaded over Nyssa, building quickly.

Ceril's attack wasn't a snare—it was a bomb.

"Shit," she breathed.

She whirled around and rushed at Medias to shield her, shards of her azure magick sparking to life all around her as protection. The ball exploded behind Nyssa, lifting her off her feet. She crashed into Medias.

TWISTED

Quinn's head bobbed up and down as she fought to stay conscious, the blackout hood suppressing her senses. The only thing that cut through the haze was the excruciating pain radiating from her back, oppressive and searing. Even the light cotton shirt that Aryis had helped her into was torture against her skin.

She struggled to put one foot in front of the other while she was dragged along, jostled between two of Ceril's lackeys. The assassins wrenched at her arms to keep her on her feet, which pulled her skin. She screamed soundlessly into the blackout hood, the agony of her flayed back turning her vision white. Her captors continued to yank her along, even as her body went limp. Though she fought to hold on to consciousness, her head lulled forward.

Quinn jolted to attention when the ground vibrated under her feet. Seconds later, the earth quaked again and her world tumbled. Pain, hot and searing, laced through her. The fingers of her captors seized on her arms before falling away, and she crumpled to the ground without their support.

She lay there, for how long, she didn't know. Everything was slow...so slow. Her thoughts. Her body. She commanded her fingers to move, grasping at the wet, cold snow. Underneath her, the ground rumbled once more.

What the hell is happening?

Quinn pawed at the blackout hood, trying to find the locked clasp. The cold metal sparked against her fingers—a weak ward that only calmed when its key was near. She almost wanted to laugh. How many times had she endured a zap of pain from a ward before she suppressed its power? This one was tame by comparison, but her hand fell away anyway. There was no getting through the lock without the key.

She lay on her side, too tired to move. *Get up. Get up. Fight.*

The notion was mad. She couldn't see or hear anything. Her magick was far beyond her reach thanks to the damn void collar. And her body ached.

But she still had what Nyssa had taught her—Ithais-Toru. If Nyssa were blind, magickless, and ready to drop from exhaustion and pain, she would still fight. Her stubbornness would allow nothing less.

Quinn moved slow, intent on climbing to her feet, but hands caught her elbow and kept her still. An explosion of sound assaulted her and the faces of Ina Ruggen and Athen came into quick focus in the dim dusk light. Her blackout hood was in his hand, its lock crushed.

"Athen?" she whispered.

He smiled down at her, and her heart leaped with hope, something she hadn't felt in weeks. A trickle of blood ran from his nose. Who could hurt him like that?

"Let me get this off of you," he said, shattering the void collar around her neck. Her magick flooded back through her body, its energy making every nerve in her body quiver.

Then she felt something else. Something she'd yearned to feel and embrace again when she was alone with her desolate thoughts in her room—the warm glow of Nyssa's presence. The warmth of their soul-bond spread through Quinn's chest brought a weak smile to her lips.

"Nyssa?" she croaked, her throat parched from screaming into the hood.

"She's here. Alive. Just knocked around a bit," he said.

Quinn followed his gaze. Nyssa lay close by, Medias hovering over her.

A loud crash drew all their attention. A massive stone giant, twenty feet tall if Quinn were to guess, burst out of the back of the house. It stomped its feet as it strode toward them, shaking the ground with each step.

"Well, I see the Justiciars' snaring spell didn't hold," Athen mumbled with mock surprise. He shot to his feet and took off toward the construct. Roaring his defiance, he crashed into the giant, flesh meeting stone. Each of Athen's punches crunched against rock, driving the thing back. The giant swung at Athen, and the force of the blow sent him sailing through the side of the house.

Moments later, he emerged from the rubble, shaking off a layer of wood and brick debris. Pure determination settled on his face, and he met the giant again with his fist. There was little skill to the clash—just fists, powered by tremendous strength.

Quinn struggled to her feet and turned to the airship. Her stomach sank to the ground.

It was already in the air.

If Ceril got to Skystrand and found that Alabaster Book, he could do untold damage from the shadows, influencing anyone in power to do his bidding. And Quinn knew in her gut that he would come after her.

Enslave her.

Finding a small reserve of energy, Quinn loped after the airship, picking up speed. A few dark wraiths flew with it.

Shadow wound around her hands—her magick wasn't at full strength, an effect of the void collar, but perhaps she had just enough power to do what was needed. She ignored the bracing winter air and the sound of the fight behind her. She ignored the pain lacing across her back. If she let it, it would cripple her.

I can stop it.

Quinn picked up her pace, pain making her lightheaded. *Now.* She had to do it *now.* She stilled, focusing, and held out her hand. Shadow swirled around it and Quinn concentrated the power of her magick into a fine point. She would have one shot at taking the ship down. The crew on board would go down with it, but they had thrown their lot in with Ceril—their lives were no longer innocent, not in the least.

Her arm started shaking, the power building and building, shaping a bolt of darkness so sharp and deadly it would splinter the ship apart and kill everyone on board.

"Quinn, stop!" Medias called out from behind her.

Quinn ignored her and kept building up energy. She needed to stop Ceril. To end him. While he was alive, she would never be free. Neither would Nyssa.

Hatred, pure and cold, twisted up in Quinn's chest, her heart pounding. Her arm vibrated from the force of the magick, shadow surrounding it, pulsating with a dark, violet light. She braced herself and did her best to steady her arm. She would have one chance at this, she couldn't miss. There wouldn't be another—

Medias's shout pierced through the winter chill. "Aryis is on that ship!"

Quinn unleashed a guttural scream. She jerked her arm down, letting the shadow bolt loose. It sailed woefully off target into a distant cluster of trees. Everything inside her quivered, and she dropped to her knees, doubling over from pain and exhaustion.

"Quinn," a soft voice said.

Nyssa sank down next to her and pushed the hair away from her face. Quinn melted into Nyssa's warm touch, resting her cheek in her palm. She grasped Nyssa's jacket and held on tight, the woman's verbena scent curling around her.

"You're here," Quinn murmured, trying to keep the tremor out of her voice. She was so close to breaking.

Nyssa's blue eyes blazed with a cold fire that made Quinn's stomach tighten. "I would have torn through the fucking world to find you."

Nyssa moved to embrace Quinn. But Quinn shrank from her touch. Even shifting a wee bit made her moan in pain. "No, my...my back."

Nyssa sucked in a breath. "What did he do to you?"

Quinn dropped her eyes from Nyssa's face. "That doesn't matter right now. We have to get to a ship. Ceril knows where the book is."

"We'll get him," Nyssa replied. "I swear, I won't let him hurt you again." Quinn tried to sink into her confidence and live in it, if only for the moment.

"I could use a little help here!" Athen yelled across the back courtyard. He had the stone giant pinned to the ground—or at least what was left of it. One of its arms was missing and a leg was shattered below the knee. But it still struggled under Athen's grip.

"How is that thing still fighting?" Nyssa asked as she helped Quinn stand, careful not to touch her back. Medias gingerly pulled Quinn's arm over her shoulders to support her.

"Go," Medias said. "I've got her."

Nyssa hurried over to Athen and the construct, lightning forming around her fist. "Athen, I've got this. A little twist to its magick ought to stop it."

He let go of the construct's remaining arm and moved away. Brilliant threads of blue lightning sank into the giant's body, its surface crackling with azure radiance.

Nyssa gritted her teeth, frowning. "It's resisting my magick. I don't know how."

"Let me know if you need help," Quinn offered as she and Medias made their way over to them.

"I just have to put a little more effort into it," Nyssa replied. Her shoulders tensed, and a burst of energy flowed through the threads of her magick and into the giant. It shuddered once before stilling. And then began to crumble back into small stones.

Athen rubbed the back of his neck, wincing. "Thanks for that assist."

"And the wraiths?" Nyssa asked.

"There were only a few to take down, but we lost Justiciar Prakis, I'm sorry to say."

Nyssa nodded, her gaze solemn.

Quinn took stock of her surroundings. She had been so focused on one thing—stopping Ceril. A small contingent of Justiciars gathered close to Ina Ruggen.

Medias stood next to her, holding fast to her arm, giving her support.

Quinn bowed her head. "Thank you, Medias." She had been so close to taking down Ceril's retreating ship. Doing so would have condemned Aryis to death. She wouldn't have known until it was too late if Medias hadn't stopped her. And she would never have been able to look Nyssa or Athen in the eyes ever again.

Aryis...

Shit.

Quinn eyed Athen. He scanned the back courtyard, the obvious change in his expression driving a dagger through her.

"Where's Aryis?" he asked, his voice hollow.

SKYSTRAND

Aryis sat still in her blackout hood, the familiar gentle rocking of an airship beneath her. She massaged her fingers into her knee, its usual dull ache now a throb she couldn't ignore.

Someone tugged on the hood and pulled it off. The world, dark and muted, flooded back in, motes of dust dancing through the single shaft of light leaking through the only porthole in the cabin.

Efla stood over her.

"Where's Quinn?" Aryis asked.

"Mind your business," Efla growled in response. She looked disheveled—something was wrong. The way Aryis had been snatched up and hurried aboard the ship had been suspicious, but the hood prevented her from seeing or hearing anything that had happened.

She's cagey, Tajal rumbled.

"She's an asshole," Aryis replied, not caring if she drew Efla's ire. "Where is Quinn?"

You put some bass in your voice, Little Bird. I'm sure that will sway this woman.

The assassin didn't answer, but the look in her face told her what she needed to know. Quinn wasn't on the ship.

"She got away, didn't she?" Aryis grinned, her heart leaping. Dare she hope?

That's preposterous. How could she get away? With a void collar and that blasted nightmare hood they put on you two, there's no way. I couldn't see a damn thing!

Aryis let out a chuckle. She couldn't help it. A feeling of certainty rose in concert with her hope.

"Nyssa, right?"

The way Efla's eyes darted to her face and away again cemented it—Nyssa had found them. She let out a laugh, half relief, half joy.

"Of course. I knew she'd find us."

And what exactly did Blacksea do for us? Nothing. She rescued Quinn, not you. I'm making a note of this.

"You're an idiot!" Aryis proclaimed.

The insult—meant for Tajal—was met with a backhand from Efla across Aryis's face.

Her nose throbbed, but she didn't care. Quinn was free. Nyssa had found them. Was Athen with her? The prospect of seeing him again made Aryis's heart sing. Whether they met again as lovers or friends or distant acquaintances that once shared a wonderful slice of time together—she just wanted to know he was safe.

Efla looked around the room once before taking her leave, locking the door behind her.

Aryis let out a huge breath of relief. "Nyssa will find us."

Why are you so certain?

She huffed out her exasperation. "You have got to be the dumbest Ancient God of the bunch. You spent a month in the Realm of Shadows rifling through my memories and emotions, but you have learned absolutely nothing aside from Nyssa's nickname for me. What are you even doing in my head besides wasting my goddamn time with your inane questions and shitty observations?"

Y-you...you're a mere child flailing about the universe. I've been alive longer than you can fathom. How dare you? I will—

"I am beyond caring about your threats. Anything you could do to me, I've already faced in some way or another, and I'm tired. Just...tired. You wanted to experience my emotions and see what mortal existence was like? This is it, Tajal. It's joyful and ugly and confusing and wonderful and painful and so much more that's impossible to describe. It's everything and nothing at any given time. You want to pin it to a board and know exactly what it is, its shape and form. The look of life, the taste of it, the smell of it, how it feels when it slips over you in all of its exceptional, terrible glory. Except you have no capacity to *truly* understand. So stop wasting my *fucking* time."

Tajal went silent. Before, she would have feared he'd hurt her in retribution for her impertinence, but now, she couldn't give a fuck. There were far larger issues at play than a curious god running around her head. Ceril with access to a book of soul magick was a more chilling prospect.

Finally, Tajal spoke up. *I'm not an idiot.*

"Then why do you keep questioning everything? Doubting the people I love?"

How do you know when you are loved?

The question made Aryis pause. "I don't know how to explain it. You just...know."

It feels so distant, this love. It's jagged and shifty. The few times I can touch it, the feeling escapes. I can't make it...stand still.

The tone of his voice had shifted, growing soft and pensive. Aryis almost felt sorry for him, an Ancient God powerless in the face of love.

"This is what you wanted, isn't it? To get closer to whatever's haunting you?"

I thought I wanted this, but your emotions are sticky. And irritating. I can feel them echoing through me, but they're not mine. Where...where are mine?

Aryis sighed. She was exhausted. "Figure it out. I don't know what more I can tell you."

Well, you're useless.

"Then leave me."

I'd be alone again.

She swallowed. "You're not my responsibility."

If I left you now, burnt away the little bit of me stuck inside of you, then you'd be alone too.

"I suppose I'll have to be okay with that."

Tajal didn't respond. How terrifying he had been the first time she saw him, an expansive dark mass rolling toward her and her friends in the Realm of Shadows, threatening to swallow them up. And when he wound his dark power around her, trapping her with him, she felt certain she was dead. He dove deep into her mind, stirring her emotions around, poking at her to see what he could bring up. His curiosity was a horror, twisting her up into a confused, lost mess.

Now, he was the very least of her concerns.

The sight of Skystrand in the distance took Aryis's breath away. Its tall spires rose into the dawn sky, the architecture reflecting the tastes of its designer, a magickless man named Lerner Grast. He was famous for having lofty ambitions that he turned into reality with the aid of the Empire's engineering and enchantment guilds—the Mercier Society and Ellanholme.

Sky cities had once been the pinnacle of Imperial decadence, taking years to build and almost constant spellweaving by mages with power that Aryis could only dream about.

When the first city fell, the rest of the cities were abandoned in a panicked exodus. The enchantments that had kept them in the air proved to be weaker than expected and costly to maintain. The cities that remained in the sky lay fallow for centuries. Over time, almost half had fallen, crashing to earth. The rest would eventually suffer the same fate.

Skystrand was all glass and metal, its round, soaring spires catching and reflecting light at any time of the day. As the city grew closer, Aryis spotted the signs of decay—shattered windows, unfettered ivy growing up the sides of what were once pristine edifices, crumbling brick and stone, and tarnished, weather-beaten metal.

Squinting in the sun, Aryis looked above the city, trying to spot the Dawn Beacon—the key clue to finding the lost book's location. The Beacon, a giant crystal star suspended above the city that reflected the light of the day, was gone. It must have fallen, shattering in the city below, no witnesses to its demise.

You mortals sure waste a lot of time on shrines to your egos, Tajal grumbled.

Aryis couldn't disagree. "A beautiful tribute to future failure."

A laugh rumbled out of the woman standing next to her.

"Areshi sky cities. Built just to eventually fall. Quite a monument to the arrogance of our ancestors," Suvi said.

"The will to build them far outstripped the ability to maintain them," Aryis replied.

"They're going to make you find that book, you know."

Aryis glanced over at Suvi. Aside from the black eye now turning a sickly shade of yellowish-green, she had managed to put herself together well, maintaining her regal air even without a crown.

Aryis inhaled deeply, drawing energy from the prickliness of the icy air. "I won't do it."

A heavy sigh left Suvi. "I hope you stick to your convictions."

Suvi's words surprised Aryis. "Why? Ceril plans to pick the Empire apart. I would think you'd revel in that."

Suvi turned her pale-green eyes on her, a seriousness in her gaze that set Aryis even more on edge. "That book was hidden for a reason. It should have been destroyed. Do you not understand this by now? My family didn't keep our magick to ourselves because we wanted power, we did it because it's *dangerous*. But that isn't the history of the Schism that you're taught in your Imperial schools. Eliza Rell's failure wasn't turning against the Empire, it was not throwing that book into a bottomless pit."

Aryis glanced at Suvi. "You're lying."

"Or you hold incorrect beliefs about my family due to a highly biased retelling of Areshi history."

As a scholar, Aryis had always tried to possess a healthy dose of skepticism, but she had to admit, she didn't question Imperial history much. Historians were not supposed to color facts with opinions—or change them completely.

But the past year had taught her painful lessons on trust.

"I grow tiresome of your naïvety," Suvi said. "You are going to be a resounding failure as Queen."

Tajal laughed. *Ruthless. She would be an interesting head to roll around in. Do you think she'd mind?*

Aryis met Suvi's insult with a shrug. "We'll likely die here today, so I couldn't give a right flying fuck about how tiresome you find me, bitch."

Aryis, you still astonish me. A valiant and righteous reply. Should I ever need you in an argument with my brothers and sisters, will you—

"Shut the *fuck* up. You are an unwanted, impotent parasite." Hot rage shot from the base of Aryis's spine to her face. If Tajal was going to remain useless, she didn't care about offending him now. Screw his ire. All his bluster amounted to nothing—he was a scared child who poked at her and ran back into his dark corner. She had reached her limit with the worthless so-called god.

Suvi narrowed her pale-green eyes. "Who, exactly, are you talking to in that head of yours?"

Aryis answered plainly. "No one of interest."

Rude!

"Quiet," their nearby assassin guard said.

Across the deck, Ceril approached, flanked by Temo and Efla. "Time to find our lost treasure." He practically beamed at the two of them. He must already consider himself the victor, only one step away from the lost Alabaster Book. A book he intended to use Aryis to find. She wouldn't help him, no matter what he did.

She steeled herself for what came next, though her insides quaked.

Loose gravel crunched under Aryis's feet as Ceril led them up from the sky docks to the outskirts of Skystrand. Weeds grew up through the cracks in the pavement, the streets jagged with fractures like haphazard stained glass. The spires she'd admired at a distance now soared overhead, the wind whispering between the buildings, creating an eerie sense of emptiness. She understood now why the sky cities were rumored to be haunted.

White birds fled in flurries, causing Aryis to flinch—the only sign of life in a city abandoned for centuries. Ceril led them to a massive park near a squat building, its three domes of glass half shattered and overgrown with ivy. Perhaps it once served as a conservatory or arboretum, but now, it sat fallow. As they drew closer, the middle of the park changed. Row upon row of small black plaques extended on both sides of the path they followed.

I don't like it here, Tajal remarked, his voice a low rumble.

Aryis looked closer. Graves. They stood in the middle of a cemetery, not just a park.

She shivered from the top of her head to her toes.

"We shouldn't be here," Suvi muttered from beside her. "This is cursed ground."

Despite their circumstance, Aryis's curiosity was piqued. "Cursed?"

"Abandoned souls. They should be in the earth at rest, not up here."

Ceril turned to them. "You have been profoundly disappointing, Suvi. You cry about lost souls when you should be vibrating with excitement to see the Rell legacy reborn here today."

Tajal spoke quietly, *Mortals shouldn't be playing with magick they don't understand.*

"My family locked this magick away for a good reason," Suvi said, disdain weaving through her voice. "You should abandon this folly."

"Those who dare push boundaries are reined in by the likes of the Justiciars or the Lythrosii. Fear holds the world back. Why should I be restrained from utilizing my talents?"

Suvi chuckled. "You sound like some of my idiot ancestors, now long dead. The smarter faction of my family won out, sealing our work away from opportunists like you."

A sour anger overtook Ceril's face. He strode over the cracked pavement to sneer at Suvi. "You are a shadow of your family. A coward."

"I am a pragmatist. And this magick you're playing with doesn't add beauty or power to the world, only takes from it."

He ran his pale-blue gaze up and down Suvi, smirking. "I will not be lectured by you, a failed queen brought to heel by a lowborn child of pirates."

Aryis seethed. "Nyssa has more worth in a fingernail than you have in your whole body."

She expected an outburst of anger, but Ceril merely sighed. "Prepare them."

Efla closed in on Suvi, drawing a dagger. Suvi sneered and drove her fist into an assassin's kidney as he tried to grab her. Two more seized her arms. "Don't do this, Anelos!" the fallen queen seethed. She struggled in the assassins' grasp but couldn't stop Efla from making a deep slice across her palm. Blood filled the wound.

Suvi continued to fight against her captors, but was quickly subdued by a vicious backfist across her face. Efla yanked Suvi forward and smeared Suvi's hand across Aryis's face, the warm blood dripping down her cheek. Efla unlocked the void collar affixed around Aryis's neck. The moment it was gone, a wave of nausea rolled through her, her whole body flushing with heat, making sweat prick up on her forehead. Her magick flooded back, an unwelcome sensation, given her predicament.

"Now you have her blood. Trace it to the book," Ceril ordered.

Aryis's eyes darted about. Efla, Temo, and their Rule brethren watched.

"No."

Ceril moved toward her, a whip unfurling from his fist, the tip of it dragging lightly in the gravel. "This isn't a choice."

Aryis, do as he says and end this. You can't win. He'll kill—

"No," she spat.

In a blur of motion, the whip cut through the air and sliced open the skin across her collarbone. The shock of the blow caused her to stumble back. Blood beaded along the slash, then surged out, staining her white button-down shirt.

Aryis, he's going to kill you. I am concerned. I have grown to slightly appreciate your existence.

"Let him kill me," she said.

You haven't thought this through. You can't endure this pain!

"Yes, I can," she hissed.

Then perhaps I can't endure it. I don't like this at all. Your pain is unpleasant.

"Then fucking do something."

Ceril narrowed his eyes. "Who are you talking to?"

I...cannot intervene.

"Cannot or will not?" Aryis replied.

Does it matter?

Aryis took a deep breath and steadied herself, fearing her leg might buckle beneath her throbbing knee. "You're a fucking impotent coward."

Ceril drew the whip back. She flinched and put her left arm up to block the blow. The skin on her forearm burst open, and she cried out, clutching the wounded arm to her chest.

Please, just give him what he wants.

"He shouldn't have this magick. You said it yourself!" Aryis hissed below her breath.

Don't you care about your own mortality?

Efla wrenched Aryis's arm and drove her to the ground. Aryis's knee crunched against the gravel, forcing a cry out of her. Tears brimmed in her eyes.

What are you doing? Is this a lesson for me? Are you trying to show me how far you'll go for some foolish heroic ideal? I don't like it. It makes you stupid and illogical.

"You don't understand," she said.

Ceril scowled at her.

Then explain!

"I can't explain love."

Efla chuckled. "I think she's gone insane."

You have gone insane. You'll let this man strip the skin off your bones. Why?

"If I give in, he'll do far worse to those I love. And you're content to watch. You're not incapable of learning, you're just a shallow, frivolous god, forgotten as time passed you and your ilk by," she whispered.

Love isn't worth your life!

"My life is nothing without it," she mumbled.

"Call your magick forth and find the book," Ceril demanded.

Aryis shook her head.

"Get her on her feet."

Temo and Efla pulled her up. Ceril approached and wrapped his whip around her throat, tightening it. "Track the book."

"No," she choked out.

The pressure around her throat increased until she could no longer breathe. Her body bucked while Efla and Temo struggled to hold her between them.

Ceril's face grew dim as her vision contracted to a small window. "Track the book."

Aryis, do as he asks or you die here!

She fought to breathe, to free herself. Her eyes rolled back.

Tajal's voice boomed in her head, the only thing that cut through the growing dull. *Aryis!*

It would be so easy to give in. But promises had been made. She wouldn't go back on her word. Not now.

Not ever.

She stopped struggling.

You goddamn foolish woman.

Something brushed against her face. Not something. Her own hand. A strange, distant, familiar tingle of magick sparked at her fingertips—

Suddenly, she was sucking in ragged breaths, her throat free of the whip. Her vision returned from a small pinpoint, and Ceril's face came into focus. A ribbon of red magick wound around her outstretched blood-stained hand.

"No," she whispered, trying to draw back her magick.

You wanted me to help. You don't get to dictate the terms.

Tajal had taken control of her magick. Of her.

"Stop!" she coughed.

I'm not going to let you die.

The glowing red ribbon danced in the air, and she could feel the connection forming between Suvi's fresh ichor and the hidden Alabaster

Book, its ink infused with Rell blood. Her magick surged through her veins, not at all in her control.

"Not like this! Please!" she cried.

Ceril narrowed his eyes. What would he do if he found out an Ancient God was running around in her brain? Aryis had no idea what Ceril could be capable of, but she had to keep Tajal a secret.

I warned you about displeasing me. Your death would greatly displease me, Little Bird.

Aryis watched helplessly as her ribbon of magick darted forward, seeking its goal.

"Temo, follow it. Bring me the book," Ceril said, pointing after the trail of red.

Temo nodded and disappeared in a waft of smoke, reappearing over a hundred yards away, heading closer to the city's core. He disappeared again when the ribbon bent around a building.

Minutes passed, her magick weaving through the city. How strange it was to feel it working, threading toward the book, but not be in control of it at all.

Aryis let out a gasp when she felt her magick reach its target. A few moments later, that target's place in the world shifted. Blinking across the distance, drawing closer. Finally, Temo reappeared next to Ceril. He held out a black leather-clad book, unadorned by filigree or title.

"Shit," Aryis breathed.

"Where was it?" Ceril asked.

"There's a small library on the other side of the city. It was up inside a fireplace," Temo replied, brushing dust off his jacket.

Ceril snickered. "A mundane place for an extraordinary treasure." He took the last Alabaster Book in his hands, holding it gingerly. It was thin, not like the others in the set. A sheen of magick rippled across its cover.

Efla grabbed Suvi, yanked her toward Ceril, and forced her bloody hand on top of the book to unlock the ward protecting the tome. Whirling threads of golden magick spun around the book before dissipating in the air. Efla shoved Suvi away as Ceril opened his prize. Slowly, he turned its pages, scanning the contents.

No one moved or made a sound. His assassin lackeys kept their eyes moving, scanning their surroundings, watching for threats. As if anything in this long-dead city stirred.

Ceril strolled over to a half-crumbled cement bench and sat down, his attention firmly planted on his new acquisition.

Suvi glanced over at Aryis, her face bloodied and her gaze solemn. "Do you know what you've done?"

Aryis's mouth went dry.

Don't listen to her. You're still alive.

"You've fucked us," Aryis whispered.

Your corpse offers nothing to the world but rotting flesh. You can only fight back if you're alive, Aryis Devitt.

Arguing with such an infuriating, obtuse idiot was fruitless. Aryis returned her gaze to Ceril, who stared intently at the Alabaster Book. Efla waited patiently, watching him. He quickly rifled through the book, scanning page after page until he stopped and ran his finger down one particular page, studying its contents for a long minute. Scowling, he snapped the book shut. Aryis flinched at the sound.

Ceril rose to his feet. "We have to go to Arcton."

Efla inhaled a deep breath. "Arcton was crawling with Justiciars, guards, and adepts ready to defend the manor. I'm not sure it's—"

"We're going to Arcton!" he snarled. "I need the Spire of Heaven."

"I don't understand."

Ceril held up the book. "There's an enchantment in here that's *quite* interesting, and with it, I can use the shard to create Ancient Magick."

Efla and Temo exchanged a glance.

Ceril smirked. "I won't need to fear a god when I can become one myself."

CLASH IN THE CITY

Athen gripped the rail of the Cloud Crasher, his eyes on the city above them. They had approached low, Anna eking every last bit of speed out of her ship that she could, her expert skysailing skills making up time in pursuit of Ceril and his assassins. She read the currents and threw caution literally to the wind, parts of their journey rather turbulent. Even with a tonic to settle her stomach, Nyssa had been miserable.

Athen's gaze was glued to the docked airship. With any luck, Ceril wouldn't have any idea they were close until their boots were on the ground.

A sharp *crack* drew Athen's attention. Part of the rail broke away, the wood splintering in his grasp. He didn't realize how hard he had been squeezing.

A light hand came to rest on his shoulder. Quinn peered up at him. "She's alive, Athen. I know it's cold comfort, but Ceril needs her alive."

He nodded, turning his attention to Skystrand. "How are you feeling?" He and Nyssa had held Quinn down while Reece applied healing disk after healing disk to her back. They burned through six mending her wounds, and she passed out halfway through, but she was on her feet again after resting the through night, though paler than usual. She was a strong woman in the face of that pain, earning her even more of his respect.

"I'm alive," Quinn responded. "Sore as hell and not looking forward to seeing a healer to really fix it properly, but...I'm alive."

A voice spoke up behind Athen. "Nonessential crew are secure in the interior."

"Got it," he replied to Nyssa. Medias and Reece stood beside her.

He looked across the deck of the ship. Only a few crew remained in order to spot a good place to disembark. Their boarding party, Justiciars and Ina included, were also waiting, prepared. The boat was an old decommissioned warship that Anna's family had bought and converted into a luxury ship, but it had the underpinnings of a vessel that had seen battle. And they'd need to lean on its sturdiness if things got dicey.

"I've reached out. I can sense a cluster of souls on the edge of the city," Quinn said, "but it's hard to tell how many. The magick of the city is old and powerful, hard to push through. It...it almost sings, its power so beautiful and complex."

"You're pushing your limits. You and Nyssa aren't fully rested, your magick is weaker."

Nyssa sighed. "Pain in the ass, this magick. There's being tired, then there's this...magick exhaustion. Can't say I like it. But we'll be ready."

"Okay, you know the plan. Scatter them, secure Aryis, scoop up Ceril, pick off the assassins," Athen replied. He would be the first off the ship, followed by the others. He claimed he could withstand an initial attack. Truth was, he wanted to get to Aryis first. He would do anything to get her back. *Anything.* His love spilled into the space left by her absence, looking for somewhere to go.

Nyssa put a hand on the small of his back, almost leaning against him, and her presence was a comfort. An odd reversal of their usual roles. She was the hothead, and he would talk her down. Now, his anger boiled under the surface, and she seemed to sense it. "We'll hit them with everything we've got. I'll drain every last bit of my magick to make sure Aryis is safe. You have my word."

"Thank you," he replied. "Both of you."

"You're family. So is Aryis. We look out for each other. Bloody our knuckles and blades for each other. Always."

Athen met Nyssa's gaze. Those azure eyes were resolute, and he found comfort in them. He needed her strength in this moment.

Anna tromped up to them, her goggles affixed to the top of her head and her one-size-too-big overalls rolled up to reveal worn, dull boots. "Grab hold of something. I'm going to kick in some boost to bring us level with the city. Wait for the safe fall enchantment to deploy when we get up there." She pulled down her goggles, their dark tint obscuring her pale-blue eyes.

"Take your positions!" Athen called out, scanning their small cadre of Justiciars. Nyssa, Quinn, Medias, Reece, Ina, and the others gathered close to the railing, crouching down and grabbing hold.

Anna climbed up to the bridge, pulling the door closed behind her. The helm's house contained a large, curved window that gave Anna an excellent view of the sky before her. Athen kept his eyes on her and when ready, she gave him a nod.

"Brace for ascent!" he yelled.

A heartbeat passed. Then they shot upward, feeling heavy as the cold air pressed down on them. The old ship groaned beneath them. Nyssa turned white and clutched the safety handles on the railing. Athen put a hand on her shoulder. She hated flying, donning a brave face when he knew she was quaking inside.

The bottom of the city grew wider and wider, expanding until it filled Athen's field of vision when they quickly rose to meet it. The Cloud Crasher jutted to the side a bit, changing its course to continue its ascent. They slowed down and passed a thick expanse of steel and stone—the foundation of the sky city where most of its floating enchantment was embedded in runes specifically designed to amplify and retain magick. But it was only a matter of time before the enchantment would decay to the point of giving way to gravity.

The Cloud Crasher slowed further and further, finally popping up next to the city, close to the sky docks where Ceril's ship was moored. Anna cocked the ship, tipping to the side and moving over the outer edge of the city.

Athen stood, peering over the side of the ship, desperate to spot Ceril. Wherever he was, Aryis would be nearby.

"There!" Medias yelled.

A group of people gathered in a park, its greenery unruly and over-grown.

The deck navigators signaled the bridge. The Cloud Crasher banked quickly, Anna using the last of the ship's propulsion to move closer to the park until they were almost on top of the group below them. The crew rushed to the rail, wooden tubes in their hands and extra tubes stuck into their belts.

"Fire!" Athen shouted.

The crew let loose their attack. Glowing orbs shot out of their tubes with a shrill whistle, and the air next to the ship exploded with bright colors and thundering *booms* that shook the vessel.

Next to Athen, Reece raised the crossbow she had scrounged up from a storeroom. She loaded it from the small quiver of bolts strapped to her waist, then set her eye behind the sight and let a bolt fly. It struck the ground a foot away from a retreating assassin.

"Impressive," Medias intoned. Earlier, she had tried to insist that Reece stay below deck, hidden and safe, but Reece had silenced her with a glare.

The men and women on the ground scattered. The distraction worked. It was Anna's suggestion to use the ship's store of fireworks used for birthdays and holidays. The fireworks were harmless, but the assassins couldn't know that.

Athen spotted Ceril, two assassins closing in on him. "There!" he shouted, pointing.

Ceril disappeared.

"Fuck," Athen said under his breath. Their enemies had a teleporting assassin—he was going to be a pain in the ass, forcing them to play hide and seek to find Ceril. But that wasn't Athen's concern. He'd leave Anelos to Quinn and Nyssa.

He scanned the fleeing assassins, recognizing Suvi Rell in their midst. And behind her, a sight that made his heart jump.

Aryis. She's alive!

"Deploying safe fall!" a crew member called out, pulling a lever set beneath a panel on the deck. The enchantment roared to life, glowing bright orange. "Safe fall away!"

Athen didn't wait—he vaulted over the rail. The ground came up fast, and he landed with a grunt, rolled once to disperse the impact, then took off in a sprint toward Aryis. She was struggling against two assassins, staggering one of them with a punch she put her full weight behind. A burst of pride ripped through Athen. Suvi tried to kick the other assassin, but she got her legs knocked out from under her for her trouble.

Athen charged the man attacking Aryis, smashing him in the chest with a punch that sent him flying. He hit the ground with a thud and didn't move. The other assassin lunged at Athen, dagger in hand. The blade deflected harmlessly off of Athen's chest, and he grabbed his attacker by the jacket and tossed him over his shoulder with a growl, not caring where the man landed.

Aryis spun around. "Athen?" she breathed. She flung herself at him.

He caught her and wrapped his arms around her. "You're safe now," he murmured next to her ear, his heart beating wildly.

"I knew you'd find us."

Her grip on him tightened, and he could have stayed there for a great, long while, just holding her in his embrace. But he pulled away reluctantly and eyed Suvi, who backed away from him. "What do we do with her?"

Aryis put her hand against his chest. "She comes with."

"Back into a cage?" Suvi replied. "I don't think so."

"Well, you can join these poor souls, then." Aryis gestured to the grass beyond the paved walkway they stood upon.

Athen glanced around, realizing there was more than overgrown trees and bushes in the park. In his haste, he hadn't noticed the gravestones dotting the ground, small plaques embedded in the dirt.

The hairs on the back of his neck rose. A crack of lightning shot past him, hitting a fleeing assassin near a three-domed building. Athen flinched, pulling Aryis close. "I brought reinforcements."

Nyssa, Quinn, and a group of nine Justiciars ran up, Ina and Medias trailing behind them. Nyssa strode up to Aryis and threw her arms around her.

"Good to see you safe, Little Hawk," Nyssa said, pulling back, seizing Aryis's face, and planting a kiss on her forehead.

Aryis approached Quinn. "Ceril has the book. I'm sorry...I—"

"This damn fool led him to it," Suvi spat.

"I didn't. It wasn't..." Aryis stiffened and shook her head.

"Ceril has ways of extracting what he wants," Quinn said, her eyes troubled. "He hurt you, didn't he?"

Aryis nodded.

Athen stepped back and finally took a good look at her. The skin on her upper chest was split, and blood dripped from her left hand from a cut on her forearm.

Athen ground his jaw. "What did he do to you?"

Aryis swallowed but didn't answer.

"Get her back to the ship," Quinn said. Her eyes began to glow, shadow seeping off of her. "We'll go after Ceril."

A low chuckle wafted their way, the sound unnatural. Athen shuddered.

Ceril stood at the edge of the park in the distance, flanked by an assassin.

Shadow exploded out of Quinn in Ceril's direction, her face a mask of pure hate. Her magick struck Ceril with an ear-splitting *boom*, shaking the ground beneath their feet, red sparks flying in all directions.

A wave of shimmering darkness rushed back toward them, hitting Athen and his cohort. A buzzing sensation moved through him. Quinn and the others cried out, sinking to the ground in pain.

Ceril stood unharmed, surrounded by a translucent red bubble. A shield? But one that did more than just block magick—it seemed to reflect it.

Ceril eyed them, his lips moving. He held up a hand and began spell-weaving, his gestures jerky and efficient, not one wasted motion.

"Stop him," Suvi breathed, stumbling up to Athen. "We're surrounded by graves. You have to stop him now!"

Brilliant purple threads hung in the air in front of Ceril. He teased forth more magick, building a swirling web of energy and filling the air with a pulsing thrum, the sensation diving deep into Athen, making his bones ache.

Athen let go of Aryis and broke into a sprint and covered the distance to Ceril. He slammed into the red barrier with all his might and staggered back. Delicate strands of energy flickered all around him. He reared back and smashed his fists against the magick. With each massive punch, the wall sparked and wavered, but it held.

Ceril stopped casting and spread his arms apart, the purple threads spiraling around his hands. A moment later, they shot out in all directions and dove into the dirt under their feet. The ground began to rumble.

A smile spread across Ceril's face.

"Fuck," Athen whispered, backing up, the drone of magick humming through him.

All around him, decayed hands burst through the dirt.

Wraiths.

The shrieks of the newly created creatures chilled his blood as they crawled forth, twitching from their graves. Their yellowish-white eyes almost glowed in the stark sunlight. Some bodies were more intact than others. Few were more than bone with hunks of flesh.

Wraiths were bound to their master. If Athen could get through the magick shield and to Ceril, he could end things. He spun around, only to find Ceril gone.

"Dammit!"

The ground rumbled as wraith after wraith emerged, dirt cascading off their blackened bodies. Once out of the ground, they turned to Athen and quieted. Poised. Waiting.

Nyssa's voice cut through the silence. "Athen, run!"

He ran.

High-pitched shrieks assaulted his ears, the *whoosh* of dozens of leathery wings taking flight making his heart pump.

A wraith dove in his path, and Athen lowered his shoulder, roaring as he drove his body through the creature and left it in his wake.

A blur of wraiths rushed toward him.

Flashes of bright cobalt lightning streaked past him as he ran, Nyssa doing her best to fight off the wraiths. A few dropped dead, their flesh sizzling from her attacks, but most were merely slowed.

Nyssa's magick was waning.

The Justiciars joined her in the fight, and Athen chanced a glance behind him. Pops of light and plumes of fire met the wraiths head-on, giving him a little more breathing room while he sprinted toward the Cloud Crasher.

His heart was nearly beating out of his chest by the time he reached Nyssa and the others. He had been so focused on getting to them as quickly as possible, he hadn't noticed the wraiths had stopped trying to kill him.

"What are they waiting for?" Nyssa asked.

The creatures took to the air, filling the sky with undead monsters. They circled, watching.

Athen wasn't about to stick around and find out. "Back to the ship. Now!"

Quinn shook her head. "No. We go after Ceril."

"Back to the ship," he insisted. He pointed up at the wraiths. "We can't fight them all. Not with two gods at half power."

Not waiting for her response, he scooped Aryis up in his arms. "I know you're not helpless, but that knee will slow you down, so no protests!"

She wrapped her arms around his neck. The others turned, each racing back to the ship. Nyssa lingered, waiting for Quinn.

"Quinn, come on!" Aryis pleaded.

Athen understood how badly Quinn wanted to stop Ceril, but he didn't have time for her shit. He landed a heavy hand on her shoulder. "Lose in the moment, but win the day," he said, repeating a lesson Eron had once taught him. When Quinn didn't move, he leaned in. "I'll drag your ass back to the Cloud Crasher myself."

With an angry grunt, Quinn turned and ran. Nyssa and Athen followed.

CLASH IN THE SKY

Aryis fell to the deck of the Cloud Crasher, her arms burning from clutching onto Athen's back as he climbed the ladder up to the hovering airship. She could barely feel her left arm. Her knee throbbed.

Well, this day went to shit, Tajal grumbled in her head.

"Sever the ground lines!" a woman shouted. "Shield the sails. Hopefully, the damn enchantment still works."

"Aye, Captain!" several crewmen cried.

The woman ran past, heading toward the bridge. "I'm getting us out of here."

Athen bent over Aryis. "You okay?"

"Yeah."

Still alive, Little Bird. You're still alive.

"We are," she mumbled.

Athen barked out, "Get Suvi Rell into a secured room, deckie!" Two of the ship's crew scrambled over and grabbed hold of Suvi, who tried to yank out of their grasp.

"I'm not going to die in the bowels of some airship!" she spat.

"Throw her overboard," Athen replied. "Never mind, I'll do it." He grabbed hold of Suvi's arm.

Suvi shrank away from him. "You are being hasty."

He shoved her toward the deckhands again. "Take her below. Tie her up, lock her in, got it?"

The two men nodded and hauled Suvi away, who was now far more compliant.

The deck tilted below Aryis, the airship moving with a small burst of power. Athen grabbed ahold of her to keep her steady.

The spires of the city zipped by as they departed, the sails beginning to shimmer, a ward taking hold to protect the fragile fabric.

Athen picked Aryis up and placed her on the steps leading to the observation deck. Intensity radiated off of him, though he appeared calm. It was one of the qualities Aryis admired about him—his ability to keep everything together, keep everyone together, when things were going to hell.

Medias crouched next to her.

"I would suggest you head below deck, as you're injured, but I know you'd refuse."

"Damn sure I would."

Medias pulled a weapon off of her belt and pressed it into Aryis's hand. It took Aryis a second to recognize it. *Talon*. She wrapped her hand around the hilt, finding it a comfort. "Thank you."

Medias rose to her feet, joining Reece at the railing and brandishing her own dagger. Reece tried loading a bolt into her crossbow, her hands shaking. Medias grasped her trembling hands. "Breathe," she said, offering a rare smile meant to reassure.

Aryis, Tajal rumbled, an unmistakable note of worry in his voice. *Skystrand.*

She turned her eyes back to the city. Dozens of wraiths swirled in the distance, their wings beating in unison.

Aryis held her breath.

Inhuman cries pierced the air, and the wraiths began peeling away from each other and heading toward the Cloud Crasher.

"Incoming," Athen yelled.

Aryis drew Talon, tucking the sheath in her belt. She was in no shape to fight, but she had no choice. None of them did.

Please note before you die that I did everything I could to save you.

NO END

Nyssa sprinted to the back of the airship, Quinn on her heels. The wraith horde drew closer, their shrieks growing louder. She called forth her magick, and shadow began coiling around Quinn at her side.

"There's too many," Quinn said, her voice flat.

"Eyes up, Emerrath. Be fierce," Nyssa replied, trying to bolster Quinn's confidence.

Quinn nodded, her glowing emerald eyes not showing any fear.

She looked at Ina and the Justiciars surrounding her. "Protect the sails at all costs."

The wraiths flew above them, diving toward the ship. Magick flared all around Nyssa, the Justiciars rising to the challenge. The buzz of power made her skin vibrate.

She flung bolts of lightning, chaining her attacks to hit more than one wraith when possible. Shards of shadow, honed to a razor's edge, tore through the creatures. They screeched as they died, some dropping onto the ship.

A wraith darted through their defenses, crashing into a Justiciar. It ripped into the poor woman's neck, killing her instantly. Another landed and lunged at Nyssa. She spun to the side, drawing Winter's Bite and slicing through its throat in one smooth motion.

In a blur, she found herself slammed into the deck, another wraith on top of her. She grabbed its leg and sent a shock of pure electricity through the beast. It shuddered before falling toward her, forcing her to roll out of the way.

Nyssa gasped for air. Ina stood above her, sword shearing off the arm of another attacker. The thuds of feet on the deck made Nyssa's blood run cold. More of the monsters were landing, pulling their attention away from protecting the ship. Others darted in the air above them, trying to tear into the sails. They held together, their usual gossamer sheen replaced by sparks of the silvery protective veil that clung to the airy fabric.

They won't hold long.

Nyssa stood and released a wave of lightning, striking the closest wraiths attacking the sails. Those caught in the web of her lightning screeched and tumbled away from the mast, flailing and falling. She was surrounded by wraiths, some dead, some writhing, some struggling to get back up on their feet. Others screamed and snapped their jaws as they advanced.

More of the monsters fell to Ina's blade, her face covered with bright crimson from a deep cut in her temple. Nyssa pulled Quinn backward with one hand and sliced the arm off a wraith with her sword as it scrabbled to claw Quinn into its clutches.

The creatures were relentless, pushing them back toward the main deck. Nyssa almost tripped over the body of a Justiciar, his eyes still open, staring at the sky as the sun blazed down, offering no warmth.

Above them, the wraiths ripped at the sails, the protection veil holding like a thin layer of armor. It was the only thing stopping them from shredding the delicate fabric that kept the airship aloft.

Nyssa kept up her attack, but these wraiths were harder to bring down than the others.

She ran back to Athen and the Justiciars, who were fighting their own battle on the main deck. Athen and Medias stood against at least ten wraiths. Reece was on the steps with Aryis, firing her crossbow at one of the monsters at it came at her. The bolt hit its mark in the shoulder but didn't stop its advance. Medias slid over, white magick flashing from her hand, blinding the wraith, slowing it just enough to drive her dagger into its neck.

Nyssa caught up to a wraith moving toward Athen, ramming her sword into its lower back and forcing it to the ground. Its wings flapped wildly, and she twisted the blade, severing its spine. She didn't wait for it to stop moving. She yanked out Winter's Bite and found the next one, slicing through its neck before it had a chance to sink its claws into Quinn, who was fighting off an enemy of her own.

Athen aided Quinn, pulling the wraith away and heaving it over the side of the ship. He yelled at Nyssa, "Any ideas?"

She was at a loss. "These wraiths are stronger and our magick is flagging. We're trying, but we can't get them away from the sails."

"Shit," he breathed.

The monsters kept coming. There seemed to be no end to them.

A STALWART EMPATH

Reece fell back against the steps, a wraith bearing down on her and Aryis. Half the skin on its dark, twisted face was missing, exposing a yellowing skull underneath. It roared and snapped its fangs at her, its milky white eyes fixed on her.

She fired her crossbow directly into its face. The shot was driven by pure panic, no time to aim. The wraith wavered, then tumbled off the side of the stairs, the ass end of her bolt sticking out of its cheek. Her hand flew to the quiver, her fingers desperately searching for another bolt.

The quiver was empty.

Reece scrambled down the steps and snatched up a sword that lay in a dead Justiciar's hand. She almost dropped it, not accustomed to the weight of the weapon. Medias backed into her, driven back by two wraiths. Magick burst from her fingertips, and the wraiths clutched their heads, crying out.

Without thought, Reece shot forward, plunging the tip of her sword into the abdomen of one of the wraiths. She yanked it back out, almost falling on her ass. The wraith screamed and stumbled away like a drunk. Medias drew her knife across the throat of the other beast, and it fell without a sound.

"Get below deck, now!" Medias shouted.

"No," Reece replied.

"You'll get yourself killed, woman!"

Reece shook her head. She wasn't leaving her friends and the woman she loved with this mess—

A cry from above startled her. Medias jumped in front of Reece, shoving her back against the steps. A wraith dove into Medias from the sky. She slammed to the deck, and the wraith rolled over, popping up onto its feet. It trained its putrid white eyes on Reece.

Medias struggled to her feet.

Reece rushed to her side, the sword quaking in her hand. "I've got you."

"Get to safety," Medias slurred, blood running down her face. "Please."

"I'm not leaving you."

"Above us!" Aryis yelled from the steps behind them.

Shrieks filled the air. Wraiths circled over their heads, filling the sky with menace. They weaved around the mainmast and more landed on the deck, closing in on their small ranks.

A DESPERATE GAMBIT

The sound of leathery wings filled the air. Aryis limped up the steps, collapsing against the front of the bridge, pressing her back up against its cold metal. The ship was being overwhelmed by monsters. Her fingers were slick with blood...her own.

Aryis, get below deck. You'll get torn apart out here!

"It's too late, Tajal."

Once the wraiths destroyed the sails—and the groans of the dying protection enchantment signaled they were close—the ship would plummet to the earth.

And once they fell, no one could stand in Ceril's way. He would tear the Empire apart.

The shouts and screams of her friends turned her stomach with mortal fear. On the deck, Quinn and Nyssa were surrounded by a throng of wraiths. They defended the ship, but their magicks were waning as they drove themselves to exhaustion.

Athen fought next to them, swinging his fists, his glance cast often toward Aryis. His energy, too, was flagging. But he'd die on his feet, ever the honorable warrior, of that she was certain.

Medias and Reece fought below her at the foot of the stairs. Medias was injured, and Reece could barely hold the tip of her sword up.

They were all going to die today. Everything they'd been through would be rendered meaningless by the treachery of a small, hateful man.

Aryis shivered, her blood-soaked shirt offering no warmth. She grasped Talon in one hand and tried to flex the other, her hand stiff. The cut on her forearm barely hurt anymore.

"Will you even care when I die, Tajal?" she asked, rueful.

What is a mortal life to me?

The cold cruelty of his response ignited a fire inside her. "You wasted my time, you coward."

The insult drew silence. *Good.* The useless god would soon only have himself for company.

He had imposed himself on her and given nothing back. Fucking useless asshole god...

Aryis let loose a sharp exhale and raised her numb left hand. The one with a remnant of Tajal embedded in it.

Useless? Perhaps not.

A desperate situation called for a desperate act.

Aryis exhaled, closed her eyes, and let her magick flow. She curled her left hand into a fist as best she could and summoned her magick. Everything in her body went cold. She gave a tug.

Aryis.

A smile formed on her face. Now she had his attention. She tugged again, meeting resistance.

Aryis, stop.

The sparks of white magick began to swirl around her hand, speeding up and expanding. As she continued to exude power, strands of black appeared, threading with her bright-white energy and glowing with a deep-violet light.

Stop!

Blinking familiar objects to her was easy, a mere thought and a tug. It was easy with books, even Winter's Bite. But what she wanted now fought against her. Aryis opened her mouth and let out a scream, putting every bit of will and magick to bring something forth into the world that didn't belong there.

She met resistance.

And that resistance met Aryis's rage. She threw away all caution, gritted her teeth, and yanked.

Hard.

Black smoke began to form and spiral in front of her, sparks of dark light bursting into the air. The thick smoke hovered a moment, then imploded, leaving behind a shape. Aryis blinked at the figure that loomed over her. It had a human form, but it wasn't human. Anything but. She stifled a scream.

"What did you do?" Tajal asked, turning toward her.

Aryis stared up at the Ancient God of the Realm of Shadows.

Countless puss-yellow eyes floated on tentacles that formed the god's head, rotating in all directions. He pulled on the lapels of the tuxedo he wore. "Quite the donnybrook here, Little Bird."

"Help us. Please," she breathed.

"Why should I?"

"I'll stay with you in the Realm of Shadows. Forever."

Tajal's gaze snapped down to her, all eyes moving in unison. He conjured a ridiculous top hat out of the black mist surrounding him and bowed to her. "A rather compelling offer. I accept."

Tajal lost his semi-human form and spread out in a mass of swirling black smoke and tentacles, eyes rising and sinking all over his body as he moved. He swelled and overflowed from the bridge, like wax melting down a candle. His dark mass expanded, eyeballs and tentacles growing out of the blackness and rolling onto the deck, curling up the mainmast, and reaching out for the wraiths. Tentacles darted out, impaling three wraiths and pulling them back toward his body, where his eyeballs split into fanged mouths and tore the undead creatures apart.

Aryis sat back and watched the horror, bile rising in her throat. "What have I done?"

BOOM!

Aryis screeched, the loud explosion making her jump.

A large gossamer sail flapped in the wind, tattered. It sparked and popped, its silvery material trying to repair itself.

And failing.

The Cloud Crasher jerked forward and trembled.

The wraiths had breached the protection enchantment.

Tajal was too late. *She* was too late.

The bow dropped in one violent motion, and Aryis was thrown forward. She tumbled down the steps and slammed into the deck next to Reece. Dazed, she began sliding toward the bow of the ship. A hand grabbed the back of her jacket.

"Hold on, Aryis!" Reece hissed.

A TUMBLE

Nyssa dodged a wraith's strike, its claws grazing her jacket. She drove her sword up into its neck and twisted the blade as she withdrew it. The wraith fell. She heaved a breath and kept Quinn at her back, feeling her presence.

"Nyssa!" Quinn yelled.

Nyssa whirled. Her mouth dropped open. *Impossible.*

A confusing black mass of eyeballs and writhing tentacles spread across the deck and curled around the ship's masts, ensnaring wraiths and...eating them? Nyssa shook her head.

"What the hell..." she whispered. *Is that...*

Beneath her feet, the Cloud Crasher shuddered violently.

Shit.

The ship tilted forward in one sudden motion. Nyssa toppled over and slid down the deck, losing hold of Winter's Bite. She clawed for purchase, her innate fear of heights flipping to panic.

A hand caught her.

Athen.

He held onto the railing that surrounded the stairs leading to the entertainment deck. Quinn almost slid past before Nyssa grabbed her, sinking her fingers into the fabric of her jacket. Quinn turned on her side and seized Nyssa's leg, holding on.

The sensation of speed coupled with weightlessness made Nyssa's heart leap into her throat.

An airship falling from the sky wasn't survivable.

Wraiths tumbled past, wings flapping desperately to take flight and getting tangled in each other in their mindless panic. Their screams mirrored Nyssa's terror.

"Hold on!" Athen yelled. "The ship will stabilize when the sails repair themselves."

If *they repair themselves.*

It took more than just the sails for the ship to fly—a complicated, interdependent system of enchantments functioned in concert to keep aloft, catch air, and sail the winds. If one system failed, the others weren't strong enough to keep the Cloud Crasher in the sky.

Nyssa cursed under her breath, lamenting ever asking Aryis how airships worked.

Athen pulled Nyssa closer to the rail. "Grab hold. You and Quinn."

Nyssa did as she was told, not releasing her death grip on Quinn, who scrambled toward the railing and wrapped her arm around it.

"Reece!" Athen yelled.

A moment later, Reece's voice broke through the wind. "Here!"

The voice came from above their position. Nyssa strained her neck. High above them, Reece and Medias clung to the ropes tied around a bollard near the bridge. Reece had a tenuous grip on Aryis.

The Cloud Crasher shuddered again, the bow dipping even lower, and they gained downward speed. The sails weren't repairing themselves. Not quick enough. And the wraiths were still doing their damage.

"Get them off the sails!" Aryis screamed.

Nyssa's eyes shot to the mainmast. The dark mass full of eyeballs and tentacles expanded, spearing wraiths out of the air, plucking off their fleshy wings, and tossing them aside, some dead, some still moving.

Undeterred, more wraiths attacked, one diving through the mainsail.

A large, metallic groan made Nyssa's stomach twist.

The sound of magick failing.

The ship dropped again, then tilted suddenly to the starboard side, sending Nyssa, Athen, and Quinn swinging, colliding with one another as they clung to the lower deck guardrail, their feet pointed toward the starboard rail. The Cloud Crasher leaned into its listing dive, spiraling down, its descent slowed only by the tenuous hold of the remaining enchantments.

Nyssa's eyes were drawn to the starboard rail. The top of the bright orange safe fall enchantment flickered, still deployed off the side of the ship from their attack on Skystrand. Beyond it, the sky. And then, in the far distance, the earth. Her heart pounded wildly in her chest at the sight.

Hold on, hold on, hold on!

Screeching wraiths dropped and skidded down the sloping deck, crashing into the starboard railing. Their momentum carried them over the side, tumbling over the metal lattice. The railing shuddered.

An incoherent shout from Reece made Nyssa's heart leap into her throat. A wraith had landed in their midst. It grabbed at Aryis as it began to topple backward. Aryis planted a foot in its chest.

The wraith reeled back, slamming into the deck and skidding down the slanted surface.

"No!" Reece screamed.

Aryis slid behind the wraith. She had slipped out of Reece's grasp.

The wraith hit the railing, its broken wings tangling in the metal slats. Aryis hit the railing next to the beast, her head cracking against the metal.

She went limp.

The wraith twisted toward her, its claws aimed for her stomach—

A spike of onyx shadow shot out from Quinn's hand, impaling the wraith's head. The shadow fell away, and the deadly creature collapsed.

"Hold on!" Athen yelled. He let go of the guardrail and slid down, hitting the safety rail. Then he climbed up the rail and grabbed hold of Aryis.

Shadow wrapped around her limp body. "I've got her," Quinn yelled.

Athen released her, relief on his face.

His head snapped up, and suddenly, a wraith rammed into him from above. Athen and the monster fell off the edge of the ship.

He was gone.

"No!" Nyssa choked. Her heart dropped. Desperate thoughts pinged around in her head. One thought burst through the others.

"Quinn, save the others!"

"What?"

Nyssa grabbed Quinn for a moment. "Trust me."

Before she could answer, Nyssa let go and slid down the deck. She braced her feet, trying to slow her descent. The starboard rail came up quick, and she turned her body, slamming into it. The impact knocked the wind out of her, but it didn't impede her momentum.

Nyssa tumbled off the ship.

Into the vast winter sky.

Quinn screamed her name.

FREE FALL

Nyssa plummeted through the sky.

A scream caught in her throat and stayed there, unwilling to release. Her thoughts seized up. The wind howled in her ears and buffeted her eyes so badly she had to close them.

She fell end over end.

Again.

And again.

And again, until her mind grew heavy and her limbs light.

A shrill scream snapped her mind back to awareness. *Reach out. Reach. Out!*

She pushed through her panic and exploded with power. The sky's magick filled her vision. Instinctively, she flattened her body, arms out. The way the deckhands of the Cloud Crasher did when they dove off the ship. She stopped tumbling ass over head, finally able to focus on finding Athen.

There. A glowing soul. Falling below her.

She shot her hand out, a rush of electricity flowing toward Athen. She wrapped her magick around him. Alive. He was alive.

A long column of bright orange magick buzzed next to her—the safe fall enchantment. She gritted her teeth, shooting out another stream of lightning, hooking her magick into the enchantment.

This is insane, this is insane, this is insane...

Nyssa locked the world away, drawing on the last of her reserves. Drawing on the lessons Fontaine had taught her.

Concentrate. Focus.

She latched onto the two magickal signatures. Centered them in her mind. Only them.

This has to work.

In one last explosion of power, Nyssa yanked Athen and the safe fall enchantment toward her.

Athen's essence flew at her. As did the column of magick still attached to the ship, its bright-orange glow bending in her direction.

Nyssa sucked in a breath as Athen and the enchantment rushed at her, about to converge in one point in the sky. Converge too fast, she realized.

No!

Nyssa braced herself before crashing into Athen. A cry of pain died on her lips.

DESCENT

Athen fell, his body settling into a slow rotation toward the green and brown earth beneath him. As the ground approached, he closed his eye and accepted his fate. His thoughts settled on Aryis. He hoped she would forgive herself and live a good life. And that Nyssa would look after her.

A shock of pain ripped through him, yanking him back into the moment. The pain was familiar—Nyssa's magick.

He was suddenly jerked backward, the strange sensation of falling replaced by an even stranger feeling of being slingshotted back up toward the ship. He twisted his head in time to see the impossible—Nyssa rushing at him, her lightning flowing around her like a river.

"Shit," he hissed.

They slammed into each other.

Athen grabbed ahold of Nyssa, pulling her into his arms. She was unconscious.

I'm not falling?

He was no longer plummeting toward the ground. He was still falling, but slower. A faint orange glow surrounded them, protecting them from the wind and gliding them down toward earth.

The safe fall enchantment? How the fuck...

Athen risked a look down. Below them, a vast forest raced up to greet them, the canopy of trees visible and distinct. In a few seconds, they'd be knee-deep in branches.

He tensed. They were still falling too fast. His gaze shot back up to the ship in the distance high above him. It was still listing to the side, spiraling down. At its rate of speed...no one would survive.

His heart sank.

A deafening drone washed over him before the airship shimmered, the air around it growing dark.

Athen sucked in a breath—his gut screamed that something was wrong. He wrapped his arms around Nyssa's limp body.

The Cloud Crasher disappeared.

They fell.

DISPLACED

Quinn's heart pounded in her chest. She had watched helplessly as Nyssa fell off the Cloud Crasher. Panic and despair wrestled in her mind, threatening to overtake her. Render her useless.

"Trust me."

Those words pushed past the hopelessness. There was no one in the world she had more faith in than Nyssa.

It had to be enough now.

"Save the others."

"Hold on!" she cried.

Quinn tapped into what little energy she had left, hoping she could do as Nyssa asked. Shadow billowed out of her, and she wrapped it around herself and the railing she held onto. Extending her magick, darkness spread across the deck like an ocean wave, seeking out every glowing orb of life.

Aryis was already secured. Darkness shot up to Reece and Medias, tethering them to the ornate railing that lined the stairs up to the bridge. She coiled her shadow around the remaining Justiciars and Ina, latching them onto the boat, sinking barbs of darkness into the wooden deck to secure everyone.

She held on tight to the cold metal railing, trying to maintain her focus as the last of the wraiths slid past, their fleshy wings useless against the bracing winds as the ship descended toward the earth.

If the vessel didn't slow down, they'd all slam into the ground.

A high-pitched whine grew louder and louder, the sound of an enchantment straining to do as designed. The sails above her head sparked, the edges of each tear glowing like hot embers. Quinn whispered a soft wish, shivering in the cold air as it buffeted her body.

The shimmering sails began to stitch back together.

"It's working," Quinn breathed, hope lighting in her chest. "It's working!"

The glowing red borders of the fabric flickered and burned out, and the repairs were blown apart again by the wind.

The Cloud Crasher groaned underneath Quinn when the enchantments tried and failed to right the ship and get it sailing again.

The stress on the ship could tear it apart.

A black mass spilled down the mainmast, eyeballs roiling in its darkness—a darkness that met her own as the mass oozed around Aryis.

Quinn gasped when the black thing touched her magick. A deep cold shocked her, making her clutch tighter to the rail. She closed her eyes and concentrated, tightening her grip on all the living souls on deck. She couldn't lose her focus or she'd lose them.

Energy pulsed through her, a strange but familiar presence pressing into every part of her body. His presence was unmistakable, even though she'd only felt him once from a distance in the Realm of Shadows.

Tajal.

What was he doing here? Had...had Aryis *summoned* him?

A voice echoed in her head, loud and all-encompassing. The voice of a god. *Why does the ship still fall?*

"The enchantments have failed!" she yelled.

Shoddy work.

Quinn choked out a breath. "Help us."

But I already did. Did you not see me pluck the wings off—

"We're running out of time!"

Seconds passed, stretching into an eternity that Quinn didn't have.

Across her unlikely connection with Tajal, Quinn felt a pang of long-ing. Of concern.

The Ancient God spoke again. *Mortal time ticks and ticks and ticks. It's meaningless.*

Quinn swallowed, grasping hold of Tajal's strange, errant emotions that cascaded over her, and took a desperate gamble. "Not to her. Not to Aryis."

The black mass rolled across the deck, eyeballs bobbing up and down like bubbles of a wave washing onto shore, their surfaces splitting open like mouths, revealing countless fangs.

Tajal smiled a thousand smiles, and the ship began to vibrate, losing its place in the world.

SHADOW

Aryis startled awake. Cruel, searing pain was the first sensation to greet her. She let out a sharp cry of pain and tried to move, but found herself restrained.

"Aryis, stay still, please," a soft voice requested.

A dark form moved over her, offering a smile—Quinn, with worry behind her eyes.

"Wha-what's..." Aryis tried to sit up, but a hand pressed down on her chest.

"I said, stay still, let the healing disk work," Quinn said.

"Stubborn bird," a low voice rumbled, vibrating all around her, coming from everywhere and nowhere at the same time. Unmistakable. Tajal.

"You hush," Reece said.

Did Reece...did Reece just hush Tajal? "Am I dreaming?" Aryis asked through gritted teeth.

"No," Reece said, her face coming into focus opposite Quinn.

"The ship," Aryis mumbled. "We were falling."

"Not anymore, thanks to me," Tajal replied, an undeniable touch of pride in his tone. "You are welcome. I do accept gifts and adulation."

Aryis closed her eyes, her mind trying to race, but tripping and stumbling as the pain from her chest and forearm—not to mention a roaring headache—made it impossible to form complete thoughts. But one thing didn't escape her notice. She was *alone*. No one else hanging about in her head. "Explain. Please."

"I saved you!" the Ancient God boasted. "You weren't even awake to see it." A low, quaking sigh filled the space around her, waves of echoes rushing away and toward her. Her eyes flew open. The darkness around her wasn't Quinn's shadow. She was someplace familiar. Someplace awful.

"I have a feeling we're not the ones who need to provide an explanation," Medias said from above Aryis, giving her a pointed stare.

"Shit," Aryis whispered. She slowly realized she was lying on the deck of the Cloud Crasher. Familiar faces surrounded her. As did Tajal's eyes. So many eyes...she did her best to tamp down her fear, akin to the fear that had gripped her when he once trapped her in the Realm of Shadows, enveloping her, feeding off of her.

"Shit indeed," Quinn replied. "But Tajal can wait—"

"Excuse me?" he said.

Quinn hummed out a groan of annoyance. "You can wait until we get Aryis sorted. I thought you wanted us to help her?"

Aryis held her breath. If Quinn pissed Tajal off, he could just dispatch them all with barely a thought. Nyssa was usually the one they had to rein in, but Quinn was chippy. She wore a pain on her face that made something inside Aryis ache.

Aryis let out a breath. "Athen?" she asked. "Nyssa?" She looked to Quinn and Reece for a reply.

The sullen expression on Reece's face made her heart bottom out.

Aryis forcefully sat up, pushing their protests away. "Where's Athen and Nyssa? Where are they?"

Quinn swallowed, her eyes full of tears. "Athen fell off the ship. Nyssa jumped after him. She said—" Quinn's head dipped forward. "I didn't have enough magick left in me to save them and everyone on the ship. I hope they're alive. If they're not alive, I..."

Grimacing, Aryis tried to stand. "Help me up, please." Before Quinn and Reece could move, black tentacles slid underneath her and raised her to her feet, steadying her.

"Thank you," she breathed.

Tajal's many eyes blinked at her and split in half to smile, revealing pallid gray fangs. She shuddered at the sight.

Aryis limped to the starboard rail and looked over its edge. The ship was surrounded by a roiling darkness, tentacles and eyeballs rising and falling like the waves of a very strange sea. Stars twinkled overhead, illuminated by a dark-purple light. She turned back to the deck of the Cloud Crasher. Light orbs hung in the air, glowing dimly, fighting valiantly to part the dimness of the Realm of Shadows. The air held a constant low hum, and Aryis wondered if it were Tajal's doing, or if he was simply the caretaker of a realm that seemed hauntingly alive.

A small group of people stood huddled near the mainmast, including Reece, Medias, and Quinn. Ashcloak Ruggen was there too, along with six Justiciars, their usual stoic appearance replaced by wide eyes and an undercurrent of fear that Aryis didn't need to be an empath to sense.

All around them, Tajal moved and shimmered, his tentacles gathering the bodies of wraiths from the ship. Aryis watched curiously as the Ancient God wrapped his darkness around a wraith and absorbed it into his expansive body. He swept across the deck, clearing it of the creatures.

The tentacles began to twist, weaving together to create the rough form of a man. The shape stepped forward, detaching from the rest of the mass. More shadows swirled around it before dissipating to reveal Tajal.

Tajal floated toward Aryis, doffing his top hat. "You are better now?"

"Yes," she grumbled. She glanced down at her forearm and chest. Red magick still clung to her skin, the remnants of the healing disk. It had done its job. Painfully. Her knee throbbed, though it was a dull ache—one she had grown far too accustomed to enduring. "Where's the crew? Are they safe?"

"They're below deck," Quinn replied.

Aryis scanned the Justiciars. Four were missing. "And the other Justiciars?"

One of their number turned his eyes to her. "One lost at the manor you were held in. The other three fighting the wraiths."

She swallowed. "Where are their bodies?" Justiciars honored their dead with ceremonial burials—they would go to great lengths to recover the bodies of their fallen companions.

The Justiciars didn't respond.

Medias answered for them. "I believe they went overboard."

"I'm so very sorry, Justiciars." A few of them nodded their heads to her.

An older woman stepped forward. By the looks of her, and Athen's stories, Aryis knew she had to be Captain Anna Legrand.

"Where the hell are we?" Anna asked, her eyes boring into Tajal. "I don't know who you are, but I want our—"

"Tajal the Curious," he replied, doffing his top hat. "And I—"

"Take us back. Now." Anna planted her fists on her hips.

Aryis put her hands out, trying to head off Tajal's anger. He had the power of a god and, often, the temper of a toddler. "Please, let's just calm down and sort this out."

The woman turned to her, narrowing her eyes. "You must be Aryis Devitt. Athen has spoken of you. At length. I hope you are truly worth this trouble."

Quinn stepped forward. "Tajal, can you return us all to our realm? We need to get back to Athen and Nyssa. They—"

"Stop your incessant jabbering!" Tajal bellowed, his voice filling the Realm of Shadows. The others were quick to cover their ears. "I saved your flimsy ship from crashing into the ground and splintering into a million little pieces. Your bones are all inside their body where I'm told they belong. Show some gratitude, mortals!"

Aryis put a hand on his arm. The fabric of his sleeve vibrated under her fingers, like a thousand bees contained by his tuxedo jacket. "Tajal, thank you."

Tajal turned all of his eyes to her. "I've attracted the attention of the others. My brothers and sisters will have words for me. How angry they had been the last time I wandered into your realm..." He bristled. "Koras and Narileh have their little playthings and not one of my brethren admonished them. I dare them to speak against me now. I will see their words turn to ash."

Swallowing, Aryis screwed up her courage. "Take us back."

Time ticked by slowly. Aryis became acutely aware of her ragged breathing and her heart threatening to beat out of her chest. She had no power here in his realm, none of them did, and being at the god's mercy felt like balancing on a razor's edge.

Finally, Tajal reached up and stroked her cheek, his hand a mass of small tentacles. "So fragile."

The Cloud Crasher began to rumble under Aryis's feet. Shadows crept over the sides of the ship and rose up into the air, encapsulating the Cloud Crasher in a sphere. A deep, throaty drone filled the air and reverberated in her chest, down her arms, and into her legs. Her knee protested and she stumbled, but Quinn and Reece were quick to steady her.

"Are you watching?" Tajal asked, his eyeballs parting in the middle of each to give her a toothy grin.

"Yes," she breathed.

Her world flooded with light.

LIGHT

Nyssa groaned, roused by an incessant tapping on her forehead.

"Wakey-wakey!" a low voice rumbled.

Her eyes snapped open. Multiple sickly yellow eyes stared back at her.

Nyssa shot upright and yelped from a sudden sharp pain in her right forearm. Broken, if she had to guess.

"Wha-" she sputtered, groggy. Her head pounded mercilessly.

The many eyes continued to stare at her. It was unmistakably Tajal, wearing a...tuxedo? She took a deep breath and released it, trying to vanquish the desire to panic. *I was right...he was on the ship. But how?*

"You look terrible," Tajal said, pressing closer.

Nyssa pushed his 'face' away, her hand sliding against mushy eyeballs. Her stomach roiled at the slime her hand came away with.

A groan next to her grabbed her attention. *Athen!*

She pulled herself over to his prone body. "Hey, big man."

His eye slowly opened, its golden orb finding her. A smile spread across his face. "You're alive," he mumbled.

She helped him sit up. "You okay?"

Rubbing the back of his head, he nodded. "Yeah. For the most part. The branches broke our fall."

"And my arm, I fear."

Athen's attention went immediately to Tajal. "Is that—"

Raised voices startled them.

"Come on, at the ready." Athen lumbered to his feet and pulled Nyssa up next to him. Bodies moved in the trees and she steadied herself. She didn't have much fight left in her, but if Ceril's assassins were coming to finish them off, she and Athen would give them hell.

As the bodies drew closer, a warmth spread across Nyssa's chest. She gasped, hope flooding through her.

Quinn burst into their small clearing, about a dozen expressions crossing her beautiful, flushed face when her eyes lit upon Nyssa. She took a hesitant step forward before rushing at Nyssa.

"Blacksea, you insane fucking woman!" She crashed into Nyssa and wrapped her up in her arms, breathing into the crook of Nyssa's neck.

"I'm okay, Freckles. I'm alive. Careful though, I'm a bit beat up." She pulled Quinn's face up and gave her a long, gentle kiss, reveling in the warmth of her soft skin.

Quinn's brilliant green eyes brimmed with tears, and she quickly wiped them away. "How are you alive?" She looked over to Athen. "How are either of you alive?"

Nyssa let go of Quinn. "I just sort of improvised. I made Athen and I crash into the safe fall enchantment, and it caught us."

A rush of air left Quinn, and she shook her head, a bewildered smile adorning her gorgeous face. "You're insane."

Nyssa shrugged. "Yeah, but it worked." She donned a crooked grin and gave Quinn a wink.

"I have several questions, especially about him," Athen said, his voice low as he nodded at Tajal, who was busy examining the bark of a tree. "But most importantly, where are the others?"

"Right here," Medias said, stepping through the trees, her arm around Aryis. Reece followed them.

Aryis gasped. "Athen!"

Athen rushed forward, pulling her into his arms. "I've got you," he whispered.

"I thought you were dead."

"I'm a little bruised, but I think I hurt the trees falling through them more than they hurt me."

Next to Medias, Reece let out a trembling sigh, covering her mouth, her eyes welling with tears.

Medias took a deep breath and strode over to Nyssa and Quinn, giving Nyssa a once-over. "It's good to see you again, Blacksea."

Nyssa laughed and pulled Medias into a one-armed hug. Medias cleared her throat, trapped in the embrace, but she returned the gesture.

She let go of Nyssa. "I would prefer to not have the gods I'm supposed to be watching over take very ill-advised risks. You both—"

"Risks?" Reece grumbled before giving Nyssa and Athen hugs. "You're one to be lecturing Nyssa about risks when you keep risking your own damn life."

Nyssa sat down on a nearby tree stump. She groaned as she tried to move her right arm. "Anyone have a healing disk? My arm is broken."

"Oh, let me!" Tajal said, darting toward her.

Nyssa recoiled from him, holding a hand up, weak sparks of lightning serving as a warning. "Can someone *please* explain why the *fuck* Tajal is here?"

Nyssa sat still on a deck chair on the Cloud Crasher and kept her eyes locked on Tajal. Anna cracked a healing disk and pressed it to her skin. Pain raged through Nyssa's forearm. Anna had used up the ship's healing supplies, dipping into her own emergency stash, mumbling her intention to finally drop some gold marks on hiring a healer onto her crew.

Clenching her teeth and doing her best to not make a sound, Nyssa focused on Aryis's story. Tajal floated behind her, his eyes blinking out of rhythm with one another. Nyssa suppressed a shiver. Everything about the Ancient God unnerved her.

More unsettling, perhaps, was the familiar ease with which Aryis dealt with the tentacled god. They had, for lack of a better word, a rapport.

How had she kept him a secret and not gone mad with Tajal forever chattering in her head? And how had he not simply devoured the woman as he took from her?

"I didn't mean to lie to you all," Aryis said, continuing her tale. "But Tajal made it clear that your lives were forfeit if I told you he was in my head."

Tajal floated toward Quinn, instantly drawing Nyssa's ire. She tensed, ready for a fight.

"This one thinks you do nothing but lie," he said, circling Quinn, his body becoming more elastic, coiling around her like a cobra.

"That's not true," Quinn said, appearing unconcerned about Tajal's proximity. "Aryis and I have...healed some of our wounds."

"A reconciliation! How delightful!" Tajal applauded as his voice dripped with sarcasm. "You mortals are like the sails of this ship...fragile and subject to moving any which way the wind blows. Inconstant. In flux. Confusing."

His eyes scanned the deck of the ship. The crew was scurrying about, handling repairs and giving their small contingent a wide berth. The journey back to the Cloud Crasher had been slow, but Tajal had relocated the ship from the Realm of Shadows to a bit of open land nearest to where he sensed Nyssa and Athen to be.

Quinn relayed what had transpired upon the ship after Nyssa dove after Athen. Aryis explained how she yanked Tajal from the Realm of Shadows to help. She then further disclosed the situation she had been dealing with for months, having the god rolling around her mind.

Thinking back, Aryis's behavior had been odd at times, but Nyssa attributed it to her trying to fit back in with their group of friends, as well as her penchant for talking to herself.

Reece frowned. "This explains why you never felt settled. I thought it due to your unease after your...actions." It was nice of Reece to not say *betrayal*, but they all knew what she referred to.

Tajal turned his attention to the empath. "You didn't feel me?"

"Oh, I do now. And I have to block you out. But that sliver of you that Aryis carried inside of her? No."

"Why are you blocking me out?" he asked, sounding almost...hurt.

"I have never held my face underneath a raging waterfall, but I liken your emotions to doing so."

"And what emotions do you feel?"

Reece scowled. "That's the problem. I...don't know."

Tajal took a deep breath, his whole body expanding. Nyssa tapped her finger against her thigh. They needed to extricate Aryis from Tajal's grasp and his seemingly endless curiosity.

"What do you want with Aryis?" she asked.

The god moved toward her, his body resembling that of a snake before it re-formed into the shape of a man. "I thought experiencing life with a mortal might help me understand these fleeting emotions that haunt me from the edges of the world."

Nyssa scowled. "I don't understand."

Tajal shrugged. "Neither do I. Not yet."

"Not to be inhospitable, but we've been through a bit of an ordeal. You're a headache I don't need," she said.

"You are, as always, extremely rude. You will one day come to regret—"

"Stop," Aryis said quietly from her seat on a battered wooden crate. She stood up. "It's time, Tajal."

"Time for what?" Athen moved to her side.

She looked at him, her eyes betraying a deep regret. "I...I can't..."

"Wait...how did you get Tajal to help us?" Nyssa's mind raced back to her own bargain with Tajal, trading the memories of her parents for Aryis's freedom. A breath left her. "What did you promise him?"

Aryis shook her head. "Nothing I wouldn't give a thousand times over to make sure you were all safe and alive. He's...taking me back to the Realm of Shadows."

"What? For how long?" Athen asked, a strain in his voice.

Her lips parted but she didn't say anything, her eyes filling with tears.

She isn't coming back.

Silence fell over them all.

A loud groan rumbled out of Tajal. "You are all so tiresome. Perk up those forlorn faces." He darted toward Aryis.

Athen moved between them, his fists balled up. Nyssa exchanged a glance with Quinn—they were all ready to fight. But Aryis pulled Athen back. "It's okay," she said. She stepped forward, extending her hand to Tajal. "I keep my promises."

Nyssa shook her head and stood, calling her magick forth, weak as it was. "Aryis, this isn't happening."

"Nyssa, I'm asking you to stop fighting. Just this once," Aryis said, her eyes steady. Unafraid.

Tajal's eyeballs rotated in all directions, gazing across their gathered cohort. Nyssa braced for a confrontation—there was no way the god was taking Aryis back to the Realm of Shadows forever.

After a few moments, Tajal reached forward and grasped Aryis's hand. "I've had...fun?...but I fear you'd just get in the way. Because you're so disgustingly soft and breakable, you'd likely perish in a day or two. Far more trouble than you're worth, I'd say."

Aryis gaped at him. "I don't understand."

Tajal's face zoomed close to hers. "I'm releasing you, Little Bird." He let go of her hand. "I'm sure we'll see each other again. Sometime soon. Or later. Or thereabouts." He plucked an eyeball off one of the stalks that comprised his head and tossed it in the air. It hovered for a moment, then began to spin, growing darker and bigger until it resembled the portal to the Realm of Shadows created by the Hummingbird that Aryis stole from the Wayland Conservatory.

Tajal bowed, tipped his top hat to Aryis, then stepped through the portal. It collapsed with a high-pitched squeal.

Aryis stumbled back and sat down hard on her wooden crate. Her face was blank.

Athen crouched down next to her. "You promised him your life?"

She blinked at him. "I didn't know what else to do. He wouldn't have saved us if I didn't offer him something in return." She pressed her hand against his chest.

Athen covered her hand with his own, holding it to his heart. They shared a soft smile that gave Nyssa hope. Maybe they hadn't fully found their way back to each other, but their hearts were bound together, that was eminently clear.

Aryis turned her attention to Nyssa. "We have to get to Arcton as soon as we can. Ceril is going to use the Spire of Heaven to make himself a god."

"Wha-what?" Quinn asked.

"He found a spell that uses the Primalith Shard to turn regular magick into Ancient Magick. I think he intends to change his *own* magick."

A breath left Quinn. "That's...not possible, is it?"

"Theoretically, maybe? The Rells had the Spire of Heaven to study for years. Maybe they figured out a way to draw out its power, sync up types of magick until they resonate, and change them?"

Nyssa rubbed her face, anger and frustration settling in. She wanted to scream. "How dangerous would he be if he achieved this theoretical change?"

Aryis furrowed her brow. "There have never been Cursed Gods with ethereal magick. Only corporeal—only able to manifest facets of one power. Well, I suppose you two break that rule a little. But someone with access to all the spells Ceril knows *and* the power of Ancient Magick? Turning a cemetery into an army of wraiths will be trivial compared to what he could do. And soul magick means he can control whomever he wants. What if he controls Decia or Safin? Or...one of you?"

Quinn glanced at Nyssa, her face going dark.

"Captain, when can we get back in the air?" Nyssa called out to Anna, who was squinting up at the mainmast. Two deckhands swung from ropes connected to the yardarms, pulling the thin sails taut. The edges of the slashes in the fabric glowed red, slowly mending the fibers back together.

Anna walked over, running a hand through her spiky white hair. "Good news is the sails are starting to self-repair. Bad news is they're repairing slower than usual. They were due for an enchantment refresh, but I put it off. This is my fault, I'm sorry."

Nyssa clucked her tongue. "What would've happened if you weren't at the helm when the sails gave way?"

Anna frowned, her bottom lip protruding. "Hard to know exactly, but the ship could have capsized, maybe even started tumbling stern over bow."

Nyssa perked up an eyebrow and tried to smile through the fear that gnawed at her upon learning the news about Ceril's aspirations to become a god. "The sails will repair themselves a bit slower, but I know you'll get us up in the air and to Arcton as fast as possible. But your skills as a helmswoman and captain saved our collective asses, Cap." She clapped Anna on the back. "I owe you a drink when all this is over."

Anna's frown disappeared. "When all this is over, we'll drink ourselves into the next week." She nodded, patted Nyssa on the cheek, and hurried back to the mainmast.

A stiff breeze picked up. The pine trees surrounding the clearing swayed, and Nyssa shivered. Something felt off, and her mind clicked to what it was. She reached over her shoulder, finding Winter's Bite gone from its sheath. "Fuck," she whispered. "My sword. I lost my damn sword."

"I got it," Aryis said. "Help me up." Athen pulled her up, and she held her hands out. They began glowing with a golden light, and after a few moments, Winter's Bite appeared, showers of sparks falling from the sword.

"Fucking brilliant," Nyssa sighed. She carefully took her sword from Aryis and gave it a once-over. Its blade was stained with the black blood of wraiths, but other than that, it was fine. She leaned it up against a crate. It would need a good cleaning later.

She wrapped an arm around Aryis's shoulders and leaned in to kiss her temple. "Thank you. For everything."

Reece took Aryis's hand. "Come on. We could all use a bath, a hot meal, and some sleep. Especially you two," she said, pointing to Nyssa and Quinn. The suggestion implied what they all knew—she and Quinn would have to be at their very best to take on Ceril now that he had access to magick they didn't understand.

"Oh, and we should check on Suvi to make sure she's still tied up and miserable," Reece added with a smirk. She led Aryis away to head to the cabins below deck, trailed by Medias and the remaining Justiciars.

Ina lingered, her back straight and her chin up. "I will use the ship's messenger bowl to inform our forces at Arcton to ready themselves for Ceril. The Citadel's runes can hold him off for a while, but he'll likely know weak spots to get inside. I will also let the Emperor know of what transpired."

Nyssa held up a hand to stop Ina before she left. "Ina...Ashcloak Ruggen, tell our people at Arcton to not throw their lives away. Ceril will cut through them like paper. Just hold him off if they can but be smart. And tell Safin to stay far away. He needs to stay safe, and that means being nowhere near Ceril."

Instead of rebuffing Nyssa's advice, Ina nodded, then hurried off.

Turning, Nyssa came face-to-face with Athen. He braced her shoulders. "Now that we have a moment, can we talk about you jumping off a perfectly good airship? Are you fucking insane?"

She shrugged. "Your invulnerability has limits, big boy. And falling off an airship is one of them." A wave of melancholy washed over her as he peered down at her. "I...I couldn't let you die." She cleared her throat. "Next time, try not being so damn clumsy. I can't be diving after your foolish ass all the time."

Athen leaned over and kissed her forehead. "I love you too, idiot." He straightened up and swiped at his eye. "Go clean up and rest. We'll reconvene in a couple hours to talk strategy."

His Ashcloak tendencies were showing. He would have made an excellent leader in the Emerald Order. Nyssa hated that his association with her cost him his place in the guild. He left her to follow after Aryis, giving Quinn's shoulder a squeeze as he passed.

Quinn stood silent, watching Nyssa.

"I need a bath, as does Winter's Bite." She nodded towards her sword, smiling at having it back in her possession. "And food. And sleep."

"Yes," Quinn replied. "We need to be ready for Ceril."

"We will be."

An unsettling cloud dimmed Quinn's face. "It ends at Arcton."

Nyssa truly hoped Quinn was right. The toll that Ceril had taken on them both wore them down. And there was a tension between the two of them ever since Arcton and that damn nightmare.

Quinn's pain had turned her distant. Silences stretched longer. Touches didn't linger.

Nyssa had learned to give Quinn space. To be within reach, but not overbearing. But her heart ached.

RETURN TO ARCTON

*T**his is a trap.*

Nyssa kept on alert as she trod deeper into the forest next to the Citadel, moving toward the dark column of smoke emanating from the trees.

It had taken days to get back to Arcton, but they'd landed only an hour behind Ceril's ship by Anna's estimation, having made good time on the merchant vessel thanks to her flying skills and the Cloud Crasher's old bones as a warship. Thankfully, Ina's communication back to the Citadel had worked—the Justiciars and guards who remained at Arcton were prepared for Ceril's ship, ready to protect the guild at all costs.

Once the Cloud Crasher landed, Nyssa and the others were quickly debriefed. Apparently, one well-aimed fireball from a Justiciar had ripped through the merchant ship's sails and forced it to make an emergency landing in the dense woods.

The only problem was that no one had emerged from said woods...so Nyssa and her motley party of Justiciars, Citadel guards, and friends decided to cautiously go after Ceril and what remained of his assassins. Aryis and a few Justiciars were sent into the Citadel to make sure the adepts, Masters, and staff hunkered down deep in the Spine and didn't try to be heroes. At least for the moment, Nyssa didn't have to worry about Aryis's safety along with everyone else's.

Nyssa's gaze flicked upward, keeping watch on the sky for wraiths. A column of billowing black smoke hung in the distance, giving them a rough location of their enemy's downed ship.

"Is it too naïve to hope that no one survived?" Athen asked from beside her.

Nyssa scanned the trees, Winter's Bite at the ready. The air vibrated around her, buzzing with ambient magick. It had to be the Spire of Heaven, its presence stronger since the last time they were here.

She kept her off-hand close to the rucksack slung across her chest, close to the void collar nestled inside, handed to her by one of the Justiciars to use on Ceril. The irony wasn't lost on her. Not long ago, the Justiciars were eager to latch a collar around her neck before the Empire saw fit to detach her head from her body. Now, they were tenuous allies.

"Let's assume that Ceril and the others are alive," Nyssa replied. She cast a glance around her. Ina, the Citadel guards, and the Justiciars spread out, carefully traversing through the trees, on high alert.

Quinn and Athen moved next to Nyssa, with Reece following close behind. There had been no persuading her to stay on the Cloud Crasher or go with Aryis, so Medias stuck close to her.

The forest sprawled before them, thick and green, making it difficult to see in the dwindling daylight. Thanks to a day exploring the Citadel grounds weeks earlier, Nyssa knew that if she continued forward and veered to the left, she'd eventually reach the entrance to a large mountain valley that opened up to a lake. And if she continued right, she'd quickly find the narrow path that led to the cliff's edge. The same cliff's edge that Quinn had stepped off of and into a safe fall enchantment to escape the Citadel more than two years earlier.

Quinn stopped and leaned against a tree, a scowl on her face.

"Are you okay, Emerrath?" Medias asked.

"The Spire...feels like it's calling to me."

Medias placed a hand on her own chest. "I feel it too."

Interesting that Medias could sense the shard. The bit of Ancient Magick she possessed seemed to attune her to the Spire's magick more than any of the others. The low buzz of the Spire had become a constant drone since they'd landed. Something was different about how it felt—urgent, almost. The pull of the Primalith Shard was also draining, as if the magick contained in the Spire were dueling with their own.

They continued forward, Nyssa's eyes darting from tree to tree. The hairs on the back of her neck stood up, and she held up a fist, signaling everyone around her to halt. Something pricked against her expanded senses.

Figures moved through the trees in the hazy distance.

Nyssa released her fist, spreading her fingers and lowering her arm until her palm was facing the ground. She and her cohort quickly slid behind trees for cover.

Reece crouched behind the tree to Nyssa's left. "Something's not right here," she said, keeping her voice low. "Those are Rule assassins waiting for us, but they feel...off. They're...cold. I...I don't know how else to explain it."

Quinn's eyes flashed with green energy. "I can't tell how many there are...there's something strange making it hard to pinpoint magickal signatures."

Nyssa tapped into her magick and expanded her senses, understanding what Quinn meant. Instead of the soft glow of souls, there were only muted flickers of magick in the forest ahead of them.

The air quivered, like the surface of water disturbed by a stiff breeze. A second of silence hung in the air. Assassins crept closer, appearing and disappearing behind trees, the waning light hiding them.

"Circle up!" Ina commanded. Medias pulled Reece behind a tree.

"Got your back," Athen said from Nyssa's left. Quinn stood at her right as they formed a defensive circle to keep the assassins in front of them.

A chill wind whipped through the woods and the pines swayed, drifts of snow falling off their limbs. Nyssa and the others waited, their breaths hanging in small puffs of fog.

Finally, the remnants of Ceril's Obsidian Rule traitors attacked, rushing at them wordlessly from the trees ahead. Athen shouted and fell into a group of them, swinging his fists, sending one flying into a gnarled tree with a dull *thunk*.

The rest of their cohort whirled into action.

Nyssa drew her sword as an assassin lunged at her. The woman's face was blank—devoid of anger or hate or fear. She moved with deadly purpose, a dagger arcing up toward Nyssa's throat. Nyssa twisted away, her sword slicing through the assassin's forearm. The detached hand landed with a thud, its dagger rolling into the snowy grass.

Nyssa slid back, ready. No sound came from the assassin, nor did she seem to be affected by the loss of her hand. Instead, she turned her eyes to Nyssa, her face remaining still. A quick glance to the other Rule attackers raised Nyssa's hackles—each of them wore the same emotionless gaze. What had Ceril done to them?

Her attacker advanced toward her again. Nyssa drove Winter's Bite into the woman's stomach, but the assassin didn't stop trying to get to her, her remaining arm outstretched, fingers scrabbling in the air like spider legs.

Nyssa held steady as the woman inched forward, impaling herself further on the blade.

"What the fuck?" Nyssa hissed.

In a blur of motion, Quinn was next to her, driving the tip of her sword into the assassin's eye. The assassin jerked once before sliding off Nyssa's blade and slumping to the ground.

"Remember what Aryis told us about what happened at Wayland?" Quinn said. "I think this is the same thing."

"Ceril did this to his own allies?" Nyssa asked. *What depths wouldn't that monster sink to?*

A low whistle seized her attention. She threw up a protective web of lightning in front of her allies. An arrow struck the translucent blue magick, bouncing off and falling harmlessly to the forest floor.

A figure stepped out from behind one of the trees far ahead, and Nyssa's blood ran cold.

Efla Eld'on, a crossbow in her hands, smirked at Nyssa across the distance between them.

Nyssa let loose a guttural roar and sent a streak of lightning at the assassin. The bolt fizzled halfway to its target. *How?* Efla disappeared behind the thick trunk of a nearby tree.

Quinn gripped Nyssa's arm, pointing to where Efla had disappeared. "We need to stop her."

Nyssa shook her head. "Ceril is our focus, and that bitch could be trying to split us up."

"Efla will do anything to help Ceril succeed—I don't know why, but she's devoted to him. If she's loose, she's a threat."

Sweat ran down Nyssa's back, the Spire of Heaven pressing against her senses and resonating through her like a feverish ache.

"We've got this, Nyssa!" Athen said. He reared up to his full height and clapped his massive hands together. "Which one of you assholes is next?"

The assassins turned to him, like moths to a flame.

Quinn looked to the tree line. "Go."

Nyssa stepped to Quinn and kissed her. "I'll be back...then we go after Ceril. Together," she whispered. "Wait for me."

"I promise," Quinn said, shadow winding around her.

Nyssa took off running to the woods, the warmth in her chest receding as she drew farther away from Quinn.

Nyssa didn't stop or look back—she needed this. She *needed* Efla on her knees, begging for her life. Needed to see the fear in her eyes, the understanding that a reckoning was upon her right before Nyssa clamped a void collar around her traitorous neck.

QUINN'S CHOICE

Quinn watched Nyssa disappear into the trees, then turned her attention back to the problem at hand. Bodies whirled in the dim light, clashing against one another.

Ina, Justiciars, Athen, Medias, Reece...how many would survive the day? Quinn ground her teeth, the cold thought of any of them dying by Ceril's hand leaving her hollowed out.

An assassin stalked toward her. She wound shadow around him and jerked her arm forward toward a tree—

But her magick dissipated into the atmosphere.

What the...?

Athen shouted and tackled the assassin as he lunged at Quinn.

"Something's interfering with my magick!" she said. It had to be Ceril's doing. It would explain the strange sensation coming from this area of the woods. Just what had he learned from the last Alabaster Book?

"Stay behind me and use what Nyssa taught you," Athen said, one hand wrapped around the assassin's throat.

Flashes of light popped in the air around her, Medias doing her best to keep the assassins at bay. Ina and the others were holding their ground as the Rule assassins attacked from the trees and retreated, dragging the fight out.

Still, there was no sign of Ceril.

This is a distraction.

There was only one place he could be, and she and the others were wasting precious time with his underlings.

He wants us away from the Spire of Heaven.

She turned, her eyes drawn up to Beckwit Tower.

He's there.

Quinn turned back to the fight, her friends and allies battling to stop a threat greater than the Empire had faced in decades.

Athen, Medias, Reece, Aryis...none of them questioned what they needed to do, selflessly throwing their lot in with her and Nyssa. They were risking their lives, but Ceril was cunning and ruthless. He'd cut through every last person she cared about.

Every last person she *loved*.

Narileh's words rang in her ears—*there are some battles only Cursed Gods can fight.*

She needed to face Ceril and end this.

Alone.

There was no way Quinn was going to let Ceril hurt anyone she loved. She burst into a sprint, leaving Athen, Medias, and the others behind, breaking her promise.

I'm sorry, Nyssa.

Quinn darted through the trees and ran toward the Citadel, her name shouted in the air after her, yelling for her to wait. She had enough of a head start that they couldn't stop her.

The cold air stung her lungs and stiff evergreen limbs clawed at her as she weaved her way through the woods. She doubled her efforts when she reached the tree line and Arcton was in view.

Her legs burned by the time she got to the Citadel's back garden and slipped through the double doors into the sprawling mansion. Once inside, she hugged the wall and stilled, listening.

The main foyer was dark and empty. The flames in the fireplaces were low, not having been fed and stoked to prepare for the evening. While Quinn held no love for Arcton, she hoped its current residents were safe and would stay that way. And she hoped Aryis was with them, tucked away in a protected vault.

After taking a deep breath, Quinn pushed off the wall and jogged into the main hallway, following it until it branched off toward the antechamber at the bottom of Beckwit Tower. She took the corner and nearly ran right over Aryis, who jumped and let out a little yelp.

"Quinn? Where are the others?" Aryis asked.

Quinn looked around. No guards were stationed outside the entrance to the stairwell that led up to the Spire of Heaven. "Are you alone?"

"Yeah, First Master Ludov and the others are down in the vaults. They've closed off the Spine."

Quinn grunted. "It's Citadel protocol. You should be with them."

"There's no way I'm hiding away when the rest of you are risking your lives." Aryis narrowed her eyes. "You didn't answer my question—where are the others?"

Ignoring her, Quinn strode toward the door at the end of the hall.

"Did you see anyone go up in the tower?"

"I just got here a minute before you did," Aryis called out, limping after her. "Athen...Nyssa...are they okay?"

Quinn swallowed down her fear. "They're handling the last of Ceril's assassins and will follow." *They'll be okay. They have to be...*

She hurried to the door at the end of the antechamber, trying the knob. It didn't budge. She tentatively called her magick forth, hoping the dulling effect out in the forest was temporary. She extended her hand and shadow drifted out, strong and powerful. Relief flooded through her and she turned her attention back to the door.

Swirling spirals of purple magick shimmered on its surface. Powerful wards to keep everyone out...trivial to Ceril's growing power. She narrowed her gaze and focused on the ward keeping the door firmly shut. The magick in the enchantment was ancient, though now it had another sheen of magick on top of it...Ceril's reinforcement.

Quinn sent strands of dim shadow into the door and wove her magick around the ward. It resisted at first, but with some effort, she was able to suppress its protection. She tried the handle again and the door opened for her. Beyond its threshold was a stone stairwell that wound up to the top of Beckwit Tower.

Taking a deep breath, Quinn slipped through the entrance and glanced back to Aryis, who moved to follow.

"I'm sorry," Quinn said, shoving her away.

Quinn slammed the door closed with a bone-shuddering *thud*, then cut her magick off, allowing the ward to spring back to full power.

From the other side of the door came Aryis's muffled voice, "Quinn! Don't do this!"

No one could get through the door...no one except for Nyssa. It was time to put an end to Ceril.

ERON'S HONOR

Every last ounce of common sense within Nyssa was screaming at her, over and over again.

This is a trap.

This is a trap.

This is a trap.

Still, she slipped through the trees, her eyes darting back and forth. Leaving the others wasn't easy, but Quinn was right. They had no idea what Efla was planning or the damage she could do. They couldn't risk it. So Nyssa continued to track her, heading toward the cliff face.

The Spire of Heaven's presence reverberated through her chest, almost pulling at her. Nyssa stopped and steadied herself against a tree. Calling on every last bit of concentration she could muster, she recalled Fontaine's words— *"Find the calm in the chaos."*

Nyssa pulled forth her magick to sense what lay in the woods, grateful that it was no longer glitching from whatever enchantment Ceril had used to slow her and Quinn down back near the crashed ship. That damn Rell spell book was making him far more powerful—but the true threat lay in the unknown. What other spells were in that Alabaster Book? A book so dangerous Eliza Rell had hidden it away from the world.

The forest buzzed with magick of its own, the soft energy of the trees pulsating low and strong. Small glowing souls flitted about. *Birds? Squirrels?*

Nyssa exhaled when she found what—or rather who—she was looking for. The bright light of Efla's soul moved away from her. And she was alone.

Pushing off the tree, Nyssa cut off her magick, muting the intrusive thrum of the shard in the distance, and bisected the woods to get to the trail that led to the cliff.

What was Efla playing at? She had to know she couldn't stand toe-to-toe with Nyssa.

Movement past the trees ahead made Nyssa freeze.

Something bit into her thigh.

Nyssa whirled behind a thick trunk, hissing from the sting of pain. A crossbow bolt was stuck in the bark of a tree behind her, vibrating slightly from its impact. There was a thin, neat slice in the side of her leather pants, blood oozing from the gash beneath. A mere graze, but it could have been worse. She'd made herself an easy target, her bright-blue magick undoubtedly drawing Efla's attention.

Nyssa slid down and leaned over to take a quick peek. A soft whistle made her duck back just before bark splintered on the other side of the tree. Growling, she rose to her feet and stepped out into the open, throwing up a web of lightning to block another shot.

In the distance, Efla sprinted through the trees. Nyssa gave chase, finding her way to the footpath. Efla turned to let another bolt fly from her small crossbow, this one sailing way off its mark into the underbrush on the side of the trail.

Ignoring the cut in her leg, Nyssa sped up, hurling a narrow thread of lightning at the assassin, careful to ratchet back her power. *Capture, not kill.*

Her attack went wide.

"Fuck," she hissed.

They reached the small clearing at the mountain's edge, and Efla whirled around to face her.

A hard lump formed in Nyssa's throat as the assassin grinned a wolf's smile at her. For the past two years, she'd seen that grin in her nightmares, standing over Eron's dead body wearing her face.

Efla spread her arms wide. "It's just you and me now, Blacksea."

Nyssa stepped into the clearing, lightning rippling across her skin. The Spire of Heaven buzzed at the edge of her senses.

"You have a lot to answer for, murderer." She reached into the rucksack strapped across her chest, fingering the void collar within.

Efla's eyes drifted to the bag. "Are you going to arrest me?"

"You killed my father. I'm going to see to it that you spend the rest of your days in prison."

"You murdered my brother!" Efla spat, her face a mask of rage. "You deserve everything that's coming to you."

Indignation bubbled up. "Tann met the consequences of his actions. Now you're going to meet yours."

Efla tossed her crossbow to the side and cocked her head, the air around her shimmering. Suddenly, Eron's face stared back at Nyssa. "Do you miss me, child?"

A surge of heat shot through Nyssa's body. She drove her fist forward, lightning flowing from her hand. Her aim was true, the bright-azure bolt striking Efla in the chest.

The woman didn't fall. She locked eyes with Nyssa, her face changing back to her own, as flickering blue lines lit up her chest, forming intricate spiraling patterns in the leather jacket she wore. No, not *just* leather. Nyssa realized there were interwoven plates embedded in the leather.

Armor?

The glowing lines grew brighter.

A streak of lightning flew from Efla, blasting Nyssa in the chest. She fell back, hitting the ground hard. All the breath fled her lungs.

"How…" she choked out, gasping for air. Efla's armor not only seemed to absorb magick, but let her harness it?

A shadow fell over her.

Efla bent down and dug into Nyssa's rucksack. *The void collar!*

Nyssa grabbed the assassin's wrist. A shock wave of energy exploded at their contact, driving Efla back with a yelp of pain. The woman wavered on her feet, her armor lit up, pulsating with azure power.

Nyssa rose to her knees with a grunt. Efla put her hand to her chest, and the energy flowed out of the armor, coalescing around a thick, black ring she wore around her middle finger. She flung her hand out, blue magick exploding forth.

A charge of lightning struck Nyssa's chest. The strike doubled her over, her hands clutching at the dirt and rocks. Her heart shuddered as she tried to push herself up and failed, collapsing back to the ground. Her magick sputtered across her skin and dissipated.

Boots crunched against leaves and stones. "Every single day since you murdered Tann, I've dreamt about killing you."

Nyssa turned her head. Efla hovered over her, her armor and that ring on her right hand pulsating with power. "How does one kill a god?" she asked. She opened her fist, the ring glowing bright blue, and flicked sparks at Nyssa. The little bits of energy hit her with a sizzle. "Do you like what Ceril made for me?"

Efla dug her fingers into Nyssa's hair and lifted her head up. Lightning began to spin around the ring, and the assassin smashed her fist into Nyssa's face, sending a shock wave crashing through her.

Nyssa fell to the dirt and curled into a ball, twitching. She tried to move, to do anything other than cough up blood, but the pain and the electricity coursing through her veins made her sluggish.

Efla circled her. "Once you're dead, I'm going to leave you here on this cliff. Birds will pick the flesh from your bones." She planted a boot on Nyssa's shoulder and pushed her onto her back. "I'll be a godslayer and you will be forgotten, Blacksea." She straddled Nyssa and wrapped her hands around Nyssa's throat.

Nyssa seized the woman's wrists, gasping for air, but Efla bore down, magick crackling off her ring. Searing pain thrummed through Nyssa. She kicked her legs and wrenched at the assassin's wrists, trying to gain purchase, but her fingers seized up from the electricity leaking off the armor.

Pure hatred burned in Efla's eyes.

Nyssa opened her mouth, trying to draw in air. Hot tears streamed down the sides of her face. She was going to die here, her own magick turned against her.

Leaning closer, Efla sneered, "I can't wait to watch Ceril turn Quinn into his plaything."

No!

Nyssa bucked one more time, but it did nothing. She was weak and powerless again, like a child, her bullies raining down their fists and indignation on her.

But Eron...Eron had taught her how to fight back. To use everything at her disposal. To persevere.

Her fingers scrabbled against the sword belt over her chest, finding her throwing knives. She slipped one out of its sheath and plunged it into Efla's gut.

With a yelp, the woman let go of Nyssa's throat.

Nyssa bolted upright, grabbing hold of Efla's chest plate and driving her forehead into the woman's nose. The assassin rolled off her and scrambled to her feet, blood streaming down her lips and chin.

With a snarl, Efla reached down, found the small blade embedded in her abdomen, and pulled it out, dropping it to the dirt. She balled up her fist, blue sparks sputtering around the ring she wore. The armored plates in her jacket dimmed, no longer glowing with power.

The cold winter air burned Nyssa's lungs as she took big, gulping breaths. She turned on her side and pushed herself up to her knees, using every precious second to regain some strength. Her magick still reverberated through her, her nerves jumping with pain.

Nyssa gritted her teeth and reached into her rucksack, taking out the void collar. The metal was dull and cold in Nyssa's hands.

"You'll never put that on me," Efla sneered.

"You're right," Nyssa replied, looking out toward the edge of the mountainside. With a flick of her wrist, she tossed the collar off the cliff. "One of us dies here."

Hate curled Efla's lip as she drew her daggers from her belt and lunged at Nyssa. With no time to think, Nyssa drew Winter's Bite from its sheath and met the attack, blade against blade, from her knees. Efla's daggers slid off Nyssa's sword, and she spun away. The tip of Winter's Bite sliced along the bottom of her jacket, sparking against a plate of armor.

Efla attacked again. Nyssa swept the backside of her sword across her body to block the blow. The dull side of Winter's Bite collided with Efla's left wrist, and she cried out, dropping one of her daggers and staggering backward.

Nyssa slowly got to her feet, keeping her eyes on the assassin. Her arms ached just from holding Winter's Bite, the buzz of her magick shuddering through her body. Exhausted, she lowered her blade and took a defensive stance, holding up her hand and beckoning Efla to attack. "Come on, you fucking coward," she spat. "Come and take your revenge for your worthless brother."

Efla fell upon Nyssa again, howling with rage. Nyssa let Winter's Bite drop to the ground and slid forward, closing the distance between them. Efla's dagger arced down, and Nyssa blocked the blow with her wrist, quickly twisting her arm around Efla's forearm. Nyssa punched the assassin in the throat with her free hand.

Efla choked and staggered back, gasping for air. Her eyes went wide.

Nyssa balled up her fists. "Come on, traitor."

The assassin swayed on her feet as silence hung in the air between them.

"Come on," Nyssa whispered, knowing she had the woman beat.

Efla whirled and sprinted for the cliff's edge. Before Nyssa could react, the woman jumped.

Nyssa scrambled forward, stopping at the two short metal stakes that sat at the edge of the cliff. She crept forward and peered over the side. Hundreds of feet below, Efla disappeared into the clouds surrounding the mountain top, enveloped in the aura of the safe fall enchantment.

Nyssa roared with rage.

Swallowing down her fear, she backed up and prepared to jump.

But an unexpected calm washed over her.

No.

When you save others, you save yourself.

Eron's death had left a massive hole in Nyssa's heart, but one that was healing bit by bit every day. He had taken her in, raised her, helped her channel her anger. And she would avenge him. One day.

"I'll find her again. I promise," she whispered before retrieving Winter's Bite. She spun for the forest, breaking out into a run, back to Quinn and the others, back to the fight, the Spire of Heaven still humming in the distance.

THE SPIRE OF HEAVEN

Quinn wound up the stairs to ascend Beckwit Tower, her eyes trained to the eerie faint blue glow above her. The Spire's pull was undeniable, her chest buzzing like a nest of hornets. Her heart beat hard and fast, but she kept going, her fingers lighting upon the rucksack slung over her shoulder and resting against her hip. A void collar lay inside.

The sides of the tower were a smooth, black marble, cold to the touch as she pressed one hand on the wall to help guide her way up the dim ascent. Carved symbols ran along the wall, her fingertips brushing across them, an electric thrum of magick vibrating from each indentation laced with old enchantments. Whatever their purpose, Quinn couldn't say. No Citadel adepts were allowed near the tower.

As the top of the tower grew closer, she slowed, cautious. When she reached the landing, there was a narrow, curved hallway to an interior chamber and the source of the blue glow.

The Spire of Heaven awaited.

Quinn took a deep breath and followed the curve of the corridor until it opened up into a large room. Waves of magick washed over her from the bright azure shard in the middle of the room. The Spire of Heaven resembled a massive jagged crystal emerging from the stone floor, at least thirty feet tall. The remainder of the shard was embedded deep into the mountain, veins of its magick running parallel to the Spine below the

Citadel's main library. It pulsated slowly, each beat thrumming through her, making her fingers and toes tingle.

She approached the monolith, its surface translucent, but the interior of it moved as if alive. Sparkling luminescent motes of light flowed through the crystalline structure. The closer she got, the faster the motes moved.

"Beautiful, isn't it?" Ceril stepped into the shard's circle of light on the opposite end of the room.

Shadow coiled around Quinn, and she hurled razor-sharp spikes of darkness at him.

Ceril raised his hand. The spikes stopped cold, suspended in the air before bending toward the Spire of Heaven. Quinn tried to pull them back, but she was no longer in control. Ceril whispered the words of a spell and a pulse of purple energy flew out of his hands, enveloping her spikes and forcing them to sink into the shard. The motes of light flared brightly before settling back down.

Ceril stepped closer to the Spire of Heaven. "I can feel it changing me," he said, touching the surface of the shard, its glow fully encasing his hand. The motes within the structure broke free, flowing up and down his arm. He took a deep breath. "Gods can be forged by the will of man."

"What did you do?" Quinn growled.

A smile curled up his lips. "I attuned myself to the Spire of Heaven. Took a few times to get the resonance right, though." He flicked motes of light toward a corner on the opposite end of the room.

Quinn gasped. Bodies lay in a heap in the corner. Dark, twisted husks coated in dark-green leather. Obsidian Rule assassins.

"You killed them?" she whispered, tearing her eyes away from the bodies.

"Technically, the Spire of Heaven did."

She took a step back. "You're a monster."

Ceril glowered at her, poison in his gaze. "You were just like me once, your life stripped away from you. Now I'm taking what I deserve, like you did."

"I took back control over my own life. We are not the same!" Heat flooded through Quinn.

He waved his hand, a dismissive gesture he'd used countless times with her, usually in response to her cries of pain and protest.

Quinn would not be dismissed now. She opened the bag at her side and pulled out the void collar. "This ends here." Her magick unfurled around her, darkness spreading out at her feet, swirling toward Ceril.

She collapsed her shadows in on Ceril.

The room exploded in bright-blue light. Cold, excruciating agony radiated through her body. Grunting, Quinn lunged forward and grasped Ceril's wrist. She let her power flow again, this time aiming to extinguish every last bit of magick within him. The instant she tried, it felt like sheets of ice were being driven up her arm. She gasped and let go of him, sinking to her knees. The void collar slipped out of her hand, clanking against the stone floor.

Ceril smirked and bent down to pick up the collar. He ran a finger along its edge, chanting. The metal glowed white for a moment before the collar tumbled out of his hand and fell to the floor, shattering into pieces.

"Your Ancient Magic is quite useless against a reflection spell. Simple, yet elegant magick." He swept away from her and approached the Spire of Heaven, placing his hand on the glowing surface. The Spire pulsed under his touch. "I enchanted Efla's armor with the same spell, to aid her in getting revenge for her brother's death. Blacksea's likely dead by now."

No...

Quinn roared with fury and sprang to her feet. She drew her sword, arcing the blade down at Ceril's arm.

It struck his wrist and shattered.

The impact vibrated back through Quinn's forearms, and she dropped what was left of her sword, gasping in pain.

Ceril pressed his palms together, mumbling a spell. The air shimmered. Before she could move, a column of light ignited, surrounding her. An invisible force wrapped around Quinn's neck and constricted, lifting her up onto her toes. She clawed at her throat, gasping for air, and tried to use her magick, but it backfired, sending waves of icy pain up her arms.

A low laugh rumbled out of him. He watched her struggle, his eyes not leaving her face. "You're so young and still have a lot to learn in order to stand against me, girl."

Ceril turned to the shard and edged closer to it. Its blue magick flowed out and encircled his wrists, then elbows, then all the way up his arms. "Once my transformation is complete, I shall turn you into my slave. You *will* become the weapon that was promised to me. And I'll have you destroy anyone who seeks to stop me."

He stepped into the Spire of Heaven, disappearing into its azure glow.

Quinn tried to scream, but the vise around her throat tightened. Her vision began to darken.

No.

She gasped for air, struggling to stay on her toes. The restraint enchantment around her neck buzzed against her skin. She wrapped her shadow around it, feeling the edges of the spell with her own power. As she poked, Ceril's enchantment responded, punishing each attempt to attack it with icy stinging shocks. Ceril had infused all his spells with some sort of reflective magick, but she had no other recourse but to push forward, to try to escape, pain be damned.

She sank her magick into the enchantment. Tears sprang to her eyes, but she persisted, doing all she could to concentrate. Every movement of her power inside the invisible noose around her neck sent a thrum of agony through her. Was this how others felt when she used her magick on them? Every time she got close to suppressing Ceril's enchantment, she slipped, the sharp, biting pain shaking her focus.

It can't end like this...

Swallowing back bile, Quinn stilled her mind, falling back on Fontaine's training. The low drone of the Spire quieted. Her world shrank down to the tight grip around her neck and her own magick. She steeled herself. How many times had she willed herself to ignore the pain while living at Arcton? Or as Suvi's captive? Pain was a familiar friend. Pain was easy.

She focused on the enchantment around her neck and wrapped her shadow around it. Enduring the agony—like cold spikes shooting through her body—she tightened her power, sinking it into Ceril's enchantment, trying to extinguish the trap.

Her magick met resistance. Quinn almost relented. She pushed herself, forcing her shadow into Ceril's enchantment, bit by bit, trying to pry into the shifting energy.

The moments ticked away, the corners of her vision darkening. If she passed out before she could negate the restraint around her neck, it was over. Everything she had endured would be for nothing.

Tears sprang up in her eyes, rolling down her cheeks. *Come on...*

She gritted her teeth and made one last, tenacious push, forcing her shadow to shatter Ceril's spell. The pressure around her neck disappeared. Sucking in air, Quinn sank to her knees. The Spire of Heaven glowed brighter than before, the dark shape of Ceril within the heart of the shard now hardly visible. She willed herself to stand.

I have to stop this. Stop him.

Quinn stumbled toward the shard and extended her hand, touching its radiant surface.

Her world went white.

The shard trapped her hand, weaving its energy around her fingers. The sensation wasn't warm nor cold. Nor painful. It was...*other*. A roar enveloped her completely, loud and insistent. The sound was beautiful and melancholic, the sound of lost love, of pleasure, of agony, of laughter, of—

Quinn reeled from all the emotions it spurred, its low, wailing drone burying itself into the center of her chest and making her whole body vibrate.

The Spire's energy kept moving through her, a strange visitor that made her feel like she was being evaluated. In that moment, she panicked, remembering the bodies in the corner. Were they, too, examined and found lacking? What if the Spire found *her* lacking?

Quinn tried pulling her hand away, but the Spire wouldn't let go. Her heart began to pound in her chest. She had just rushed forward and touched the damn thing, not thinking of the consequences. What a fucking ridiculous way to die.

Make it count. At least make your death fucking count!

She tried to negate the shard's magick where it made contact with her skin, cursing under her breath when nothing happened.

If Ceril wanted her as his slave, he would make it happen, and she had just trapped herself. Her stomach turned to acid at the thought of hurting Athen, Medias, Reece, Aryis...those who took her in, trusted her simply because *Nyssa* trusted her.

And Quinn couldn't even fathom what Ceril would make her do to Nyssa. She refused to believe Nyssa had fallen to Efla...she had to still be alive.

Quinn's mind raced, scattered in a million panicked directions. How had she been so careless, rushing in to stop Ceril without a plan? And she'd lost the one weapon she could possibly use to stop him when he destroyed the void collar.

The void collar...

A desperate thought struck her and she lifted her head up, resolute, and pushed against the Spire. It greedily swallowed her up to her elbow. If she couldn't get the shard to let go of her, then she'd give herself to it.

Quinn dove into the Spire of Heaven.

THE POSSESSED

Reece crouched down, back against the tree as she had been ordered, watching her friends wade into battle. Watching the woman she loved fight off assassins.

And losing.

An assassin backed Medias up, striking blow after blow. Explosions of white light hit the man, but he barely flinched. Reece sensed nothing from him. He was null—as if dead inside.

The assassin kicked Medias in her chest, sending her sprawling to the forest floor. He didn't relent, closing in on her fast, his dagger ready to strike.

Reece jumped to her feet and took off in a sprint, crashing into the assassin before he could slice Medias open. They both tumbled to the ground, Reece stunned from the impact. It wasn't her best move, but it was the only thing she could think of in the moment.

The assassin's gaze snapped to Reece, his cold eyes locking with hers. He spun over onto his hands and knees and crawled toward her, grasping onto her ankle, digging his fingers in as he pulled her toward him.

Reece kicked her legs out in a panic, catching him in the chin. He swiped at her, the tip of his dagger slicing into her shin. She cried out from the sudden hot sting of pain. Hands wrapped under her arms and lifted her to her feet and she spun around to face her attacker, fists up, ready to fight.

Medias put up her hands. "It's me!"

Reece's attention flew back to the assassin, who hobbled to his feet. The expression on his face had never changed. No sign of pain. Of hate. Of...*anything*.

The assassin lunged at Reece, but Medias interceded, blocking his dagger and driving her own blade into his chest. Unfazed, he stared at Reece, reaching for her as blood gurgled out of his mouth. It took him a second to stop moving. His eyes never closed as he died on his feet.

Medias pulled her dagger out of his chest, and he tumbled over. "Come on!" She grabbed Reece's hand and ran toward the thick trunk of a tree, pushing Reece against it. "I told you to stay put!"

"I'm not going to sit back and watch you get hurt!" Reece replied. "Are you okay?"

Medias whirled around, her head on a swivel. "Where's Quinn?"

"I don't...I don't know." Reece had never taken her eyes off of Medias, scared to death for her. Now, she let her magick flow, searching for the glaring emotional signature of a Cursed God. And she found it. "I think I know where she went..." She glanced up at the tower.

"Damn it," Medias seethed, following Reece's gaze. "Ceril must be up there too. What is she thinking?"

Movement made Reece suck in a breath. An assassin stalked toward them. "Medias!"

Medias stepped up, sweeping her arm around Reece and pushing her behind her.

The body of another Rule adept flew through the air and collided into their assassin, sending them both tumbling across the snow and dirt on the forest floor.

"Hey, assholes, over here!" Athen shouted, one meaty hand wrapped around the throat of an assassin. He picked her up and slammed her into the ground. The other two assassins untangled themselves from one another and diverted their attention to Athen, rushing at him. Athen braced for contact, swinging a fist into the chest of one as the other crashed into his legs.

"We have to help him!" Reece said.

"As if you could," a voice hissed. A wave of hate hit her before a fist did, and she crumpled to the ground, stunned from the blow.

"Reece!" Medias cried out.

An assassin appeared behind Medias and struck her in the lower back. She dropped to a knee with a grunt, clutching at her back. He moved quick, delivering a crushing fist to Medias's jaw. She fell onto her back, barely moving.

The assassin stood over Medias. Quinn had warned them about this one—he could travel short distances in the blink of an eye. He grinned down at Medias and unsheathed the dagger he wore strapped to his thigh.

Reece fumbled around, her fingers scrambling through the snow, towards a rock. Fear drove her to her feet, stars still in her eyes, her head filled with a fuzzy, distant drone. She threw her rock at the assassin, hitting him in the shoulder. "Come on, you bastard," she mumbled, egging him on. A wave of his anger crashed into her senses as he turned to her.

I'm an idiot.

The assassin smirked, then disappeared in a gust of blue smoke. His anger jumped locations in an instant, and he reappeared next to Reece, burying a fist in her stomach. She gasped for a breath and swung her dagger at him, finding nothing but air. His laugh rang out right next to her ear and she flinched. He reappeared again, this time behind her, slicing his dagger across her lower back. Reece cried out and stumbled forward.

Medias climbed back to her feet, wobbly. "Reece," she slurred, a trickle of blood dripping from the corner of her mouth. The assassin appeared over her shoulder.

"Behind you!" Reece yelled.

Medias turned in time to barely block the assassin's dagger, the blade slicing into her forearm.

He disappeared again.

Reece hobbled over to Medias. "Are you—" A prick of anger popped up to her right. She turned and thrust her dagger into the air next to her, driven by desperation and pure instinct. The weapon sank into flesh with a sickening squelch, the assassin materializing to take it in the gut. She twisted the blade and wrenched it back, hot ichor splashing her hands.

The assassin choked out a ragged breath and sank to his knees. He raised his eyes to Reece, his mouth moving, but no sound coming out.

An arm wrapped around her shoulders and pulled her back. Medias's voice buzzed in her ear. "You're safe."

Reece kept her eyes on the assassin, and he stared up at her. Blood pooled around his knees. He wasn't like the others—his emotions weren't dull at all. He must have been spared Ceril's enchantment to turn him into a mindless, emotionless murderer. His anger was now gone, replaced by an almost peaceful resignation to his fate. Reece shivered as the feeling waned, drifting off into nothingness. The assassin slumped over on his side, his eyes still.

She let out a held breath, tearing her eyes away from the body to find Athen and the others had dispatched the rest of their attackers. Assassins lay scattered on the forest floor. One or two moved, but the rest...Reece couldn't sense them. A Justiciar and a few Citadel guards lay dead too.

Athen had his arm around Ina, and the remaining guards and Justiciars pulled in close.

"No prisoners?" Medias asked Ina, who winced and leaned against a tree.

"No. The assassins...they wouldn't stop. Like they were possessed," the Ashcloak replied.

"Ceril's doing," Athen said. "He did the same thing to the students at Wayland." He looked around. "Where's Quinn?"

There was no mistaking the emotional signature of a Cursed God, strong and powerful, even across distance. "The tower," Reece breathed.

"What?" he snapped.

"I think she's trying to stop Ceril."

Athen shook his head. "Nyssa is going to kill us for letting her slip away."

Reece turned her attention to finding another god, opening up her senses. "She's coming."

They all turned in the direction Reece indicated, and Nyssa emerged from the trees not a minute later. She looked shaken up, a trickle of blood running out of her nose, but she was alive.

"Where's Efla?" Athen asked.

Nyssa's jaw tensed. "Escaped." Her eyes took a quick scan of their number. "Where the fuck is Quinn?"

"The tower," Reece said.

"What? Why did you let her go alone?"

Reece shook her head. "She took off while we were fighting."

"Can you sense her?" Nyssa grabbed Reece's shoulders. "Tell me she's alive."

Reece closed her eyes and relaxed her control. She didn't have to search for Quinn—the woman's emotions slammed into her.

Fear. Wave after wave of fear was all Reece could sense coming from the distant tower. Her stomach dropped. "Something...something bad is happening to Quinn."

Nyssa broke into a dead sprint toward the Citadel.

"Follow her!" Athen shouted, taking off after her.

Reece grimaced, unable to keep Quinn's emotions at bay. Besides the fear, Quinn's hate burned through Reece, dark and ugly.

"We're running out of time," Reece whispered.

Medias grasped her hand. "Let's go."

STILLNESS

Quinn slowly exhaled the breath she held, trying to find herself in the vast darkness dotted with stars, but her body was weightless, almost meaningless in this place, inside the Spire of Heaven. She was filled with a sense of connection to a nothingness that stretched in infinite directions, spanning time. It felt real and impossible all at once.

She closed her eyes.

Find yourself...

Calling upon her magick, she tried to ground herself in her own darkness, a shadow that at times seemed endless. She opened her eyes to find her shadow flowing out of her, dissipating. Trying to control it was fruitless—she was now a part of the Primalith Shard, its Ancient Magick far eclipsing her own.

"Ceril!" she called out.

The hairs on her arms rose at the sound of her own voice echoing back and forth, the effect not unlike what she experienced in the Realm of Shadows. Except here, inside the cosmic shard, she had never felt more alone or so far away from every single person she cared about.

Athen. Aryis. Medias. Reece.

Nyssa.

I have to save them. Save her.

A crackle of magick startled her. A lone glowing star drew her attention. No, not a star. It was him. She could sense him.

"Ceril!"

Another sound echoed all around her, Ceril's voice making her simmer with a deep, cold hate. "Quinn."

"Come get me, you bastard," she whispered, slipping her hand into her rucksack. She grabbed two small orbs, scavenged from Hannah's Whisper before they left the ship. Taken just in case she ever needed them. She gripped one in each hand, ready.

The distant dot moved toward her. She braced herself.

In a heartbeat, Ceril was in front of her. But he was different. Altered. Younger. He glowed, a purple sheen of magick encasing his skin.

A god. Like her.

"It's time for you to become mine," he said. He wove his fingers together and began mumbling a spell.

Before she could move, a wave of purple magick burst forward, engulfing her, her muscles tensing and freezing.

Paralyzed.

A tingly warmth crawled over her skin and, to her horror, started to sink into her body.

Unable to move, she dug deep and tapped into her magick. She gritted her teeth and struck back, meeting the heat of Ceril's magick with the cold of her own power, fighting for control.

Fighting for her life.

She gasped at the energy flowing through her, her heart beating as Ceril's magick threatened to envelop her own. Bit by bit, his power sank deeper.

Ceril stared at her, his face a mask of concentration. She wasn't making his bid for control over her easy, but she was losing. If she hadn't used so much of her magick trying to escape, she might have had a chance. Her world would shatter if she succumbed to him. And he would run rampant, destroying everything she loved.

The strain of keeping him at bay was draining her. She needed to break free, to get closer to him. There was one last gambit to try.

She stopped resisting, dropping her magick.

Ceril gasped, likely not expecting her to give up. *Good*.

"Smart decision, girl," he seethed, his shoulders sagging for a scant moment.

A moment of *weakness*.

Quinn drew on every last bit of power and exploded with magick, burning what she could of his power out of her. She lurched forward, her body her own again.

"This ends for you now!" Quinn howled.

She slammed her palms together in front of Ceril's face. The orbs she held shattered. Black dust exploded in the air all around them. Quinn breathed in, her lungs filling with Coldlight dust. She held up her hands, the shadow magick leaching out of them, disappearing.

Ceril's eyes went wide. His face changed, its newfound youth fading, giving way to age. The purple magick on his skin sputtered and then vanished. He tried to weave a spell, but nothing happened. "What did you do?"

Quinn reared back and rocked him with a punch to the face. A satisfying crunch of bone—his nose had broken. He wobbled forward and grabbed her wrist, his grip like steel.

The interior of the Spire shimmered, revealing glimpses of the room beyond, its magick flickering like a candle. The air within the Spire thickened as she moved, halting her progress. She had used her last bit of strength to stop Ceril and now she was trapped, like an insect in amber.

But they were *both* trapped.

The anger on Ceril's face gave way to something new—fear. He opened his mouth, gulping for air.

Quinn tried to turn her head, bend her fingers, anything, but moving became impossible. The air became too thick to breathe, and she choked, desperate for air. She strained her muscles one last time, trying with all her remaining might to move even an inch. Nothing happened—she was ensnared completely, drowning in the Spire of Heaven.

Nyssa...

I'm so sorry...

Though her lungs began to burn, Quinn stilled her mind, refusing to panic, and closed her eyes. She had gotten the chance to finally live because of Nyssa. Not only live but thrive and grow...and love.

Thank you.

A coldness washed over her as the Primalith Shard's magick recharged, its power buzzing against her skin, singing an ancient song of the stars that once gave it life. Tears gathered under Quinn's closed eyelids and rolled down her cheeks, leaving an icy trail of mourning.

Of longing.

An explosion of warmth spread through Quinn's chest. Her eyes shot open.

A deep growl of thunder assaulted her ears as arms wrapped around her waist.

"Hold on, Quinn, I've got you," Nyssa's voice roared.

Jagged shards of lightning surrounded Quinn, filling her vision. The thunder grew louder, as if amplified by the Spire of Heaven as she was violently yanked backward.

Suddenly, she tumbled out of the shard and hit the cold stone floor of the chamber, gasping for air. Nyssa lay next to her, panting and bloody. Violent coughs wracked Quinn's body, the Coldlight dust heavy in her lungs. She struggled up to her knees and spit out thick, black fluid.

"Nyssa?" Quinn breathed.

Nyssa let out a deep, pained groan and smiled. "Hey, Freckles."

Quinn raised her eyes to the shard. The Spire of Heaven shuddered, its once-smooth flow now twitchy. Large, black streaks marred the fast-moving blue magick like poison.

She turned her attention to the other body on the chamber floor.

Ceril.

He had dug his fingers into her wrist before they became trapped—the bastard had held onto her as Nyssa pulled her out of the ancient Primalith Shard.

He struggled to his feet, stumbled over to the chamber's nearest wall, and slid down it with a grunt until he hit the floor. He locked eyes with Quinn and raised his head high, his lips streaked with black dust and blood dripping from his broken nose. Breathing heavily, he moved his hands and mumbled the words of a spell.

But nothing happened.

His hands fell to his side, shoulders slumping.

Quinn looked back at Nyssa. She had come alone, but it was only a matter of time before Athen and the others would follow. And the Justiciars would take Ceril away as the Empire demanded. They'd make him stand trial—it would be a great spectacle—and "justice" would be served in the minds of many.

But Ceril was too dangerous, even as a prisoner.

Quinn retrieved the hilt of her shattered sword from the floor, a foot of blade still attached. She struggled to her feet, lungs burning.

"Quinn..." Nyssa said, her voice soft.

Turning back to Nyssa, Quinn steeled herself. "I'm ending this now, even if that means I lose you. I can't take the chance that he'll hurt you again."

Quinn closed the distance to Ceril. His eyes, now full of fear, never left her face as she sank to her knees next to him. He raised his hand to stop her, but she swatted it away.

She pressed her hand against his shoulder, pinning him to the wall. Holding his gaze, Quinn slowly slipped the jagged, broken remnant of her sword into Ceril's chest. His mouth fell open and a soft, desolate sound escaped his throat.

"How small you become the moment you die," Quinn whispered.

She tilted the blade upward and pushed it into his heart, as Nyssa had taught her. Ceril's eyes went wide. Quinn remained still, watching the monster who had tormented her for years die by her hand.

Ceril's head lolled forward, and Quinn exhaled. She let go of the sword hilt, warm blood coating her hands, then she moved aside and collapsed against the wall.

A calmness washed over her.

It was *done*.

She closed her eyes.

A minute or two passed before distant voices began to grow louder and louder.

Quinn took a deep breath, knowing judgment was coming.

Footsteps thundered into the chamber, and a moment later, Quinn felt hands on her. She opened her eyes and Medias filled her vision.

"Are you hurt?" she asked.

Quinn shook her head. "Help me up?"

Medias pulled Quinn to her feet and steadied her. Her legs felt like rubber.

Athen got Nyssa standing, supporting her. "Are you both okay?"

"Yeah," Nyssa replied.

"Is everyone safe?" Quinn asked.

"Yes," Medias said, giving her shoulder a light squeeze. "Everyone's safe."

Quinn looked around the room. Reece had her arm around Aryis, supporting her. Ina stood by the entrance to the chamber while the Justiciars had spread throughout the room, shooting furtive glances at the Spire.

"Anelos is dead," Ina said, her eyes drifting down to Quinn's bloody hands.

"I ended him," Quinn said. She let out an exhausted breath. "As long as he lived, he was a threat to us all."

Nyssa turned toward the Justiciars, dim lightning sparking across her skin. "If you're going to arrest her, you'll have to go through me first."

Ina glanced at the Justiciars. Quinn had admitted to killing Ceril intentionally, and she would say the same to anyone who questioned her, head held high. The only judgment she feared was Nyssa's.

Quinn took a breath and waited for her reckoning. No one moved.

After a moment, Nyssa looked to Quinn and nodded, her gaze unwavering. Behind her, the Spire of Heaven flickered, the streaks of black from the Coldlight bombs barely visible in its brilliant-blue interior. It had restored itself, as if she and Ceril had never disrupted its ancient slumber. A mere blip in an otherwise endless existence.

Exhaling, Quinn left the chamber and didn't look back, descending into the Citadel.

A FORGOTTEN QUEEN

S uvi pressed up against the door of her stateroom aboard the Cloud Crasher. "I need a healer."

Someone shuffled on the other side. "You were checked out already."

"I...I think I have internal injuries. I'm pissing blood." She closed her eyes. "Please, help me."

Time dragged by as she waited for a reply. Finally, "Stand away from the door."

Suvi did as she was told. "Okay."

A key jangled in the lock and the door swung open. The deckhand charged with guarding her door stepped in. "I'll take you to see the Cap. She has the healing disks."

Suvi winced and grabbed at her side, her legs buckling. "Help," she whispered.

The deckhand rushed to hold her up.

Suvi kicked him in the crotch. Inelegant, but effective.

He doubled over and gagged and she took the opportunity to grab a vase off a side table and crush it against his skull. The man collapsed to the floor. Unconscious or dead, she didn't care. *Cage a queen and see what happens!*

She yanked a dagger off his belt. It was aged and nicked up—a working person's tool and a poor replacement for her family's dagger, but it would have to do. Pulling on a winter cloak, she flipped up its hood.

How short-sighted of Blacksea and her ilk to leave a goddamned queen guarded by a bunch of soft, luxury airship personnel who were far better suited to transporting her bags and pouring champagne.

Idiots. Suvi smirked and slipped out the door.

A DESERVED PEACE

Nyssa splashed water on her face in one of the ground-floor bathrooms and stared at herself in the mirror. The tired ache in her bones was written all over her expression, and she let out a resigned sigh. She wasn't going to fault herself—it had been a long fucking day.

To top it all off, Anna had relayed bad news from the Cloud Crasher: Suvi was nowhere to be found. A search of the grounds yielded nothing but a pair of footprints in the snow leading to the forest. She had likely taken the same route Efla did off the mountain.

Another problem for another day.

Nyssa slipped out of the bathroom and strode down the main corridor, heading for the Great Room where her friends were waiting. Conversations hushed when she entered. Arcton adepts, Masters, guards, and Justiciars milled about the tables and chairs spread through the room, picking at platters of food that the kitchen had scrounged up.

During her first stay at Arcton, most of the guildies and Citadel staff avoided her. Now, some nodded at her or offered smiles. Not exactly a warm reception, but better. She'd take better.

It had been a few hours since Ceril's death. The Citadel's two healers had worked tirelessly to attend to those who had the worst injuries, with a third Arcton adept weaving a few healing spells he had learned from his mother. He'd shyly tended to Nyssa's cuts, apologizing for his shaky hands. While getting seen to, kept watch over Quinn as one of the guild healers took care of her. Quinn kept her eyes down and spoke to no one. Nyssa had given her space and didn't follow when she disappeared from the infirmary.

And to tell the truth, Nyssa had needed time to sort through her own thoughts before diving into a conversation with Quinn.

Nyssa spotted her friends huddled in the far corner of the room and headed their way. Fires crackled in the four large fireplaces in the massive room. Lush, scarlet carpets with woven patterns of ancient runes spanned the floor. Athen, Aryis, Medias, and Reece looked worn out, but they were smiling and laughing—a welcome sight. A few plates of food sat on a low table in the center of their chairs. Nyssa bent over to grab a hunk of bread.

"Where's Quinn?" she asked.

Athen nodded to a set of terrace doors. "Out in the garden."

"She...say anything?"

"No. We figured we'd give her space."

Quinn had gone after Ceril on her own, something that Nyssa had to work through, but she had also saved them all. She'd caught him before he was able to do real damage. When they were all in the infirmary, Quinn had also shared that Ceril had intended to enslave her and use her as his weapon. The very idea of it made Nyssa's blood run cold.

She glanced to the windows facing the garden and chewed on her bread, not realizing how famished she was. She sat down and grabbed a few pieces of cheese when Ina approached, nodding to the group.

"We are arranging a return to Cardin in the next few days aboard the Cloud Crasher," she said. "The Emperor is very keen to see you all at the Sun Palace."

Worry ate at Nyssa, and she couldn't ignore it. Quinn had killed Ceril, disregarding Safin and Decia's orders. "What about Quinn?"

"The Justiciars and I were discussing how to proceed in light of Emerrath's actions. None of us feel any sort of justice would be served by taking her into custody at this time."

At this time.

Nyssa scowled. "Do Safin or Decia intend to arrest her when we arrive in Cardin?"

"That I cannot say. But I did stress in my communication with the capital that it's perhaps in everyone's best interest not to...incite the anger of any Cursed Gods."

Not the response Nyssa had expected. "You looking out for us, Ruggen?"

The Ashcloak took a deep breath. "I pledged my life to protect the Areshi Empire and its Emperor. And the Empire was protected today from a very dangerous man. A man who killed First Master Greye, who I held in the highest of regard. As far as I am concerned, we are aligned on this issue, Blacksea."

Nyssa blinked, unable to come up with a proper response, but Athen saved her by popping up onto his feet and extending a hand to Ina. "You do us all proud, Ashcloak Ruggen," he said, "even though Nyssa and I are no longer counted among your ranks."

Ina shrugged. "An honor code is an honor code, regardless of title." With a curt nod, she turned on her heel and walked away to join a table of Citadel Masters.

"I don't understand her," Nyssa mumbled. Ina had spent years tormenting her at the Emerald Order. Now she was standing shoulder to shoulder with Nyssa in solidarity?

"Yes, you do," Athen replied, dropping back into his chair. "Eron was her teacher too, you know. We all share that."

"I suppose we do." How odd it was to find a bit of peaceful ground with her old bully. Nyssa leaned over and squeezed Aryis's forearm. "How are you feeling, Little Hawk?"

"Like I've been battered between rocks and left for dead. So pretty fantastic, given the alternative," she replied, beaming. Nyssa caught a glimpse of the old Aryis in that moment. It was a welcome sight.

"Your knee?"

Aryis gave her injured knee a rub. "I'm going to seek out a healer in Cardin to see if I have any recourse and at least have a brace fashioned."

"And after, we can go shopping for a proper cane," Athen said, giving her a wink. It was still something he was incredibly bad at, his one remaining eye not exactly adept at the task.

Aryis laughed at him, and they shared a warmth between them that Nyssa hadn't seen in a long time.

Reece sat silent across from her, sipping on a steaming mug, and Medias sat on the arm of her leather chair, an arm draped lazily over the back of it, her fingers resting lightly against the empath's shoulder. Seemed there was more than just a friendship there, but Nyssa resisted the urge to poke and prod and see what shades of red she could make Medias turn. Another time.

She stood, glancing out the glass doors. A fire burned in the distance in the center of the garden.

"Here, some sweetened tea," Reece said, filling two mugs. "Take one out to her."

Nyssa swallowed, hesitating. "How is she?"

Reece shook her head. "I haven't intruded into her feelings. It's not proper, not after what happened."

"Understood." Nyssa picked up the mugs, took a deep breath, and headed toward the terrace doors.

Quinn stared into the embers as flames licked away at the cedar logs in the fire pit. In all her days at Arcton, she had never sat in the garden like this, at night, beside a warm fire. She simply wasn't allowed.

She turned her eyes up to Beckwit Tower. The constant drone of the Spire had receded, though it still pulsed ever so gently on the edge of her senses. Had she, by stepping inside of it, made herself known to it? Nyssa had remarked how she barely felt the shard herself. Its scant presence came as a relief now, like a splinter had been removed from her finger and only a dull ache served as a reminder of the pain of the past.

When Quinn left the infirmary and came out to the fire pit, no one moved to join her. She welcomed the solitude. She needed space, and everyone seemed more than willing to give it to her.

The moment she killed Ceril loomed over her. There was no undoing her actions—actions that the Justiciars might consider a crime. Ceril was meant to be arrested and brought back to Cardin.

But an arrest and void collar meant nothing to a man who likely had allies who could help him escape as the Empire prepared for trial.

No one would have been safe.

And something darker within Quinn had called for revenge, to make the man pay for everything he had done to her.

"Hey."

Quinn lifted her head to find Nyssa across the fire, two mugs in her hands. The shadows from the flames danced across her face, making it hard to read her mood.

She moved around the fire and took a seat on the bench next to Quinn, handing her a mug and bearing a gentle smile—one Quinn felt she didn't deserve. Sitting by the fire pit for the last hour, she'd tried to envision this conversation, but everything in her head and heart felt muted.

"Sweetened tea," Nyssa said, putting her mug down beside her, eyes on Quinn. But she didn't say anything.

Quinn put her mug down without taking a sip and gathered her courage to say her piece. "I realize that I didn't act with honor today, but I'm not sorry for what I did."

A scowl haunted Nyssa's features. She leaned forward, her gaze demanding every bit of Quinn's attention. "Listen to me. When I found Efla at the edge of the cliff, I felt nothing but rage. Blind hate. And I struck out at her, fully intending to eradicate her from this earth after what she did to Eron. Her armor was the only thing that saved her." She exhaled. "I'm not better than you—or more honorable."

Quinn ground her jaw. "But you are. And I don't think you deserve to carry the burden of my actions. I'll accept whatever judgment the Justiciars have for me."

"They're not going to do anything. And once we get back to Cardin, I'll make sure you're safe from Safin and Decia. I'll talk to them—"

"No, Nyssa." Quinn swallowed hard, her heart on the verge of breaking at what she had to say. "I'm not going back. It's...it's best we part ways. You can get a fresh start, maybe even stay in the Empire with your friends."

In a flurry of movement, Nyssa hauled Quinn to her feet and twisted her fists into her jacket. Her eyes were full of anger. And tears.

"Part ways? After everything we have been through together, you think it's best if you leave me?" Nyssa asked, her chest rising and falling with quick, sharp breaths.

Tears sprang up in Quinn's eyes. "I dishonored you."

"No. You *saved* us," Nyssa insisted, her brows furrowing.

"It...it wasn't just about ending a threat. I wanted revenge."

Nyssa swallowed hard. "Quinn, I know. And you deserved revenge after what he put you through."

"But I killed him knowing I could lose you," Quinn said, lowering her eyes.

Nyssa put a finger under her chin and lifted her head back up. "You will *never* lose me. I promise."

Quinn couldn't tear her eyes away from Nyssa, no matter how ashamed she felt. Her heart beat hard, but that warm, unyielding glow in the middle of her chest calmed her. It always did.

"You deserve peace, my love," Nyssa said, her voice a gentle rumble.

My love. The words made Quinn inhale a shaky breath.

Nyssa took Quinn's face in her hands, a soft smile gracing her beautiful face. "I will never judge you for what you did, but I know from my own experience that you need to reconcile your actions in your own heart. That might not be easy, but I'll be here for you." She leaned forward and placed a soft kiss on Quinn's forehead. "I'll never leave you, Quinn Emerrath. I love you too much to even fathom being without you. If you were ever lost to me, I would burn everything down around me to find you again. *Forever entwined.*"

Nyssa's love—powerful and unyielding—was a force of nature, just like the woman herself. Her touch, gentle and warm, made Quinn feel safe, unleashing something in her she could no longer hold back. Tears came, hot and plentiful. Nyssa wrapped her up in her arms and let her weep. Quinn grabbed hold for dear life, afraid of spinning off the earth, her emotions tumbling chaotically and her aching heart thundering in her chest. There was nothing Quinn wouldn't do for Nyssa.

Nyssa let her cry for a good long while. Quinn's tears slowed and the ache abated, a sense of loving calm overtaking the churning chaos. The tension released from her body.

Nyssa was Quinn's peace.

CLEANSING FLAMES

Medias drew closer to the window and glanced outside. Nyssa sat with her arm around Quinn at the fire pit—at least Quinn no longer seemed to be crying. None of them were entitled to interrupt that moment. That needed to remain between Nyssa and Quinn. "Can we go out there yet?"

With a grumble, Reece sidled up next to Medias. "I hate doing this."

"I know and I'm sorry to ask you to intrude by reading their emotions, but I'd rather not interrupt them if they're arguing."

"Understood." Reece stilled. Moments later, a smile sprang to her lips. "I think we can venture out."

Athen helped Aryis to her feet, but Medias stepped in front of her before she could move toward the terrace doors. "Are you sure about this?" she asked in a hushed tone.

"Entirely sure?" Aryis replied. "No. Which is why we make this decision together."

Medias moved to the side and gestured toward the doors. They followed Aryis outside as a group, Athen casting a glance back at Ina and the Justiciars. They were about to make a decision without any Imperial input or approval. Medias had expressed caution, her old Justiciar impulses kicking in.

They wound their way through the gardens, Aryis's cane clacking against the flagstones leading to the fire pit. Nyssa and Quinn smiled at them as they approached. Both had obviously been crying, but they looked at peace with one another. It made Medias's heart a bit lighter to see them like that.

"Sorry to interrupt," Aryis said, "but we have something to discuss."

"Away from the prying eyes and ears of the Empire," Medias said, handing Quinn a small wrapped package. "Here, a bit of grilled chicken and flatbread. You haven't eaten a thing today."

Quinn accepted the package with a smile, and Medias patted her on the shoulder before taking a seat next to her.

"Our Sentinel delivers food. Good to know," Nyssa said with a wink.

Medias hummed out a disgruntled sigh. There was only more of this teasing to come for the foreseeable future. But she didn't...hate it.

"What do we need to talk about?" Nyssa asked. "It's getting incredibly late and we're both about to drop from exhaustion."

Aryis took a seat opposite them, leaned forward, and began casting her magick. Athen moved behind her to block the view from the Citadel. After a moment, bright-white sparks fell from Aryis's hands and a book appeared.

"Is that..." Nyssa lowered her voice. "Is that the sixth Alabaster Book?"

"Yes. It was secured in the Night Vault. I have a bit of a tenuous connection to it thanks to Tajal taking over my body and finding it for Ceril."

"What are you going to do with it?" Quinn asked around bites of her sandwich.

"Well, that's what we're here to discuss with the two of you. Ludov intends to leave it locked up in the Night Vault with the rest of the Alabaster Books. The other volumes have spells that are already out in the world, in some form." Aryis peered down at the book, her palm resting on its cover. "But this book...it messes around with soul magick. I was thinking we should destroy it."

Medias was confident it was the correct decision, but they were all in this situation together now, and the choice wasn't one person's to make alone. The destruction of Imperial property and a key volume containing rare magick was not a casual undertaking. Ludov would not be pleased, neither would Decia, but Medias felt sure she could smooth over any issues.

"I take it all four of you are of one mind?" Nyssa asked.

"We are," Athen replied.

"We don't know what kind of consequences we'll face in Cardin for Ceril's death when we return." Nyssa sat for a moment, then shrugged. "So I don't see how eradicating that piece of shit book from existence will do much more harm."

Medias almost rolled her eyes. Typical response from Nyssa, but they still needed one more person's approval. All eyes turned to Quinn. She handed the remnants of her food to Nyssa and stood.

"It won't burn," she said, extending her hand out to Aryis. "If it's like the other volumes, the paper is protected by an enchantment."

"You're sure?" Aryis replied.

Quinn chuckled—the first genuine sign of lightness Medias had seen from her since her rescue in Dennbury. "I may have tried to burn the other Alabaster Books once when Ceril wasn't looking, but I didn't have this magick back then," Quinn said. "Give it to me."

The book was handed over, and Quinn's shadows emerged, her eyes glowing green. It was, as always, an impressive sight to see a Cursed God's magick. Quinn wrapped her darkness around the spell book and closed her eyes. Several seconds later, she opened them.

"The protective magick is no more," she said.

Aryis shook her head when Quinn tried to hand the book back to her. "I think you need to see this through."

Quinn regarded Aryis. "You know, you're alright, Devitt."

A bright smile spread across Aryis's face. The energy between the two women was far different now. Forgiveness never came quick or easy, but it was a cleansing force, one that Medias took comfort in.

Quinn moved over to the fire. A scowl crossed her features for a scant moment before she tossed the book into the flames. The fire flared and licked at the pages of the book, curling them up and turning them black until they dissolved into ash on the wind.

The six of them watched in silence as the book burned.

After a while, Quinn stood up, took Nyssa's hand, and they returned to the Citadel. Athen and Aryis followed shortly thereafter, leaving Reece and Medias alone, staring into the fire.

Medias had hoped for a moment alone with the empath.

It took an hour or two after the battle against Ceril's cohort for the reality to sink in—she was very close to dying this day. Facing her own death didn't scare her. She had been raised as a Justiciar at Ambershine to not fear death. Seeing Reece in danger, though, brought up feelings she couldn't ignore or deny. Or suppress any longer.

Reece stood and stretched. "Oh!" she said, wincing.

Medias popped to her feet, quick to Reece's side. "Are you okay?"

"Yeah, just sore. I should be used to getting beaten up by now."

"I wish I could keep you safe," Medias murmured.

With a scowl, Reece replied, "You're not responsible for my well-being. I am."

"Well, you're not doing a good job of it."

Reece stepped back, her scowl deepening. "Excuse me?"

Medias ground her teeth. "You take too many risks. I wanted you to get below deck when the wraiths attacked the airship. And today, you were told to stay back, but you ignored that as well."

"You have some nerve talking about taking risks when you do the same." Reece stood, the naked moonlight illuminating her silver hair and dark eyes. Stunning as ever.

Medias hummed out an annoyed sigh. "Now wait—"

"I won't stand here and be lectured when you put your life in danger trying to protect me. You have no business risking your life for me."

Heat flooded through Medias. How could Reece think for a second that Medias wouldn't protect her no matter what? "Your audacity knows no bounds, empath. If you'd listened to me, you would have been safe."

Reece pinned her in place with her dark gaze. "But you wouldn't have been. Do you honestly think for one moment I'm going to leave your side in a fight?"

Any response would have withered on Medias's lips if her mind could have conjured a sufficient reply. Except there wasn't one. She knew, deep in her bones and with every last flicker of her soul, that Reece would never waver in her loyalty. Or her love. The heat rising in Medias no longer sourced itself from her anger.

Reece crossed her arms, punctuating her argument. A gesture of protest that was equally endearing and maddening.

Medias sighed. "I'm trying to be rational here."

"I'm sick of these excuses, Medias. I don't need—"

Medias growled out her frustration, quickly grabbing Reece to kiss her.

Reece gasped against her lips. But she pressed against Medias, her hands lighting upon her waist as she returned the kiss, her lips soft and giving. Reece's grasp tightened, as if she needed to hold onto Medias to ensure the moment was real.

Delicious seconds melted away, and Medias forgot about her aches and pains, her heart lightening of the burden of denial, having fought so hard against what must have been fate. Not that she had ever seen this in any of her visions, but nothing felt as real or inevitable as her love for the empath.

She broke the kiss. "You are an exasperating woman," she said with a smile, one that she felt down to her toes. A smile of unrestrained love.

Reece breathed softly, her lips parting. She reached up to move an unruly strand of hair from Medias's eyes. "I can't do this if you only want sex. I love you, but I won't lessen myself just to be with the part of you that you'll give me."

Medias shook her head. "I am giving you everything I am," she replied. She wanted there to be no doubt as to her feelings. "I love you and I want to give us a chance to be together. If you'd still have me, that is. I haven't exactly been uncomplicated to deal with of late."

Her heart thumped in her chest as she waited for the answer.

"You already know my feelings, Medias. And they haven't changed one bit. I love you too."

Medias dipped her head, her short curls cascading around her face.

Reece reached up and gently stroked her cheek. "You are going to have to get used to me fighting by your side."

A chuckle escaped Medias's lips. There would be no talking Reece out of risking herself for those she cared about, that was certain. "Fine. Then you will let me teach you how to fight."

Reece cocked her head. "I've...seen you fight. That wasn't one of your best disciplines at Ambershine, was it?"

Another arrow to Medias's pride, though Reece was correct. "Fine. Then you will let Athen teach you how to fight."

"I think he can teach both of us a few things." Reece pulled back and took Medias's hand, interlocking their fingers. "Are you ready for this?"

Medias pressed a kiss against Reece's temple. "Not in the slightest. Be patient with me?"

"I will treat you like Ox."

"W-what?"

Reece beamed a beautiful smile up at her. "A little succulent plant that gave me fits for months. I never knew how much water or sunlight he needed. So, I took it slow, got to know him, his idiosyncrasies, and practiced patience. Now, he's a happy plant."

Ox. She named a plant *Ox*.

How ridiculous. I...I love it. "Interesting."

"I talk to him about you."

Medias shook her head with a low chuckle. "Of course you do."

Reece squeezed her hand. "I love you, Sentinel."

Medias smiled, the fullness invading her heart quite a new feeling. But a welcome one. "I love you, empath."

A RULER'S THRONE

Nyssa leaned back in her chair and swirled the hay-colored honey whiskey in her tumbler, giving it a sniff. Her mouth watered before she even took her first sip. It went down smooth, the sign of a very expensive—and dangerous—liquor.

She had scrounged up the bottle from a drink cart while perusing the books adorning the shelves around the room. One book in particular grabbed her attention, and she pulled it down and slipped it into her jacket. Recompense for what the Empire had put her through.

Small, folded paper animals dotted the table in front of her. She had discovered a stash of them in a drawer where she sat and put them out on display. Perhaps she shouldn't have snooped, but she couldn't stop herself from examining every nook in the room.

Nyssa smiled at the little gathering of animals—she still had the Kraken that Safin had slipped into her pocket months earlier. It now sat in the journal she hid in an inner pocket of her jacket, along with Quinn's drawing of her eyes she had taken off the wall of Arcton and the chromoimage of her and Eron.

The door at the end of the room opened. "You're in my chair, Nyssa. My throne, to be exact." Emperor Safin walked into the room, accompanied by a small cadre of six Justiciars and Ina. Arch Justiciar Decia and Safin's mother, Lyra, followed them in.

Nyssa didn't like how armed his entourage was but kept a calm demeanor. "This is your throne?"

"One of them."

"Oops." She shrugged. "Comfier than I would have expected."

Safin strode through the room to where she sat at the head of a long wooden table. The war room, as she was told when brought here by Palace guards to wait to see him. For a so-called war room, the space was inviting. Warm, rich wood covered the walls, and the decorations looked carefully curated. She imagined that one vase alone would finance her life for a year.

"And you're drinking my liquor?" Safin asked, raising an eyebrow as he drew closer. Nothing in his tone belied annoyance. Actually, he seemed lighter than ever.

"And a fine whiskey it is."

"Aged for twenty years in honeyed barrels. Velonin bees, to be exact," Lyra Vonner said. She walked over to the drink cart, picked up the same bottle Nyssa had chosen, and poured herself a drink. "At least you have good taste."

The backhanded compliment didn't bother Nyssa. A compliment from the woman was still a compliment, no matter how it was framed, and was a far cry better than her open hostility toward Nyssa in Ocean's Rest.

I guess saving the fucking Areshi Empire garners some favor with these rich bastards.

"Where is Quinn Emerrath?" Decia asked from the other end of the table, her hands clasped behind her. From a distance, she resembled Medias. Similar posture. The same annoying, haughty grace and intimidating stare.

Nyssa swirled her glass again. "Quinn is on a ship hidden offshore, ready to disappear into Unbound waters should I not return by dawn."

Lyra and Decia shared a glance. Nyssa sipped her whiskey. *No, I don't trust your Imperial asses.*

Safin's brow knit up. "Do you think I'm a threat to her?"

"You ordered Ceril to be captured. Quinn killed him. You can see how we might think you or your Justiciars would have a problem with that."

Safin draped his long arms over the chair closest to Nyssa. "I won't arrest her. Nor will any of my Justiciars or Ashcloaks. As far as I'm concerned, Quinn dealt with an Imperial traitor as she saw fit."

While his words came as a bit of relief, Safin wasn't the only person she had to worry about. He faced pressures from all angles—the Sun Council, Decia, guild leaders, even his own mother. While he might not wish Quinn harm, he could be strong-armed into seeking justice. He was a young Emperor, barely months into his reign.

Nyssa placed her glass on the table and tapped her finger against it. "I want your promise—your word—that Quinn and I are safe from you and the Areshi Empire."

"You have my word."

Quickly checking the other faces in the room, Nyssa didn't get the sense that he was lying, though she wished she had Reece's empathic abilities, just to be sure.

Perhaps Safin sensed her trepidation. He moved closer and offered his hand. "I promise." They shook on his promise, but he didn't let go. Little sparks of purple magick encased his hand, winding up Nyssa's arm. "May I?"

"Wha—ow!" Her forearm pulsed with a sharp pain before it was flooded with a warm sensation that dulled everything else.

"Your arm wasn't healed properly. I amended that issue for you." He gave her a bright grin and let go of her hand.

Nyssa rubbed her arm. "A little warning next time?"

"I find the pain isn't as bad if it's a surprise."

The nagging ache in her forearm had dissipated. She had to admit, he was an excellent healer, if a bit stunted in his bedside manner.

She asked, "Any word on Suvi Rell?"

"Unfortunately, not yet," Decia replied. "We will find her in time. The price we put on her head will draw interest."

Wasn't so long ago that Nyssa had a bounty herself, from both the Empire and Suvi, but that was thankfully no longer an issue. Nyssa hoped that remained the case.

Lyra sat down at the other end of the table. "What are your plans, Blacksea?"

"Are you asking because you're scared I'm going to hang around and fuck things up?"

The woman frowned. "As usual, a colorful response. I'm merely curious to know if we need to assign extra security. For your protection. And ours."

Nyssa chuckled. "No. Quinn and I are going away to spend a few months on holiday. We need some rest."

"Well-deserved rest," Safin said. "But do come back for my Ascension ceremony in six months' time."

"You're postponing it for six months?"

He nodded. "With everything that's happened of late, having a grand party now seems a bit crass."

"And expensive. And garishly opulent," Decia intoned from her spot next to the door.

"Ah yes, Decia hates a good party," Lyra drawled, winking at her son. They shared a smile that made Nyssa happy. It was the first time she'd witnessed a more casual rapport between the two. Lyra was always so buttoned up and formal, but Safin needed a lighter touch at times.

"The decision to postpone is wise," Decia said, unfazed by Lyra's gentle teasing. "With the Lythrosii sending an entourage, it's best we not have drunken laggards lying about the Palace."

"The Lythrosii are coming here?" Nyssa knew the Areshi Empire, as did most nations, had a relationship with the secretive sect. They functioned much the same as Arcton Citadel, curating collections of magick, but with a major difference: they weren't restricted by national borders. Lythrosii agents hunted down rare relics anywhere. And they dealt with forbidden magick with lethality.

"A visit from the Lythrosii is customary upon a change in rulers," Decia replied. "But I suspect expressing their respects to Safin is not the only reason for their journey. Word of the Alabaster Books has spread, including the rumor of the sixth volume. It will be hard to convince them that the sixth book was destroyed, let alone gently telling them no when they ask to take possession of the remaining volumes."

Nyssa leaned forward. "Can they do that?"

"They certainly can," Lyra answered. "We'll have to navigate them expertly. The last thing a new Emperor of the Areshi Empire wants to do is capitulate to a foreign entity and hand over precious Imperial assets."

"And if they insist?"

"We say no with more conviction until they accept our answer. The Empire has had a very collaborative relationship with the Lythrosii over the years, and we'll remind them of that fact." Lyra raised her glass and downed the rest of her whiskey. "We've moved the Alabaster Books from the Night Vault and secured them deep within the Citadel, behind more wards than likely necessary, but Decia insisted."

Nyssa finished off the rest of her drink, lamenting that she couldn't snag the bottle and take it back to the Whisper while no one was looking. She pushed away from the table and stood.

"I should get going. I have a few people to say goodbye to before I leave," she said.

"Will you come back? For my Ascension and maybe stay for a bit?" Safin asked.

Nyssa smiled at him. "I never miss a good party. All that free booze needs to be drunk. Drank?" She shrugged as Safin laughed. "As far as what's after our little respite, I can't say. It's hard to know where we can be safe. Quinn and I still have this to contend with." She pointed at the Mark of the Unworthy on her chin. "And this." She let her magick flow for a moment, energy crackling on her skin before she pulled it back.

"You saved my life...more than once," Safin said. "I can offer you the peace of mind that I'll welcome you here in the Areshi Empire. Even though you and Quinn have revoked your citizenship, I still consider us allies. And your pardon stands."

"That's kind of you, kid. I'm very pleased you didn't turn out to be an asshole."

"Show the Emperor respect!" Decia hissed.

"She just did, Arch Justiciar." Safin extended his hand again. "Thank you, Nyssa. And thank Quinn for me. I'm sad she's not here."

Nyssa shook his hand and started toward the door. "Are you sure Quinn and I are welcome back to the Empire? Won't the Sun Council grouse about it?"

"I think the Sun Council will have enough to worry about in the immediate future." He gave her an odd little smirk. "Take care, Nyssa."

A GREAT HOUSE

Reece paced across the deep-gold rug in the East Library of the Sun Palace. She and Athen had been summoned by Imperial invitation, showing up on a crisp white card bearing impeccable penmanship. Reece had insisted that Aryis and Medias join them. Aryis tried to beg off, saying she was intruding, but Athen took offense to that notion.

Aryis browsed the bookshelves, excitedly mumbling to herself and marking up her little notebook. "Ooo! I haven't read this one," she'd occasionally exclaim. Athen would softly laugh and smile to himself as he kept his eyes on her.

Medias took up a post in a corner, doing as she had always done. Watching.

Reece, however, couldn't calm her nerves. "Are we in trouble?" She halted her pacing. "Did they do something to Nyssa?"

"If they did, I would know," Athen said. "She's got a messenger orb on her set to make a beeline to me with one word."

"Smart," Reece replied, absentmindedly gnawing at her thumb. Nothing since their return to Cardin had indicated they were in any danger, but she left her walls down to make sure, tuning in to all the emotions around her. So far, they'd only been met with a great deal of curiosity and, at times, admiration, but nothing nefarious.

Yet.

Athen got up from his chair and wandered over to a small table full of bottles along the wall. "A drink to calm your nerves?"

Reece shook her head and resumed her pacing.

"Medias?" he asked.

"No, thank you."

The door to the library swung open, and an unexpected visitor entered.

"Mother?" Athen said.

Lilliana Fennick crossed the room. "It is so good to see you both again. Safe." She didn't hesitate to sweep Reece up in a crushing hug. They were rare, but Reece relished each one.

Lilliana moved to Athen and embraced him. "You need a shave."

"Mother," he admonished.

"Why are you in Cardin?" Reece asked. "Are you okay? Is everything okay in Ocean's Rest?"

Lilliana raised an eyebrow. "Reece, everything is fine. I was called here by the Emperor."

No sense of doubt or worry came off of her, and Reece huffed out a breath and relaxed a bit, tucking her magick back in. It had been exhausting sensing emotions all day, remaining vigilant for someone who might have ill will toward any of them.

"Why were you called to the capital?" Athen asked.

"Emperor Safin has extended House Fennick an invitation to join the Sun Council."

Athen chuckled. "Very funny. You're kidding, right?"

"I am absolutely not kidding about this," his mother replied. "Seems you and Reece made quite the impression."

Reece let out a little breath of air. *House Fennick...on the Sun Council?*

"That's...that's wonderful!" Aryis said, joining them. "Think of all the things you can accomplish!"

"Navigating the egos and politics of the Great Houses is going to be a complex undertaking," Lilliana replied. "A perfect challenge for my daughter."

The gaze of everyone in the room fell upon Reece.

Her mind reeled. "I'll take that drink now."

FAREWELLS

"**B**lacksea, a word please." Decia's voice trailed down the corridor.

Nyssa waited for the Arch Justiciar to catch up with her. The halls of the Sun Palace were still bustling with activity, even as the night wore on. Nyssa felt the eyes of passersby on her. Would she ever get used to the extra attention? Some of it bordered on gawking at times, making her feel like a carnival oddity.

Decia drew closer and came to a halt a few feet away, clasping her hands behind her back. Nyssa tensed.

"I know you and I have very little to say to one another outside of Imperial business," Decia said, "but my interest here is a personal one. My daughter...I don't know what being a Sentinel means or what will be asked of her, but will you look after her well-being?"

Nyssa bowed her head, searching for the right words. Words that wouldn't come out as angry or bitter. "Sometimes I think the universe is laughing at me, shoving the daughter of my parents' murderer directly in my path. Medias would call it fate." A rueful smile graced her lips, thinking of the strange turns of her life. "She sacrificed everything to follow a different calling, and now it seems she's stuck with me and Quinn. And I'm honored to call her my friend."

Decia blinked, wavering for a scant moment. "I'm scared for her."

Nyssa stepped forward. "You ripped my parents from me, and I will never forgive you for that." She tamped down the anger building at thinking of what the Empire had done to her mother and father. "But I regard Medias as family now, and I will take care of her. That is a promise."

"Thank you."

Nyssa turned quickly to hide the tears rising in her eyes. With Kalla and Ceril dead, there were only two people left alive responsible for her parents' fate, and Decia and Lilliana were untouchable.

Without another word, Nyssa walked away from Decia knowing she'd never have revenge.

Now to find Athen and the others back in the guest quarters. Wherever the hell they were. The Sun Palace was too damn big. She stopped at intersecting corridors, frowning as she tried to get her bearings.

"Miss Blacksea?"

Nyssa looked around, searching for the source of the voice.

"Ma'am." A shiny silver orb whizzed past her head and stopped, bobbing in the air.

"You found me."

"House Fennick has requested your presence in the East Library."

Nyssa laughed. "How very formal. Which way is the East Library?"

"It's in the north-east wing of the Sun Palace, past the Rahl Collections Room, named after Rahl Areshi, the Empire's fifth Emperor and a prolific collector of historical—"

"Uh, can you just take me there? I'm a bit turned around."

The orb bobbed up and down. "Of course, Miss Blacksea. Would you like a curated journey to the East Library or silence?"

Nyssa shrugged. "Chat me up."

She followed the silver orb through the Sun Palace. As they passed rooms, paintings, and statues, the orb would share a tidbit of knowledge about the items. It was an enthusiastic narrator. Although it was an automaton like The Curator at Arcton, she believed that the little constructs had personalities. Their creators—this one's probably long dead—wove bits of themselves into their enchantments. Quite the legacy.

When they finally reached the East Library, Nyssa had gotten a fairly good lesson on the early days of the Empire, its Emperors from House Areshi, and the art created during those times.

"Thank you...what do you call yourself?" she asked.

"Eos."

"Well, I appreciate the tour, Eos."

"Thank you for not eradicating me, Cursed God," it said as it casually zipped away.

Nyssa chuckled and walked into the library. Her mood darkened upon seeing Lilliana Fennick. All of House Fennick was here, it seemed.

"Nyssa!" Athen said, raising a bottle in the air at a small drink cart, its glasses tinkling. "What did Safin have to say? Do you want a drink?"

"Yes to the second question," she said, walking over to the couch next to where Athen was pouring drinks, recalling her conversation with Safin as best she could. When she concluded, she added, "The key here is that we're safe. We all are. Me, Quinn, the rest of us."

"A positive outcome, considering," Medias said from the corner.

"That's the goddamn truth." Nyssa took a long draw of the clear liquor Athen poured for her. It burned before turning sweet with an aftertaste of honey and licorice.

Safin would be a good ally to have in the future—especially not knowing what the future held. What did Cursed Gods do day after day when not on the run and fighting for their lives? Nyssa smiled. She couldn't wait to find out.

She noticed Reece seemed withdrawn. "Are you alright?"

"Oh, the other news of the evening!" Athen said, beaming. "Guess who is now on the Sun Council. We are!"

The news was a shock. "House Fennick? But...how?"

"There was an empty seat with the dissolution of House Notario, and the Emperor extended an invitation to me," Lilliana replied.

"House Fennick...among the Great Houses?" Nyssa gave it a thought for a moment. "Oh, that's gotta piss them off something fierce. Explains why Safin said the Sun Council would have other things to worry about instead of a couple Cursed Gods."

"Reece looks like someone just kicked over her favorite plant because Lilliana has named her as House Fennick's representative on the Council," Medias said, a slight twitch of a smile on her face.

Nyssa burst out laughing. The notion was *delicious*. An empath among the leaders of the Great Houses? They would squirm, no doubt. "That's fantastic."

"You find it hilarious," Reece groused.

Immediately feeling bad, Nyssa put up her hands. "No, I'm not laughing at you. I'm just picturing how the other Houses are going to cope. I think you're perfect for the job."

"She is," Lilliana said, walking over to sit next to Reece. "Safin needs someone strong on the Council, and that's you. You'll shake them all to their very core, especially those who seek to undermine him."

"I...I don't want to be away from Ocean's Rest. I have a life there. Everyone I care about is there." She glanced at Medias. No one in the room could miss the look.

Lilliana leaned back and sipped on the drink Athen handed to her. "You will be in Cardin a couple times a year for a few weeks at a time. The Sun Council can't stand to meet more often than that. You'll spend the majority of the time in Ocean's Rest, and I'll need your help more than ever. And you won't be alone when you come here. Pol will be your advisor and, Athen, I trust I can count on you to be her personal guard?"

"Of course," he responded.

"What does this really mean, though?" Reece asked. "All the Great Houses existed far longer than us before they were elevated to their status."

"Save for House Devitt," Aryis interjected. "Remember, before we left the Empire, we had an at-large seat and my mother served as the sitting Council member. The only time there was a thirteenth House on the Council."

Nyssa glanced at the clock in the back of the room, realizing her time in Cardin was drawing to a close. A tender from Hannah's Whisper would be waiting at the docks in half an hour. She stood and stretched, her back popping.

"Is it already time?" Aryis asked.

"Yeah, Little Hawk. I have a boat to catch."

Aryis, Athen, and Reece crowded around, each taking turns giving her a hug.

She smiled at Aryis. "I'm going to miss you."

Aryis's eyes filled with tears. "I'm sorry for everything I've ever—"

"You need to stop apologizing to me," Nyssa interrupted, poking her in the arm. "You look after everyone, will you?"

Aryis wiped her eyes and nodded.

"And you," Nyssa said, turning to Reece, "are going to be the brightest goddamn star in the Sun Palace."

Reece didn't hide her emotions and started crying. Aryis wrapped an arm around her. "Don't mind me," Reece said, "I'm just a bit overwhelmed."

Nyssa rocked back on her heels. "Medias will keep an eye on you, so I'm not worried for one second."

Reece laughed through her tears and shot a look at Medias, who stepped out of the shadows in the corner and gave Nyssa a nod.

"I will see you to the docks," she said before quickly giving Reece a warm smile.

Nyssa nodded, then looked up to Athen. "Walk me out, big man?"

Athen accompanied her out into the hall, shadowed by Medias.

"It's going to be weird without you around," he said, looking a bit sad.

Fighting a pang of melancholy, she took a deep breath. "Quinn needs some time to recover from everything that's happened." Nyssa knew that at some point Quinn's anger and guilt were going to work their way out of her system, and she needed a safe place to fall. "We're planning on being away for three months. Then back to Ocean's Rest."

Reece had extended House Fennick's hospitality to Nyssa and Quinn, offering them a residence at Ocean's Keep. It was a generous offer, but Nyssa didn't know if she could stomach living under the same roof as Lilliana. Without money, though, they didn't have many options. It was something she'd have to discuss with Quinn.

"I'll miss your idiot face," Athen replied. "And I could use an assistant trainer to get my Lion's Guard in fighting shape."

"Uh, assistant trainer?"

He shrugged. "Assistant to my assistant, that is. So, Brick's assistant."

Nyssa let out the most dramatic sigh she could work up. Athen gave her another hug. "You take care of yourself, big man."

"Goodbye, Blacksea. See you in three months."

"We have a messenger bowl if you need us."

Athen nodded and, with a wave, went back into the East Library. Nyssa watched the door close and lowered her head. She'd only be gone for a little while, but she still felt a longing wash over her. A couple years on the run, in hiding, left her feeling ready for a place to settle and call home. Somewhere close to her chosen family.

"Let's go, Sentinel," Nyssa said, taking off.

"This way, Blacksea," Medias sighed, walking in the opposite direction.

The ride down to the Cardin docks was quiet. Nyssa stared out the window of their motorized rickshaw, a courtesy of the throne, and watched the bustling crowds moving in and out of bars, restaurants, and shops.

At the docks, they exited the vehicle. The whispers and looks started, and a small following gathered while they made their way to the boat slips. The moon poked in and out of the clouds, and Nyssa reveled in the last of winter's chill in the air. As soon as they drew closer to the water, the familiar sounds of ships and the sea filled her with energy. The briny wind whipping in from the open sea made her shiver and reinvigorated her.

"Oy, you out for a stroll or you gonna get your ass moving?" a voice called out. Yuha crossed her arms and scowled at Nyssa as they approached.

"I've missed you too," Nyssa said.

Quinn poked out from behind the large woman.

"Quinn?"

"I had to make sure you were safe," Quinn replied.

Nyssa didn't hesitate to pull her into her arms. "I'm here, Freckles. And we're fine. I'll tell you all about it back on the Whisper. Wait until you hear about the Sun Council's newest problem."

"Let's get going. Elias is wearing a rut in the deck with worry that Decia would have you in chains. And Fontaine is...well...dancing naked. Again."

Nyssa laughed. "We'll be right there, Yuha. Give us a chance to say goodbye to our Sentinel."

Medias stood straighter. "I feel like I should be...going with you. To...I don't know...do whatever a Sentinel is supposed to do?"

"We'll be fine," Quinn replied. "You need to spend some quality time with Reece."

A scowl overtook Medias's face.

"Everyone knows," Quinn continued.

Nyssa leaned in. "The walls on the Cloud Crasher are thick, but not that thick."

It was too dark to tell, but Nyssa was certain Medias was in the midst of turning a bright shade of red.

Quinn stepped forward and gave Medias a hug. "I told you."

Nyssa scowled. She'd ask Quinn about that later.

She squared up to Medias. "Thank you...for everything. We'll figure out what being a Sentinel means for you when we get back. I envision some foot rubs in my future."

A chuckle emanated out of Medias. An odd and welcome sound. "I will, strangely enough, miss you both."

Nyssa pulled the woman into an embrace. "You make your father proud, Medias."

Nyssa felt Medias's breath hitch. "You too, Blacksea."

They watched Medias walk back down the pier before returning to the tender. Yuha sighed impatiently, making Quinn chuckle. After they got underway, Nyssa turned to glance back at Cardin. Time away to heal, mentally and physically, would be good for them both, but she'd miss everyone dearly.

"See you guys soon," she whispered.

EPILOGUE: THE CURSED GODS

Nyssa stripped off her sweater and tossed it on the pillow in the corner of the main room. Spring was nipping at the tail end of winter, and Nyssa was already lamenting the coming heat.

"Is that sweater dirty?" Quinn asked, glancing up from her book.

"Yes."

"Then put it in the hamper in the bathroom."

"But it's not *dirty*-dirty," Nyssa replied. She watched a wave of frustration work its way across Quinn's face. It was kind of fun, she had to admit.

"Then put it in your dresser," Quinn said.

"But it's not *clean* enough to go back into the dresser."

Quinn blinked. "I-I…" A rush of air left her, and she shook her head. Tossing her book aside, she got up and stretched. "I'm going to meditate on the dock."

Nyssa watched her leave the house, admiring the view. She put a pot of water on the stove, heating it up for tea. The tin that Koras's Sentinel, Cyphon, had given them was proving to be the perfect gift. It refilled itself magickally and the tea inside was always delicious, altering subtly in taste from time to time.

Their teacups were arranged neatly on the counter, their handles facing the same direction. A sugar bowl sat next to them, its spoon in perfect alignment, along with a folded tea towel. Quinn's doing.

While they had roomed together on the Whisper, Nyssa only noticed Quinn's tidiness in passing, and she hadn't said much about Nyssa's personal habits. Now, they were starting to see what it would truly be like living together. Adjustments would have to be made...but the sweater could be picked up later.

The two of them had settled into a comfortable routine on Monk's Cove. Nyssa resumed Quinn's Ithais-Toru training in the mornings, and the afternoons were spent meditating or reading Sakei's book, *The Way of Ithais-Toru*, "borrowed" from the Sun Palace.

There was peace to Sakei's philosophy, a stillness of the heart that Quinn sorely needed. And so did Nyssa after everything that had happened. Reading the passages again and discussing them with Quinn made Nyssa feel closer to Eron in some strange way.

In the last few days, Quinn had begun opening up more about her upbringing at the Citadel. At first, she was dispassionate, as if discussing the weather. But over time, she peeled back the layers of emotions that had built up over years. There was a darkness there that Nyssa recognized as similar to her own—a deep anger that could fester and turn into cancer.

Growing up, Nyssa used her anger to fight back against the adepts at the Emerald Order who bullied her. Eron had taught her how to channel her anger using Sakei's teachings, and Nyssa would do the same for Quinn. She would help turn that anger into a strength.

Ceril's cold disinterest had burrowed to the depths of Quinn, making her feel unworthy of existing. Quinn had told Nyssa in muted tones that the disdain and dispassion were, in many ways, worse than being whipped. Because at least in that moment, Quinn felt seen.

There was more work to do, and Quinn certainly needed more time to heal, but her demeanor had lightened after her stark honesty.

Nyssa peeked out the window to make sure Quinn was on the dock before returning to their bedroom. She started digging in her bottom dresser drawer, pulling out the gift she had gotten Quinn. Elias had picked it up in Ocean's Rest while finishing repairs on the Whisper, and they had successfully hidden it from Quinn, storing it in the bottom of Nyssa's trunk when they were dropped off at Monk's Cove.

She walked through the house and went outside. The chill in the air had far less bite to it than when they'd arrived two weeks ago. Quinn would soon be in her element, enjoying the warmer weather and swimming in the cove. When Nyssa grumbled at the change in seasons, Quinn pointed out that since they were alone on the island, they could skinny-dip without fear of being caught. Turned out to be a very convincing argument on Quinn's part.

Nyssa leaned over, plucked a wildflower from the edge of the porch, and strolled down the dock. Quinn sat cross-legged, stacking river rocks with her shadow magick. An exercise in fine control, she had called it, but it seemed meditative for her as well. She would sit and practice for hours. Anything to bring about stillness was welcome.

Nyssa bent over and tucked the wildflower behind Quinn's ear, giving her a peck on the top of her head. "I have something for you." She handed Quinn a long, thin leather pouch.

"What's this?"

"Open it."

Quinn opened the end of the pouch and pulled it back, revealing a black scabbard holding a sword.

"I asked Brick's wife to make it for you months ago. I'm very happy with it, she's an amazing swordsmith."

Quinn popped to her feet and drew the sword with a gasp. Its blade caught the light, and Nyssa admired the etching that lined its flat edge—entwined deer antlers. Its cross guard had similar engravings. She had given Becks all the specifications, including the antlers to represent Koras.

"If the length or the balance are off for you in any way, Becks can remake it. But we worked hard to get it right, given your height and how you fight with a blade."

"Is this sun steel?" Quinn whispered.

"Of course. I'm not going to get you a piece of shit that'll shatter when it meets a stiff wind." Nyssa grinned. "Take a few practice swings."

Quinn stepped back, assuming a casual stance. She lifted the sword up, paused, then moved through the first few steps of the Bamboo Form, modified for a sword as Nyssa had taught her.

As she flowed through the form, the smile on her face widened.

Finally, she stopped and sheathed the sword. "It's perfect." She drew close to Nyssa and tugged at the collar of her shirt, pulling her in for a kiss. When they parted, Quinn's touch lingered on Nyssa's lips and she desperately wanted more.

"Hold this." Quinn handed her new sword to Nyssa and then started unbuttoning Nyssa's shirt, her smile turning suggestive. "Let me thank you properly," she murmured, slipping a hand inside of Nyssa's shirt and finding a very pert nipple.

Nyssa hummed with anticipation. It took their journey on the Whisper to regain an intimacy that wasn't tinged by their experiences at Arcton. They were both cautious with one another at first, but since stepping back on Monk's Cove, sex had become rather frequent. Having the island to themselves was proving dangerous. "Should we take this inside?"

Quinn raised an eyebrow. "I thought you liked the cold?"

A challenge? Nyssa gently placed the new sword down on the dock and threaded a finger through Quinn's belt loop, pulling her closer until their bodies pressed together. "I do like the cold, but let's see how long you can stand it, Freckles." She dipped her head to the hollow of Quinn's throat, drawing a moan out of her. Nyssa slid her hands to Quinn's belt, undoing the buckle and pulling the leather end out. She undid the first button, then the next. "I love you, Quinn."

A sudden strong presence of magick pricked up against Nyssa's senses. It felt familiar.

Quinn flinched and pulled back, her face scrunching up. "What the hell is that?"

Shit.

The air began to flicker and spark, giving way to a familiar dark oblong portal.

Nyssa braced for a fight, lightning dancing across her skin. Next to her, darkness coiled around Quinn.

Two women tumbled out of the portal and onto the dock.

"Stay on your side of the Shimmer!" a deep voice boomed, unmistakable. Tajal the Curious.

Just as fast as it had appeared, the portal collapsed on itself and the oppressive press of magick was gone.

Tajal had dumped two strangers in their midst, then fucked off back to his realm. Nyssa growled—he had ruined what was going to be a perfect day.

The two women scrambled to their feet and turned toward Nyssa and Quinn. The tall one gasped. The short one with the strange arm reached for her daggers.

Quinn didn't hesitate. She curled her darkness around them, trapping them before they could attack.

Nyssa stepped forward, lightning arcing across her fingertips, ready to strike. "Who the fuck are you?"

EPILOGUE: THE FALLEN QUEEN

Suvi Rell turned her nose up at the disgusting stench hanging in the air. The tangy scent of sweat mixed with dank cigar smoke and stale beer would have twisted her stomach if it wasn't becoming all too familiar. A fact she lamented with every dim bar she entered, looking for a drink and a victim.

How many of these bars and seedy hotels had she been forced to frequent in the weeks trudging through the cursed Northern Wilds? And further, forced to get by stealing coin like a common pickpocket. No one in the Wilds seemed to have much money, so she was stuck with staying at establishments that featured thin blankets, lukewarm coffee, and noisy neighbors.

The whole experience was distasteful.

She made her way through the crowded bar, careful to keep her hood over her eyes and scarf tight to hide the void collar still clasped around her neck. Her patience was at an end, but she was hopefully about to turn her fortune around. However she had to do it.

Suvi approached a table in the back corner. The woman sitting there looked up with not even a flinch of surprise.

Shaylin Vance leaned back and laughed. "Well, hello, Princess."

"Vance."

Shay's eyes scanned the bar before returning to Suvi. If the bitch made a commotion, Suvi would be back in Imperial custody.

The pirate causally placed her dagger on the scratched-up table.

A threat. How *cute*.

"You've got a price on your head, and Ceril, the dead bastard, never paid me." Shay narrowed her eyes. "How about I get my cut now? In more ways than one?"

Suvi didn't flinch. She had been threatened by far better people than this lowborn pirate. Not waiting for an invitation, she pulled out a chair and sat down, leaning in. "I have a job for you."

Shay pursed her lips and leaned in as well. "Not interested." She reached for her dagger.

Suvi grabbed her wrist. "I can pay you five million gold marks. Is my bounty anywhere near that amount?"

A flicker of interest crossed Shay's face, her purple eyes widening for a moment. Idiots like her were easy to read and easier to manipulate when driven by basic desires like lust, gluttony...or greed.

"Five million gold, eh, princess? What sort of job we talkin'?"

The offer wasn't real. She would slit Shay's throat when all was said and done, but right now, she needed the pirate.

Suvi inhaled. "I want my goddamn crown back."

Acknowledgements

Writing a book is no small feat. Inspiration comes from a myriad of sources. For me, it's a weird mix of kung fu movies, Miyazaki's films, Radiohead, powerful women, the sound of falling snow, and the gentle, warm hue the light takes on just as the sun is setting. Aside from inspiration, writing a book well takes far more than just the lone author. A number of people contributed to this book being written, edited, and out in the world.

I want to thank the small army of people who helped me make this book and The Blacksea Odyssey shine: Max Gorlov, L.R. Friedman, Chinah Mercer, Zoe Markham, and Chris Yarbrough.

I'm eternally grateful for my friends, close and far, especially the FBC Crew, Duy, Lucia, Cal, Scott, Dan, Niecy, Merritt, Jo, Aimee, Meagan, Kirsten, Cristina, Brandi, and Dani. The support and encouragement is priceless. Love all of you guys!

And lastly, thanks to the two biggest people in my life:

Joe, a trusted mentor and my biggest supporter. Navigating life with someone who is always rooting for your success is priceless. I love you, big bro!

Lisa, my girlfriend, though we both know that's in insufficient term for what you mean to me. Finding you at this stage in my life was the biggest surprise. I'm so happy I took a chance and went on a date with a nerdy Trekkie who loves hockey. I love you, woman!

What's next for Nyssa?

You can keep up to date on all upcoming stories, novellas, and novels by signing up for my newsletter at www.javodvarka.com.

This trilogy is just the beginning of the Blacksea Universe. Nyssa's adventures will continue—there are other gods out there that aren't so nice, remember? There will be another trilogy or two in the future, featuring Nyssa, Quinn, and the rest of their amazing friends.

There's a spin-off or two in the works. The next project is code-named The Dragonfly and The Viper. Are these the two that show up during an inopportune moment on the dock with Nyssa and Quinn. You'll meet Wyeth and Sivaar in their own story.

And don't forget about Suvi and Shaylin. Suvi has a crown to reclaim and Shay has a "Princess" to torment as they embark on their own adventures. There are worse things out at the sea than a cruel ex-Queen and her sociopathic pirate sidekick.

And finally, a request. Reviews from readers like yourself are the life blood of indie authors, so if you would kindly take a moment and leave a review for this book, I would be eternally grateful.

About the author

J.A. Vodvarka is an adult fantasy author, combining action, humor, romance, and unique world-building to create epic fantasy stories with a ton of heart. The Blacksea Odyssey trilogy features strong, sensitive, kick-butt women in a semi-modern setting.

Her writing is inspired by: a childhood spent watching kung fu movies, Toshiro Mifune's swagger, a splash of Hayao Miyazaki's mysticism, her 5000+ comic book collection, and a love of fun, smart, and complex female characters who appreciate a fine dessert.

Originally from Illinois, J.A. received a degree from UIUC in English and American Literature and Creative Writing. J.A. currently resides in Houston, Texas with a surly French bulldog, Emmitt.

Connect with J.A. Vodvarka on her site: www.javodvarka.com or on social media: linktr.ee/javodvarka

Content warning

All my books are intended for an adult audience (18+). *Unyielding* contains graphic violence, body horror, death, torture, profanity, gore, physical abuse, and explicit sexual scenes.

Please email me if you have any questions about the content warnings – blacksea@javodvarka.com.